FEATHERS

floating

THROUGH

EMBER

Book Two of the Adrift Series

TRINITYDUNN

Copyright

Cover design by Twisted Plum LLC

I dedicate this book to my mother.

Thank you for always believing in me.

THE ADRIFT SERIES BOOKS (IN ORDER):

Book 1: More of Us to the West

Book 2: Feathers Floating Through Ember

Book 3: Remnants on the Tides of Time

Book 4: A Reflection of the Sky on the Sea

(Coming Winter 2022)

Prologue

"Ally?" he breathed, and I could feel my knees begin to buckle.

Chris... he was alive. He was alive, and he was standing in front of me and I couldn't breathe... I couldn't speak... the words stuck in my throat and I stared dumbfounded up at him. He was dressed strangely and he had an odd new scent... and how the hell did he—

"Ally," he repeated, wrapping his arms around me and pulling me against him. "My sweet, beautiful, Ally. I knew you were alive," he whispered, laying kisses against my temples and cheeks until his mouth covered mine.

"I knew it was you I saw..." He kissed my shocked lips again and again, smoothing his hand over my hair to cup my face. "I knew I'd find you here." He pressed his forehead against mine. "I'm so sorry for how long it's taken me to get to you."

Before I could get a handle on the situation, he covered my lips again with his, pushing past them and pulling me up on my toes as he frantically reacquainted my mouth with his. His kiss was desperate and deliberate. His hands moved frenziedly over my face and arms as he pressed deeper. I could feel his tears drip down my own cheeks.

'Chris... he's alive! How?'

Slowly, my body recovered from its shock and I let my arms wind around him, let my senses rejoice in the familiarness of his hands on my face, of his lips over mine, of his body moulded against me.

Just as soon as the relief had come, it disappeared, and a panic set in. Guilt washed up into my throat as he pulled me closer; as his mouth grew warmer. I was kissing my husband, but I had an unrelenting feeling that I was doing something wrong. He was familiar, but a complete stranger at the same time. He was mine, but he wasn't. I was two different women standing there at that moment; one that was betraying her fiancé by kissing another man, and another that was utterly relieved to find her husband still alive.

He pulled back, holding my face in his hands as he inspected me. "I knew you were alive," he said softly, his eyes watering as they focused on each of mine. "I wouldn't stop looking. I knew you were out here somewhere. There's so much I need to tell you... so much I—

"I knew it wasn't no damn storm!" Jim shouted behind us. "Didn't I tell ye?"

"Ally," Chris evened out his voice, his expression shifting to solemn. "There's a lot you need to know before you get on that ship. Is there somewhere we can go? To be alone?"

I was trembling, but I nodded.

"The others... they'll need to hear it too." He looked up from me for the first time to take in the other survivors. "We've created identities and backstories for you all."

He didn't wait for me to respond, but turned to a tall soldier at his side. "Buy us some time for me to tell them everything?"

The soldier bowed his head. "I will."

"Come." He turned me back the way I'd come. "Before the captain catches up to us."

Dazedly, I led my husband back up the trail toward our island home... toward my home with Jack.

Where was Jack? I could hear the others joining us; could hear Bud pressing them all to stay quiet until we were clear of the other men, but I couldn't hear Jack. My face was ice cold, my mind was racing, and my vision was tunneling. I felt like I was going to be sick.

"You alright?" Lilly whispered, locking her arm around mine when she'd caught up to me.

I shook my head, still incapable of speaking. How did he get there? How could I possibly tell him everything that had happened since I last saw him? How could I tell him about Jack... about the baby... how could I ever look him in the eyes again? And Jack... where was Jack? What the hell was I going to—

"This is far enough," he instructed, forcing me to turn back toward him.

Seeing those familiar green eyes as I turned forced my racing mind to quiet and allow my heart to take a moment to process his presence. He truly was a beautiful sight to take in right then. He was the same man I'd fallen in love with and yet, he was changed.

His nose was a little different. It had a slight dip in the bridge, and his eyes seemed heavier... older... His mouth was framed with thick, dark stubble.

He wore a loose white shirt under an open vest and overcoat, a large sword hanging at his side and down his legs which were well defined in the black breeches and stockings...

He towered over us all, and he was thinner than I remembered... He looked tired... Tired, but beautiful... and alive... and suddenly I needed to wrap my arms back around him... to hold him and show him how glad I was he was alive. I hadn't given him that... I owed him that in this moment before it would all crumble... before I told him about Jack.

My eyes burned as I watched him wait for the group to gather around him. He held a new air of authority that I hadn't seen in him before, and as his eyes met mine, I felt my heart flutter just a little.

"We don't have much time," he said. "What happened to us... it wasn't just a plane crash. We've come out of that storm in..." He took a deep breath. "1773... well, 1774 now."

PART I

This is where I leave you.

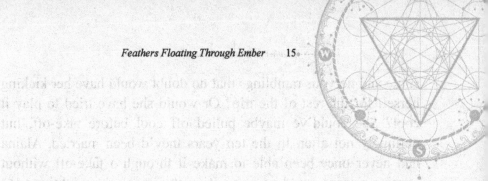

Chapter One

Chris

Chris had just drifted into sleep when the dull thump returned to torment his lower back. He took his forty-seventh deep breath of the trip, reminding himself that it was merely a child and spinning around in his seat to shout obscenities would be heavily frowned upon by the dozing travelers surrounding him.

He stretched his back straight, yawning, and rolled his head from one side to the other, his neck cracking as he did so. Leaning into the aisle, he glanced toward the front of the plane and smiled.

She was probably dead asleep and far more comfortable than he was—that is, if she wasn't too busy smiling at Jack Volmer.

When he'd passed them on the way in, he'd laughed at the pure irony of the situation. Of all the people in the world for Alaina to be seated next to on their belated honeymoon, it *had* to be Jack friggin' Volmer.

In the early days of their relationship, she'd drooled over the man every time she'd come across a rerun of *Fairview Nights* on television. Oh, and once she'd stumbled upon the channel, far be it for him or anyone else to even consider touching the remote. It didn't matter that she'd seen every episode at least a hundred times. If Jack Volmer was on tv, she *had* to watch him.

He tried to picture her expression when she'd sat down next to her childhood crush. Would she have had the awkward, toothy smile and nervous ramblings that no doubt would have her kicking herself for the rest of the trip? Or would she have tried to play it cool? She could've maybe pulled off cool before take-off, but definitely not after. In the ten years they'd been married, Alaina had never once been able to make it through a take-off without causing a scene, and he was positive any image she might've tried to paint of herself would've been obliterated once she began her routine hyperventilation.

The child behind him kicked his seat again, this time with enough force to physically cause him to lurch forward.

'That's it!' He thought to himself and stood to glare down at the little pudgy boy. The kid—no more than four or five—had slid almost all the way down in his seat to allow for the length of his chubby legs to be pressed against Chris's backrest.

His parents occupied the two interior seats beside him, their heads rested against each other as they slept peacefully, unaware of the havoc their offspring was wreaking in the absence of supervision.

Chris said nothing, but stood scowling at until the child recognized the danger and straightened, his lips forming a small pout that made Chris feel a slight ping of guilt for it.

He glanced around the dark quiet of the airplane, then looked back down to his tiny seat, and his knees protested at the thought of returning to it so soon. Instead, he decided upon an impromptu trip to the first-class bathroom to get a glimpse of Alaina's either blundering attempts at flirtation or sleeping situation.

He moved toward the front of the airplane with only the dim blue light that shone into the aisle from random device screens to guide him, and was stopped short by a tug at his arm.

"Sir," whispered a woman behind him, the slightly rolled "r" instantly giving away a Latin accent. He turned to find a beautiful flight attendant raising her dark brow in his direction. "The restroom in front is reserved for first-class passengers only. I am afraid I have to ask you to use the one in the back, please."

He frowned, glancing up from her to the vacant restroom in the rear before he leaned down to whisper back, "There's someone in the back and I need to go now. Besides, my wife is in first-class and I want to check on her. I'll be quick." He winked. "I promise."

She narrowed her eyes to inspect him. Twisting her lips to one side, she shook her head. "Hurry up. I can't have all these passengers thinking they can just bat their eyes at me and go up there whenever they want."

He smiled as she turned her attention toward a woman at her side who was *'too chilly,'* then swayed with the plane as he slowly made his way toward his wife.

He could make out her curls spilling over the side of her seat, and his heart warmed. The past few years had been hard on her. She needed this trip away from their life; away from their problems. He was determined to make it perfect for her.

He couldn't wait to see her face light up when she stepped into the over-water bungalow he'd upgraded them to.

"Will you please turn that off?" A frustrated female voice hissed to the man at her side when Chris crossed into first-class.

"Get yer hands off my display, woman!" The man retorted, smacking her hand away from his view, evidently mesmerized by the on-screen flight path.

"I can't sleep with that on," she whined miserably.

"Well, it sucks to be you then, don't it? I'm watchin' this."

Chris smirked, and as he moved past them to stand in front of the restroom door, he noticed Jack Volmer's display was also turned on. Earbuds pressed into his ears, Jack was absorbed in a movie while Alaina's head was bent to the opposite side, her mouth wide open in a deep sleep.

'So attractive, Ally.'

He chuckled to himself as he heard her distinctive snore, pulling the bifold door to the restroom open and glancing once more in her direction before he stepped into the brightly lit box of a bathroom.

Quietly closing the door behind him, he stared at his reflection in the mirror. *'I'm just as good-looking as Jack Volmer,'* he assured himself. *'Aren't I?'*

He laughed at his ridiculous insecurity, turning to face the toilet. *'Whatever. He might have the looks, but I could definitely take him if I had to.'*

The plane rocked, forcing him to seize hold of the handicap rail and the sink to catch himself before he could fall backward to bust through the door.

Straightening his legs, his ears filled with a high-pitched buzz, dizzying him before the ringing turned to complete silence.

He blinked at himself in the mirror and shook his head, attempting to clear his hearing, when, without warning, the plane shifted and for a fleeting moment, he was weightless—euphoric and floating freely.

Before the sensation could completely register, he was plastered to the opposing wall with such force he was sure his bones would break beneath the pressure holding him there.

The lights flickered, creating a strobe effect that grew less and less frequent as the plane sped downward. He stared at his mortified reflection in the flashes of light, trying to rationalize what was happening while his body fought against the gravity cementing him against the wall.

'Oh God, we're crashing,' he realized as the light stopped blinking, cloaking him in an utterly silent blackness. *'Ally, I have to get to Alaina!'*

His arms and legs were like lead. With all his strength, he fought to reposition himself, contorting his body down to the floor to wedge between the wall and the vanity.

"Ally!'" He cried out loud despite his lost hearing, "Please God, please, please let us be okay. Don't do this now. Please, please don't do this now!! ALLY!!"

Could she hear him? If he shouted loud enough, would she know he was right there, crashing just a few feet from her?

The plane shook as it picked up momentum; the velocity smashing his head against the wall. "I promise I'll do anything you want if you just keep her safe. Don't take her. Not yet. Please let her be okay. Let *us* be okay."

He turned himself to one side, bracing his forearms on the cabinet and the wall as he fought to position his legs in the same way, shaking with the effort of holding himself upright against the force. *'We're going to die... No... we can't die. Not like this.'*

"Ally!" He cried out again, still unable to hear his own voice or anything around him.

"ALAINA!" He persisted, reaching up to grab the handicap rail as the plane vibrated.

Could he get to her? Could he crawl to her seat to look into her eyes just one last time?

He adjusted his position, turning his body against the pressure trying to force him back against the wall. *'I can't die like this. Please, not yet. Let me get to her. Let me see her.'*

The vibration of the plane grew nearly unbearable as it picked up more speed, and a feeling in his gut told him they were close to crashing. He took one last deep breath, squeezing his eyes closed. Just as his body tensed for impact, the plane's trajectory slowed, and his stomach danced with the sudden change in momentum.

Once again, an overwhelming sense of weightlessness washed over him as he floated upward. "This is it. This is how I die. I'm going to die."

With all the air he had left in his lungs, he cried out one last time. "ALLY!"

Then his mind went as quiet as his ears, and he hovered in a blissful state of oblivion.

"Mr. Grace..." He heard Alaina whisper. "Wake up and show me how a husband kisses his wife..."

He grinned, assured in that moment he was safe in his bed and she was lying beside him.

Had he dreamt it all? He was sure he'd roll over and see that look in her eyes—the one she always had when she said those words; that look that begged him, *'come get me.'*

God, he hadn't heard those words in so long. He'd waited so long to hear *those* words.

Just beyond her in the darkness, there was a steady sound, like a tide washing into a shoreline; in and out with such perfect tempo, his shoulders eased even further.

In and out... In and out...

As his mind came alive, he identified the sound as his own breath, loud in his ears. "Ally..." He reached for her but came up empty.

'What happened?' he wondered, new noises accompanying the cadence of his breathing, their static growing louder and louder until it overwhelmed him.

"Al," he whispered, "what is that?"

'Water... Water?!'

He opened his eyes to the blackness around him and recognized the flooding of water pouring into the bathroom to climb up his legs.

"Ally?!" He screamed, launching himself up off the floor to push at the door handle. It was jammed on its mangled track. "ALLY!!"

He curled his fingers around the edge of the door and jerked with all his strength, water hitting his knees as he bent the top half of the door open by a few inches.

In a flash of lightning through the crack, he could see a large male body at the exit door across from him. Hanging lifelessly from the man's arms was the outline of a woman, and he could just make out the shape of Alaina's coveted Renaud boots on her feet. "Alaina!"

The water was pooling around his waist, and he hurled his body into the door.

'Was she moving? Is she alright?'

He leaned back against the sink and kicked over and over. The door shuddered with each blow, but the surging water made each kick less effective.

'She has to be alive... that's why he's carrying her out... He wouldn't bother if she wasn't... she's alive and I have to get to her.'

He inhaled deeply, turning his shoulder as he launched his full weight into the door, tumbling out into a cascade of rising water.

He fought against its current and headed toward the exit, a flash of lightning revealing a raft just outside filled with bodies. "Alaina!" He cried out, tears filling his eyes as his heartbeat raced. He turned back to check the seat she'd been in, and his stomach danced when he found it empty.

"Help me!" a frantic female voice called behind him. "¡Ayúdame! Somebody help me! I'm trapped!"

He peered once more out the plane's exit to see, in a spark of lightning, the raft wavering in the turbulent ocean. He could see people moving on its surface.

'I have to get to Ally,' his heart argued.

"Please," the woman begged, desperation forcing her voice to crack, "someone please help!"

'Dammit. I can't just leave someone to die here.'

And despite his mind begging him to leap out the door and onto the raft, his body turned toward the voice.

"Keep making noise," He ordered, wading through the intensifying rush of water in the direction of the cry.

"I'm here! Over here!" Her thick Spanish accent rang through on her rolled 'R' as he drew closer.

"Where?" Lightning flashed again through the open exit door and he glanced back toward the raft. She was on it. She had to be safe, and he would get to her.

"I'm stuck! Help me! I can't move!"

Blindly, he extended his arms forward, reaching toward the voice as the water reached his chest. The voice ahead of him was starting to choke.

His fingers curled around something solid, and her labored breathing was now loud in his ears.

"I'm here," he assured her, his other hand feeling around the large cart that held her pinned.

She choked and gasped while he pulled at the unmoving cart beneath the water, the chilly waves now at his throat.

"Come on!" he shouted in frustration, bracing his legs against the wall to jerk the metal, tipping his head to the ceiling for air as the water reached his ears.

He felt the cart dislodge and reached down to feel for her, locking his fingers around a petite wrist to pull her upward.

She came up with a gasping inhale, her arms splashing in a panic.

"Wait! Wait!" she cried as he pulled her toward the exit. In the flickering of white lightning, he caught her reach back to where she'd been to pull something off the wall. "Go!" she urged him.

As the plane sunk more rapidly, the rushing water pushed them backward with every attempt to cross the door's threshold. He tried once, then again, and then again, each time the influx of water shooting them back toward the restroom.

"We have to wait until the door fills." He coughed, filling his lungs to float above the water in the bit of air left near the ceiling. "There's a raft out there..." His mouth sunk beneath the saltwater momentarily, "we have to get to it."

He kept the fingers of one hand clutched tightly around the woman's wrist while he gripped the overhead bin with the other and waited for the sound of rushing water at the door to cease.

'I have to get to Ally.'

As he waited, memory of the pudgy-faced boy in the seat behind him returned and he glanced back toward his seat for the first time. Another strike of lightning revealed the entire back of the plane had vanished, leaving only an endless rolling ocean spilling into the gap where it once had been.

Where was the rest of the plane? Where was the little boy? His heart sank in his chest as the child's pouting face flashed through his memory.

The stream of water at the door quieted, drawing his attention back to the task at hand.

"Take a deep breath," he commanded the woman, "and kick your legs as hard as you can when we get on the other side. The plane will try to pull us down with it. We have to fight to get above the water. Understand?"

"Sí," she said, inhaling loudly.

He pulled her under the water, gripping the frame of the door to propel them out into the sea. He kicked his legs violently, feeling their bodies being pulled downward despite his attempts to swim to the surface.

Disregarding his implicit instructions, he felt the woman's legs wrap around his waist. He kicked harder with her added weight and then was surprisingly jerked upward by the inflating of her life vest between them.

They surfaced in a collective gasp for air, both of them choking against the rolling waves that pushed them high into the storm.

He scanned the pulsing ocean around him, and as one long bright burst of lightning lit up the sky, he could see a dot of yellow far ahead on the tumbling surface.

"There!" He screamed, "The raft! It's there!"

The woman clung to him, her arms and legs wound tightly around his upper body as she spun her head to look behind her, then forward, then back again.

"Land!" she cried out just before a wave spilled over them, forcing them deep under the water. He wrapped his arms around her, holding on to her for dear life as he kicked his legs toward the surface.

They sputtered and spit as their heads emerged, and he searched again for the raft as the woman attempted to swim in the opposite direction.

Again, he saw the yellow of the raft moving further away from him. "We have to get to them!" He fought against her pull to swim with the tide. "The raft is this way!"

"NO!" She pulled his face to look at her, her expression frantic in the strobing storm. "There is land! Look there!" She turned him so he could see a small shadowy outline of earth against the ocean's horizon.

"My wife—

Another rolling wave poured over them, pushing them and holding them deep down beneath the surface. He clawed at the ocean, his legs fighting as his breath threatened to run out.

He gagged on the air when he finally was able to inhale again, and she pulled him in the direction of land, straining to swim against the waves that dragged them further out to sea.

"No!" he argued, tugging her back. "My wife is on that raft. I have to get to her!"

"¡Oye! ARE YOU CRAZY?" she shrieked. "We can't catch them! We'll die. There is land just there. They will see it too!"

"NO!" He fought to stay afloat as they rode up a swelling wall of water, his stomach rising with it to sit in his throat before they dropped back down. "I CAN'T LEAVE HER!"

"Well, I can't help you!" she snapped. "You want to die out here? FINE! I will not die here with you. I'm going to the land!"

She unwound her legs from him and moved to swim away.

With one hand on her life vest, he glanced between her and the ocean behind him.

He couldn't risk losing Alaina. Not now. Not when they were on the verge of finally mending their broken relationship. Despite his mind's warning against it, he let go of the woman and turned his body.

"YOU FOOL!" she shouted, panic filling her voice. "You will die! Please don't do this!"

Without the life vest, his body sank down so only his head remained above the water, and he fought against the pouring rain to breathe. "I HAVE TO!"

He began to swim, a wave pulling him in and gushing over him.

He kicked and propelled his arms with all the strength he could muster, the pressure of the swell overpowering his body and moving him like a rag doll beneath its force. For a moment, his head surfaced and he inhaled, then was pushed down again to flail helplessly.

His lungs protested for oxygen and he felt the saltwater fill them when he could hold it no longer.

'No, please! Please! I can't drown here! I have to see her. Please, not yet!'

He reached up, kicking endlessly to survive, his body beginning to fatigue when he felt a hand grab hold of his to pull him back to the surface.

He choked and spit as the woman wrapped her arms and legs around him once again. "You stupid man!" She sobbed loudly near his ear. "We have to get to land! Please come with me. They will see it when the sun is up! Please! Please don't leave me!"

He glanced back at the wall of eddying ocean and could no longer see the raft. Too tired to argue, he surrendered, curling his arms around her as another wave lifted them up and back down.

Chapter Two

Chris

Chris clung to the woman as they established a routine out of kicking their legs against each wave, wrestling with the tide's momentum to keep the island within view.

Each new swell would drag them upward and backward, and they would paddle down the front of the wall, enduring the painful crash of the succeeding wave as it pushed them underwater long enough to pass over.

He squinted in the darkness with each rise of the water to search for the island through the enveloping rain. As the lightning came less frequently, he struggled for a sense of direction, knowing only that the island was opposite the tide and blindly swimming against it.

"I can't keep going like this," the woman panted. "My legs are tired."

His body clenched as he prepared for the next crashing wave, and he clutched her against him as they submerged. Coming up for air, he held her tighter, leaning into her ear. "You have to keep fighting. The storm will die down. We'll make it. Keep going."

'We have to make it. And they have to see it. Oh, please God, let her see it.'

She sobbed as they rode up again, and he could feel her body fatiguing against his as he swam them both down the opposite side.

He inhaled, squeezing his eyes shut as they were once again drowned beneath the ocean's force.

It was only her life vest that kept them re-surfacing. Over and over they battled the surge, both of them exhausted and holding onto each other as the unrelenting ocean swallowed them and spit them out.

The simple effort of breathing seemed more and more insurmountable with each crash of water over their heads; every break for air growing shorter so his lungs felt as if they might collapse waiting for the next.

When his body wanted to give in, he pictured Alaina and held the woman tighter, kicking his legs as he wept silently into her shoulder.

Each roll of the chilly water over them felt like an onslaught of punches, bruising every inch of his body, and the longer they fought, the worse each blow became on his shivering skin.

After what played like hours of fighting, he noticed the wind dying down and the thunder quieting. The rain was reduced to a light drizzle, and although the waves grew smaller, they continued to command them, dragging their almost lifeless bodies out to sea to kick their way back.

"It's almost over," he promised, his eyes and throat burning as he held her against him. "Can you see the island?" He was shivering, both from the exertion of the fight and from the cool water.

"No," she said defeatedly, her body going limp against him. "I see nothing."

"Keep looking." He paddled them against an oncoming wave, determined to swim over it rather than to ride it up and swim down. Relief washed over him when he made it through. The waves were diminishing to a much more manageable state. He could make it if he could muster up the strength to keep paddling.

"Everything hurts," she whimpered. "I can't go anymore."

"It's alright," he said, using his arms now in conjunction with his kicking legs. "I got us now. All you need to do is search for it. I'll swim for both of us. You hold on and look for the island."

"¡Oye! I can't see anything!" she asserted. "How am I supposed to find the island when I can't even see you?!"

"Keep looking. It's got to be this way."

Their voices were strangled and hoarse, and as the storm disappeared and the water calmed, they reduced to a low whispering.

"What's your name?" he asked, more to distract his mind from the exhaustion filling him than out of sincere interest.

"Maria Amelia," she uttered. "What's yours?"

"Chris Grace." He weakly pushed one heavy arm forward. "What time do you think it is?"

"We were almost halfway there," she mumbled against his shoulder as he propelled his other arm. "Maybe four or five in the morning?"

"That means the sun will be up soon." He could feel his muscles dwindling, his legs tiring as he tried to keep moving them against the pull of the ocean.

She, too, was losing energy. Her body trembled against his and her grip around him was starting to slip. He adjusted his stroke to loop one arm around her back and tread water with the other. He couldn't risk losing the only life vest in his current deteriorating state. "We'll be able to see it soon. It has to be close."

"Mmhmm…" she muttered.

"Maria, stay awake," he urged her. "Keep your eyes open."

"How do you know my eyes *aren't* open?" she scoffed, her teeth chattering as she attempted to tighten her legs around him. "Why are we stopping?"

"I can't keep going and the waves have calmed down." He could feel his own muscles shivering. "If the sun is coming up soon, we should save our energy to swim toward the island once we can see it. I don't want to risk swimming in the wrong direction."

Beneath his chin, he could feel her head moving, growing more frantic as she looked around them. "We can't just sit here. We have to keep moving. What if a shark comes?"

His shoulders slumped. "I have to stop for a while." Every bone in his body felt heavy beneath the water. "We'll be fine."

"How do you know we'll be fine?" she snapped, squirming to inspect the water as if she could see through the blackness. "Are you bleeding? Am *I* bleeding? Sharks can smell blood from a mile away! We have to keep going!"

Her question struck him, and he wondered for the first time if he had been injured. His adrenaline had been too high to notice if he were. It was entirely possible that they were both covered in blood. More than just possible, he thought, it was extremely *probable* they were both severely injured after a commercial airplane crash. "I'm sorry." He trembled, gripping her tighter. "I have to take a break."

"If my boyfriend were here, he would swim all night if he had to!"

"Would that he were," he retorted, closing his eyes to get a sense of the condition of his body. "What's his name?"

"David." She said the word in its Spanish form, pronouncing it "Dahveed" and she began a feeble attempt to backstroke. "He will come find me."

"I hope so." He could feel a little pain in the back of his head.

"He will," she assured him. "He's a very powerful man, my Dahveed. When he finds out our plane has crashed, he will pay whatever it takes to send the whole army to search for me. He works for the CIA, you know."

"Does he now?" Chris stifled the urge to call out the very evident fabrication, deciding it wouldn't benefit either of them to bicker, and he resigned to rest his chin against her shoulder. "He sounds like a real catch. For both our sakes, I really hope he does send the... army."

She sighed, giving up on the backstroke.

"Does anything hurt on you?" he asked as she wound her arms back around him. "Can you tell if you're injured?"

"I don't know yet." She yawned. "I think probably, though."

"Same." He echoed her yawn. "My head hurts. I think I might've hit it on something."

She nodded against his shoulder. "My ankle hurts… and my back… and my arms… and my head… everything hurts."

He closed his eyes to remember the crash—the sudden loss of hearing… the force that held him to the wall… fighting to pull himself upward before impact… The feeling of floating just before it all went black…

"Did you notice the plane slow down just before we hit the water?"

"No," she said, adjusting her head to face away from him. "I don't remember anything. I was standing in the aisle one minute and the next I was trapped in a sinking airplane and Frank…" She growled at the memory. "He moved right past me to open the door and just left me stuck there, calling for him."

"Frank?"

"The stupid pilot." She repositioned her arms to fold them under his as they floated on the water's surface, the occasional flicker of lightning far off in the distance, the single reminder of the storm that had ripped them from the sky.

"I've been flying with him for years and that sonofabitch just walked past me… like I was nothing!" She broke off into a much more sinister tone then, raising her voice to accentuate her outrage. "Ese hijo de puta, comemierda! Let me see his stupid ass again! I'll make him so sorry he didn't turn around to help me!"

With her sudden raised voice, the dull ache at the back of his skull grew stronger and he could feel his eyes getting heavier with a headache. He reached up to inspect the damage. It was tender. He brought his fingers to his lips and tasted the metallic tang of blood.

'Great,' he thought. "That can't be good."

"What is it?" she asked. "Is it your head? Is it bad? Don't you dare die and leave me out here by myself!"

"It's fine," he assured her. "If it were bad, I'd be dead already." As he said the words, though, he grew more anxious, his heart beating in his throat. What if it was bad? What if the only thing keeping him alive was adrenaline? Now that it was wearing off, how long could he go on?

She loosened one arm to feel his head for herself. It seemed odd to have a complete stranger touching him with such informality. "You're bleeding. This is too thick to be water." She swept her hand through his hair with growing concern, her fingers prodding for a wound and causing needles to stab at his eyes. "Where is the damn sun?!"

Behind her head, he could see the faintest hint of an orange glow creeping up the horizon. "It's there." He sighed in relief, scanning the still dark ocean for signs of the island.

She unwound her legs from him and they both paddled their legs so they bobbed in a circle, each of them searching the horizon.

They spiraled endlessly and silent and he'd begun to worry they'd drifted too far when he saw the blackened silhouette of land against the indigo skyline.

"There!" He spun her so that she could see it. "Do you see it?"

"I see it!" She squeezed him, shaking with tears of relief. "How far do you think?"

He circled around to look again. "Maybe a mile?" He laughed hysterically, hugging her to him. "Doesn't matter if it's ten. I'll get us there. We're going to make it!"

Energy suddenly restored, he pulled her legs back around his waist and began to paddle with all his strength, arms and legs propelling them forward. With each stroke, saltwater poured into his mouth, forcing him to spit and choke, but he wouldn't be deterred. He pushed onward at a steady pace.

He needed water and food. He needed Alaina. The people on the raft would see the island, too. They would come. They *had* to. He'd be with her soon, and he would never take their time together for granted again.

He wondered if they'd already seen it. Could they be on their way? He paused to look around for the raft. In the growing morning light, the island should've been visible for miles. Surely the storm couldn't have carried them so far?

Seeing no signs of them, he continued. They would see it, however far out they were. It would be unmistakable as the only dot on this vast ocean. Once on the island, just to be safe, he'd build a fire to help guide them in… He'd load it up with greenery so they could see the smoke even if they couldn't see the land.

The raft would have supplies on it. It would have water, flares, a first-aid kit… They would be alright.

He swam harder.

But his mind raced. What if the storm *had* carried the raft too far?

Being so close to where the airplane went down, he was sure rescue would see the island right away, possibly within the next few hours. With the advantage of a helicopter that would certainly accompany the search party, he would then be able to search the parameter. The raft would still be near enough to find.

They were getting closer. He could see the palm trees and the white sand in the growing light, a grouping of thicker trees just beyond the shore.

It was a small island, but it was land and after spending hours in the water, his body was desperate for its stillness. His heart skipped a little when he looked down into the water and could see what appeared to be the bottom. He tested his proximity by lowering one leg and was delighted when he felt the sole of his boot touch solid ground.

"We can walk from here," he whispered, releasing his grip on Maria for the first time in hours.

She warily disentangled her limbs from his torso, testing the ground for herself with one hand clamped on his wrist. "AH AH AH!" She winced, leaning into him as she spat water.

"What? What's wrong?"

"My ankle!" she wailed, "I can't stand on it! Oh, OW OW OW!"

"Okay, it's alright." He hooked an arm around her waist to pull her alongside him as he trudged through the sand with only his head and neck above the surface. "Just keep your feet up."

"Something touched me!" she shrieked, curling herself around him. "Go faster! Go faster!!"

"I'm going as fast as I can," he groaned as she folded her arms around his neck, burying her face against his cheek.

"Maria, you do know that there are more than just sharks in the ocean, right? It's probably just a fish."

She made no move to release her death-grip around his throat.

"Oh God. You're bleeding a lot." She touched the back of his head gingerly, then flinched again and squeezed him tighter, jerking her legs up toward the water's surface. "What's that? Something big touched me! It could be a shark! Your blood could be attracting them!"

"We're almost there," he promised, picking up his speed as best he could, ready to be free of her.

He was beyond tired. The island was within reach, but he could feel his limbs weakening. His arms were numb beneath her weight, and his legs were growing heavier with each step. His head ached and his throat was dry. With burning eyes and a trembling body, he pushed himself forward.

'Just a little further and I can rest.'

'No... I have to make a fire,' he reminded himself. *'I can't rest until we have smoke. I can't risk Alaina not seeing it. And then we'll need water. We've swallowed too much saltwater... we're probably already dehydrated.'*

He trudged onward. *'Just a little further, then fire, then water, then sleep.'*

The sun hit the horizon at his back and lit up the small island before them. It was picturesque. Bright white sand crawled up from the clear blue water into a thick tree line of palm. He couldn't wait for Alaina to see it. Under different circumstances, this island could've served as a far superior backdrop to the honeymoon they had planned.

"You don't look right," Maria observed, snapping him out of his zombie-like state to look down at her.

In the almost full daylight, and now in waist-deep water, she was fully out of the water in his arms, allowing him to inspect her for the first time.

She was undoubtedly beautiful, he noted, as if she'd been pulled from a magazine. Her long dark hair, soaked as it was, curled in waves that framed a heart-shaped face. Her dark brown eyes sat beneath thick lashes and her petite nose was dusted ever so slightly with freckles.

She frowned at him. "You look like a dead man. Are you going to fall over?"

"I'm fine." He scanned her for signs of injury as he carried her knee deep in the water, noticing she was missing a shoe.

He didn't remember when or how, but she'd removed the life vest at some point, holding it now in one hand behind his back.

Her white collared shirt had come untucked and hung loose beneath the navy blazer of her stewardess uniform. Miraculously, the red and blue scarf remained secured around her neck, and her pencil skirt, although drenched, still seemed perfectly intact.

She clicked her tongue. "You've got blood all down the side of your head. You can't die on me and leave me alone out here to fend for myself, Chris."

It was the first time she'd said his name, pronouncing it "Kreese," and he smiled at her.

"I'm not going to die." He lowered her to her feet, keeping one arm around her waist to help her hobble through the ankle deep water. "Where are you from, anyway?"

"All over." She limped alongside him, keeping her eyes on her feet. "I was born in Cuba, migrated to Spain, and then, after a long immigration process, moved to Miami on a visa."

As the ocean gave way to dry land at their feet, they both collapsed onto the beach, breathing heavily. He closed his eyes and let his cheek rest on the warm sand, feeling his muscles melt away.

'Fire, water, then sleep,' he reminded himself.

He opened his eyes to find Maria face down in the sand beside him, her legs and arms sprawled out behind her.

"I've got to get a fire started," he groaned, granules of sand around his mouth blowing with his breath and sticking to his lips. "So the raft can find us."

"MMHMM," she mumbled into the ground, not moving.

He dragged himself to sit up, his muscles protesting at the movement, and scanned the ocean for signs of them. With nothing but blue as far as his eyes could see, his heart sank in his chest. *'Where are you, Ally?'*

Chapter Three

Chris

"Everything on this goddamn island is wet!" he growled, his hands shaking as he continued his attempt to force a friction fire out of two pieces of bamboo.

He'd seen it done on a survival show—Alaina loved to watch them—and they'd made it look so damn easy. He gathered what he could for tinder from the tree line, and he'd found the driest pieces of wood that were available. For a solid two hours, he'd been pushing one piece over the other, false hope washing over him with every fleeting sign of smoke. Sweat beaded from his forehead and dripped down his nose to land on the bamboo. His hands callused and were starting to bleed. His overworked muscles shook around him, but he continued to push. He *had* to get a fire... for Alaina.

"I'm thirsty," Maria whined next to him. She'd done nothing to help throughout the process, but had opted instead to sit beside him to watch and complain.

"And these stupid mosquitoes!" She scratched her neck and arms. "¡Ay coño!" She smacked at the invisible creatures. "They are driving me crazy!"

He could feel the little bugs hovering around the wound on his head, but he couldn't stop to swat them away.

'Infection is the number one cause of death in a survival situation,' his mind cautioned him, venturing off to play a warning from a survival expert on one of the various documentaries. *'You need to wash and dress any open wounds before they can get infected.'*

He shook it off, pushing the bamboo as small teasing wisps of smoke began to waft from between them. He moved the wood faster, ignoring his trembling body's need to fall over.

"¡Oye! What's taking you so long?" Maria scoffed, swatting at the cloud of gnats around her face. "Dahveed would have had three fires burning by now! Maybe you're not doing it right."

'Shut up, shut up, shut up!' he thought to himself, setting his jaw and using the outrage to force the bamboo harder.

More smoke. It was growing thicker and more steady. He dared not stop now.

"I've never seen a fire made like this... Aren't you supposed to spin it?" she continued. "Wouldn't it be faster to spin it?"

Faster... faster... faster... Almost there...

SNAP.

The bamboo split in half in his hands. Quickly, he folded over what remained to search for an ember, blowing at the still smoking wood like he'd seen on tv. Almost instantly, the smoke dissipated to leave him blowing the sand around it up into his face.

"See!" Maria scolded. "I told you you weren't doing it right! But you don't listen!"

The fingers on both his hands curled tightly around the halves of bamboo still in them, and his muscles stiffened as he rose to glare at her.

"What?" She frowned at him. "Don't be looking at me all angry. It's not my fault you broke the stick."

He couldn't form words. Kneeling at the side of her, he squeezed the wood harder, trembling with the effort of keeping his cool.

In his mind, he'd launched the bamboo at her, delivered several choice words, then stormed off. He imagined the shocked look on her face as he left her there in the sand to deal with the fire herself.

But Chris wasn't the sort of man to explode at a woman. He took a deep breath and rose to his feet, dropping the shards of his attempt onto the sand and looking down at his sweaty, blood-soaked hands. With as much calm as he could muster, he managed, "Why don't you see if you can open one of the coconuts that are on the ground over there while I try again?"

She laughed loudly. "Mi amor, have you ever *tried* to open a coconut with just your hands? It is impossible."

"It's not impossible," he assured her.

He needed water. His throat was tight with thirst and his mouth felt like it was filled with cotton. He'd sweat out what little hydration was left in his body and he could feel himself weakening by the second.

Plucking a coconut up off the sand, he shook it near his ear and smiled as he heard the sound of liquid inside. He spent several minutes attempting to open it by banging it against a rock before he was forced to stop by the stars that filled his vision.

He shook his head and exhaled, closing his eyes to attempt to steady himself. "Check your pockets. See if there's anything useful in them."

"I don't have any pockets on this stupid uniform," she informed him as he dug into the pockets of his jeans.

He came up with his Illinois driver's license, a twenty-dollar bill, a shattered cell phone, and a quarter.

Growling, he tossed the contents to the sand near Maria's feet and surveyed his surroundings. "See if you can get the phone to turn on while I go search for water or something sharp to break that with."

Maria rose on one foot, careful not to put her weight on the bad ankle, and she teetered on the single leg, reaching for him. "I'll come with you."

"You should stay here," he instructed, purposely moving away from her grip. "I can move faster without you. Find some dry wood while I'm gone."

"I'm not staying here by myself!" She hopped toward him, latching onto his upper arm. "We don't know what else is on this island! I don't want to be alone."

He scanned the empty beach and the noiseless tree line. "Maria, I assure you, there's nothing and no one else here. This is barely even an island."

He gazed out through the trees behind them, seeing a hint of ocean on the other side. "I'm guessing it's a mile across at best. I won't be far. Stay here and rest."

"No," she insisted. "Kreese, I'm scared and I want to come with you."

He could feel his shoulders tensing. He'd been fortunate to have found Alaina for a wife. She was always so independent. At times, her independence made him feel like less of a man that he wasn't needed in more of a protector sort of role, but now, as Maria quivered at his arm with even the sound of the wind in the trees, he was grateful.

Groaning, he turned them into the trees, moving through the thick brush at a snail's pace with Maria affixed to his bicep.

Once under the canopy, he was glad Maria had chosen to come strictly for the little bit of hydration they could get along the way. The storm had left the leaves dripping with bits of residual rain water and he encouraged her to drink from the leaves as they passed. Each leaf could produce a minuscule sip, but it was more than they'd had, and his throat rejoiced with every drop.

Defeated after searching the full expanse of the island and finding no additional source of freshwater or sharp object, they headed back toward the beach.

"Look!" Maria said, releasing him to hop to one side and kneel at a puddle on the ground.

"Don't drink that!" He shouted as she lowered her face toward the edge.

"Why not?" She frowned up at him.

"Because it's contaminated. See those mosquitos? They lay eggs in there. You'll get sick. That needs to be boiled before we can drink it."

"Well, since *somebody* doesn't know how to make a fire," she rolled her eyes, "I don't really have much choice, do I? We'll die if we don't drink water soon. I can't be sitting here all day waiting for a fire."

"Maria," he shook his head, "if you drink that, you could get diarrhea and then you'd be even more dehydrated than you are now."

She inspected the puddle, tilting her head to one side. "It's only been a few hours since the rain. How sure are you this will make me sick?"

He ran his hands through his sweat-soaked hair, groaning. "Pretty sure. Everything I've ever learned about survival is that you don't drink stagnant water."

She scratched mindlessly at a bite on her calf as she considered it. "Will this water kill me?"

He sighed. "I don't know, but if it did make you sick and we couldn't get more water, then yes…"

"There is water in coconut, no?" She looked overhead at the palm trees that grew in abundance around them. "If we drink this, yes, we might get sick, but it would give us the strength to open coconuts… to build a fire. We can't do nothing like we are. I can barely stand up."

"I'm telling you Maria," he warned as she lowered her face down, "you're going to be sorry if you drink that!"

Ignoring him, she drank… and drank… and drank… relief washing over her body when she sat up and exhaled with an "ahhhh."

"It's so good, Kreese," she pressured. "You should have some. It tastes fine." She lowered herself again to take more.

'Don't even think about it,' he said to himself. *'You know better.'*

"Oh God," she moaned, slurping. "It's so damn good."

He moved toward her despite his best interests; his mouth desperate for the moisture the puddle offered. *'You know better, Chris!'*

He knelt down beside her as she hummed in ecstasy between each swallow. He knew he shouldn't…

"It doesn't taste funny at all?" he asked, knowing damn well that it didn't matter what it tasted like… this was a bad idea.

"No," she breathed. "It's delicious."

'Rescue will be here soon… it'll be alright… Rescue will probably be here before we even have the chance to get sick,' he told himself.

He knew the risks, every bit of warning signal firing in his mind at once, but he drank anyway and the water was delicious. His entire body came alive as he swallowed, the hairs on his arms and legs standing to attention.

They both hunched over the puddle, drinking until they were full. At last, they sat on their butts on each side of it. He waited for signs of poison. How long would it take? He needed to get back to work on the fire… for the sake of Alaina. They'd been away too long. What if rescue was on the way? What if Alaina was on her way?

"Okay." He extended his hand to Maria and hauled her up with him. "I'm going to start over with the fire and you are going to work on the coconuts. We're gonna be alright but I need your help."

She made a sarcastic sound. "Oye, how am I supposed to *work* on the coconuts? You couldn't even do it! It's impossible to open them without a knife."

He wrapped an arm around her for support as they limped toward the beach. "Did you see the rocks off to the side of where we came ashore?"

"Sí." She frowned up at him.

"Well, I think we could wedge a coconut down in them so it can't move, then drop a heavy rock onto it a few times. That should loosen it enough for us to peel it open. While you're doing that, I'll start over with the fire."

"I don't know if I should be hobbling around those rocks on one leg, Kreese. My ankle doesn't look so good."

He looked down then at her elevated foot, noticing its discoloration for the first time. It was still wedged inside her solitary shoe, turning shades of blue and swollen around the folds of the little black pump.

"Jesus Maria," he scolded. "You should've at least taken the shoe off!"

"I don't wanna touch it. It hurts too much!"

"I'm taking it off as soon as we get back. We need to wrap that."

"Don't talk to me like I'm a child!" she spat back. "Like you're any better? Your head is busted open, and you got bugs crawling around up there eating your brains!"

"I'll deal with it after I get a fire. I have to get a signal so the people on the raft can see us. My wife is with them and I need to know she's alright."

"How do you know your wife is on the raft?" She tilted her head to one side, raising an eyebrow.

"I saw her." He kept his eyes on the ground ahead as they reached the clearing leading to the beach. "Through the door of the bathroom. I was stuck, but I saw a man carrying her out when I pulled the door back."

"YOU!" She released him, stumbling backward as recognition washed over her face. "You're the man with the wife in first-class!"

He blinked at her.

"You're the reason I was out of my seat! You did this to me!" She motioned toward her swollen ankle.

He groaned, leaning his head all the way back on his shoulders. "How was I supposed to know we were about to crash?!" He could feel his patience with her dwindling. "I'm also the reason you're *off* the damn plane, remember?!"

She narrowed her eyes at him. "I would be on that stupid raft right now if I hadn't gotten up out of my seat to deal with you! I would've never gotten stuck!"

He remembered the gaping hole at the back of the plane, the pudgy child that was kicking his seat gone with it. "You came from the back of the plane! The back of the plane was GONE! You'd be dead!"

She quieted then, frowning to herself as though she were trying to remember.

And suddenly he was standing at his seat on the plane, staring down at the little plump boy with his legs pressed against the seat. Guilt washed over him and pulsed in his throat.

The last human interaction the kid had before his death was Chris glaring down at him... He remembered his little innocent face washed over with fear as he'd straightened. He'd scared him and that was the last experience the poor child had. What kind of man was he to be frightening children? Who had he become lately? He'd never been so cold in his life. When had he gotten so bitter? Why was he so angry at the world?

"Come and take this shoe off then." Maria's demanding voice forced him back to reality. She'd sat down in the sand and stuck her leg out in front of her as she scratched at her cheek. "And then we'll wrap your head so whatever brains you got don't fall out."

His hands were raw and every muscle in his body burned when he laid down on his back in the sand that night to surrender.

He'd spent the entire morning and evening attempting to make a fire. Twice, he'd been able to produce an ember only for the wind to put it out.

He'd scanned the water endlessly. There'd been no signs of the raft or rescue. Wherever Alaina was, she couldn't see him. Even if he got a fire started now, she wouldn't see it.

'Show me how a husband kisses his wife.'

He could hear her voice as clear as if she were lying beside him. He focused on the image of his wife, begging for sleep so he could meet her in his dreams, but Maria's movement nearby kept him awake as she swatted at the mosquitoes and scratched the bites they left behind. They bit him too but he was too exhausted to fight them.

Earlier, when they'd returned to the beach, he'd pulled her shoe off and wrapped her ankle in fabric torn from her blazer. In turn, she'd cleaned the wound on his head, dressing it with her scarf.

He hadn't spent a lot of time with the opposite sex outside of his wife, and it had felt strange to him to have another woman's hands on him in such a way.

He imagined it would've felt strange even outside of the circumstances. Alaina had never been one to play caretaker. As Maria had treated him, he'd laughed to himself, remembering a time when he'd smashed his thumb with a hammer and Alaina had blanched and nearly fainted at the sight.

His head properly cleaned, and the injury determined to be non-lethal—in their non-professional assessment—he'd gone straight back to work on the fire. Hours and hours, he'd pushed until his body could go on no longer.

He'd removed his shirt as he worked in the sweltering heat and could now feel the sting of a painful sunburn spread over his chest, arms, and shoulders, nagging him with every hint of movement against the torturous surface of coarse sand.

"Kreese?"

He cringed at the sound of his name on her lips. The upward cadence in her voice told him she was going to ask him, yet again, for something.

All day he'd had to stop and help her with the coconuts—which of course meant that *he* cracked all the coconuts—or escort her to the tree line to pee because she was scared, or help her move to the shade... then back to the sun... then back to the shade. Of all the people in all the world to be stuck with, how had he managed to be stranded with *this* woman?

"What?" He sighed.

"I'm scared," she whimpered. Her fingers curled around his forearm and she tugged, his skin boiling at the touch. "Put your arm over me?"

He jerked free of her. "No. I'm right here. Go to sleep."

"Kreese..." She whined pitifully. "Please. I'm scared."

"I'm not cuddling with you, Maria. I'm a married man." He rolled to face away from her, a motion that caused his entire sunburnt body to pulse. "Go to sleep."

"Ay Dios mío. I know you are married, estúpido. I'm not asking you to make passionate love to me, am I?" She pulled at his bicep and he winced. "I'm scared. Just put your arm over me. It's not going to hurt anybody and it'll make me feel safe."

He growled. "You're driving me crazy, do you know that?" He rolled to face her, regretfully draping an arm over her. "There. Happy? Now, go to sleep."

"Gracias," she said, rolling onto her side to curl her face into his chest.

Once again, he closed his eyes, conjuring Alaina's voice back to his mind.

'Show me how a husband kisses his wife...'

But Maria pushed the voice further away as she flinched her leg against the onslaught of mosquitos attacking them. Then she kicked... then flinched... then kicked again... and again.

"Maria!" He groaned. "For the love of GOD! Knock it off and go to sleep!"

"I can't help it! They won't stop biting me!"

"They're biting me too," he said through gritted teeth, "but you don't feel me writhing around like a lunatic, do you?!"

"Maybe you don't taste as good or something. They're eating me alive!" She uncurled an arm to spit and swat them away from her face, her legs spasming again. "Besides, you have pants on and I don't. They're getting all up in my chocho!"

He chuckled at that, despite his frustration with her. "Your what?"

"It's not funny! I can feel them crawling up my skirt!" She convulsed again.

"Just... try not to think about them," he advised, attempting to separate his lower body from hers. "They'll be doing that all night and if you keep squirming, neither of us is going to sleep for the second night in a row."

She sighed, curling her entire body uncomfortably against his.

He closed his eyes, taking a deep breath.

She twitched and tossed, turning opposite him, then back. He tightened his arm around her in an attempt to settle her and she shook with the effort of being still.

'Show me how a hus—

"I can't take this no more!" She shouted, rearing up and scratching frantically at every piece of her body. "Kreese, I can't live like this!!"

"What do you want me to do?" He sat up beside her, pressing his palms over his face to pull the skin of his cheeks down in aggravation. "I can't make them stop."

She scratched her hair, messing it wildly, then her face, arms, and calves. "I don't know! But I can't just lay here and not think about them!"

'I could just knock you out...' He thought, laughing to himself.

She stopped scratching and scanned the length of him; her face lighting up with an epiphany. "Give me your pants."

"My pants? Have you completely lost your mind?!"

"Do you want to go to sleep or not?! Give me your pants so they aren't eating my legs! You have underwear on under there, yes?"

"Yes, but—

"Yes, but nothing. They are biting me more than they are biting you." She held her palm out toward him. "Give me your pants and I will let you go to sleep."

Did he want to sleep or did he want to stand his ground? He didn't know Maria well, but he knew her well enough to understand there would be no sleeping if he didn't give her exactly what she asked for, and he was far too tired to go a second night without sleep.

"Fine, but I swear to God, Maria," he stood to unbutton his jeans, letting them fall to his ankles and step out of them, "if you so much as turn once you've got these on, I will pick you up and throw you in the ocean. Understood?" He held the jeans out to her.

She rose to balance on her good foot, one hand bracing his outstretched arm as she unzipped her skirt with the other. "Don't look."

He huffed and turned his head, gritting his teeth. *'Why me? Why her?!'*

"You know..." He could see her out of the corner of his eye attempting to balance as she slid her bad foot through the leg of his pants, then collapsed on her butt in the sand to slide the other in. "You are a very crabby man."

"And you are a very obnoxious woman," he retorted, careful not to look at her as she laid back in the sand to pull the pants up, catching just a glimpse of her figure before it disappeared to swim in his jeans. "You're welcome for the pants!"

He lowered himself back down onto the sand, suddenly chilly in only his boxer shorts.

"My hero." She laid down beside him, pulling his arm beneath her so she could curl into his side. "Much better."

"Goodnight, Maria," he grumbled, lowering his other arm over her.

"Goodnight, Kreese." She snuggled into his burning side.

Within minutes, he was asleep, dreaming of Alaina.

She was with him on the island... running toward him from the raft that now sat on the shore. Her beautiful, wonderful, perfect face was lit up in a smile and his eyes watered at the sight of her. He ran toward her, promising God he would never take another moment with her for granted, meeting her halfway between the ocean and where he once stood. She plunged herself into his arms and he squeezed her tightly to him.

"SHIT!"

"What?"

"¡Coño! Ah Shit!!"

Maria scuffled out of his arms. He blinked his eyes open to find her haphazardly running in the moonlight, ignoring the broken ankle as she beelined toward the ocean.

"What the hell is she doing now?" He griped to himself, sitting up and rolling his head from one side to the other. He made a move to call out to her when his stomach rumbled thunderously and he felt the vibration of illness rippling through his intestines.

"Oh, God…"

He leapt to his feet and ran in the opposite direction—toward the cover of the trees.

Moisture teased the back of his mouth… growing thicker…

"Oh God, oh God, oh God…"

He flung his boxers off without mind to being seen as he ran faster toward a large shrub at the edge of the tree line. Once safely behind it, he doubled over, his stomach in knots as the rancid water wreaked havoc on his insides, making its way out whichever direction it could.

In between waves of sickness, he shouted down toward the beach, "I FUCKING TOLD YOU!!!" Then he vomited miserably.

"It's not my fault you don't know how to make a fire, estúpido!" She called back, her voice barely audible.

He could hear her retching at the water and that gave him a little gratification despite the knots pulling and grinding his stomach.

'Good. Hope she's up all night with it. Maybe I'll get some peace and quiet tomorrow.'

He curled miserably over as he emptied himself to dry heave in the dirt.

There was more, he was sure, and he laid on his side, curling into a fetal position.

'This is as bad as it can get. You've shit on yourself… and now you're lying in it… like a fucking animal. It has to get better from here, right? It can't possibly get any worse. Rescue has to come find us… they can't be far away.'

He closed his eyes as his body trembled, praying he could fall asleep and wake feeling better. He pictured Alaina at the beach again… focusing on that image… willing his eyelids to grow heavy…

He was sure he slept for at least a few minutes before he woke to another round of sickness.

"Kreese?" Maria called up to him at the sound of his coughing. "Are you alive?"

"No," he shouted back, squeezing his eyes closed as he fought the acid still lingering in his throat. "Leave me alone."

"Kreese, I need to tell you something…"

He spat into the sand. "What?"

She paused. "I—"

"What, Maria?"

"Nothing. Nevermind." Her voice grew smaller and more timid.

"For the love of Christ, what do you want??"

"I…" She gagged loudly. "I think I ruined your pants."

Chapter Four

Chris

He felt a dull, scratchy object being pressed repeatedly against his forehead and squinted his eyes against the sunlight, saying up at the silhouette of a woman standing over him, her hair blowing gently with the morning breeze.

He raised one palm up to shade his eyes and found Maria, nose buried beneath her collared shirt as she poked him with a long stick.

"Kreese..." she whispered through the fabric, her dark eyes wide. "Are you alive?"

"Yes." He frowned, smacking the stick away and trying to get his bearings.

"That's good, because you stink like the dead. I thought for sure I would have to bury you."

Memory of the night before returning to him, he lowered his hand to cover his exposed self.

"Go back to the beach." He blushed, glancing down at his filthy, naked body. "I'll.." He cleared his throat. "I'll just go wash off..."

Her eyes slowly scanned the length of him.

"Maria!" He sat up, hugging his legs to protect himself from her judging eyes. "Go back to the beach!"

"Don't be such a baby about it." She rolled her eyes. "I've seen a naked man before." She giggled, wisely taking a step back before she added, "just never one covered in his own shit!"

Through gritted teeth, he hissed, "Go back to the BEACH!"

"I'm going, I'm going." She snickered, her eyes lingering a moment more before she turned to limp away. "I found something on the shore, by the way," she added over her shoulder. "A suitcase from the plane. Maybe you could find some pants in there."

She disappeared then.

"Jesus Christ," he muttered under his breath. He did stink. He could taste it on his tongue. The odor was strong enough to make him gag and spit to one side. He needed to wash off, and he needed to get back to work on the fire. He glanced down at his hands, both of them caked with dried blood from the broken calluses that coated his palms.

He rose to stand, covering himself as he peeked over the shrub. Maria was sitting on the sand, halfway down the beach with her back to him, inspecting the contents of a large suitcase.

"COVER YOUR EYES," he called down to her.

"Mi amor, there is no sense in hiding now. I have already seen ALL OF IT." She grinned back at him and winked. When he made no move to come out of hiding, she rolled her eyes and grabbed a shirt from the suitcase to drape over her face. "There. Happy?"

He tiptoed onto the sand, angling his bare bottom away from her as he kept both hands over his privates. Plucking up his boxers on the way, he watched her shyly while he side-stepped down to the water, splashing into it where he collapsed to scrub every inch of his skin.

"IS THERE SOAP IN THAT SUITCASE?!" He shouted up the beach to her.

"Sí." She waved a toiletry bag over her head. "Come and get it?!"

"THAT'S NOT FUNNY."

"No?" She raised on her foot, limping down to the water's edge. "How about now?" She held the toiletry bag out toward him so he would have to expose his body to retrieve it.

"Maria," he shook his head, "I'm really not in the mood for this."

"Fine," she huffed. "You're no fun. Catch." And she tossed the bag high in the air, forcing him to leap out of the water to catch it before it went over his head.

She grinned proudly and turned to hobble back.

Dressed in fresh underwear and khaki shorts that were one size too big, Chris wrapped his hands in a t-shirt and prepared to attempt a new fire. Beside him, Maria held a dress against her body as if she were shopping. "You think this would fit me?"

Not looking up from the tinder he was positioning in the crease of the split bamboo, he grunted. "Don't know. Don't care."

She clicked her tongue and stood, limping toward the trees. "I'm gonna try it on."

"Whatever."

He tested his grip on the edges of the bamboo, adjusting the fabric of the shirt to protect the calluses.

'You can do this Chris,' he assured himself, taking a deep breath in. *'You are a man and you are going to make fire today.'*

He balanced the second half of bamboo against his stomach as he knelt. Taking one last deep breath, he began, pulling and pushing the wood over the other, counting in his head to gradually increase his speed every thirty seconds.

Small signs of smoke began to appear around the edges, and he grew more determined. Up and down, up and down, and the smoke grew thicker. *'Keep going... keep going...'* he encouraged himself, excitement filling him as the heat radiating off the wood kissed his wrists.

He saw the ember's warm orange glow amid the plume of smoke dancing off the tinder and he folded over to blow gently until a flame erupted.

Tears in his eyes, he quickly and carefully lowered the tinder onto his pile of twigs, adding larger pieces and eventually thick branches once the flames grew stronger.

"AHAHAHAHA!!!" He rose and laughed deliriously as Maria came out of the trees. "FIRE!!!!" He raised both arms victoriously. "I MADE FIRE!!!"

"Took you long enough," she said smartly, dropping her uniform into the case.

He wanted to be angry with her remark, but was too ecstatic. He grinned at the growing blaze, shrugging her off. "I made this," He said to himself, his chest held higher for it.

"So what now, superman? We still don't have no water."

He turned to her, finally noticing her updated appearance.

She'd changed into a white and pink dress that clung to her body and flowed out at the waist to sit on her knees. Her breasts, he noticed—the only thing he *really* noticed,—looked as if they would spill out of the delicate neckline at any moment, the size of them seeming to make the tiny spaghetti straps strain with the effort of holding them in.

"¡Oye!" she scolded. "My eyes are up here. Don't be looking at me like that. Dahveed would kill you."

"Oh, believe me, I am certainly not looking at you like *that*. I was simply trying to figure out how long those straps can hold up. That dress is very obviously too small for you."

She gasped. "It is not! You're an asshole!"

He chuckled. "Stay here and don't let that go out. I'm gonna go get the rest of the water from that puddle to boil. Then I'll head down to the shore to see if I can catch us a fish."

She held the dress out at her thighs, inspecting her body. "You really think it's too small?"

He glanced at her breasts where they threatened to spill over the top. "Yep."

She growled. "Some gentleman you are!"

He grinned, collecting a piece of bamboo and hurrying off into the trees.

Beaming with pride, his smile remained affixed long afterward and, as he came up on the puddle, his cheeks burned for it. Kneeling at the edge, he submerged the bamboo to fill the topmost chamber with water. If only he had a knife, he could fill *all* the chambers... He sighed. It would have to do. He would come back and keep coming back with bamboo until the puddle was gone.

He spent the morning doing just that, becoming so focused on the task that he nearly forgot about his circumstance were it not for the periodic stabbing sensation at the back of his skull to remind him.

He was pushing a piece of bamboo down into the last of the water when he heard Maria shriek loudly. "KREESE!!!" She screamed. "COME QUICK!!"

He dropped the bamboo and bolted toward the beach, coming out of the trees and panting. "What is it? What happened? Is it the raft?"

"Crab!" She pointed to the ground where the largest crab he'd ever seen stood with its two massive pinchers pointed toward them.

"Jesus!" His eyes grew wide. "That's a coconut crab." He laughed, looking around them for a weapon. "I've read about them, but I never thought I'd actually see one! Look at all that meat!"

She cowered slowly away from it. "Look at its little evil eyes! El diablo!"

Chris lowered himself to pick through the stash of firewood, careful not to spook it. He came up with a long branch that was thin enough to break. Positioning it over his knee, he snapped the branch, smiling as the break produced the desired sharp edge he was hoping for.

He inched toward it. It truly was a massive creature. Dark red on top and white on the bottom, it was intimidatingly large and creepy. Looking like a hermit crab the size of a raccoon, he was just a little threatened by it. It danced with him for a moment before he mustered up the courage to stab his makeshift spear down into its body.

For the second time that day, Chris was filled with an overwhelming sense of masculinity. He raised the giant crab, its legs still moving slowly on the edge of his spear, and he grunted with his chest pushed outward. "I have made fire, and I have caught dinner!"

Maria raised one of her dark brows, "Very impressive superman, but you left out that you shit yourself today too."

As the sky turned shades of red, they sat together in front of the fire, the massive crab roasting over it and starting to whistle as the pressure expanded the meat inside.

"Why haven't they found us yet?" Maria asked, scratching her calf. "We're right here next to where the plane crashed. They should have found us by now. I don't understand what's taking so long!"

Chris stretched his legs out in front of him. "I don't know. Maybe we went off course? Stop scratching those. You're making it worse."

"We didn't go off course." She scratched her neck and arms roughly. "And don't tell me what to do. It itches."

"If you keep scratching, you'll have open sores that could get infected out here, and then I'll have to deal with you whining about that. Put a sweater and pants on."

"I don't whine," She scoffed, rummaging through the suitcase beside her. "Maybe I'm allergic to these mosquitoes or something. These bites itch more than normal ones." She smacked her palm hard on her forearm, attempting to kill one. "¡Los odio! Stupid little assholes!"

She shoved her legs into a pair of oversized sweatpants and laid back in the sand to pull them up under her dress. As she sat up, she looked out over the water in front of them. "We should hear the helicopters searching for us. Or see other airplanes. Or even the rescue boats far out to sea. Where the hell are they?"

She pulled a men's sweater over her head, her upper body swimming in it as the grey fabric formed fold after fold when she'd popped her hands through the sleeves. "They would have sent them within hours of the crash and they would've come here."

A thought occurred to him, and he wasn't sure if it made him happy or terrified. "What if rescue found the raft? What if they assumed they were the only survivors? Maybe they're not looking for us?"

"Your wife wouldn't keep looking for you?" She tilted her head to one side.

He shifted uncomfortably. "I don't know… she didn't see me. She probably thinks I'm dead."

"Dahveed would never stop looking for me, nor I him in that situation. I would have to see his dead body with my own eyes before I gave up on him. You don't think she would do this for you?"

The fire popped loudly, a steady steam escaping the crab as he pondered the question. Would Alaina assume he was dead and go on with her life? Would she be relieved that he was gone? He hadn't been what she'd wanted in a husband—he knew that—but would she grieve his death or celebrate her freedom from their crumbling marriage?

"Did you love your wife very much?" Maria asked, the question entirely too personal for his liking.

"Of course I *love* my wife very much! What kind of question is that?"

She curled her arms over herself, nestling into her sweater. "Easy superman. It's a simple question. Lots of men stop loving their wives after a while. I was just wondering, since you weren't sitting next to her, if you are one of them."

"No, I am not," he said pointedly.

"And did she love you very much?"

"I think so," he huffed. "Why are you asking such personal questions?"

"Just curious. Why do you say you *think* so and not you *know* so?"

He ran a hand over his face. "This isn't really the setting and I don't know you well enough to be talking about the inner workings of my marriage."

She smirked. "That's the best person to talk about your marriage with, estúpido! You don't know me and, after we are rescued, you will never see my beautiful face again. You can tell me anything and know it will never come back to you. What else are we going to talk about, eh? Maybe you want to talk about how I found you this morning with your little—"

"Alright!" He placed a hand up to silence her. "Jesus…"

How did this woman manage to get under his skin in such a way? "My wife and I were—*are* fine, we just had a rough couple of years."

"Why? What happened?" She lowered her legs to stretch them in front of her, leaning back on her hands.

Chris wasn't a *"sharer."* He never opened up about anything… ever. He was wandering into unfamiliar territory and it made him fidget. "We… ah…" He scratched at the back of his neck.

"Stop scratching, you'll make it worse," she mocked. "What happened that you had a *rough couple of years* with your wife?"

"She ah…" He frowned, surrendering to share what he'd never spoken out loud to this complete stranger. "She got pregnant a few years ago… She had this condition that made it almost impossible to get pregnant so, once she was, we were just so excited that we forgot the pregnancy didn't necessarily mean we would *have* a baby… especially with her condition."

He gazed into the fire, remembering it all. "The doctors all tried to warn us… but as she got closer and closer to the due date, it became harder not to be excited. We bought all the baby stuff… cleared out the guest bedroom to make a nursery… read all the books… They still kept warning us we could lose it… and I told myself I was prepared to handle that if it happened… but I wasn't."

He blew out a little shakily. "The baby came early, and it lived for a few days… There was no amount of warning that could've prepared us for what came after. They don't warn you about the anger you feel; the need to blame someone—*anyone* for the loss. And you would think no one could blame *her*, right? But *I* did. Instead of grieving the loss of my child, I grieved the loss of my wife and resented her for it. She was in pain but I just wanted her to bounce back... to be who she was before it happened... and my need for her to be normal drove her away. She couldn't even be in the same house with me. She left. When she came back, I resented her for leaving me when *I'd* lost my child, too. She was angry with me for being angry with her... And then there was just this strain between us that we never got the chance to fix."

Blinking free of his daze, he rose up to pull the crab from the fire and set it on the ground beside him to cool.

Maria pursed her lips. "You say your baby lived for a few days, yes? Why do you call the baby an *'it'* and not a *'he'* or a *'she?'*"

"It's easier not to think of her as a *her*... as a real human that was created from me..." His face flushed. "I don't know, it sounds stupid when I say it out loud."

She shook her head. "That's not stupid. It hurt you too, superman, and she left you. That's not fair. No matter what, you don't leave the person you're meant to love. Especially not then. Men can hurt just as much as women, and it is a woman's duty to stay beside him, even when she is hurting. She shouldn't have left you. You are right to be angry with her."

He shook his head. "I'm not angry with her. I haven't been angry with her in a long time."

"It's okay to be angry, Kreese. Who am I going to tell?"

"I'm not angry." His shoulders tensed. He was done with this conversation. He wasn't going to sit there and make Alaina out to be a monster. He'd already painted her in a terrible light and regretted it.

"Yes, you are." Maria nodded. "Otherwise, you wouldn't have opened up our first conversation about your wife with *'we had a rough couple of years.'*"

"I'm not angry at my wife, Maria." He held up a hand before she could retort. "Enough about me. What about *you* and your CIA boyfriend? Where's his army, huh? Did you love him very much? Did he love you very much?"

She tilted her head back in a dramatic laugh. "Mi amor, there are no words for the love I share with my Dahveed. He would kill anyone who stood in the way of me. And he would never walk away from me. Every day he reminds me how much he loves me… tells me how beautiful I am… kisses me like I am the only woman in the world whose lips can satisfy him. And believe me… they do *plenty* of satisfying. Every single day, to be exact. There would be no doubt in his mind of whether or not *I* love him."

"Sounds almost too good to be true," Chris noted, rolling his eyes. "How long have you been together?"

She smiled. "I met him when I was sixteen and we have been inseparable for the twelve years since that day."

He broke off one of the crab's legs, inspecting the contents to be sure the meat was fully cooked before handing it to her. "Twelve years and still not married?"

"Well," she stuttered. "He… it's… it's his job… they could use me against him. He chose to keep me a secret from them so I could be safe. He's always protecting me, my Dahveed. One day soon he will retire and we will be married."

Unconvinced of the actual existence of David, Chris pried further, breaking off his own section of leg. "What does David look like?"

She mindlessly pulled a piece of crabmeat from the leg and held it to her lips. "A lot like you… Muscular and tall with dark hair… but he's bigger, and he has darker skin. His hair is cut shorter than yours and he has brown eyes."

He shook his head and sighed, even more convinced David was a figment of her imagination. He pulled a long strip of crabmeat out of his own piece and took a bite. The meat melted like butter in his mouth and he held it there, savoring the warm, delicate flavor; the perfect blend of salty sea with a hint of sweetness.

"What does your wife look like?" Maria asked with her mouth full.

He smiled. "She's gorgeous. She has this long red hair that goes on for days. It's curly—which she hates—but the days when she doesn't straighten it are my favorites. It's just so perfect the way it lays around her face and spills down over her shoulders. And her face—my God. I could never see another woman without seeing something wrong with her face in comparison. Alaina's proportions are just... right. You know? Her eyes are both blue and green with hints of gold, spaced the perfect distance from each other and from her other features... and she's got this cute little button nose with freckles. And big full lips that most women spend a fortune in botox trying to create for themselves."

Maria's face lit up in recognition. "Oh, I think I saw her! She was in first class next to that handsome actor, yes?"

"Yes."

"Why were you sitting so far away from her? And why did you let her sit next to such a handsome man?"

He chuckled. "We missed our first flight and couldn't get seated together. And I'm just as handsome as he is!"

"Kreese," Maria bit off another chunk of meat, moving it to one side of her mouth. "You are a handsome man, for sure, but if *that* man were here with me, I would have stripped naked on the first night and done anything he asked of me."

"Oh?" Chris laughed out loud at that. "And what about your *undying love* for David?"

"That man," she swallowed, "would have me saying *'Dahveed who?'*"

He shook his head and cracked another leg from the crab while Maria pulled one pant leg up to her knee to resume her scratching. "Seriously, Maria, you have to stop scratching!"

"Look at this!" She shoved her calf directly in front of his face. "Look at these bites! I can't help the scratching. I'm being eaten!"

Her leg looked awful. It was a mess of small and large welts and they covered nearly every inch of skin. Her claw marks danced across several areas, leaving some of them to break and leave small streaks of red over the surrounding bumps. It resembled more of a rash than mosquito bites. "Oh my God. Maybe you *are* allergic. I've never seen bites do this to a person."

"See! I told you!" She returned her leg to its rightful position and slid the sweatpants down to the ankle. "I am in hell."

"The smoke from the fire should help." He frowned, trying to remember hearing anything about a natural deterrent for mosquitoes on the survival shows. "Are there any socks in the suitcase? Maybe you should put some on and tuck your pants into them? Sleep with the hood up and tied on that sweater?"

"Maybe." She sighed, looking over into the suitcase and plucking up a pair of tightly rolled socks. "Kreese?"

He'd shoved a large piece of crab meat into his mouth and his cheeks bulged out. "MMM?"

"If I were your wife… *if you were Dahveed I mean…*" She frowned as she stared into the fire. "You would come look for me, right?"

There was a hint of self-consciousness in her tone that made him momentarily feel sorry for her. He shrugged it off, grinning when he'd finished chewing. "Well… if you really satisfy him *every single day*, then yeah… I guess so."

She crawled over to him and nestled herself into his side, draping one of her arms over his chest.

Dumbfounded, he froze, holding both of his arms up and pausing mid-chew to frown down at her. "What are you doing?"

"I am sad and I want to go home." She squeezed him painfully harder than he'd imagined she could be capable of. "I need to be comforted, and you are the only person here. Hold me."

"Maria, come on, this is inappropriate." His arms hovered in the air and he glanced at the crab leg still in one of his hands, wanting a bite but not daring to move until she was detached.

"Comforting a sad woman is inappropriate?" she scoffed, curling her legs in to rest against his thigh. "We are not naked. Just hold on to me so I know I am not alone out here."

"Maria—

"It will keep me from scratching. Please?"

He rolled his eyes and lowered his arms, ignoring the awkwardness of her body against his as he bit into his crab. He'd never remembered anything tasting better. He closed his eyes and took another bite.

"Oh my God, Kreese," she groaned, her eyes closed tight. "Could you chew any louder?"

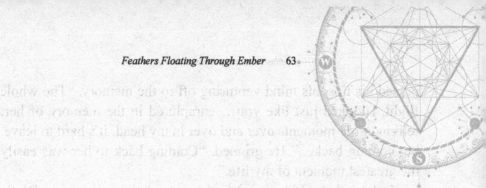

Chapter Five

Jack

There was something about Bud that made Jack Volmer less uneasy on the water. The man had a sense of wisdom about him that put Jack's mind at ease.

Two days into their journey, they were in the middle of nowhere on a raft surrounded by blue ocean and blue sky as far as the eye could see.

With only a compass and two paddles to head west against the wind, Bud's calm demeanor made Jack feel like they were somehow on the right path to finding Ua Pou. They *had* to find Ua Pou... for Alaina's sake.

Bud sat at the front of the raft, holding the compass in one hand and Zachary's journal in the other, while Jack sat in the back, facing him as he used both oars to paddle them in the direction Bud instructed. Navigating against the wind, they kept their makeshift sail down for the journey, hoping to use it on their return.

"It's hard to leave her for the first time." Bud smiled at him.

Jack blinked from his daze, wondering how long they'd gone on in complete silence.

"Alaina." Bud winked. "I see your mind going to her. It was the same for me with Bertie when I left for Travis air-force base all those years ago; not knowing if I'd ever make it back to her..." He pursed his lips, his mind venturing off to the memory. "The whole flight, I looked just like you... enraptured in the memory of her; reliving little moments over and over in my head. It's hard to leave, but coming back..." He grinned. "Coming back to her was easily the greatest moment of my life."

Jack smiled. "If I can make her even half as happy as Bertie was with you, I'll consider it a win. What was it like out there, anyway?" he asked, feeling ashamed that he'd never asked Bud about the war before that moment.

"Nam?" Bud raised his eyebrows. "Oh, well... I didn't experience it like most men did, you know. I was deployed in late 1970 and taken prisoner by April of 1971."

"You were a P.O.W.? You never mentioned that before."

Bud double checked the compass in his lap before returning his focus to him. "With so much life to make up for it, it's but a distant memory, hardly worth mentioning."

"What happened?"

Bud's eyes moved past him as he remembered. "Our platoon was heading through the jungle toward an L.Z. and we got off course. It's a tricky thing to navigate a foreign jungle in the middle of the night. Most of us were barely eighteen years old and, to say we were shaken up after three days of continuous combat, would be an understatement. We'd killed men, many of us, for the first time in our lives, and we'd just witnessed our brothers being slaughtered. We were terrified."

His fingers moved over the compass, drawing idle circles as Bud scanned the horizon. "By nightfall, no one knew who was alive and who was dead, and so we all focused strictly on getting to the L.Z. before morning. Thick mud and heavy rain made the trip slow going and multiple times we had to veer off course to avoid floodwater. Somehow, we ventured too far into enemy territory. It didn't take long for the bullets to start flying. Out of the twelve men making the journey, two of us survived the night to be taken prisoner."

Jack pulled the oars at a steady rhythm, listening intently. "Where'd you go? I've heard horror stories of P.O.W.'s getting tortured over there. Was it as bad as they say?"

Bud nodded. "They shipped us out to Hanoi and threw us into interrogation. We were taught in training to give the *'big four and nothing more,'* which is our name, birthdate, serial number and rank, so that's all I would give. Naively, we assumed we would be treated with civility under the Geneva Convention... but the United States never declared war in their eyes, so we were not protected. Instead, we were treated as criminals; tortured for hours in ropes and chains, starved, and thrown into solitary confinement for even looking at a soldier the wrong way."

He sighed. "But I can't complain. I had it much easier than a lot of the men who were locked up with me. Many of them had been imprisoned for years before I even arrived. They called our prison the *Hanoi Hilton* because it was such an improvement over their former camp. I can only imagine what they must've gone through. Most of the men in my cell spent those early years locked up in tiny brick rooms with no windows, no ventilation, and strict rules that kept them silent. They rarely bathed, and they were nearly starved to death. A few of them were tortured within an inch of their lives."

He shook his head. "I took my share of abuse, but I can't hold the P.O.W. title with any sense of entitlement—not after hearing about their experiences. Those men were the *real* prisoners of war. I only caught a glimpse in comparison. And after it was all over... Well, even with the torture, the P.O.W.s still had it better than the men stuck in the thick of the fighting... the ones who never made it home, or the ones who made it home missing limbs or half their faces, or so mentally drained that they went mad. I only saw combat for those three days before I was imprisoned and the images still haunt me... there were some men who saw nothing but. I can't imagine what that does to a person."

Jack met his eyes. "Jesus, Bud, I'm so sorry."

Bud waved it off, checking the compass and squinting over Jack's shoulder. "I had an amazing life to make up for those bad couple of years. I had Bertie, and I'd have done it a thousand times over just for ten extra minutes with her by my side."

He could relate to that. There was nothing he wouldn't go through, no amount of pain or torture he wouldn't withstand to be able to return to Alaina's side. He'd never been in love; had never understood the hype until he'd laid eyes on her. Everything before her now felt like a distant memory, as if he'd seen it in a movie but never actually experienced it... It seemed strange that anything could've meant enough to make him sad or angry or happy before he met her.

"Do you believe them?" Bud asked after several minutes of silence.

"Believe who?"

"Jim and Magna." Bud stared down at the journal, smoothing his fingers over the cursive. "Do you think there was more to it than just a storm?"

In the ten months that had passed since they'd crashed, he'd read the old journals over and over, pondering his own theories about the strange storm that struck both their plane and the old merchant ship back in 1928.

Jim was convinced they'd hit a Pacific Ocean version of the Bermuda Triangle, and Magna had all kinds of thoughts about Hawaiian legends and time travel.

Jack, however, was a realist and whatever theories his mind tried to create as a means to explain their circumstance, he was able to rationalize himself back into reality.

"Oh. Well..." He frowned. "I *can't* really believe them, can I? If any one of those theories were true, where would that put Alaina in her condition? Where would that put our baby? They could both die without a real hospital. Without a real doctor..." He cleared his throat. "Do *you* believe it was more than a storm?"

Bud nodded, looking out over the ocean and squinting his eyes, forcing the deep wrinkles around them to become that much more defined. "I don't mean to scare you, son, but I do. We should've seen ships... or an airplane. Should've seen *something* after all this time. I don't know what to believe, but I know something isn't quite right. I can feel it. A strangeness about the air. You don't feel it?"

He shook his head. Outside of Alaina, Jack hadn't noticed much of anything. Even while crashing, he was consumed by her.

Where the others remembered strange lightning and silence, he'd remembered Alaina's expression. She'd looked over at him with a uphoric gaze that made him instantly calm. He remembered, in a flash, something had struck her head and he'd watched the blood spill over her eyes in slow motion. He remembered reaching for her, and then it was all a blur. He didn't remember the actual crash, nor did he remember unfastening his seat belt, but he could still see his hands unfastening hers, could still feel her body in his arms as he carried her out.

"Bertie felt it too," Bud added, shielding his eyes from the sun to look just beyond Jack. "She had a sense about things…"

He checked the compass, glanced at the map, and then back out. "She wasn't the type of woman to stretch the truth, or express a feeling that didn't stem from something legitimate. If Bertie said she felt something, I believe it."

The afternoon sun was beating on his shoulders and his arms were getting tired, but he pushed on, as he'd done since they'd set out. "What did she think?" Jack asked, forcing the oars forward and back. "She never said anything about a strange feeling to me. I always assumed she was like me and didn't buy into it."

Bud smiled at him. "Bert wouldn't have said anything to you. She wouldn't want to cause you any more concern than you already have. I don't want to worry you now, but since we're headed away from a place we're familiar with, I think we ought to be prepared for any wonder of strange things when we come upon someplace less familiar."

Jack raised an eyebrow, rowing steadily. "Such as?"

Bud peered past his head again, closing the journal. "Such as those oddly shaped canoes coming toward us."

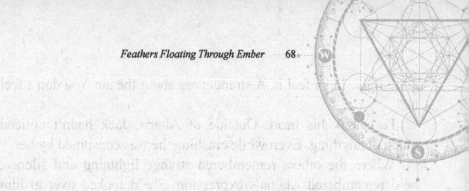

Chapter Six

Chris

Chris held a large rock over the water, waiting for signs of movement below its surface.

He counted the days. Every morning when his eyes popped open, his mind said the number as if to remind him of his forgotten existence. That morning was day sixty-two. Sixty-two days stranded, and in that time, rain and food were limited. They'd been unable to keep more than a few ounces of rainwater from each storm, and they both had lost a significant amount of weight.

His skin was in a constant state of burn, tight and dark against his dwindling muscles. Along with his mouth, his entire body felt dry and his weight, despite its diminishing, grew heavier on his bones with every passing day.

They'd built a small shelter at the edge of the trees; a lean-to out of bamboo and palm fronds that was just big enough to sleep the two of them. The raised platform and enclosed walls helped keep some of the sand flies off them, but even the smaller number of them tormented Maria's body. Her legs were covered in bites.

Two months on the tiny island with Maria had been a bigger challenge than the survival itself. There was nothing to do outside of attempting to catch fish, searching for another crab, cracking coconuts, or waiting for rescue. And wherever he was, she was right there beside him to nag, gripe, or insult everything he did.

She was wearing him down in ways he'd never experienced, and he didn't like the man he was becoming. His patience with her had dwindled to almost nothing and as a result, they were frequently at each other's throats. He screamed at her sometimes. He'd never screamed at a woman; had never been the type of man to even argue with a woman. But with Maria, argument was unavoidable. Words he'd never used to insult another human had poured from his lips, and where he should've regretted them instantly, he instead prided himself on having delivered them. She made him crazy, and he despised her most of the time.

Other times, in contrast, and particularly at night, he actually liked her. At night, the fighting would stop, and she would curl into his side in the shelter. Forced to cuddle for warmth, there was an intimacy in their touching bodies that softened them both. They talked about life and were decent to each other the minute the sun went down. As time dragged on with no signs of rescue, they had even become friends.

The forced proximity and friendly nighttime conversation married with the loneliness of being stranded together had created, in him, an unspoken—*and unwelcome*—attraction toward her. As much as he loathed the woman during the day, she radiated a seductiveness that lured his dreams to her at night.

Her curves, her hips... the way she moved them through the day as if she were purposely trying to provoke him... stranded and forgotten as they were; it was torture. He hated himself for it. He was ashamed of the thoughts that taunted him, ashamed of the way his eyes lingered on her... of the things... the desperate and urgent things he did to her in his dreams.

He wouldn't act upon it. He would never act upon it with Maria, of all people, but it was making him less of the man he was and more into a monster he couldn't recognize.

Sixty-two days stretched on like sixty-two years with nothing but Maria to keep him occupied. He was tired and longed desperately for the comfort of his own bed and his own wife lying next to him.

And if he wasn't thinking of Alaina, his mind was almost always on food. He was starving.

After several days limited to coconuts, Chris had remembered a trick he'd seen on television where a survival expert created a fish trap with small pieces of bamboo stuck in the sand inside calf-deep water.

The fish, lured by bait—which Chris had in the form of coconut and snails—would swim into the bamboo funnel and, for whatever reason, had a hard time navigating back out. If he could lure them in, he could smash them with a rock.

He spent an hour creating the little trap and stood patiently in the water, a large rock held out, waiting for the arrival of his dinner while the late afternoon sun beat down on his bare shoulders.

"This is not how to catch fish, Kreese," Maria informed him from the beach at his back.

He cringed. Even the way she would say his name made his blood boil.

"Are you really going to stand here all day?" she berated. "You can't catch nothing just standing there... except maybe a sun burn. This is stupid. If Dahveed was here, he would have caught the whole ocean by now!"

He could feel his muscles tensing, his entire body fighting the urge to spin around and launch the boulder at her instead, but he held the rock steady and focused his attention on the water, attempting to drown her out.

She groaned, sitting down on the rocks to comb her fingers through her hair. "None of the fish seem to care about your little trap, Kreese. Maybe they don't like coconut." She laughed.

"Maybe they're not coming because you never shut up," he hissed through gritted teeth, his arms beginning to shake beneath the weight of the rock.

"Or maybe they are all watching you thinking, *'look at this stupid man and his little rock!'*" She smirked, stretching her legs and leaning back to let the sun shine upon her face.

A shadow of movement in the water caught his eye, and his heartbeat quickened. As the fish swam into his trap, his arms tensed and his palms tightened around the rock, waiting for the right time to drop it. The fish inched cautiously toward the bait.

Maria huffed. "Dahveed would have made a spear… why don't you make a spear? I think a fish would swim away from a rock… You're just wasting energy."

He drowned her out and licked his lips as the fish closed in on the bait, pecking at the white fruit, completely unaware of its impending doom.

'1…2…3!'

He dropped the boulder and, amid the dying ripple, he saw the fish scurrying out of the way. Unable to find the path out, it circled back toward him. He leapt onto it in a frenzy of splashing water, grabbing it in his fist once—twice—then successfully locking it in his grasp on the third attempt.

He raised the fish out of the water, drenched from head to toe, and spun to face Maria, shaking it at her. "HA!! Look at that!!! Can *Dahveed* do that??!!!"

She hid a smile as she inspected his prize. "You call that a fish?" She made a gesture with her fingers to signify size. "Es tan chiquitito! Looks like a little baby minnow… Maybe you could use that as bait to catch a real fish!" She chuckled.

"AH HA HA HA!" He echoed her laugh dramatically, then looked back at the fish in his hand and grinned. "You're right… definitely too small for the both of us. The rock is still there if you want to catch your own." Smiling proudly at himself, he moved past her toward their camp.

"You wouldn't dare!" She limped after him. Her ankle had healed awkwardly in their time stuck on the island, and she walked with a slight limp.

"Oh, but I would!"

"Kreese!" She panted behind him as he purposely picked up speed. "I am only joking. It's a… a nice fish. It's a perfectly good size! Kreese!"

He spun around then and doubled back. "I'm not sharing my fish with you, Maria. I have given you everything. Food, water, shelter, even my own damn pants —which you ruined by the way, forcing me to wear these stupid looking shorts that barely stay up —and you have not had the decency to thank me even once! NOT ONCE!! You want to be a bitch to me? That's fine. You can find your own food tonight!"

Instead of the usual explosive reaction he'd come to know from her, she halted, her expression turning ice cold as her eyes narrowed into small dark slits. When she spoke, her voice was low and steady. "What did you just call me?"

He'd struck a nerve. *Finally.* She'd been dancing on his since they'd arrived. He smiled, tilting his head to one side. "A bitch, Maria. I called you a biiiiiiiiiiiiiiiiitch."

"Oh, you're a funny man now, huh?"

As ready as he was to go toe-to-toe with her again, his attention was pulled from her developing tantrum to the sky behind her head.

There were clouds,—giant white ones with peaks that pointed high over their rounded bottoms, stark bright against the endless blue canvas they spotted. Far off on the horizon, he saw a blur of grey connecting one of them to the water below it… rain.

"Rain!" He blurted, interrupting whatever insults she was delivering and pointing at the sky behind her.

Maria slowly turned to follow his gaze and shook her head. "We've seen this before and it missed us."

He could smell the hint of ozone now. It was coming.

"Not this time. That's going to hit us." He spun around and rushed to camp, depositing his fish near the shelter before hurrying to collect every piece of bamboo he had to position them in the sand for collection beneath a giant funnel of fat leaves.

Maria followed behind him. "You're going to get your hopes up again for nothing, superman. Do you remember the last time?"

He *did* remember the last time. There had been a massive storm on the horizon that day. Lightning skidded over the water and it had come so close he could hear its thunder. He'd run all over, just as he was doing now, to gather anything and everything to use for water collection, only to watch the storm veer away from them and dissipate over the ocean to the east.

He hadn't reacted well.

In truth, he'd thrown a full-on tantrum, kicking the shelter so it caved in on one side and breaking several large pieces of bamboo into small shards.

Maria hadn't tried to console him—she wasn't the type—instead she'd teased him for it.

"Some big man you are," she had said, "hitting things that can't hit you back!"

He felt a single cool drop of rain land on his eyelid and his heart raced in his throat. He shook with excitement. The water he so desperately needed was nearly there. Perhaps, he thought, if he were relieved of his thirst, the thirst for other things might also become subdued. Maybe he could start to resemble his true self if he could just drink something other than coconut water…

Another droplet bounced onto his arm, then another on his cheek, and he felt the coolness of one on the crown of his head. He tilted his head back in relief and opened his mouth just as the heavens poured their monsoon down upon him.

He let the downpour consume him, cementing his hair to his face and his clothes against his skin. He held his lips parted and his eyes tightly closed and let it fill his mouth as the static of its steady falling filled his ears and erased the world around him.

Maria was there. He could feel her arms wind tightly around his waist, and she shook with tears of joy.

"Kreese! We are saved!" she sobbed, clinging to him as she tilted her head back to take in the rainwater.

The exposed skin of his torso, already on high alert from the beads of water springing every hair to attention, became acutely aware of the thin fabric separating her upper body from his. He took a step back from her, but his eyes could not be pulled away so easily.

The white and pink flowered dress, now drenched and cemented against her body, left nothing to the imagination. For a single fleeting moment, he forgot about Alaina, forgot about the crash, forgot about survival altogether as his eyes scanned her slowly; as his eyes followed the thin fabric of her dress where it clung to outline her breasts, stomach, thighs and...

She cleared her throat. "¡Oye! You going to paint a picture of me later, pervertido? Close your mouth and—

She caught sight of something just past him, and her expression changed. "The fire! The fire!!" And she bolted toward camp.

Fists clenched at his sides, he turned, and his heart sank as he saw the billowing white plumes of smoke where his fire once sat. He sprinted toward it and could hear the hiss of distinguished flames where Maria knelt over the coals, searching for an ember still left alive.

He collapsed next to her. "No, no, NO!" He dug frantically through the ash, lowering his face to blow, praying to see a hint of orange glow. "Please, please, don't go out! Don't go out! Oh God, please!"

"You stupid man!" Maria scolded over the deafening downpour, bending down to blow on the coals and send wet ash into his eyes. "This whole time you're running around knowing a storm is coming and you never think to grab a piece of the fire and put it in the shelter?!"

He searched the ash, turning logs for signs of smoke, desperation filling his body and causing it to tremble.

Maria straightened, giving up on the fire to direct her anger at him. "How you gonna cook that little baby fish now? You stupid, stupid idiota! If you weren't so busy thinking with your d—

"SHUT UP!!" He rose to his knees, his fingers curling tightly into his palms. All of it boiled over then. The sexual tension, the thirst, the hunger, the guilt and the sheer direness of their predicament; it all rose to suddenly explode from him.

"SHUT UP, SHUT UP, SHUT UP!" He growled and stood to pace, letting the downpour drench him. "DON'T YOU EVER SHUT UP? EVER??! JESUS CHRIST, I CAN'T DEAL WITH YOU ANYMORE! You sit on the beach and spit orders and insults and you don't help. Why didn't *you* think to save the fire? While I was busy getting the bamboo so you would have something to drink, why didn't you *do* SOMETHING?! ANYTHING?! I'm so sick of your attitude. Sick of your mood swings. Sick of your stupid voice constantly in my ear!"

She stood up quickly to face him. "Oh? It's me with the mood swings, yeah? ¡Estúpido comemierda! Don't you dare accuse me of having mood swings when it is *your* mood that swings with the wind! You forget that I know who you are, Kreese. Who you really are! And you are not this perfect man you walk around here pretending to be. You walk around here with your chest puffed out like you're some big man. Like you're better than me! HA! But I know the real you. *I* know whose name you cry out for in your sleep and it is not your wife's!"

He reached for her then, the fingers of both his hands wound tightly around her upper arms and he shook her hard. He couldn't form the words he wanted to say. There weren't enough curse words to deliver the amount of venom he needed to cover his guilt, so he growled loudly and shook her again.

"You gonna hit me, big man? You're so tough to grab onto a woman. Go ahead and hit me. Do it. I dare you! Hit the biiiiiiiiitch!"

His chest heaved, and he held her there as he battled to get ahold of his anger.

"No? You scared to hit me then? You chicken shit man! Or maybe you don't want to hit me at all… Maybe you want to do something else to me, yeah? That's it, isn't it, superman?" she taunted him, lowering her voice as the rain poured over her face. "Tell me what it is you do to me in your sleep that makes you cry out my name instead of hers."

He trembled with the need to break something. He could feel his grip tightening and released her before that *something* became her. He spun away from her to punch the hard bamboo of the shelter's back wall.

"Oh, yes, go ahead and break the shelter again so we are forced to stay in this rain. Such a big strong man you are! *'Oh, Maria…'*" She teased, moaning mockingly as she followed him around to the front of the shelter. "That's how you do it in your sleep. *'Oh… Maria!'*"

He needed to get away from her. Never in his life had he laid his hands on a woman. He hated himself for having touched her at all and he could feel his anger getting away from him, pushing him to contemplate the unimaginable.

"*'Oh, Maria!'*" She continued, following at his heels as he hurried toward the trees, the wet sand sticking to his bare feet and ankles, slowing him in his attempt to retreat.

"Come on, Kreese. Show me what makes you say these things." She grabbed hold of his arm, launching herself to stand in front of him and block his path. "Don't run away now, big man. Not when you are so close to having all your dreams come true!"

She wouldn't relent, and she continued on her tirade despite the warning his shaking body should have given her. "Go on, put your hands on me. That's what you want! Why, though? Eh? Your perfect wife with the little perfect face and hair for days don't look at you like the big man you are? Is that it?"

She raised her eyebrows, placing her palm on the center of his chest to prevent him from moving past her. "Yes, that is it. I see it in your face. So you want to put your hands on a woman and show her how big and strong you are. You don't have any power over her, so you want to overpower me. Yes?"

The anger rose to form a knot in his throat. There was truth to her words, some bit of him exposed, and he didn't like it. He hadn't dreamt of Alaina in weeks… hadn't heard her voice at all. Instead, he'd been consumed by a sense of defeat and an attraction to this awful woman stuck beside him. "Let go of me."

"No." She narrowed her eyes. "I want you to show me who you really are."

"Take your hand off me," he insisted, his jaw clamped so tight that his teeth ached.

"No. You do not get to run away from this." She reached up, grasping his chin in her palm and pulling his face inches from her own so she could meet his eyes. "Look at me and understand these words, Kreese. *I* am not a woman to be abused by *any* man. I will not be beaten or grabbed or used to make you feel better about yourself."

The rain poured down on her, plastering her hair against her temples as she raised her voice louder. "I will not kiss your ass every time you do something out here. If you catch a fish, it is not for me to bow down at your feet just so you will share it with me. We are both stuck on this stupid island. It is our jobs to take care of each other, not keep track of who is doing more and shove it in the other's face."

She blinked the rain from her eyes, her chest heaving. "You and I are not the same, and so we fight. We will continue to fight because of who we are. Because of where we are… because fighting is all we have to do to pass the time. But today—*this*—this was not fighting. Today I saw darkness in you that I have seen in other men, and I cannot live with this. Not from you. Not from my superman. You will not touch me like this. You will not look at me like I am an object to be used at your will. Not ever again. This is not who you are, and I would live on this island by myself before I let you become that to me. I will not live here and be afraid of you. Do you understand?"

He swallowed the lump from his throat and nodded.

She released his face and crossed her arms over her chest. "Good. Now I need you to be a man and stop with this stupid tantrum you are throwing. Come build a new fire so we can eat your little fish."

For an hour, he attempted to salvage the fire before he gave up. Unsure if it would be safe to eat the fish raw, they took small bites throughout the night.

The rain would not relent, and neither of them slept for the leaking shelter. Every part of them, the shelter, and the island was soaked through by the time the morning came. Still, the rain persisted, keeping them trapped inside the shelter to shiver.

"Look at this!" Maria growled, breaking the hours of silence between them to shove her foot into his lap. "¡Lluvia maldita! The bottoms of my feet are falling off!" She spread her fingers wide and flipped her palms up, presenting them to him as well. "And my hands too!"

Her palms and the soles of her feet had pruned and turned white with the dampness. She retreated her hands to pull at a piece of skin. "I am falling apart!"

"Stop peeling it off," he said. "Leave it alone."

She proceeded to pull a large strip of thin skin off and held it between her fingers, snarling as if it were an alien life form. "I am decaying."

"Seriously, stop picking at it."

"Don't tell me to stop picking at it. You think I don't feel you picking your nose at night?"

He sighed, lying down on his back and folding his hands beneath his head, relieved to find her in playful spirits. "I don't pick my nose at night."

"No?" She scoffed, crawling in to lie on her back next to him, resting her head in the crook of his armpit. He noticed her skin was warm and wondered if she wasn't running a fever.

"What else would you be doing with your arm wiggling around all crazy up there? Poking your eye out?" She held both hands up over their heads, turning them slowly against the small bits of light shining through the cracks in the bamboo over their heads. "I know you are picking your nose. You don't have to lie about it."

He closed his eyes, ignoring her bored attempts to bicker.

"One time, you picked your nose for a whole hour on the beach when you thought I wasn't looking."

"I don't pick my nose, Maria."

"Yes, you do. And it was a whole hour. You know how I know this? I counted. I counted all the way to an hour thinking, '*Oh my God, no wonder he don't have any brains left!*'"

He smiled and shook his head. "I see what you're doing, and I'm not going to bite. I'm not in the mood to argue."

"Who's arguing? I'm just saying that you pick your nose..." She turned her hands over, then back. "*A lot.*"

He stood his ground, opting to stay silent. With his eyes closed, he could feel her peeling her hands; the constant jab of her elbow in his ribs, a dead giveaway. "Stop picking at it. You're going to make it worse."

She sighed, lowering her hands to rest them on her chest. "Tell me something, nose-picker."

He chuckled softly. "Tell you what?"

"I don't know. Something. *Anything.* Before I die of boredom."

"What would you like to know?"

"Tell me this," her tone turned more serious. "When was the last time your wife made love to you?"

And there it was. He'd been waiting all night for her to address it. She'd read him like an open book, calling out his innermost thoughts and feelings and exposing them for what they were. He wouldn't fight her if she wanted answers. There was no sense in it. She'd already seen him. More than anyone ever had, she'd seen right through him and she deserved an answer for the way he'd treated her... for the way he'd looked at her. "I can't even remember, it's been so long."

"Hmmf." She mumbled into his bicep, curling herself into his side to shiver. "So it was not the island or me or the fire that made you act like a crazy person."

He nodded, turning on his side to wrap an arm around her. "That doesn't make it alright." Her temperature was definitely rising. "I'm sorry," he whispered, meaning it. "I never should've put my hands on you. I think this place is turning me into a monster."

She snuggled closer, folding her arms up near her face. "I have known many monsters in my life, Kreese. You are not one of them."

He scratched the back of her head. "Someone hurt you before?"

She nodded against him. "Sí. Many times."

His heart stung. He'd seen her as an object himself, dreamt of her in ways he was ashamed of, and he could only imagine what a worse man might've done to her. "Do you want to talk about it?"

"No." She shivered more fiercely as the wind howled through the shelter's frame, her teeth chattering beneath him.

He squeezed her tighter. "I'm sorry, Maria. I'll never let myself get so angry again."

She sighed. "Why didn't you fix it with her? You love her. You should have done something."

He took a deep breath, quivering himself as the rain grew chillier on his skin. "I don't know... After the baby, and after she'd left me... I guess I just stopped seeing her as my seductive, sexy wife, and she became something else... Something changed between us after all that hurt. You know? I loved her still, with all my heart, but I can't explain it... I just couldn't touch her that way... couldn't view her as someone I needed to touch. And I let it go on because I was so sure whatever it was would go away on its own at some point. It had to... It was just the pain... and the pain would go away at some point and we'd be us again. I've never said that out loud, and it sounds stupid... Does that make any sense at all?"

"That sounds like an awful lot of words to say you weren't attracted to your wife anymore."

"No, no, it wasn't that." His cheeks flushed. "She's gorgeous, of course I was attracted to her."

"Kreese, you can *find* a woman attractive and still not be attracted to her. It's okay to say it out loud."

He frowned. Was that really it? Had his resentment for Alaina's leaving caused him to lose all attraction for her? Is that why he couldn't bring himself to touch her the way he knew he needed to?

"Say it and you will feel better."

He shook his head. "No, that's not entirely it. I *was* attracted to her... but I was attracted to the *old* her and I just wanted that person back. Before it all happened, she used to crawl into bed and whisper in my ear, *'Show me how a husband kisses his wife.'* And I keep hearing it now... over and over in my mind... I keep picturing her face hovering over mine with that smile every time she'd say it and I'd open my eyes."

He shivered against the rain dropping on his arms and squeezed Maria tighter, longing for Alaina to be in her place. "I can't even remember the last time she did that. I think, maybe deep down, I was waiting for those words… craving those words."

Maria's fevered body trembled harder. "How *does* a husband kiss his wife?"

He closed his eyes and could see Alaina the first time she'd said it. It was the night after their courthouse wedding and she stood in front of him in the little white dress she'd picked out at a thrift store, looking more stunning than he'd ever seen her with her hair pulled up in loose curls that had begun to come undone and tumble toward her shoulder. "However she wants to be kissed in that moment. Sometimes she just wanted something tender and sweet to remind her she was loved… other times, she wanted something else entirely… it was all in the eyes…"

"Hmmf." Maria shifted a little in his arms and grew quiet. After several minutes of silence, she tapped on his chest. "Do you want to hear my confession now?"

He rested his chin on her head. "*You* have a confession?"

"Sí. And like you, I've never told anyone. Do you want to hear it or not?"

"Sure."

She took a deep breath and pulled herself from him so he could just see the glossiness of her eyes in the bits of sunlight that shone through the rain. "There is no Dahveed."

He laughed. "I know that."

Her eyebrows shot upward. "I went too far with him to be believable, yes?"

"Just a tad." He smirked. "The CIA bit is a little hard to digest."

"I will give him a different job next time." She laid her head back against his chest and sighed. "When I was a child, everyone was always telling me how beautiful and perfect I was, and how lucky I was to be born so pretty. I thought it was a gift, you know… to be prettier than the other girls… but I was still a child when I learned it is a curse. The first time it happened…" She swallowed, mindlessly drawing a circle on his chest with one finger, "…it was my father's uncle. I was too little to understand what he was doing wasn't normal. I was too little to fight. Do you know what I am talking about?"

He tightened his arms around her small body, gently combing his palms over her hair. "Yes." He knew exactly what she was talking about, and as much as the woman drove him crazy, he cared about her. The thought of any man taking advantage of her, especially so young, enraged him.

She inhaled deeply. "We had moved from Cuba to Spain after my mother died so my father could go to school there. He wanted to get a degree and come to America. He said I would have a better life if he could just get us to America. So we moved to Barcelona to live with his uncle. He attended school through the day and worked late into the night to earn his keep, which left me alone with his uncle most of the time."

She flicked a bug from his shoulder. "My poor father had no idea the man was a monster. I didn't know either... I didn't understand what he was doing."

She sighed. "I never told my father, even once I did understand... It would've broken his heart. And the older I got, the more I understood just how many men there were like my uncle. I was always too little to fight a man, and there were many men who saw me as something that wouldn't fight back. So... one day I created Dahveed. I made him big and tough; a man who could lift five-hundred pounds and kill with his bare hands. A man to be afraid of. I thought, who would dare to hurt a woman that belonged to such a man?"

He shook his head and squeezed her tighter.

"And it worked." She combed her fingers over his exposed chest hair. "It worked too well. I have never known a man that would make me feel safer than Dahveed... until I met you."

He tensed. "Maria, I—

"Cállate, I don't mean it like that estúpido. I know that you love your wife and I want you to be with her. I am only telling you that you *are* a good man and not a monster. I knew you wouldn't hurt me. Deep down, I knew you would *never* hurt me. Even though you have thought it, you wouldn't do it. I have never known a man, other than my father, that I could be so certain of my safety with. And I am telling you thank you… for making me feel safe… for being my real life Dahveed. I am *finally* saying thank you… for everything. And that is all."

He didn't know what to say. He'd never imagined her thanking him for much of anything, and *this* gratitude rendered him speechless.

He hated the world for what it had done to her; the *'many men'* who had made her create an imaginary defender. Maria was difficult, obnoxious, and even mean on occasion, but it was the world that made her that way. It was abuse and evil men with thoughts like he'd had that day that made her cold and uncivil.

He'd wrongfully lusted after her, knowing he could never love her. But he cared about her, and he would never hurt her. For as long as she was a part of his life, he would do his best to make sure no one could hurt her again. "I'm sorry."

She turned then, bending her elbow to rest her cheek on her fist and hover over him. "Your wife. You said you saw her…" She glanced down at her finger where she scratched at a splinter of bamboo with her nail. "I've been thinking about that. It was so dark, Kreese. How do you know it was her you saw?"

"The boots."

"Boots?!" Maria looked at him incredulously. "You are so sure your wife is alive because you saw boots?! You know how many people wear boots in March?!"

"Not just any boots." He smiled. "Renaud boots. She had to have them and one year for Christmas, I went to twenty-two different stores in search of that one specific style in her size. Apparently, everyone wanted that particular boot that year. Since I'd seen them in every size but hers and was so dead set on buying that exact pair, there'd be no mistaking them for anything else."

She twisted her lips in thought. "If *everyone wanted that boot*, how do you know it wasn't someone else with the same boots?"

"In the couple of rows of first-class seats that were left?" He shook his head. "It was her. I *know* it was her."

"Hmmf." Maria laid back down, resting her very hot cheek against his arm. "I've never met a man who would go to twenty-two stores to buy a woman boots. You really love her, yeah?"

He smiled. "Yes. I really do."

She exhaled heavily and frowned. "Twenty-two stores... and she left you? No wonder you are angry with her."

"She had her reasons. We lost a child."

"SO? That's not a reason to leave a man who loves you so much. Unless you don't love him. Did she stop loving you?"

"No."

She shook her head, rolling on her back to inspect her hands again, poking at a piece of skin near her thumb. "I don't understand your life, Kreese. You love her, she loves you... She left you but came back to you... what's the problem then?"

He shrugged. "I don't know."

She peeled off another thin piece of skin, rolling it between her fingers. "Maybe you just make things too complicated. Life is over like that." She attempted to snap her pruned fingers and winced. "It's stupid to waste so much time complicating the good things so they become bad."

He smiled at the simplicity of her very profound explanation. They *had* spent far too much time overcomplicating their relationship. He'd wasted years being angry... letting himself stay angry and not doing anything about it even when he knew he should.

Maybe he *was* still angry.

All of a sudden, the rain stopped and bits of sunlight shone down through the crevices overhead, warming his arms in the small places it touched.

"Maria," he whispered. "It stopped raining."

"Oh, good." She yawned. "You can go start me a fire now. I might as well be warm and hungry." She grinned. "God knows you can't catch me a real fish!"

He chuckled. "Come on, smartass." He pulled her upward. "Let's get you in the sun to warm up."

He crawled awkwardly toward the opening, his hands and feet stinging where they, too, had become raw from the constant wetness, and he came out to squint his eyes against the blinding sunlight.

Feet planted on the damp sand, he extended his hand down to her. She grabbed hold, and he nearly jumped out of his skin when he heard a male voice shout behind him.

"You there! Sir! What on earth are you doing out here?"

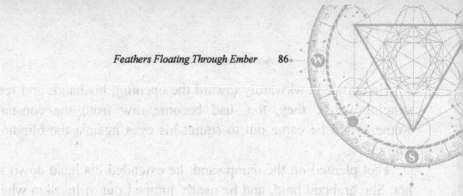

Chapter Seven

Chris

He turned toward the voice, dropping Maria's hand as he sprinted for the large group of uniformed men approaching from the beach. "OH THANK GOD, WE—"

"HALT!" The frontmost man shouted, stopping his approach to place a hand on his hip. "Stop, I say!"

"WE WERE ON THE PLANE!" Chris continued, ignoring the man's order and running full speed toward them, waving both arms over his head. "WE WERE IN THE CRASH! HAVE YOU FOUND THE OTHERS? ARE THEY WITH YOU?! ALAINA, IS SHE WITH YOU?!"

The man drew a long sword from his side, as did many of the surrounding men, the ringing of the sliding steel echoing in his ears. "COME NO FURTHER!"

Chris stopped suddenly, noticing for the first time the two massive wooden ships that sat far out in the water and the group of men paddling to shore from a smaller dinghy, all of them clad in brightly decorated navy breast coats with white breeches and cinematic quality tricorn hats.

'What... the hell...'

The man in front held his sword steady, the sun shining off the thick steel blade. "Your name, sir. And how have you come to be so far removed from civilization?"

Chris noticed a powdered wig beneath his hat, and an air of authority as the other men held out their weapons, glancing from Chris to him for guidance as to what to do next.

Chris blinked at the man and frowned. "I…" His eyes darted between the man speaking and the two who stood to each side, all of them observing him as if he were naked and growing hair from his eyeballs.

"I… Our…" He glanced back at the ships on the ocean, then to the group of men who remained near the smaller boat, and shook his head. "Our plane crashed. We've been stranded here for months… there are others. My wife is out on the water somewhere still."

"Your… plane?" The man sounded the word out as if he'd never heard it. "I'm afraid there must be some sort of language barrier, sir." He made no move to lower his weapon, a suspicious scowl remaining affixed to his face. "I don't recognize your accent. Pray, where are you from?"

Chris narrowed his eyes at him. "What is this?" He looked back toward the ships. "Is this some kind of joke? Do you have any idea what we've been through? This isn't funny!"

At his raised voice, the men steadied their weapons, a few of them moving closer.

"¡Oye!" He heard Maria shout from behind him, growing closer. "What the hell are you doing?! Why are you pointing guns at him? ¡Estúpidos hijos de puta! Put those down!"

As she reached his side, he extended his arm, stopping her before she could reach the group of men, half of which adjusted their weapons to point them in her direction. Slowly, he pulled her to stand behind him, widening his arms to keep her shielded.

The man in front lowered his sword a few inches and bowed his head. "Madam." He scanned her slowly, then Chris. "Forgive me, it seems I have forgotten my manners. Captain James Cook at your service. And you are?"

Maria, in her feverish state, pushed past Chris to straighten her back, stepping forward and ridiculously presenting her folded hand to the man. "Maria Amalia. Tell these idiotas to put their knives away!"

A man with dark hair that had been standing to one side of the captain removed his hat and diverted his eyes, leaning in to whisper to his superior. The captain eyed Maria, then whispered back, sending the man scurrying down the beach quickly.

"Why are you dressed like this?" Maria demanded, her head rotating from side to side as she took in the growing number of uniformed men filling the beach. "What is going on?"

The captain raised an eyebrow at her, tilting his head to one side. "I should ask the same of you madam."

They stood in awkward silence, inspecting each other until the man he'd sent off sprinted back to his side with a younger soldier at his heels. The captain kept his sword pointed at Chris.

"Is it she?" he asked, looking at Maria.

The young man removed his hat, revealing dark hair and brown eyes that scanned her face before growing wide. He bowed. "Aye Captain," the man said with his head still lowered. "I know with all my heart it is she."

When the man straightened, the captain removed his own hat, taking Maria's hand and bowing before it, the powdered wig sliding forward as he did so. "Your Grace!" He straightened and spun to face the men around him. "Lower your weapons! It is the duchess of Parma!" His eyes returned to her, humility washing over his pointed features. "Forgive me, madam! I had no idea!"

Maria tilted her chin upward. "It is nothing," she said snobbishly, removing her hand from his grip and standing straighter still.

Chris grew more impatient with the charade. "We really don't have time for this! We need to get help. There are at least ten other people lost out there!"

"Your Grace," the captain continued, dismissing Chris altogether as he moved closer. "What are you doing so far from Parma?"

She stepped back to Chris's side and folded her hands neatly in front of her, keeping her chin held high as she attempted *poorly* to play along. "What are *you* doing so far from Parma?"

Chris leaned in to whisper. "What are you doing?"

Not breaking her gaze with the captain, she hissed through her teeth, "Are you so stupid that you don't see something strange has happened to us? I am doing whatever I have to. I am not staying on this island for another second."

The captain swallowed, returning his hat to his head. "I have been commissioned to lead a scientific expedition on behalf of the Royal Society. This is no place for one such as yourself. I must assume you have been forced against your will. Are you in some sort of trouble?"

He raised his sword again, pointing it at Chris's throat and taking a step forward so Chris was forced to place both palms in the air. "Who is this man? What has he done?"

Maria raised her chin. "I am in trouble because I am trapped here with you silly men pointing your little knives at us. This man has done nothing. And how do you know *I* wasn't on a scientific expedition too?"

"A *duchess* on a scientific expedition?" Cook scoffed, keeping the pointed edge of his sword within inches of Chris's throat. "I've never heard of such a thing! Madam, I assure you, you are safe now. I must ask again, what are you doing out here? Has this man taken you captive? Who is he?"

"He is eh…" She frowned. "He saved my life."

Unable to contain his aggravation, Chris interrupted, rolling his eyes. "That's enough of all this! She is not a duchess and you are not… whoever you're pretending to be. We should be calling for help! I have to get to my wife!"

"Sir." The captain smiled warmly, lowering his sword into its sheath at his hip. The men around him lowered their weapons in response. "You needn't be afraid for the Duchess's safety. No harm shall come to Her Grace among my men. Parma is not an enemy to the crown and therefore you should not feel it incumbent upon yourself to conceal her true identity."

He looked back to Maria. "I have been bestowed by the Royal Society many fine jewels and silk gowns for my travels. We shall have you out of this garb and back to yourself straight away."

"Thank you." Maria looked all-too-pleased at the term *"fine jewels"* and beamed proudly up at Chris, whose eyes pleaded with her to stop.

Twisting her lips to one side, she turned back to the captain. "We did see the others on the ocean after the crash. We've been stuck here for two months and we are worried about them. They must be close by. Will you help us search for them?"

Captain Cook frowned. "Two months is a very long time to be on this ocean. Forgive my saying so, but they are very likely perished by now. I cannot deter from my course to search for the dead, madam. I can, however, offer you passage if you would be so kind as to travel with me. We are traveling first west and then back to the south and east. If your companions *are* alive, it would only be that they themselves came across another island or a local fisherman. Since it is my duty to map out the land on this voyage, we shall be stopping frequently and it will present you ample opportunity to inquire as to the whereabouts of your comrades should they have survived."

Maria leaned into Chris and whispered, "They might be crazy, but they could get us off this island. We can send help once we get somewhere."

A third dinghy was being pulled ashore and a new group of men noticed them as they set a strange tripod tool onto the sand.

Chris was uncomfortable. He didn't like the idea of traveling with this group of clearly delusional men. It seemed cruel that anyone would insist on role play finding them stranded in such a way—more than cruel, it was absurd! It was—He looked around him at the growing number of men in costume, three highly decorated ones walking up the sand toward them—eerie.

"I don't like this," he whispered back as Captain Cook turned to speak in hushed tones with the approaching men. He noticed they all stood a little differently—taller—and every one of them adorned an intricately detailed sword at their hips. The waist coats were finely sewn with brass buttons on each side. The costumes were exhaustively detailed and the ships too… thousands of feet of rope wove in and out of the massive masts atop real wooden planks; it all seemed surreal. The sails were rolled up for docking, but even deflated as they were, he could see the discoloration of wear on them. How long had they actually been sailing these old ships? He shook his head. "I don't like this at all."

The three men joined their circle and a man with short dark hair removed his hat. "Your Grace." He bowed to Maria. "Captain Tobias Furneaux."

This man had a darkness behind his smile that made Chris a little uncomfortable.

She once again extended her hand, looking outrageous in her oversized sweatshirt as she stood tall and allowed him to kiss it.

Chris didn't like the way he lingered over her hand; didn't like the way his eyes scanned her body as if he were attempting to see through the clothing to what was beneath.

The man straightened and eyed Chris dubiously with his nearly black eyes. "My men, First Lieutenant Joseph Shank, and Sergeant Albert Harris."

The two other men bowed their heads to Maria.

"You must be exhausted," Cook interjected, offering his arm to her. "I insist we get you settled into a cabin at once, your Grace. I will have my men prepare my own cabin for you. I shall send for a basin and the finest clothing onboard. Would you be so kind as to join me in the great cabin for supper this evening?"

She nodded, taking his offered arm.

He shifted his focus to Tobias. "Tobias, you must join us as well! Come! Let us get the duchess settled in on the Resolution and find suitable sleeping arrangements for her… man."

"His name is Chris," she stated matter-of-factly. "I would like him with me at all times." She glanced between the two captains, then helplessly back at Chris. "I cannot get on a ship full of strange men and feel safe if he is so far away from me."

"Of course!" Cook smiled at her and focused his attention on Chris. "You must sup with us as well, sir. Is he a guard then?"

Maria slowly nodded her head. "Yes, he is *my* guard. But I mean that I cannot sleep with him so far away from me."

Tobias frowned. "Surely you cannot expect him to share a cabin with one such as yourself? Your propriety will surely be in peril."

She unfolded her arm from Cook and stepped backward, crossing her arms over her chest. "I know this man and I know he will not harm me. I do not know your men." She nodded at the crowd of soldiers standing at the waters edge staring up at her. "Surely, there is something you can do?"

Cook scanned Chris who was all but seething as the conversation stretched on. "I'm afraid we are short on accommodations as it stands... But for you, your Grace, I can offer him the secretary's cabin. It shares a wall with yours so both your propriety and peace of mind may remain in-tact. I shall order it cleared straight away."

"Fine." She sighed, looping her arm back through his. "As my *guard* has mentioned, we have been trapped here for a long time. Tell me, Captain. What is the date?"

Cook smiled, leading her toward the shore. "It is the tenth day of June, my dear, 1773."

Aboard the ship, Chris sat down on the bed in his cabin—if you could call it a cabin. It was a tiny room, resembling more of a closet than a "cabin."

He had to duck if he stood and the bed was merely a cot along one wall, too short to support his full length so his feet would be forced to hang over the edge.

They'd placed a small table near the cot with a basin and pitcher. Beneath the cot was a metal pan that he could only assume, based on its pungent odor, was a bedpan.

The ship as a whole held the same foul stench and it had gagged him immediately upon entering the lower deck. He recognized it as a combination of sweat and human waste, and was reminded of a time he and his mother had visited her aunt in a nursing home. Everything in that nursing home stunk like piss and old feces. The ship had the same odor only it was amplified and thick; so thick it stung his nose so he was forced to breathe from his mouth.

The boat rocked on the water and made his stomach uneasy. Everything about the situation made him uneasy; the stench, the role-playing, the way the others looked at them; he was tempted to dive overboard and swim back to the safety of the island.

But Maria was here. She was here with all her sexual energy on a boat of at least a hundred men; all of them making their intentions known as their mouths opened and their heads turned when she'd boarded. He overheard several whispered obscenities and more than one had mentioned the bad luck of having a woman onboard.

He laid back on the cot with his legs bent over the edge to stare at the worn wooden beams over his head. What the hell was happening? Could it even be possible that they'd come out of the storm in a different time? There *was* that strange moment before impact... And it seemed odd that so many men would be role playing in such a dire circumstance.

But if they *had* somehow travelled back in time, what would that mean for Alaina? Was she on a ship somewhere too? How would he ever manage to find her if she'd been rescued already? Was she safe?

He remembered seeing her legs dangling lifeless from the man who carried her. Was she alive? If she'd made it to a ship, and if they were in a different time, would the men look at her the way these had looked at Maria? Without the luck of a duchess's name, would she be treated differently?

No... it was all too impossible. It was much more likely that this was all some kind of a sick game. Perhaps they were all part of a strange cult that worshipped and lived out the past?

On the other side of the wooden planks separating his cabin from hers, he could hear Maria's temper flaring.

"And what the hell am I supposed to do with this?" she spat. "Do you expect me to do this myself? Send me my guard right now."

"Your Grace? Do you think that is appropriate? A man?" A male voice argued, prompting Chris to roll his eyes for the millionth time.

"I didn't see any other women on this ship so I think it is *only* appropriate. I am certainly not having one of you do it! Send him to me and make sure he has a fresh change of clothes as well!"

Chris turned his head to glance at the pile of "clothes" they had brought for him. There was no way in hell he was putting any of them on.

"Sir," a man called from just outside his door. "Her Grace is calling for you. Sir?"

Blowing out, he rose from the bed, momentarily forgetting his circumstances and smacking his forehead on the overhead beams. "DAMMIT!"

He pressed one palm to his throbbing head as he pulled the door open to glare at the short fat man that stood on the other side. "I heard her."

He took the two creaking steps to her doorway where Cook and Tobias still stood. "Christopher." Cook nodded his head. "I'm afraid we have no maids on board to help her Grace dress. I know it is beneath your rank, but she is insisting you do it."

"Of course she is." Chris pushed through them into the large cabin, noticing its lush furnishings, oversized bed, tea and biscuits, and window overlooking the water.

"I've called for an early supper. The great cabin is just there." Cook pointed to a set of French doors on his left. "If there is nothing else you'll be needing, your Grace, we shall take our leave."

"I am fine. Go," she snapped.

At this, he warily closed the door and Chris listened to their voices as they disappeared down the hall.

"Kreese…" Maria's eyebrows shot upward and she lowered her voice to a whisper as she moved close to him. "Who are these men and why does everything smell like shit? I can't breathe because it stinks so bad! Do you think we are really in 1773?"

He shook his head. "No. I think these people are crazy and I'm not sure that we're any better off on this ship with these delusional men than we were stranded on that island."

"But look at these clothes!" She spun around to present an elaborate cream gown that hung near the window. "Look at this detail!" She ran her finger over the breast of the jacket where pink roses were finely embroidered. "It is too beautiful to be a costume... And this ship!"

She smoothed her palm along the engraved wood encasing the window. "It's real. A *real* wood ship this far out to sea? And so many men in costumes and speaking proper English? With all that they *know* we have been through after a plane crash... after being stranded for so long with no food and water?" She clicked her tongue. "One of them would think, *'no, this isn't funny for these people.'* Someone would have broke and called for help. Don't you think?"

"Who knows what crazy people would and wouldn't think?" He ran a hand over his face, noticing his reflection in the small vanity just beyond the dress. He looked beaten. Dark circles sat beneath his eyes and his beard had grown to nearly an inch. His hair was disheveled and his skin was a dark shade of red. Would Alaina even recognize him if he stood before her now?

Maria looked at him through the mirror. "You see now what I have had to live with these past few months, mountain man? You look like shit."

He half smiled at her reflection. He *did* look like shit. "Oh, and you look so much better, *Your Grace?!*" He sighed. "I don't know what they're after, but I don't want to play this twisted game with them."

"Mi amor..." She motioned to a small stool that sat at her vanity, pushing the sleeves of her sweatshirt up to her elbows as she opened the drawer to pull out a folded straight razor. "Come. Sit."

He followed her orders and she stood behind him to tilt his head back, combing her fingers through his hair. "I think this is not a game. All of this... it's too real to be a game. All of these men... It's too many for them all to be crazy. The details, the stink, all these antique things around you... I think maybe we are somewhere else... somewhere before. I don't know how, but I believe we are *really* here. And I think we should play along until we know more. Yes?"

He closed his eyes as she poured a small amount of water over his hair, catching it in the basin, then setting it in the floor to scratch his scalp. The smell of roses filled his nostrils to mask the stagnant odor of human filth that had affixed itself to his nose hairs.

"You're not serious. You can't really believe them," he whispered. "It's insane. These men are clearly insane and who knows what they'll do to us once we sail away from that shore. Maybe we should just swim back to the beach. As much as it sucks there, we'd know we're safe."

"And what about your wife? If we are really back in time like *I* believe we are, we will probably never see another ship again. We would be trapped forever, just the two of us. There would be no rescue. No one searching for us and no one searching for her. This is the only chance we're going to have to look for her. You would give this up and live forever on that stupid little island with no water, never knowing what happened to her?"

He huffed. "No."

"Well then..." She glanced scandalously around the room before she pulled her toiletry bag out from the pocket of her sweatshirt, producing a small travel sized canister of shaving cream. "Play along and be nice. For the sake of your wife, eh? Did they give you clothes too?"

He rolled his eyes as she filled her hand with cream. "I don't know that I would call them *clothes*."

She lathered the cream into his beard, focusing on her fingers as she moved over him. Wiping her hands on a towel she then placed on his chest, she grinned mischievously as she unfolded the straight razor. "You will wear them... After you help me figure out how to wear that!" She tilted her head in the direction of the dress hanging at the window before she brought the straight razor closer to his throat. "Maybe they are insane, but maybe not. Either way, we are off the island. We will have to play along until we figure it out."

He eyed the razor as she ran a fingertip over the blade's edge. "Have you ever used one of those?" he asked, swallowing. "That looks dangerously sharp."

"Have *you*?" She pointed it toward him.

"No."

"Well, shut up then. It's supposed to be sharp." She came around to the front of him, tilting his head back as she bent over him. "Now," she whispered, her face hovering a foot over his, "don't move."

As if she'd done it a thousand times before, she swept the razor over his cheek and jaw with such precision that he smiled in relief.

"So you *have* done this before." He raised an eyebrow.

"Sí." She rinsed and repositioned the razor. "I used to do this for my father."

He waited for her to remove the blade before speaking again. "Where is your father now? Is he still alive?"

"No." She gently pushed his chin upward to shave down the length of his jaw and throat. "He died last year. A heart attack."

"I'm sorry."

"You didn't kill him." She dipped the razor into the bowl at his side again, returning to slide it smoothly over the opposite cheek. "I wish he were here to tell us what to do... what to believe. He would have known. He always knew what to say and what to do. You would have loved him—everyone did. He is the only man *I* have ever truly loved."

Chris raised an eyebrow, catching the slightest hint of gold speckle in her brown eyes when she leaned closer to shave his upper lip.

She pulled the blade down gently, noticing the question that remained on his features and shrugging. "I have not been lucky enough in my life to meet someone worth loving. Thank God though…" She glanced around the room. "How would I ever get back to them now if I had?"

He rolled his eyes as she ran the blade over his chin. "We have not magically travelled through time, Maria."

"No?" She focused on her hands as she moved down his jaw. "What point is there in a bunch of grown men sailing the ocean in an old ship in costume? Do you think they sail from island to island searching for stranded people just to trick them?"

She scoffed. "And just how often do you think they would find someone? And what would they do once we reach civilization and find it is just as it was? If we have not magically travelled through time, what other reason could there be for this ship and these men?"

He held his breath as the razor moved down his throat. "What reason do serial killers have for the things they do? Or cult followers? Not everyone is so cut and dry. People do strange things all the time without a reason."

"I disagree." She rinsed the blade and set it aside, folding the towel in half to smooth it roughly over his face. "Serial killers kill because it excites them. Cult followers follow because they need to believe in something. This… there is no reasoning to it." She stepped back, admiring her work. "¡Oye! You don't look like a hairy ape anymore!"

He ran his palms over his smooth cheeks and checked his appearance in the mirror, looking up at her reflection when he'd finished his inspection of her work.

"Maria, I don't like this. It doesn't feel right. Taking away the fact that they're in costume and acting strangely, there are no other women, and the men on this ship… the way they look at you…"

"Sí, I know," she interrupted, turning to rummage through the stack of undergarments neatly piled to one side of the dress. "I always know. I have always felt the eyes on me. But what choice do I have? I cannot go back to the island, and I have you to keep me safe, no?"

She plucked a strange garment from the pile and held it in front of her. Two strips of patterned fabric were sewn onto a string of lace. She tilted her head to one side. "What do you think this is for?"

He rose from the stool to stand beside her. "What if it is a cult of serial killers then? What if they get some strange excitement out of making people believe in time travel just before they kill them?"

She held the garment out to him. "Well then we will find out soon enough, no? Would you rather we died on that little island?" She frowned at the fabric in her hands. "Seriously, what the hell is this?"

He took it in his hands and stretched the lace to hold it against his waist. "It's pockets."

"Am I supposed to wear *all* of this?" She pulled the corset top from the pile and held it against her breast. "I think I might suffocate, no?"

"You really want to go along with this?" He glanced back at the door. "We could steal one of those little boats and try to get away on our own."

She shrugged, inspecting a pair of stockings against the light from the window. "And what direction would we go? With no food and water? How far do you think we could make it before we would die? I know you are scared—

"I'm not scared," he corrected proudly.

"It's okay. I am scared too, but I don't think we have any other option than to go along with this. Now..." She looked back down to the pile. "What do I start with, you think?"

Giving in to her, he set his mind only on the task in front of him. For the better part of a half hour, they laid out the garments in various orders, creating a silhouette of a person on the bed as they puzzled over the lace and fabric until they had found a use for each item.

"I am supposed to do all this every day?" Maria huffed while Chris stood behind her threading the lace through her stays. "It will take an hour to get it all off! And you will have to do it day and night. I can't reach!"

"Are you sure you don't want to go back to the beach?"

She winced as he pulled the stays tight. "¡Ay Dios mío! Not so tight! My tetas are going to explode! How am I supposed to breathe in this stupid thing?"

"You wanted to play this part, *Your Grace*. I'm simply doing it like I've seen it done in movies. Okay, you're laced... next piece."

She moved stiffly to the pile and grabbed the stockings, sitting down on the bed and frowning as she attempted to bend to reach her foot. "Kreese..." she grunted. "I cannot bend... I cannot bend over! You're going to have to do this, too!"

"I told you to do the stockings first!" he reprimanded, kneeling down in front of her. "Why would a person even need these? Everything's going to cover them anyway!"

She slid her shift and slip up above her knee, fidgeting as he bunched the stocking. "Kreese... I, eh... How high up does this go?"

He raised his shoulders and held the stocking out so she could slide her foot into it, slowly working the thin fabric up over her knee with plenty more stocking left in his hand. "Higher than we thought..." He blushed, looking up at her.

"I will do it from there, gracias." She held the fabric of her slip pinned against the bed, preventing him from moving any further. "You can start the other one..."

His eyes went wide and he teetered backward. "Oh my God! You're not wearing anything under there, are you?"

"You really want me to add underwear to the twenty pieces of clothing I'm already putting on? No. And anyway... I couldn't wear it even if I wanted to. I haven't had underwear since that night... after we drank the water. There was no underwear in the stupid suitcase! Who doesn't pack underwear when they go on vacation?!"

He laughed, picking up the other stocking and gathering the fabric to present it to her other foot. "Gross."

"Do we really want to talk about who came out of that night more *gross*?"

He cleared his throat, pulling the stocking up her leg to her knee. She quickly adjusted both stockings and tied lace around each before she stood. "Okay... I think the pockets and the butt-pillow thing go on now."

He snorted at the word "butt-pillow" but it was the best descriptor they could come up with to describe the little padded ring that tied around her waist.

The dress laid out came with two petticoats, and he helped to lower each one over her head and tie them around her waist. They finished off with a long jacket which he pinned to her stays. She stood fully dressed before him and held her arms out. "Well? Do I look like a duchess then?"

He hid a smile. "I suppose. Although I don't think a duchess would wear her hair... *quite* like that."

She spun around to glance in the vanity mirror at the waves of tumbling dark brown hair that matted in spots. "I will braid it. You go get dressed. The captain mentioned pork and I am starving."

He began to turn when she grabbed his hand. "Kreese?"

Turning back toward her, he noticed her eyes had begun to water ever so slightly. "What if we can never go back? What if we are stuck in this time forever?"

He swallowed.

For the first time, as he stood staring at Maria in her elaborately detailed dress in front of the antique wooden backdrop of the cabin, he considered the possibility that they'd somehow travelled back through time. With no way of knowing how they'd arrived, there would be no way to get back.

Where could he take Alaina so she could be safe? And Maria... He wouldn't be able to abandon her, not here. Once they realized she wasn't the duchess, what kind of danger might she be in?

"I'll figure out a way to get us home."

He turned toward the door, frowning. *'I have to.'*

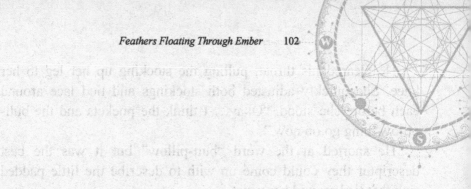

Chapter Eight

Chris

Inside his tiny cabin, it took Chris nearly an hour to dress himself. He'd banged his forehead, jabbed his elbows and stubbed his toes on several occasions as he struggled with the countless buttons, pins, and layers of his own formal attire.

All the while, his mind raced. He began to notice the finite details for himself, the intricate hand-carved trim around the doorframe, the detailed embroidery on his own clothing, the straw mattress and coarse bedding, all of it making a case for the theory of time travel.

'But time travel is impossible.'

Mounted on one wall was an old oil lamp, its brass still bright and shiny. On a small wooden table that was affixed to the wall just below it, there was a box labelled *"sulfur matches."*

'...but time travel is impossible,' he reminded himself, pulling at the cuffs of his shirt where they spilled out from his jacket sleeves. He could only imagine how absurd he must look. With no mirror to confirm, he shrugged and ducked out of his room to tap on Maria's door.

She pulled the door open, her hair braided and pinned up to make her long neck and cleavage that much more accentuated. Encircling her throat, she'd fastened a necklace; three rings of small pearl beads wound down to a large and bright ruby that hung at its center.

His mouth began to drop open when she burst into laughter. "¡Oye! Tan guapo!" she howled, dragging him into her cabin and closing the door, bent over as much as she could bend with uncontrollable hysteria. "You look so stupid!"

"Shut up," he growled, stepping to her vanity to check his appearance for himself. Catching his reflection, he hid his own laughter. Clad in fold after fold of white ruffles housed inside a turquoise-grey breast coat with matching breeches, and all lined with a gold leaf pattern, he indeed looked stupid. He gazed down at his white stockinged calves and silver-buckled shoes that were too small for his feet and sighed. "I hate myself for this."

Maria stood next to him, admiring herself in the same mirror. "¡Míranos! We are quite the pair, no?!" She burst into laughter again, laying her head against his shoulder. "What are we going to do if we have to look like this every day?!"

She grinned at his reflection in the mirror, reaching up to adjust the kerchief knotted at his throat. "Kreese... I think maybe you shouldn't say much at dinner." She dusted off his shoulder, straightening the edge of his jacket. "Let them talk and don't be moody. If they kill you, I will have no one."

He frowned. "I have to know what's going on. Where we are... Where we're going... Who these people are. You want me to just sit there and be silent all night and not ask questions?"

"Sí. It is what a guard would do, no? And you are all I have left in both of these worlds... If I lose you, I will have no one to protect me—no one to talk to who knows the things I know. I will die if you die. So just be quiet. Don't tell them who we are. Don't tell them where we are from. Play along and be my obedient guard. Just until we figure out what is happening and who we can trust, yes?"

A rap at the door made them both jump.

"Your Grace," a muffled voice called from the opposite side. "Supper is prepared."

"I am coming," she announced, glancing back at their reflections to whisper. "Promise me, superman. Promise you won't get yourself killed by saying stupid things."

He groaned. "But—"

"But nothing." She shook her head. "I will die if you die. And your wife will be lost forever. Promise me... promise *her* you'll be quiet."

His shoulders slumped in resignation, and he nodded. He would stay silent for Alaina's sake.

"Good!" She looped her arm through his and spun them toward the door.

Down the hall a few steps, Chris opened the set of French doors for Maria to grandiosely make her entrance into the candlelit room. The two captains, along with several other men, stood from their seats around the long wooden dinner table.

"Your Grace," Tobias bowed to her as a servant rushed to pull out a chair beside him, encouraging Maria to be seated. "I have heard tales of your beauty but I'm afraid the tales have fallen short. I am truly humbled to be in the presence of such fairness."

Captain Cook smiled warmly. "Your Grace, you have made the acquaintance of Captain Furneaux. Might I introduce Sir William Hodges, the ship's artist, Sir Johann Reinhold Forster and his son Georg, the ship's naturalists, my nephew, Isaac Smith, master's mate, and Lieutenant John Edgecumbe—he is in charge of the marines on our journey." The men surrounding him bowed their heads.

Tobias presented the men across the table from him. "And you've met First Lieutenant Joseph Shank, and Sergeant Albert Harris."

"Your Grace, it is an honor." Joseph bowed, a few strands of his dusty blonde hair sliding loose from its ribbon. "You truly are the most handsome woman I have ever seen. I was sorry to hear about your most unhappy marriage."

Chris made his way to the opposite end of the table and the lot of them sat collectively with Maria.

'Stay quiet... stay quiet.'

The servant appeared at Maria's side to pour wine into her glass, then moved silently around the table to pour a hefty amount into Chris's.

"Who told you my marriage was unhappy?" Maria raised an eyebrow, smiling flirtatiously as she raised her glass.

James Cook laughed. "Your Grace, there are few of us who have not heard tales of your beauty, valor, and unwillingness to marry the Duke of Parma!"

Chris could feel the frustration already welling in his stomach. He didn't buy it, but he couldn't put together a reason for such an elaborate hoax. Still, he listened carefully for any sign of a break in character that might expose them.

She sipped her wine. "I would love to hear these tales for myself! It's not every day you get to hear what the world has to say about you."

The French doors opened, cutting conversation short, and several servants spilled into the cabin with platters, circling the table to serve salt pork, peas, cabbage, sauerkraut, and bread.

Chris's mouth watered as he waited for the others to pick up their utensils. He was starving and the idea of eating something other than fish or coconut made his whole body chill in anticipation.

He followed the other men's lead in placing his napkin into his lap, but was sorely disappointed when not a single one of them picked up their silverware.

"I've never heard an ill word spoken, your Grace." Cook tipped his glass toward her as the servants exited. "The world is quite fascinated with your many accomplishments."

"If it is all good things, then now I *have* to know what they say! Come. We'll make a game out of it! Tell me the stories you have heard that you *think* are true and if they are not, you must…" she glanced around the room, "…finish off your wine!"

Chris admired her cleverness in that moment and took a sip of his own wine, noticing it was much stronger than any port he'd ever tasted. For as much as he appreciated the tactic, he also detested her timing, as he stared down at the glistening piece of pork that was begging him to eat it.

"*I* will play your game, your Grace." Isaac smiled across from him. Isaac and Georg were the youngest at the table, both looking to be in their very early twenties with full, youthful cheeks. Isaac had a sense of entitlement about him in the way he sat and held his drink that made Chris wonder if he'd been raised rich. He held his glass up and spoke loudly. "I heard a tale that the duchess of Parma holds many gala parties and she invites both noble and poor guests alike, making sure that all guests, no matter their place in society, are served the same meals."

Maria grinned at this and tipped her glass in his direction. "This is true."

Joseph Shank, who was seated on her left, sat straighter, his cheeks already beginning to redden from both the wine and from the evident blush being next to her inspired.

"I heard a tale that the duchess of Parma fell in love with Prince Charles of Zweibrücken, and despite her wishes to be married, was forced by her mother to marry Ferdinand of Parma instead!"

Maria squinted her eyes and twisted her lips to one side. "Yes. This is also true."

Chris's stomach growled loudly, and he glanced around the table to see if anyone had heard. Dammit, why was no one eating?

Tobias raised his glass. "I heard a tale that the duchess of Parma single-handedly freed Parma of Austrian and Spanish influence, severing all diplomatic ties so Parma could keep its independence."

She sipped her wine again and Chris noted her glass was already nearly empty. She would need to slow down, *especially* if she wasn't planning to take a bite anytime soon. "This is truth."

Next to him, Sergeant Harris, who had remained silent, lifted his glass and cleared his throat, raising his salt and pepper eyebrow dubiously. "I heard a tale that the duchess of Parma often sneaks out unaccompanied, disguised in male uniform to gamble on the officers' club."

Maria scoffed at this. "No. That does not sound like something I would do. Drink!"

As Harris tilted his glass to his lips, Chris gave up on waiting and picked up his fork and knife, noticing the fork consisted of two long prongs, resembling a skewer more than a fork. He dug the prongs into the meat, slicing a hefty chunk, and began to bring it to his watering lips when Tobias grinned in his direction.

"Christopher, surely, as her guard, you would know best! Have you ever caught her Grace dressed as a man to roam the streets unaccompanied?"

"No," Chris said flatly, forcing a smile and attempting to ignore the juicy pink meat that beckoned him where it hung on its skewer mere inches from his lips.

"Not even once?" Tobias poked, evidently flirting with Maria as he leaned closer to her to speak in Chris's direction.

"Not once," Chris said, his annoyance with the situation growing by the second.

"Because..." Chris set the skewer down on his plate as Tobias continued. "I, too, have heard this very tale. I shan't say I believe it, but nonetheless, I have heard it told by many men."

Maria finished off her wine and the servant who'd been lingering near the French doors quickly appeared to refill it for her.

"¡Oye!" she scolded Tobias playfully. "Stop listening to men who have nothing better to do than make up stupid stories about great women!"

"Here, here!" Cook agreed, raising his own wineglass. "A toast!"

Chris sighed and raised his wineglass alongside the others, the aroma of the pork driving his stomach mad.

"To the good fortune of the company and generosity of the Duchess of Parma! May her valor continue to be ever mighty, and may her long life be one of good health and good fortune! To the duchess!"

"To the duchess!" The entire table echoed, all taking a drink before finally settling down to pick up their own utensils.

Maria eyed the sauerkraut on her plate with a snarl as she pushed it away from her pork.

Tobias, next to her, leaned in. "Captain Cook insists on serving it nightly. I haven't the stomach for it either, my dear."

Cook straightened. "It's certainly not suited for royalty, but it keeps the crew from developing scurvy."

Tobias rolled his eyes, pushing the vegetable away from his own pork as he sliced into it.

Chris let the warm salty meat take over his tastebuds, holding it in his mouth to savor it. Mixed with the split pea concoction, it was gloriously comforting; like a taste of home he desperately needed. He was reminded of a meal Alaina's mother made with pork and black-eyed peas and wondered if he'd ever see any of them again.

Lieutenant John Edgecumbe, who was seated diagonally from him, cleared his throat. "Your... Grace..."

Chris's heartbeat quickened. This man knew. He could tell instantly by the tone. Would he expose them? What would happen if he did?

"Where were you headed before your shipwreck?"

"Oh... ah..." She fidgeted in her seat. "We were on our way to see... Tahiti."

"Tahiti?" The lieutenant frowned. "Surely you must mean Otaheite? But what would you know of Otaheite? So few have been there outside of the great Captain Cook." He smiled fondly in the captain's direction.

At that moment, Chris recognized the name. Captain James Cook had sailed the southern hemisphere, being one of the first to navigate the islands of the Pacific. He'd read about Cook once and how the man mapped the southern half of the world and discovered Hawaii.

He'd remembered seeing portraits of him and peered down the table to try to remember the paintings in his textbooks... The man who sat before him *did* seem familiar; his long rounded nose and quizzical brow, his hazel blue eyes and the way his lips seemed to hold a half smile even if he was scowling... it looked very much like the man he thought he'd remembered.

Assuming he was who he said he was, could Chris use his knowledge to gain Cook's trust, or, if he wasn't, could he use that knowledge to expose him?

As Maria fumbled for an answer, Chris muttered. "She has only heard the stories of it and wanted to see it for herself."

The entire table looked in his direction then, and he could feel his ears reddening as his nerves caught up. The statement had fallen from his lips, which meant he was officially playing their game. He couldn't back out now.

Slowly, he used what knowledge he had of Captain Cook to invent a story that might suffice. "There were two men leading the expedition on behalf of the duke. They were to explore the Southern Pacific for new lands, map them out and report back."

He held his chin higher, hoping the story would stick. "The duchess wanted to come along and with all the scandal and gossip surrounding the marriage, the duke was all too happy to send her away for a while."

Captain Cook frowned. "Why would the duke of Parma wish to have a map of the Pacific? What intention could he possibly have for it?"

Chris shrugged. "He wouldn't tell *me* that, sir. I was simply sent to watch over the duchess. I only know because I overheard the men talking about it before we shipped off. I can't say what he wanted it for."

"How peculiar." Cook pursed his lips, looking down at his plate and back up. "Did they create anything? Were any sketches salvaged from the wreckage?"

Chris saw an opportunity and took it.

"I'm not sure. When the ship wrecked, Her Grace and I were separated from the others. We saw several men on a raft, and my wife was with them. We couldn't get to them. They might have been able to salvage what they had. They were good men, sir. I'm sure they'd be more than happy to share their findings with any person who would offer them rescue. Assuming you can help us find them."

Cook considered it, peering at his food for a moment. "There are not many places outside the direction we are headed that they could've found themselves."

He sliced a piece of pork, holding it over his plate. "If they are alive, we will come upon them. Forgive my intrusion, Christopher, but what was your wife doing aboard the ship in the first place?"

"She is my maid," Maria interrupted. Smiling proudly at Chris as she took another sip of her wine.

Lieutenant Edgecumbe's attention remained on him. It was evident he was unconvinced as he narrowed his blue eyes and tilted his head to one side. "Tell me, is it common practice in Parma for a guard to marry a maid? Or speak on his duchess's behalf? Or dine at her table as though he were her equal? Forgive me sir, but your manner does not suit any guard I have ever come across."

Maria's eyes met Chris's as if to say, *'I told you to be quiet,'* and she set her wineglass down loudly. "And when was the last time that you visited Parma, sir?"

"I've not spent much time in Parma, but I daresay this man is no guard at all but merely masquerading as one. And my apologies, Your Grace, but I suspect you of colluding to keep his identity concealed yourself."

Chris could feel his heart beating in his ears. He should've stayed quiet. Even though Maria's story was falling apart, he should've remained silent and let it. Now he may have put them both in danger.

"And what if I am?" Maria smiled provocatively. "If I am hiding his identity, then I must have a reason. If I say he is a guard and you don't believe me, why should I care what *you* have to say about it? If I have told you something, then it is because that is all I am willing to tell. I have no reason to tell you anything else!"

Captain Cook laughed at that. "You give your opinion very decidedly, madam! Come, John, let us not spoil the night with unnecessary interrogation. The duchess and her *guard* are our guests on this ship and should be treated as such! Let us speak on more happy matters."

He turned toward Maria. "Your Grace, I myself visited Otaheite only recently on my first expedition. I've never come upon a more beautiful landscape and am delighted to be headed back in that direction. We are on course to stop there very soon."

As Cook exchanged pleasant stories of his first trip, Chris could feel John's gaze upon him. The candles burned low as the evening turned to night and conversation carried on. All the while, Chris remained silent, avoiding the stare of the man seated diagonal from him, and drinking more than he should've in order to avoid another misstep. His head was swimming by the time they all rose to say their goodnights.

"Your Grace," Cook bowed as Chris escorted Maria to the door. "It is my pleasure to have you as my guest on board. If there is anything you need and it is within my power to provide, do not hesitate to ask."

He pulled a lit oil lantern from its hook on the wall, handing it to Chris before he smiled at Maria. "I bid you both good night."

Chris leaned a little too heavily against her as he led her the few steps to her door and pulled it open.

"Kreese," she hiccuped, covering her mouth with both hands as she glanced toward the back cabin to see if anyone had heard. She lowered her voice to a whisper. "You'd better be sober enough to help me with this stupid dress. Come." She dragged him inside and pushed the door closed behind her.

She laid her head against the door, closing her eyes and taking a deep breath. "I told you not to say anything," she breathed. "Do you believe me now? That we have gone back in time?"

He set the lantern on the bedside table and swayed with the rocking ship, landing heavily on his butt on the straw mattress.

"Well," he extended his hand to her, "if we haven't, then we have stumbled upon a whole lot of James Cook fanatics."

She took his hand, and he pulled her to stand in front of him in the light so he could find and remove the pins from her jacket.

"You were right, I should've stayed quiet." He squinted his eyes as his palm smoothed over the jacket's folds and he pulled the first pin, then the second. "I know you said you don't remember the crash… but…" He blinked heavily to stop the room from spinning. "Think hard. Do you remember anything strange?"

"I told you. I was standing in the aisle, and then I was thrown to the front of the plane and I woke up trapped under that food cart." She twisted her lips to one side. "There was a bright flash of lightning… I remember that from right before… and I remember thinking something happened to the cabin pressure because I lost my hearing."

"How many pins did we put in here?" He leaned closer. "You would think clothes would be easier… not harder!"

She combed her fingers through his hair as he worked up both sides, slowly releasing the tiny needles until the jacket loosened. "I lost my hearing too," he huffed. "It doesn't make any sense. How could we end up—"

He hiccuped loudly.

"Mi amor," she slid the jacket off, resting both palms on his shoulders after it hit the floor, "you did not tell me you were a lightweight!"

He tried to keep his focus on his fingers and not the spinning room as he untied the first petticoat around her waist. "The lieutenant… he saw right through our story. Assuming we are somehow back in time, we should probably come up with a backstory… for when we're separated."

She slid one hand up his jaw to tilt his face up to her. "I don't think you will be able to remember it if we did, mi borracho. You are drunk."

He shook his face free of her grip, reaching both hands around her waist to untie the back strap of the petticoat. "Well, it's no wonder I'm drunk. What else was I going to do all night? You just kept talking, and I was stuck there wondering how the hell we were going to get John Edgecumbe off our scent… Wondering if they are all lunatics or if we really are back in time… And if we are, wondering how the hell we got here… How the hell a storm pulled us through time… wondering how we're ever gonna find Alaina… asking myself whether or not we could ever be able to go home… Wondering where I could take you both if I can't get us home… or what purpose I could serve in this time. How we would ever be able to live… what I might have to do if they find out you aren't the duchess before we can escape this ship."

"Oh," she grinned, stepping out of the first petticoat as his fingers returned to untie the second. "so drunk Kreese likes to feel sorry for himself, eh?"

"I'm not feeling sorry for myself," he said through gritted teeth, closing his eyes as her fingers returned to his hair. "I just…"

He could feel tears wanting to come as she scratched over his scalp and the lump in his throat grew heavier. "I just want to go home. I want to wake up. I want to hold my wife in my arms and have her tell me this was all a very bad dream."

"Is that what a good woman should do?" she whispered, leaning over him to smooth both palms over his crown. "Hold you like a child in her arms and rock you until you are done feeling sorry for yourself?"

As he reached back to untie the second knot, he rested his forehead against her midsection, folding his arms up to hold her, desperate for just a moment of comfort.

"Oye. Look at me." She grabbed a handful of his hair to pull his head back. "I am not her. Do not make the mistake of pretending I am. *I* will not rock you in my arms because you are not a child. You are a *man;* a man who makes fire and kills giant crabs with his bare hands; a man that fought the ocean and won. I need you to be a man and get us both out of this bad dream. Understand? Now stand up and unlace this top."

He nodded, clearing the lump from his throat.

She turned her back to him as he stood, presenting the intricate laces he'd weaved hours prior. "We've been through worse, mi amor. *Much* worse. We'll get through this just like we got through the crash and the storm and the stupid island. I will deal with the handsome lieutenant."

For a single fleeting instant, his heart stung at the word "handsome" on her lips. He shook his head free of the bizarre feeling and pulled the laces, attempting to keep his eyes focused on his fingers as he swayed with the ship. He leaned closer and lowered his voice. "Maria, what will I do if they sail us away from the safety of the island and turn on us?"

"You are superman." She sighed as the corset loosened. "You said you will figure it out, and so you will. You never gave up on the island, no matter how hard it got. If we were thirsty, you found water. If we were hungry, you caught us food. If we are in danger, you will find us safety. Do not give up on me now."

Chapter Nine

Jack

Jack stood and spun to face the several makeshift rafts and canoes that were rapidly approaching them. Standing atop them, he noticed the men were heavily tattooed and dressed in only a fabric dressing covering their groins. They wore elaborate headdresses with boned necklaces around their necks, and each of them had bright red feathers woven into their long dark hair.

They called out in what sounded like low grunts to each other as they grew nearer, holding their oars outward and upward.

Jack's heartbeat quickened. This was not the help he was anticipating. This looked more like danger. He looked from them to Bud, who he'd deferred leadership decisions to since leaving the island; insecure in his lack of experience after learning so much about Bud's. "I don't know about this. What do you think we should do?"

Bud tilted his head to one side and inspected them as they drew closer. "Nothing we *can* do but try to communicate as best we can with them… get a sense of where we are, who they are, and where we can find help. They had to come from somewhere… that means there's land nearby. Act natural and calm."

Jack nodded and watched in trepidation as the canoes pulled up alongside theirs. The men grunted and studied them, unabashed, as two of them boarded the raft to examine its architecture.

One of the large men seemed fascinated with Jack's size as he placed both hands on his shoulders and smiled, grunting to the other his approval.

"We're looking for help," Jack said slowly as the man pulled at his hair, hoping one of them might understand. "There are more of us on an island not far from here. Do you speak English?"

The man inspecting him was clueless as to what Jack was saying and continued with his survey, squeezing his bicep and grinning wider, continuing to express his approval to the other man.

The other man was rustling through their food stash, investigating the smoked grouper and inventory of coconuts. He spoke in quick, low tones to a heavily tattooed man still on one of the adjacent canoes. The man nodded in response and reached down to produce and present them with fresh mango and kiwi.

Hesitantly, Jack took the fruit, forcing a smile despite his raised anxiety. "Do any of you speak English?"

The man in the canoe grunted and said, "You, come." Then he motioned behind him to indicate the direction he wanted them to follow. "English." And he formed the outline of a man with his hands.

"There is someone there who speaks English?" Jack attempted to clarify.

The man made a noise deep in his throat, growing frustrated as he pointed at Jack and back to the horizon behind him. "You. Come," he reiterated. "English."

Something bizarre was definitely going on, Jack noted as the man who'd been prodding his bicep moved on to touch Bud's patchy beard.

Even the native tribes in these areas should've been more civilized than this. There hadn't been truly indigenous people in this area for hundreds of years. Surely, these men had been exposed to tourists over the years. They *had* to be familiar with more civilized culture.

He observed the man in the canoe, and was reminded of the journal and the *'demon'* Frankie had claimed to have encountered nearly a hundred years earlier. The man was covered nearly from head to toe in tattoos, giving him the appearance of being *'black as tar.'* Could it be possible that Frankie had run into the same tribe all those years ago?

The man in the canoe spoke to the men aboard their raft, sitting to take his oars and turn in the direction he'd insisted they follow. The tribesmen in the adjacent canoes took their places to follow as the smiling man sat down beside Bud and pointed, instructing them to paddle with the others.

The second man sat alongside Jack, picking up one of the oars and speaking in his native language as he motioned for Jack to pick up the other.

Reluctantly, Jack took the oar, and they rowed, following the leading canoe.

"What are your names?" Bud asked the man beside him, pointing to himself and saying, "Bud." He then pointed to Jack. "Jack."

The man beside him grinned, a seemingly common act for him, showing off his straight teeth that were only slightly discolored as he held his fist to his chest. "Ahomana."

The man next to Jack echoed the gesture, holding his fist to his chest. "Kaikoa."

It was hard to tell the two apart. Both Ahomana and Kaikoa were large men, their muscles well defined despite the tattoos that covered them, leaving only small bits of reddened brown skin to show between the intricate ink.

Both of them had long black hair and almost black eyes. Kaikoa had a slight streak of silver hair in the front and it was the only real differentiator between the two. Jack assumed they were brothers; they were too close in age to be father and son.

The man in the leading canoe was even larger, and his tattoos were slightly different. He held an air of authority over the others, despite looking younger, and seemed a bit more standoffish than the two smiling men aboard their raft. Jack pointed ahead at him. "And his name?"

Ahomana narrowed his eyes and shook his head, not understanding.

Jack put his fist on his chest. "Jack." He pointed out again to the man leading them. "Name?"

Ahomana's smile returned. "Tamatoa."

They paddled on then, Jack stiff with anxiety as Kaikoa and Ahomana spoke in their own language to one another, both of them looking from each other to him.

It was obvious they were impressed with his build and conversing about it as though he were on display for their amusement. The fact that they were so enamored with his physique made him that much more uncomfortable.

Bud was calm, as usual, and used a soothing voice as he spoke to Jack. "We are going north now."

He glanced at the compass, then looked out toward the sun, holding his fingers up against the horizon. "It's roughly 3p.m., we need to keep track of how long we travel north."

Jack nodded, glancing to his side at Kaikoa. "This doesn't seem normal, does it? For them to be so far removed from civilization?"

Bud looked at the two men and smiled. "Nothing about the past ten months has been normal. Why should this be any different?"

"Do you think they can understand us?" Jack eyed Ahomana suspiciously.

"Maybe," Bud said, keeping his voice even. "Maybe not. Might be best we just keep our heads down until we get to this English-speaking man and can get an understanding of who they are and where we are."

"And what they want with us," Jack added, shaking his head. "You don't think we could really be..." He cut himself off, rowing steadily as he contemplated the various theories they'd all tossed around. It was too far-fetched to assume they'd somehow been transported through time or space... Wasn't it?

"I do," Bud answered, not needing the rest of the question to understand its meaning. Jack respected Bud, and the idea that a man he thought so highly of, particularly for his level-headedness, could so easily believe in such a ludicrous theory made him second guess his own disbelief. "But it doesn't matter what we think," Bud continued. "The theories... we will know soon enough, won't we?"

They rowed for another hour, opting to remain silent, before the small black silhouette of land appeared on the horizon. As the surrounding men began to converse with excitement, Bud once again held his fingers up against the sun. He then turned toward the land, extending his arm all the way out in front of him with his thumb held up. He closed one eye, then opened it and closed the other.

"What's that you are doing?" Jack whispered, curious.

"Trying to get a gauge of distance to determine how fast we're going. If I can figure out how fast we're moving and we find rescue, I'll have an idea of how far we'll need to travel south before heading east. Once we're close enough to be able to guess how big the island is, I should have a rough estimate of how far we've traveled. Would you say we've maintained this speed the whole trip?"

Jack nodded. "I think so."

"Good." Bud repeated the process, closing one eye and then the other with his thumb still held out. "That island is about three miles away. It's almost 4:00 now. If we make it there in an hour and a half—which is my best guess at this speed, then we're traveling at two miles an hour... which would mean, to get back, we'd need to go south for four miles, then east for... almost sixty-five miles."

"You'll have to teach me how you do that." Jack smiled, cautiously removing the smile when Kaikoa looked over at him.

"Don't seem so put off by them," Bud offered. "They are just people, after all. Even though they look different, they're made of all the same stuff we are. We just need to find a way to communicate. It'll be alright."

"Not all people are made of the same stuff... *mentally,*" Jack said. "What about your captors in Vietnam? The ones who tortured you... *they* were not like us."

Bud shrugged. "A man cannot be blamed for the circumstances he is presented with. The Vietnamese viewed us as intruders and did what they felt they had to do to protect themselves... just as we would have done in the same situation."

"You really think *we* could torture someone?"

Bud lifted an eyebrow. "Have you forgotten Phil?"

He smiled and shook his head. "A man is capable of all sorts of things when he perceives a threat. These men are no different. If they see us as a threat, we may be in trouble, but if we treat them as friends... we should be welcomed."

They paddled on, and as they grew closer and the island grew larger, they found several lush green peaks towering high into the clouds, similar to their own single summit, seated in the center of a larger island, several miles wide.

They'd gone northwest... this wasn't Ua Pau, perhaps it was Nuku Hiva? Or perhaps they weren't anywhere near the Marquesas, but rather, they were actually somewhere closer to Hawaii. Jack wished he knew more about the Pacific islands to be able to identify them.

As they came into the shore, native people crowded its beach, loud high-pitched notes of welcome being chanted. The group on the shore all held a similar look to the men on the boats; tattooed with minimal coverings and feathers. The women were topless, with dark skin and black hair. They, too, were covered in black ink and bright red feathers.

Maybe, Jack thought, as the two men hopped off their raft to tow it into the beach, they *had* entered some kind of parallel universe. The island was much too large to have gone unsettled for this long.

The men along the shoreline rushed the canoes and pulled Jack and Bud into the knee-deep water, all of them smiling in greeting as they inspected their guests; prodding at Jack's chest and squeezing his bicep similar to the way Ahomana had done.

They spoke in their native tongue as they crowded around him, all of them poking, pulling, or squeezing him.

"English?" he asked, praying one of them would be able to understand. "There's someone here who speaks English?"

"English," a very large man beside him repeated, wrapping a heavy arm around his shoulders and guiding him onto the shore.

The man presented a young naked woman to him, who immediately laid both her hands on his chest and smiled up at him.

"You speak English?" he asked her as she smoothed her hands upward and out over his bare shoulders.

She responded only in her native language, evidently clueless, as two more women joined her to grope at him while a new wave of men formed a circle around them.

"I'm sorry," he fidgeted nervously, trying to remain neutral as he shrugged off their advances. "I really need to find someone who speaks English. We need help." He searched around the unfamiliar tattooed faces that surrounded him for signs of Bud. "Bud? BUD?"

"I'm here." Bud laughed from the other side of the wall of bodies. "Stay calm. We're alright. Remember, we are friends. They are simply greeting us. Let them."

One of the women slid her hands down over his jeans and he flinched, turning his body away from her as another woman cupped his face between her hands and grinned.

"English?" he repeated, raising his voice a little as another woman tugged at his hair.

A thick voice rang through the group, and Jack recognized it as Tamatoa pushing his way through them. "English." He nodded and grabbed Jack by the forearm. "You. Come." He turned and pulled him behind him, setting off on a path that led into the thick brush toward the center of the island.

They walked for nearly a half mile through thick rolling jungle. All the while, the group of men and women surrounded him, speaking excitedly as they took every opportunity to touch him.

They came to a clearing in the forest where a large community of bamboo huts sat. Smoke rolled from several small fires on the breeze and brought the scent of meat to his nostrils.

"Here." Tamatoa tugged Jack to stand in front of a short muscular man, his tattoos faded on his wrinkled dark skin. "English."

The old man grinned and whistled loudly. He turned to shout instruction to a group of men that stood around a nearby fire. The group obeyed whatever order was given and disappeared into the woods.

The old man turned back and nodded as he slowly scanned the length of Jack, expressing his approval with Tamatoa as they waited for the other men to return.

It didn't take long for two large men to appear with a stout man in tow between them. The man was covered in dirt and dried blood, his clothing ripped and dirtied to a point of being indistinguishable as any one style of cloth. He walked with a limp and his hands were tied in front of him. The rope at his hands was attached to the man in front. From where Jack stood, it was evident the man was white only by the bits of pink on his fingers where the mud had caked and crumbled off.

As they drew closer, the man kept his head down while he stumbled barefoot across the sandy dirt to where they stood.

"English," Tamatoa instructed, pushing the man hard toward Jack.

"You speak English?" Jack asked, thoroughly concerned with the man's treatment and ever the more cautious of the group around them. He noticed that the man was missing two fingers where his hands were tied in front of him and there was blood on the rope that was too red to be from an old wound.

What had happened to this man? Why were they treating him this way? Would they suffer the same fate?

The man nodded but didn't look up.

"Where are we? Who are they? We need to call for help. Do they have a way to get in touch with an American Embassy nearby? What happened to you? Why are you tied up like this?"

The man shook his head and took a deep breath. "Jack," the man said, his voice cracking as he choked on the words. Slowly he rose his chin from his chest and the familiar blue eyes of Phil Ramsey met his, causing him to stumble backward a step.

"You're going to die here," Phil said, looking warily between Jack and Bud with the one eye that wasn't swollen closed, "unless you do exactly as I say."

He then looked up at the old man and nodded. "Yes. It is him."

Chapter Ten

Chris

It'd been a little over two weeks since they'd boarded the Resolution. From the stern of the ship, Chris had watched in trepidation as their little island disappeared over the horizon.

Every day since, he'd woken with a sense of doom, wondering if that was the day the ship's inhabitants would turn on them. Every night, he and Maria would dine with Captain Cook, Isaac, Johann and Georg Forster, William Hodges, and the ever-suspicious Lieutenant Edgecumbe.

It was exhausting to see so many unfamiliar faces and to have to remember, not only their names but also all their unfamiliar customs and formalities; the bowing, the posture, the right and wrong times to speak during dinner, and, most confusing, who he should and should not speak to onboard according to his stature.

Aboard the Resolution were ninety seamen and eighteen royal marines. All of them seemed suspicious of him and overly interested in Maria, but, always being next to Maria, he was unable to go out of his way to seek answers among the men since most of them were "below her title."

Even if he could easily approach the men on board, he wouldn't have the time. Captain Cook had given Maria every elegant gown onboard and Chris had painstakingly spent a half hour every morning getting her dressed in a casual gown, then another hour to undress her and re-dress her in formal dinner attire.

He, too, had been provided with more casual clothing for daytime sailing, but was always forced to change into one of three formal outfits for dinner. He spent more time getting them both dressed than he did anything else.

While he remained unconvinced about their circumstance, every day that passed made it less and less conceivable that these men were faking.

Despite the tension between them, and their suspicion of each other, he'd grown to like Captain Cook and Johann Forster.

James Cook had a positive and welcoming enthusiasm about him that made it hard not to desire his friendship. Johann was incredibly smart and beyond titles and ranks. He spoke to whomever he wished and addressed everyone as his equal. He had a pleasant and down-to-earth demeanor that was a breath of fresh air among so many stiff and official men. As time went on, Chris found himself "playing along" more often than he questioned his surroundings, almost accepting his newly found circumstance as reality. *Almost*.

That afternoon, he stood on the bow of the Resolution, glancing back to the accompanying ship, The Adventure, as the salty breeze cooled his warm skin. Beneath the layers of his clothing, he'd worked up a sweat and enjoyed the moments above deck to lavish in the fresh air. The ship was otherwise stagnant and muggy; the stench of sweat being no wonder to him now that he'd been layered in the thick fabrics they offered. His only saving grace was a stick of deodorant that he and Maria secretly shared, and even with it, he could smell his own sweat.

Rumors of an outbreak of scurvy aboard the Adventure had begun to circulate and he wondered how much additional stench might be added with a sick crew. With every passing day, Captain Cook was increasingly concerned for the well-being of Captain Furneaux and more anxious to arrive in Tahiti to seek out the fruit and water that were required to get their malnourished bodies well again.

Something just beyond the sails of the Adventure caught his eye and pulled him from his thoughts… something dark against the blue horizon… smoke.

"SMOKE!" he shouted out to the men around him, pointing. "We have to go there! It could be my wife! It could be the others!" His heart began to race with excitement. "We have to tell the captain!"

A nearby seaman with matted hair and black teeth peered out at the water. "Och, nay. We can't go there, lad! Those are the devil's lands! No man will sail near them and come out wi' his head." He chuckled.

"But my wife…"

The man shook his head, spitting to one side. "If your wife landed there my boy, she is your wife nay more!"

The man laughed, revealing bits of tobacco wedged between his rotten teeth. "Have ye never heard the tale o' the devil's lands?" He leaned closer, smacking a hand on Chris's back as his eyes grew wide. "They lure ships in with smoke, and many o' great men have turned toward her shores. And those men would be showered with feast and drink the like they'd ne'er seen—such strong drink they can hardly stand upright by the night's end. Oh, but that's when they turn the demons loose. They wait til' you're so liquored up ye canna see straight, then they slaughter ye, one by one, until they've made a feast out of ye. The rest, they lock up for their next meal. They're cannibals, the lot of 'em. Ye dinna want to be caught anywhere near those three islands."

Aggravated with the superstition, he looked back toward the quarterdeck where Maria stood next to James Cook. "That's ridiculous. We *have* to get closer. I have to know it's not her."

He stormed past the man toward the captain, ignoring the continued shouts of warning in his wake.

"Captain!" he yelled up as he ascended the several wooden stairs to join them. "There's smoke out there." He pointed toward the single black cloud far in the distance. "Please sir, it could be my wife."

James Cook smiled warmly at him, then pulled out his telescope to scan the horizon. Slowly lowering the brass spyglass, he shook his head and his expression told Chris that he, too, despite his intelligence, was afraid of the same stories. "My sincerest apologies, Christopher. I cannot sail near those lands."

Maria frowned between them. "Why not?!"

Next to the captain, Isaac stood straighter, raising one of his auburn eyebrows. "Your Grace, they call those the devil's islands. The natives there are cannibals. Isn't that right uncle?"

Cook sighed and nodded, flashing Chris an apologetic look. "I can see you do not believe it. I considered the tales fallacy and folklore myself. I assure you, I would not be convinced until I had seen it with my own eyes. On our first voyage, my eagerness for precision forced me to disregard the crew's warning and I turned toward the smoke. It is no fable. We had to open fire upon them, and even then, gravely outnumbered by the hundreds, they managed to pull several crewmen off to their shores before we could escape."

"Couldn't we just get a little closer?" Maria asked, curling her fingers around Cook's bicep. "Just close enough to see through your little scope thingy?"

Cook closed his eyes and took a deep breath. "Would that I could my dear, but even despite the legends, I must get the men aboard the Adventure to Otaheite before they begin to perish. They'll need refreshment and fruit. I've word that Captain Furneaux is bed ridden and I cannot add any more risk to the lives of those men. I must get them to safety where they can heal. To turn now would add several days to our journey and would likely result in the death of several more men."

Chris glanced back toward the smoke. "But if it's them... if you're wrong..." He looked back to Cook. "Let me take a boat and paddle out. I'll take the risk myself. I have to know if it's her."

"Christopher," Isaac interjected, "you are not listening. We cannot be expected to wait idle with the men aboard the Adventure in such peril already. My uncle is afraid of no man, and so, if *he* says he will not sail toward it, there is just cause."

"Then don't wait," Chris pleaded. "Give me a small boat to paddle out and leave me."

"Kreese," Maria scoffed, "are you crazy? You cannot do this! What if your wife isn't there and you are taken and eaten? Who will find her then?"

Chris shook his head, desperation filling him. "You said you were sailing west and then back east. I could plan for it. I could paddle back out."

"Forgive me." Cook lowered his eyes. "I cannot, in good conscience, send you off to your death." He raised his palm as Chris moved to argue. "However, I can see that you shan't be deterred. I will offer you this promise. If along our journey we come upon no word of your wife, in exchange for your continued service to Her Grace on this ship, I vow to you that, upon our return, we shall circle back from our southern path to sail nearer to the devil's shores. I must get my men healthy and cannot turn the ships now."

"Uncle! You cannot make such a promise! It is surely suicide!"

Cook raised his chin to his nephew and kept his eyes fixed on Chris. "There are many islands on our route. It is more likely, God willing, that she is safely landed upon any one of them."

Lieutenant Edgecumbe approached Cook from behind to whisper something in his ear and Cook bowed his head to Chris. "My apologies. I must attend to more pressing matters and I must beg your leave. I know it is not what you want to hear, but you should consider that she is likely not there at all. Your Grace." He bowed to Maria and followed the lieutenant to the lower deck.

Chris's heart beat in his throat as he looked back out at the horizon. What if it was her? Could he jump off the boat and swim toward it? He'd fought the ocean before, could he manage again?

"¡Estúpido! ¡Idiota!" maria hissed, rushing to his side to punch his arm with her bony knuckles. "And what would I do if he would have said yes? Eh? You gonna get on a boat and disappear and leave me here with these men? Leave me stuck in this time with no one?!"

His cheeks burned with the frustration and emotion that was boiling inside him. "But it could be them... She could be right there... within my reach."

Maria scoffed. "Or she could be on the next one and then you will be someone's steak dinner for nothing!"

He shook his head, his eyes remaining focused on the smoke as it gradually moved further from reach. "It's so close to where we were, Maria. How much further away from us could they possibly have drifted? What if she's there and the story is true? What if she's in danger and trying to call for me?" He tried not to imagine her being imprisoned, tortured, murdered... "I could get to her... I could find a way to get back to you."

"¡Te morirás!" Maria spun to face him. "She is not there so take it out of your stupid little brain. You heard the captain. He saw it himself! If she *is* there, she is dead and then you will die for nothing!"

"But if she is alive..."

"¡Oye! Are you listening to yourself? Two months? Your wife could fight off hundreds of cannibals for two months and then make a fire to signal you? ¡No seas ridículo! Is she some kind of super human? Mi amor, if she *is* there, she is dead. We will pray she is not and keep looking. ¿Sí?"

"But..."

"No buts. It is done. We will keep looking and if we cannot find her, the captain will bring you back here to be a steak dinner then."

He skipped dinner and supper that night. He'd assisted Maria in getting dressed and then promptly returned to the ship's deck to stare at the blackness of the horizon behind them where the smoke had once been.

He pondered whether or not he could sneak off with a boat once the captain had gone to bed. He battled between an obligation to his wife and an obligation to Maria. He couldn't put her life at risk by bringing her with him, but he couldn't leave her alone with these men either.

He also couldn't risk losing Alaina. The island was close enough to where he'd been that it made sense she'd be there. How could he, in good conscience, sail off without investigating?

"I can hear your thoughts, sir." A playful German voice said just behind him. "And forgive my saying so, but you are wrong."

Chris turned to stare into the pale green eyes of Johann Forster, who was holding an oil lantern and leaning casually against the ship's netting. His reddened cheeks sat high around a knowing smile. "Look there." He straightened to point in the opposite direction where a very faint warm haze shone on its horizon. "Do you see now? They are trying to lure our ships."

Chris glanced between the two opposing horizons as Johann set the lantern on a hook and stepped forward to present him with a chunk of bread and cheese.

"A hundred years ago, a Portuguese ship came upon a man floating in the ocean, bloodied and beaten and nearly dead. The man told the tale of the devil's islands... how they had lured his ship and he'd watched as his lifelong friend was sacrificed. Under cover of night, he stole away and swam until he could see the land no more, determined not to be used himself for their next ritual. He floated on the ocean for days before he was recovered. The men aboard the recovering ship grew to like the man and swore to avenge his comrade. On their return route, they sought out the islands and were never heard from again. No ship will sail anywhere near those lands. The captain's curiosity on the first voyage placed him closer than any man has been since and it nearly met him the same fate."

Johann pushed the offered cheese and bread until Chris took it, then joined him to lean over the ship's wooden rail. "We are not all bad, Christopher, especially the captain. Our journey is long and it would suit you well to know you are not among enemies. The captain is incapable of looking ill upon any man. He would not keep a man from his beloved without just cause and it pained him to do so today. He spoke of nothing else over supper. It is his duty to take into consideration the health of all of us. He could risk losing a whole ship in the pursuit of one woman."

Chris let out a long breath and stared out at the night sky. "Johann..." He cleared his throat. "Is it real, all this?"

Johann looked him over and raised an eyebrow. "Precisely what are you referring to in the question? The ship? Oh yes, it's real. The ocean? I'm afraid it too is very real. Scurvy? The devil's islands? All real as well, so far as I am aware."

Chris shook his head. "That's what I was afraid of... This isn't some elaborate hoax then?"

Johann laughed. "I'm afraid you have piqued my interest now, dear boy! Pray, what kind of hoax might you think the humorless royal navy capable of carrying out on one such as yourself?"

He tore off a piece of bread and held it between his fingers. "You wouldn't believe me if I told you and it doesn't really matter. What matters is that those flames are within a reasonable distance to where you found me and could very well be my wife... What kind of husband would I be if I sailed away now? If I believed this story over the much more realistic probability that those flames are someone signaling for rescue? How would I ever be able to live with myself if I didn't jump off this ship right now and swim in that direction?"

"Neither the captain nor myself would have cause to lie to you about the danger those islands hold. And jumping off this ship now would do your wife no good. You'd never make it anywhere near those flames."

He tilted his head to one side and shrugged. "But I can see we've not yet earned your trust and these words hold little value to you now. If it were my own wife lost at sea, I shan't say I'd feel much different."

Johann looked out over the water and back at him. "I have to admit, Christopher, I have misjudged you, and for that, I must beg your forgiveness."

"How so?" Chris bit into the stale bread, keeping his eyes on the trailing horizon.

"I'm afraid the duchess of Parma has a reputation for laying with men who are not the duke. I regarded your circumstance as a failed attempt at running away together and the story of your wife and others was merely a masquerade to hide an underlying scandal. Your willingness to abandon Her Grace today made it clear that an undying love for the duchess would be an unlikely cause for your journey. While I still find your story to have holes in it, I can see now that your wife is indeed real."

Chris swallowed the bread and winced as its staleness scratched his throat. "She is *very* real... and she is the only thing in this world that matters to me. I am lost without her and I'm terrified that if I don't inspect every sign of life on that water, I might lose her forever. If I don't get to her and she gets on another ship, where would she go? What would she do? She didn't see me in the storm... What if she thinks I am dead? How will I ever find her?"

"If you thought she were dead, where would *you* go? Perhaps she would go home?"

'Home,' he thought. *'Home is gone. There's no home to go to...'* To go to America now would put them in the middle of a gruesome war with the British within the next few years. Surely she would know that if she, too, boarded another ship. With the same knowledge as he, where would she go?

"I don't know." He sighed. "Are there many ships that would sail through this area she could board?"

"There are many trade routes between the islands," Johann assured him. "Within the fortnight, we shall arrive in Otaheite. The captain has developed friendships with the chiefs and kings there. He can inquire as to whether or not they have come upon anyone matching her description."

He followed Chris's gaze to the horizon trailing the ship. "The captain has vowed to return here if we do not find her. He is a man of his word. You should know the islands in this area are bountiful in fruit and should the legends prove wrong, you will likely find your wife just as she was upon our return. After all, you survived on an island much smaller than those."

"How long will you stay there? In Otaheite? Do you think I might be able to board another ship from there? To come back and inspect for myself while the men are healing?"

"Not from there, dear boy." He patted his back. "Outside of their limited trade, it is still a very primitive civilization when it comes to travel. But our return shall be swift. We sail to the west only a little further, then to the southeast in search of the Terra Australis, which the captain does not believe we will find. I beg of you, be patient. If she is indeed alive, the captain will locate her. His vow to circle back from our southern path is no small feat for so great a man as he."

"How long before we return?" he asked, his shoulders slumping in defeat.

"Only a few months."

Chapter Eleven

Chris

Whatever lingering apprehensions he had about the year were obliterated the moment the ship sailed into the shallow waters around Tahiti.

He could see the unmistakable peak of Mont Orohena high in the clouds as they turned toward its shores, but all signs of civilization, tourism, and the twenty-first century were completely removed.

He knew from his month of planning the trip that the coast should have been lined with hotels and over-water bungalows. He knew he should see cruise ships docked to one side and beaches lined with tourists clad in brightly colored bathing suits. Instead, he saw an infinite nature and a native people gathering on its sands who blended perfectly against the backdrop.

Where there should have been bright white sales of modern-day sailboats floating just outside its turquoise sandbars, he instead saw the sails of primitive wooden canoes, their rustic fabrics made from animal hides, bamboo, and palm; all of them loaded with various colorful fruits and sailing toward the two ships.

He'd been anxious to reach Tahiti. Despite his conscious mind becoming more and more persuaded they'd travelled through time, his subconscious had held onto the hope they would reach civilization—*real civilization*—and, once returned to it, he would be able to revisit the site of the crash to search for Alaina with a helicopter or a plane.

Standing now on the bow of the ship and looking out at the wilderness before him, his heart shattered. There would be no helicopters or planes... no elaborate search and rescue. The concept that she might be lost forever ate away at him along with the fact that, if he somehow managed to find her, he would never be able to take her back to the home they'd built together. They would never be the people they'd once been... would never see their families or friends again. They would be forever changed and trapped here with no identity and no purpose.

As the canoes drew closer to the ship, the men around him grew louder and more raucous. The midshipmen had joined the upper deck. These were the lewd and raucous men that were generally forbidden to surface. They were a rough group of brutish, foul-mouthed soldiers and sailors that Chris had been warned to steer clear of.

He followed their attention out to the canoes. Most of the women aboard them shone exposed breasts, which prompted obscene gestures and roaring excitement. The men leaned over the railing to wave and blow kisses, shout vulgarities, and beat loudly on the wooden planks of the ship's side.

'Maria.'

His heartbeat quickened. He'd come up early that morning when he'd heard shouting and left her sleeping. Never leaving her side for longer than an hour unless she was with the captain, he panicked that he'd left her alone for so long.

The men aboard the ship couldn't be trusted in such a heightened state, and he worried they might already have a mind to barge into the room of the single woman onboard. He spun on his heel to head back below deck.

He didn't knock, but pushed through the door in a panic, scanning the room for intruders.

She screeched and pulled the blanket up to her chin where she still laid in her bed, unharmed. "¡Ay Dios mío! You scared the shit out of me! What the hell do you think you are you doing?"

He sighed, letting his shoulders relax as he closed the door behind him and leaned against it. "We've arrived in Tahiti."

"And?" She lowered the blanket and sat up. "Are there people? Is it back to normal?!"

He shook his head. "There are people, but it is *far* from normal. I'm afraid we really are stuck in 1773."

She collapsed onto her face in the bed and groaned, balling her hands into fists in her hair. "I'm so sick of living in this stink. I want to go home!"

He slid down the door to sit on his butt on the floor, curling his knees into his chest. "Me too. But I don't see how we'll ever be able to get back now."

She sat up suddenly. "No." Flinging the blanket to one side, she flew out of the bed, marching over to stand above him.

"Get up from this floor. You are not giving up. *We* are not giving up. We will find your wife and then we will find a way home. I will not live in this stinking place forever. I have things I want to do with my life!"

"How?" He ran a hand over his face hard. "How will we find my wife? How will we get home? We don't even know how we got here! Hell, for all I know, Alaina might still be in our time! She could very well be sitting in our home right this instant waiting for me to return! What if it wasn't the crash that brought us here but something in the water?"

She crossed her arms in front of her. "So what? You want to just give up then? You want to just sit in this stinky floor with these stinky men on this stinky ship and give up? You are very ugly when you sulk and you are too handsome a man to be doing this all the time. Get up."

"I really thought it was fake. Even with all the dinners and bowing and clothes and details, I really thought we'd get here and it'd be normal again; that I'd be able to go home, and that Alaina would somehow be there."

"Well, you can't do nothing about it from there. Get up. I need to get dressed and talk to the captain."

He shook his head. "You need to stay here, as far away from those men as you can possibly be. The midshipmen are up there. They're all worked up and you're not safe out there."

"¡Oye! I am not going to hide away in this little depressing room while there is fresh air out there. I want to see this world we have come to, and how will we look for your wife from in here?! Get up estúpido!"

The ship lurched heavily, forcing her to fall over onto the floor in front of him. Loud shouting echoed from the planks over their heads and he heard men running across the deck as the ship rocked again to send her sliding across the wood floor, landing against his chest.

"¡Ay coño!" she cursed, trying to lift herself up off the floor. Before she could raise to her knees, the ship rocked again in the opposite direction.

He wrapped one arm around her, pulling her to him as he held the other out in preparation of impact against the opposing wall they slid toward. They landed against it with a crash, sending a tray of biscuits to spill out over them.

Again, there was shouting overhead and the thunder of boots running from one side of the ship to the other. Beneath them, he heard a loud creaking and felt a vibration in the floorboards under his legs. They'd come too close in the shallow water and the men above were scrambling to turn the ship around.

He reached up and grabbed the window ledge above their heads, but was unable to get a strong enough hold before they were once again pulled toward the door. This time, they tumbled to land lying on the floor, he on top of her, with their sides wedged against the door.

His arms still wound tightly around her, he braced for another shift, holding her head against his shoulder as he stiffened his forearms against the floorboards.

"Are you trying to suffocate me?!" she nagged against his shoulder when no further movement came, wrestling against his death grip to free her face.

Slowly, he let his muscles relax and unwound his arms from her, balancing over her on his forearms.

She let out a long exhale as she laid her head back against the floor with a thud, then grinned mischievously up at him. "I have never seen you from this angle, mi amor."

She lightly traced his jaw with her fingertips and the grin widened. "I hope you keep the lights off when you sleep with your wife! You are not so handsome from here!"

Despite himself, he laughed at that. "Thanks asshole." But when he moved to disentangle himself from her she clasped his face between both her palms.

"No, wait," she said, smiling sweetly up at him as her eyes searched his. "If we really are stuck here together, there's something I need to say to you…"

She eased her grip slightly and smoothed her thumb over his cheek, tilting her head to one side as she inspected him. The gentleness in her touch made him momentarily close his eyes. He'd needed just a moment of tenderness… a single moment of comfort to make him feel like it would all be alright. He let out a long sigh as her palm moved along his jaw.

"My superman," she said softly. "You are *definitely* ugly from this angle!" She released his face and burst into playful laughter.

She wiggled out from beneath him to peek out of her small window. "Come and get me dressed now so we can go and search for your wife." She grinned as he tried to recover himself. "The sooner you have someone else to pine after, the better!"

"I'm not pining!" He blushed, standing and straightening his clothing.

"Oh, that's good then." She giggled. "Because you couldn't handle a woman like me."

When they'd ascended on deck a half hour later, the scene before them was chaotic. Captain Cook was at the helm, shouting between the men he was ordering to help navigate and the ones who had abandoned all their duties in order to grope the native Tahitian women who'd flooded the ship's deck.

"Stop those men!" Cook ordered to a soldier near him as a group of native men made their way past Chris to head toward the lower deck. "Take your hands off that woman!" he shouted to another who had pressed a young woman against the netting to run both hands wildly over her exposed skin. "You there! Get a man down in that water this instant to search for the anchor!" His head snapped to the opposite side of him. "Lieutenant! Send word to the Adventure to come no closer!"

A group of male and female natives surrounded him and Maria. They reached for the fabrics on her dress, grabbing at the necklace around her neck, and several of the women began to touch her hair. Chris pulled her into his arms and took a step back, shielding her from their grip as they pursued.

"Christopher!" the captain shouted, several more native Tahitians spilling over the side of the ship's rail to board as he did so. "This is no place for the duchess! Go with Lieutenant Edgecumbe to the Adventure and keep her away until I send word!"

Beside the captain, a native man tugged at the sword on his hip, diverting his attention back to his attempts to maintain order.

Lieutenant Edgecumbe pushed through the madness with a pistol pointed at the natives surrounding them. "Back up!" he demanded, forcing his way through to grab Maria's arm. "Come, both of you."

He led them toward the back of the ship, pointing his pistol to clear the way of natives and pulling seamen off the native women as he passed. "Animals! All of them!"

Chris held Maria closer as they moved rapidly. The lieutenant grabbed a man by his hair to launch him to one side where he'd unfastened his breeches and prepared to thrust himself upon a distressed woman. She scurried away quickly before he could recover.

"PREPARE A SLOOP! And make haste!" the lieutenant shouted ahead of him, prompting a group of men to begin hoisting a small boat on one side of the ship.

A massive blast shook the ship and nearly deafened Chris's ears, forcing him to jump and squeeze Maria tighter.

"Worry not," Lieutenant Edgecumbe assured him as they approached the ship's rail. "Warning blasts from the cannons is all. They'll shoot them over their heads to ward them off. Your Grace," he peered down at Maria where she'd buried her face in Chris's chest. "You'll want to take every precaution to stay close to your guard, the captain, or myself. Trust no other man aboard this ship. Propriety is lost on them with so much to lust after. It will only worsen on land. The captain will have them flogged, but they will return to do it again. It seems the reward outweighs the punishment."

He motioned for them to climb down into the sloop. "The natives will not harm you, but these men might. Even the soldiers should not be trusted. Christopher, you will need to remain with Her Grace even at night—*particularly* at night."

Chris nodded and climbed over the railing. Feet planted in the smaller boat, he reached out to steady Maria with his hands at her waist, pulling her down into the boat alongside him.

Lieutenant Edgecumbe, three soldiers, Johann, and Georg climbed into the sloop and the men above began to lower them down. Chris could feel Maria trembling beside him, and he placed a hand over hers to steady her.

"They will settle," the lieutenant assured her, noticing Chris's hand over hers. "Once the initial excitement has worn off, they will all settle down. No harm shall come to you, I swear it."

"Is it always like this?" she asked. "When you come upon land?"

Lieutenant Edgecumbe sighed and nodded. "Men are peculiar that way; even a gentleman can lose sight of decency when he is overwhelmed with temptation."

"Not I," Georg beamed proudly at Maria, his long auburn hair coming loose from its knot in wisps to blow against his face as the sloop grew closer to the water. "I will assist the men in looking after you, Your Grace."

She smiled at the young man. "Gracias."

"Do they speak English?" Chris asked, cautiously watching the canoes where they'd stopped to float in the water after the cannon blast. "How do you communicate with them?"

"There are always a few among them who can manage enough English to serve as translators. We will seek them out before the night's end and the Captain will ensure you be granted an audience straight away to inquire about your wife."

Once the small boat hit the water, the three soldiers stood, rocking the sloop as they untied the ropes. Grabbing the oars from the boat's floor, the three men and the lieutenant sat to begin rowing them toward the Adventure where it sat far out in the darker water.

"Kreese," Maria leaned into him to whisper, "promise you will not leave me alone out here with these crazy men." She kept her eyes focused on two native canoes that pursued them to one side.

"I promise," he whispered back, squeezing her hand where it sat beneath his.

The canoes caught up to slide along each side of the sloop, and a woman outstretched her arms to present them with a basket overflowing with assorted fruits.

"Ay, she is so beautiful," Maria marveled as Chris accepted the gift from the woman.

The woman said something in her own language and smiled warmly at Maria before sitting back in her own canoe. On the opposite side of them, a large man responded in the same language, his voice low and thick. He grinned at the group of them, offering his own basket full of fruit and nodding for one of the soldiers to take it.

Maria looked at the lieutenant. "They don't want anything in return?"

His mouth curled up on one side. "Oh, they do. We will shower them with gifts just as soon as there is order and they know this.

Mostly, it is supplies they want for building, but the captain has all manner of gifts to bestow upon them."

"Hmmf." Maria stared at the woman, whose eyes seemed fixed on the emerald necklace around her neck. "Can I give this to her?" she asked, placing her fingers on the pendant.

"It is yours to do with as you please, Your Grace."

Maria smiled and rose, unclasping the necklace and extending it out toward the woman. "Here. You can have it."

As the woman apprehensively took the necklace, Chris noticed one soldier on their boat staring at her naked breasts. The soldier's eyes remained fixed until Maria returned to her seat, where they promptly shifted to zero in on Maria's cleavage.

The expression on the man's face made Chris blind with rage and he kicked the man's shin hard.

"That is the duchess you are looking at," he reprimanded, sitting straighter and acting the part of a dutiful guard. "Keep your eyes off her."

The man glared at him, resting a hand on the hilt of the sword at his hip. "You forget your place, sir. You hold no power over me here."

"Mind your tongue, Officer," Lieutenant Edgecumbe warned. "He may not have power over you, but *I* do and you will show respect in the presence of Her Grace."

The man continued to glare, his palm remaining rested on his sword until the two canoes paddled past them and back to the waters between the Resolution and the shore.

When they reached the Adventure, they were hoisted up, and climbing over the edge, they found a scene significantly different from that onboard the Resolution.

Nearly all the men were pale with reddened eyes, barely the strength among them to stand; most of them sat or laid on the wooden planks of the deck. It was a quiet and eerie setting as the men sat awaiting word on how or when to approach the island that would offer them the nutrients they needed to heal.

Georg leaned over the railing to pull a basket of fruit onto the deck. "These will help," he announced, taking the second basket from his father to place next to the first. "There is plenty more coming. Eat! Your bodies need it."

As much as the men could "hurry," they did toward the baskets, rapidly emptying them of their contents.

"Where is Captain Furneaux?" Lieutenant Edgecumbe asked the surrounding men.

"He's in his cabin sir," a seaman near the helm announced between noisy bites of guava. "He's been wrought with sickness and unable to get out of bed."

Johann inspected the ship's deck from where he stood still on the sloop. He looked at Georg. "Lower me back down. I shall retrieve more fruits for the crew. Officer Evans, join me? Georg, my boy, you stay here and watch over the duchess." He winked at Chris then took a seat, his head disappearing over the rail as the soldier climbed back over.

Chris and Maria sat on the quarterdeck, leaned up against the ship's mast as they waited and watched helplessly while the Resolution struggled to turn out of the shallow water.

Johann made several trips to and from the shores with fruit and freshwater. They observed as Captain Cook went ashore to speak with the natives, and witnessed as several crews from both the Adventure and the Resolution made trips back and forth.

Maria, despite her desire to join the men, was instructed to stay onboard the Adventure until they'd docked in Matavai Bay.

She was provided a small cabin and Chris slept on the floor with his back against the door.

After two days of sitting idle, Captain Furneaux became well enough to walk and join them on deck, and word came that they were moving to Matavai Bay where they would finally be able to go ashore.

By the time the two ships were anchored, night had fallen, and deciding it was too late to lower the scoops, they were instructed to once again remain upon the Adventure until daylight.

Too anxious to go below deck, most of the crew sat or laid on the floor of the top deck, including Maria and Chris.

"Mi amor," she whispered as she yawned and laid her head on his shoulder. "What if it really was something in the water that brought us here? What if your wife is still in our time? How long will we look for her?"

He closed his eyes. "I don't know that I could ever stop."

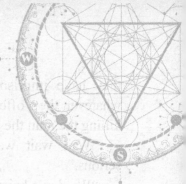

Chapter Twelve

Jack

Jack's mouth dropped open. "Phil?" He blinked hard. "Where... when—I don't understand... How did you get here?"

"Whatever you do, don't—where's Kyle?" Phil's eyes grew wide as he scanned their surroundings. "Do they have Kyle? Please, *please* tell me he's not with you."

"No, it's just the two of us," Jack said cautiously. "We came in search of rescue."

One of the two guards spoke, frowning and pushing Phil hard in the center of his back.

"I've already told you it's him." Phil glared at the man. "I don't understand what you want."

The guard raised his voice and repeated the words he'd previously spoken, bringing a hand to Jack's shoulder as he swung the other around in front of him in an attempt to illustrate the words he was saying. He then touched Phil's hand where his fingers had been cut off and pointed at Jack.

Phil let out a long exhale. "Okay look... There's a boy, Michael... He's the only one among them that speaks English. I don't have the time to explain it all, but he believes we are gods sent from the future to battle their enemies. You are the God they are looking for. They will hold a ceremony in your honor... they'll offer you food, drink, and they'll want you to fight one of the men they have imprisoned from a rival tribe. You'll have to take whatever they offer... do whatever is asked of you... including killing the man they'll force you to fight. If you don't—

"Wait wait wait..." Jack shook his head. "You can't be serious."

"We don't have time for me to explain. They'll take me back any second. If you don't kill the man, they'll know you're not a god and they'll not only imprison you, but they will likely kill us all. If you play along, they might leave you to walk free and then maybe you can help us get out of here. Bud won't stand a chance. They'll lock him up within hours."

"Phil, this is insane. I'm not going to—

"Whatever they offer you, you take it," Phil insisted. "Women... food... drink... take it and smile. Whatever they tell you to do, you do it. You are a god... don't give them any reason to think you aren't."

"But—

"I have seen them rip a man limb from limb while he screamed. I have seen them place those limbs on the fire and eat them while the man—dying slowly—was forced to watch. These people..." Phil glanced nervously around them. "Fighting is their way of life. War, strength, masculinity... it is everything. They do not think like us. Show them you are strong and they will worship you for it. Offend them in any way or show any ounce of weakness, and we will all die here."

Behind them, Jack could hear a large group forming in the distance. He could hear the tuning of several deep drums as they were prepared for a ceremony. "This is crazy. How do you know all this?"

Phil took a deep breath. "Look, I know you and I are not friends. I know my face is not a welcome sight to you, but I am telling you the truth. You are the only hope I have to get out of here. They're going to test you to see if you are the god they have been searching for. If you don't pass their test... we're all dead. Including everyone on that island."

Jack swallowed. "What do you mean *'everyone on the island?'*"

"Jack," Phil pleaded as the guards began to turn him back in the direction they'd come. "We are not in our time. These are not people who can be reasoned with. Do whatever you have to. For Alaina. They know about the island... They were searching specifically for *you.* If you die, it's only a matter of time before they find our island and they die too."

Jack looked nervously toward Bud, whose normal calm expression was washed over with anxiety.

The two guards ushered Phil back. "You have to believe me!" Phil called back as Tamatoa draped a heavy arm across Jack's shoulders and turned him toward the sound of the drums. "Don't do anything to make them doubt you! And do not trust Michael!"

In front of them, the drums beat loudly around a roaring fire where a massive gathering was waiting for them.

As they drew closer to the fire, they were joined by a heavily decorated, large man. He wore an elaborate cloth draped around him with several boned necklaces hung from his neck. Beside him, dressed in a similar fabric, was a young and very scrawny white boy.

"I Michael," the young man stated, smiling sweetly to show his crooked teeth. He was young, perhaps fifteen at the most, and his accent was a strange tone of spotty British. "And you Jack, *God of War.* Phil tell us of your greatness and we excited to welcome you here. This man great chief, Uati, and he offer you friendship."

The large man bowed his head and smiled.

Jack's mind raced and repeated, *'do not trust Michael.'*

Was Phil telling the truth or was he up to something? Surely he wouldn't be lying... not with all that had appeared to have happened to him here?

"Come and eat." Michael extended his arm to a seat around the fire. "We all friends."

"Phil," Jack began, sitting down as Michael stood in front of him, ushering the women to gather food on his behalf, "he told you where to find me?"

Michael grinned. "Oh yes. Phil said we find more gods from future if we go east... and here you are."

Jack tilted his head to one side. "How old are you?"

Michael's crooked smile widened as he lowered his tone. "I not know. Uati took me as son when I very young. He not know English words. If you god, I beg, take me away with you."

Jack nodded, choosing his words carefully; cautious of Michael's trustworthiness. "Phil says I will have to fight someone? To prove I am a God?"

Michael kept his pleasant expression, glancing back to Uati, who watched him proudly from a seat higher than the others. "After eat, they give you warrior weapon and you fight against Uati enemy. You must win. They give you many gift for win."

"Phil told Uati *I* am a God?"

Michael shook his head. "Phil say you all fall from sky. I pray for God send help. I know it you. We tell him fight and he say he not fighting god. You are fighting god. Please win. Please fight enemies so you take me home. Uati people at war with Kahurangi people for hundred years. Uati believes that god of war is only way to put end to fighting so Nikora people live in peace."

"And what if the god of war does not want to fight for the Nikora people?" Jack raised an eyebrow. "What if he does not like being tested?"

The corner of Michael's lip twitched in a smirk. "Then Nikora people kill you. If you not *Nikora* God, then you not keep alive, understand?"

Jack nodded. "What happened to Phil's fingers?"

Michael laughed at that, glancing back at Uati and translating in the native language. Uati laughed thunderously in response.

Michael shook his head as he turned back toward Jack, still chuckling. "Uati make Phil fight anyway, even though he not fighting god. Man cut Phil fingers off before he even raise sword. Uati think it not right to kill Phil in case he really is god and get angry. He lock him up and look for you."

Uati grinned and held his large palm up, then demonstrated the chopping off of a finger by bringing his other hand down over it and curling his pointer finger inward.

"So Phil didn't kill anyone?" Jack asked.

Michael curled over in laughter. "No. Phil like woman. Maybe old man better fighter than Phil."

Jack glanced at Bud and back to Michael. "This fight... tell me how it will work."

Michael sat down beside him, handing him a bowl filled to the brim with meat. "You choose weapon. Enemy get same weapon. You fight. One man still alive."

Jack's stomach turned into a knot. Phil had been telling the truth... they expected him to kill someone. How could he possibly bring himself to do it? To kill a stranger? He glanced around the fire at the strange faces that were all watching him. He wouldn't be able to fight them all... And Alaina could be in danger if he gave them any reason to continue on with their search for the island. "And if I choose not to fight?"

Michael bit into his own meat. "Then Uati kill you *and* friends and go find women for new wife."

Jack took a deep breath, staring down at the bowl in his lap. "How many women does Uati think are out there?"

Michael chewed noisily to one side. "Phil give all names of gods." He raised a finger as he said each name. "He say Anna healer and Lilly pretty. He say Alaina sing and Magna look like Nikora people. He say Bertie old and Izzy like baby. Uati take all for him. He take men too. Phil say Jim hunter and Bruce cook. This..." Michael pointed at Bud. "This Bud. He god of wisdom. Uati want him teach English words."

Jack swallowed hard. He'd listed them all and in detail... All but Kyle, he noted.

"Eat," Michael encouraged him. "You need strength for fight. I want go free."

Jack stared at the charred meat overflowing from the clay bowl in his hands. Again, he thought of Phil's warning and of the limbs of a man that had been thrown into the fire and eaten... He could feel bile rising in his throat. "What is it?"

"Phil fingers." Michael said, staring at him straight-faced. "Another man pain give god of war strength."

Jack dropped the bowl to the ground and shuffled backward onto his feet.

Michael burst into laughter. He looked up at Uati and spoke in their language, holding his fingers up and pointing at the bowl. Uati and all the spectators around the fire erupted in laughter alongside him. Michael stood and placed a hand on Jack's back, wiping tears from his eyes as he attempted to catch his breath.

"I joke Jack. It only pig." He grinned, pointing to the charred remains of a carved boar that sat to one side of the celebration. "I only joke. Just pig, see. No fingers Jack. I tell truth now." He chuckled, picking up Jack's discarded bowl and handing it to him. "Eat."

Jack held up a piece of meat, his stomach protesting at the thought of eating anything this group offered.

"Jack," Bud said softly from his seat beside them. "I'm so sorry, son. You're going to need to eat it if we want to stand any chance of getting through this."

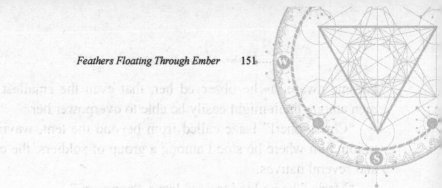

Chapter Thirteen

Chris

On the shores of Matavai Bay, they spent hours setting up medical tents for the men of the Adventure. Chris and Maria helped in getting the sickest of the men to the tents and distributing much needed fruit and water while Captain Cook, after learning of a recent civil war that removed the former king and killed their former translator, sought out a new translator and the prince.

Chris kept a wary eye on Maria at all times. While the men of the Adventure were being brought to shore, many of the men from the Resolution disappeared deeper into the island, pockets loaded with nails to exchange for sexual favors from the Tahitian women.

He wondered how long Maria would be safe among the men. Even once they had left Tahiti—or rather, *especially* once they had left Tahiti, how long before they began to look at her the way they were looking at the Tahitian women? He didn't like the idea of returning to the ship to sleep with a wall separating them; with a door that could be barricaded to prevent him from entering should some of the men get the wrong idea.

He watched her as she lifted a man's head to pour water into his mouth. Her fingers seemed frail where they held the glass and her arms, suddenly so thin, appeared as though they could break from the weight of the man's large head. She lowered his head and pet his hair. She wasn't muscular or strong physically and he became aware, as he observed her, that even the smallest of the men among them might easily be able to overpower her.

"Christopher!" Isaac called from beyond the tent, waving him to join him where he stood among a group of soldiers, the captain, and several natives.

"Maria," he nodded toward Isaac, "come on."

She set the glass down on the table beside the bed, whispering softly in the man's ear before she hurried to walk alongside him toward the group.

"You're awfully friendly with that one," he noted as they began up the sandy path.

"That's because he is going to die," she said simply. "I am not *completely* heartless, you know."

"Would you be so friendly to me if I were going to die?" he teased.

"Jealous?" She raised a defiant eyebrow at him. "And no, I would kick your ass for doing whatever you did to be dying when you have promised to get us out of this mess."

He smirked at that, straightening his back as they joined the men.

"Christopher, this is Hitihiti." Isaac presented a dark-skinned man with black hair that curled around his face. "He will serve as our translator while we are here."

Captain Cook cleared his throat, his eyes focused on Maria. "King Otou has fled to Oparre. Apparently our cannons frightened him yesterday. We are invited to join him in the morning and I wish to make a strong impression by presenting him with Your Grace's presence as well. He will appreciate the honor."

Cook motioned to a large man at his side. "This is Maritata. He and his wife have agreed to escort us to Oparre. Christopher, you must join us as well, where you may inquire about your wife and the other survivors. Maritata assures me that if anyone on this island should have word of them, it would be king Otou."

Isaac placed a hand on Chris's shoulder and turned him to the opposite side. "Christopher, you've met Lieutenant Edgecumbe. He and the Royal Marines are taking the Forsters to Point Venus to set up an observatory and encampment there. The encampment will be heavily guarded and no one would frown upon a guard sharing a tent with his duchess in a foreign land. It is my recommendation that you take her there for the duration of our stay. Lieutenant Edgecumbe will assure his marines treat the duchess with the utmost respect and they can be trusted over the officers and seamen aboard the ship. We can call for her things to be transported with the others.'"

The lieutenant bowed his head. "No harm shall come to the duchess among my marines, I can assure you."

Chris glanced at Maria, who was speaking through Hitihiti to the wife of Maritata and smiling. He nodded. "If you think it's best, then we will go there."

Lieutenant Edgecumbe flashed his teeth in a wide smile. "Very well then. Corporal Beard," he addressed a man standing to his left, "have the duchess's cabin emptied, and a tent provided that will sleep both she and her guard comfortably. Spare no luxury in making her quarters suitable for the royalty she is."

"Aye sir." The man saluted and set off with a group of others toward the beach.

Chris turned his attention back to Isaac. "Have they mentioned seeing anyone?"

Isaac nodded. "Aye. There was a Spanish ship arrived here just before us. According to Maritata, there was sickness aboard the ship so many of the locals were kept separated. However, the king spent much time with its captain and will have insight as to the ship's inhabitants. They sailed out just a few days ago."

Chris could feel his pulse suddenly race. Could it be possible Alaina was aboard a ship that was so close to him? He couldn't help but smile as fresh hope washed over him for the first time since he'd seen the smoke, and he looked around the island surrounding them with a new sense of optimism.

He notice the sheer beauty of an undeveloped Tahiti; its rolling green and lush volcanic peaks that soared high into the clouds unobstructed by modern-day tourism, and the white sand at his feet that crawled out to the still turquoise water, perfectly undisturbed outside of where the men had come ashore.

He'd made it to their destination… might she have been there too? Could she have had her feet in this very same sand just days prior?

Suddenly giddy with excitement, he didn't know how he could wait until the following day to speak with the king; didn't know what to do with himself. "What can I do? Can I help in some way?" he asked the lieutenant.

The lieutenant glanced at Maria. "Maritata and his wife have agreed to take Sir William out to explore more of the island for his paintings. I am sending a few of my men along with them. After so much time at sea, the fresh air could serve the duchess well."

They'd spent the day at a beautiful waterfall buried deep in the island where William set up his easel and canvas to paint infinitely. By the time they arrived back at Point Venus, the sun had set and the landscape was spotted with white canvas tents, several guards patrolling its boundary.

Greeting them at the entrance was Lieutenant Edgecumbe. "Your Grace," he bowed. "I hope your adventures met your pleasure this day. My marines have spared no amenity in erecting your sleeping quarters. Come and see for yourself."

He looped his arm around hers and led them to the center of camp where a massive tent stood amidst the small ones, surrounded on all sides by marines.

He pulled back the single flap at its center to expose a candle-lit interior lined with extravagant rugs, trunks, and tables overflowing with fruit and biscuits. They'd even gone so far as to disassemble and reassemble her bed in its center. One tall oval mirror sat on one end next to her vanity, which was overflowing with jewels, brushes, combs, and lavender.

Tucked away to one corner, he found a straw cot set out on the ground for himself.

"Does it suit Your Grace's approval?" the lieutenant asked self-consciously.

She grinned. "It is perfect! I don't think I'll ever want to go back to that tiny cabin on the ship again!"

Lieutenant Edgecumbe beamed with pride. "You may be relieved to know we've acquired a young lady to assist you with your dressing, madam, so you may not be burdened with your guard having to do so during your stay."

A young, smiling Tahitian woman dressed in a white fabric that resembled a towel wrap appeared at the entrance to the tent.

"Wonderful." Maria forced a smile. "She will not be sleeping in here as well, will she?"

The lieutenant laughed. "No Your Grace, most certainly not. You may call for her at your will and she shall be provided to you. Christopher," he diverted his focus to Chris as the young woman joined Maria near the mirror, "you are unarmed, sir. I've been instructed to provide you with sword and pistol and have done so. You will find both just there." He pointed toward a sheathed sword and pistol laid out on a trunk next to his cot.

"Thank you," Chris said, wondering if he would give himself away by having to use either of them and having no idea the proper way to even hold them.

"If there is nothing else," the lieutenant bowed, "Christopher, let us speak outside while Her Grace is undressed."

Chris looked back to where Maria sat at the vanity, the young woman already pulling pins from her hair.

"Worry not. No one shall breech this tent while my men surround it. We will only be just outside."

Slowly, he turned to follow him outside.

In the moonlight, he could just make out the lieutenant's expression as it turned solemn, and he leaned in to whisper. "You are no guard, of this I am certain."

He peered around them to make sure no one was listening. "I have been observing you these past weeks and there would be no convincing me otherwise. Whatever you and the duchess do behind this canvas is of no concern to me or my men. Your secrets shall be safe. However, her wellbeing has been entrusted to me and I must know you are quite capable of defending her should a threat arise."

He unsheathed his sword and held its hilt out toward him. "Take this."

"Oh… I…" Chris stuttered, taken aback.

"In my experience, gentlemen rarely know how to hold a sword, and you, sir, strike me as a gentleman. Disprove me by taking this sword and striking me with it."

Chris's heartbeat quickened, and he hesitated, taking a step backward from the offered weapon.

"It is as I thought, then." Edgecumbe smiled and returned the sword to his hip. "Do not be distressed, I've no cause to expose you. I am merely testing you out of necessity. Our journey is long, and with little exposure to the opposite sex past this island, I'm afraid the men onboard will become increasingly agitated. I offer you my friendship and discreet instruction in exchange for your influence with the duchess and the captain. I've no intention of remaining a lieutenant for long and would like the command of my own ship upon our return. You will need the skills I have to offer if you intend to keep the duchess's propriety intact by the trip's end." He winked. "Her *presumed* propriety, that is."

Chris straightened. "The duchess and I are not… involved."

The lieutenant raised an eyebrow. "Again I say to you sir, it is of no account to me or my men either way. Do you wish to accept my offer or not?"

Reluctantly, Chris nodded. "How? When?"

"I must presume the duchess is aware of your… lack of experience wielding a sword?" He tilted his head slightly. "Since you cannot be expected to leave her, it is my recommendation that I instruct you under the cover of night within the confines of this tent until you become more familiar. Once you are better versed, we may call it *'sparring'* and continue in the open where no one would suspect you."

"And when do we start?"

"Tomorrow night." The lieutenant glanced around again. "I'll be expected to patrol this first night and you will need rest after such a long day. While you are visiting the king tomorrow, I shall stock the tent with wooden sparring swords and come up with a clever excuse for my presence within the tent on the coming nights. I can see you are wary of me, and I would expect nothing less. It is my wish for us to become friends and I hope to earn your trust throughout this endeavor."

Chris was indeed wary of him, but the thought of having a friend in this place, particularly one so close to him in age, was appealing. He might even be able to use it to his advantage in acquiring some sort of job or home if they couldn't find a way back to their own time. "Thank you."

The native woman silently exited the tent to stand between them, promptly cutting the conversation short.

The lieutenant bowed to him. "I shall bid you goodnight then."

Chris returned the bow. "Goodnight."

Back inside the tent, he crossed over to the bed, where Maria lay staring up at him. She grinned, folding her hands beneath the back of her head and wiggling happily. "I like it here. I think I might have to stay so I, too, can walk around topless without these stupid corsets to suffocate me."

He laughed and sat down on the edge of the bed to remove his boots and stockings. "The lieutenant knows I'm not a guard. He thinks I am your *gentleman lover*." He bounced his eyebrows at her as he pulled off one stocking to flex his aching foot.

"He wants to train me to fight in exchange for a good word from you to the captain. I think it's a good idea." He pulled the other stocking off. "If I can make a friend here, perhaps I can eventually tell him who we really are... find a way back or at the very least a purpose while we are stuck here."

Maria frowned. "Or maybe you just exposed yourself and this man is going to run straight to the others to tell them we're liars!"

He shook his head, standing to remove his jacket and vest. "I don't think so. He seemed sincere."

"¡Oye! You need to tell me before you make these types of decisions."

"I didn't make the decision. I was exposed before I said a word. To have refused his offer would've put us in more danger, I think."

"Hmmf." She turned on her side to watch him as he unfastened the buttons on his breeches. "So you are my lover then?" She grinned.

He rolled his eyes. "Johann thought so too... I'm wondering if most of the men think the same."

"It might not be so bad to have them think so. It at least gives them some reason you do not act like a guard. They must all think you are such a lucky man to have such a beautiful woman!"

She flicked her hair dramatically as she stretched and posed. "Come then, lover." She patted the bed next to her. "With all these sexed up men running around, I will feel better if you are next to me."

He stared at the bed. In truth, he'd missed sleeping next to her; not for any reason other than the single bit of comfort it gave him to hold on to someone. On the island, half asleep, he would often forget he wasn't holding onto Alaina in the comfort of their own bed, and despite the heartache that followed in the acknowledgment of reality, the peace those fleeting moments offered had always been worth it.

He blew out the candles around the tent and climbed into the bed, leaning over the bedside table to blow out the last.

She curled naturally into his chest, draping an arm over him. "Oye. Did you see that fat man going at it with that tiny woman on the trail today?" she whispered, giggling. "With his big bare ass jiggling for the whole world to see?!"

He laughed out loud. "How could I miss it? She didn't seem to mind it much though."

"¡Sí! She was making some interesting sounds, eh?!" She buried her face to chuckle against him. "I have never had a man prompt those kinds of noises out of me before! Maybe I need to look for a big fat man, no?"

"Maybe they know something we don't." He grinned.

She snuggled closer. "Don't give me any ideas superman, I might go find one and then where will you sleep?"

"Where will I sleep, anyway?" He sighed. "Once we find Alaina... Where will we go? You heard about the Spanish ship that was here? Tomorrow I'll find out if she was on it. And if she was... I'll have to figure out where they were going and how I can get there, then where to take you both after."

"What if we come back here?" she asked, sliding her body even closer to his. "It is so beautiful and so much simpler, I think, than anywhere else might be. We wouldn't need to worry about jobs or titles or where to live... I could find a fat man to make me happy." She laughed, moving her hips against him.

"What are you doing?" He stiffened. "Stop doing that."

She giggled. "I can't help it. After seeing that big hairy man, I'm all worked up!"

"Well, be worked up over there." He nudged her away from him.

"Oh, come on," she teased, pressing her body back against his. "Be my gentleman lover! Give them something to talk about in the morning!"

"Seriously, Maria. Knock it off."

She sighed, propping her head up on her palm to look down at him as she stilled her body. "You don't crave it at all?" She combed over the exposed hairs on his chest where his night shirt hung open. "The physical connection to someone else?"

He cleared his throat and flattened her palm over his chest. "Not at the moment, no. I will have it soon enough when I find Alaina."

"Alaina," Maria repeated dryly, falling over to lie flat on her back beside him. "You are so obsessed with this woman. She had better be the most amazing creature I have ever laid eyes on!"

"I promise you, she is."

She propped herself back up. "Kreese... if she thinks you are dead, how long do you think she would wait before she decides to look for someone else?"

A stab of jealousy ran over him and he frowned at the thought that any man could possibly have his hands on her. "I… I don't know. How long would *you* wait?"

"For you?" She smirked. "With all your attitude and swinging moods… I would run into the arms of the next man instantly!"

He turned to face her and propped himself up. "Seriously, though… you're a woman. Do you think she would wait?"

Maria sighed, extending a hand to smooth it over his cheek. "All women are different, mi amor. Some of us need more than others. You should know what your wife would and wouldn't need and how long she might wait before searching for it. If a man offered her comfort after so long—it's been, what, four months now? Would she take it?"

He knew exactly what Alaina needed, and it was the affection he didn't give her. She'd craved it—begged for it even at times—and still he'd refused her. Now, as far as she knew, he was dead, and she would be free to find the affection she so desperately wanted. He didn't think she would wait long if someone willingly gave it; if someone spoke the words and touched her the way she'd wanted him to. Regret welling in his stomach, he laid back down.

"Oye, superman, I did not mean to upset you. If she loves you, no man will matter when you return to her."

He swallowed hard. "What if she *is* with someone? What if some other man has his hands on her right this very moment?"

Maria made a "tsk" noise and laid back down against his chest. "Look at us, mi amor. We are laying together now and we have not been so unfamiliar with each other. We have cuddled many nights together, have even thought impure thoughts about each other, and still you love her, no? A woman is no different. Sometimes we just need to be touched—to *feel* loved—while we wait for the real thing. It doesn't always have to mean something."

He closed his eyes and took a deep breath. "I cheated on her once, you know."

She gasped. "Why did you cheat on a woman you love so much?"

"Same reason, I suppose… I needed to be touched… to feel loved while I waited for her. It was when she left. I'd drank too much and ended up in another woman's bed. I couldn't go through with it—didn't actually sleep with her, but I did enough to hate myself for it. It broke Alaina's heart too."

"You told her?"

"Couldn't keep that kind of thing hidden from her. It added to the tension between us, though, and at times, I wished I'd never said a word. It meant nothing to me, but it was everything to her. I even tried to justify it by accusing her of sleeping with someone else while she was gone. Deep down, I knew she hadn't… but I needed some reason for my resentment of her… some excuse to explain why I couldn't touch her."

"Hmmf." Maria draped her arm back over his chest. "You think too much. Maybe you could learn more than just how to fight on this island. Maybe you could watch the people here… how they live and love without overthinking everything. Then you might not be so difficult to deal with."

"I'm not that difficult."

"Yes, you are and you know it, mi amor. I feel sorry for your wife that she has had to deal with such a difficult man for so many years! And one who is so ugly from underneath too!" She snickered loudly.

"Shut up." He chuckled, sliding his arm around her. "Apparently not so ugly to stop *you* from having impure thoughts about *me*."

"Do not flatter yourself, mi amor." She curled into him. "I am lonely. I've had impure thoughts about the captain, most of the crew, and even the big hairy fat man on the trail today."

Chapter Fourteen

Chris

The next morning, the camp outside their tent was bustling with excitement as they prepared to set off on their journey to Oparre.

Chris, too excited to sleep in, woke early and immediately went to the sword near his cot. He spent hours in the dark of the early morning attempting to hold and swing it properly. He was a strong man, he knew, but the weight of the sword had surprised him, and he wondered how strong he might be in comparison to the men who wielded them with ease.

Fastening it to his waist, he practiced walking with it at his hip, pacing from one side of the tent to the other, adjusting his stride to prevent the sword from swinging too much.

"You are a very strange man," Maria stated from the shadows around the bed. "How many times are you gonna walk back and forth like this?"

He straightened and cleared his throat. "How long have you been awake?"

"Long enough to know you are a weirdo."

"It's not like I can just strap this thing on and walk like it's natural," he hissed, moving to the bedside. "Nobody suspects you of anything, but all of them are suspicious of me. The less awkward I can appear, the better."

"If you don't want to look awkward," she snickered, sitting up in the bed to inspect him, "you should probably wear some pants!"

He unsheathed the sword single handedly, as he'd practiced several times, holding the pointed edge toward her. "Eh?"

"Yes, very scary superman." She yawned. "Take your little knife over there and cut me some fruit."

He returned the sword to its sheath and glanced down at his bare legs. "I need to get dressed, and so do you. You'll have enough people to serve you later. For now, you can get your own fruit."

"Asshole." She yawned again, stretching her arms over her head. "I wonder what the king of Tahiti is like? Ooh, I wonder if he needs a queen? I could get used to being royalty."

Chris smirked and plucked his pants up from the trunk beside the bed. "Would you marry just for that?"

"In this time and place?" She rose from the bed to tiptoe over to the table of fruit, snagging a banana. "What else am I going to do? You will find your wife and I will be alone to fend for myself."

He sat on the bed to pull his stockings on. "I wouldn't abandon you, Maria. I'll take you wherever we go."

"You say that now, mi amor, but things will change once you find her. You will not see me the same as you do now and I will become a burden to you."

"Who's feeling sorry for themselves now?" he teased. "You could never be a burden to me."

"We will see." She stepped into the full-sized mirror and turned from one side to the other. "Ugh. I am too skinny now."

It never ceased to amaze him how quickly she could shut down a conversation once she was finished having it. She turned to look over her shoulder and pulled her shift against her skin. "Look at this. My butt is almost gone."

"I'm not looking at your butt, Maria." He stood to button his vest and refasten his sword at his waist. "Should I call for the woman to come dress you? From the sounds outside, they'll be wanting to leave soon."

"Her name is Fetia," she corrected, turning back to push her breasts upward and check her cleavage. "I guess so."

Chris stepped out of the tent to find Lieutenant Edgecumbe standing to one side of its opening. "Lieutenant." Chris bowed his head.

"Christopher!" The man smiled.

"The duchess would like to get dressed now."

"Very well." The lieutenant spun to address a man at his side, who swiftly disappeared in search of Fetia. "Christopher, we are friends now, are we not? You may call me John."

Chris noticed the man had a desperation in his voice at the word "friends," as if he were starving for someone to talk to. He imagined it must be difficult for a lieutenant to find real friendship when he outranked most of the men onboard.

There was something about him that seemed trustworthy and Chris looked forward to learning more about him in the coming nights."And you may call me Chris. Have you come up with an excuse for our training then?"

The lieutenant smiled back at him. "Oh, aye. I've told them the duchess, after witnessing such vile behavior onboard the Resolution, has requested an additional guard inside the tent at night to allow for you to sleep a few hours before you stand watch over her." He examined the sword at Chris's hip.

The young Tahitian woman appeared, her arms loaded with fresh flowers and a basin filled with water. She smiled up at Chris and the lieutenant as they opened the tent flap for her to enter.

"A very delightful people, are they not?" the lieutenant observed as the woman disappeared into the tent. "I can't say that I agree much with such open fornication as their customs allow for, but they are quite refreshing in their good nature to be so surrounded by. Always smiling and in such happy moods. It is hard not to smile ones self in such a place, is it not?"

Chris nodded, glancing up to the shore where Maritata and his wife stood among the seamen who were loading several cutters and canoes with gifts for the king.

The lieutenant followed his gaze. "Rumor onboard the ship is that you lost your wife at sea. Do you think the king will have word of her?"

Chris sighed, watching as two men struggled to corral the goats onto the cutter. "I really hope so."

"We found *you* so close to this place," he offered. "It is very possible she could have made it here by now. Perhaps she is still among the people?"

Chris could feel the excitement of the idea dancing in the pit of his stomach, but he urged himself not to get his hopes up. "That would be amazing if she were. I really don't know what I'll do if I can't find her soon."

"Have faith. I shall have my men inquire as well. Even if this king has no word, the next may well have seen her. Before our departure, we shall be visiting the adjacent land and its leaders, and there are several more stops along our journey before we turn south."

"How familiar are you with this area?" Chris asked, looking over at the lieutenant. "Have you sailed it before?"

"Indeed, I travelled with Captain Cook on his first voyage as well."

"Have you ever heard of anything... strange... happening in the water? Ships disappearing or people appearing seemingly out of thin air?"

The lieutenant's lips curled upward in amusement. "I can't say that I have heard that tale specifically!" He laughed. "Although there are many sailors' superstitions about all manner of strangeness in the water. I've heard of sirens that mesmerize you with song and pull you overboard to drown, massive monstrous beasts that can swallow ships whole, and strange lights beneath the sea... why do you ask?"

"Oh... just a story I heard someone telling on the ship." His cheeks flushed, and he looked back out to the beach. "Curious if anyone else had heard of it is all."

"I wouldn't spend too much time listening to sailors' tales. If you spend enough time at sea, your mind can make fantasy out of just about anything."

They stood silent then and Chris wondered why he hadn't thought to spend more time below decks with the sailors seeking out folklore. They'd spent much more time on the water than the soldiers and might have heard stories similar to his own. Perhaps they might even know how to get to the spot he'd come through.

Slowly, his mind started to formulate a plan. If he could find the right story; if he could get to Alaina; if he could befriend the lieutenant and convince him of who they were; if the lieutenant could become a captain leading his own ship… perhaps he could get them back… someday.

"¡Maravilloso!" Maria swung out of the tent, showing off her very elegant blue silk gown as she spun a circle in front of them. "What do you think? It is beautiful, no?"

"You are divinity itself if I have ever seen it!" The lieutenant beamed, bowing before her offered hand.

"You're going to be hot," Chris observed. "Are you sure that is what you want to wear all day?"

She scoffed. "Yes, I am sure this is *what I want to wear all day.* I am perfectly capable of choosing my own clothing!"

"It's your life," he stated. "But it's going to be a long day in the sun."

"I will worry about myself, thank you." She rolled her eyes and returned to her flirtations with the lieutenant. "What time do we leave, Lieutenant?"

"I believe they are only waiting for you, Your Grace. Shall I escort you to the beach?"

"Oh Sí, yes, please! I am anxious to meet this king!" She looped her arm through his, turning to stick her tongue out at Chris before leaning back into the lieutenant. "Such a fine man you are! And so handsome too!"

Chris followed just behind them, hoping his stride appeared natural with the added weight of the sword at his hip.

They arrived at Oparre after a grueling half hour in the sun on the canoes and cutters. Chris could feel the heat radiating off Maria from her silk dress, and he noticed the beads of sweat where they formed around her hairline and bust. She was stubborn, and he wondered how long she could refrain from complaining strictly out of pride.

When they came ashore, they found the king clothed in a white fabric and seated under a large tree with a group of native men and women surrounding him.

As they grew closer, it became clear that none of the people around the king wore any clothing at all. Maria noticed as well, her mouth dropping open as she stared.

"Maria," Chris hissed in her ear, "don't stare."

She closed her mouth and blinked, but her eyes remained fixed on a very muscular man who laid on his side, one knee bent upward to support his arm and show off every bit of his manhood where it rested against his outstretched leg.

"Seriously, stop staring," he insisted. "They might take offense."

"Oye!" she whispered back as the king rose to greet the captain ahead of them. "A man with a thing as big as *that* doesn't put it out there if he doesn't want a woman to stare at it!"

"A duchess wouldn't stare."

She snapped her head to look over at him. "Jealous, mi amor?" She turned her attention back to the man who met her gaze and smiled up at her. "Look at that thing. It's so much bigger than yours, no?"

"No, as a matter of—

"And this!" Captain Cook waved his arm toward Maria, "It is my honor to present to you, Her Grace, the Duchess of Parma."

Hitihiti translated to the king and the tall dark man tilted his head to one side, inspecting the length of her until a grin formed on his lips. He was as tall as Chris, well over six feet, and his dark hair, like most of the men, curled around his face.

"Your Grace," Captain Cook smiled at her. "This is King Otou."

The man stepped forward and leaned down to press his nose and forehead against hers. "Manava. O te hoê ïa tura," he said in a deep, thick voice.

"King says," Hitihiti spoke beside him in an equally deep baritone. "Welcome. It is great honor."

Maria smiled up at Otou. "Tell him that *I* am the one who is honored. It is so beautiful here."

Hitihiti leaned in to translate, and Otou beamed with surprisingly white teeth. He spread one arm toward the shade of the tree where the others sat and he spoke, waiting patiently as Hitihiti translated, "Come… sit."

The lot of them joined the small group and Chris was careful not to make eye contact with the nude women seated across from him as they stared unwavering back at him. Maria, however, made no move to remove her eyes from the man who still lay on his side beside them.

As introductions began, he noticed the man and Maria were exchanging a language of their own, raising eyebrows and exchanging mischievous smiles.

"Knock it off," he whispered down to her.

"¡Cállate!" she whispered back, not looking away. "I am not doing anything."

The captain and the king thankfully didn't appear to notice and spent an hour speaking about the previous trip and people who were no longer with them, the civil war which had killed the previous king, and Cook spoke at length about the greatness of the new ship, begging Otou to come for a tour.

They spoke about the gifts the captain had brought and the captain refused several gifts offered in exchange, explaining that he was not there to trade, but to make friends. Chris waited for his chance to ask his own questions, but Maria grew impatient as the temperature continued to rise.

"We are looking for our friends," she blurted out the moment there was a break in conversation, wiping the sweat from her brow. "And I am curious if you might have seen them? Maybe on the Spanish ship that was here before us?"

Hitihiti turned to speak lowly to the king, and the king responded, looking quizzically back at her. "King says he sees many on this ship. How will he know your friend?"

Chris cleared his throat and motioned his hands over his head and down his shoulders. "She has long red hair, very white skin."

Hitihiti translated, and the king frowned for a moment and shook his head. He responded with a few short noises. "King says he sees no woman. Only man."

Captain Cook saw the defeat in Chris's shoulders and gave him an apologetic look before turning back to Otou. "If we cannot find her along our journey, we shall return. If she comes to arrive here while we are at sea, would you tell her that her husband is coming to retrieve her? Keep her here in your care?"

Hitihiti struggled to translate this, breaking to think of the right words before Otou interrupted, speaking in detail before Hitihiti had the chance to relay. "King says how you lose a woman? And is she... er..." He pointed to Maria. "Important? Like duchess?"

Maria nodded, speaking before the captain could. "Oh yes. She is *very* important. *More* important than me." She smiled at the captain. "We hit a storm and our ship sank. We lost her but we know she is alive."

Again the two of them discussed before Hitihiti nodded to Maria. "Yes. King says he keep this woman for you. He will give her good care."

Maria smiled at him. "Thank you. You are a great man."

No translation was needed for King Otou to understand her meaning, and he bowed his head to her, flashing his teeth once more. He motioned to a woman at his side, one of the three who had been staring at Chris, and spoke through Hitihiti.

"King says, this is his queen. She is happy to have duchess here. She say you very beautiful. King says tomorrow we have hog."

"Delightful!" Captain Cook exclaimed. "We would be honored if the king would join us aboard the ship in the morning. We have many more gifts for him there and we shall be happy to join him here for dinner."

Hitihiti frowned. "King is Mataou Poupoue. He... eh... no guns..."

"Assure him that no guns shall be fired upon his visit. I shall make certain of it."

Otou rose, Hitihiti along with him, and he motioned toward the boats, evidently implying their visit was over. He spoke a few words as they all rose to their feet, then turned with his wife to walk the opposite direction.

"King says he will think on offer to come to ship. Thank you for many gifts."

Once back on the cutter, Maria shifted uncomfortably, pulling at the neck of her dress and fanning herself. "Oye, it is too hot," she muttered. "I think I might die."

"Your Grace," Captain Cook turned to face her, "I am indebted to you for making such a fine impression upon the king this day. Your company was well received and I think we have secured a lasting friendship with the king as a result. Thank you, my dear. Please, join me and Captain Furneaux aboard the Resolution for a celebratory dinner before returning to the encampment?"

"Oh," she frowned, prompting Chris to hide a smile. "I'm really very tired from the heat today."

"Aren't we all, madam?!" He snickered. "I must insist. I shall order a bottle of our finest port opened for the occasion and we will have you back to your tent within an hour's time!"

As it was, an hour's time turned into three as the captains Cook and Furneaux replayed all the day's events, recounting word-for-word every conversation over an extended dinner and drinks.

The longer they celebrated, the hotter the cabin became, and the hotter it became, the more frequently he observed the servant filling Maria's drink.

The sun was setting in the large window behind him, and he was anxious to get to the tent to begin his training with Lieutenant Edgecumbe. Despite the day's lack of news on Alaina, the lieutenant had given him hope that the people on the neighboring islands might know more. He also needed every opportunity to become closer to John Edgecumbe in order to build the foundation of his plan to return home.

"I should really get the duchess back. It'll be dark soon," he announced, setting his wineglass on the table and standing.

The others stood with him. Captain Cook took Maria's hand in his and bowed. "You're right. We have kept you far too long, Your Grace! I must bid you goodnight! Thank you for such a wonderful day!"

She wobbled a little as she stood and hiccuped. "It wa-as my pleasure, cap'n."

The captain laughed loudly. "Indeed, I believe we have kept you *far* too long this night! Isaac, send for a few marines to escort Her Grace and Christopher both safely back to shore. Worry not over your wife, dear boy. I will stop at nothing to assist you in your endeavor to find her. Your Grace," he smiled fondly, "do get some rest."

"Thank you, captain." Chris bowed properly, then folded Maria's arm around his to support her where she'd nearly fallen over. "Goodnight."

He followed Isaac out to the upper deck, where two young soldiers helped them into a sloop and Isaac lowered them down.

Maria curled into Chris's side and stared at the two men as they waited silently to hit the water. "I know wha-at you are thinking." She sneered at them. "You are thinking *he* is my lover." She hiccuped loudly.

Chris's cheeks reddened, and he smiled at them. "Her Grace has had a bit too much port and sun today."

"Silence!" She ordered, giggling at her own raised voice. "And you are thinking what a lucky man he is to be the lover of such a beautiful woman, no?"

The boat hit the water and the two men raised to disconnect the ropes, careful to avoid Maria's eye as she continued her rambling. "You are thinking, how could such a stupid man become the lover of so great and powerful a woman?!"

"Shut up, Maria," he hissed.

"Do-on't tell me to shut up, *guard*." She chuckled as the men took their seats across from them and began to row toward the shore. "This is what you are thinking, yes?"

"No, Your Grace," one man said nervously.

"PFFFFT." She sat up straighter. "You lie. Everyone is thinking this, no?"

The other soldier shook his head. "Certainly not, Your Grace."

"Maria, stop," Chris whispered, squeezing her hand hard where it sat beneath his jacket.

"¡Aye Coño!" She jerked her hand free to massage it with her other and glare up at him. "Estúpido." She returned her attention to the two baffled soldiers. "He could never be my lover, you know. He is much too ugly."

"I do not think him ugly at all, Your Grace." One soldier smiled at Chris.

"No?" She looked up at him. "Well, that's because you have never seen my real lover, Dahveed."

Chris rolled his eyes as Maria proceeded to describe in detail the exact man they'd seen earlier that day with the king. "Now that," she giggled, "that is a *real* man."

Much to his relief, the boat reached the shallows, and the two soldiers hopped out of the sloop to pull it onto the shore.

"Shall I escort you into camp, sir?"

"No, thank you." Chris ran a hand over his face as he stood and lifted Maria into his cradled arms. "I've got it from here. Goodnight."

"Goodnight." The two soldiers said in bewildered unison.

He carried her up the sand toward camp, relieved for the darkness that had fallen around them that no one else might see her drunken stupor. "You are ridiculous," he hissed once he was outside of earshot, stopping to set her on her feet.

"I am ridiculous?" She swayed and hiccuped. "*You* are ridiculous. Look at you... standing there all proud... like you're going to do something about it."

"Maria, I need you to take a deep breath and try to sober up now. The lieutenant is going to be at the tent soon and I can't risk you saying something to expose us."

Again she hiccuped loudly. "Us?" She scoffed. "There is no *us*. There is you and there is your wife and that is all there is."

He groaned. "I don't have time to argue with you about this right now. I've already told you I would never abandon you."

"Why wouldn't you?" She stumbled backward, and he promptly caught her. "You don't care about me. Not really. You *deal* with me because you are stuck with me. Once she is here, you will not want to *deal* with me anymore."

"You're drunk. You know that's not true."

She stumbled again, latching onto the arm that still steadied her. "Women don't like me, Kreese. Your little wife will not like me and so I will become a burden. She will steal you away and I will be forgotten here. You will abandon me like everyone else in my life has abandoned me."

Chris rolled his eyes and bent to scoop her back up. "There's obviously no reasoning with you while you are drunk. I'm not going to leave you anywhere, you pain-in-the-ass woman. Now, I'm taking you back to camp where you will hopefully be passed out before the lieutenant gets there."

She didn't fight him, but curled into his chest and sighed. "Do you love me, Kreese?"

"Not at the moment." He moved cautiously through the dark toward the lights of the encampment's fires, his eyes scanning every bush and tree as he became aware of the danger they might be in if too many drunken men found them on the beach alone.

She grew heavier in his arms as she slipped slowly toward sleep. "But you do love me sometimes? Not like you love your wife... but you love me, yes?"

He blew out, squinting to make out movement ahead of them near the camp's entrance. "Yes, Maria."

"Say it."

"Say what?"

She yawned. "Say you love me."

A figure was moving toward them in the shadows from camp, and he tightened his hold on her. "Someone's coming. Be quiet."

She hiccuped. "I will be quiet when you say it."

Through gritted teeth, he managed, "Fine. I love you. Now, shut up."

She hummed happily, and he could feel her body go limp as she almost instantly lost consciousness.

As he came closer to the camp's entrance, he found it was the lieutenant walking toward them; his appearance disheveled and his expression somewhat frazzled. "Chris!" he whispered, gazing down at Maria in his arms. "What's happened to the duchess? Is everything quite alright?"

"She's fine." He adjusted his grip on her. "Too much sun and entirely too much wine is all."

"Oh, very well. I was concerned for her after the day I have witnessed here. Shall I call for Fetia to undress her?"

Chris glanced down at her lifeless body as she began to snore ever so softly. "No, I think it might be better if I do it. She's out cold and that tiny woman wouldn't be able to move her."

He chuckled a little as her mouth fell open. "I don't think we will need to worry about disturbing her, though. What happened here today?"

The lieutenant walked alongside him through camp, the subtle sounds of men who had secured a trade for the nails in their pockets seeping from the tents as they passed. The lieutenant glanced at Maria to assure she was sleeping. "Something quite grave indeed. I'm afraid I don't know quite how to put it."

He looked around self consciously, then back to Chris. "Might I speak openly with you about something?"

Amused at the disorder the normally very orderly lieutenant appeared in the midst of, Chris nodded. "Of course."

Arriving at the tent, the lieutenant pulled back its flap to usher them inside the candle-lit room. "And you won't repeat what I have to say?"

Chris held in a laugh at the man's fidgeting as he carried Maria to the bed and laid her across it before turning back to him. "Your secrets are safe with me, John."

The lieutenant swallowed, then leaned in to speak softly. "I'm afraid I've been... molested."

Chris did laugh out loud at that, regretting it as John's face appeared even more distraught. He cleared his throat and adjusted his expression. "How so?"

"Maritata's wife." He looked around them. "She... well... she had her way with me very much against my will! I made every attempt to plead with her to stop, but she would not! I've never had a woman do such things... and once she started... I couldn't find the strength to stop her. I'm afraid I am quite tormented as to what I should do now. Do I inform Maritata of his wife's ill-doings? Do I tell the captain? Surely he would have me flogged for it! Am I condemned eternally for having engaged in such sinful behavior?"

Chris tried to make his amused expression seem solemn. "Did you have sex with her?"

"Certainly not! *I* did not do a thing... *she*, however... did several... things."

"Well then." Chris smiled. "Surely you would not be condemned eternally for something someone else did to you against your will? I think your soul will be just fine. As for Maritata and the captain, would telling them do any good for anyone?"

John frowned. "No. I suppose not."

"Then let it be for now. Avoid her whenever possible. You haven't done anything wrong."

The lieutenant nodded, focusing on Maria where she lay lifeless on the bed. "Should I leave you to undress the duchess and return later then?"

Chris looked over his shoulder at her. "No. I think it's best if I let her sleep it off for a while before I attempt to touch her. She might claw my eyes out if she wakes to find me removing her clothing..."

'Or attempt to molest me,' his mind added. *'Who knows with that woman.'*

"Besides," he shook his head, "I don't think she would appreciate waking to find both of us seeing her in only her shift."

The lieutenant laughed at that, looking once again in her direction. "She is quite beautiful, Chris. There is not a man among us who has not noticed."

He snapped himself from his stare to spin around and kneel at the trunk beside Chris's cot. Hidden behind it, he pulled out two wooden sparring swords, handing one to Chris. "Come, let us begin. You'll need all the training you can get before we are back at sea with these lustful men."

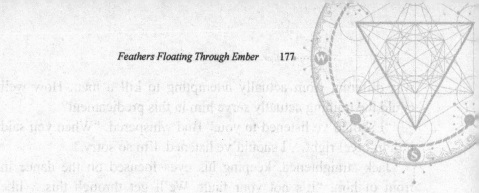

Chapter Fifteen

Jack

Despite his nerves causing his stomach to turn, Jack managed to get down a few pieces of pork throughout the ceremony. As he picked at his food, the drums beat louder and the men stomped and shouted in a tribal dance.

They tensed their muscles and moved together as one in a perfectly stiffened rhythm with the drums. Through their movement, they illustrated a battle and the death of a man. They illustrated fierceness in themselves as they roared loudly into the skies around them. In dance, they painted a picture for the fight to come.

Jack could feel his heart beating in his throat as the evening drew onward and the theatrics grew more intensified. He kept telling himself that he would do whatever he had to do for the sake of Alaina... But could he? He'd been so ready to kill Phil when Phil had thrust himself upon Alaina, but could he kill a complete stranger? Could the knowledge that these people could harm her be enough to force his hands to tighten around another man's throat?

That's how he imagined doing it... with his hands. He didn't think there was any weapon he could use better than a native, and so when the time came, he would choose his hands in the hopes he could overpower his opponent with sheer strength. He'd been trained on how to fight for his various acting roles... but acting was different from actually attempting to kill a man. How well could the training actually serve him in this predicament?

"I should've listened to you," Bud whispered. "When you said it didn't feel right... I should've listened. I'm so sorry."

Jack straightened, keeping his eyes focused on the dance in front of him. "It's not your fault. We'll get through this... like everything else. We have to. Besides, they could've found the island before we found them."

"It's not an easy thing to do... killing a man," Bud whispered. "If I could trade places..."

"I know."

"You can't think of him as a man," Bud continued. "You have to think of him as your enemy. Focus only on what needs to be done and know that if you do not do it, he will kill you. He will kill Alaina... he will kill your child. He is not a human, but a job... an obstacle. He is the death of everyone you've ever loved and you must defeat him. He is not a person. He lives only to kill you and the ones you love. He has been training his whole life to kill your family. Do you understand?"

Jack nodded, swallowing hard.

"Everything you've ever been taught to feel about killing needs to disappear. You need only think about that baby... You would do anything to protect your child. And this is what needs to be done. He will kill your baby if you do not kill him first. He will kill Alaina. You need to see his hands on her in your mind. You need to know that it's his life or hers in your hands. His life means nothing up against hers."

The drums stopped then, and the crowd looked over at Jack.

"Drink," Michael instructed, handing him a clay bottle filled with liquid.

He sniffed its contents and, identifying it as a heavily fermented fruit concoction, raised the bottle to his lips and took a hefty swig.

"It time now." Michael grinned, standing.

Several large natives approached then, each of them carrying two identical weapons. One man held broadswords, another held long wooden spears. A man beside them held two very sharp daggers while a fourth held out two antique looking axes.

"Choose weapon," Michael said.

"Hands," Jack said, holding up his fist to illustrate.

"Very good." Michael grinned, turning to the crowd to inform them of Jack's choice. They all cheered in response and followed as Michael led him to a clearing on the opposite side of the fire. At the clearing, Uati sat in a throne-like wooden chair placed up several carved steps to oversee the events. "Uati will raise hand. Then fight. Understand?"

Jack took a deep breath, trying desperately to prepare himself for what needed to be done and settle his heart from beating out of his chest. "I understand."

The crowd created a circle of bodies around the clearing, lighting torches in the dimming light. His hands were shaking, and the spit in his mouth was growing thick. He hopped on the balls of his feet from one side to the other, shaking out his arms and tilting his head from one side to the other to warm his trembling muscles.

'Breathe,' he reminded himself, inhaling deeply. *'This needs to be done... he is not a man... he's not a man... I have to do this.'*

'How will I do it?' he wondered, his eyes darting from one face to the next as he waited for an opponent. *'Do I charge first? Do I let him come to me? I have to get him on the ground... get my arms around his neck... Will I be able to hold him tight enough? What if he's stronger than I am?'*

The drums began to beat again, this time a slow and steady march of war, and his already racing heart quickened. He bounced from toe to toe, trying to clear his mind... to prepare for something that no man could've been prepared for.

How had it come to this? How had they arrived here? Why? Why couldn't he have just stayed on that island? Built a bigger ship or let Anna leave? How could he have left Alaina there?

He saw the man being pushed through the crowd. In the fading evening light, his dark tattooed skin made his snarling teeth and glaring eyes that much more pronounced as he approached. He focused on Jack with an unwavering stare, growling as he stiffly punched his own chest and entered the circle.

Jack stared back and envisioned the man's hands on Alaina... his dark fingers curled around her delicate neck... and immediately rage burned in his lungs. He could do this. As he looked into the dark black pupils of his eyes where the fire reflected inside them, he didn't see a man, but instead, a monster. He could kill a monster. He had to.

The man shouted out a monstrous high-pitched battlecry, but Jack didn't blink. He stared, unmoved and waiting for the man to charge.

He didn't look up for Uati's signal. He didn't care... He would wait and he would use every ounce of strength he had to do whatever he had to do to kill this man. Then he would take Bud and get the hell off this island. Rescue be damned. He would go back to the island and he would never leave her again.

He didn't remember the charge... didn't remember his reaction or the reactions of the crowd around them.

In a flash, he was rolling on the ground with the man in his arms. There were blows and scratches. He clawed and punched at whatever he could as the man wrestled with him in the dirt.

As they rolled to one side, the man curled his arm around Jack's throat, and Jack reached up to try to dig his fingers into the his eye sockets. Coming in too low, he hooked his fingers into his mouth instead, then used his other to try to force the jaw open and broken.

He pulled the top and bottom half of the jaw until he felt it crack and the man screamed out. In that moment, the man's arm loosened, giving Jack the opportunity to roll and wind both arms around his throat, squeezing the life out of him, his muscles trembling with the effort.

The man reached up to claw and scratch at Jack's face, pulling at his hair, digging his nails into the skin, urgently searching for a way to regain control. Jack held tighter, turning his face to shield his eyes from the man's clawing fingernails.

He could feel the man's body weakening beneath his force, and he watched as his arms flailed and clawed at his forearms, desperately trying to work free. As he waited for the flailing to stop, his mind returned to him and the monster in his arms became a man pleading for his life.

"I'm sorry," Jack whispered, squeezing his eyes tightly shut as the man grew weaker still. "I'm so sorry."

He could feel his eyes burning beneath his closed eyelids; tears welling in them as he tightened his arms around him and the man stopped fighting. "Please forgive me."

He squeezed tighter, keeping his eyes closed as he felt the man's pulse slow to a stop against his forearm. Even then, he didn't let go. He held him, tears dripping down his cheeks. "I'm so sorry," he repeated over and over.

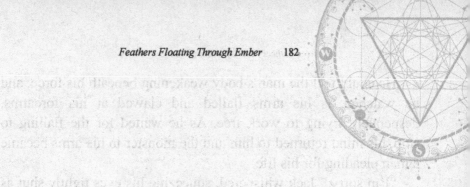

Chapter Sixteen

Chris

Chris, as luck would have it, was a natural with the broadsword. He and Lieutenant Edgecumbe spent hours in the tent sparring, quickly transitioning from the wooden swords to real ones.

With Maria too hungover to join the following days' events, they informed the captain she'd fallen ill, and they used the next several days to train around the clock inside the tent.

The lieutenant was instantly impressed by how quickly Chris had picked up the skill. Even Maria complimented him on how natural he appeared with it.

He enjoyed the feel of the sword in his hands and couldn't remember the last time anything had given him so much gratification. He'd thought that construction had been his calling, had always felt a sense of accomplishment in doing so, but this… this level of satisfaction was unlike any other he'd felt in his life. Even when John Edgecumbe had finished the lessons and his arms were too fatigued to lift the sword, Chris continued to practice.

The lieutenant had also made a gift of a small dagger to Maria and dedicated their breaks in training to showing her how to use it. He was becoming a friend to them both, sharing stories of his upbringing and his aspirations to become a captain himself. Chris liked him and was sure someday soon he could tell him the truth about who they were... hopefully long before they'd landed somewhere that would expose Maria for not being the actual duchess of Parma.

Chris wanted nothing more than to stay at the camp and continue to train. That morning, however, they would be revisiting king Otou on Oparre again. Since the king had no answers regarding Alaina, Chris was unconcerned with the constant niceties the Captain felt obliged to pay the young king and was anxious for them to move on to the next island.

The captain had insisted on Maria's presence—had even come around to check on her well-being the night before and, as a result of him seeing her health restored, they were unable to refuse.

He waited outside as Fetia dressed Maria and was pleasantly surprised when Maria appeared in a flattering cream colored dress with bright white and pink flowers weaved into her hair.

The dress exposed her arms and fit snugly at the breast and waist, its small embroidered bits of rose-colored flowers popping off the fabric. Her hair was woven into multiple braids that wound upward to flow out into curls high on her head, the little flowers making her dark hair seem that much darker.

"You look amazing," he blurted before he had the chance to think better of the statement.

She raised an eyebrow at him and smiled. "Oh, I know. I wonder if that handsome man will be there again today? Speaking of handsome, where is the lieutenant?"

He shook his head as she curled her arm through his and they started toward the boats. "Maria, you really shouldn't flirt so much. What will you do if one of those men shows up in the middle of the night wanting something more?"

"*Those* men?" she scoffed. "I would throw you out into the dark and do whatever they wanted!"

"Seriously Maria." He stopped to face her. "You could be putting yourself in danger. You really should make yourself seem less..." He glanced down at her cleavage where it swelled atop the neckline of her dress. "...accessible."

"Be quiet idiota! I am not hurting anybody and John showed me how to defend myself if I need to! Where is John, anyway?"

He rolled this eyes, turning them back on the path. "He's already on the boat."

She hopped with excitement. "He is coming with us today?"

"Yes."

"Good! I like him."

He nodded. "I know. I do too. I think he might be able to help us find a way back… once we're better friends and can tell him the truth."

"Do you think he will believe us?"

"Not yet." He sighed. "But in time, once he knows us better… maybe. From what he's been telling me, I think there's a good chance he'll be given command of his own ship once we return to England. Maybe we could convince him to take us back to the spot of the crash… try to search for whatever it was that brought us here… I plan to spend more time below deck talking to the sailors. They tell lots of stories and maybe one of them has heard of something similar?"

"It is a good idea. What will I do while you are down there?"

"I've thought about that a lot. I think it'd be best if I began eating dinner with them. You would be safe in the great cabin with the captain."

She snarled her nose. "I don't know how you will eat down there. It smells like shit… like more shit than the rest of the ship even."

He chuckled. "I'll manage."

On this trip to Oparre, the king set up food and festivities which went on for hours.

As the afternoon turned to evening, he ushered them all to a small pavilion which would serve as a stage for a native performance.

Otou insisted Maria and the two captains join him to sit at the front of the pavilion, encouraging Chris to remain at the back with the other soldiers and servants. Natives and members of their group filled the space between them so there were at least a hundred people gathered in anticipation of the show.

Three drums began to beat steadily, and a group of men appeared in the center of the stage. Bursting through them in dance was the queen, who remained topless but sported an intricately tasseled red skirt.

The drumbeat very gradually swelled, and the group dance began. The men contorted their bodies at strange angles in unison as the queen began a hypnotic movement of her hips, winding her arms up over her head and out as her lower body vibrated with the speeding drumbeat.

Chris fell into a daze watching her.

As it so often did, his mind went to Alaina. He tried to remember the last time she had moved in such a way to seduce him. It had been years since she'd even attempted...

He wondered if he'd been purposely remembering only the good things in order to drive himself forward in his search for her. Had he forgotten the years of arguing that followed the good years; the years of hurt tthey'd inflicted on each other before they'd boarded the plane?

He'd stopped hearing her voice before they'd even gotten on the ship; had stopped dreaming of her altogether. Part of him wondered now if the resentment had returned. The crash and their separation had put her up on a pedestal, but now that the shock had worn off, he found the frustration was still there.

She'd left him. Regardless of why she'd left, she left and then she came back to constantly accuse him of being unaffectionate. She, too, was unaffectionate. But she'd just expected him to do it all—expected him to be the one to reinitiate all physical contact after going so long without it.

Maria was right... he *was* still angry with her, and as he watched the woman move across the stage, he became more angry. If she had put in just a little more effort... if she had taken at least some of the blame upon herself... maybe they never would have boarded that plane. Maybe they'd have found happiness in the home he worked so hard to build her... in the *life* he'd worked so hard to give her.

He loved her, but God, he was angry. He wanted to find her and shake her and scream at her for wasting so much of their lives; for being so selfish in their relationship. He wanted Alaina back—*his Alaina*—the person she'd been before they'd lost the baby... before he'd had to walk on eggshells around her.

The queen smiled at him and he tried to remember the last time Alaina had actually smiled at him? Was *his* Alaina even still there anymore, or was she forever replaced by the new one? Would it matter that he was angry? Would it matter if she took some of the blame? Could they ever be the people they once were?

As the people around him began to applaud, he was pulled from his trance, and realized, upon looking to where she'd been seated, that Maria was gone. His throat tightened as he scanned the dimming landscape around him. '

You idiot! ' he berated himself. How long had she been missing? How had she gotten up without him noticing? Where in the world could she have gone to?

"The duchess," he said hysterically to the soldier standing to his right. "Did you see where she went?"

"Aye, sir." The man nodded and pointed to the trees in the distance. "She went that way some time ago. She looked as though she might've been ill."

"Fuck," he grumbled under his breath, racing past the soldier toward the trees.

Once within a reasonable distance from the group to do so, he began calling for her, first in a hushed voice and then growing louder as he made his way into the brush. "MARIA?!"

Panic swept over him the deeper he went with no answer. How could he have taken his eyes off her? In this place where he trusted no one? In this place where *everyone's* eyes were on her?! "MARIA?"

He heard a sound ahead of him and began to jog, noticing the sound was that of a woman sobbing. "MARIA??!!"

He ran faster, ignoring the sharp branches and vines that scratched and whipped his arms and face as he increased his speed, terrified of what he might see ahead as he drew closer and the sound of the cries became distinctively Maria's.

With the sun setting behind him, beneath the canopy, it was nearly dark and he almost missed the clearing were it not for a hint of her bright cream dress catching the corner of his eye.

He turned quickly and dashed into the opening where she knelt on the ground and sobbed loudly, Lieutenant Edgecumbe at her side with both arms wrapped around her shaking body.

"What happened?" he panted, falling to his knees in front of them. He noticed that Maria's hands and the front of her dress were covered in dark red blood, as was the lieutenant's attire. Her hair had come loose from its pins in most places and was matted with twigs and leaves poking out from several spots. The front of her bodice was loosened to expose her shift where it had been ripped. "Who did this?"

"I called for you," she sobbed, shakily holding her bloodied hands in front of her. "Over and over and you did not come."

He tried to take her outstretched hands in his, but she pulled them away and buried her face in the lieutenant's shoulder.

"John, what happened?" he demanded.

John pointed to the lifeless uniformed body lying on the ground a few yards away from them, rocking her softly as she clung to him. Chris stared at the dead soldier, then back to them.

He'd never seen Maria cry. Not really. There was a stab of pain now in his heart as he watched her crumble in John's arms. It should've been him there on the ground consoling her, and he longed to wrap his arms around her... to carry her back to the tent and hold her... to promise her no one would ever touch her again, to beg her forgiveness for not being there to prevent what he assumed had just happened.

"We can't take her back like this, nor can I return with blood upon myself," John said quietly, glancing around to be sure Chris wasn't followed. "That is a sergeant from the Adventure. They'll be looking for him and I'll have to do something with his body before anyone can find it."

"Tell me what to do." Chris straightened, trying not to break himself as he watched Maria shake harder with tears.

"Go back to the group and inform the captain that Her Grace's illness has returned. Tell him, *discreetly*, that she's made a mess of her dress and to avoid embarrassment in front of the king, I have offered to escort her back to camp myself on a small cutter. While you are doing that, I'll hide him so I may return later and dispose of his body. I need you to insist he keep the group there long enough for us to steal away with her before they can see us. Meet us at the beach when you are through."

Chris swallowed hard. "Maria…"

She would not look at him.

"Maria, I'm so sorry."

"Go," John urged. "We haven't the time to waste. She is safe now, I assure you."

Chris stood and stared a moment longer, longing to touch her just once, to make sure she was still whole, to let her know he was there and he was sorry. Knowing he couldn't in that moment, he nodded and turned back toward the theatre.

He trudged through the brush toward their group, cursing himself over and over. He had failed. In every way he could fail, he'd failed. How could he have taken his eyes off her?! With all he knew about these men in this place, how could he have let himself become so distracted?

'There is no us,' he could hear her saying. *'There is you and there is your wife and that is all there is.'*

At the time, he had considered her words drunken and dramatic ramblings, but here they were, just days later, and he'd been so entrenched in his thoughts of Alaina that he failed to do the only thing he had promised her he would do. He'd abandoned her even before he found Alaina. Now he would spend the rest of his life regretting it.

Back at the small theatre, a new group had appeared on the little stage, seemingly more comical than the last as the audience erupted with laughter at the appearance of a small man boasting a powdered wig, an apparent imitation of Captain Cook.

Chris made his way through the crowd to the captain. "Captain," he whispered in his ear. "the duchess has grown ill again. I'm afraid she's gotten sick on her dress and is embarrassed to return. Lieutenant Edgecumbe has volunteered to take us back to camp, and she insists you all stay and enjoy the festivities."

"Most troubling news indeed." Cook shook his head and frowned. "I should not have insisted she come today when she was so recently recovered from her sickbed. Offer Her Grace my sincerest apologies. Shall I send a few men to assist you with the cutter?"

"No, sir." Chris smiled. "She is quite humiliated as it stands and wouldn't want anyone else to see her this way. It's hard enough for her that Lieutenant Edgecumbe has seen her in such a state."

"You are right, sir. I wouldn't want to add to the duchess's discourse by exposing her to any additional audience. Do express my apologies to Her Grace for having forced her out this day."

"I will."

Chris shook with the effort of remaining calm as he stood and made his way back to the boats. It took all the willpower inside him not to run.

As he approached the cutter, he found Maria already inside. John had removed his bloodstained jacket and was standing at an angle to keep her bloodied dress shielded from view.

Chris jerked his own jacket off his shoulders as he hurried down the beach and onto the boat, covering her with it as he sat down beside her.

"Take that oar there," John ordered, not giving him the moment to apologize again. "We'll need to make haste."

He followed the order, and John sat down on the opposite side of Maria. Collectively, the two of them rowed out of the bay, hoisting the small sail in order to move more quickly once they were out of the shallow water.

Maria trembled beside him, and he leaned in to whisper. "Maria, I'm—"

"We will not train this night, as I'm sure you are already aware." John pulled the oar to turn them toward Point Venus. "I'll need to return as soon as possible to figure out what to do with the body."

"How did this happen?" Chris said finally, anger catching up to his sorrow. "Why didn't you tell me you were going off?" He looked past her to John. "And how did you end up out there?"

"I saw her run toward the trees with her hand covering her mouth. I assumed she was ill and did not want to intrude upon her being sick. When she did not return for some time, I took it upon myself to inspect the situation and had only come upon her moments before you did, sir."

"I killed him," she said in a far off voice, staring straight ahead. "I killed a man."

"*You* killed him?" Chris looked at her tiny body where it shook beside him.

She nodded slowly. "Sí. It all happened so fast." She kept her eyes focused far ahead of them and trembled harder. "One minute, he was on top of me and he was trying to…" Her voice hitched and she shook it off, straightening her back. "…but he didn't because the next thing I knew, he was lifeless and the dagger in my hand was full of his blood."

Relief washed over Chris at the knowledge that the man hadn't been successful.

"You did exactly what I taught you to do," John reminded her. "What happened is not your fault."

"But I murdered someone." Her eyes welled with tears and she began to tremble again.

Chris smoothed a hand over her back only for his fingers to bump into John's, where his hand was already there doing the same. Both men pulled away from her, carefully avoiding each other's eyes.

Chris cleared his throat. "Could we just tell the captains what happened? The man attacked the duchess! She shouldn't be expected to just let him, should she?"

John shook his head. "Duchess or not, the murder of a marine would not be taken lightly at the hands of a woman. Even if it is justified, I'm afraid it would not go unpunished. And that was Furneaux's man. Captain Furneaux is not known for being lenient with his punishment. She could risk being flogged, imprisoned, or even hanged."

"Hanged?!" Chris's mouth dropped open. "For defending herself?"

"I'm afraid so. That's why I must return most immediately. Her attire must be completely disposed of as well. Burn it when the encampment is asleep."

"I will. What will you do with the body?"

John shrugged. "I'm not entirely sure. I will figure out something."

"Why are you doing this for us?" Maria asked, looking up through her tear-filled eyes at him. "You barely know us. What will happen to you if you are caught with his dead body?"

"My fate would certainly not be so dire as your own, madam. As his superior, I can justify my actions as self defense, accuse him of attempted harm upon myself. I should be flogged for it and returned to duty."

Chris frowned. "Why not save yourself the trouble and do that in the first place, then?"

John tilted his head to one side and smiled. "Because a man, no matter how angry he might be, would not willingly stab another man where the duchess has stabbed the sergeant... unless some sort of... *other* activities might be involved. I dare say I might be in a great deal more trouble among my men should I confess to inflicting such a wound."

Chris cautiously moved his hand over her shoulder. "I'm so sorry. I should've been there."

"I still don't understand why you would do this for us." Maria repeated, shrugging Chris's hand from her.

John straightened and looked ahead at the sky where it had turned indigo. "When you have been at sea for as long as I, it is rare to come upon friendship. One longs for someone to talk to as the months drag on. I believe I have found true friendship among you and it is of value to me. I hope that, in assisting you in this endeavor, you will come to value mine as well."

Chris leaned forward to look past Maria at him. "We cannot thank you enough for this, and your friendship was already very much valued by both of us."

They had reached the shallows at Point Venus, and Chris followed John's lead of jumping out of the boat to pull it ashore. "This is where I leave you." John bowed to them. "I must return straight away. I shall call upon you both in the morning to inform you the task is done."

Maria stood in the boat and reached a hand out to place it on his cheek. "Thank you, John. For everything."

He smiled sweetly and stared for a moment, exposing an underlying fondness for her that Chris assumed was the true reasoning behind his willingness to assist them. "It is my honor to serve you, Your Grace."

She allowed him to assist her out of the cutter and stood on the shore as Chris helped him push it back out into the water. They stood side by side in silence and watched as he disappeared into the shadows.

As soon as he was gone, Chris turned toward her. "Are you angry with me?"

"Not everything that happens in this life is about *you*," she managed, her words evidently forced against the tears she was so desperately trying to hold back. "No. I am not angry with you. I am angry with myself."

She turned toward camp, wrapping the jacket around herself and taking a deep breath. "Come on, before someone sees me like this."

He reached to take her arm in his, and she flinched. "I do not want to be touched right now."

"Maria, I—

"You are sorry. Yes, I know." She sniffled, trembling with the effort of not breaking down again. "I don't want to talk about it right now. Okay?"

He swallowed the lump that formed in his own throat and nodded.

Silently, he walked alongside her through camp, avoiding eye contact with the other marines. Every sniffle from her felt like a stab through his chest, and by the time they reached her tent, he felt like he might die from the heartache inside him.

The tent's candles had already been lit in preparation of their return and she crossed over to the trunk by her bed to pull out a new shift. "I don't want Fetia in here tonight, understand?"

"Yes," he said softly, shame filling him as he stood and awaited instruction as to what to do next.

She moved to the standing mirror where she removed the coat and inspected her disheveled appearance and blood-soaked hands. She looked up at his reflection after several minutes and straightened. "Come and take this off me then."

He went straight to stand behind her, his shaking hands fumbling with the laces of her stays. They didn't speak a single word as he loosened the corset and untied the petticoats, but only watched each other's reflections in the mirror.

When she stood in only her torn shift, his hands hovered in the air between them, unsure of what to do next. Finally, he spoke, his voice hoarse and coming out in a choke. "Are you hurt?"

She stared at his reflection for a long while until her lip quivered and her eyes watered. "Yes, I am hurt." Then she broke, letting the tears fall. "I am hurt in every way."

He wrapped both arms tightly around her, burying his face against her shoulder to hide his own tears. "I'll never ever take my eyes off you again, I swear it! God, if I could take it back... If I could fix this..."

"It's my fault," she sobbed, turning in his arms to rest her face against his chest. "I knew I shouldn't run off on my own! I have always known not to run off on my own! Why do men do this to women? Do you know what it's like to live your life unable to do anything on your own out of fear that a man might do this to you?! To never be able to feel safe walking alone? To never be able to make a decision that doesn't involve other people being there to watch out for you?!"

He smoothed his hands over her hair, wincing as the leaves and twigs still tangled inside it served as yet another reminder of his failure to watch over her. With one arm still holding her against him, he began to pull them out.

"My whole life, I have never had a man kiss me out of love... or touch me out of love... it is always this. Do you know what it's like to hear so many fairytales about men; to know that it exists for other women and to only know the darkest sides of them yourself? Is there something wrong with me?"

He very softly pulled her away from him and shook his head, smoothing his hand down her hair to rest it upon her cheek and tilt her face to look up at him. "There is *nothing* wrong with you."

And he surprised himself by the depths with which he meant the words; by the sudden longing inside him to give her just a moment of fairytale to erase her pain.

Her breath hitched as she inhaled and big tears spilled over her cheeks. "Yes, there is!" Her voice raised an octave as she fell apart again. "I am a murderer now!"

"You are not a murderer." He grazed his thumb over her cheek where he still held her face. "You defended yourself against a monster, and that's not something you should ever cry about. If anything, you should be proud of yourself. Never again will you need to be afraid to walk alone. Besides, if you hadn't killed him, *I* would have. Do you think *I* am a murderer?"

She sniffled. "No."

He knelt to pick up the clean shift from the floor where she'd dropped it at her feet. "Here. Put this on and sit down there." He motioned to the vanity before he turned his back to allow her to change."I'll wash your hair and we'll get you in bed. Did you bring your toiletry bag out here with you?"

"Sí," she uttered. "It's under my pillow."

"I'll get it. Take that shift off and I'll burn it with the rest."

He retrieved the little bag and returned to find her seated at the small table, watching his reflection in the mirror. He grabbed the wash basin and bowl from the table, then circled around to kneel at her feet. "Give me your hands."

He tore a strip of cloth from the old shift and poured water over it, producing the bar of soap and lathering it into it.

She held her hands out to him, watching him as he took each and scrubbed the blood from her fingers. "It is not your fault, you know," she whispered.

He kept his attention on her knuckles as he pushed the cloth over them. "Yes, it is. I had one job out here and I failed to do it."

"Mi amor, it is *I* that had one job out here, and that was to stay next to you. *You* have to search for signs of your wife, learn to fight, make friends and earn their trust, try to find us a way home, come up with all the plans to get us there, worry about finding a job or a home if we don't get there, and on top of all that, you have to make sure I am dressed and taken care of every day. You told me to be less accessible, and I didn't listen. You told me to stay beside you and I didn't listen. *I* am the one who failed us. Not you."

He stood, avoiding her eyes as he moved behind her with the basin to pour it over her hair. Gently, he massaged shampoo into her dark waves and focused on his fingers instead of her gaze through the mirror in front of them.

"I wasn't so sick I couldn't tell you, superman." She sighed. "The truth is… I wanted to be followed into the woods today… by John."

He looked up at her then, baffled at the confession. "By John?" He frowned, his fingers freezing in place against her soapy scalp.

"Yes, *by John*. I see the way he looks at me sometimes and I thought…" She looked down at her lap where she fumbled with the fabric of her shift.

"Well, I knew he was watching me, and I thought if I ran into the woods to be sick, he would follow to help me… I thought maybe I could start to make him fall in love with me… I thought… maybe if he loved me and he thought I loved him, he would believe us… he would be more willing to help us."

She looked up at him, new tears in her eyes. "But someone else was in there... and John didn't come... and it is all my stupid fault."

"John?" He repeated, blinking hard. "And what were you thinking of doing with *John* if he followed you like you wanted?" He could feel his pulse in his throat.

"I don't know," she admitted. "I just thought if he helped me, I could touch his arm and tell him how wonderful he is... make him feel good... make him start to develop feelings..."

He didn't understand why he was suddenly upset, but he was. He was almost angry about it. "Is that what you want? You want John?"

She frowned at his shocked expression in the mirror. "I want to help! I feel so helpless here that you have to do everything while I just sit and look pretty. I thought I could help. And besides, John is a good man. What would be so wrong with me wanting him, anyway?"

He focused back on her hair, massaging the soap through. "Nothing, I guess."

"Are you afraid I will love him and we will abandon you?"

"No." He knelt to pick up the basin and bowl.

'*No...* ' he repeated in his mind, trying to make himself believe it, but deep down, he was afraid of that very thing. He was terrified she would love him. Jealous at the thought of the two of them together in the bed he'd shared with her while he slept in the tiny cot in the corner alone. "Tilt your head back."

She obliged, and he rinsed her hair, combing his fingers through until the basin was emptied. He moved to fetch the remnants of her old shift to dry the ends of her hair with.

"You don't want me to love him?" She kept her eyes focused on him in the mirror.

"I didn't say that." He wiped his own hands with the shift and turned to add it to the pile of clothes to be burned.

"But you are thinking it... Why don't you want me to love him?" She spun in the chair to face him.

"It's nothing, Maria." He didn't look back at her, but folded the blanket down on the bed. "Come on, it's been a long day. You should lie down."

She stood then and took his hands in hers. "Oye, if you tell me not to love him, I won't."

"You can do whatever you want," he whispered, keeping his eyes on his feet.

"Hmmf." She let go of his hands and crawled into the bed. "You are staying with me, aren't you? I cannot sleep alone tonight."

He looked at her then, his mind racing as he struggled to get a handle on the emotions that had come seemingly out of thin air to plague him. "I have to burn these clothes first. I'll be right out front. As soon as they are burnt, I will come lay down with you."

He knelt to pick the clothes up from the floor and turned toward the entrance, his cheeks on fire.

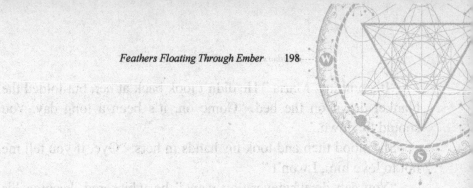

Chapter Seventeen

Chris

He burned her clothes and stared into the flames until they became ash, all the while trying to work out his own mind. Why should he care if she wanted John? He was married and his heart was set on finding Alaina.

But why then did he want to scream *'Don't love him!'* the moment Maria had promised not to if he'd only asked it of her?

Why did the feel of John's hand on her back make him shake with jealousy? When had he developed any kind of feelings outside of attraction toward her and how had it taken her interest in John for him to notice?

How would it be fair for him to ask her not to love someone else when he himself loved another... had been in search of her every day since their arrival? It's not like he was going to abandon his search for Alaina now... Alaina was everything to him... But why was he so bothered by Maria's interest in John?

When he couldn't find the answers, he went back inside to crawl into bed, fully clothed, beside her. She was asleep and moved only slightly when he laid down.

In the light of the single candle that burned beside him, he watched as her face shifted in dream. How beautiful she suddenly was to him with her long dark hair spilling in waves around her sleeping face. The longer he inspected her, the more he hated every man who'd ever laid hands on her; even John.

He stared at her lips and loathed any man who'd ever placed his upon them... to have kissed her without the love she deserved... the love she so desperately wanted in her life... it made him cringe that he couldn't go back in time to prevent them all.

His mind played out the events of the day and he wished he could've been there to stab the soldier himself... to catch him just before he'd touched her... To have had the gratification of killing him for himself... of preventing yet another moment of the hurt she'd grown so accustomed to in her life.

Life hadn't been fair to this little strong-willed woman who suddenly held his heart captive; whose mere existence in bed next to him made him want to cry for reasons he couldn't explain.

He listened for signs of anyone else who should come seeking her out. He almost hoped another would come so he could defend her; so he could show her the lengths he would go to to make sure she was safe.

'Don't love him,' he begged her in his mind, watching as she curled her hands up toward her face and frowned in her sleep. *'Please don't love him.'*

How he longed in that moment to kiss her the way she needed, to touch her with the tenderness she craved, just once.

'But you are married,' he reminded himself. *'And you would hurt her worse with tenderness than any man ever has with force. You love Alaina more.'*

'More...' His mind echoed the word over and over.

Did he love her? When had that happened? *How* could he have let it happen?

He'd always hated the stories of men who'd taken a mistress and strung them along... he'd always thought them the worst kind of men to so selfishly waste the hearts of the women they took for granted. But now, a part of him understood. He wanted her; loved her, even. And he loved Alaina. He wanted them both differently— *desperately*, and the thought of either of these women with anyone else tore his heart in two. It was unfair; it was selfish, and he was just as bad as any other adulterous man for thinking it, but he couldn't help his heart racing as he laid there really seeing her for the first time.

She was beautiful.

Sure, she was difficult and snarky on the surface, but beneath that, she was stunning. This woman was all the things he'd wanted Alaina to be; attentive, caring, inspiring, and real. She said what she meant, and she did what she said. She held nothing back. If she was sad, she cried. If she was happy, she laughed. And if she was in trouble, she would fight to the death if she had to. What he wouldn't give to fight for her.

He watched her for hours, listening for sounds of any man who might come to hurt her again, when in the dim light of morning, long after the candle had burned out, she blinked her eyes open.

She stared back at him in silence for a while before she slid her hand across the bed to place it over his. "You have never looked at me like this before, superman."

He took a deep breath and stifled the words that lingered in his throat. *'Don't love him.'*

He didn't want to hurt her; didn't want to selfishly keep her from finding her own happiness; didn't want to have these feelings when he had a wife he was anxious to be reunited with, but her hand over his made void all the things he didn't want and only heightened the things he did.

A small smile tugged on her lips, and she searched his eyes as she moved her thumb over his wrist. "I am alright." She glanced at her fingers where she interlaced them with his and pressed their palms together. "I am safe now."

He could feel his pulse quickening, his heart begging to have what his mind had thought about all night. He couldn't—*wouldn't* act on it, but he couldn't stop himself from thinking it.

"Maria, I—

"Your Grace?" John Edgecumbe called softly from just outside the tent. "Are you awake?"

Chris quickly rolled off the bed and stood near his own cot, straightening his clothing just as John came through the tent's opening.

"Oh, good. I thought I heard voices." He gazed at Maria where she lay still in the bed, an act which made Chris stiffen with jealousy.

"I've come to return this to you." He presented the dagger he'd gifted her and placed it on the table. "And to inform you both that all has been taken care of and you needn't worry yourselves." He returned his attention to Chris. "Have you discarded the clothing?"

"Yes. I burned them." Feeling guilty for envying someone who'd done so much for him, he stepped forward and extended his hand to the lieutenant, taking the man's hand in a firm handshake. "I have no idea what we would've done without you. I don't know how I will ever be able to thank you enough for all that you've done."

John placed his free hand on Chris's shoulder. "It is the least I could do for such fine company." Upon the release of his shoulder he looked back toward the bed, his expression softening. "Your Grace, are you quite alright? Is there anything I can do for you?"

She sat up, pulling the blanket up to cover her shift. "It is *I* that should be asking if there is anything I can do for *you*. You have done too much already."

He smiled fondly at her. "It is my honor, madam. I'm afraid I should be inclined to do any manner of things if only in pursuit of Your Grace's happiness. The captains are preparing for another trip to Oparre today. Shall I tell them you are still unwell?"

Maria glanced between the two of them and tilted her head. "Neither of you has slept at all because of me. Yes, tell them I am still very sick and then I want you both to get some sleep. I can't have the two men I trust in this world falling over."

"Yes, Your Grace. I shall inform him straight away." He turned to Chris. "Perhaps once we are rested, we could spar for an hour or two?"

Chris nodded. "I would like that very much."

"Very well then." John bowed to them both, his eyes lingering on Maria for a moment too long. "I shall call upon you in a little while."

As soon as John exited the tent, Maria rose from the bed. "Oye, before you go to sleep, I need to get dressed. I don't want to be stuck in only a stupid shift all day." She opened the trunk to rummage through it, and Chris took two long strides back toward her.

In his mind, he grabbed her hand and spun her round, sliding his palm up to cup her face and smooth his thumb over her cheek just before he pressed his lips to hers.

In reality, he stood shaking with restraint, his heart nearly beating out of his chest when she turned to face him.

She slowly inspected him and raised one eyebrow. "You are tired." She grinned. "And you look like shit."

She motioned for him to lie down and he obliged, keeping his eyes on her as she crawled in to sit at the head of the bed beside him. "And I can see that you are stuck in your big stupid head."

She combed her fingers over his hair. "Go to sleep now... I will be right here when you wake up... I will not leave your side again, I swear."

He curled his arm around her waist where she sat and smoothed his thumb along the side of her ribs, the familiar lump returning to his throat as he whispered, "I should've been there. Are you sure you're alright?"

"Shhh." She scratched gently at his scalp. "It is all over now and I am fine."

Her nails scratched and combed in a subtle rhythm, forcing his eyes to grow heavy and his arm around her to slowly go limp.

He fell asleep almost instantly and found her in his dream. He was standing where he'd just been, only there was no guilt, no nagging voice in the back of his head to tell him to stop as he brought his lips to hers.

There was no second guessing as he lowered her down onto the bed to interlock his fingers in hers and press their palms together while his mouth moved against her own, showing her all the depths with which she already possessed him. There was no time travel, no Alaina, and no John in his dream to stop him. There was nothing save his body pressed against hers; her mouth under his and a desire to show her the love that had been so foreign to her in her life.

Up and down he moved gently with her, his desire for her only growing stronger; his appetite for more pushing him deeper; his hands moving over her skin with the need to touch every inch of her as his lips remained locked with hers.

He could feel his body trembling, all the anticipation building up inside him, and he pulled her body closer, begging for the release he was on the precipice of. Instead of release, he found his arms suddenly empty, her body disappeared, and he woke with a jolt in a panic.

He blinked in the dim light of the tent, his entire body damp with sweat. As he let out the breath he'd been holding, he looked around for her... but she was gone.

He leapt out of the bed and bolted to the entrance, where he stopped short when he heard her laughter just outside.

"Aye, no." She was saying happily. "I have always wanted to see the world... to travel. So much beauty to see in this life to waste so much time in one place."

"That's why I am so anxious to captain my own ship," John's voice echoed back. "I wish to explore it all. To go where no other man has been, just as Captain Cook is doing now. I wish to spend as much time in any one place as I desire, without another man to tell me when it is time to move on to the next."

"Perhaps you will take me out on your ship one day," she offered sweetly. "I do not want to ever go back home."

"I should be honored to take you with me. But why ever wouldn't you want to return home?"

"There is nothing there for me anymore."

Chris's heart sank at the words. She did not mean Parma, and this was not an act. She meant *home*, and she didn't want to go back because there was nothing for her there. If he could find a way back... would she go?

"Where shall I take you on my ship?" John asked. "Perhaps you wish to be returned to Zweibrücken and Prince Charles?"

"No," she said. "I think I would like to go wherever you are."

Chris closed his eyes and let the words sting. *'Alaina,'* his conscience reminded him. *'You have no right to feel this way because you have Alaina... because in the end, you will choose Alaina, because you love Alaina.'*

"You would let the people of Parma think you are dead?"

She hesitated and let out a long sigh. "John, there is something I think I need to tell you now—

Panic washed over him to replace the envy, and Chris hurried out of the tent before she could say more, finding the two of them seated on the grass side by side, both of them leaned back to rest against their palms as their heads tilted up in unison to stare at him. He noticed the fingers of her hand were near enough to his that they were touching, and he couldn't seem to focus on anything else.

"Mi amor," she giggled. "It looks like you have finally gotten some sleep! Oye, that hair!"

He ran a hand over his head, realizing his hair had been standing straight up in several places. "I…" He cleared his throat. "How long have I been asleep?"

She grinned. "For a long time. It is almost time for dinner. I have told the captain we all will join him on the Resolution. John sent Fetia to dress me already… You made a lot of interesting noises in your sleep and did not seem to notice us!"

He glanced back at the tent and blushed, remembering what he'd been doing in his dream and feeling suddenly exposed. Snapping back to reality, he turned back. "Are you sure you're up for it? After everything, you don't want to—

She made a "tsk" sound and waved her hand to dismiss it. "I told you before, I am fine. Now go and change. You cannot go to dinner in the clothes you had on yesterday." She leaned ever so slightly toward John and smiled. "We will wait for you."

'We.' He stared at their hands where she'd raised her pinky finger to place it over his.

John was a good man, and he didn't want to loathe him at that moment. John could make her happier than he ever could. He wanted that for her. But in that moment, he wanted *her* more. Swallowing hard, he nodded. "Maria, can I have a quick word?"

"I'll be right back." She grinned at John, then hopped up and followed him back into the tent.

Once deep inside and out of earshot, she swung around to whisper. "I told you I'm fine. I don't want to keep—

"That's not what I want to talk to you about. I heard you two talking. I brought you in here to tell you we can't tell him yet. It's too soon."

"But I don't want to lie to him anymore," she said, looking back toward the tent's opening.

"It's too soon, Maria."

She nodded. "Fine. I won't tell him… but I won't lie to him much longer. It's not fair," she huffed, meeting his eyes. "Did you need anything else?"

He swallowed as his mind screamed out to her. *'Yes. There are a thousand more things I need to say to you. I wish that we were still on the island; wish that I had just one more day there uninterrupted to say all the things that I need to say to you… To work out all these things that are going on in my head…'*

But he only shook his head.

"Get dressed then. I'm hungry." She spun around to retreat to the tent's exit.

Having grown accustomed to the fresh air at camp, the stench of the ship was overpowering the minute the sloop was hoisted to the top deck, and he understood why Otou was so hesitant to come onboard himself.

Upon exiting the sloop, John curled Maria's arm into his to escort her to the great cabin. Chris walked directly behind them.

Every touch of her shoulder against John's ate away at him, every tilt of her head and smile in his direction was a dagger through his heart.

He followed silently, staring at the one single wisp of curl that had escaped its pins and ran down the nape of her neck to taunt him. That one single wisp teased him as it glided softly along the skin he so desperately wanted to touch.

"Your Grace!" Captain Cook beamed at her as they entered the cabin. "You are looking as beautiful as I have ever seen you! Pray, how are you feeling?"

"Much better." She smiled as she took her seat. "I'm so sorry for leaving so soon yesterday. I hope I didn't spoil the night."

"Not at all, my dear." He sat down at the head of the table as Chris took a seat opposite John and Maria. "We departed just shortly after you did."

Chris noticed John stiffen, and he could almost hear his thoughts. Could they have caught a glimpse of Maria's blood soaked clothing out on the water? Had someone seen him coming back? Had they noticed him with a dead body in tow? Could Maria be in danger right now? Chris cursed himself for not asking more details about what exactly John had done with the body.

"We had a most pleasant visit, and the king sent several parcels of fish for our dinner and no small amount of fruit for our men! I must say, though," he frowned, "he appeared quite troubled by the gift of my broadsword. I wonder if I needn't apologize for having forced it upon his person?"

"I'm sure it is fine," Maria said cooly, sipping her wine the instant the servant had finished pouring it. "The men on the Adventure seem to be doing much better, Captain Furneaux. I am curious when we will set sail again?"

Tobias raised his glass to her. "Indeed, they are! I am much indebted to these fine people for assisting to bring them back to good health. I've word that you yourself assisted as well? Thank you, Your Grace. I believe we shall move on to Huahine in a few days. Isn't that right Captain?"

Captain Cook nodded. "Tomorrow we shall say our fairwells to the king in preparation of our departure on the following morn. We will spend a few days on Huahine and then embark to Raiatea before we are back out on the open water again. Have you already grown weary of the landscape, Your Grace?"

"No. It's so beautiful here, I could stay forever. I just worry about our friends." She stared at Chris. "I am anxious to see if anyone from the other tribes has had word of them."

As she kept her eyes locked with his, he wondered if she'd read his thoughts, and if there wasn't an undertone to her words. She'd always had a way of seeing through him on the island. Could she see him now? Did she know the torment he was in? Was this her way of saying *'we need to find his wife before he acts upon these thoughts and breaks my heart?'*

"And most understandably so! I am most anxious to inquire as to their whereabouts myself." Cook tipped his glass to Chris. "And to meet this fine wife of yours, who the duchess claims," he winked at Maria, "is more important than even herself!"

'Add another nail to the coffin, why don't you?' he thought, his mouth growing suddenly dry. He raised the wineglass to his lips and took a hefty drink.

He looked down at the fish on his plate and tried to picture Alaina. He tried to conjure her face, tried to make out her features, but came up short. All he could see was Maria.

He couldn't understand his sudden obsession. In all the days and nights they'd spent together, he'd never seen anything but Alaina's face in his mind. He'd barely noticed Maria next to him.

Now, threatened by the possibility she could develop feelings for another, his mind couldn't focus on anything else. He couldn't hear Alaina's voice, couldn't recall her taste or smell, couldn't even remember what her skin felt like under his now that Maria had been there.

'This is ridiculous,' he told himself, trying to rationalize it. *'It's all some kind of weird infatuation from being stranded together so long. You want her all of a sudden because you might lose her and that is all. You love Alaina. It's nothing... In a few days, it'll pass.*

You have to let this go. You have to focus on what matters: finding Alaina and getting home.'

Throughout dinner, he attempted to distract himself by conversing with Johann about the upcoming stops and the people they'd met on each island during their previous trip.

He tried desperately to seem interested in Johann's promises to assist him in seeking out Alaina, but his eyes kept dancing back to Maria, where she smiled at John; where she laughed at his stories and touched his arm.

He battled to keep his attention off her lips every time she brought the wineglass to them or flashed her teeth in a wide, perfect smile.

Over and over, he told himself to let it go; that it was nothing; that he couldn't really love her; and over and over his heart failed to listen, growing more jealous as she and John leaned their heads closer in private conversation.

"Your Grace," Captain Cook wiped the corners of his mouth with his napkin and folded it on the table, signifying the dinner was done, "I wouldn't dare to impose any burden upon you after yesterday's events, but if you are feeling quite up for it, I'm sure King Otou would appreciate you accompanying us on our final trip to Oparre tomorrow."

Maria smiled. "Of course I will come!" She yawned. "I have to say goodbye to him and thank him for hosting us in this beautiful place!"

"Most wonderful." He placed his hand over hers on the table. "I can see you are quite exhausted. I shall call for a sloop to escort you back. I wouldn't want to keep you late this night and risk you falling ill again in the morning."

Maria stood, which prompted the entire table to stand with her. "Thank you, *Captains*, for such a wonderful dinner." She smiled up at John. "And for making sure I am so well taken care of throughout this trip. The lieutenant has been a great friend to me. I hope he will be recognized for all he has done here."

Captain Cook's face lit up, and he met John's gaze. "His fine treatment of Your Grace and the excellent manner with which he has led the marines on our journey will most certainly not go unrewarded, Your Grace!"

"Good." She grinned, curling her arm around John's. "Goodnight gentlemen. I am looking forward to seeing you both in the morning."

Once again, Chris followed behind Maria and John as they made their way back to the sloops, and once again his anxiety piqued as she leaned into him, sat beside him on the boat, and continued to let him escort her through camp to their tent.

Part of him wondered if she was purposely trying to drive him mad... if she knew all the ways he wanted her and was using John to show him just how much she was worth... Or perhaps she was disappointed that it hadn't been him to come and rescue her. Perhaps she was torturing him with John as a means to get back at him for letting the sergeant lay his hands on her. He couldn't blame her for that. He deserved far worse.

Inside the tent, John unsheathed his sword and held it toward Chris. "What say you, Chris, care for a bit of sport before we retire for the evening?"

Maria giggled and sat down at the edge of the bed to watch them.

Chris, needing an outlet to relieve his frustrations, accepted by drawing his own sword, very much aware of her eyes on them both.

John smiled and lunged toward him to be met with the loud crash of Chris's sword pushing him backward. "Excellent form!" he replied, caught a little off-guard by the strength with which he was met. "You would make an excellent marine!"

Again, John lunged forward, and Chris spun out of the way to counter his attack and be swiftly met with John's blade ringing as the steel of both swords were held tightly against each other.

"So it's a fight you're after then?" John grinned. "Very well, but be warned, I shall offer you no mercy!" He spun out of the stance to swing his blade low and was met again by Chris's defense.

"Very excellent, indeed." He beamed with pride, frowning a little at Chris's sudden determination. "But…" He swept his leg, forcing Chris's feet out from beneath him and causing him to fall back on his butt. "You have forgotten your stance."

As he charged forward to deliver his sword at Chris's throat, Chris rolled to one side and back up on his feet to nearly bring his own sword to John's before the ringing of steel sounded once again and John pushed him backward.

"Not quite, Chris." He grinned, then raised his eyebrows, glancing at Maria. "Perhaps you would do better if I were to impose a threat upon Her Grace?" He started toward the bed, prompting Maria to giggle wildly.

Chris sprang for him, wielding the sword over his head and meeting John's blade where he spun around to block him. Blades held over their heads, they came face to face, their noses inches apart. "Indeed," John whispered. "Much improved."

"Is that all you got?" Chris sneered.

John shook his head. "Not even half, sir. Would you like to see *all* I've got?"

Maria's attention was on them. He could feel her eyes watching as his muscles shook to overpower John. "If you can handle it," he smirked.

In one quick sweep, John guided their joined blades to the floor. "I assure you, Chris, I can handle it. Can you?" He turned quickly and returned with force.

Over and over, they danced around the tent in a roar of clashing steel, both of them growing more ferocious in their attacks on the other; both of them with something to prove to the woman who watched them.

With every swing of his sword, Chris envisioned Maria's pinky finger dancing over John's, his arms around her in the woods, and the smile that lit up her face every time she looked up at him.

He then pictured the last woman he'd lusted after when he'd cheated on Alaina; imagined his hands on her naked skin and let the disgust push him further. He swore he'd never put himself in the position to cheat on her again… but here he was… and this time, there were feelings attached… was this not worse?

They battled silently, their expressions shifting from playful to vicious the longer the fight went on. Mentally, Chris fought a silent battle himself, caught between his jealousy of John and his desire to be reunited with his wife.

'You can't tell Maria any of it. Not ever,' he told himself. *'You have to let it go.'*

The blades grew heavier, and they gradually slowed, taking longer gaps between their pursuits of each other to catch their breath, until, when both men were unable to even hold their swords upward, John laughed. "I think that is enough for tonight, don't you?"

Chris nodded, panting where he stood with his blade held down, both his arms vibrating with fatigue.

"Your Grace," John managed through labored breaths, "I think it is safe to say that any man who should find himself standing between you and this man would be swiftly stricken down. I've not seen any man take so naturally to the sword as Chris has." He extended his hand and shook Chris's. "Excellent fight, sir."

Chris smiled at him and waited for him to sheath his sword before he did the same. "One day, John, I *will* win."

John laughed heartily. "And I am looking forward to that day most ardently!" He bowed to him. "I'm afraid I am exhausted and must bid you goodnight before I am embarrassed at the fragility you have plagued upon my arms. I shall send for Fetia to come and get Her Grace undressed and will call upon you both in the morning."

Chris walked John out of the tent and waited as Fetia entered to undress Maria.

In the cool night air, he centered his thoughts on Alaina, and he pictured the night before they'd boarded the plane.

They'd stayed up all night; both of them terrified they might oversleep and miss the flight. It had been an uncomfortable several hours leading up to their departure. They'd been silent with one another, finding menial last-minute tasks to do around the house instead of conversing. It was as if they were both waiting to arrive in Bora Bora before they could even attempt to reconnect. What would've become of them had they landed safely at their destination?

He had to find a way to get back to her... to fix this. He couldn't let his proximity to Maria pull him away from his wife.

As Fetia exited the tent, he reentered, and the once familiar tent seemed foreign, leaving him uneasy as he hurried to the corner to undress.

His arms were so exhausted, he barely had the strength to unfasten the buttons of his vest. He kept his eyes on his hands as he undressed shyly, avoiding the awkwardness of being alone with her.

Unsure of what to do once he stood in only his long shirt, he looked finally at her and was taken aback to find her sitting up in the bed, beaming with amusement.

"That was quite a show you put on, mi amor. I thought you were going to kill each other." She tapped her palm on the bed beside her. "Are you going to come to bed or are you going to stand there acting strange the whole night?"

He sighed. He didn't trust himself to sleep next to her. Not now; not with the thoughts that returned to plague him by simply looking at her. He couldn't trust his dreams not to venture back to where they'd been; couldn't trust his body not to respond to them if his arms were around her; couldn't trust himself not to say the wrong thing in the night. "Maria, I think I should—

Gunfire erupted just outside their tent, followed by the shouting and running footsteps of several men. "BLOODY MURDERERS!" He heard a man shriek loudly, forcing him to spring to the table with renewed strength to hold his sword out toward the tent's opening.

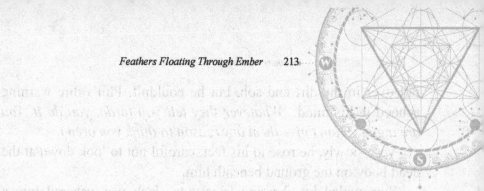

Chapter Eighteen

Jack

Jack sat in the dirt with the man wrapped in his still tightened arms as the crowd around him cheered loudly.

Slowly, he opened his eyes but dared not look down. He scanned the rejoicing crowd until his eyes landed upon Bud.

He could see in Bud's expression all he'd done… He could see the disappointment, the apology, the acknowledgement that what he'd just done would never leave him; that he would relive it, remembering new details every time, for the rest of his life. He loosened his grip and felt the lifeless body fall to the dirt.

"Victory!" Michael shouted, placing himself in the center of the circle beside Jack. "You win. You are god of war." He placed a hand on Jack's shoulder, tapping lightly. "Stand."

Uati rose from his wooden throne and descended the steps to join Michael in the circle. He smiled as he spoke in his deep, thick baritone, then motioned for Jack to follow as he turned toward the community of huts.

"Come," Michael translated, tugging on Jack's upper arm to encourage him to stand up. "Uati have gift. You not want make him wait."

But Jack didn't think he was capable of standing. His adrenaline was wearing off and his knees were weak. He could feel a chill running across his skin with the need to vomit. He wanted to fall over in the dirt and sob, but he couldn't. Phil's dire warning echoed in his mind. *'Whatever they tell you to do, you do it. You are a god... don't give them any reason to think you aren't.'*

Very slowly, he rose to his feet, careful not to look down at the dead body on the ground beneath him.

Surrounded by cheering tribesmen, Jack was ushered into a hut, the interior lit by a single torch stuck in the ground near the entrance. Uati said something and turned, leaving Michael and Jack to sit on the straw filled fabrics inside.

"He bring you woman." Michael leaned in to speak softly. "You take her."

"I can't do that." Jack shook his head. "I'm sorry, I can't."

"You must," Michael insisted. "It will be great insult."

"Really, I can't," Jack pressed. "I have a woman and this isn't right."

"No matter." Michael put his hand up. "You take woman then you set me free. Take me be with mother and father again. I want go home. I have many woman." He grinned. "It only take little time and done. Feel good."

"That's not the point," Jack persisted. "There must be some other gift he can give."

"You say his gift not good, he say you not god. He be angry. Kill Phil for lies. Woman not so bad. Just little time." Michael presented him with a large clay jug. "Drink and you feel good."

Jack sniffed the contents to find an even more pungent fermented fruit odor emitting from the bottle. He inhaled deeply and took a drink.

Deep down, he knew he couldn't sleep with a woman, but maybe she could be reasoned with. She probably wouldn't want to sleep with him either... was probably going to be forced there against her will... maybe she would work with him to make them think something had happened.

He brought the bottle to his lips again and tilted it back, chugging the vile liquid. Hopefully, this would work. He observed Michael's innocent face. "You're too young for all this. How old were you when you came here?"

"Five." Michael nodded, plucking a fig from a tray of fruit in the center of the small room. "I wait for father come back. He not come. You take me back to him."

Before he could elaborate, Uati returned. He pulled behind him a petite woman wrapped in white fabric. He spoke to Michael, smiling proudly at Jack.

"Uati give you best woman. She not have man before."

Uati pushed the girl in front of him, presenting her to Jack.

Jack's stomach dropped. She was young; younger even than Michael. Her large dark eyes sat over youthful cheeks, unstained by the tattoos the rest of the tribe wore over their faces. He could see tears welling in them and felt even more disgusted than he had when presented with the man he would kill.

"She's a child!" Jack blurted, noticing the room had begun to blur and shake around them.

"You take woman," Michael said pointedly, his face distorting to wobbling lines as he stood and moved with Uati toward the entrance. "We wait there. Just little time."

Jack blinked hard as his vision doubled. "I…" He stifled a burp and felt his body going numb as he struggled to stay upright. "What—What's going on?"

"We wait," Michael repeated. "Drink make you ready." He disappeared into the night, letting down the fabric covering to the entrance and leaving Jack alone with the girl.

Jack placed a hand on the ground behind him to stop his wavering, then held the other up toward her as she began to come closer. "No, stop. This…" His eyes grew heavier and his speaking slowed as the room's temperature rose to burn his cheeks. "It's not right. I won't do this."

He struggled to remember his original plan. He could feel his body tipping over but forced himself upright. He couldn't let anything happen. With his eyes closed, he felt her hands softly rest on his shoulders as she came to sit in front of him. He reached up and grabbed her wrists, removing them. "No."

What was it that he was going to do? Sleep… he could sleep. Oh God, he needed to sleep.

She pushed his already toppling body over so he laid back on the heavenly soft pillows. "No," he repeated, forcing his eyes open. "I won't do this."

With every bit of willpower and strength he could muster, he pushed her away, then rose up on his hands and knees. The world around him was a pulsing haze of orange and brown lines. He couldn't see straight, but he knew he had to get out. He crawled blindly away until the orange lines turned to blue and the warmth of the fire turned to a cool breeze on his face. He was out of the hut. He crawled further, his limbs growing heavier and heavier until he was sliding across the dirt on his belly.

He heard Michael's voice. "You not Nikora God." And then the world went black.

Groggily, Jack blinked his eyes open to find himself still cloaked in blackness, only the ground beneath him was now cold, damp stone.

"What have you done?" Phil hissed from nearby in the darkness, his words bouncing off the stone walls around them.

"Where..." Jack shook his head. "Where am I? Where's Bud?"

"He's here." Jack could hear Phil's movement as he came closer. "Sleeping like you were. What happened? Did you fight? Did you do everything I told you?"

"I fought," Jack whispered. He tried to lift himself up, but the world around him was spinning too fast and he lowered his heavy head down to the cool dampness of the rock floor.

"So how did you come to be locked down here, then?"

"They brought me a girl. I couldn't."

"I told you to take whatever they offered! You couldn't swallow your pride for a few minutes and take the woman to save us all?"

"She was a child."

"Child or not... we're dead men now. We're never getting off this island. They would've let you walk freely among them if you'd taken her. You would've been worshipped... given anything you asked for. Including a boat!"

"They were never going to let me leave." Jack curled his knees up toward his chest to relieve the cramping in his abdomen.

"They might've let you send some of us away... Including Bud."

"How is Michael?" A male British voice asked from the opposite side of the cell. "Did you see him?"

"Shut up, Jacob," Phil spat hatefully. "Michael's the reason we're all down here."

"Who's that?" Jack asked.

"My name's Jacob," the voice said. "Michael is my son."

Chapter Nineteen

Chris

Had they found the body? Were they exposed? Was John in trouble? Was Maria at risk? Could he fight them off if they came for them? Would they be able to hide?

These are the thoughts that raced through Chris's mind as he stood just inside the tent's entrance, listening to the ongoing commotion while he held his sword steady.

On the other side of the fabric, he could hear men fighting and a woman screaming. One group of men shouted in Tahitian as the other screamed accusations of murder toward them.

Maria appeared behind him, placing her palm on his back. "What do we do now? What's happening?" she whispered nervously.

"I don't know," he whispered back. Keeping his blade pointed at the entrance, he turned to look at her. "But I can't leave you to find out."

"Do you think they found the body?" she breathed, sliding her hand into his free one.

"If they did, they'll think the natives did it…" He looked down at their entwined fingers. "You can't say anything. Not a word. Even though it was justified, you can't say anything. Promise me you won't?"

"But—

"But nothing, Maria." He squeezed her tiny palm in his. "There's you and me out here, and the only thing that matters is that *we* get home. Nothing else is more important. Not the sergeant, not the captain, and not these people... they're all in the past... they're not real."

"They *are* real, Kreese."

"Not to us, they're not." He pulled her behind him as he heard the shuffling of feet coming nearer to their tent.

"What about John? What if he is in trouble? He's not real to you?"

"No, he's not." He guided her backward as the footsteps grew closer, focusing his eyes and the pointed edge of the sword on the tent's entrance, ready to attack anything that came through it.

"He is real to me," she said softly.

His muscles shook as he tensed in preparation for a fight—a *real* fight. Could he fight a soldier? Would he be able to keep her safe if they flooded the tent?

As the shouting intensified outside, it became increasingly evident that the soldiers were intoxicated, and, outnumbered as they were, he realized he needed to get her out of there fast. Even if they didn't accuse Maria of the murder, once they'd found whatever fight they were looking for, they might come in search of something else... something else that was limited within the confines of the encampment...

"Grab my pants and a robe for you," he whispered. "We need to get to the ships."

"We should wait for John," she insisted. "He is probably out there right now... he'll come for us."

"Just do it," he hissed.

She scurried toward the back of the tent to grab her robe just as he heard John's voice shout loudly outside.

"Officers! Lower your weapons this instant! What on earth do you think you are doing?"

"Sergeant Harris has gone missing sir," another man slurred. "Been missin' since yesterday! I jusss know one of these savages did somethin' to him! Filthy bastards won't admit to it though!"

"Lower your pistols, I say," John ordered. "You haven't sufficient evidence to support this claim, and these people have offered nothing but kindness to us. Besides, it is common knowledge that Sergeant Harris takes heavy to the drink. He may just as well be lost on the island. Private Evans, go and fetch the surgeon to care for this man's wound. You unhand those men, and Officer Taylor, you and your men lower your pistols this instant."

"I told you he would come," Maria whispered, circling around to stand at Chris's side and lean her head against his shoulder. "I knew he would. They haven't found the body... We are alright."

"Sergeant Harris wouldn't jusss go wandering off..." The man continued. "Even if he were gone with the drink. You know that."

"Lower your weapons or I shall have you all in irons, sir," John said calmly.

"I'll do no such thing." The man hiccuped. "I wanna' know where my sergeant is. And this man knows... look at him. He's hiding something."

"I give you my word. I shall search for Sergeant Harris myself the instant the sun rises. You may join me, if you'd like. If we do not come upon him, then we shall bring the matter to the captains to handle accordingly. Now lower your weapons and return to your tents. That is an order."

This was met by a series of low groans, profanity, and mumbling between the men. After several minutes of less animated argument, the sound of retreating footsteps signified the situation was deescalating.

"Mi amor," Maria swept her palm down Chris's arm to rest it over his where he still held the blade out toward the opening. "We are safe now."

He stared down at her hand over his. "We won't be safe until we get back home," he said, lowering the sword to face her. "You're not safe here."

Outside, he could hear John speaking to someone new. "Help me get him on his back."

"The captain demands to know what's happened out here." A new voice said with authority, grunting as there was a shuffling against the sandy ground. "He's let the drunken behavior go on long enough and won't tolerate any more. He wants swift punishment for any misconduct this evening."

"Men from the Adventure, sir," John informed the stranger. "Sergeant Harris has wandered off and they've accused the locals of having a hand in it."

"He'll want them all dealt with for injuring this man. Which men?"

"Taylor and his regiment."

The man growled in response. "Taylor has had a hand in plenty of disorderly conduct since our arrival here. The captain will be pleased to see him dealt with. Let us tend to his wound and then we must collect the men responsible."

As the voices outside grew quiet with the effort of dressing whatever wound was inflicted, Chris felt a sense of momentary safety, and his shoulders relaxed.

"This look you are giving me," Maria squinted up at him where he hadn't realized he'd been staring at her the entire time. "You have been giving me this look all day. What is going on with you?"

"Nothing." He quickly looked down at his feet. "I should get dressed and see if John needs help."

"Oh, no." She grabbed his wrist as he turned toward his cot. "John has men to help him out there. Do not mistake my accent for stupidity, mi amor. Something is off with you. Tell me what's going on."

"Nothing," he repeated, knowing that if he looked her in the eyes, she would see through him just as she was almost always able to do.

"*Nothing?*" She scoffed, tightening her grip on his wrist. "You think I can't see you are jealous of him?" She nodded toward the canvas John stood on the opposite side of. "This is not nothing, and I'm not going to stand here and act like it's nothing. What do you want?"

He blew out, still staring at their feet. "I want to go home and worry about normal things; bills, laundry, or what to eat for dinner... not whether or not I can kill a man if he comes in here lusting after you or if they find out you aren't who they think you are."

"That's not what I meant, and you know it. You are looking at me different than before. This is not loneliness and an innocent fantasy to pass the time… this is something else. What do you want *from me*?"

"Nothing," he said again. "I just want to get you home."

Selfish thoughts were one thing; acting upon them was another, and he would not be selfish with this woman, not when he damn well knew his wife was out there somewhere. He took a deep breath and turned away from her to collect his breeches from near his cot.

"I told you, John doesn't need your help," she said softly. "Come to bed. He would have come in here if he wanted you."

She had a point, but he didn't know what to do with himself. He couldn't go near her without his heart racing; couldn't think clearly when she was so close to him. He couldn't *come* to her bed and be trusted to keep his secrets. "I should probably sleep over here…" he motioned to the small cot on the floor, "…in case he does come."

"Hmmf." She waved him off, crossing the tent to blow out the candles.

As the room around them grew pitch black, he listened to the men outside as they set out in search of Officer Taylor and the others. He could hear their voices growing further away and heard the protesting of Taylor as they took him into custody far in the distance.

"Earlier," he said into the blackness, "you told John you never wanted to go back home. Did you mean that?"

Suddenly, he felt the straw mattress dip beneath his legs as Maria crawled onto the small cot beside him. "Spying on me now, eh?" she whispered, entirely too close for comfort.

"What are you doing?" he breathed. "I told you, I—

"Shut up, estúpido," she hissed, pulling his arm to one side to nestle into his shoulder. "I am not deaf. I heard you. Put your arm over me."

He sighed, letting the tension in his shoulders ease as he let his arm fall over her and the familiarness of her body forming against his settle his mind.

She hummed softly. "And what I said earlier… *not that it's any of your business*, but I've realized there's no way to get home… and so I must force myself to seek out a future here."

"I promised you I would find a way home. And I will."

"Oh, you will?" She adjusted her position to lay her head on his chest and drape an arm over him. "How? How exactly are we going to get back there? I have been thinking about this. We are in Tahiti. *Tahiti.* It took us two weeks sailing from the *east* to get here. We didn't go off course. We just went down… no warning. And we were nowhere near where they found us on that flight path. It is a big ocean, and we came through time somewhere completely different from where we went through. How would we ever know where to go to get back?"

He hadn't thought about their location in that way. Had never thought to question that they'd come out in a different part of the ocean than where they had been flying. "I don't know, but we can't give up looking for it."

She took a deep breath. "Why not? Life will never be the same for us, mi amor, whether we go back or not. We are different people than who we were when we crashed. I killed a man…" She tightened her arm over him. "I killed a man and I don't feel anything. I don't feel any remorse at all, only the fear of being caught. How can I go back as this person? How could I go back to a normal life knowing I killed someone?"

He frowned as he considered it. What would it be like to go home? After all they'd been through to survive, would he ever be able to return to his job; to the mundane simplicity of everyday life as if it all hadn't happened?

"What if I changed history?" she asked. "What if everything we do here changes the world we once knew? What if I killed the great-great-grandfather of someone important? Have you thought about that? What if every second we are here, we are changing something there? What if we prevent someone from being born?

What if we accidentally prevent our own families from meeting… or your wife's? Would we just disappear? Would she? Who disappeared when I killed that man?"

He could hear the panic forming in her voice. She'd said she felt nothing, but it was clear that it was consuming her. "It's alright," he whispered, combing his fingers over her hair. "We don't know that we weren't supposed to be here. Maybe we were meant to do everything we've done. Maybe our presence here created the world as we know it. It could be that the man you killed would've spawned something evil in our world. We can't know either way, but questioning everything we do in order to get home won't do us any good."

They laid silently for a while after that and Chris pondered her words. What if they were unknowingly rewriting history? How would he know if he'd run into an ancestor of Alaina? He didn't know much about either of their lineages to know the last names… what if she disappeared? What if he did?

"Kreese?"

"Yeah?"

She sleepily drew a circle on his collarbone with her finger. "We would not even be friends in the real world, you and me… You know that? But out here… we are stuck together and after all this time, you are forced to care about me."

She paused, flattening her hand over his chest as she took a deep breath. "Do not confuse this for something it is not. You are married. And as a married man, you should have no reason to be jealous of John. Understand?"

"I'm not jeal—

"Understand?" she repeated with authority.

He nodded. There was no sense in arguing with someone who was able to see through him so clearly. And she was right. It didn't matter that he was falling in love with her. He already loved Alaina. Alaina was his home and his heart. She was out there somewhere, and that should've been all that mattered.

Should've been.

The truth was, though, simply knowing Maria had changed him. When she looked at him, she saw him like no one ever had. In only a few months, she knew him deeper than anyone. And he knew her.

Loving her was so much more than circumstantial. It was unavoidable. Maybe they wouldn't have been friends in the real world, but maybe they were meant to find each other here. Perhaps they were not rewriting history, but history itself was bending solely so she could influence his own future. What if he was destined to be with her and needed to be sucked through time to see it? He hadn't given her a second glance on the airplane... What if he was supposed to?

"Ahem."

Chris tightened his arms around Maria's sleeping body as he blinked his eyes open.

In the dim morning light of the tent, he could just make out John standing at the entrance, a look of disappointment washed over his features as he stared down at the two of them in the cot.

"Forgive me," he said softly, looking down to his feet when Chris's eyes met his. "I do not mean the interruption, I just—

Maria came alive and scurried quickly out of Chris's arms to stand in only her shift between them. She ran a hand over her matted hair. "It's... it's not what you think. You're not interrupting. Come in. Come in."

He looked up at her, then immediately back down at his boots. "My apologies, Your Grace. I shouldn't have barged in. I... I didn't want to wake the others."

"Really," Maria stammered, "it's nothing. I got scared is all with the gunfire last night. Come in."

He kept his feet planted at the entrance and continued. "Chris, I'm afraid I must ask for your assistance."

Chris pushed himself up to sit, forcing his hand through his hair as Maria fidgeted nervously in front of him. "Maria, put a robe on. You're making the lieutenant uncomfortable."

He blinked hard to clear the sleep from his eyes and focused on John. "What is it?"

"The sergeant." John spoke quietly, careful not to look up at either of them as Maria hurried to the bedside to force her arms through a silk robe.

"We depart tomorrow and they want to send out a search party this morning. I am to lead that search party. It appears they won't relent until he is discovered. We need to find him and it needs to look like he had an accident. I have a plan, but I need your help."

Chris nodded. "Whatever you need me to do, I'll do it."

John glanced shyly at Maria, then back to the ground. "I took the body to the waterfall in Oparre. He's wedged behind a rock at the base of the fall. The men knew he was there with us and will most assuredly want to search the area. It needs to look like he fell... Needs to look like the wound was inflicted by the rocks there. Sergeant Harris was known to be clumsy when he was gone with drink. It's a believable story. The problem is... I won't have the time to do it. The party is expected to leave soon. I'll need you to move the body while the captain and Her Grace are bidding farewell to Otou. I can start the search out here to give you ample time to slip away."

"You want me to leave her *alone?*" Chris glanced at Maria and back to John. "After what happened the last time we travelled to Oparre?"

"I'll stay next to the captains," Maria assured them, desperate for John to make eye contact with her. "I promise I won't leave their sides. They won't let anything happen."

"I understand what I'm asking of you." John straightened his back and finally looked at Chris. "Would that there were any other man I could trust... but there is not."

Trust. He saw the devastation still on the man's features. It was no secret that John was infatuated with Maria, and he'd stepped into the tent to find the only friend he had—*the only man he trusted*—curled up in bed beside her.

Chris's cheeks flushed. "I'll do it. How far is the fall from Otou's residence?"

John glanced behind him to make sure no one could overhear. "To the east of where we found them by less than a kilometer. He's a large man, and it was a struggle just to get him that far. You will be invited to accompany Her Grace and you shall have to come up with a reason to excuse yourself." He cleared his throat. "Might I have a word with you outside? Fetia is waiting."

"Alright." Chris stood, grabbing his breeches from the table and stepping into them.

John opened the flap to the tent to allow Fetia to enter. She smiled up at both of them as they exited.

Outside, as Chris was still lacing his breeches, John spun around to come face to face with him. "Who are you?" he asked through gritted teeth.

Taken aback, Chris frowned and stepped backward. "I—What do you mean?"

"Who is she?" John narrowed his eyes. "I know she is not the duchess, and I had hoped to earn your trust enough that you would not feel it incumbent to conceal your true identities from me. Again, I ask you sir," he placed a hand on the hilt of his sword, "who are you?"

"John," Chris said calmly despite his suddenly racing pulse, "Of course she is the duchess—

"I have met the duchess of Parma. While the likeness is uncanny, I knew almost immediately it was not she. In the beginning, I took you for spies and had the inclination to earn your friendship and expose you. I know now you could not possibly be spies and despite myself, I'm afraid I've..." His expression softened as he looked back to the tent. "...become quite taken with her. I've no intention of exposing either of you, but I must know who you are. I must know I can trust you. After all this..."

"You can trust us," Chris assured him. "But if I told you who we are, you wouldn't believe me."

John glared at him. "It makes no difference if I believe you. I cannot be expected to bestow my good faith in someone who will not return the courtesy. Who are you?"

Chris's shoulders slumped in resignation. "Fine. I will tell you everything, but..." he glanced up at the large search party approaching from the opposite side of camp. "But not now... tonight. I'll tell you everything tonight. I promise."

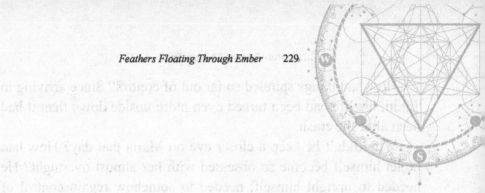

Chapter Twenty

Chris

The cutters, overloaded with gifts for Otou, finally set off for Oparre a little after 8AM.

Chris's stomach was in knots as they rowed away from the shore. How would he explain his disappearance to the captain? Surely, it would take longer to move the body than a bathroom break would allow for.

Could he play sick? No… Maria had already used that excuse too often. Maybe the captain wouldn't ask… even the more distinguished soldiers disappeared with pockets full of nails during the trip; perhaps the captain would simply think he'd gone off to do the same. It wouldn't matter that the captain thought less of him if it meant keeping Maria safe.

She sat silently beside him and hadn't made eye contact with him since the morning's events. He wondered if she was somehow angry with him for allowing her to sleep in his cot.

'Of course she would be mad at me. It's Maria. Everything is always my fault,' he sulked, letting himself grow increasingly frustrated. *'Doesn't matter that I told her not to crawl in bed with me… Doesn't matter that I wanted to sleep separate for the sheer purpose of him not finding us in bed together… in her eyes, I should've done more to stop it… And… I probably should have.'*

How had things spiraled so far out of control? Since arriving in Tahiti, his life had been turned even more upside down than it had been after the crash.

Why didn't he keep a closer eye on Maria that day? How had he let himself become so obsessed with her almost overnight? He needed to upright himself; needed to somehow regain control of their situation; to regain control of himself.

The cutters turned into the banks of Oparre to find them almost entirely desolate, save for two men standing at the water's edge. Hitihiti hopped out of the boat to speak with them as the soldiers pulled the boats onto the sand.

"Captain," Hitihiti said as they approached, "king is scared off by gunfire last night. He move his family someplace safe."

The captain's normally pleasant expression turned cold. "Blasted imbeciles!" He adjusted his scowl and straightened his back, smiling warmly at the natives where they had cowered away from him.

"Do they know where he's moved to? I must apologize for the behavior of my men. I ordered all responsible parties in irons. I need him to know this behavior is not representative of the admiralty nor has it gone unpunished."

Hitihiti nodded. "It is far walk for you."

Captain Cook smiled. "I don't mind a good walk. My legs could use the exercise after being so long at sea!" He turned toward the other soldiers. "Come along! Gather the gifts!"

The group followed the natives onto a trail that led through the thick brush of the island's jungle. About ten minutes into the trek, they came upon the waterfall, and Chris held his breath as they passed, his focus on the large boulder at its base behind which he knew the sergeant's body would be found.

"How magnificent!" the captain marveled, stopping the group as he stood to admire the scenery. He smacked a hand hard on William Hodge's back as the artist joined his side. "Perhaps, upon our return, you should spend a day here to paint such beauty!"

William smiled. "It is marvelous indeed. I'm not sure I could ever pull myself away."

The captain grinned. "Do you not think it the most beautiful wilderness you've ever laid eyes upon, Your Grace?"

Maria nodded, inspecting the same rock Chris was; assuredly trying to make out whether or not any of them could see any hint of the sergeant's body behind it. "It's very beautiful."

"You do not seem so impressed!" Cook teased. "Surely, I must visit Parma if a sight such as this falls short upon your eyes!"

She shook her head. "Oh no, I think it is breathtaking. I am just anxious to see Otou. I feel so guilty for leaving the other day without saying goodbye. And now I feel more guilty we have scared him and his family."

"Worry not, Your Grace. We shall repair our good standing with the king. But you are right. We mustn't dally. Let us continue! Perhaps, once we have righted our reputation with the king, we might spend more time here before we return to the ship."

They continued through the dense vegetation. They walked for what felt like miles. As more time and distance passed, Chris grew more anxious. How would he explain himself now? So far from the waterfall, it'd take a significantly longer amount of time than he'd originally thought. And there was no way to warn John of the delay... did he still have time to excuse himself, make it there, move the body, and return before the search party found it?

As if she'd read his thoughts, Maria slipped something into his hand.

"Oh, no!" she shrieked, calling the attention of the captain and crew. "My earring!" She held her ear and spun in a circle, then looked up at Chris. "I must have dropped it on the cutter! They are my favorite gift from the captain. Please go search for it! Please?! Please?!"

"Your Grace," Captain Cook placed her arm through his and flashed Chris an apologetic look, "surely you can't ask this man to walk all that distance for an earring? There are many others I can offer you."

"Why can't I? I love these earrings! There is no other pair like it and I don't want to risk losing it forever! Please? Oh, please go find it!"

'You little genius,' he thought, smiling at her. "It's no problem at all, Your Grace." Chris bowed to her.

"Oh, thank you! Thank you!" She grinned, resting her head against the captain's shoulder. "I couldn't bear to lose it!"

Captain cook sighed and shrugged. "Women are most particular creatures when they've set their mind on a thing. I shall watch over her in your absence, sir. Hitihiti says it's just a little further along this trail. Do you think you shall be capable of finding your way?"

Chris nodded. "I'll catch back up."

He turned the opposite direction and headed back down the trail. Glancing over his shoulder, he waited until the group was out of sight before he began to sprint.

'Please don't be there yet... please,' he begged, running faster.

What he wouldn't give to have the convenience of a cell phone in that moment... a simple text to say *'need more time.'*

Where was the search party now? Were they close? They'd headed out an hour before his departure... could they be on their way to Oparre in that moment?

He ran harder.

Assuming he could get through the next several hours, how was he going to convince John that they were who he said they were? Was there any bit of history—*nearby history* he could quote to prove it? Maybe the maps Captain Cook was working on? Maybe he could point out some discrepancy on the maps to prove himself...

He turned with the path and could hear the rushing water of the fall just ahead of him.

His mind raced.

If the soldiers found it before he did; if they were there this instant, would his sudden appearance incriminate Maria? What would he do if they saw him? How would he explain himself?

He could see the waterfall ahead and ran even faster toward it; his lungs beginning to burn.

'No soldiers. Good.'

A large boulder sat at the base of the waterfall, its blast spilling out over it.

He couldn't very well return soaked. Quickly, he removed his shirt, stockings, and shoes. Hopefully, his pants and hair would dry before he'd gotten back.

Barefooted, he climbed over the smaller rocks and navigated through the semi-cool water to the edge of the largest one.

And there it was. The body was wedged awkwardly between the boulder and the cliff face the water spilled off of. Its eyes were wide open and the skin had turned shades of blue and grey.

Chris gagged loudly from both the stench and the action as he reached into the crevice and wrapped his fingers around the corpse's wrist.

He pulled but the body was stuck. At some point, bloat had set in and the sergeant's body had expanded almost double in size. Chris took a deep breath, holding it as he wedged himself in alongside the dead man.

He gripped the man's jacket with both hands, pulling hard to wiggle him loose. He pulled once, twice, then on the third attempt, the body spilled over onto him, forcing a single terrified shriek to escape his lungs as they fell out of the crevice.

"There! I knew I saw movement!" A man shouted from the trail, forcing Chris's stomach to turn over on itself. "What have you done to Sergeant Harris?!"

He stiffened with the cold, lifeless body still pressed against him, and he couldn't find any words to explain himself. He stared in shock as the search party ran toward him, his mind going completely blank.

"Take your hands off him this instant!" A man shouted as he raced through the water and over the rocks. "What have you done?!"

"I…" He looked down at the corpse and back up. "I…"

Nothing… there was no excuse he could dream up fast enough to explain how he'd come to be miles from his own party, half wedged in a crevice with the sergeant's dead body in his arms.

"What kind of sick bastard are you?" the man spat, jerking the sergeant's body out of his arms. "What did you do to the sergeant?!"

"I... I found him," he stammered. "I was coming back to search for Her Grace's earring and... and I saw an arm."

"Liar!" another soldier shouted as he caught up to the man's side. "You killed him! You killed him and you came back to hide the body! Look at him! He's been dead for days! Lieutenant!!!"

"What's happened here?" John asked with authority, flashing an apologetic look in Chris's direction.

"I found him," Chris repeated. "I saw an arm... I... I didn't kill him."

"You found him?" John asked, glancing from the body to Chris. "And just how did you come to find him in such a remote location?"

"The duchess lost her earring on the cutter... We were headed inland to visit Otou. He and his family were scared by the gunfire last night, so he wasn't at his home. She sent me back down this trail to search for it. I saw an arm and decided to investigate."

The man kneeling over the body gasped, hobbling backward in a splash of water as his eyes grew wider. "He's been stabbed in the cock, sir! What kind of monster are you?!!"

"I didn't do this," he repeated, taking a step back as the other soldier lunged toward him.

"Calm yourself, Officer," John said, stepping between them before he could grab hold of Chris. "If the man says he found him, we mustn't be so quick to accuse him of lying. It is up to the captain to decide what is truth and what is not."

"If he didn't do it, then that whore of a duchess did! You know she's been known to indulge in all manner of foul behavior!"

"Aye!" The soldier who'd been kneeling over the body came to stand on the other side of them. "And she went missing the night of the theatre, too. Said she was sick! This is a woman's wound!"

"You forget that *I* was the one who escorted Her Grace back, Officer," John reprimanded. "I'd have known if she'd been involved in any foul play."

"Oh you would, would you?!" the man scowled. "You're just as bewitched by the little whore as the captain! I said it when we found her; told everyone to steer clear of her. I called it! She's an enchantress… a witch! You can see it in her eyes! I know she did this! And she's got that man under her spell too, out here to cover it up!"

Chris balled his hands into fists. "The duchess didn't do this. She is never out of my sight."

"Just what an enchanted man would say of his master!"

"We don't have any evidence to support this claim," John argued. "It could just as well be that the sergeant met his end at the hand of any one of these natives. Perhaps he thrust himself upon the wrong woman."

"If that's true, then how did he get wedged in that cave there?" The man spat to one side. "You want me to believe one of these little native women is strong enough to lift the sergeant? I'm no fool. That devil woman did this and sent this man to hide it. There's no other reason for him to be out here."

"He said he was sent back to retrieve the duchess's earring when he came upon the suspicious sight," John attempted to reason. "We should confirm his story with the captain."

"Oh, aye?" The man shook his head. "And do you often lay down *your* sword before you go to inspect something suspicious? No! Look at him! There's no reason this man would disarm himself if he didn't know what was here already!"

John closed his eyes and took a deep breath. "Sir, can you explain why you are without a weapon?"

Again, Chris's mind drew a blank. His heartbeat quickened and his cheeks flushed. "I… I…" The other men of the party grew closer, surrounding him now on all sides. "I wasn't thinking clearly. I thought… the duchess might have me beaten if I returned to the king in soaked clothing… She… she really is very strict about appearances, and the sword, I—

"Liar!" a young soldier behind him shouted. "Lieutenant, have this man arrested at once! I will go and inform the captain so we may take the duchess into custody to be tried for her murderous crimes!"

"No!" Chris shouted as the men closed in on him. "She didn't do this!"

"Lies!" The first soldier sneered. "Everything you say is a lie. You are under her spell!"

John's eyebrows shot upward as he watched helplessly while the men pulled Chris's hands behind his back.

"Officer White, go and fetch the duchess," the soldier behind him ordered.

"I'm telling you, she had no hand in this!" Chris argued as he tried to wiggle free of the men gripping him. Panic filled him as the soldier marched past him toward the path.

"Alright! I confess! I did it! I killed him! The duchess has no knowledge of it!"

The man stopped, spinning back toward him. "You expect me to believe *you* stabbed him in the cock?"

Chris nodded. "When the duchess got sick... I caught him in the woods with it in his hand... watching her while he... touched himself. It's my job to protect her from any threat. I saw this as a threat. I didn't think it would kill him. And when it did, I panicked. I was afraid she could be implicated. I hid him here... and then I came back today to make it look like an accident."

"Lieutenant?" The man looked at John. "What will you do with him?"

John's shoulders slumped. "I shall take him to the ship and place him in irons until I've spoken to the captain as to what to do. We cannot hang a man for protecting his duchess from a perceived threat... the captain will decide what punishment is necessary. Officer White, you will go and inform the captain of what has happened here."

"Lieutenant—

"That is an order."

"Aye sir."

John calmly stepped behind Chris to replace the men who'd held him captive. "I shall escort him to the cutter. Gather Sergeant Harris so we may give him a proper ceremony."

The men scrambled in all directions as John urged Chris to march forward, leaning in to whisper. "I'm so sorry."

Chris nodded. "What will happen now?"

"I will beg the captains to be fair. Because it is one of Furneaux's men, it will be his decision. He will not kill you for protecting her, but he'll have to punish you for attempting to conceal it. I warn you again, sir, Captain Furneaux is not known for being a gentle man. You should've kept quiet. I could've convinced the captains that a native was involved."

"They wouldn't believe it. Their minds were made up."

"The captains think too highly of Her Grace to believe she would've had a hand in it. They would've believed her over the officers. I could've handled this."

"I didn't know what else to do."

John sighed. "I know that... I am truly sorry. Rest assured, I won't let any harm come to her. I swear it."

Chris closed his eyes. "This morning... what you saw... it really wasn't what it looked like. She..." He took a deep breath. "She doesn't want me. She wants you."

He felt John's hand tighten over his wrists. "It is of no importance right now. What is important is that you get your story straightened out so you do not implicate her or I in any way. It is too late for you, but I cannot keep her safe if they become suspicious of me. I escorted you both to camp that evening. How were you able to stab a man so close to us without my knowledge of it happening? How were we unable to hear you? You'll need these answers before you are questioned."

"I covered his mouth... approached him from behind... Didn't get any blood on me."

"Good." John pushed him forward. "What did you stab him with to have been so close?"

"Fuck..." Chris shook his head. "I had no way to stab him that close."

"You used *your* dagger," John said. "It is your dagger, not hers. No one knows she has it. Is it in her possession now?"

"I don't know."

"Tell them you gifted it to her afterward... out of fear that someone might come upon her again. I'll need to speak with her... make sure she can confirm this story if she is questioned."

"How? When will you get a chance between now and when they come to question me to be alone with her? If she finds out, she could very well confess to it herself!"

"You're right..." John let go of his wrists. "You'll have to hit me."

"What?!"

"Hit me and run. When they catch you, you can say you were worried for her safety after all the men said here. Hit me. Hard. It'll make your punishment slightly worse, but it'll give me time to warn her while everyone is searching for you."

"John, I—

"Do it before they see us."

Every bit of emotion inside him had piqued in that moment. His whole body shook as his nerves caught up. He couldn't let her mess up the story. Surely if she found out he was taken prisoner, she'd start running her mouth. She might even incriminate herself if she was angry enough. With a lump in his throat, he balled his hands into fists. "Keep searching for my wife if I can't, okay?"

"I will. Now do it!"

With all the strength he could muster, he spun around to punch John in the face, feeling the crunch of his knuckles against the eye cavity, but not stopping to look before he sprinted into the trees to head back up the path.

He heard the men shouting; heard John sending orders at them to search for him.

"OFFICER WHITE!" John shouted up the trail. "COME BACK AT ONCE!"

"What the hell for?" Officer White yelled back from further up the trail. Chris stayed near enough to the trail to listen, but far enough in the thickness of the trees to remain hidden.

"That sonofabitch escaped!" John continued. "I need you to help the men search. The bastard blackened my eye and I can't see well enough to search myself! I'll go inform the captains of what has happened here. My return shall be swift and I expect him to be in custody by then."

"I knew he was trouble from the minute I laid eyes on him! Didn't I tell you?!" Officer White boasted, his voice getting closer. "You want me to shoot him?"

"No," John instructed. "No one is to shoot him. Otou is afraid of guns and the captain will be none too pleased to have more gunfire. Take him into custody and keep him here until I return. I shall deal with him myself."

While John headed up the trail, the voices grew quiet and he only heard the sounds of crackling leaves as the men spread out in search of him. He needed to hide long enough for John to get far ahead of them. Running would give him away. The ground was too noisy.

There was a downed tree a few yards from where he stood. He crept over to it and wedged himself into the small gap between the trunk and the ground, pulling leaves and palm over the opening to keep himself concealed.

He closed his eyes as he heard their footsteps cross over him.

His hand throbbed where he had punched John. He flexed his fingers, wondering if Tobias would be as generous with punishment as he was sure Captain Cook would've been.

They both seemed to like him... surely they would understand why he'd stab a man in such a way. They adored Maria. Perhaps they would imagine themselves doing the same and forgive him. Or perhaps they would turn on Maria...

"He went this way, I'm sure of it!" a man shouted just outside his hiding place. "There's footprints just there."

'Not yet... not yet,' he pleaded in his mind as their footsteps grew closer. He needed more time... John couldn't be far enough yet. It had taken him almost twenty minutes sprinting at full speed to get down here... how long had it been? Five minutes? Ten? Not long enough.

Still barefoot and without his shirt, he stiffened with every tickle of bug that crawled over his skin; and with the soldiers standing inches from his face, every bug that resided beneath the tree seemed to crawl over him, daring him to flinch and expose his location.

Once found, they were going to beat him, he knew. It'd been a long time since he'd been in a fight. When was the last time he'd been in a real fight? High school? Yes. Freshman year. It was Brian Dawson. He remembered the chubby red-faced senior who'd been twice his size coming barreling toward him, jealous over the girl who stood at his side.

Brian Dawson had hit him right in the nose that day and he hadn't felt it. Adrenaline, he supposed, as he'd returned the punch and knocked Brian flat on his ass in the hallway.

This wouldn't be like that… This would hurt.

These men were brutal and they would beat him within inches of his life. He would have to let them and despite all the urge to fight back, would have to show restraint to avoid a worse punishment. Perhaps, if he was bloodied and beaten already, Tobias might show some mercy on him when it came time to decide his fate.

"I still think that witchy duchess of his had a hand in it," the man above him said. "I don't like her… not one bit. Glad I'm not on the same ship as her, but still I'm scared she's cursed us all!"

"Pfft," the man next to him teased. "I've a few things I'd like to do to that duchess if I could get her alone." He laughed loudly, and Chris could just see the lewd gesture in his mind.

"That's not funny, Henry. You don't want to put your willie anywhere near that witch. Did you see what she did to poor Albert?"

"Oh, come on, you don't really think she'd do such a thing?"

"I wouldn't be putting my cock close enough to find out!"

Again they laughed out loud and Chris took the opportunity to swat a bug from his face.

"Hey, do you think that servant of hers is really laying with her?"

"That's what they say. He's a braver man than I if he is. You can see it in her eyes that she's evil—*pure evil*. I'm tellin' you, she's a witch if I've ever seen one. She's got him under her spell. Maybe she didn't kill Albert, but she sure as hell has that boy so enchanted he'd kill him for her! Hell, she might have all of us under her spell too! I might go kill someone if she wants him dead and not even know I was doing it!"

"That's absurd! She can't bewitch you if she's never touched you!"

"She touched my shoulder once."

"No, she didn't!"

"God as my witness. I felt chills run down my spine."

Chris stifled a laugh. These were the men who were about to beat the life out of him and they were terrified of little tiny Maria.

"What are you two doing?" a deep voice commanded. "You're supposed to be searching for him not dallying around!"

"There's footprints right there," Henry said. "Look. They stop right here. He's got to be around here somewhere."

Chris squeezed his eyes closed as the new soldier said the words he'd been waiting for.

"Aye, did you look under that tree, you dumb twats?"

There was a rustling of leaves, and then daylight shone into the small hole. He held his breath as he felt hands on his arm and didn't fight as those hands tightened around him and yanked him out of his hiding place.

Just as he'd suspected, the moment his body emerged, all three men brought their wrath down upon him, showing no mercy as they delivered blow after blow of fists, knees, elbows, and feet to every inch of his body.

As best he could, he curled into a fetal position, attempting to protect his face and ribs as word got out that he was found and more soldiers joined the one-sided fight.

He felt his ribs bruising, felt his eyes swelling, and in one hard blow, felt the crunch of his nose breaking. This was nothing like Brian Dawson. He felt every single punch and kick; all of them with the force of a metal baseball bat against his exposed skin.

"Maybe I ought to cut off *his* cock... see how he likes it? Eh?" One man teased, unsheathing his sword to point it at Chris's groin. The other men laughed around him.

"Charlie, you got any rope? Let's string him up!"

This was met by more cheers from the surrounding men.

"Alright, alright, settle down." A new voice joined them... a familiar voice... a *German* voice. It was Johann Forster and Chris sighed in relief. "What's happening here?"

"He killed Sergeant Harris," one of them responded. "Stabbed him right through his manhood!"

"Oh?" Johann said cooly. "Well, I imagine Sergeant Harris must've been doing something quite troubling *with* his manhood to have deserved to be stabbed through it, wouldn't you say?"

"He murdered him and came out here to hide the body. We caught him! Then he punched Lieutenant Edgecumbe and ran away!"

Johann made a "tsk" noise. "And no wonder. Look at what you've done to this once handsome man! You've rendered him unrecognizable. Lieutenant Edgecumbe is not harmed. I passed him on my way down. This is punishment enough, don't you think? Christoph, are you not sorry now for what you have done?"

Chris nodded, keeping his eyes closed and his face shielded.

"There you have it, boys. He is sorry. You can back up now. If you beat him any more, you might stand your own trials for murdering a royal guard. Back up. Go on... Shew."

Chris listened as the men moved back a few steps and felt the thud of Johann as he sat down on the ground near his head. He placed a hand on his hair and patted softly. "Are you alright, dear boy?"

Chris inhaled painfully, his ribs on fire. "I'll be fine." He squinted one eye open. "What are you doing down here?"

"Oh... you know me. My curiosity, once piqued, cannot be pulled away so easily. I saw John Edgecumbe with a swollen eye and thought I might come and take in a bit of the show to finish out my stay here. I must say, I was much surprised to find *you* at the center of it."

"How well do you know the captains?" Chris asked, closing his eye to ease the pounding in his skull.

"Fairly well," he said casually. "Why do you ask?"

"Will they have me hanged for this?"

"Nah," Johann laughed. "Everyone knows Sergeant Harris was an *arsch mit ohren*... Do you know what that means?"

"No."

"It translates in English to *'ass with ears.'*" He snickered. "Pray tell, what on earth was this *arsch mit ohren* doing that caused you to kill him in such a manner?"

Chris exhaled, his shoulders relaxing. He needed to tell the same story over and over until he believed it as truth. "He was watching the duchess while he touched himself. She was alone in the woods when I found him hiding in the bushes nearby."

"I see." Johann pushed a wet piece of fabric over Chris's face. "And were you sure he would have launched himself upon her if not for your involvement in the situation?"

"Yes."

"Well, then." Johann dabbed lightly at the blood around his nose. "I certainly can't say I wouldn't have done the same thing. Why didn't you just tell the captains in the first place instead of trying to hide it? Would've saved you quite a bit of trouble."

Chris sighed. It's what he'd wanted to do, but John had been terrified of their reaction. Now they'd made things worse. "I didn't want anyone to think the duchess might've had a part in it. She didn't know, and I didn't want to scare her. And I wasn't sure how they'd react..."

"Hmmf." Johann sat quietly for a moment. "You were merely doing your duty. You are surrounded by men whose customs you are unfamiliar with. No wonder you should be afraid to confess to killing one of them. I can't say I'd feel much different even now if I were faced with the same circumstance... Even with our years together, I am a foreigner to them as well and—

"KREESE!!"

He heard her far up the trail and immediately forced himself to sit up. Every muscle and bone in his body protested, but he sat up and opened his eyes to the blurry world around him.

"KREESE!" She shouted again, her voice getting closer. He could hear her feet on the leaves and the rustling of her skirts as she sprinted nearer.

"Get away from him!" she ordered, grunting as she most likely pushed her way through the crowd of men. "Stand back! Get back!"

And suddenly she was there, kneeling in front of him, her eyes full of tears. "Kreese..." Her eyes darted from his eyes to his nose to his body and back, her hands shaking in front of her as she debated whether or not to touch him. "Are you alright?"

He forced a smile. "I'll be fine. I need *you* to do everything the lieutenant tells you to and everything will be alright. Understand?"

She nodded.

"Your Grace," Captain Furneaux said sternly from the trail behind him. "You need to join the others on the cutter now."

"He was only doing his job." She stood, sniffling and wiping the tears from her eyes. "You can't kill him for doing the job he was ordered to do!"

"Your Grace, I assure you, *I* will not kill him. There are, however, laws we must abide by, and I cannot let his duty to you overshadow the laws of the admiralty. A punishment must be delivered."

"You won't kill him?" She crossed her arms over her chest.

"No, Your Grace. I'm not going to kill him."

She stood taller. "I don't understand what gives you the power to punish *my* guard. Shouldn't it be my responsibility to deliver punishment to my own servant?"

"My apologies, Your Grace, but it is under my leadership this crime occurred and therefore it falls upon me to deliver just penalty."

"Well then, I must be present when that penalty is decided," she demanded. "I need to know what you intend to do with him so I can figure out what to do with myself. If you plan to strip me of my only guard, I'll need to make arrangements for a new one. Won't I?"

Two men stepped directly in front of Chris and he squinted up against the blinding daylight to make them out as the Captains Tobias Furneaux and James Cook.

"He should be flogged with the others. Two dozen lashes," Tobias said with a darkness in his tone. "Then placed in irons for thirty days—no, sixty. I think that is more than fair, given that he has taken the life of one of my sergeants. What say you, Captain Cook?"

Captain Cook frowned down at Chris, then offered what appeared to be an apology in his expression before he straightened. "Do you not think that a bit excessive?"

"He has killed one of my best men, Captain. I do not think it nearly excessive enough."

"What does this mean, *flogged*?" Maria spat hatefully.

Tobias laughed. "Surely you are privy to the act of flogging? Perhaps you call it by another word? He shall be whipped across the back, madam, publicly. It will leave a mark or two, but it shall heal and the men will view the scars as payment for his crime. Come. Let us take him back to the ship. The flogging will be swift and the ship's surgeon will clean him up before he is placed in irons."

"And what will I do for sixty days with no guard? With no one to help me dress? Eh? Are one of you going to come to tie my stays each morning?"

"Lieutenant Edgecumbe has offered to guard you at night," Captain Cook assured her. "We shall give him the secretary's cabin until Christopher is returned. You may remain close to myself through the day. We will offer Fetia compensation to join us on our journey to assist you in dressing and return her with Hitihiti on our trip back. Come. There is no sense in arguing now. It is already decided, Your Grace. Let's get it over with."

At the ship, his arms were tied over his head as the soldiers and shipmen lined up behind him to take in the theatrics of his punishment.

His nose whistled as he struggled to breathe through it and his eyes were so swollen, he could barely keep them open. He almost looked forward to sixty days of rest after what had already been the worst beating he'd ever taken.

He could hear Tobias behind him and he stiffened the exposed muscles on his back in preparation of the *'two dozen lashes'* he boasted to the crowd behind him he would give.

He took several deep breaths and gritted his teeth, staring out at the ocean just as the first stroke was delivered.

Nothing could've prepared him for the pain of it. That one single swing of several knotted cat 'o nine tails lit his back on fire as it tore into the flesh.

"One…" Tobias shouted as Maria screamed deliriously from the crowd.

Again he braced and the claw of the whip scraped across his back, this time digging deeper, pulling at the already torn flesh from the first blow.

"Two…"

"Three…"

"Four…"

He stood straighter and set his jaw, determined not to break. He would not show weakness in front of these men. Soon enough, he would be let out, and they couldn't see him as a man to be easily broken.

"Five…"

"Six…"

"Seven…"

He winced with each strike on his skin, but dared not cry or pass out. He would heal, and they would remember. Perhaps the image would be enough to keep them far away from Maria's cabin.

"Eight…"

"Nine…"

Each lash seemed to grow more violent, and he could feel the muscles tearing beneath the whip. Suddenly, in place of the ocean, he saw Alaina. She was right there in front of him, holding his face between her palms.

"Twelve…"

"Thirteen…"

"Fourteen…"

It was the first time he'd been able to see her face in months and tears did form in his eyes then. The comfort of seeing her was more than he could bear. He hadn't realized just how much he'd missed her until that moment. He blinked the tears away, but kept his eyes fixed on hers. "Ally," he whispered. "You're here."

"Fifteen…"

"Sixteen…"

There was something in her expression that was changed; different. His focus danced between each of her hazel eyes. "Are you alive? Are you safe?"

"Seventeen…"

She smiled softly and nodded, her expression calm and collected.

"Eighteen…"

His back was ripped to shreds. He could feel every slice on his skin, but as his vision began to blur, her grip on his face tightened, and she forced his eyes to stay open.

"Nineteen…"

"Twenty…"

He winced, tears threatening to fall down his cheeks as his body trembled. "I have gotten so lost without you," he whispered so low it couldn't have been audible.

"Twenty one…"

"Twenty Two…"

She held his face tighter, steadying him as his muscles shook. "I've let my mind drift away from you... and I'm so sorry."

"Twenty Three..."

This lash hurt the worst and his mouth opened as if to cry out when she placed her lips over his. Instantly, he was filled with relief and he closed his eyes to let her comfort fill him.

"Twenty Four..."

He let himself remember the sensations of her mouth as Tobias stopped counting and he felt the whip come across his back over and over in a mad rage, each lash becoming more violent than the last.

"That's enough!" He heard Captain Cook call out as Maria screamed just beyond him. "We agreed to two dozen! What are you doing?!"

Still, the whip came down more ferociously and he could feel himself giving way to the pain, losing the feel of Alaina with each piercing whip across his back; with the sounds of Captain Furneaux's delirious laughter.

"I said it is enough!" Captain Cook ordered, his voice growing closer.

Another slash and he could feel the burn of his muscles shredding. He tried to hold on to Alaina, but she was gone, and in her place was someone new; someone softly caressing his cheek.

"Mi amor," Maria whispered as the struggle of men attempting to settle Tobias sounded behind him. "You are a *man;* a man who makes fire and kills giant crabs with his bare hands. Do you remember? I need you to be a man and get us both out of this bad dream. Understand?"

One final blow forced his eyes open. Alaina and Maria were gone, and there was only an endless ocean before him. He let his head fall forward then, his body going slack in the ropes that held him as the crowd behind him fell dead silent.

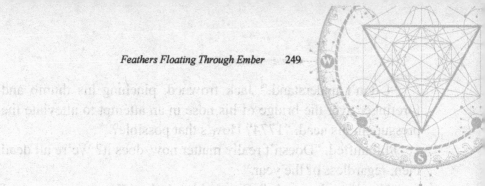

Chapter Twenty One

Jack

Jack propped himself up against the stone wall behind him, every muscle in his body feeling like lead as the poison wore off. "Why do they think we're gods?" he asked Phil.

"Because I told them about the plane," Phil muttered.

"And how exactly does that translate to us being gods?"

"Because there are no planes in 1774," he said nonchalantly.

Jack blinked hard, and he heard the groan of Bud nearby as consciousness found him as well.

"What do you mean, *1774?*" Jack asked, reaching in the darkness for Bud until he felt an arm. "You alright?"

"I'm fine," Bud whispered, sitting up and scooting backward to place himself between Jack and Phil.

"The year," Jacob said. "It is 1774."

Phil cleared his throat. "I thought they were just removed from the world... When I explained to them what an airplane was and the date our airplane had crashed, I became the *'man from the sky... a god sent from the future to help them win their war with the Kahurangi.'* It wasn't until I landed myself down here that I understood why the airplane must've seemed like something godly."

"I don't understand." Jack frowned, pinching his thumb and forefinger over the bridge of his nose in an attempt to alleviate the pressure in his head. "1774? How's that possible?"

Phil huffed. "Doesn't really matter now, does it? We're all dead men, regardless of the year."

"Not if we're gods," Bud said calmly. "We can get out of this... We just have to be smarter than them. Tell me what you know."

"What I know?" Phil spat hatefully. "I know you beat the shit out of me, put me on a canoe, and left me to die on that ocean... and then these people picked me up and are dragging that death out by cutting me up, one piece at a time!"

"Kill the theatrics," Bud retorted. "You know what you did, and you deserved worse than what we gave you. We're here now. And if you'd like us to take you with us when we escape, you'll tell us everything you know—start to finish. How they found you, where they found you, how they treated you, what they like, dislike, and what their weaknesses are. What are they afraid of? What do they want? Whatever you know, you'll tell us."

"They dine upon their enemies," Jacob said, not allowing Phil the moment to respond. "They pride themselves on being the greatest warriors. In their culture, they capture and keep their enemies. They consume them. It's considered the ultimate triumph to consume the soul of their enemy... If you have made an enemy of them, I daresay you may meet the same fate. They often bring Kahurangi men and women to this prison, break their legs, and bring them out to watch as they kill and eat each prisoner. They want power. To humiliate a man by slaughtering his woman gives them power. To consume the soul of a man who stands against them gives them power. To devastate another by forcing him to watch gives them power. I shiver at the thought that my Michael may too be joining in their rituals now that they have taken him as one of their own. How did he look when you saw him? Was he well?"

"He seems okay," Jack said softly. "He doesn't know you're here. He asked me to help him escape so he could go home to you."

"Aye," Jacob agreed. "I've not been let out since they captured me. I think they might be keeping me to use against him one day should he turn against them."

"If you've never been let out," Jack observed, "how do you know so much about them?"

"When I was taken, I thought for certain they had killed my Michael. I was desperate to know whether or not he was alive. Each time a Kahurangi tribe member was brought down, I worked tirelessly to learn as many words as I could. Over time, I learned to converse with them. The Kahurangi are not cannibals. They are peaceful people. They want no part in the wars they are forced to fight with the Nikora. They only want to live on their side of the island in peace. They converse willingly, offer up everything they've come to know of them."

Jack shivered as he remembered the man he'd held in his arms; the feel of him convulsing as he'd squeezed the life out of him. He'd been a peaceful man forced to fight for his life... and he'd lost. He'd lost for no reason at all.

Bud cleared his throat. "How often do they bring them?"

"Frequently... it is rare that there are not at least two in here alongside me."

Bud nodded. "So we should expect more—and soon. Tell me Jacob, how did you come to be here?"

"Oh... ehm... well..." He cleared his throat. "It was 1764 and a dear friend of mine, John Byron, was granted command of the HMS Dolphin. He was to sail into the Pacific Ocean to New Albion and search for the North-West Passage. I had hoped to be one of the first Englishmen to settle in New Albion, so he agreed to escort my wife, Michael and I there on his voyage. One night along our journey, we saw flames on the horizon. We thought we might find much needed supplies on an inhabited island. Uati was unable to communicate with our translator, and many of the soldiers expressed concern, even with Uati's happy manners. They would not leave the ship and therefore, John Byron would not either. Still, Uati's smiling face and peaceful demeanor fooled many of us into accompanying him onto the island. Once on land, it was over. There were more than twenty captured along with me before Captain Byron could pull anchor and escape. They killed all but myself and Michael... including my wife."

"I am sorry for your loss," Bud said. "I've only just lost my own wife a few days ago."

Days... Between navigating the ocean, arriving on the island, killing a man, and being taken captive, Jack felt like they'd been gone for a month instead of mere days.

"Then it is I who must be sorry for *your* loss, sir," Jacob said.

"It's alright," Bud assured him. "Now... you say Uati was unable to communicate... So he keeps Michael as a translator... Michael mentioned that Uati begs him to teach him to speak English but he refuses... So we know Uati wants to learn English... and he hates the Kahurangi. He worships power... and he thinks we are gods... Do the Kahurangi speak the same language as the Nikora?"

"Yes."

Jack tilted his head to one side, intrigued. "You have a plan already?"

Bud laughed. "I'd hardly call it a plan... but I have an idea." He could hear Bud shuffling to sit up straighter. "Phil, you told him you are not a fighting god... so what kind of god are you then?"

Phil sighed. "He didn't ask. He threw me in here when I couldn't fight and hasn't bothered to ask me anything about myself... Only questions about how and where he could find a fighting god."

"Alright that's good." Bud paused in thought. "Jacob, how long before they return for one of us?"

"Have they killed the Nikora they brought out earlier?"

Jack cringed as the man's face flashed through his memory. "Yes."

"Then you have a few weeks before they bring the next."

"I can work with that," Bud assured him. "I'll need you to teach me as much of their language as you can. Late nights, early mornings... I need to know how to speak with ease. Can you do that?"

"Yes. Of course. Can you remember it all?"

"I'll have to. When they come, I'll offer to teach Uati English in exchange for time... I'll tell him I am a god of wisdom... I assume he'll take me up on this offer and allow me out for spans of time... I'll learn the landscape... find weaknesses in their defense... figure out a plan to get us out of here."

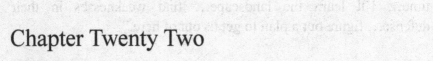

Chapter Twenty Two

Chris

He didn't know what he'd been expecting when they'd said *'sixty days in irons,'* but it hadn't been the dark and bottommost corner of the ship; his only company several pigs kept a few feet from where his arms were chained to the wall.

The ship's surgeon had come down with him and "tended" to his wounds. This mostly entailed coating the scrapes on his back with salt which intensified the pain for days after the event.

With no light whatsoever outside of the lantern that would be carried with whichever shipman was assigned to bring him his meal for the day, he had no sense of time. He wasn't sure if it was day or night; if he'd been locked down there for a few weeks or only a few hours.

There were no other prisoners, no guard, no one to talk to in the blackness; no sound whatsoever outside the occasional grunt and squeal of the nearby pigs. With no human interaction, it didn't take long for his mind to play tricks on him. He heard Alaina's voice first, as clear as if she had been sitting next to him.

"Have you stopped searching for me, love?" she asked, and he jumped in the darkness; the clarity of her voice making him ponder whether she was actually there with him.

"No," he attempted to respond, but his voice cracked from the lack of use.

"Shh. It's okay. I'm here," she cooed. "Are you hurt?"

"Yes." He tried to sit up so the could be sure she wasn't there, but his body was too weak to support itself and he laid back on his side. The beating and the lack of food had rendered him defeated.

"Do you love her?" These were the words that convinced him he was hallucinating and he relaxed a bit with the knowledge she couldn't actually see him in such a state.

"I didn't mean to."

"But you *do* love her?"

"Not the way I love you."

"OYE!" Maria's voice appeared in the darkness, as if the reference to her had summoned her existence. "What do you think you are doing? Sit up. You are not some little baby."

"I can't," he breathed.

"So… what? You just going to lay there this whole time, eh? You going to let your muscles disappear so you are half a man when you come back to me? Get up estúpido and act like the man you are."

"Leave him alone," Alaina protested. "He's in pain. He needs to heal. Can't you see his back is torn to shreds? He needs to rest. It's okay, love. Close your eyes."

"Oh, and you know what's best for him, yes? Is that why you leave him when he is in pain? Is that why you leave when he needs you the most? What are you doing down here anyway, you selfish woman? He doesn't need to be babied. He needs to be pushed. Sit up, mi amor. Sit up and work your muscles. Those men will still be out there when you are released. You need to be able to fight if the time comes."

"Don't listen to her, love. She doesn't know you like I know you. Close your eyes and rest. You can build up your strength when it stops hurting."

He squeezed his eyes closed, begging his mind to be quiet. He knew what his subconscious was doing and, in that moment, he wanted no part in it. He just wanted to sleep.

"Oye, superman, you've slept too much already. You need to get up. How you gonna find this selfish little wife of yours if you give up now? And what will you do if you come out of here looking like a stupid toothpick with noodles for arms and someone comes to attack me? You gonna let John be the hero now? Eh? You want John to be the one I run to? How you going to lift your sword if you can't even lift these little baby irons?"

This forced his eyes open. The chains on the shackles clanked against the ground as he slid his hands up near his face to push his torso upward. Everything hurt. His back, ribs, and arms all protested, and he wanted to collapse back down to the floor.

"Don't you even think about laying back down!" Maria ordered. "Sit up on your butt right now or I will never speak to your stupid ass again!"

Slowly, he slid his knees forward and rose his body off the floor, leaning back to sit up on his butt. "There. Happy?"

"Sí! Now, you do whatever you have to do to keep yourself from falling apart. Sit-ups, push-ups, whatever. You have already lost your mind—sitting here talking to no one—don't lose your body too!"

Then it went quiet again, with only the movement of the nearby pigs to remind him he wasn't entirely alone.

As time crawled past, he forced himself to follow Maria's orders, making a routine out of push-ups, sit-ups, squats, and arm curls to keep his muscles from diminishing.

He couldn't keep his mind from slipping, though. He would hear Alaina or Maria almost always. He could hear them as clear as if they were there beside him in the straw; as if he could reach out and touch them.

They frequently argued the same way they had the first time, each making a case for themselves and why they were more superior to the other.

He had been listening to one of these arguments when a new voice appeared among them.

"Christopher Michael Grace... Birth date, May eighteenth, nineteen eighty-five... Height, six foot three inches..."

Chris felt a hand smooth over his shoulder and he jumped, his chains clanking loudly as he sat up and opened his eyes to find

Johann seated beside him, a lantern hung just over their heads. "Johann? You're here?"

Johann smiled playfully. "It appears that way, doesn't it, my boy?"

"Mari—the duchess. Is she alright? Is she safe?"

"She's as boisterous as ever! Angry with every man aboard that she's not been allowed an audience with you and she's no qualms in letting every single one of us know about it, too. Tell me…" He held out a small white card, turning it against the lantern light to reveal it as Chris's Illinois driver's license, his eyes wide with wonder. "What is this?"

"Where did you get that?" he asked self-consciously.

"It was in your coat pocket. I returned to the fall to collect your belongings… I've been studying it for some time and I cannot fathom why you would have such a thing in your possession."

"It's… it's nothing," Chris huffed, remembering he'd placed it there to support his claim for when he would try to explain himself to John.

"No…" Johann grinned and turned the license from side to side, the hologram glistening with the lantern light. "I don't think *this* is nothing. I have told you already about my curious nature. And this has held my curiosity captive for some time now. As a scientist, I must think a little differently; ponder that which most men would overlook… This… I have worked it over and over in my mind and I must know if it is real."

Chris half laughed. "And what would you do if I told you it was? Would you believe me?"

"Oh, but that is why it has taken me so long to come down here and ask. I thought a lot about the possibility you would say it was real. And…Well… I cannot come up with a reason *not* to believe you, and so I must. I would like to know what this world looks like in the year two thousand seventeen. I would like to know how you came to travel backward and if it is possible to move forward the same way."

Chris shook his head. "I don't know. It was an accident. And I have no idea how I'll ever get back."

Johann's eyes grew even wider. "But you did come through time?"

"Yes."

"How?"

Chris shrugged. "We were traveling across the ocean, and we hit a storm... I woke up in the water... didn't feel any differently; didn't know we'd crossed through time. We floated to that island and you found us. That's all I know."

"How close to your island did you cross through?"

"Maybe within a mile or two? I'm not sure."

"This is most exciting. I cannot stay since I am expected to join the captain for drinks in the great cabin. I've only come down for this answer, but here." He reached into the breast pocket of his coat and pulled out a napkin, extending it to him. "I will come back often with more questions and you must tell me all about the future!"

Johann stood as Chris unwrapped the napkin to find a large, shimmering chunk of salt pork. The glands on each side of his jaw burned painfully at the promise of something other than stale bread. "Thank you."

"Thank *you*," Johann beamed, unhinging the lantern from the wall. "I will bring more to exchange for your stories. I must know everything there is to know."

"Johann," Chris stopped him before he could turn to leave. "How long have I been down here?"

Johann raised his eyebrows. "Fourteen days, I believe."

It was hard to differentiate reality from dream. Days would pass between visits from Johann.

He'd told Johann as much as he could about the future, about historic events that happened in between—the upcoming war with America and the United States that would form... He'd spoken at length about the plane crash, always having to tell it over and over so Johann could analyze every detail. He'd told him about his plans to search for the way back once he'd found his wife and the two different locations he'd come through.

At least, he *thought* he'd told him all that. He couldn't remember if he'd dreamt the visits or if they had actually occurred. Johann's voice and image appeared just as vividly as Maria and Alaina did. The only difference between them was the taste of salt pork on his tongue, but even that couldn't be trusted. He was losing his mind.

"Kreese?"

He was leaning against the wall with his eyes closed and he grinned. It had been a few days since he'd heard Maria's voice. Alaina had been taking up much of his thoughts lately, interrogating him about the collapse of their marriage. It was a relief to hear from someone else.

"Maria," he whispered.

"Mi amor, it stinks so bad down here."

He laughed. "I know."

"Oye, and you stink too!"

He opened his eyes to be sure it wasn't real. Finding himself still shrouded in darkness, he sighed. "How are you? I've missed you."

"You have?"

"Of course I have."

"I miss you too. I hate the stupid captain for doing this to you! How is your nose? And your back? Are you hurting?"

He smiled. "I'm fine… aside from hearing voices and going a little crazy." He smoothed a finger along his nose. "And I think my nose might've healed funny. It feels a little more crooked than it was before."

"If they have ruined your beautiful face, I will kill them all," she whispered, her voice so close he could've sworn he felt her breath on his cheek.

He opened his eyes again to the complete blackness around him.

"You're not really here." He frowned. "I'm dreaming."

"You are, eh? And do you often dream of me, superman?"

He smiled. "I dream of you all the time."

"What do we do in these dreams?"

He closed his eyes. "Talk mostly. I miss the sound of your voice."

"Oye, maybe you *are* going crazy down here if you miss the sound of *my* voice. But you are not dreaming tonight. I am here, mi amor."

He opened his eyes, both panic and excitement washing over him. It was too dark to even see his own hand in front of his face, and he couldn't be sure his mind wasn't playing more tricks on him. "Where?"

"Here." She laid her hand over his and he nearly jumped out of his skin at the touch, his chains clanking noisily as he straightened.

"Maria," He breathed, unable to stop the tears that poured from his eyes. "You're really here? What are you doing down here?"

"Of course I am really here, estupido." She squeezed his hand. "How could I not come to see you? After all you have done for me? I have tried so many times to come, but Tobias left some of his men to make sure the captain would carry out your punishment. ¡Esos feos bastardos! They wouldn't let me see you." She reached out to run her fingers over his cheek. "Are you alright? He hit you so hard... so many times. Everyone is still talking about how brave you are to not cry out."

"I'm alright," he whispered, his throat hoarse. "You really shouldn't be down here. If they catch you—

"I don't care. I had to make sure you were okay. I had to know you are not down here suffering because of me. Tell me the truth. Are you alright? Are you hungry? Are you hurting? What can I do?"

He winced as he sat up straighter. "I told you, I'm alright. But... John... before we left... he said he knew you were not the duchess. I don't think he will hurt you, but—

"I know, and this is why I *had* to see you tonight." She moved closer, crawling to sit beside him and rest her head against his shoulder. "I am going to tell him who we are. I will tell him everything. He loves me, I think. But to keep us safe, he will have to love me all the way." She ran her palm up his bicep. "Kreese, I am not the type of woman to torture a man. He is a good man and I... I could love him too."

Now the tears fell fiercely down his cheeks. He was grateful for the darkness that she couldn't see the torture inflicted in him.

John was good. He would be good to her. She deserved the kind of happiness John could give her, and he wouldn't dream of placing himself in the way of that, but he couldn't help the hurt it would leave inside him to let her go.

"Mi amor, I have told myself over and over that I am being ridiculous, but I need you to tell me there is nothing else for me."

"What do you mean?" he whispered, knowing what she meant but selfishly needing her to say it just once before he turned her away forever.

She draped her small arm across his chest, squeezing him as she nestled her head against his neck. "Tell me there is nothing between us. Tell me it is all in my head and I am a stupid woman for thinking it. Tell me you love only your wife and that if I give my heart to this man, I will not regret it. Tell me there is nothing for me to go home to and staying here with him is the right thing for me to do."

He cringed at the sound of his shackles as he raised his fingers to pet her arm where it clung to him. He cleared his throat, letting his tears fall freely as he forced the words. "I have nothing to offer you, Maria. I love... *only* my wife."

At this, she pressed her lips against his cheek. "It was selfish of me to ask it, but I had to..." She let go then, sitting back on her bottom to lay her head against his shoulder and sigh. "You are my best friend, Kreese. I owe you my whole life for everything you have done for me, and I will miss you for the rest of my life after I get you and your wife home."

He panicked at the thought of leaving without her. Far-fetched as a way home might've been, in his mind, that was where they were headed. "You don't have to stay... What if we brought him back with us?"

She laughed, casually combing the hairs on his forearm. "Can you imagine John Edgecumbe in the future? With all his good manners... they would eat him alive." She curled her knees into his chest and cuddled up against his side. "No. It would make more sense for me to stay here. I have nothing to go back to, anyway. No family... no purpose... Here, I could travel the world with him— this untouched and beautiful world—and I think I would be happy."

Chris took a deep breath, wiping the tears from his cheeks as he rested his head against hers. "Johann knows. He's been coming down more and more frequently to talk about the crash and the future... He's trying to come up with a plan to help us get back."

"Sí. I know. He told me." She yawned, adjusting her legs against him.

"Maria, you should go back up... before someone comes looking for you."

"I know," she said softly, not making any move to stand. "But I don't know if I'll be able to sneak back down... and I miss you so much. You still have a month left before we get to Queen Charlotte Sound, and I am bored to death without you. All day, I am forced to sit in my room with no one to talk to but Fetia... who doesn't speak any English and just smiles at me. Yesterday, I told her she looked like a chihuahua and she nodded and smiled. How stupid! The only time I have company is during breakfast or dinner and then I am forced to tell these lies I can hardly keep track of... If I am lucky, Johann volunteers to escort me to my room afterward and gives me a few minutes of truth before he opens my door for me to leave me alone again."

"What about John?"

"Aye, John." She sighed. "He is so... polite. He will not come to my cabin or be seen alone with me for fear that the others might talk. The only time he will speak with me is if we are at dinner or on the top deck. I hope by telling him the truth, maybe he will be less gentlemanly... If he knows we don't live by the same rules in the future, maybe he will spend some time alone with me."

He shuddered at the thought of John sneaking into her room once the others had gone to bed. He'd always been so sure John's honor would keep him from touching her. But then again… there was that moment with Maritata's wife… While John had been mortified by the act, he hadn't stopped her. If Maria insisted… if she made the move, would John be capable of turning her away? She wasn't exactly one to shy away from touching another.

"Tell me something about Alaina," she said sleepily, evidently reading his thoughts and needing to remind him of his decision. "Something to make me love her as much as you do."

"Oh, eh…" His mind went completely blank. All he wanted in that moment was to wrap his arms around Maria and shut out the world… Talking casually about Alaina was the furthest thing from his mind. "I don't know… She's… What do you want to know?"

"What do you guys do? What makes her smile? What made you fall in love with her? Something… Anything. Just talk to me."

He wanted to… but after so much time with his mind consumed by Maria, memories of Alaina suddenly felt distant. "Can we talk about something else?"

She raised her head from him then and he could feel her frowning even in the blackness. "Why don't you want to talk about her? On that island, you wouldn't shut up about her!"

He blew out. "I don't know… being down here… your mind does things to you. When we crashed, all I could think about were the good things… and since I've been down here, all I can do is play out the bad memories over and over."

She kissed his shoulder before laying her head back on it, and his stomach floated to his heart and back.

"You are scared to find her?" she asked.

He laid his head against hers. "I don't know… It's strange to feel this way. I knew her so well, but in the end there, we were complete strangers. I know it's only been six months, but I have changed so much in such a short time. Has she? Will we even recognize each other?"

He locked his fingers in hers where her hand sat in his lap. "I am terrified of the man she'll see when we do find her. I am not the same person she married. What if she doesn't like who I am anymore? What if she hasn't liked the person I am in a long time? What if we're both just holding on to the people we once were?"

Maria squeezed his hand in hers. "No one is the same person they were yesterday. Life changes us all. She would be a fool not to see the man you are now and love you that much more."

"Your grace?" A voice called from far down the hall. He saw the faint glow of a lantern heading toward them in the distance. "Your Grace? Are you down here?"

"I have to go," she whispered, rising to her knees and pressing her lips softly against his for a fleeting moment, an act which caught him completely off guard.

"Thank you," she breathed, resting her forehead against his. "For everything you have done for me. I promise I will find a way to make this up to you. We'll find your wife and I'll make sure we figure out a way for you both to get home. And you will see, she will love you more than ever for the amazing person you have become."

And just as quickly as she'd appeared, she disappeared.

The guard, he presumed one of Furneaux's men, patrolled dutifully, shining the lantern into every corner of Chris's prison before giving up and retreating back the way he'd come, leaving Chris alone in the darkness with the taste of Maria still on his lips.

His hands were shaking when Alaina's voice appeared beside him.

"You swore you'd never do this to me again, love."

He frowned. Had Maria ever really been there, or had he imagined it all? Devastation and anger filled him. His hands shook harder, and he let the words he'd left unspoken spill out into the darkness.

"I haven't *done* anything to you. I'm here, aren't I? Do you have any idea what I've gone through to be here? I worked my ass off to give you everything you ever wanted, then sat alone in the house I built *for you* waiting for you to come back, mourning my daughter alone... I took ownership for not being affectionate when it was you who stopped trying! I boarded that plane, screamed for you as it crashed, and fought the damn ocean to try to get to you. Did you ever even look back to see if I was there? I lost the skin off my hands attempting to make a fire to signal you. I've been beaten, chained, and starved, and still I will keep looking for you. Still, I will keep you at the top of my mind, love you enough to let her go... to never say the words to her because they are reserved exclusively for you. She is the only light in this blackness, but instead of basking in that light, I choose to be tormented by your darkness. I have *done* nothing to you."

"Oh, but you have!" she shouted. "Look at you! You've made me into a monster! Look at the voice you have given me compared to the one you have given her... Do you hate me now? Are you letting your feelings for her make you hate me? I was here first... but because I am not here now, you hate me."

"I don't hate you."

"You are *my* best friend, Chris," she whispered. "And I am yours. When we crashed, you remembered all the best parts of our relationship. Then you developed feelings for her, and you have remembered the worst. Love, we are not just the good or bad parts. We are so much more than that. And you know that... You know that because it was my face you saw when that whip came down across your back. It was *my* lips you kissed to silence the cries of pain. Remember *us* and come back to me. Come and find me and let's get back to being us again. What we have, it's not like everyone else. You don't get to give up on this. Remember?"

Those last words echoed over and over, turning into his own voice as he'd said them once to her before the world around him went as quiet as it was dark.

Chapter Twenty Three

Chris

Over the next several weeks, he volleyed between his love for Alaina and his developing feelings for Maria. The two women occupied his thoughts day and night, their voices ever present beside him.

The ship had made a few stops along the way. Those were the hardest days. Long gaps of time would pass between Johann's visits when they were stopped, leaving him to repeatedly question whether or not Maria was with John on whatever island they'd arrived upon; to wonder if she was safe, if she was alive, if the locals on any given island were kind... He tortured himself with the question around whether or not she had fallen in love with John yet... and if she had, what they might be doing about it.

He spent an equal amount of time thinking about Alaina. Who was the man carrying her out? Could it have been Jack Volmer? What would she do stranded with her childhood crush in the 18th century? Could they be off on a ship somewhere pretending to be husband and wife? If she thought Chris was dead, could they actually be *acting* as husband and wife?

In all the time he spent down there, he'd never once thought about their actual predicament; about time travel or a path home; about his parents or his job, or what going home might be like. He only thought of Alaina and Maria, the guilt of loving them both spinning their images in his mind so they were almost always in the arms of another.

If he was not imagining them elsewhere, they were there with him, pitted against each other in a battle over which one of them was best suited for him. It was unfair he felt the way he did. Unfair to both of them, and he didn't deserve either of them. Despite the torment it brought him, he preferred the images of them happy with other men to the sounds of them vying for his love.

Sleep was indistinguishable from reality. In the darkness, it was hard to tell what he'd imagined with his eyes open and what he'd dreamt with them closed. The only times he was ever certain he was awake was when he would force himself to exercise or when Johann would visit with some bit of food to wake up his tastebuds.

As he sat pondering whether he was awake or asleep, a loud crack of thunder outside jarred him completely conscious.

Almost instantly, the waves lifted and rocked the ship violently. Chained to the wall in the deepest parts of the ship, his body was rigorously hurled against the wall, then out to the fullest length of his chains, threatening to rip his arms from their sockets.

Much like the ocean had tossed his body like a rag doll during the first storm, the waves outside the ship slung him to and fro, his wrists and forearms burning with the hold of his shackles. There was no amount of shifting or positioning he could do to brace for each wave; no place to grab onto save his chains, and all he could do was pray.

"Please, God," he begged, his body smacking the wood wall hard. "Let me get out of this… let me make things right."

He could hear the thunder; could hear the seamen scrambling to keep the water out of the ship, and it was only minutes after it begun that the water began to rise where he was held. The pigs screeched in protest as they, too, were knocked around their pin; he could smell their filth rising with the water around his ankles.

"I know I've not been perfect, but I made a vow to her and I've done my best to honor it. I'll do better. I'll put Maria out of my mind if that's what you want."

The ship lurched heavily forward, forcing him down on his butt in the rising water as the pigs squealed loudly.

"Is that what you want? Tell me what you want! Why did you bring me here? What am I supposed to be doing?!"

Another loud crash of thunder sounded overhead, and he was forced against the wall with his shoulder so violently that he cried out in pain. "ARE YOU EVEN THERE? HAVE YOU EVER HEARD ME?"

Again, he was stretched out, his elbows clicking at the sudden pull. "ALL MY LIFE, I HAVE TRIED TO BE GOOD. I HAVE TRIED TO DO WHAT I THOUGHT YOU WANTED! BUT WHEN I HAVE ASKED YOU FOR HELP, YOU ARE NOWHERE TO BE FOUND! I ASKED YOU TO SAVE MY DAUGHTER... TO SAVE MY RELATIONSHIP... TO SAVE ALAINA... AND WHERE WERE YOU?!"

He curled into a ball as he was pulled backward, landing with his shoulder and knee against the wall. "WHERE IS SHE?! WHY ARE WE HERE?! SAY SOMETHING!! ANYTHING TO PROVE YOU CAN HEAR ME!"

Another loud crack of thunder sounded outside as he was pulled outward. "Please," he sobbed. "Tell me what I'm supposed to do out here. Where I'm supposed to go to find her—*if* I'm supposed to find her... Give me some kind of sign. Show me how to get them home... *if* I'm supposed to get them home."

This time, he was pulled so quickly, and with so much force against the wall, he didn't have the time to brace, and he smacked the wood with his head, the impact forcing his eyes closed.

He could hear the water rising around him, could feel the pull of the ship, but it felt more distant somehow... he knew his body was being flung around the small space, but he was detached from it.

"Wake up, Mr. Grace," Alaina whispered. "And show me how a husband kisses his wife."

"This is what you want, then?" he continued on his tirade at God. "Isn't this what I was doing? I never touched Maria. I didn't tell her how I felt. I have been searching for Alaina all along! I don't understand what you want!"

"Love, who are you talking to?"

He opened his eyes and there she stood, clear as day, across from him in the hotel room in Minnesota where they'd once driven all night to visit her niece in the hospital.

He blinked hard at the clarity with which she appeared to him. She was standing with a coffee in one hand, snow falling in the window behind her head, the bright white snowflakes of the snow storm mixing with the sunlight to shine into the room and highlight every orange, gold, red, and amber curl in her hair where it tumbled loosely down her shoulders. "What's going on?" He demanded.

"Maddy's feeling better. They took her off the oxygen this morning. They're saying she could go home as soon as next week. You should see her. She's all snuggled up with every single stuffed animal she owns in that hospital bed. Just as happy as she can be that everyone's here to see her."

He remembered the conversation that came after that sentence, and he wondered why he'd been brought to this very moment. Was this his sign?

She sat down on the bed beside him, placing the coffee down on the burgundy and green carpet at her feet. "Chris, I don't want to do this anymore. This whole... I don't know... fake marriage we're doing."

'You think our marriage is fake?' He heard himself saying, and he cringed now at the defensive stance he'd immediately taken with her that day. He'd known what she meant, but had chosen to take offense instead of talking things out.

"Well, it's certainly not real," she replied, frowning up at him. He could see now the desperation in her eyes as she searched his. She wanted to fix it. He saw that now, but he hadn't seen it then. She placed her hand over his. "I'm not blaming you for the past few years. We both let it become this way. I'm asking you whether or not you want to fix it. What happened the other day... that was not making love... hell, that wasn't even sex. I don't know what that was, but we both know it wasn't us. And if that's it… If that's all we've got left of us… I don't want that for the rest of our lives."

'So what then, you want to divorce me? Is that what you're saying?' He'd said then, rising from the bed to stand.

What an idiot he'd been. Looking at her now, he could see all she wanted was to reverse time; to go back to the way they had been before Evelyn. He'd wanted it too, but instead of fixing it right then and there, he'd gotten upset.

'Jesus, Alaina, you're gonna divorce me because we had bad sex?'

"Chris, you're not listening to me, love," she begged, her eyes filling with tears. "This isn't about sex. I'm telling you we can't live like this. I'm telling you I want to figure it out; fix it. I'm not attacking you, I'm pleading with you. We stopped looking at each other, we stopped touching each other… We have to do something about it."

That day, her tears had made him angry. *'Are you kidding me?'* He'd shouted down to her, not noticing she was falling apart. *'Like I've done nothing? Who drove eleven hours up here and then back every single weekend just to make sure we held this together? Who waited in our home for months by himself for you to come back?! And now… What? It's my fault we're not this perfect couple anymore? It's my fault you hate your life? You think I didn't see it? We didn't break us. You broke me!'*

"Chris, please," she sobbed. "I know I didn't react well. I can't go back and change any of it. All I can do is apologize for it and try to move forward. I'm asking you if you still want to be with me, and if you do, how do we fix this?"

Her eyes were swollen and red, her nose had moisture beneath it. Her hair was frazzled where she'd been running her hands through it incessantly as she tried to make her case.

Why hadn't he done something? He was right there, wanting the same things she did, and all he had to do was curl his arms around her. All he had to do was drop down to his knees and hold on to her, kiss her, hell, anything but what he did!

'Is this about Doug?' He'd asked shamelessly.

"Doug?" Her expression hardened, and she rapidly wiped the tears from her cheeks as she rose from the bed. "What does any of this have to do with Doug? After all that's happened, you're still accusing me of having an affair?"

He could see it now in the way she stood, swaying a little with her hands balled into fists, she was just barely keeping it together. She'd carried a child inside her broken little body for seven months. All that time, she'd known she could lose it, and still she'd held out hope.

She'd gotten to know Evelyn like he never could over those months... Then she sat in the NICU, not sleeping, watching every single breath Evelyn took until she stopped breathing altogether.

Then she'd completely lost it and returned to a negligent husband who chose to be defensive instead of understanding. He felt the hairs on the back of his neck stand as he heard the words he said next.

'If the shoe fits, Alaina.'

Her eyes narrowed into slits, and she crossed her arms over her chest. "You don't know me at all anymore, do you?" He watched as a single tear rolled down her cheek. "Have you ever known me at all? Tell me, Chris, what is it that keeps you coming home to me? Is it me, or is it just the time you have invested in me? Do you stay with me because it's more convenient than starting over? Why are you with me? You don't touch me, you don't talk to me, you don't even look at me... and you obviously don't trust me... so why are you with me?"

'I'm with you because I love you.' He'd said hatefully. *'Like I have always done. I have given you everything, dammit. And now you want to question whether or not I love you?'*

"Do you, though?" She asked, tears streaming down both cheeks. "Or do you love an idea of me you've created in your head?"

She held up her palm. "Do not answer that until you've had time to think about it. Ask yourself what you really know about me... If you even know me at all or if you're holding onto an idea of who you want me to be. Ask yourself if that's why you can't look at me like you used to. Ask yourself if I am disappointing you every day because I am not living up to the idea you have. I'm gonna check into my own room for tonight... to give you time to think. Uncle Bill says we should head home tomorrow since there's a break in the weather... If you're not ready to have a mature conversation about this before then, we'll deal with this when we get home."

She plucked her coffee cup up from the floor, spun on her heel and disappeared, leaving him standing in the middle of the hotel room.

He'd spent the entire night that night debating her question; asking himself if he really knew her at all. He hadn't made any move to stop her, and they spent the entire trip home avoiding speaking to one another.

When they'd gotten home, they both returned to work, and she'd dropped it. He'd never brought it up. It wasn't until she'd suggested the honeymoon that she mentioned fixing their relationship again.

He sat back down on the bed. Why had he been brought to this exact moment? Was he supposed to see what he did wrong or ask himself that question again?

Did he know his wife?

Did she know him?

He stared down at the green and burgundy rug, noticing the hints of gold that spiraled through the floral pattern. Why couldn't they just talk? Why had they never learned how to have a real argument? Why was one of them always left alone with their problems unresolved while the other stormed off? Is this what he was supposed to notice?

"I don't understand," he said out loud. "Why did you show me this?"

The room around him shook violently, and he fell hard off the bed against the wall, blinking to find himself back awake in the darkness of the ship's prison cell, water pooling around his calves as he was pulled away from the wall again to be held only by the shackles at his wrists.

He could feel his body weakening, every muscle in his body growing sore. "I was a bad husband. Is that what you want me to say?" He shook his head. "But I wasn't a bad husband... I was good to her. I was wrong that day, yes... And I should've fixed it... but I wasn't bad to her. Do you want me to say that I don't know her? This isn't helping me! This wasn't the sign I was looking for!"

The ship swayed, and he was once again slammed against the wall.

Feeling utterly defeated, he nodded, letting his body go limp. "If I am supposed to fix it, I will. I promise. But help me get to her... Help me understand if that's what you want me to do."

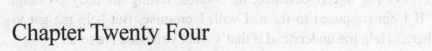

Chapter Twenty Four

Chris

He woke to the captain and two soldiers standing over him.

"It has pained me day and night to have done this to you," Captain Cook said down to him. "I would have done the same if I were faced with the decisions you were. Forgive me for having carried out Captain Furneaux's most harsh punishment. It was not without my own suffering."

He straightened and cleared his throat, continuing as the two soldiers knelt to remove the shackles on his wrists. "We have arrived at our destination and I'm afraid we've lost the Adventure in the night. We shall await her arrival here and gather provisions in the meantime before our long journey south. The duchess is anxious to have you returned to her service. I've arranged fresh clothing and soap for you, but I'm afraid you'll need to submerge in the ocean for some time to wash the stench off."

"Thank you, Captain."

"These men will assist you up and take you out to the new encampment once you are bathed and dressed. No harm shall come to you. The men of this ship recognize that you have served your sentence for the crimes committed. If any man raises a hand to you in the name of vengeance, you have my consent to strike him down."

Chris nodded as he stood, stars momentarily filling his vision as he did so.

"I see you took some damage in that storm." The clicked his tongue, inspecting the side of Chris's head. "We'll have you fixed up and fed before we join the others."

One of the soldiers extended his arms to Chris, a pile of folded clothing neatly stacked in them and topped with a bar of soap and a straight razor.

He took the clothing and let the three of them lead him to the stairs. It felt amazing to move more than a few feet in one direction and his legs rejoiced in the exercise.

As they ascended to the top deck, the captain broke off to join the ship's master in the great cabin, and he emerged with only the two soldiers. The sunlight hit his face, and he squinted to let his sensitive eyes adjust to the brightness, but basked in its warmth.

"It was quite impressive the way you handled the flogging, sir," one of the soldiers said. "Never seen anything quite like it. The men have spoken of very little else since."

"They have?" Chris noticed his skin had grown pale and, despite his daily exercises, he'd lost a significant amount of weight.

"You've become a bit of a legend, sir. It's said that no man has ever taken more than six lashings from Tobias Furneaux without crying out. Certainly never seen a man take nearly three dozen and not make a sound. My name's Edmund Thompson and it's an honor."

"Oh... um... thank you."

The soldier on the other side of him cleared his throat as they approached the sloops. "And mine's Owen Collins. If you've ever a mind to join the navy, you have a place with us. We all heard about how you found Sergeant Harris. None of us liked him much as it were. Rest easy that the men of the Resolution surround you in support. If the Adventure returns and any man aboard has an ill word to say, you'll find that the extent of the navy would strike that man down on your behalf."

Chris smiled at that, carefully climbing over the ship's rail onto the sloop. "I appreciate the kind words. I'm afraid I might need the help after being locked away so long. If I had a mirror, I don't think I'd recognize myself."

"Aye, we'll fatten you back up in no time." Edmund grinned. "There's not a man aboard who wouldn't share his rations with the legendary Der Mutige; the man who stood tall and made not a sound as the flesh was torn from his back until the whip cut into his bone!"

Chris laughed as they lowered the sloop. "Der Mutige?"

Edmund nodded. "Aye. That's what they call you now."

He smiled and shook his head. He'd never had a nickname before and liked the sound of it. "What does it mean?"

Edmund shrugged. "Not a clue, sir, but I think it's something good."

"Might I see it?" Owen asked shyly. "Your back?"

Edmund kicked Owen's shin. "That's rude!"

Chris smiled. "It's alright. I wasn't planning on bathing with the shirt on, anyway." He pulled the shirt off over his head and turned. "How bad is it?"

"Christ," Edmund breathed. "It looks like you've been chewed up by a beast and spit back out!"

"Does it hurt?" Owen asked.

Chris pursed his lips and shook his head. "Not anymore. But it did for most of the time I was down there." He rubbed the back of his head. "Everything else hurts worse at the moment after the storm last night. Worth it though. It feels good to be out."

"Tobias Furneaux is ruthless," Owen snarled. "When I saw it was he that would be whipping you, I thought for certain you were a dead man. We've heard stories of his harsh punishments. Never seen a man smile while he was doing it. I've seen my fair share of floggings, but never like that."

When the sloop hit the water, Chris stood to leap into it.

"You're gonna jump in here?" Edmund laughed. "You don't want us to take you a little further out... some place a bit more private?" He glanced toward the nearby shore.

Chris shook his head. "No. This'll be just fine. I can't stand my own stink any longer." He dove headfirst into the water, pulling his bottoms off once his head resurfaced.

"You're going to need this," Owen teased, tossing him the bar of soap. "You *do* smell like the dead."

"What do I do with these?" Chris raised the filthy breeches out of the water.

"Leave them to stink up the ocean," Edmund said. "They'll never come clean now."

Chris scrubbed every inch of his skin, scratching the soap into his pores. His back burned with the saltwater and soap, but he scrubbed anyway. He'd lived in filth for too long.

He joked casually with the two soldiers as he lathered himself over and over until he was sure the odor was gone. He then focused on the two inches of beard that had overtaken his face, shaving blind until his skin felt smooth. He crawled back into the canoe naked, and dressed unabashedly in front of his new admirers.

He had no idea what he would be stepping out of those chains into and he was relieved to find friendship.

"Do you remember me, sir?" Edmund asked shyly.

Pulling a shirt on over his head, Chris frowned. "I'm so sorry. I don't."

"I delivered you and Her Grace from the ship one night." He smiled. "I believe Her Grace had had *'a bit too much port and sun'* that day."

"Oh! Yes, I remember you now!" Chris shook his head and smiled at the memory. "She was not her best self that evening!"

"Can I ask you something?"

Chris knew what he would ask by just the expression on his face. "You want to know if I am *indeed* her lover? No. I am not. She's aware of the rumors and enjoys making me uncomfortable when I have pissed her off."

Owen punched Edmund's shoulder. "See! I told you! Der Mutige has far too much honor to bed a married woman! I never believed it for a second, sir!"

"I do believe she will be anxious to see me, though. If she finds out I am out of chains and did not immediately come to see her, she might kill us all. Probably best we head in that direction."

Edmund chuckled as he reached down to grab the oars. "Scared of the lady, are you?"

Chris ginned. "Oh, yes. Any man who isn't afraid of *that* lady is a damned fool."

The two soldiers rowed the canoe toward the vast shoreline. Chris took a deep breath of fresh air and admired the towering green cliffs of the coastline before them.

"We heard you are searching for your wife," Owen noted. "Every man has been instructed to inquire on your behalf while you were away."

His wife... in the darkness of the ship's hull, Alaina's voice was like a knife. He knew it was his subconscious trying to justify feelings for Maria he felt guilty for, but still, the experience had left a sore spot associated with her image. How would he feel if she greeted him on the shore? "Any word of her?"

"Not yet, sir."

There wouldn't be word of her this far from where he'd landed, he knew, but he was even more anxious to find her; to fix the mental image he'd created of her during his months imprisoned. "Can I ask you gentlemen one other favor?"

"Anything!" Owen all but bounced with excitement, causing Edmund to shake his head with embarrassment.

"It's going to sound strange, but I heard a legend about a place in the ocean where ships vanish out of thin air. I'm fascinated by the story and have been searching for anyone else who's heard it. Can you ask around for me? See if any of the other soldiers or seamen have heard something similar?"

"I certainly will!" Owen grinned.

"OYE! Let go of me!" Maria shouted from the beach, drawing his attention to the shore about fifty feet in front of him where she pushed past three officers to run splashing into the water. "Kreese!!" She yelled as she attempted to run against the heavy skirts of her bright yellow dress.

Chris winked at Owen and Edmund and hopped into the waist deep water.

"Are you crazy?!" He called out as he hurried toward her. "You're going to ruin your dress!"

"I don't care about this stupid dress! They didn't tell me they were letting you out!" She bounced through the water until she reached him, then lunged her full weight upon him, wrapping both arms around his torso as she buried her face in his shoulder. "Estúpido idiota! Don't you ever leave me again!"

He folded his arms around her and squeezed. "You're making a scene, *Your Grace*."

"Shut up, I don't care!" She sobbed, clutching him tighter. "I missed you."

"I missed you too," he whispered, smoothing a hand over the crown of her head.

"You're too skinny now!" She pulled back and inspected him. "Look at this!" She pinched his side, "you got no fat lef—¡Ay Dios mío!" She gasped, looking up at his face. "Your nose *is* crooked!"

Self consciously, he reached a hand up to touch it and she slowly formed a grin as she watched the realization wash over him that her visit that night hadn't been a dream at all.

"Oye," she raised an eyebrow, "but it makes you less ugly now from this angle." She laughed, smashing her cheek against his chest as she hugged him once more. "I will kill any man who tries to take you from me again! Come!"

She released her death grip on him to clutch his hand in hers. "There's so much I need to tell you, but first I'm going to have to feed you." She pulled him behind her as she turned toward the shore. "You look ridiculous so skinny. And then I'm going to fix that stupid hack job you did on your face. Who the hell taught you how to shave?!"

On the shore, Captain Cook provided him with a breakfast of bread, jam, salt pork, eggs, and, much to his surprise, fresh oranges. Maria paced impatiently next to the table while he devoured it. Before he'd even finished chewing the last bite of pork, she snagged his arm and dragged him out of his seat toward camp, explaining to the captain she wouldn't have anyone else hog him that day.

Up a narrow path surrounded by thick woods, she pulled him to a large encampment, and she led him to a canvas tent at its center. Inside, the decor looked almost identical to that of the previous camp and she spun around to face him the minute they were safely hidden from view.

"Let me see what they've done to you," she said softly, sliding both palms down his sides and gripping the bottom of his shirt to pull it untucked.

"Wait…" His heartbeat quickened, and he felt his cheeks flush with an unexpected sense of shyness. He placed his hands over hers at the base of his shirt. "I—

"Don't you dare fight me." She frowned up at him. "I have had nightmares about that day every night since. Let me see it."

"But…" He sighed, opting not to fight as she pushed the shirt upward, and he helped her by pulling it over his head as she hurried around to the back of him.

She gasped. "Ay, no… Oh, Kreese…"

He closed his eyes as her fingertips lightly danced over the multiple scars that spanned the length of his back. "Ese hijo de puta, comemierda! I will kill that man!"

He stiffened as her fingers worked upward, reminding himself that he swore to put her out of his mind; swore to stop obsessing over her. Even despite his promise to God, he couldn't help his body's reaction; his hairs standing at attention as her fingertips lightly danced over his muscles. "He kept hitting you harder and harder every time, mi amor…"

She traced the lines from one side of his back to the other, up and down his spine, illustrating the magnitude of the scarring left behind. "Like he was angry you didn't cry out…"

Her fingertips ran over his skin and sent a shiver through his body. "Like he needed the satisfaction of making you cry out so he kept going harder… Kept rearing back further…" She traced a long line near his shoulder blade, then another in the center of his back.

"His face. I have never seen a man so determined to hurt someone else." She traced his spine, and she rested her forehead against the center of his back. "I'm so sorry," she breathed. "It's all my fault and I'm so sorry!"

Slowly, he turned around and her eyes filled with tears as her hands slid over the exposed ribs in his abdomen. He watched her expression shift from apologetic to angry. "Who told you to take credit for his death? Eh? Who told you forcing me to watch you be beaten almost to death was better than taking the beating myself?! You will never do this to me again. Not ever. We will run and hide and live forever in the woods if we have to before I'll ever let anyone do this to you again.You don't get to make these types of decisions without me. Okay?"

He nodded. "I won't."

She placed her hand over his heart, sighing as she stared at her fingers where they smoothed over the hair on his chest. "Well…? Are you going to ask me about John then?"

He took a deep breath, swallowing the jealousy that didn't belong in his throat. "Did you tell him who we are?"

She smiled and nodded, sighing as she did so. He could see it in her expression as she looked up at him that she was truly happy. "Mi amor, he is… the fairytale I have always dreamt of. I never thought I could have it… Real love… But he loves me." She swooned, resting her head against his side. "Kreese, he loves me so much it makes me want to cry. Do you know what I mean?"

He looked down at her, wanting to cry himself. "I do."

"And he believes us. He and Johann meet in my cabin every night and we talk about the crash and ways we might find a way back." She motioned to the chair at her vanity. "Sit."

He let her lead him to the chair and sat, attempting not to notice her fingers when they slid over his exposed shoulders and up into his hair.

"Oye!" She frowned down at his head. "Your head is bleeding." She pulled the hair to each side roughly, inspecting his skull.

He reached up to touch the spot she was looking at and she grabbed his wrist, pulling it up to her eye level. "Jesus Kreese! Your wrists are all bruised too!"

"The storm got a little rough down there last night," he said to her reflection. "I'm fine."

She made a 'tsk' sound and continued examining his head. "You're not fine, you fool! Your head is split open AGAIN." She placed his hand on top of his head. "Wait here. I'm going to have John get the doctor."

"No, no, no." He stood and grabbed her shoulder to stop her as she spun around. "I don't want that man anywhere near me. Can you stitch it?"

She turned slowly back around and raised an eyebrow. "You want *me* to stitch your head? Are you crazy? I can't even tie a shoe half the time! I'll go get John. He could do it."

"I don't want John to do it." He heard the envy in his voice and tried to quell it. "I'm fine."

"Will you stop telling me you're fine?!" she growled. "You sound like a damn woman. I just got you back, superman. I'm not going to lose you now because you are too proud to have someone stitch your head when you need it. I'm going to call for John. Now shut up and sit down."

He laughed to himself as he obediently sat down and watched her storm out of the tent.

"Edmund!" She shouted. "Send me Lieutenant Edgecumbe at once! Der Mutige needs him!"

He shook the smile from his face. *'No,'* he reminded himself. *'You've made a promise to God. You cannot go back to this. You cannot look at her like that... Cannot think of her like you are. This is done. You promised.'*

She returned swiftly. "Alright, while we wait..." She stood behind him and smiled at his reflection in the mirror. "We will fix this face of yours. You look so stupid."

He followed her gaze, noticing the patches of hair clumped along his jaw, down one side of his neck, and in small spots on each cheek. He ran a palm along his cheek and sighed. "What have they figured out about the crash? Anything?"

She filled her hand with shaving cream, bending to begin lathering it over his face. "I showed them on the captain's maps where we were when we crashed and they showed me where they found us... Johann has these theories about the storm. He thinks it could've been a massive event—something about space expanding — and he says there's a possibility we weren't the only ones in our time to be pulled through it. He thinks maybe more people could have gotten caught in it, and we are just the first they have come across so far out on the Pacific... But I think that is wrong. I told him, if it were worldwide, we would have run into others in Tahiti or on some of the other islands, or here. We are in New Zealand, mi amor... We would've run into others like us by now."

He could feel his heart flutter as she worked the shaving cream over his cheeks, remembering the first time she'd done it. That's the moment he'd started falling for her; that moment she'd leaned over him and he'd seen a hint of gold in her eyes.

"John thinks it is limited to one spot on the ocean." She smiled as she said his name, sliding the razor over his cheek. "Which is a theory I like better since it offers a possible way back. He's spoken nightly with the captain about being granted his own ship when we return. Captain Cook has assured him he will put in a good word as soon as we return to England. John believes he will have his own ship and he has sworn he will take us to the spot we crashed and sail between it and where they found us however long it takes to find a way home."

She moved to the other side of him, and he watched her face as she guided the razor carefully along his jaw. "Johann says that theory could be possible, but he wants to go to London just to be sure it wasn't a global phenomenon. He says there would surely be word of people appearing out of thin air as soon as we landed there."

"But if he is wrong..." She pursed her lips. "I cannot risk going to London and exposing our lies. When we find your wife, we'll need to find a safe place to stop and wait for John to return."

He reached up to gently grab her wrist, stopping her before the blade could meet his cheek. "What will you do if we find the way home? Will you stay here with John?"

She nodded, freeing her wrist of his grip and continuing down his skin. "There's no place for me there." She focused on the razor. "No place for me anywhere really... I think maybe I was supposed to die in that airplane... and you were supposed to get on that raft. If I weren't here, you would never be apart from your wife... I would never have killed that man. You never would have been beaten for it... If I had died, I wouldn't be messing up everything. I wouldn't be stealing the life John would have lived... Wouldn't be stealing pieces of you from your wife."

"You're not stealing anything, Maria. Don't talk like that."

"No? You mean letting you take credit for Sergeant Harris and spend two months down in that prison when you could've been on all those islands with us searching for her wasn't stealing you away from her? And John... He is supposed to be living a different life and I am taking that from him... I am taking it, knowing he is meant for other things. I think I am evil."

He closed his eyes and laughed as she plucked up the towel to rub it over his face. "If *you* are evil, I don't even want to know what that makes me. You are not evil. Not even a little."

She rinsed the blade and returned it to its case. "Yeah, okay. God will hold a parade to usher Der Mutige into heaven on *your* judgement day."

He smirked. "What *is* that name?"

"Johann gave it to you the day you were beaten. It means *'the brave one.'* I think it suits you... You are a saint, mi amor. Everyone can see it and that is why they all love you."

He laughed out loud at that. "You don't know what goes on in my head. I'm not a saint."

She clicked her tongue. "Shut up estúpido, you cannot convince me you are not perfect." She eyed him in the mirror, tugging at the hair near his temple. "You need a haircut too."

John rushed into the tent. "What is it? What's wrong?" He hurried to the vanity.

Chris could feel his heart shatter when Maria's face lit up at the sight of the lieutenant.

"Look at this." She roughly pulled Chris's hair to one side to show John the wound. "His head is split open."

John smiled at his reflection. "Welcome back, my friend. My deepest apologies for not having visited. Furneaux's men would not allow any man outside the servants and Johann to come down." He frowned at the wound. "Perhaps the surgeon—"

"No," Maria smoothed her palm over John's shoulder. "He says he does not want the doctor to touch him. Can *you* stitch him up?"

"Well I'm not exactly qualified…" He looked at Maria, whose lip protruded in a pout. "But I suppose, for you, my dear, I can try. Go down to the surgeon's tent and ask him for a needle and suture."

He pulled a flask from his breast pocket and offered it to Chris. "You'll need this."

"Thank you, cariño." She smiled affectionately up at him, then lowered her gaze to Chris's in the mirror. "Don't die," she teased. "I'll be right back."

At this, she raised on her toes to peck John on the cheek before picking up her skirts and jogging out of the tent. Chris watched John in the mirror as his eyes followed her out.

"So, you know everything now?" Chris asked, looking up at his reflection. "And you believe us?"

John turned his attention to the mirror, catching sight of his back and frowning down at it. "He sure did a number on you, my friend." He shook his head, unable to look away from the scarring. "I wasn't being entirely truthful about Furneaux's men. It was only Maria forbidden from seeing you. Furneaux's men couldn't be convinced she did not have a hand in it. In truth, I was ashamed to come and face you; terrified to see what my failure had done. I must beg your forgiveness. I have gone over it in my mind every night and every night I think of all the ways I could've prevented it."

"We all failed," Chris assured him. "There's nothing to forgive. It's no one's fault. And it's over now."

John nodded, keeping his eyes on Chris's back. "Chris, I must ask something of you."

"What?"

John frowned. "But first, I must know... The morning you were arrested... she came from *your* bed. I beg of you, if there is something there; if there is a history between you; if you have any feelings for her, tell me now."

"She was scared," Chris said, stiffening with the effort of keeping his jealousy at bay. "Nothing more."

He saw John's entire body relax, and they made eye contact in the mirror. "Then I must ask your permission, sir, as there is no one else to give her away. Might I ask for her hand in marriage? Surely you must know how much I love her. Forgive me for not allowing you a moment to bask in your freedom, but I'm afraid I cannot go another day without the knowledge that she might one day be my wife."

Chris envied him at that moment. He knew John would never hurt her, would love her the way she deserved, would give her a life he never could. As much as he didn't want to give her away, he'd seen Maria's face and recognized the happiness; the same delirious happiness he'd once had when he looked at Alaina, and there was no amount of envy that would prevent him from granting her that. "Of course." He forced a smile. "Of course I consent."

John sighed in relief. "Thank you. I fear I would not have been able to carry on in this life if you had not given your approval."

Chris tilted his head to one side. "But she cannot marry you now... as the duchess. How will you work around this lie we have pulled you into?"

John shook his head. "It will need to be a rather extensive betrothal, I'm afraid. I cannot bring her to London to live as my wife with so many of my men believing her the duchess. She cannot step foot on those shores, as she will most assuredly be exposed upon arrival. I will need to relocate; perhaps to the colonies. She has told me of the war's outcome. I could serve as a spy in Washington's army. I could work out a deal for land and title in this new world that will form... Create a life for her there in a place that is familiar to her."

Chris turned to face him. "But that would put you in the thick of a very brutal war. If you were to be caught, you could die, and if she is to give up everything she knows to stay in this life with you, what will she have if she doesn't have you? She has no family, no friends, no job... You couldn't risk that."

John took a deep breath and nodded. "You are right, sir. But I haven't much other choice. She will always be the duchess to these men, and these are the men that surround me in London. I cannot take her there. I do not know a place where there is another equal opportunity to start over than the colonies. You know the history. You could tell me where to go... which areas I could be safe in?"

Chris shook his head. "I learned it in school, but it was so long ago, I don't remember the details."

"We've time. Perhaps your wife will recall something? Or perhaps there are others with her that may." He ran a hand over his hair. "I see you are concerned, but I swear to you, I shall go to whatever end I must to ensure she has a happy life here."

"I know you will," Chris said honestly, reaching his hand out to shake John's. "There's no one else I could willingly leave her in the hands of. I know she will be safe... and happy."

John took his hand but stiffened. "And you are sure I am not imposing upon your own desires? I know you are married, but it could quite be that you are widowed, and if you are taken with her, I could not bear to deprive my dearest friend of his own happiness."

Chris shook his head. "She wants *you*, my friend. And I couldn't bear to deprive *her* of her happiness."

"You did not answer my question. *Are* you taken with her?"

Chris sighed. "Whatever I might've been is irrelevant. I am not a widower. I know my wife is out there, and I know that when we return to the place we saw that smoke, I will find her and have my own happiness. I might've had a moment of desire for Maria, but I have nothing to offer her. You do. I give you my word. I have never acted upon those desires, nor will I, and I am happy she has found you. *You* are what she deserves."

Chapter Twenty Five

Jack

Jack waited patiently, all of his hair standing on end. Bud's plan was working. He'd spent weeks learning to speak the language. He and Jacob worked around the clock—he hadn't seen the old man sleep once since their arrival.

For the second time, Bud was let out and brought to Uati, and as the hours dragged on, Jack became increasingly nervous Bud wouldn't return.

"I never should've touched her," Phil said. "Alaina."

"Don't say her name," Jack spat hatefully.

"Alright, I won't. But I'm still telling you I shouldn't have touched her. Shouldn't have done most of the things I did on that island. I'm not that man. I just... when I drink..."

"That's not an excuse."

"What do I gotta do then to convince you I'm sorry? I know I screwed up. I'm trying to apologize to you. I want to be a better man than I was."

"You want to get out of here and you think I'm magically going to be the one to do it."

"That's not true... well, it's true, but that's not why I'm apologizing. I know what I did now. I know it was unforgivable. And I'm telling you, that's not who I am. I would never do that to a woman when I'm in my right mind. I wasn't in my right mind. I went mad on that island."

Jack took a deep breath and shivered. They'd barely been fed and had minimal water rations. As a result, his body constantly had a chill.

"Jack, please, believe me. I'll spend my whole life apologizing for what I did. I'd give anything to have my son look at me the way he did when he was little. I'm sorry and I'm gonna make it up to you... to him, too. I've had a lot of time to think down here... about what's important. And I've realized I've been a shit person my whole life. I never really saw what mattered because I was always too busy working, and if I wasn't working, I was finding myself at the bottom of a bottle. *He* matters though. He is all that matters. And I want to make up for the shit I've put him through. I want the chance to do that."

"Phil, just stop talking now. Your life is what's important to you, not his. You're telling me this so I'll bring you with me when I leave here. Don't bother. As much as I loathe men like you, I'm not a monster. And even after what you've done to my family, I can't leave you here to die like an animal. Stop with the lies. I'll take you."

"They're not lies," he said quietly. "And I'll prove it to you."

Movement above silenced them both, and Jacob's snoring beside them stopped. Jack held his breath until he heard Bud's voice as he was flung back down into the dark cell.

"Are you alright?" Jack asked.

"I'm right as rain, son." Jack could hear a smile even though he couldn't see him.

"It's working. He's sending for me again tomorrow, and I have an idea."

Jack sat up straighter. "What's that?"

"Uati is fascinated with us. He has not given up on the idea we could be gods. He is also a man who appreciates a good bit of sport. I think I can make a wager that may set us free."

"A wager?"

"Yes, a wager. I will bet him that, should he capture three of his enemies, I, using only wisdom, and Phil, using only trickery, will defeat our opponents faster than the god of war will defeat his with strength. If I win my bet, then he must set us free and, as a token of our appreciation, we will return with more gods to defeat the rest of his enemies. If I lose, then he can do with us whatever he pleases."

Phil laughed. "Have you seen the Kahurangi? They are gigantic! How am I supposed to kill one of them with trickery? And how are you supposed to kill one with wisdom?"

"Smoke and mirrors, Phil."

Jack shook his head. "I'm with Phil on this one. How exactly is this going to help us?"

"The Kahurangi are peaceful. They don't want to fight. And we know how to speak to them. I've spent enough time with Uati to know there is no other prison cell but this one. We will make a deal with the three prisoners he brings. We won't kill them if they play along. We'll help them go free. We'll put on a show and pray it works."

Jack huffed. "Uati will know they're not dead."

"Will he?" Bud asked. "I was there when you killed that man. No one touched him for hours. They left him lying there in the dirt as they all followed you back into the village. If we put on a show and make it convincing enough, we have to hope they'll do the same, and maybe those three men will help us escape to the other side of the island."

"And what if we put on an elaborate show and they don't leave those men lying in the dirt? What if they go to inspect?"

"Then we attack. Six of us can do a lot of damage if we work together. I may be old but I've got fight in me. When it's time to choose weapons, we all choose one. We'll be armed. Six armed men against a mob of unarmed ones? I like those chances better than dying slowly in this prison cell."

Phil laughed. "You're forgetting that I'm old, fat, slow, and nearly starved to death. I can't fight them."

"Yes, you can." Bud assured him. "And I can show you how with just your hands."

Jack considered it. It could work… Uati wasn't a particularly smart man, nor were his people. They were going to die if they did nothing. Armed with a weapon, they might be able to strike down enough men to run.

"Alright. Tell me more."

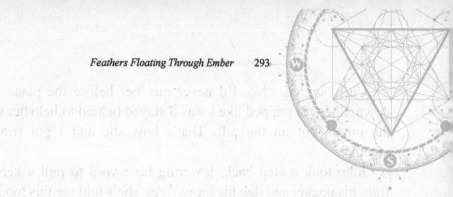

Chapter Twenty Six

Chris

"Tell me again," John managed between swings of his sword aimed at Chris's head, "about the plane."

Chris, after spending a month in New Zealand, had regained some of his weight and was growing increasingly confident in his swordsmanship. He blocked John's advance, spinning to one side to return an attack. "Which part?"

"Before the crash. Where were you going and why?"

He, John, Maria, and Johann would convene in her tent at night to discuss theories around the crash, talk about the future and the war, and discuss plans to go home. Where Johann believed every word, John always needed to hear the same parts over again, searching, Chris assumed, for holes in their story.

He imagined it was difficult to believe the truth and exposing them in a lie might seem just as feasible to John as it had Chris when he'd arrived on the ship.

"Otaheite." He dodged another oncoming attack and countered again. "My wife and I were going there on vacation. We missed our flight and got seated separately. She was in the front, and I was in the back. I'd gone up to use the privy, and that's the only reason I survived."

"And Maria. You're sure you didn't know her before all this?"

Chris smiled. "No, I'd never met her before the plane went down. She was trapped like I was. I stayed behind to help her when the others got on the raft. That's how she and I got stranded together."

John took a step back, lowering his sword to pull a kerchief from his pocket and dab his brow. "Yes, she's told me this too."

Chris could see the anxiety wash over his features. This particular inquiry wasn't about finding a hole in their story. This was about Maria... *Again.*

Maria hadn't given John the response he was hoping for when he'd proposed, telling him only that she'd *'think about it'* and every day since then, he'd grown more and more distraught by her indecisiveness.

"I tell myself she's not given an answer because of her apprehension to live a life less independent to the one she's so accustomed to... That she might be concerned for my association with the captain... or afraid I might perish in the war and she should lose the only connection she has to this time."

He frowned. "And she has just cause to worry. How will I ever introduce my wife to my men who once knew her as the very much married duchess of Parma? How can I guarantee I shall escape death while serving as a spy in this war we know very little of? How can she be certain a life in the colonies will be worth leaving her own world behind for?" He paused, tucking the cloth back into his breeches. "What if I travel with you to your future? Do you think she would have me then?"

Chris lowered his sword. "I'm afraid you'd be more out of place there than I am here."

John shrugged. "I could make it work for her. Surely there would be some place for me there? You could teach me, as I have taught you, how to act or fight or serve a purpose in that time. I would do anything to see her happy. How could I ever make her happy in a time that is not her own?"

"She loves you," Chris said simply. He'd accepted that fact weeks ago, but it still pained him to say the words out loud. "*You* make her happy. Men don't propose so quickly to women in the future. They spend a lot more time getting to know each other. Give her time to spend with you. She'll say yes. It's not like you can marry her tomorrow, anyway."

John sheathed his sword, shaking his head as he furrowed his brow. "I'm afraid time is not in my favor. Every day since I proposed to her, she becomes increasingly distant with me. She told me she loved me once—before you were freed." Chris watched John's eyes drift away in memory. "She couldn't bear to be apart from me then... But now... Now I think I may have frightened her with my offer of marriage. Have I been too forward?"

Chris returned his own sword to its sheath, his arms vibrating from the exertion of the fight. "No. She says you are the perfect gentleman."

"She talks to you about me then?"

Chris nodded. "Who else is she going to talk to?"

"Will you inquire for me as to whether or not I have misstepped in asking her so soon? Will you inform her of my torment, tell her how I long only to be with her and will give her as much time as it warrants? Beg her not to pull away from me?"

"John, I don't want to get in the middle—

John's expression washed over with embarrassment. "I ask too much when you yourself have given up your own desires to be with her so I might." He adjusted the sleeves of his shirt as he pulled his jacket back over his shoulders. "Forgive me. I have forgotten my manners and taken advantage of your good nature, my friend. I should not burden you with such things."

Chris sighed. "It isn't that," he lied. "I just don't want to get in the middle of it. It's a difficult decision to give up the life she knows there to stay here. Neither of us should push her to make it so soon when there is so much time we still have left here. We are leaving in two days for the southern continent. You'll have months before we return to the place you found us. Give her that time to spend getting to know you."

They'd waited for the Adventure for a month after being separated in the storm, but the ship never appeared. Captain Cook had been anxious to set sail, and had decided, reluctantly, they would move on without the other ship. His men were growing restless, and he didn't trust the New Zealand natives to turn a cheek to their misbehavior the way the Tahitians had. He was ready to get on with their voyage, and they would be packing up that evening.

John smiled. "I have kept you too long when we are departing so soon. You had plans to question the tribe to the east with Hitihiti today."

In addition to the soldiers and seamen who sang Chris's praises, Hitihiti had watched the beating and had, as a result, become a devout follower as well.

When Chris wasn't sparring with John or assisting Maria, Hitihiti was affixed to his hip, seeking out New Zealand natives to inquire about Alaina or stories of mysterious vanishing ships in the ocean. They'd formed a friendship in their time together, and he'd grown to enjoy Hitihiti's company.

Chris bowed his head to him. "You're right. I should get going if I want to get back to help pack up. I'll see you this afternoon then."

He spun on his heel and headed back toward the shore to seek out Hitihiti.

As much as Maria's refusal to give an answer tormented John, it tormented Chris as well. She'd sang John's praises every day since he'd been released from his prison. She never shied away from grazing his fingers with her own when she thought no one was looking or playfully flirting over dinner. She was completely swept off her feet by John and seemed excited to spend her life with him. Why hadn't she said yes, though? What was she waiting for?

His mind replayed the night she'd visited him, echoing the questions she'd asked, torturing him with the assumption that she might be waiting until they'd found Alaina to be sure she was alive; to be sure there was nothing else for her. And what would she do if they never found her? What would he?

He shook the thought from his head. Of course, Alaina was alive. He'd seen her. He knew, without a doubt, they would find her. He had been more determined than ever since his release to seek out any signs of her.

He knew they were too far for anyone to have word of her in New Zealand, but he'd remained hopeful they might find her on a ship, despite the responses to his inquiries always being no and his heart knowing she was back where they'd seen the smoke.

He had to find her; to be reassured she was alive and the love they once shared could be rekindled; to be sure he'd read the sign he'd been sent as a message to fix things instead of letting them go.

The vision of her in the hotel was ever present in his thoughts, and he could hear her asking over and over, *'Have you ever known me at all?'*

This thought remained at the forefront of his mind as he came upon Hitihiti where he stood on the beach translating a negotiation between the captain and a native chief regarding the trade of several large hogs in exchange for supplies.

Chris waited patiently for their conversation to complete, smiling when the men shook hands and the captain turned to face him.

"Good morning Christopher! I daresay we shall be well-fed on our journey south!"

"Very good, captain." Chris bowed. "I was hoping I could go to the east with Hitihiti before we begin packing up to question the tribe there as to whether or not they might've seen my wife."

"There is no need, sir." the captain beamed. "The man who has just left us is the chief of the eastern tribes. I have already inquired on your behalf and they've had no contact with anyone matching her description."

"Oh." Chris frowned.

"I've not forgotten my oath to you, Christopher." The captain placed a hand on his shoulder. "I was mistaken in my assumption she might be on one of the islands along our route, and I have kept you too long from searching nearer to where you lost her. It is my deepest wish to see you happily reunited. Would that I could bypass the Southern voyage entirely to have you returned there. I do not believe there is a continent to be found, but the society demands I explore it nonetheless. We shan't stay long in the frigid waters before we return to search for her. I swear it."

Chris nodded. "Thank you, Captain."

"It is quite intolerable down in those waters," Captain Cook informed him. "It is no place for Her Grace. You should know her health and comfort on this upcoming voyage have occupied my thoughts these past weeks. I've secured, in addition to no small amount of hogs, a collection of furs to keep Her Grace warm. The chief has assured me these furs are the warmest we shall come across. They are made from seal. He insists on presenting them to Her Grace himself. Would you be so kind as to collect her for tea on the beach as we await his return?"

"Certainly, Captain. I'll be right back"

The captain bowed his head, and Chris hurried back toward camp.

Despite his promises to God and his determination to let his feelings for her go, seeing Maria was the best part of his day. He looked forward to her banter, her Spanish curse words, and that mischievous look she always gave him, and he found himself all but running toward her tent in anticipation of seeing her face for the first time that morning.

He pulled the flap to her tent open, stepping inside, but stopped in his tracks as he found her in the middle, wrapped in John's arms, their lips locked in a very passionate kiss.

He'd known they must've had some type of physical contact in his absence, but he'd never witnessed it; had hoped even that John's sense of honor would prevent him from indulging in physical contact, but seeing it for the first time, he felt his knees weaken. He felt his whole body quiver with the devastation that suddenly filled him watching her fingers move over his cheeks, watching John's hands find their way into her hair.

Slowly, he began to back away, when she opened her eyes and forced herself apart from John.

"Kreese!" She gasped, stepping back several feet and adjusting her skirts. "It isn't—what..." She looked from Chris to John, her cheeks flushing. "What are you doing in here?"

He imagined this must've been how John felt when he'd come in to find them snuggled up together on Chris's cot that day. Much like John had done then, Chris stared down at his boots. "I didn't mean to interrupt. I'm so sorry. The captain sent me... He's asked that you join him for tea. The natives have a gift they'd like to present you with."

"Oh, of course!" She attempted to compose herself, fidgeting as she adjusted her corset, smoothed her hair where it was pinned up, and brushed off her skirts several times. She looked up at John. "We'll talk later, then?"

John nodded, smiling sweetly as he watched her leave his side to hurry out of the tent.

Chris cleared his throat, unable to look John in the eyes. "I'm sorry. I didn't realize you were in here. I didn't mean to—

"It's nothing," John said happily, his voice far off as if he was caught up in a dream.

He turned, not looking up, and followed her outside.

"Kreese," she looped her arm around his, "that was just—

"You don't have to explain, Maria. You're allowed to kiss him, you know."

"I shouldn't though. If it had been someone else that found us..." She huffed. "How did women just decide to marry someone after knowing them for so short a time in these days? With no physical connection... I had to kiss him at least once... just to see."

"So I barged in on your first kiss?" He raised his eyebrows as he looked down at her.

"The first one like that, yes... but I'm glad you did." She folded both her arms around his as they walked out of camp. "It didn't feel right."

"What do you mean?"

She shrugged. "I don't know... I *do* love him... and a few weeks ago, all I could think of was kissing him like that. I couldn't wait to really kiss him for the first time, you know? We'd had little moments... small playful kisses... but nothing passionate. And right then, it wasn't about passion for me... it was a test... it was a test to see if I could be happy with that kiss for the rest of my life. What is wrong with me? My first *real* kiss with the man I'm supposed to be madly in love with was just to find out if I liked kissing him?! Everything since he asked me to marry him is now a test for me. I wish he'd never asked it."

There was a slight bit of satisfaction in him that she wasn't enjoying the kiss the way he'd imagined seeing them in that moment, but he was also sad for her. Where she'd initially seemed so happy to have found the love she'd always wanted, there was now pressure on her to change her whole life, and he saw the weight of it beneath her eyes. "There's nothing wrong with you, Maria. You're just trying to figure things out. Did he at least pass the test?"

She raised her shoulders and let them fall. "No sé. My mind was too busy thinking: *'you're going to kiss only this man for the rest of your life, Maria. This is it forever. This is what the rest of your life is going to be like, Maria. Will this work for you forever? What if someone walks in and sees you like this? What if the captain sees us kissing? This could ruin everything.'*"

He shook his head and patted her arm. "I'm sorry. That's a lot of pressure to put on yourself. Falling in love with someone is supposed to be fun. You should let yourself enjoy it."

"I *was* enjoying it until he asked that stupid question!" She leaned heavily against him as they stepped out onto the beach. "And now it's all so... final. To stay here... to live in this time... what if he is not the one? Do you know how many relationships start out wonderful and then fizzle out? How am I to know that in a year we won't be one of them? And then I could be stuck here forever... and you will be long gone."

"I won't leave you here unless I am positive you will be happy forever. You know that, right?"

She frowned up at him. "And what do you know about happiness? Or forever? Your own marriage was in pieces when we crashed. Who's to say I won't be the same way in a few years?"

"That's a risk you take if you love someone." He heard his own words and felt them. He loved Alaina and had taken that risk willingly. Perhaps his sign from God was still coming to him. "And you work on it even if it falls to pieces. You never let yourself forget you took that risk. You do whatever you have to in order to make it work."

"Ugh," she groaned. "Can you just let me have my dramatic moment? I don't want to be inspired. I want to sulk and be miserable."

He laughed, squeezing her arm in his as he leaned in to tease her. "You are very ugly when you sulk."

"¡Cállate, you asshole!" She pinched him, then laid her head against his side. "I am going to miss you."

"Oh?" He chuckled as the captain waved them in from a small table on the shore. "So you're going to say yes after all?"

She sighed. "Probably. But not for a while. I have more tests. And that's assuming we don't all freeze to death in the arctic."

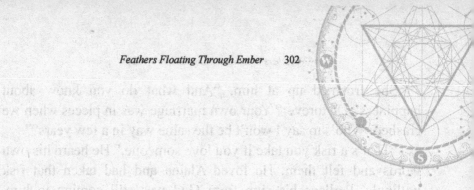

Chapter Twenty Seven

Chris

Over the course of two months, they'd watched the scenery around them change from blue to grey to white as they'd entered the Southern Pacific. The days grew cold and the nights even colder as they ventured further south.

While Maria spent most of the time curled up in her fur blankets in her cabin, finding excuses for John to join her so she could make her decision, Chris put distance between them, spending more and more time with Johann and the Captain on deck.

He was fascinated by the icy waters and the glaciers they sailed around—despite the frigid air. He couldn't remember seeing anything so beautiful, and the majestic icy scenery was a welcome distraction from the mass of emotions building up inside him.

There were days where the water was still and the glaciers reflected on its surface, transforming the water into a mirror of teal and white where the ice grew up from the ocean to meet the snow.

As they'd ventured further south than any man ever had before that time, the water that had once surrounded the bits of ice became gradually surrounded by a still and vacant desert of white where the snow laid on top of the sea. A blanket of powder laid undisturbed on each side of the ship. The air was still and quiet, and with it, the men grew quiet, the only sounds on deck were the creaking of the ship as it made its way through the cold water.

As the temperatures grew unbearable, Chris spent more hours in his cabin. Sharing a thin wall with Maria, he heard John sneak into her room every night to talk. While there was solace in hearing voices instead of the sex he was horrified they might someday have, he hated it almost as much as he'd hated seeing them kiss. He felt like an intruder to something very intimate, detesting something beautiful that was forming between them.

He'd heard every whispered conversation, despite his attempts to tune them out. He'd listened as she'd shared stories with John about leaving Cuba with her father when she was young, living with her father's uncle in Spain—leaving out the details of her abuse— and eventually coming to America and getting a job with the airline.

He'd listened to John's offers to build her a home, to give her children, and his promise to live whatever life she wanted alongside her, whether it was a simple life in the colonies or a life at sea traveling the world.

Chris would toss and turn, attempting to drown them out with thoughts of Alaina, until John would creep back out several hours after Maria had fallen asleep.

He missed her; missed the ease with which they'd once been able to speak to each other. He'd never been one to open up to anyone—even his own family—but she'd always somehow managed to get him talking. He couldn't have that with her now, he knew, not with all she was building with John, and not with them so close to turning north in search of Alaina. They would never be as close as they once were. He had to accept that.

He'd asked for a sign, and God had sent him Alaina. He had to keep himself distant for both of their sakes. He would need to devote every ounce of himself to his marriage; to making that marriage work in this place, especially if they were unable to find the way home. Who else would Alaina have in this time?

He'd been laying in his bed replaying his sign from God one morning when he heard shouting on deck above his head.

As cold as it was, he didn't even bother undressing at night. He leapt out of the bed fully clothed and shoved his feet into his boots, wrapped a wool coat around himself, and hurried out.

When he came up the steps and into the bitterly cold air, he noticed a thick fog had enveloped the ship; so thick, he couldn't see the ship's bow or the captain at the wheel nearby, where he was arguing with Johann.

"We can't go any further in this," Cook said to Johann. "The ice in the water is too difficult to navigate, and the fog is too dangerous. I can't see where there is water and where there is ice. We need to turn back. We could risk damaging the ship."

Chris joined them at the wheel, sleet and snow starting to fall lightly on the crown of his head.

Johann clicked his tongue and frowned, a few stray snowflakes landing on his thick brows and lashes as he did so. "It is not so treacherous yet. We should go a little further before we abandon our search, no?"

Captain Cook and Johann argued constantly about the existence of the southern continent. Johann, knowing Chris's secret, had of course confirmed that Antartica was there and was adamant about traveling further south in search of it each time Cook suggested turning the ship.

The captain shook his head. "We are not abandoning it. Danger aside, we are running scarce on food and supplies; we'll have to ration what we have to make it north as it stands. I believe we should return north; spend a few months in the tropics until warmer weather can settle in. This will allow us opportunity to gather more supplies and search for both Der Mutige's wife and The Adventure. We'll return once more before we travel home. What say you Christopher? Are you not anxious to be reunited with your wife?"

Chris shivered beside them, pulling the collar of his wool coat up to protect his neck. "I am, sir."

"Let us not keep this man waiting another moment longer, Johann." The captain flipped through the pages of his journal to land on a date before looking back up to Chris. "If we venture straight northwest from here, we should come upon the place we found you. I gave you my word I would search for her, and we shall leave no leaf unturned. Lieutenant!" He called ahead of him, and Chris noticed as the captain stood waiting that he too was shivering.

John appeared from the veil of fog in short order, standing straight before him, shifting from one foot to the other to keep his body warm. "Captain?"

"Inform the others we are returning north."

"Aye sir." John bowed his head and spun on his heel, flashing a congratulatory smile in Chris's direction before he crossed to the front of the ship to inform the men.

The usual sounds of excitement from the crew whenever they changed course were muted that day. There was something about the fog that made the men afraid to speak any louder than a whisper. Even Chris's own excitement about leaving the arctic felt subdued in the stillness of the frozen morning.

As the crewmen moved silently in and out of the blanket of grey mist on deck preparing to turn the ship, Chris couldn't help but hurry down the stairs to share the news with Maria.

She hated the cold and couldn't wait to leave it. He wondered why he suddenly felt more excited to see her happiness when he told her she would be warm than the fact that they were finally returning to where he'd seen the smoke to search for Alaina. He paused at her door, feeling shy as he tapped on the wood. "Maria?"

"Come in," she commanded hatefully from the other side.

He opened the door to find her scowling in the center of her bed, every blanket and fur she could find wrapped around her so only her face was exposed. "What do you want, superman? Close the door. You're letting the ice in."

"We're going north," He said softly, closing the door behind him. "We're going back to where we saw the smoke."

"Good." She sniffled, and Chris could see she'd been crying. "I am tired of being cold."

"What's wrong?" He moved to the bed to sit down beside her.

"Nothing, I am fine." She sniffed again and pulled the fur around her tighter. "I don't feel good is all."

He pressed his palm to her forehead, and she wiggled free.

"You're crying," he observed. "What happened? Did John do something?"

"No." She groaned, falling over on her face in the bed. "Of course, John didn't do anything. He is *perfect*."

He noticed a hint of sarcasm in her tone and placed a hand on her back, patting it softly. "Well, what is it?"

Slowly, she sat up, brushing the hair from her face as she straightened and blew out. And then he noticed the very strong odor of port wine emitting from her. When the nights were particularly cold, she tended to call for wine to help warm her. He smiled to himself as she swayed in the bed, realizing she was not sick, but *heavily* intoxicated.

"I am tired of this stupid place," she slurred. "Tired of these stupid people and this stupid cold and your stupid wife."

He laughed. "What's she got to do with you being cold?"

"You are so busy looking for her... I told you that you would abandon me. She is not even here yet and I never see you anymore."

He shook his head. "Maria, I wanted to give you space to be with John. I can't be barging in on the two of you like I did in New Zealand. You need your privacy."

"Oh, like you'd barge in on anything, anyway!" She snarled. "He's such a *stupid gentleman*. He *wouldn't dare* do anything improper! Oh Maria, I could never!" She mocked. "Your propriety, my dear!" She rolled her eyes. "Propriety... PFFFF. I don't want propriety. I want to *feel*. Do you know what I mean? To need to *feel* something?"

"That's just not how they do things here. You have to be patient."

"I don't want to be patient," She huffed. "He hardly even kisses me. What's wrong with kissing?" She laid her head on his shoulder. "I need to feel something, mi amor. Something more than this emptiness inside me that is eating me alive."

"You're being very dramatic this morning," he teased. "You've never mentioned feeling empty before."

"Are you not feeling empty too out here in this frozen silence? It's cold and everyone is quiet... I want to be held, want to feel warm, want to feel ANYTHING!" She looked up at him. "You feel it too, I can tell." She hiccuped. "Wanna make out?" She snickered. "It wouldn't have to mean anything. It could just be to..." She hiccuped again. "...tie us over... Eh?"

God, what he wouldn't give to kiss her just once. Drunk as she was in that moment, she probably wouldn't even remember it... but he knew he couldn't—wouldn't. He scratched the top of her head. "You know I can't do that."

"I know. But admit it, you have thought about it." She yawned, sitting back on her butt hard and nearly falling over. "I know you've had to. I think about it aaaaaall the time."

"Is that so?"

"Yes, that's so." She giggled. "Just look at those lips." She grabbed his lips and smashed them together in her grip. "I bet you're good at it."

He laughed at her. "Oh, you are fun this morning."

She brought her other hand to his lips, playfully moving them from one side to the other. "I could be more fun, you know... if *someone—anyone* would play with me."

He pulled her hands away from his face. "You need to eat something. That's obviously the wine talking and not you. Have you even slept?"

"Ugh," she pouted. "I am being ridiculous. It's this damn cold. It's making me crazy. I'm sorry." She sighed. "So... you said we are going north?"

He nodded, rising from the bed to grab the tray of biscuits from near the window and place it between them on the bed. "Yes. They're turning the ship now. We could be there in just a few weeks."

"And are you excited you will finally find her or are you still afraid of how she will see you?"

"Both," he admitted, handing her a biscuit.

She took it and held it to her lips. "What if you are right? What if she doesn't love the man you are now? What will you do?"

He grinned. "I'd get you wasted drunk and hope you'd ask me to make out with you again."

She punched his arm. "Oye, I'm serious! What will you do?"

He shrugged. "I don't know. I'd have to get over it somehow, I guess. I couldn't exactly force her to like who I am."

"Who else is she gonna' like stuck in this time? Isaac?!" She snorted, biting into her biscuit. Mid chew, she stopped, furrowing her brow. "Wait... If they've been stranded on one of those islands this whole time... they probably have had no idea we travelled back in time. How do you think she will take it?"

He shook his head. "It'd be hard for her to accept the actual truth; she'd miss her family like hell, but I think, by the time we get there, she'll be ready for some kind of strange news. She'd know something was wrong, I imagine, by now. She'd know a ship or a plane would've found them over the course of this last year."

"Can you imagine if *we* had been stuck on our island for almost a year?"

"I don't think we could've survived that long on what we had." And then he started to wonder whether or not Alaina's conditions were similar to his. Johann had assured him the Devil's islands were bountiful, but what if she was as limited in food and water as he had been? Could she still be alive or might he find her bones all that remained of her? What if there really were cannibals on her island? Or what if someone else was wearing those same boots? What if she'd been dead all along?

"She's okay," Maria said, reading his thoughts even in her drunken state. "You and I have always known she is alive... and we will find her. I can feel us getting closer to her and I have never even met her. Can't you feel it?"

He nodded. "I do, actually."

She stood from the bed and rose on her tiptoes to look out the window. "We're going to find her, and she will love you like crazy," she said softly, her breath fogging the glass on the window in front of her. Casually, she drew a smile in the fog with her pinky finger.

"I miss talking to you like this. I don't ever want any space from *you*. You are the only one who really knows me in this place." She turned to face him, swaying heavily. "Will you take me up to see this place before we leave it?"

"You'd better eat something first. You're falling over."

They returned to the deck after she'd eaten several more biscuits and drank two full glasses of water. She remained in her homespun fabrics, then wrapped two seal furs around her body to hide her missing corset.

When they'd ascended the stairs, the fog had lifted a little, and the morning sun shone through the clouds, casting a warm purple hue on the icy waters around them.

Glaciers towered over the water, blue and lavender where the light reflected on them, and the water was a still mirror beneath it all.

"It's beautiful," she whispered, her breath visible against the cold air as she took it all in. "I never thought I would see anything so perfect in my life."

He smiled, escorting her to the ship's rail to look out. "The pictures don't do it justice, do they?"

She slowly shook her head, small wisps of her dark hair blowing ever so softly with the breeze. "No… everyone should have to see this for themselves at least once. It is worth being cold."

Watching her experience it was worth being cold, he thought. Try as he might to fight it, he couldn't help but watch her face light up as she marveled at the beauty surrounding them.

"When I said I wanted to see the world," she laughed to herself, her eyes scanning the landscape, "this is what I meant.

This…" She spread her arms out. "Right here. This is the world I wanted to see."

"It is quite majestic, Your Grace," Captain Cook said, joining them at the rail, "is it not?"

She smiled, unable to look away. "It is bigger than majestic, captain. This is God's work. This is… divinity."

The captain grinned and nodded. "Indeed. Although, I daresay you will be much more pleased with the view from the bow of the ship, my dear. Come, you shall be the furthest south any person has ever been from there."

Her eyes lit up, and she excitedly turned to allow the captain to escort them to the front of the ship. Once there, with the sun to their left, they stared out at a turquoise ocean spotted with snow and ice, lit up by the sun in shades of red, orange, and lavender.

Captain Cook placed a hand on Maria's back, pushing her to the very front of the bow of the ship. "And now, Your Grace, you have made history. You are the farthest south any person has ever been. How do you feel?"

She smiled and shook her head. "Captain, it is you that should stand here. You have amazed me… to come so far south on this wooden ship… I do not deserve to be here. You do."

The captain blushed. "You are too kind, madam, but I insist—

"Neither of you is the furthest south," a voice above them called. They looked out to see Georg Forster sitting on the bowsprit, smiling widely. "It is *I* that has reached the furthest south of any man!" He laughed.

"Georg, come down from there at once!" The captain shouted. "If you fall, you will most certainly perish in these waters!"

"Not a chance, Captain!" Georg beamed. "Not until you've turned the ship! I'll have no man—or *woman*—take this accomplishment from me!"

As the captain tried to coerce Georg into joining them at the bow, Chris felt Maria's hand slip into his beneath his coat and squeeze gently.

He closed his eyes and squeezed back.

This was the end of it all. She wasn't saying goodbye to the arctic. She was saying goodbye to him before they returned north and found Alaina. She was saying goodbye to all they'd been to each other, and to the life she'd once had in a place she would never go back to. She was saying goodbye because she was going to say yes to John. She would stay in this place forever, and he understood all of that from just the squeeze of his hand.

Chapter Twenty Eight

Jack

Jack stared at his opponent in the fading evening light, holding a heavy broadsword with both his hands. It'd been almost two months since they'd first been thrown into the prison. Tonight was the only opportunity they'd have to get back to their island.

The plan wasn't perfect. Hell, it was absurd. In the 21st century, if he'd been presented with this same plan in the form of a script, he'd laugh at how ridiculous it was. But it was all they had, and the only option now to escape.

After a month of daily visits with Uati, Bud finally placed his bet and Uati happily accepted it. Within weeks, three men were thrown down into the pit and after days of planning, the ceremony began.

All three men knew they would die eventually at the hands of the Nikora tribe. With promises of a chance at freedom, they'd very slowly agreed to the performances they were all about to give.

Bud held two daggers, as did his opponent. Phil and his opponent each held axes, where Jack had chosen swords for himself and his.

All six men stood in the center of a circle of excited Nikora, waiting patiently for Uati to clap his hands together.

Jack's palms were sweating beneath the hilt of his sword. *'I don't know if you're up there,'* he prayed in his mind, feeling ridiculous for it. *'But if you are... I know how insane this must look. There's no way we're going to be able to pull this off. If you can hear me, I'm begging you. Please, help us.'*

In order for the plan to work, they needed to make it look real. All of them would hurt each other before the show was over. They'd planned to deliver non-fatal blows, even cutting each other on occasion. Mid-fight, Phil would kill his enemy first with trickery, giving the illusion he'd lost his axe and holding up his fists. His opponent would accept the invitation to fight with bare knuckles, tossing aside his own axe to allow Phil the chance to swing the axe from behind his back into the man's stomach.

They'd practiced the maneuver over and over in the darkness of the pit. Phil would need to control the swing to make it appear as if he'd dug the axe in, and his opponent, Ariinui, would need to bend over, turning away from Uati, to hold the axe in his stomach before collapsing to the ground.

Bud's performance was more difficult. Armed with daggers, the two men would dance around each other, attempting to stab one another. They'd cued their moves and responses in the dark. Bud would take a hit to his upper arm to make it appear real.

He would speak throughout, offering riddles that the man, Heremoana, wouldn't be able to understand. Once Ariinui had fallen, Bud would recite his riddle louder, balancing one of his daggers in the palm of his hand. Heremoana would be confused by the trick, particularly when Bud tossed it high into the air.

Eyes fixed upon the dagger above him, he wouldn't notice Bud as he brought the second dagger to his kidney. He, of course, would not hit the kidney, but would graze his side just enough to draw blood, allowing Heremoana the opportunity to curl his fingers around the dagger to conceal the wound and fall to the ground. His only concern was the dagger in the air. He'd need to throw it high enough to move Heremoana out of the way on the kidney shot.

All the while, Jack would need to maintain a realistic sword fight with his opponent, Tua. He knew how to swing a sword from years of training, but whether or not he could maintain against a man who'd been training his whole life was unknown. They had no way to prepare in the dark. If the sword was lost, Tua would lose his own, and they would have to beat each other until the other two sets of fighters had won their own battles.

At that point, the bet would be won, and Tua would not need to be killed. He would likely be taken to the prison where he and Jacob could overpower the guard waiting there for him.

The drums beat from one side of the circle, and Jack squeezed his eyes closed, wishing they'd spent more time coming up with alternative options.

'Please. If you can hear me. Please help us.'

He scanned the circle, noticing Michael sitting inside their inflated raft to one side, his eyes wide with excitement. Michael was another story. He'd spent almost ten years with Uati, living as a son. Jack knew the boy wanted to be with his father. If all went to plan and they were free to walk among them, Jack would need to coax Michael into the woods, where Jacob would be waiting.

Nerves on edge, he trembled in anticipation. The plan had to work. *'Oh God, please let it work.'* He stared at the flames dancing in the eyes of Tua, hoping the man wouldn't change his mind.

Uati rose to clap, Jack's entire body pulsing with anxiety, when suddenly a group of men came roaring into the circle, pointing toward the beach and shouting loudly. Uati frowned and said a few words, prompting Michael to stand from the raft, holding both hands over his head as he entered the circle.

"Uati say no fight today."

Jack noticed the circle of people immediately disassembling as they followed the interrupting group toward the beach. They'd begun to jog away from them. Something big was happening.

Uati, too, seemed more interested in whatever was going on at the beach and hurried down the steps to push his way to the front of the now running crowd.

"Men take you back now," Michael said, looking nervously toward the fleeing crowd. "You fight another day."

With the majority of the Nikora tribe moving away from them, Jack looked around them at the handful of remaining men closing in to escort them back. Bud waited as long as he could, letting the guards move in closely, before he shouted the order to attack, and all hell broke loose.

Jack pulled Michael to him, whispering in his ear. "Your father is in the prison, I give you my word. Go." He handed the boy his sword and pushed him toward the prison cell. "The guards cannot defend against a swinging sword. Get him and run for the trees just there. We'll meet you and take you both home."

Michael took the sword, staring for a moment before he bolted for the prison, while Jack launched himself upon the first Nikora man to approach him.

They rolled in the dirt in a cloud of fists and knees. The man broke loose of his grip and drew a dagger from his waist, slashing Jack's chest several times before he could roll out of the way.

Planting his feet beneath him, he stood just as the man lunged with the dagger, his black eyes fixed upon Jack's throat. Behind him, Phil swung his axe and took out the man's legs.

Without a second to spare, Phil spun around to plunge his axe into the chest of another. Stupefied by what he'd done, he stood in awe as his attacker slowly collapsed onto the ground.

"Get down!" Jack cried out, prompting Phil to drop to the ground just as Tua swung his sword to halt a club-wielding guard from bashing in Phil's skull.

He pulled Phil off the ground and placed his back up against him, dragging Tua to face another direction. "Get your axe," Jack instructed, watching as two more men approached. "You take the one on the left."

Phil was attempting to pull his axe from the ribcage it was embedded in. "Which left? They're coming from this way too!"

Beyond them, Bud and Heremoana were both wrestling with two other men, blood spraying out on the ground they moved over. Bud, as if he were twenty years old, sprang up from his own fight, leaving his opponent lifeless, and spun round to stab his dagger into the neck of the man fighting Heremoana.

Both men stood and Bud quickly crept up behind the men running toward Jack, slitting the throat of one while Jack leapt onto the other, wrapping his arms tightly around his throat.

This man was stronger than the first and bucked him off, digging a thumb into the gash in Jack's chest and forcing him to cry out. Blindly, Jack threw punch after punch, rolling the heavy body beneath him and feeling his fists land hard against the man's face.

"We have to go!" Bud shouted as Jack curled his fingers around the man's neck. He watched him claw at his forearms and writhe beneath him, his adrenaline pushing him into a trance as he pressed down harder.

Bud placed a hand on Jack's back. "We have to run. We can't fight them all. The others are coming back. Let this one go."

Bud pointed his dagger at the man beneath Jack's grip and said something in their language. Immediately, he stopped fighting.

"Come on!" He pulled Jack's arm, and they both bolted into the trees on the heels of the Kahurangi men who led them.

"Where were they all going?" Phil panted, dragging the raft behind him. "Why did they leave? What's going on at the beach?"

"I don't know," Bud said, keeping pace with the younger men despite his age, and gripping one end of the raft to pull it up over their heads.

"Where's Michael? Where's Jacob?" Jack asked, feeling his heart beating nearly out of his chest.

"They're ahead of us," Bud breathed. "Keep running."

"What's happening on the beach?" Phil insisted.

Tua spoke, taking a sharp turn. He continued to speak and Bud listened carefully, running harder as the Nikora men began to catch up behind them.

"There's a ship," Bud translated. "These men are taking us to another shore. We might be able to get to it… if we're lucky."

"What kind of ship?" Phil asked.

"Does it matter?" Bud replied. "We have to get to it if we're going to stand any chance of surviving. We'll never get off this island otherwise."

Bud was bleeding just above his eyebrow, the blood trickling down the side of his face. Jack, too, was bleeding from his chest. He could feel the cuts burning with every branch that whipped his skin in passing.

He laughed to himself despite his circumstance. He'd prayed twice in his life for God to help him. The first time, he'd woken up beside Alaina in a crashed airplane. Now, he was running toward a ship when he hadn't seen a single ship on the ocean in the entire year he'd been there.

The sun was still up. If they get to the water fast enough, perhaps the ship could still see them. "How far?" Jack asked.

"Not far," Michael answered breathlessly. Michael was tightly gripping Jacob's hand, all but dragging him along after him. "Just there." He nodded toward a sliver of blue shining through the tree line ahead. "Run faster father. Uati kill me if he catch me."

All of them were silent then, and they all ran as fast and as hard as they could, stumbling through thick brush until they'd made their way onto the sand.

Jack could see the large wooden ship far out on the water, several much smaller boats of men surrounding it. His heart both sank and skipped a beat at the sight. They were really in the 18th century; the ship confirmed it... but they had a destination and could potentially live after all.

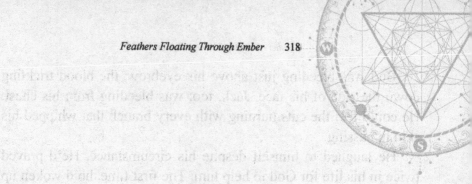

Chapter Twenty Nine

Chris

Chris stood on the bow of the ship, his eyes locked in on the flames leading them into the island. She had to be there.

After months in the frozen water, the captain had been true to his word and had navigated directly back to the place he'd seen the smoke before. As soon as they'd gotten close to the coordinates, he'd seen smoke once again, and the captain, despite the crew's apprehensions, sailed them toward it.

They were close enough that the ship could go no further and they prepared the sloops to be lowered. Chris wasted no time in hurrying toward the first one.

"Wait!" Maria called after him, clutching his hand in hers. "What if it really is the Devil's Islands? What if there are cannibals? Please, let the others go first."

"I can't. She's there. I can feel it." He pried his hand from her and climbed over the rail onto the sloop. "I have to get to her first. I have to warn her. It's alright. I'll be alright."

She glared at him. "You stupid man! You don't know what you're going into. Do you not remember the captain's stories?"

"She's here," Chris said, his hands shaking. "I can feel it."

John quickly climbed over after him, taking a seat in the center of the sloop.

"Oye! Are you crazy! Both of you?!"

John held up his rifle. "No harm shall come to either of us, I assure you, my dear. The men on deck have been ordered to fire if I fire. The cannons are loaded and ready. If there is any cause for concern, our return shall be swift. I've no intention of being eaten today."

"¡Idiotas estupidos!" She shouted, her hands balled into fists as the sloop was lowered down.

Chris scanned the vacant shoreline in the fading evening light, searching for any signs of her for the eternity it took the sloop to reach the water. "She's got to be there."

"We shall find her," John assured him, standing to remove the ropes so the soldiers could begin rowing them toward land.

His sloop held twelve men. Each one of them was terrified as they grew nearer to the shore. Even John seemed apprehensive as they all sat silently watching the beach get closer.

"ALAINA!" Chris called, cupping his mouth with his hands as he stood and swayed with the movement of the boat. "ALAINAAAA!"

Movement. There was movement ahead of them and he shook. Suddenly, she became real. What if she came running toward him in that moment? What would they say to each other? Would she run into his arms and be relieved at the sight of him? After all that had happened, would he be relieved at the sight of her?

Up until that point, she'd been a mission... suddenly, she was reality. She could be right there in front of him. And what would that mean for the rest of their lives? Would they be able to fix all they'd broken?

Like water rushing through a dam, the beach flooded with people, native people running with long canoes over their heads. Many stood on the shores waving their arms in welcome, encouraging the sloops toward them as the canoes splashed into the water.

"Cannibals," John said under his breath. "Look at the markings! Retreat at once!"

"WAIT!" Chris grabbed his arm, directing his attention to the bright yellow raft and several bodies inside it rowing toward them from the other side of the island. "There! That's them! That's the raft!"

He waved his arms over his head. "ALAINA!" He pulled an oar from one of the soldiers who'd begun to paddle them back toward the ship. "We have to get to them."

Several canoes were already in the water. Most were making their way toward the ships and sloops. Chris watched in trepidation as a group of canoes caught sight of the yellow raft and shifted their course, chasing after it and shouting what appeared to be threats as they waved weapons into the air.

"No, no, no… they're in danger." Chris looked at John. "We have to stop those men!"

John stood, pulling his rifle up and aiming it toward the pursuing canoe. The other soldiers on their boat stood alongside him, all aligning their rifles with his. "Fire," John ordered.

In a cloud of smoke, all four men began to shoot, and in response, soldiers aboard the ship began to fire as well.

Chris stood. "Don't fire at that one!" He pointed toward the approaching raft. "Don't shoot that one!!" The gunfire was relentless, and he panicked as he saw several shots hit the water around the raft. "We have to move closer to the raft. They won't fire at them if they see us moving that direction."

The soldiers rowed the sloop obediently under the order of Chris. As he'd hoped they would, those firing from the deck of the ship adjusted their aim toward the native canoes, slowing their pursuit, and they all stopped in the water when the cannons blasted over their heads.

As the raft grew closer, he began to make out the faces, searching for Alaina's among them and finding only men… He recognized one single face and his entire body trembled. Jack Volmer. Chris knew that face from years of being forced to watch him on television; had dreamt of him carrying Alaina off the airplane over and over. His shirt was open, and he was bleeding from the chest as he paddled the raft with all his strength toward them.

"JACK!" He called. "JACK VOLMER! DO YOU HAVE ALAINA WITH YOU?"

Jack paddled harder, his face distorting as he attempted to make out who was calling for him.

"DO YOU HAVE MY WIFE WITH YOU? ALAINA GRACE?"

Jack looked at Chris as if he'd seen a ghost, forgetting to row as they became closer. Close enough that John could reach out and pull the raft toward them, Jack stared open-mouthed at Chris, unblinking.

"Alaina Grace," Chris said, his eyes watering. "Is she with you?" He looked back toward the island.

And Chris nearly collapsed when Jack responded. "She's not on this island, but she's alive. I'll show you where."

PART II

The things we left unsaid.

Chapter Thirty

Alaina

"Ally?" he breathed, and I could feel my knees begin to buckle.

Chris... he was alive. He was alive, and he was standing in front of me and I couldn't breathe... I couldn't speak... the words stuck in my throat and I stared dumbfounded up at him.

He was dressed strangely and he had an odd new scent... and how the hell did he—

"Ally," he repeated, wrapping his arms around me and pulling me against him. "My sweet, beautiful Ally. I knew you were alive," he whispered, laying kisses against my temples and cheeks until his mouth covered mine.

"I knew it was you I saw..." He kissed my shocked lips again and again, smoothing his hand over my hair to cup my face. "I knew I'd find you here."

He pressed his forehead against mine. "I'm so sorry for how long it's taken me to get here."

Before I could get a handle on the situation, he covered my lips again with his, pushing past them and pulling me up on my toes as he frantically reacquainted my mouth with his. His kiss was desperate and deliberate. His hands moved frenziedly over my face and arms as he pressed deeper. I could feel his tears drip down my own cheeks.

'Chris… he's alive! How?'

Slowly, my body recovered from its shock and I let my arms wind around him, let my senses rejoice in the familiarness of his hands on my face, of his lips over mine, of his body moulded against me.

Just as soon as the relief had come, it disappeared, and a panic set in. Guilt washed up into my throat as he pulled me closer; as his mouth grew warmer. I was kissing my husband, but I had an unrelenting feeling I was doing something wrong.

He was familiar, but a complete stranger at the same time. He was mine, but he wasn't. I was two different women standing there at that moment; one that was betraying her fiancé by kissing another man, and one that was utterly relieved to find her husband still alive.

He pulled back, holding my face in his hands as he inspected me. "I knew you were alive," he said softly, his eyes watering as they focused on each of mine. "I wouldn't stop looking. I knew you were out here somewhere. There's so much I need to tell you… so much I—

"I knew it wasn't no damn storm!" Jim shouted behind us. "Didn't I tell ye?"

"Ally," Chris evened out his voice, his expression shifting to solemn. "There's a lot you need to know before you get on that ship. Is there somewhere we can go? To be alone?"

I was trembling, but I nodded.

"The others… they'll need to hear it too." He looked up from me for the first time to take in the other survivors. "We've created identities and backstories for you all." He didn't wait for me to respond, but turned to a tall soldier at his side. "Buy us some time for me to tell them everything?"

The soldier bowed his head. "I will."

"Come." He turned me back the way I'd come. "Before the captain catches up to us."

Dazedly, I led my husband back up the trail toward our island home… toward my home with Jack.

Where was Jack? I could hear the others joining us; could hear Bud pressing them all to stay quiet until we were clear of the other men, but I couldn't hear Jack.

My face was ice cold, my mind was racing, and my vision was tunneling. I felt like I was going to be sick.

"You alright?" Lilly whispered, locking her arm around mine when she'd caught up to me.

I shook my head, still incapable of speaking.

How did he get here? How could I possibly tell him everything that had happened since I last saw him? How could I tell him about Jack... about the baby... how could I ever look him in the eyes again? And Jack... where was Jack? What the hell was I going—

"This is far enough," he instructed, forcing me to turn back toward him.

Seeing those familiar green eyes as I turned forced my racing mind to quiet and allow my heart to take a moment to process his presence.

He truly was a beautiful sight to take in right then. He was the same man I'd fallen in love with and yet, he was changed. His nose was a little different. It had a slight dip in the bridge, and his eyes seemed heavier—older...

His mouth was framed with thick, dark stubble, and he wore a loose white shirt under an open vest and overcoat, a large sword hanging at his side and down his legs which were well defined in the black breeches and stockings. Towering over us all, he was thinner than I remembered... He looked tired—tired, but beautiful... and alive... and suddenly I needed to wrap my arms back around him... to hold him and show him how glad I was he was alive. I hadn't given him that... I owed him that in this moment before it would all crumble... before I told him about Jack.

My eyes burned as I watched him wait for the group to gather around him. He held a new air of authority I hadn't seen in him before, and as his eyes met mine, I felt my heart flutter just a little.

"We don't have much time." He said. "What happened to us… it wasn't just a plane crash. We've come out of that crash in…" He took a deep breath. "1773… well, 1774 now."

For the second time in minutes, my knees went weak, and I felt like I was going to be sick. This time I sat down hard on the sandy dirt as Anna collapsed to the ground beside me.

She shook her head. "They've gotten in your head… they've told you about the journals and their theories—

"I know how crazy it may sound. I didn't believe it myself," he continued, softening his voice for her. "But, it's true. I don't know quite how… but we're here. I've seen it for myself… Where there should've been civilization and technology, there is nothing. There are a few who know and can be trusted, and we're searching for a way to get back. Johann has a theory—

"Wait." Anna straightened, swallowing and blinking the tears from her eyes. "Who are you and why should we believe anything *you* have to say?"

"My name is Chris Grace. I was on the plane…" He looked at me, "…with my wife, Alaina. One of the flight attendants and I tried to catch up to the raft, but we couldn't. Her name is Maria and the others think she's a duchess. We've played along with a story she formulated to get this far. As far as they know, you were all traveling on a ship with us. Lilly?" He looked around the group.

"I'm Lilly," she answered shakily from behind me where she stood with her shins supporting my back.

He smiled at her and chills ran over my skin. I never thought I'd see that smile again.

"Luckily, the men aboard the Resolution are not familiar with the extended royal family," he said. "As far as they know, you are a lady and a cousin to the duchess. You and your husband will need to act as sophisticated members of society. You have a deaf daughter, Isobel. I don't have time to teach you both the customs, but Maria and John have agreed to show you when you are alone. Bud and Johann have developed your backstory, and we'll go over it soon. You'll need to stay quiet until then. No one could expect you all to socialize after being stranded here for a year."

I swallowed. We'd all played with theories of time travel and wormholes, but in the back of my mind, it was a means to pass the time and any day we would be met by a plane or a helicopter coming to our rescue; any day we would go home to our families.

Suddenly, I longed for my mother like I hadn't since the first day we arrived on the island. Would I ever see her face again? Would she ever curl her arms around me and make me feel that comfort only a mother could offer? How I needed that sense of comfort right then... and motherly advice.

"Members of society?" Jim scoffed. "Are ye' crazy? There ain't no way anybody in they right mind's gonna' take me for some kind of genteel!"

"You'll need to stay quiet," Chris instructed. "Until we can work out the accent. Just sit straight and act like you're above the company."

"Ally," He continued, glancing behind him to make sure no one was coming. "You will stay with me, but we're servants to the duchess... I'll attempt to keep you from serving anyone. The ship is short on cabins as it stands. Not being members of society, they're giving my cabin to Lilly and Jim... The lieutenant has offered us his."

He ran a hand over his face. "The rest of you are shipmen, servants, and crew to the royal family. You'll sleep below deck. You'll need to keep your heads down and speak as little as possible until we've got our stories straight."

I opened my mouth to speak when a flash of movement in the corner of my eye caught my attention. Izzy bolted past us down the trail, leaping up into the arms of...

"Jack," I breathed.

One syllable. One cracked word from my lips was all it took to give me away. I saw it in my husband's eyes as he looked suddenly down at me. He knew me well enough to recognize the meaning behind the name.

The first word I'd spoken was a name he'd hoped would be his... I'd said it with the same sense of relief I should've greeted him with... And I saw devastation wash across his dark features for a single fleeting moment before he blinked it away and continued.

"We'll…" He cleared his throat. "We'll be on the ship for some time. The captain is searching for Antartica. We'll make our way back to the west and down before returning to England."

"England?!" Anna shouted. "Please, please tell me this is some kind of sick joke! You're not serious! It's not possible!"

"Neither is surviving a plane crash." He shook his head. "I'm so sorry. Bud has told me about your son. I know you are anxious to get back to him. And I really do wish I could say to you this has all been a bad dream…"

As he spoke, my attention was torn between him and Jack as Jack slowly made his way to our circle, his arms wrapped around Izzy while his gaze remain fixed upon me.

"… but I assure you, it is not," Chris continued. I could see him struggling beneath his words to work out what had happened as his eyes darted from me to Jack. "The lieutenant is a friend and has agreed to take us from England back out on his own ship when he is given one. He swears he'll sail between the place we came through to the place we went down in search of any possible way back. We won't give up looking for a way home. We won't give up on your son. I promise. But you'll need to be patient, and you'll need to play along. If we want to get back, it's going to take time."

Anna stood and looked from Chris to Jack. "Jack… tell me it's not true."

Jack rocked Izzy gently to one side. "It's all true."

"And where in the Sam Hill *you* been for two months?" Jim scolded, noticing Jack for the first time and stomping toward him. "Ye' said two weeks when ye' shipped off… we been worried sick. Christ almighty, ye' look like shit."

"He's been with me." My stomach sank as Phil stepped out of the shadows to stand at Jack's side.

Jim gasped, stopping in his tracks. "What the hell—

"We don't have time for explanations," Chris said loudly as our group began to stir at Phil's sudden appearance. "It'll have to wait until we're on the ship. I've arranged for us all to meet in the great cabin to get you fed and filled in on the details of the captain's trip. In the meantime, keep your heads down and play along. Stay quiet and do not tell a soul who you really are."

Before he could say more, a large group of soldiers and an elaborately dressed woman caught up.

"Christopher!" A man at the head of them smiled. "You must introduce me immediately to your beloved wife!"

Chris finally looked at me and motioned for me to stand. I did so, my knees threatening to betray me as they shook beneath my dress. "Captain, this is my wife, Alaina. Alaina," he met my eyes and I could see the familiar hint of suspicion beneath them, "this is Captain James Cook."

Captain James Cook... I knew the name. He'd discovered Hawaii and died there. I had done a report on him in high school. Could I remember the details of that report and research? Could I remember important dates and events? Could this really be happening?

Captain Cook hurried to take my hand in his, bowing before it. "Mrs. Grace, it is an honor to finally make your acquaintance. Chris has spoken of little else since I came upon him. He has been unrelenting in his determination to seek your whereabouts. I cannot recall ever having met a more devoted husband than yours."

As he rose, he inspected my appearance. Could he see the slight swell in my abdomen? Could Chris?! His eyes scanned me slowly and then the rest of the group as he released my hand. "Do not be overly concerned with your appearance. We understand you have been stranded here for some time. There is no shortage of garment onboard the Resolution. We shall have you all fed and clothed by the night's end!"

He smiled at the group. "I know you must all be anxious to return home, and I wish I could offer more immediate accommodation, but it is incumbent upon me to complete my mission and so I'm afraid you must be burdened to travel alongside me for a time before you are returned to Parma."

He searched our circle, his brows furrowing as he turned toward the woman. "Your Grace, pray tell, which is the Lady Lillian Jackson?"

"I am," Lilly said snobbishly, and despite the predicament, I couldn't help but stifle a laugh as both she and Jim straightened their postures. "And this is my husband."

"Lord James, Lady Lillian." The captain extended his hand to Jim, smiling warmly. "It is an honor."

Jim awkwardly shook the captain's hand, standing stiff and not saying a word in response as Lilly curtsied.

"Cousin, I've missed you!" The woman said to Lilly, extending her arms to welcome her into her embrace. Lilly obliged, letting her pull her into a hug, and as the woman held her, she turned toward the captain.

"Oye, Captain, my people are very obviously exhausted. Maybe we can take them aboard for a real meal while you and William explore the island? My cousin and her husband are much skinnier than when I last saw them. They're going to need a good dinner and a few days to recover."

"My apologies, sir!" The captain held Jim's hand still in his and covered their grip with the other. "I have forgotten my manners! Of course, you most assuredly must be weary after so long forsaken upon this island. Come!"

He released his grip, and I saw Jim finally exhale when the captain turned to his men. "Lieutenant, you and Christopher escort these people to the Resolution. Make no small effort to ensure they are all fed, clothed, and offered every accommodation we can give to make them comfortable. Lord James, perhaps when you are rested, you might be so kind as to accompany me and a few of my companions as we explore this island? It is unrivaled in beauty and I've a desire to see more of it before we depart."

Jim stood straighter still and nodded, emitting the most uncomfortable and forced "yes, alright" I'd ever heard.

They'd ushered the lot of us onto a small boat that carried us to the ship. Crammed together as we were on the small canoe, my hand shook inside Chris's as I looked up at Jack. He hadn't taken his eyes off me.

Once on the ship, we were separated. Chris escorted me below deck where the others broke off down opposing corridors. I watched behind me as the lieutenant led Jack in the opposite direction, longing for one moment alone with him to explain all that was going on in my heart. The walk to our own small cabin felt like an eternity, my mind torn between replaying all the events of the past year and rejoicing in the feel of my hand inside my husband's.

I had to tell him everything and it couldn't wait. He'd seen me pregnant before and would surely notice the belly as soon as the excitement of finding us had worn off.

Inside the cabin, Chris closed the door and instantly his hands were back upon me, running over my face and down my arms.

He pulled me into his embrace and kissed the top of my head, squeezing softly as he ran his fingers through my hair. "Are you alright?"

Being in his arms felt like stepping into my my old house. I was home, but it wasn't my home anymore. It was comforting and familiar and wonderful, but it was also temporary. Soon enough, he'd know the truth and I would never be there again.

"I thought you were dead," I said quietly, resting my cheek against his chest as his palms swept down my back. "They said the back of the plane exploded. How did you survive?"

"I wasn't *in* the back of the plane." He rested his chin against the top of my head. "I came to the front to see you."

"I... I didn't know..." I swallowed, stuttering as I tried to wade through the guilt of not having noticed to find the words I had to say to him. "There are things I need to tell you... Things that have happened... Love, I thought you were dead, and I—

"We don't need to talk about it right now," he said, knowing what I was about to say would change everything about the moment. "Not yet."

He slowly stood back and held me in front of him, inspecting me. "Everything that's happened before now…" He shook his head and took a deep breath, "…we'll figure it out. We can't be blamed for the things we have done to survive. I have been no saint myself. My thoughts… I—it doesn't matter. We're together now and that's all that matters." He smiled. "I've missed you so much, and I hadn't even realized until I saw you coming toward me on that trail. Ally, everything before—we wasted so much time… I will never ever take a moment with you for granted again."

I'd missed him, too. His sudden reappearance had awakened a frenzy of emotions. I wanted to sink into his arms and stay there indefinitely, but I also wanted to wake up and find myself restored to my room in the cave with Jack lying beside me; all of this a very vivid dream.

Him being alive… what it would mean… the decisions I would need to make… I didn't want to shatter this moment; didn't want to confess so soon, but I didn't want to drag this out… or to have him hear it from someone else… or see it and know before I could explain. "I need to tell you—

As if he would never be able to again, he hurried to push his lips against mine, then pressed our foreheads together and whispered, "we won't have much time to get our story together before the captain returns. Let's get you dressed and meet the others in the cabin. Everything else can wait until tonight."

"Chris," I breathed, my eyes watering as I said his name. "Love, I don't think this can wait."

He slid his thumb over my lips and cheek. "You forget I have known you for more than a third of our lives, Al. I know what you have to say, and I'm begging you to let it wait."

He knew me well, and he knew there was something between me and Jack, but he didn't know the extent of it. I couldn't look at him; couldn't get dressed in front of him until I'd said all that he needed to know. We couldn't fall back into the life we once had;

couldn't hold things in and let them form silence between us like we had before. I wouldn't—*couldn't* be that woman again.

He turned to a stack of garments on the bed, pulling a white cotton piece from the pile before turning back to me. "We've got to come up with all of your identities before the captain gets back. There'll be plenty of time for you and I to explain everything that's happened this past year. There's not much else to do on this ship than talk. Here." He held the long shirt up toward me. "Take off that dress and put this on."

I'd known him for more than a third of my life, and yet, I became immediately shy at the idea of getting undressed in front of him. Dark as it was in the tiny cabin, the candles lit the room enough to highlight the bump in my belly. I looked down at my body, acutely aware that I would be completely naked when I gathered the nerve to pull off the dress I was wearing.

"Don't tell me you're afraid for me to see you." He grinned. "Al, it's me, not some stranger. I've seen you naked before, and plan to see you naked plenty more before we're dead."

I was completely lost. Had it been Jack in front of me, I'd not only have stripped, but I'd have ripped his clothes off in the process. This was my own husband returned from the dead; my beautiful, wonderful Chris, who I'd longed to be intimate with for so long before boarding that plane, and yet the thought of being naked in front of him now suddenly terrified me.

He let the shift fall to the floor. "It's me, Ally... Have you forgotten me?" He wound his arms around me, rocking me gently as I felt his lips press against the crown of my head. "Have you forgotten us?"

No, I hadn't forgotten him. He was familiar. Being held by him made me feel more at home than I'd felt in all the time we'd been stranded. His arms were the same—*he* was the same. The warmth of his body made my eyes water. Everything about him was just as I'd remembered. *I* was the stranger. I pulled away slowly, forcing him to unlock his arms from me.

"Chris, I'm so sorry I'm not reacting the way you probably expected me to. I'm... I thought you were dead... and I can't just act like the past year didn't happen. I need to tell you—

"I know. It's alright," he said quickly, kneeling to pick up the shift. "Whatever happened with him... well, I don't care. We're together now. We cheated death. This is our chance to make this what it was again."

"You don't understand, I—

"I'm telling you that I *do*. You don't have to say it. And you don't ever have to be sorry for it. I love you still. We have plenty of time to talk about it. But right now, we have to go. Please... I'll turn around if you'd like... but we have to get you dressed and join the others."

I took a deep breath. If he wasn't going to let me say it, I would have to show him. Either way, he'd know the truth before we left this room. Slowly, I slid the arms of the dress off my shoulders and let it fall to the floor. I watched as his eyes slowly worked their way down my body until they froze upon my midsection.

I saw the acknowledgment in his eyes as they moved no further. Dazedly, he looked back up at me. "How long?"

"Somewhere between seventeen and nineteen weeks," I whispered, trembling as I crossed my arms over my chest. "Maybe more..."

He nodded, swallowing and handing me the shift. "I think maybe this *can't* wait... I'll tell John to go ahead without us." He placed a hand on the doorknob, then turned to look back at me, his expression softening. "Don't... don't go anywhere? I'll be right back."

He disappeared and left me standing alone and naked in the center of the cabin. I pulled the shift over my head and sat down hard on the small bed, taking my first opportunity alone to process all that had just happened.

1774... How? How was that possible? What could've caused it and how in the world were we ever going to get back? We needed to go back... didn't we?

Chris.

Despite myself, I felt my lips form a smile. He was alive… he was feet away from me down the hall of the ship, and I couldn't help the tears that slid down my cheeks with the knowledge. And Jack… Jack was alive too. At least there was that. Both the men I loved were safe… they were alive… and they were with me. Soon enough I'd have to make the decision between them, but in that moment, I let myself just be happy they were both alive.

Chapter Thirty One

Jack

Jack sat with Phil, Bud, and Maria around the large table in the great cabin, waiting anxiously for the others to join them.

He needed to find a way to get Alaina alone; needed to tell her everything that had happened on that island, everything he was feeling; needed to let her know he loved her.

He needed to fight for her; to let her know he wouldn't let her go unhappy; wouldn't willingly give her up unless he knew it was what she wanted. He needed her to know he would love her still even if she didn't choose him, and that there was nothing he wouldn't do for her and their child.

How would he get her alone now that they were on the ship?

He glanced across the table at Maria, who sat quietly fiddling with the fabric of her cream dress in her lap. He noticed the way she'd looked at Chris on the trip between islands. Was she thinking the same? Could he lean on her to separate them long enough for him to steal Alaina away to a dark corner of the ship; long enough for him to say what he needed to say; to kiss her just once more should she decide to remain with Chris?

Lieutenant Edgecumbe rushed through the double doors, startling them all from their stupor. "Jack, sir," he said with authority, motioning to the hall just outside while his other palm rested on the hilt of his sword. "A word, if you will."

Hesitantly, Jack rose from the table and followed him out to the dimly lit corridor, searching down the hall for signs of Alaina.

John closed the double doors behind them and turned to speak in a hushed voice. "I do not presume to be privy to the goings-on of the twenty-first century, however, I can tell you that in this century it is quite unlawful to covet another man's wife. I have come to bid you warning. Now that she is arrived safely among us, you are ordered to stay away from her. You will not speak directly to her, sit or stand within close proximity to her, or attempt to touch her in any way lest you be placed in irons, sir. Do you understand?"

Jack tilted his head to one side. "This is an order directly from Chris?"

"Aye, sir, and as he is my closest friend, I intend to see punishment carried out should you choose not to obey."

"Is he not man enough to give this order himself?" Jack could feel his ears reddening as anger worked its way up from his chest. "He hides behind you to do his bidding for him? If he doesn't want me near her, let him tell me himself!"

The lieutenant smiled slightly, raising an eyebrow. "Sir, I assure you, there are few men in this world I would call more *man enough* than he. I should warn you, it would be ill advised to pick a fight with him. You will undoubtedly lose. He has gone to great lengths and made many sacrifices to be reunited with his wife. I understand you mistook her for a widow, and no blame for actions taken under this misconception can be placed upon you. However, any further attempt to undermine their marriage will be noticed by the men upon this ship. Christopher Grace is held in high regard among these men, and not a single one of them would shy away from defending his honor. Heed my warning, sir, and keep yourself away from her. Find another. She is taken."

"So, what then? He's just going to force us apart?" Jack could feel his pulse racing. "What if he's not what she wants anymore? He's not going to let her decide?"

"She is taken," the lieutenant repeated, turning back toward the double doors. "It is already decided."

"Nothing is decided until she says it is. Where are they?" Jack demanded. "If he won't come tell me himself, I'll go to him."

"I presume, after so long apart, they are reacquainting themselves with one another." He smirked.

"And what about the duchess?" Jack added, crossing his arms.

At this, the lieutenant spun back around, gripping the folds of Jack's shirt to force him against the wall. "What about her?" he seethed, his eyes burning a hole into each of Jack's.

That was it, wasn't it? Jack noted. The lieutenant wanted Maria for himself, and knowing she pined after Chris, he would do whatever he had to in order to make sure Chris was happily reunited with Alaina, if for no other reason than to keep him away from Maria.

"Ay!" Jim hollered from down the hall, releasing Lilly's hand to jog toward them. "What the hell's goin' on? Get yer hands off him! Break it up!"

The lieutenant released him, but kept his glare affixed as he hissed, "Stay away from *both* of them."

"What's goin' on, Hoss?" Jim caught up, placing himself between the two and eyeing Lieutenant Edgecumbe dubiously. "Where's Alaina?"

"Alaina is with her husband." The lieutenant straightened, adjusting the sleeves of his jacket. "I was simply informing Jack that he needn't seek her company now that she is reunited with her beloved."

"That ain't fer you *or me* to decide, now is it?" Jim scoffed, turning himself to stand beside Jack. "Now, as far as any of us knew, that man's been dead for a year, and a whole hell of a lot has happened since then. They got plenty of business to sort between the three of 'em and it ain't no one else's place to get caught up in the middle."

"Chris has asked me—"

"Don't matter. You and me both are gonna' stay the hell out of it." He took Lilly's hand in his as she and Isobel joined them, both wearing embroidered silk gowns. "Let's get this over with. "

As the lieutenant opened the doors, Lilly reached up to touch Jack's cheek with her free hand, smiling sweetly as he attempted to settle his heaving chest. "It'll be alright, you'll see," she whispered. "She loves *you*."

Jack took a deep breath and followed them back inside the cabin, glancing over his shoulder for signs of Alaina. She did love him, that much he knew, but was it enough?

Lilly, Jim, and Isobel took a seat next to Maria as Jack took his own closest to the entrance.

Bruce, Anna, Kyle, and Magna stepped into the cabin. While the others found their seats, Kyle froze in his tracks once he'd spotted his father at the far end of the table.

"Kyle," Phil rose, "I can explain everything."

"Don't speak to me," Kyle said pointedly. "There's nothing you can say that'll make things right between us."

Behind him, Jacob and Michael slid through the doorway and around him to sit down beside Bud; Michael staring at what was left of Kyle's arm as he did so.

"Kyle," Phil pleaded, "I swear, I'll never touch another drink so long as I live. What happened... it wasn't me... It was the alcohol. I promise, I'll make it right."

"I've heard that before," Kyle managed, pulling out a chair next to Jack.

"I've said that before," Phil acknowledged, sitting slowly back down. "But this time, I mean it."

John pulled the two French doors closed and moved toward the head of the table. "We haven't much time. Let's get started."

"We're still missing two." Jack glanced behind him through the glass down the hallway.

"Chris will apprise Alaina on all she needs to know." John offered him a wry smile. "They will not be joining us. Bud, why don't you start?"

"Jim," Bud straightened, not giving Jack the opportunity to respond. "Johann and I have come up with your identity. You are the Governor of the Duchy of Milan in Austria and Lilly is your wife. Because the others are not familiar with the area, the accent can be explained as relative to the region where you grew up, but please try to curb it when you are speaking with anyone not in this room. You are the youngest son of Charles III, the Archduchy of Austria."

"I can do an English accent," Jim said matter-of-factly.

Bud staunched a laugh. "Is that right?"

"Sure is." He grinned. "Been makin' fun of 'em my whole life. I can handle my own, thank ye' very much."

Bud stared at him for a moment before blinking heavily and focusing his attention on Lilly. "Lilly, you are the daughter of Frederick Christian, Elector of Saxony and Duchess Maria Antonia of Bavaria. Memorize those names. The two of you are recently wed and now live in Milan. Jim, I am your valet. Lilly, you are not to address me as grandpa, understand?"

Lilly nodded slowly, squeezing Jim's hand where it sat under hers on the table.

Again, Jack looked through the double doors. What were they doing? Was he holding her against his will, or was she there willingly? Would she be kissing his lips right at that moment? Were Chris's hands on her? Were his hands on the skin that covered his child?

"Bruce, you are Lilly and Jim's personal chef," Bud continued. "Anna, you are Lilly's midwife, sent along to look after Isobel and, in case she gets pregnant along the way. Kyle... you and Phil are sailors from Parma. Magna, since you speak French, English, and Tahitian, you are the ship's translator. The captain—Frank, who died on our ship, brought you from Otaheite to Parma after his first voyage. Jack and I were the ship's masters and charged with mapping the area. Understand?"

Anna frowned, running her fingers over the carvings on the edge of the long table. "I still don't understand. How did we get here?"

"We don't know yet," John answered. "Johann—he's on the island with the captain still—he has some theories, but we can't be sure. It is miraculous, to be sure."

Her eyes darted around the room, all of it elaborately decorated with what would be antiques in her own time. "If we don't know how we got here… how in the world are we supposed to get back?"

John unrolled Zachary's map and placed it on the table, pointing to a spot not far from their own X markings. "There was an island here. This is right where the plane went down. We found Chris and Maria here. And this…" He slid his finger up, "this is where you were just before the plane went down. I promise you, madam, I shall devote my life to finding the way back. We will sail it over and over if we must."

She touched the spot on the map where his finger had just been. "Who's to say that, even if we were to find whatever brought us here, we would be able to go back to our own time? What if it only goes backward?"

Bud laid his hand over hers. "There's only one way to find out. Maybe… just maybe… we can go back to the exact moment we crashed. Maybe it'll be as if we never left."

"That's not everything," Maria added, glancing at the double doors. "Because of who we're pretending to be, we can't go back to England with them. We need to figure out where we want to stay until John can come back for us. We're close to where we crashed here. Do we stay near the crash site and wait, or do we go closer to England where there may be civilization?"

"Could we stay *here*?" Kyle asked naively. "On our island? We know it is safe. We have food… water… we know how to survive here."

"No," Michael said. "They come for you."

"Who?" Kyle frowned at him.

"Uati," Michael said as if everyone should've known the name.

Jim squinted in his direction. "You-what-now?"

Jack sighed, turning fully away from the doors to give his attention to the table. "The people who held us captive. Phil told them where to find us. It's a longer story than we have time for right now. They know where to find us, and they'll be looking for Michael. We probably should leave as soon as possible."

"We can't just leave it so soon!" Lilly's eyes watered. "We're going back, right? Gramma... I have to say goodbye to her... I thought we were going back to show the captain the island! I thought I'd have time to say goodbye!"

"We ain't goin' nowhere without ye' gettin' a chance to say goodbye, baby girl." Jim smiled at her. "I promise." He looked back toward Jack. "Now we got a whole ship loaded with soldiers and guns. And I saw great big 'ole cannons stickin' out the side of it. We got time to pack up our things and say goodbye, don't we?"

Michael looked up at Jacob. "What if Uati find us?"

Jacob shook his head. "We're safe now. They can't take on *all* these men. You saw how quickly they retreated when the captain started firing the cannons."

Anna ran a hand over her face. "If this really is all true... if we're really back in time..." She looked at Jack. "Alaina... she can't—

Jack cleared his throat, flashing Anna a look to silence her. "We'll need to decide as a group what we do from here. We're not making a decision without *everyone*."

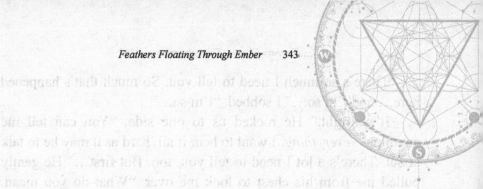

Chapter Thirty Two

Alaina

I sat on the bed, staring at the door. Then I stood and paced the couple feet of the small room. Then I sat. Then I stood.

In the span of two minutes, I relived my entire relationship with Chris; the ups, the downs, and everything in between. I experienced every sentimental moment over again, every kiss, and every bit of happiness we'd once shared. I then lived through every word of every argument we'd ever had, every moment I'd been left feeling neglected and untouched. I remembered the crash, the complete emptiness of waking on the raft with him gone; the instant I accepted him as dead and the horrible loss I felt inside afterward.

Chris was alive. For all our ups and downs, my husband was *alive.* I owed it to him to be relieved.

Suddenly, the door opened, and I threw myself into his arms and let my tears fall as I held him as tightly as I could.

"You never felt gone," I wept. "I thought I was just crazy. Everyone said it was impossible. And I died, and I saw you and I saw Evelyn... and even then I had to convince myself you were really gone. I forced myself to accept you were dead and move on... But you never felt gone. Not ever."

He swept his hands down my hair. "I'm right here," he whispered.

"There's so much I need to tell you. So much that's happened here... and I'm so..." I sobbed. "I'm so..."

"It's alright." He rocked us to one side. "You can tell me anything—*everything*. I want to hear it all, hard as it may be to talk about. There's a lot I need to tell you, too. But first..." He gently pulled me from his chest to look me over. "What do you mean, *'you died?'*"

I sniffled and laughed a little. "Oh... There was a boar."

"A boar?"

I smiled. "I don't even know where to start."

He led me to the bed where we both sat and he pulled me into his embrace. "Start with the crash."

From start to finish and every detail in between, I told him about the raft, the island, about Jack, about the family we'd built among the other survivors. I told him about Phil, the boar, Kyle, Bertie, and all about Lilly and Jim. I told him about the pregnancy and all the risks I was well aware of.

In turn, he told me all about his time away. He told me about Maria and their island and all the mixed emotions he'd felt toward her, about the smoke he knew was our signal fire, about Tahiti and Captain Furneaux, about the arctic and learning to fight with a sword, and all the theories they'd come up with to try to explain our disappearance.

The ease with which we both were able to speak to each other was comforting. In the years leading up to the crash, we'd lost that openness. It had been gone for so long I'd forgotten how honest we'd once been with each other.

In the beginning, we'd never held secrets from each other. We knew each other so well that secrets were pointless to keep. By the time we'd gotten on that airplane, it felt like all we had left were secrets.

"Do you love her?" I asked.

"No," he said sharply.

I sighed. It was the first time Chris had ever blatantly lied to me.

"You're lying." I looked up at him. "We don't lie to each other."

"No," he repeated in a softer tone. "Not the way I love you."

"But you love her," I said, closing my eyes as he mindlessly ran his fingertips over my arms. "It's not the same, but it's neither more nor less. It's just... an entirely different love. That's how it is with Jack. I love him, too. It's not the same, but I do. I hate to have to tell you that, but I wasn't expecting to ever have to... I loved you almost half of my life, and I've loved him for what has felt like another half. I love you both, and I know it's not fair, but I can't just walk away from him. I can't walk away from you either."

He held me tighter. "You can't have us both, you know."

"I know." I sighed, opening my eyes to read his expression. "What about you? Could *you* walk away from her?"

"You are my wife, and whatever I might've felt for her couldn't matter. I made a vow to you."

"What if she was carrying your child?"

I watched him stiffen. "That would never happen. I never touched her. Not like that. Not when I knew you were out there somewhere."

"But what if you didn't know I was out there? If you thought I had died and didn't reserve those feelings... would it be so easy?"

He took a deep breath. "Al, just because I choose you doesn't mean I'll ever stop caring about her; doesn't mean I'll just stop knowing her. She's my friend... We'll continue to be friends. Could it not be the same for you and... him?"

I could hear the distaste in his mouth as he said the word *'him'* and I knew he was trying very hard to be understanding when deep down he never wanted to see Jack's face again; when deep down he wanted to scream with frustration.

"Do you remember how quickly we fell in love? How consumed we both were with each other?" I asked, smiling at the memory.

He smiled too. "Of course."

"Even then... six months in... could you have walked away from me? Just been my friend?"

His smile disappeared. "You said it's not the same."

"I said it's a different love, yes. But the intensity with which I feel it is no different. If I'd known you were in the front of that plane; if I'd known you were still alive, I'd have never let myself feel this way, but...."

"But?" I could hear the frustration now. "Ally, it's only been what, a year? You could give up all our history for a man you've known for such a short time? And what if you wake up one day and realize it was only infatuation? I've had intense feelings too. On several occasions, I considered what it might be like to give in to those feelings, but I always came back to the history I built with you. What if you realize it was only the situation of being stranded together that made you seek comfort in each other? You would risk the last ten years of our life for that possibility?"

"I didn't say that." I took his hand in mine. "All I said was that I love you both, and I don't know what I'm going to do next. Chris, I didn't do this to you on purpose."

"But it was so soon, Al. In a year, you were able to get over ten years of us? Not only move on, but fall in love with someone else so much that you don't know what to do? I'm sorry, I'm trying to be understanding, but that does feel a little more like an attack than I want it to."

I squeezed his hand. "I can't explain what went on in my mind with nothing to do but think on that island. There are things we left unsaid... things that kept repeating over and over again and events that played over and over in my head."

I sat up to face him. "The day I suggested we go on the trip, right before, you said *'we need to talk.'* Do you remember that? You said it with a seriousness I knew was going to be divorce and so I didn't let you talk. Then we didn't talk about it at all. But for a month, I kept hearing it, wondering what you would've said. Then we crashed and over and over I asked myself if my husband was going to divorce me... if I'd finally pushed him out of love with me. That doesn't excuse the fact that I moved on, but it made it easier to seek comfort in anyone who was willing to give it."

He shook his head. "Ally, I have never stopped loving you, even when we were at our worst." He furrowed his brow. "And I do remember that day. We'd come home from Minnesota a few months before that. In Minnesota, we had that argument and we were supposed to talk… to fix things… when we got home. But you completely dropped it. Remember?"

"I didn't drop it," I snapped. "I was waiting for you to want to talk about it."

He took a deep breath. "Al, you went into recluse mode; burying yourself in your work well past business hours. You didn't give me the chance."

I surrendered to that. He was right. I was avoiding it. "I was terrified you might've realized that you didn't know me after all… I was horrified when you never called me to come back to our room that night. I was so sure you spent the night realizing you didn't know me at all and would eventually ask me for a divorce."

He took my hand in his. "No… that's not it. Al, I found the adoption papers in your office… and then I saw— Doesn't matter. After everything we'd gone through with Evelyn, and with everything that was still unfixed with us, I was going to tell you I wasn't ready for kids."

All the time on the island I had been convinced he had stopped loving me… I hadn't pushed him out of love with me, but I *had* pushed myself out of love with him in thinking so. Could I reverse the past year of damage or was it too late?

He pulled me back to him and laid his head over mine. "Jesus Al. I can't imagine what that must've been like for you… stranded with strangers, thinking I was not only dead, but that I was going to leave you. I want to be angry, but that wouldn't be fair. I was a horrible husband to you at the end… To have let things get so bad you thought I was going to leave. I'm so sorry. You deserved to be happy after all that."

"I was a horrible wife after Evelyn. I couldn't get past it and I took all that out on you. I thought you were going to leave because of how awful I was. You were never anything but great to me…

Even now," I placed my palms on my stomach, "with all this… you're still good to me."

He laid his hand over mine. "Not that good… I um… well, I might've sent John to… pick a fight with him."

I grinned up at him. "Oh, good. You are still human then!"

He squeezed my hand, running his thumb over my knuckles. "We'll never be friends, he and I. You know that."

I nodded. "I know."

He scratched the back of my scalp softly. "And if… I wouldn't… I couldn't watch you with him if…"

"I know that too."

"And if he's anything like me, he won't be able to watch you with me either." He sighed. "I won't ask you to make a decision. Not yet. I know this must be a shock and I know it must be hard. But would you stay here with me for tonight? Lay with me, let me hold on to you and pretend he doesn't exist just for tonight?"

"Of course I will." I could feel fresh tears spilling down my cheeks as he pressed his lips to my forehead. "I don't want to be anywhere else right now."

And that was partially true. There was a part of me that really wanted to choose him; a part of me that remembered all the good parts of our relationship and wanted them back. There was a part of me that wanted desperately to forget the past year; to go back to Chris and fix everything we'd broken.

The other part of me, however, was very much aware of Jack's presence on the same ship. That part of me wanted to run as fast as I could out of the room to find him. That part of me knew I could never go back; could never forget everything we'd been through on the island. That part of me understood there was no amount of history that could outweigh the connection I had with him.

As Chris tipped my head up to face him, I desperately tried to silence that part of me so the other part could rejoice in the satisfaction of his lips over mine. I tried to mute the voice that was pleading with me to stop him as he parted my lips, his once familiar taste now as foreign as a stranger. I did my best to focus only on his fingers in my hair; on the naturalness in the way his body formed against mine, but I couldn't.

All I could hear in my mind was Jack.

"Red," I heard again and again... the voice getting closer.

Abruptly, I realized I was not imagining the sound. Jack was in the hall. He was searching for me, and to save my life, I couldn't help myself from placing my hand over Chris's to stop him before he could go any further; from pushing softly at his chest so I could sit up.

He followed my gaze to the closed door of our cabin where, just outside, Jack's voice was calling for me.

"I have to talk to him," I whispered. "I have to let him know the baby's okay... He's been gone for months."

I saw his fingers curl into fists and then release before he pushed them through his hair. I was hurting him, and I hated myself for it. I touched his cheek softly.

"Love. This isn't a decision. I just... you'd want to know if it was you. There's nothing that could've stopped you from bursting through that door if it was you on the other side. Please. Let me talk to him. I will stay with you tonight. I won't make any decision yet. Just let me talk to him."

"You're tearing my heart out, you know that?" he managed, holding back tears as he stood and took the single step to the door to jerk it open.

He walked out into the darkness of the hallway and I heard him say, "You've got ten minutes." Then he turned in the direction of the stairs we'd come down, and Jack appeared in the doorway.

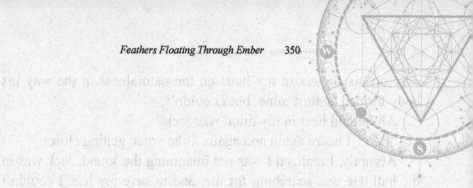

Chapter Thirty Three

Alaina

He closed the door behind him and we both stood staring at each other. I watched as his eyes scanned the length of me, inspecting my appearance as I stood barefoot in only the shift Chris had given me. I, too, was scanning him, checking for some sort of injury that could explain his extended absence.

Without a word, he closed the gap between us and reached out to push the hair from my face; the touch forcing my body to tremble with anticipation. He leaned slowly toward me, his mouth brushing against my temple as one hand slid over the swell in my belly. "The baby's alright?" he whispered.

I nodded, frozen in place as the fingers of his other hand traced the line of my cheekbone. "And you?" he breathed, his nose grazing my brow as he kissed the opposite temple. "You're alright?"

I trembled, tears forming in my eyes as he laid a kiss softly against my cheek. "I am now," I managed through shaking lips.

With a thumb against my chin, he tilted my face up to him. "Tell me to stop if—

I pulled him down to me, letting the rest of his words get lost in the kiss. He kissed me tenderly at first, his fingers dancing along the side of my throat, but tenderness wasn't what I wanted in that moment, and so his mouth inherently grew more demanding as I clung to him, molding my body against his.

"Where have you been?" I panted, pressing my lips against his before he could speak. "How are you here? Where did you go?"

"Doesn't matter. I'm here now, and I only have a few minutes to be alone with you." He lifted me off my feet with a forearm beneath my bottom as he held my face in his free hand. "Christ, I missed you," he breathed, pulling my mouth back to his once more.

With our lips entwined, I was lost in him, pulling, pushing, and grabbing at anything I could for leverage to bring us closer. He groaned, his hand curling into a fist in my hair, and as my entire body responded to him, I knew the decision was made. Relieved as I was Chris was alive, I wouldn't be able to let go of Jack. Not ever.

And at that, I held on with a new sense of urgency, pulling him until my back hit the wall so I could feel the weight of him against me. I needed him; needed *only* him. And I needed him with a hunger I had never been able to recognize.

I could never go back to Chris. I knew that as my heart danced with our bodies; as I felt the same hunger rising in him. Husband or not, the decision was made. Every single part of me belonged to this man, and there was nothing I could do to hide it.

I felt a slight tickle in my stomach reminding me we were not in fact alone, and I pulled back from him, sliding down to place my feet on the wooden floor.

"I'm sorry," he whispered, placing a hand on the wall over my head as he tried to catch his breath.

"No, no, it's not that." I kissed his lips again before leaning back against the wall to place both hands on my belly. "It's just... If it's really April of 1774..." I pursed my lips. "Well... the thing is... I did a report in high school on James Cook. 1774 is somewhere in the middle of his second voyage. He won't return to England until July of 1775 and I'm due sometime around September." I scanned the small dark room, observing the general filth that coated every surface. "We're going to have our baby on a ship…"

Jack glanced over his shoulder and back before lowering his voice. "No, we're not. You needed a hospital, and I didn't find you one." He took a deep breath. "But I'm not done looking. I won't lose you; not if it is within my power to find help. I have a map that marks the two locations of the crash. I could steal a small boat and go search for a way home. I could—

"No."

"But, the whole reason—

"I said no." I placed my hand at the center of his chest. "It's not up for negotiation. Whatever happens from now on happens to us together."

"Red, we can't stay in this place with these men. You're already showing, and it's only a matter of time before they notice. They'll know it's not his, and I don't trust them not to retaliate in some way. I won't have you giving birth in some uncivilized hut on an island, either. You need a real doctor—*real* medicine. There is nothing I can do for you now but to search for a way home."

"What do you mean *'nothing you can do for me?'* I don't want you to do anything for me. I want you to be here with me. If I'm stuck here, you're stuck here." I took his hand in mine and placed it over my stomach. "Do you feel that? Your family is here and you're not leaving us again. I can't do this alone."

I saw his eyes water ever so slightly at the feel of our child's subtle movement. For a moment, he smiled at me in amazement, then the concerned look returned. "You wouldn't be alone though, would you? Not now. Not with him being alive…"

He glanced down at his hand on my belly. "I have no right to ask you where that leaves you and me, and I won't. But I'm still the father to the child inside you, and it's my job to make sure my family is safe. I can't just sit idly by on this boat and let the risks stack up against you. I have to figure out how we got here and how to get us back."

I squeezed his hand. "Jack, we all knew, deep down, we wouldn't be returning to the world we came from. We knew something was wrong the minute we found those journals. I would've loved to go home to my family; to have this baby in the safety of a hospital, but I accepted a long time ago there was a strong probability that wouldn't happen. I will give birth in 1774, and it will be you—*not him*—that's beside me when I do."

He combed the hair from my temple and searched my eyes. "And what would I do with myself if you died during that birth and I'd done nothing to save you?"

"You would raise our son," I said simply.

"Son?" He looked back down at his hand, smoothing his thumb over my stomach. "How could you possibly know that?"

"I just know."

His brow furrowed in thought as he stared down at our hands. "The captain says we'll be in Tahiti within a week. Maria seemed to think the people there would be welcoming of us. Maybe we could stay there... I'm sure there are women who have delivered babies on the island to help Anna... We could wait for the lieutenant to come back with a ship."

"Couldn't we just stay here? We know the island... we know no one will harm us here. Couldn't the lieutenant come back here for us?"

Jack shook his head. "And what reason could we give the captain for staying here? Besides, we're not safe here anymore."

"What do you mean? We've always been safe here."

He looked up at me then and I could see a fearfulness in his eyes I didn't recognize. "There are people who will be looking for us here... if they found us, we would be far worse off than we could ever be on this ship or in Tahiti."

"What people?" I ran my hands up his chest to rest them on each side of his neck. "Jack, what happened to you out there?"

He kissed the inside of my arm. "We were taken captive. They'll be looking for us. Thanks to Phil, they know exactly where to find us. Tahiti's the safest option we have right now."

I could see the memory of whatever happened playing out beneath his eyes, and I could see he was not ready to talk about it. "Tahiti then," I whispered, raising up on my toes to kiss his lips. "I go where you go. Promise me you won't leave us. Promise you won't sneak off this ship to play out some knight-in-shining-armor role you think you need to be playing. You're right where you're supposed to be. Promise me."

He nodded, his breath growing shaky as his expression softened. "I thought I could find a way to let you go…" Lightly, he moved his thumb over my lips. "I thought I could be the better man and not stand in the way if he was what you wanted."

He kept his eyes on my lips. "I pushed you to get over his death, and now I can't even look at him. It's a strange thing to be jealous of someone whose wife you stole away from him." He shook his head. "If I went to search for a way home, you could have a chance to fix things. I couldn't come between you if I wasn't here."

He looked at me then, his eyes watering. "But if I stay… God help me, I won't be able to stop myself from standing in the way; from fighting for you—fighting him, even if you asked me not to."

I noticed, for the first time, that his upper lip was swollen on one side. Gently, I touched it. "Just kissing him felt like a betrayal to you… and telling you that feels like a betrayal to him. I love you both, but Jack… I'm *in love* with you."

At this, the tension he'd been holding inside released and he trembled with tears, bending to bury his face in my shoulder as his arms wound tightly around me. "Oh, thank God… I don't think I could've left you a second ti—

"Ten minutes is up." Behind him, the door swung open and Chris filled its frame, one hand resting on the hilt of his sword. "You can take your hands off my wife now and go back to your own quarters."

Jack spun around, shielding me behind his body. "She's not a possession for you to steal away. She's a person. I don't want to fight with you, but a lot has happened since you last saw her."

"A lot *has* happened since I last saw her." Chris echoed back. "I've been drowned, starved, dehydrated, questioned, beaten and imprisoned. I've gone through hell and given up a whole hell of a lot more to get her back. You don't get to tell me a lot has happened, I damn well know it." He folded his hand around the handle of the sword, the skin on his fingers turning white as he tightened his grip. "Leave. I'm not asking."

"Chris," I said sweetly, attempting to deescalate the situation. "Love, there's no need to fight. Not now. Not after everything we've all been through."

He didn't take his eyes off Jack, and I recognized an ensuing explosion building up inside him as his chest moved heavier with each breath. Chris had never been so short-tempered before, and it threw me off-guard.

"It's time for you to leave. There are things *my wife* and I need to discuss."

"Your wife, eh?" Jack's anger caught up to his. "Wife or not, I'm not leaving her alone with someone who is clearly unstable. Look at you. What are you gonna do, huh? You gonna stab me if I don't leave? You gonna stab *her* if I do?"

"Who the fu—"

"Both of you knock it off!" I pushed past Jack to stand between them in the small space, the three of us so crammed together I could feel the heavy breathing coming from both of them moving the curls on my head.

"No one's stabbing anyone. That's enough." I turned toward Jack. "He didn't come all this way to kill me." I spun back toward Chris. "And seriously? A sword? Can it not be enough that we are all alive and together?"

"Oh, it's enough. It's *one* too many." He glared past me. "Did he tell you how I wept when he told me you were alive; how I poured my heart out to him about all the things I was going to do better once I'd gotten you back? Did he tell you how I was ready to leap off the boat the minute I saw the flames to guide us in? And all the while, he listened with the knowledge he'd been keeping your bed warm in my absence!"

"It wasn't for me to tell," Jack said through gritted teeth.

"It wasn't? Or was it just inconvenient for you to tell since you would be risking your free ride?"

"Chris, stop it." I insisted, my voice beginning to tremble. "Both of you, please. Don't do this now."

Chris's gaze softened as he focused on me. "Forgive me. I just…" He took a deep breath. "You promised to stay with me tonight, and I'm just anxious to have some time alone with you."

I couldn't see him, but I knew every muscle in Jack's body had tensed in that moment. The words weren't meant for me. They were meant to hurt Jack; meant to instill a picture of the two of us undressed and wrapped up together in the bed, and I knew they had. Chris was being intentionally malicious, and I didn't know this side of him.

"You've got a long way until *'tonight'* buddy, and a lot more can happen between now and then," Jack assured him. "The others want to go back and spend their last night on the island, collect their things, and breathe in the fresh air before we're all stuck in the rancid air of this ship for weeks. I can't imagine it's good for a pregnant woman to breathe in the waste of a hundred filthy seamen any more than she has to."

"Good for her?!" Chris scoffed. "And what would you know about what's good for her?! Do you have any idea what you've done; the risk you put on her life by getting her pregnant?"

"Will you both stop talking about me like I'm not here?" I shouted, the baby protesting at my distress and forcing me to bend over to ease the sudden pain in my side. It was nothing, I knew, but as both men were momentarily distracted in pursuit of my well-being, I decided to remain in the position and drag it out, if only to dissolve the mounting tension between them. It was only a matter of time before they'd come to blows, and I didn't want to be caught in the middle of it.

I felt Jack's palm sweep up my lower back. "Red, what is it? Should I get Anna? Are you alright?"

At the same time, Chris was smoothing a hand down my arm. "Al, I'm sorry. I—what do you need?"

I held my stomach—even though the cramp that had caused the pain had passed and I felt just fine—and forced my words to shake a little. "Go get Anna and Lilly. Both of you go. I need a minute."

Jack bent beside me. "I can't just leave—

"Both of you go!" I insisted. "I can't handle either of you right now! Just go!"

And at that, both men, although reluctant, disappeared into the hallway and I closed the door behind them.

Chapter Thirty Four

Alaina

"Lainey, what is it?" Lilly plowed through the door first, her elaborate dress filling the small room as she hurried to sit down on the bed beside me. Anna filed through the door immediately after to kneel at my feet. I noticed both men lingering just outside.

I bent forward to whisper to Anna. "Find a way to send them away."

As I sat back up, I saw the understanding in her light features, and I hid a smile as she stood and changed from her usual timid demeanor into her commanding nurse role.

"Jack," she instructed. "I need water, cool water if you can find it, and some cloth to lay over her forehead. And... Chris, was it? I need you to go see if you can rustle up some food... fruit or something with sugar... maybe a bit of bread if you have it. Go, both of you."

Lilly took my hand in hers and squeezed as both men hurried back toward the stairs.

"What's going on?" Anna asked softly, returning to sit on the opposite side of me. "The baby—

"The baby's fine," I assured her, but my voice cracked. "I just... I don't think I can do this with them right now. It's only been a few hours, and the guilt is already eating me alive. How am I supposed to do this? Choose between them? Live knowing I'm hurting one of them? And you..." I took her hand in mine. "Please don't be angry with me anymore. I'm so sorry for hurting you too."

She squeezed my hand. "It's me that's sorry. I shouldn't have been so cold to you. I just... Well, I was so sure you were all wrong. I was terrified, not angry. I shouldn't have taken that out on you. I love you—both of you." She reached across me to place her hand over Lilly's. "We're all we've got and I'm so sorry for the way I've acted toward you both."

"We're going back to shore." Lilly rested her head on my shoulder. "Come with us. We'll make a ritual out of saying goodbye to our island... like that night with Magna when we caught our first fish. We'll tell stories about it, talk about gramma and everything that happened, and you won't have to think about all this yet."

"I can't not think about it, Lill," I huffed. "It's all so overwhelming. Take away the fact that I'm pregnant with one man's child while the other has been desperately searching for me for a year and both are ready to kill each other... We're still stuck in a whole different time with strange people and made up identities... No families to return to; no lives to go back to; no home or idea of how to get back... and me... with this condition and no real hospitals on this filthy ship... I'm horrified. How are you both so calm right now?"

Anna forced a smile, even though I knew she was fighting the same battle with time. "If we found a way through time once, perhaps we can figure out a way to manipulate it and return to the exact date we came through... like we never left... There's a scientist on this ship and his theories are far more advanced than this time should allow for. I'm excited to spend some time talking to him. Magna said it sounds a lot like the theories of relativity her daughter talked about and those won't get published for another hundred and twenty years. Right now, I have to accept that Liam hasn't technically even been born yet. It's like everything we knew is just paused. We could get there. We could go right back to that same date and it would be as if we never left."

"It's like we're in a very long dream," Lilly said sweetly. "And we'll get through it together."

I frowned. "But we'll all wake up several years older; and me with a child that's not my husband's... With a life that's completely different from the one I left with."

I shook my head. "One year is all it took to not only mourn my husband's death, but to fall so completely in love with another man that I'm barely relieved to find Chris still alive. What the hell does that make me?"

Lilly made a 'tsk' sound. "One year on this island moved a hell of a lot slower than a year in the real world. We had nothing but each other. Nothing but time to think and feel and love each other. We all experienced the island as a small eternity, and none of us are the strangers we were when we landed here. No one could understand how time worked for us unless they were right here with us, and no one should make any of us feel guilty for it. Get out of your head for once in your life. You didn't do anything wrong."

"Besides," Anna added. "that Maria woman seemed more upset about you and Chris not joining us than Jack. They've been stranded together for the same amount of time as us, and from the looks of it, time might've moved just as slowly for them. Come on. Let's get you dressed in these ridiculous clothes. There's a lot we need to learn still and a lot we all want to do before we leave this island forever."

"Ridiculous?" Lilly scoffed, standing to twirl in her elegant silk gown. "Do you see how glorious I look? I might not ever go back home just for the sake of fashion! I love this!"

Anna laughed. "That's because they made you royalty." She extended her arms to present her own brown and navy homespun dress. "You look like a princess and I look like I've clawed my way through dirt. Couldn't they have made the rest of us something a bit more exotic than servants?"

Lilly giggled. "Don't worry. I'll make up a scandal by the time we get to Tahiti. You and Alaina could be secret princesses, cousins perhaps to me and Maria… escaping the boring life of royalty to experience some adventure."

I smiled. "We're barely believable as it is. I think that might put us over the top. Let's just stick to the stories they've given us."

"Oh, come on," she teased, twisting from side to side to watch her dress flow out around her. "If we get to pretend, let's make it fun for all of us. Besides, a secret scandal could explain our strange and unbelievable behavior and give us some reason to stay in Tahiti… maybe Anna's secretly in love with a man there… Ooh! Maybe we were all on a mission to escort Princess Anna to the love of her life!"

"Let's not get carried away." Anna laughed.

I thumbed through the stack of clothing that had been laid out for me. "How the hell do I put any of this on?"

"I'll help you." Lilly clutched the pile against her chest. "I watched Fetia do mine."

Ten minutes later, as Lilly finished tying the last of my stays, Jack appeared in the doorway with a pail of water in one hand and fabric wadded up and tucked under his opposite arm. "It's not cold… but… Oh," he inspected me, fully dressed with my hair pinned up. "You're feeling better then?"

"Much." I smiled at him. "Anna says I could use some fresh air. I think I'd like to go with them back to shore. Spend tonight on the beach before we leave it."

Chris was right behind him, purposely bumping into his shoulder as he pushed through the door with a loaf of bread and a plate of guava. "I'll come with you. I want to see how you've lived all this time."

Anna took the plate from him. "Both of you need to ease up. She's in a very fragile condition and can't afford any additional stress right now. We'll all go to the beach, but whatever needs to be discussed between the three of you will have to wait. Chris, can you arrange for Johann to join us? I'd like to talk to him about his theory of what happened."

Chris nodded. "He's already on the island with the captain."

"The cave." Lilly stood suddenly. "The journals... they're dated 1928. If the captain finds them..."

"Lilly, it took us months to find that cave," I reminded her. "It's alright."

"Still." She fidgeted nervously. "We should get going, just in case."

"She's right," Jack acknowledged. "We can't risk them finding any of that stuff. There are books that won't be written for another hundred years... tools that won't be invented... and God knows what else."

"Well, let's go then." Anna said, curling my arm around hers. "We'll grab the others on the way to the top deck."

As we all pulled into the shore on a sloop, the captain hurried to greet us on the sand. "Returning so soon?"

"Oye captain," Maria looped her arm through his. "We will be cooped up on the ship soon enough. I thought we might spend a night on the island that has kept my family alive all this time... get some fresh air and sneak a peek at this beautiful waterfall I have heard of."

The captain glanced back at all of us. "A splendid idea, indeed! Lord James, I've been told you are quite the master huntsman when it comes to the hogs on this island. I've a long rifle I'd love to put to good use. What do you say to a bit of sport before we set sail?"

Jim, much to the surprise of all of us, smiled, and in the most perfect proper English, replied. "I would like that very much, captain. There's a family of them just up that trail. While the long rifle might serve well for dinner, if you've got a net and patience, we could set sail with a few of the babies."

I hid a smile as Lilly's mouth dropped open at the adjusted accent. Apparently, Jim had a secret knack for doing impressions. While his R's were a little overly southern, the captain didn't even blink at the accent, grinning in response. "Netting and patience is something we've no shortage of, my friend. We've got hog crates too. Lieutenant, have the men gather the supplies and then I would like several tents erected—one for myself as well. I think I should be much inclined to join you all this night. Johann, what say you to a bit of adventure?"

I saw Anna's attention instantly zero in on the man. "Johann." She hurried to join him and extend her hand. "I am Anna. I've been told you are well versed in the medicinal values of many plants on these islands. I was hoping you and I could spend some time together. If we're going to be at sea for some time, I'd like to collect anything I can for my mistress. She's prone to get seasick."

Johann winked at her. "Of course, madam. Captain, why don't you take young Georg along on the hunt while Anna and I do a bit of foraging? While we're at it, perhaps one of you would be so kind as to escort sir William out to the waterfall to paint its brilliance."

"I'd be happy to take him," Bud volunteered.

"Oye," Maria released the captain to curl her arm around Lilly. "Kreese. Why don't you and John take Jack and Kyle and our new friends Jacob and Michael to go hunt pigs with the captain? Leave us girls here to do more girly things... I can go help them pack, pick up some fruit for the ship, and it will give us all a chance to catch up. We have much to talk about, us girls."

Both Chris and Jack exchanged hateful glares while the captain beamed at her. "An excellent plan indeed, Your Grace! Shall we reconvene here at sundown? Perhaps these fine men and I shall return with a prize hog to feast upon!"

"Captain," Maria flirted, "If *you* are on the hunt, I will be expecting nothing less than bacon tomorrow morning."

I didn't know what to think of her. Part of me hated her without even knowing her. It was unwarranted jealousy, I knew, but it was there, and I was hesitant to trust her. I understood she was attempting to separate us all; to allow for us to go to the cave without the others, but still, there was something about her demeanor that made me think she was looking for dirt on me so she could have my husband. The same husband, I reminded myself, that I had forced myself out of love with; that I was working up the courage to tell.

As the men gathered at the water's edge, awaiting supplies to leave on their hunt, Isobel tugged at my skirt.

"What is it?" I signed down to her.

'My treasure.' She signed back, then pointed up toward the path to our cave. *'Can I get my treasure now?'*

I nodded. "The camp is a bit of a hike," I said to the others. "Do you mind if we go ahead? There's a lot to pack up before sunset."

"Not at all Mrs. Grace." The captain bowed. "I'll look forward to your return this evening. After spending so much time with your husband, I am anxious to dine with you and hear all about your time on this island. Your Grace, needn't I send an escort to accompany you?"

Maria shook her head. "Captain, we are alone on this island. I would like the freedom just this once to go for a walk unaccompanied by a man."

He laughed heartily. "Upon my word, madam, your independent nature never ceases to surprise me."

At that, Lilly, Maria, Magna, Isobel, and I headed toward the trail. I kept my eyes on Izzy as she hurried ahead of us, feeling both Chris and Jack watching as we disappeared into the canopy.

As soon as we were outside of view, Maria hurried ahead to spin and walk backward in front of me, her eyes glued to my abdomen. "¡Lo sabía! How far along are you then?"

I protectively placed a hand over my belly, looking up the trail for Magna, who had gone ahead to keep pace with Izzy. "Is it that obvious, or did he tell you?"

She raised a perfectly arched brow. "I am not stupid. I know a pregnant woman when I see one." The corner of her lip twitched as she looked back to my stomach. "Didn't take you long to move on, eh?"

"Hey!" Lilly stepped between us. "You have no right to judge her. You don't know what's happened here."

Maria grinned. "Easy prima, I am not picking a fight." She looked past her to me. "Does he know?"

"Of course he does," I snapped.

"Don't get defensive. It is only a question. He has done a lot for me, you know. He has done a lot for *you* too. I just don't want to see my friend get hurt is all."

"I didn't know he was alive," I said softly. "I don't want to hurt him… Didn't mean to do this *to* him. It just… happened. And now I don't know what to do."

She pursed her lips. "So you love him? The father?" A strand of her dark hair had come loose from its pins and she twirled it around her finger.

I nodded.

"And Kreese… he knows this too?"

"Yes."

"Hmmf." She slowed to walk beside us, staring ahead in thought. "Do you love the father more than you love your husband?"

I shook my head. "I haven't had time to even process the fact that my husband is still alive… I don't have an answer to that question yet. I'm still trying to… figure it all out."

"You do," Maria said pointedly. "If you didn't love him more, pregnant or not, you could've answered that question the minute you saw your husband."

She was right. That's exactly how it should've happened, and deep down, I knew I was *in love* with Jack. But had I only fallen out of love with Chris out of circumstance? Would that love return, or was it gone forever?

"He's a good man, Kreese." She pursed her lips, looking down at her feet as we continued up the path. "And he loves you… He talked about you every single day. In his mind, there is no one more perfect than you. You know that?"

I nodded. "But I am *far* from perfect." I motioned down to my stomach. "*Obviously.* Our entire relationship, I have let him down over and over by never living up to the perfect woman he has made me out to be in his head. And he is good. He is good in every way. *He's* the perfect one…"

"Sí. I know," she said matter-of-factly.

I could see it in the expression when she'd said his name that she had feelings for him. There was a hint of jealousy in her tone toward me. From my conversation with Chris, I had assumed the feelings were one-sided, but now I wondered what exactly had exchanged between them in our time apart.

"This isn't awkward at all," Lilly said sardonically, forcing us all to laugh.

"You know," Maria adjusted her tone to playful, opting to discuss the single thing we had in common. "I gotta hand it to you for putting up with him for ten years without killing him. I was stranded with him for two months on an island with no water and no food, and that man's mood swings were enough to make me crazy."

"Chris?" I smirked. "He's always been so patient."

"Not anymore." She grinned. "We had this little bamboo shelter I couldn't keep standing because he kept kicking it down every time he got angry. He is very moody."

"Really?" I shook my head. "I've never seen him like that. I mean, I've seen his temper on occasion… when it builds up after years of keeping it in and then he inevitably explodes… but I've never seen him kick down a wall."

"Maybe I just have that effect on people." She shrugged. "Because every day he would have a meltdown over *something*. One day it was because I spilled water, the next day it was a coconut that wouldn't crack, or he'd come randomly stomping up because he couldn't catch a fish and have a need to break something… I don't think I've ever met someone with so much anger inside them."

I huffed. "Maybe it was years upon years of being married to me that finally broke him. We weren't in a great place when we crashed. I'd been pretty awful for a pretty long time."

"Sí, I know. Like I said, we were stranded. There was not much else to do on that little island but talk." She looked around us and up toward the summit. "Our island was so much smaller than this one. Tiny. We did a lot of talking. He told me about the baby... about everything. I thought you were a very selfish woman."

"I was..." I admitted. "Maybe I still am."

Lilly groaned. "You're not selfish, Lainey."

"It's okay." Maria nudged my shoulder. "We are all selfish in our own ways. I am selfish too. You have met the lieutenant?"

"Yes."

"He asked me to marry him, you know. But... I can't. I can't let him go, either. He'd make a good husband if I could just *see* him. But I can't see him. I'm too busy looking at... someone who can't see me."

I sighed. "He sees you just fine." And those words hurt me to say out loud. More so, the hopeful expression that temporarily washed over her features destroyed me.

"Oh, no... I just meant... Not.. I..." She attempted to backpedal, blushing as she fumbled for the right words.

"It's okay. But I don't think I'm comfortable talking like this. It's all still very—"

"You're right. I'm sorry." She straightened, brushing it off. "I have never been good at small talk. Especially with women. I am too blunt and I always say too much. I'm sorry. Let's talk about something else, yes? Lilly, how long have you been married to James?"

"Jim," Lilly corrected, kicking a rock along the path. "We're not really married. Not yet, anyway. We just got engaged. We met here."

She exhaled audibly. "My grandma died here just two months ago... she's buried on the beach... and grandpa—Bud— he left the very next day. I really thought, after him being gone for so much longer than they'd promised, that I'd lost them both."

She spun to face her. "When you found them... did they tell you what happened? He hasn't said a word about it to me, but I can tell it's something bad."

Maria shrugged. "They didn't say, but when we found them, they were all full of blood being chased by strange-looking men in canoes. The soldiers and the captain call these the *'devil's islands.'* They say they are full of cannibals. The captain thinks the men chasing them were cannibals but neither of them would talk about anything but getting here."

Lilly's eyes went wide, and she looked at me. "Did Jack say anything to you?"

I shook my head. "We didn't have time."

She returned her attention to Maria. "And Phil... did they explain what the hell he was doing with them?"

Maria frowned. ""Phil is the one who stares, yes?"

Lilly crossed her arms over her chest. "Yes, and he's not a good guy. Did they tell you he tried to rape Alaina, held a gun to my head, and beat up both my grandpa and Kyle? We all thought he was dead."

Maria shook her head. "I could tell he was evil when I saw him on the canoe." She stared ahead as we came closer to the shelter and the sounds of the waterfall grew closer. "I have known evil men and there's no mistaking that look they have... a darkness underneath just waiting for the right opportunity to come out. He has that darkness... that look like he's just holding it in until he has the chance to show his true self."

Lilly nodded. "He can't stay with us. If we get off in Tahiti, he needs to stay on the ship where there are no women for him to take advantage of."

"He will be in good company," Maria noted. "Half those men have that same evil blood inside them. They've been away too long. You would do well to avoid the men on the lower decks. I made the mistake of finding myself alone with one. But I made sure *that one* could never come back to finish what he started."

"What did you do?" Lilly raised an eyebrow.

"I killed him," Maria said, forcing both Lilly and I to look at her tiny figure in astonishment. "I was not going to wait around to let him finish."

Lilly held her chin a little higher. "How did it feel? Does it bother you now?"

She raised her shoulders and let them fall. "No... I did not see him as a man right then, you know? He was something else... A monster. I don't even remember doing it, it was just a response... like... swatting a fly." Her eyes ventured off in memory. "One minute he was on top of me and the next he was dead... I am glad, though. I think men would not do these things if they saw women as creatures that would kill them for it. You know?"

Lilly nodded. "More of us should. It should be perfectly legal for a woman to kill a rapist."

Maria blew out. "Unfortunately, my crime was not—

"You are not going to believe this!" Magna called, cutting conversation short. We'd reached the cave and came upon her and Izzy crouched over a small blanket littered with items, Magna's face lit up with disbelief.

"Believe what?" I asked.

Magna raised her thick eyebrows and smiled up at me. "Her *treasure*."

I knelt down beside them, giggling as I watched Izzy thumb through the various pieces; a small wooden pony Jim had carved for her, a fabric bear Lilly had sewn her, Bertie's brown and tan hair clip, a ball of twine, her Huckleberry Finn book, two credit cards with Frank's name on them, a few quarters, and, much to my surprise, the *missing lighter.*

"Izzy!" I snatched the lighter and stared in wonderment. "Do you know how long we've been looking for this?!" I said the words, but didn't sign them. It was all over now and there was no use in scolding her for stealing something none of us thought to ask if she had. Instead, I laughed and held it up to Lilly, who immediately burst into laughter as well.

"You little brat!" Lilly teased. "All this time... she's had it!"

"Apparently!" I smirked, shaking my head as I watched Izzy hug the teddy bear against her chest.

Magna stood, glancing toward the waterfall. "They'll be at the waterfall soon. What should we do with all these books and journals?" She motioned toward Izzy's Huck Finn book. "None of the books have been written yet. And the journals..."

"They said to hide everything," I said, standing beside her. "I guess we'll take it all to the back cave, anything that wasn't made in this century... Then we'll move one of the empty casks in front of the back cave's opening. Seems bizarre that we're going to such great lengths to hide all the proof that would support us simply telling the truth."

Magna sighed. "These men wouldn't understand the truth, even if we transported them to the future and showed it to them. They'd accuse us of witchcraft and burn us at the stake."

She reached for the Huck Finn book, but Izzy snatched it first, stepping back several feet and clutching it against her body alongside her teddy bear.

"Oh honey," Lilly cooed, kneeling down in front of her to sign. "We can't take that with us."

Izzy's lip protruded, and she shook her head, squeezing the book tighter against her as she spun to one side.

"Izzy..." Lilly attempted to reach for it, but she stepped back several more feet and raised her chin defiantly. "Izzy! Come on, give me the book!"

Maria clicked her tongue. "Look at her. ¡Dulce niña! You can't take that away from her... I have been hiding shampoo and razors for a year. I will show you all the best hiding places. No one will need to know she has it."

"You have kids?" Lilly asked, looking up at Maria.

"Ay no!" She laughed. "But I have been around enough of them to know if you take that book away, you will regret it. Look at that little face! She is on the verge of a meltdown!"

"Fine, keep it." Lilly signed, standing to groan. "Why did they have to make *me* the mother? I don't know the first thing about being a mom... She doesn't even listen to me! Why couldn't they make Anna the mom?" She looked at me. "Or you?!"

"I imagine they didn't have much time to come up with the story," I said. "Although, it makes more sense that it's you and Jim... she'll be treated well as the niece of a duchess instead of a servant's daughter."

I turned to take a deep breath as I stared at our cave; at the little fire pit in front of it where we'd spent so much of our time chatting over dinner; at the little bamboo chairs Bruce and Jim had worked tirelessly to build placed around it; at the complete home we'd managed to make out of a hollow rock face. It was hard to remember the life I'd lived before the island... It was hard to picture a home with drywall, furniture and decor. The cave had been more a home to me than even the home I'd built with Chris, and I was truly sad to be leaving it.

"Do you think we should keep the wine and whiskey?" Magna asked, pulling me from my thoughts to find her knelt at a case of wine. "It is not dated... and it may help us to come with something to trade for space on the ship."

I nodded. "I think that's a great idea. And any Kolea too..." I scanned the bird cage we'd built, counting about twenty full-sized birds and another twenty or so hatchlings inside. "With their wings clipped, it shouldn't be too hard to transport them. We're adding a lot of extra mouths to feed. Anything we can bring to make us less of a burden will be useful."

Maria followed my gaze to the birds, subtly licking her lips. "Oh my God. Please tell me they taste like chicken? I haven't had anything but pork and fish for a year."

"They do," Magna assured her, stacking two cases of wine to one side with a grunt. She scanned her elaborate gown with a dubious eye. "If you'd like to grab a few of the males, snap their necks, and start plucking the feathers while we clean up inside, Bruce and I can prepare some for dinner later."

We were all expecting her to blanch at the idea of killing the birds, none of us had ever really gotten used to doing it, but instead, she pushed the sleeves of her silver gown up to her elbows, smiling as she started toward the cage. "How many should I kill?" She asked cooly, pulling a dagger from her inner skirts. "I can gut them too."

"Three," Magna said, surprised as much as I by Maria's response. "And keep the feathers, they are good for bedding... I'll get you a few baskets."

Magna produced two baskets in short order, leaving Maria to the birds as she, Lilly, and I continued inside to begin hiding all evidence of the future.

I lingered near the cave's opening, keeping a curious eye on Maria as she calmly plucked a bird from the cage, snapping its neck with an expert flick of her wrist before depositing it into a basket and reaching for another. It was no wonder to me that Chris had developed feelings for her. She was not only stunning, but from what I could tell, she was a force to be reckoned with. She was so much more woman than I could ever be... so defiant and decided for such a small person... I admired her already and had known her for less than an hour.

"She's... interesting," Lilly whispered, leaning in beside me to watch her as she snapped the necks of the second and third. "I don't know if I like her or if I'm just too terrified of her to feel any other way."

I chuckled, unable to look away as Maria casually took a seat near the fire pit and pulled one limp Kolea from the basket to begin plucking. "Me neither."

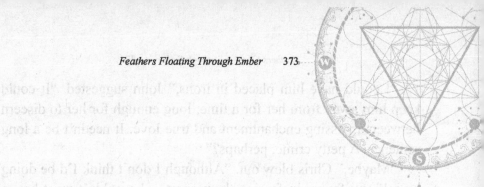

Chapter Thirty Five

Chris

Chris held one side of the heavy rope net while John held the other and they crept through the dense forestation, lagging behind the others.

"What do you wish to do about him?" John whispered, nodding in the direction of Jack.

"I *wish* to slit his throat…" He glared up at the back of Jack's head where he and the others inched cautiously toward an opening in the ground. "But I don't suppose that would do any good."

He was angry—beyond angry. He'd heard Alaina say she loved them both, but was in love with Jack. How could she not immediately let go of whatever feelings she'd had for Jack after she'd learned that Chris was still alive? After she'd learned all that he'd done and gone through to be here? How could she even begin to compare her relationship with him to their own? It wasn't fair. She barely knew the man in comparison.

Did their marriage mean so little to her? She hadn't even seemed relieved to see him, just shocked. Try as he might to see it from her perspective, he was offended. He'd given up Maria… He'd willingly let her go; had been forced to watch as she gave up any feelings she had for him to fall in love with John. And he'd done it out of obligation to his wedding vows. How could Alaina not do the same?

"I could have him placed in irons," John suggested. "It could keep him away from her for a time, long enough for her to discern between a passing enchantment and true love. It needn't be a long sentence. A petty crime, perhaps?"

"Maybe," Chris blew out. "Although I don't think I'd be doing myself any favors in forcing them apart... I wouldn't want her to choose me out of force. I want her to choose me because she wants me."

John nodded. "I know the feeling."

Maria. His gut wrenched at the thought of her. He'd pushed her completely away in the last two days, knowing he'd be with Alaina soon. He'd avoided her, keeping his mind only on his wife; only on his promises to God, fighting with all his willpower to keep her out of his thoughts. Convinced she had accepted John's offer, he'd struggled to let her go. But now he could see in the sorrow that washed over John's features, she hadn't given him an answer. Why? Despite the anger welling inside him at Alaina, a small sense of hope shone through that she might've been waiting for this very thing.

She was with Alaina now. He wondered what they might be talking about. There was little else they had in common aside from him... Would Alaina come back with a different perspective after a day with Maria? And what would Maria think of him after spending time with his wife? Would she, too, grow to resent him after hearing the other side of the story? Which one was he more worried about?

"You two..." Jim hissed, creeping up on the hole with the long rifle. "Bring that net up here and be ready to wrestle with a piglet. They're strong, so you're gonna have to fight 'em. And you four..." He looked to his side where Kyle, Michael, Georg, and Jacob held another net. "You be ready to jump on the one that comes out after. Captain..." He grinned at Captain Cook, who held his own long rifle, ready to fire. "You take the first one. Go for the kill. Me and Jack will take the second and third with a shot to slow 'em down. The babies should follow behind. Ready?"

The captain nodded and aimed for the front of the hole. Jim picked up a rock from the ground, launching it into the hole just before all hell broke loose.

The first boar was massive, and it came barreling out in a screeching fit. The captain fired, immediately silencing the creature as it fell to the ground. A second and third burst out of the opening on its heels, and Jim was able to hit one of them in the back leg. Chris and John launched their net over it where it writhed on the ground, then both men scrambled to keep hold of the edges of the net as it tried to escape.

This was not a piglet. It was a full-sized boar and with the net already tangled around it, Chris and John focused their attention only on wrangling it.

Back turned to the rest of the group, Chris could only hear the gunfire of rifles and screeching of pigs, without a clue as to what might be coming toward him as he stuck his heels in the mud and attempted to pull his two corners of the net back alongside John to very little avail. Both men were being dragged helplessly behind it.

"Get that crate open and be ready!" Jim shouted from behind them. Ahead, Isaac stared wide-eyed at the boar in their net sprinting toward him as he fumbled to pull the sliding door open to the large wooden crate.

"Isaac!" Chris shouted, pulling with all his strength to keep the pig from turning. "OPEN IT!!"

Jim bolted past them, pushing Isaac to one side, and pulling the door open. As they came in close, he reached down to grab the pig by its snout and launch it inside, letting the door slide closed behind it.

Not wasting any time, Jim hurried to the second crate to do the same while Chris stood and turned, watching as Kyle, Michael, Jacob, and Phil were dragged down the mud by their own much smaller boar.

"HOLD IT!" Jim cried, opening the sliding door on the second crate. "Don't let it go!"

But they did let it go, and it bucked and writhed in an attempt to free itself from the netting, only to tangle itself further in the knots.

Jack grabbed hold where they'd let go, the boar dragging him awkwardly on his stomach and back as he rolled through the dense brush away from the second crate.

"Got dammit!" Jim shouted, abandoning his proper English accent as he ran after them. "Dig your heels in, Hoss!"

Before he could, the pig stopped, a tangled mess of fur and knotted rope, and it turned around to charge at its captor.

Jack had been ready for it though, and managed to wrap his arm around its neck, grappling it to the ground. His face distorted as he held the pig tight against the ground. "A little help!" He cried out.

Chris made no move to assist him, but stood and observed as Jim and the captain joined in.

He noticed the captain was grinning larger than he'd ever seen as the three of them forced their weight down upon the boar and tied its legs.

The captain was laughing hysterically by the time they stood. Jack, on the other hand, seemed distraught, attempting to compose himself as Jim and the captain dragged it back up to the second crate.

"Fine save, Jack!" The captain beamed. "And Lord James! I can't say how long it's been since I've enjoyed myself so much! I thank you, sir, for indulging me this day!"

"Uncle," Isaac frowned, "you are covered in filth, sir."

Captain Cook looked down to take in his mud-caked attire and laughed heartily, smacking a hand on Jim's back. "And I haven't been this dirty since I was a child! This has been a most extraordinary day! I shall remember it always."

He wiped his hands on his breeches and took a deep breath. "Now, before we are returned to the others, Lord James. I'm not entirely sure which among your men is gentleman and which is servant. Might you enlighten me so I shan't call upon anyone by the wrong address?"

"Oh," Jim smiled, returning to his proper English accent. "I'm afraid none of us can be rightfully called by any of those titles anymore. Not after what we've been through here. Uncustomary as it may seem to you, every man and woman among us is family now. We've all been through too much to serve or order each other."

"Rightfully so. I could say the very same of many of my own men after so long at sea together. I am most eager to hear all about your time here. Come." He knelt to pick up his hat from where it had fallen to the ground. "Let us join the others at camp and share stories over this fine feast! Jack, my boy! Help me string the big one up and carry her back! We'll send the men round in our stead to collect the crates!"

As the captain, Jack, and Jim led the group in the direction of the beach, Chris placed a hand on John's arm to slow him. Seeing the instant camaraderie between Jack and the captain only heightened his jealousy toward the man. "What kind of petty crime did you have in mind?"

John laughed. "I'm sure I could dream up something. Say the word and it is done, sir."

Chris took a deep breath. "Not yet… but it's something to think about." He ran a hand over his hair and growled. "God, I don't want to be the bad guy. I'm not this person… I just… What would you do if you spent a year searching for a wife who thought you were dead only to find her pregnant by another man?"

"Pregnant?" John gasped, glancing scandalously around them. "Chris, you didn't tell me she was with child… this is most grave, indeed. Surely, I would strike him down without question for defiling my wife's good name; her reputation… You are not the *'bad guy'* here. It is he who has done you an extraordinary disservice. Even under the presumption you were dead, if he intended to bed her, he should have given her his name first."

"He gave her a ring," Chris sulked, kicking at the sandy dirt as they slowly strolled down the path. "I saw it on her right hand… She kept mine on her left though. I noticed that too. What do you suppose that means? If she loved him more, wouldn't she have replaced my ring with his?"

"One would presume..." John frowned. "But if that were the truth of the matter, mightn't she remove his ring altogether once she were privy to the fact that you were not deceased after all?"

"I don't know." Chris sighed. "You remember the smoke we saw that day on the ship not long after you found me? It *was* her. It was her, and she was still searching for me then, hoping I was still alive. If I'd gone to her then, none of this would be an issue. If I'd just insisted they give me a boat and return for me... If I'd have stole one even... If I hadn't let myself surrender to the *'devils island'* nonsense, she and I could be... we could be perfect again. She wouldn't be carrying another man's baby."

"Chris, a child that is not your own... that is no small burden to take upon one's self. If she *were* to turn him away, what might you do about the child?"

"I'd learn to love it. Treat it as my own. I'd have to."

"You could look at a child that resembled the very man you hate and love it? Chris, you are a good man, but I daresay you are giving yourself far too much credit. This child... it could destroy your marriage forever. Not just your marriage... but your reputation, your honor... You can't do this to yourself. There are ways, you know... to eliminate the problem."

"Are you suggesting we kill the baby?" Chris scoffed. "I would never."

"You're right. It was an immoral suggestion... I am only worried for you, my friend. After all that we've gone through... this is not the joyous reunion anyone could've anticipated."

"Don't say anything about the pregnancy. Please."

John raised an eyebrow. "Chris, I would never do anything to put your wife in danger. You do understand the danger she is in now, yes? More so than ever, you need an excuse to disembark. I had hoped for you all to travel further with us, but I know with certainty now, you will have to stay in Otaheite. If the men notice before she is removed from their presence... I needn't tell you that things will not bode well for her."

"We'll wait for the captain to go to bed… as late as we need to in order to speak privately tonight. With half of us servants and the other half royalty, I'm afraid we won't have another opportunity to be alone as a group once back on the ship. We'll come up with a plan tonight."

"Alright then. Before we return, there's one more thing I would like to ask you…" John said softly, squinting against the setting sun as they came out of the trees to head down to the beach. "You mentioned your wife knows of Captain Cook? Does she also know of me? Does she know if I am to return as a captain to sail the same seas as he?"

Chris shook his head. "I'm sorry. I wish she did."

John nodded. "It's quite alright. It is just very difficult to leave you all with no inclination as to when or *if* I might be returned."

"All the information she had was that Captain Cook arrives home to England in July of 1775. In July of 1776, he sets back out on his third voyage. That's all I know."

"Years then." John took a deep breath, exhaling audibly.

In the look John gave him then, he understood what went unspoken between them. He'd looked at him similarly to how Chris had looked at Jack earlier that day.

John knew Chris held feelings for Maria and he knew there was a possibility, with years before he could return to her, that Chris might refrain from fighting them now that Alaina had turned up pregnant by another. He was right to feel that way, and as much as Chris wanted to offer him a reassuring word in that moment, he couldn't bring himself to say anything. He wouldn't be made a liar.

Chapter Thirty Six

Alaina

That evening, we all sat around a fire, over which an enormous boar rotated on a spit.

The location, coincidentally, was just up the beach, not even twenty feet from the spot where Jack and I had first made love. I was painfully aware of Chris's ignorance to that fact as he sat to one side of me taking in the landscape.

It was a strange thing having my husband on our island.

Being on the ship with him was one thing, but being on the island where I'd shared a whole different life with another man was another. It was like two entirely opposing worlds were colliding and I was caught in the middle.

I sat with a plate of food in my lap, careful to keep my eyes from venturing either to my husband or my fiancé while Captain Cook spoke in detail about the hunt. Not pausing for anyone else to contribute to the story-telling, he went on to speak about the unparalleled beauty of Otaheite and how excited he was to accompany us there, then reminisced about his first voyage and the transit of Venus they all observed.

I was grateful for his stories. It was a welcome distraction from my racing thoughts.

Anna had spent the day with Johann and, when the captain finally concluded his stories, they shared their medicinal findings, although I assumed there was much more to be shared once the captain, William, and Isaac had gone to bed.

She sat close to him, and I heard her giggle at something Johann had said. It was a giddy, flirtatious laugh I'd never heard from her before. I noticed Bruce noticing it as well, and I wondered, as I glanced around the fire, just how many of us weren't a part of some overly complicated love triangle?

It was no secret that Bruce had a crush on Anna, but I'd never seen her return that interest, and I watched her as she watched Johann with the same interest Bruce had in her.

It made sense that she might be attracted to Johann. He was intelligent, and if I knew anything about Anna, it was that brains— not beauty is what attracted her. My heart ached for Bruce as he, too, put it together.

I then observed the lieutenant watching Maria. There was no hiding the affection he held for her. I could see it in the way his body was positioned to face her; in the way his face lit up in the fleeting moments where she removed her attention from Chris to acknowledge him.

Beside Maria, I found possibly the single uncomplicated relationship among us in Lilly and Jim. What they had was unbreakable. She watched him proudly as he shared our island stories, *opting to leave out love affairs and journals, of course*, in his best proper English accent.

I watched his hand casually slide into hers in her lap, and I noticed the way he would occasionally squeeze it when the story was particularly sentimental to them.

Watching Jim and Lilly, I couldn't help but glance up at Jack for a moment. I was unsurprised to meet his gaze, and he casually tilted his head to the left, toward our spot just feet from where he sat, and grinned at me.

"Tell us about the devil's island, Jack," the captain called out, pulling our attention from each other. "I've been anxious to find out just how you managed to escape."

"Oh, I don't really think—

"He man from future." Michael announced, much to my horror. "Uati think he God. Make him fight. Give him woman."

My heart dropped at the sound of *'give him woman'* and I stared without caution at Jack for an explanation.

Phil cleared his throat. "*I* told them I'd come from the future… hoping they'd think I was special enough to keep from killing."

"Very wise decision, indeed." Isaac leaned forward, intrigued. "They believed it?"

Phil nodded. "They did. They thought I must be some kind of god sent back in time to defeat their enemies. For several months, they showered me with gifts, drinks, and an endless supply of food and women. I thought I'd surely died and gone to heaven. The problem though, is that before long, the time came where they wanted me to actually defeat their enemies."

He laughed, placing both hands on his large belly. "And well, as you can see, I'm no fighter. I told them there were different kinds of gods and I was not the fighting kind." He held his hand out to show his missing fingers. "They didn't like that answer. So, threatened with losing my life, I told them I knew where they could find a fighting god… and I described Jack. They threw me down into a pit with Jacob. I had no idea Jack was already on his way to our location until they pulled me out months later to identify him."

Jack took over from there, and I couldn't help but grow anxious for him to explain the part of the story including the woman.

"You can imagine my surprise," he looked at me and then at Kyle, "to find Phil on that island. He and Michael painted a pretty clear picture for me. None of the tribe speaks English, so they explained the god part and told me to do whatever I had to in order to make them believe it. Within hours of being welcomed and fed, they presented me with a prisoner from a neighboring enemy tribe. I was to fight him until one of us was dead." He looked down at his palms, as if he couldn't believe them possible of such a thing. "So I did."

My heartbeat quickened as I imagined him there, feeling obligated to make that decision. He'd been forced to kill a man without cause and it must've been eating away at him. I could see the need inside him to talk about it, and I wondered how much pain he must have been feeling as I watched him relive it in his mind.

He cleared his throat, shaking his head of whatever memory was playing. "And then I thought I could walk free... but they brought a girl... a very very young girl, and when I turned her down, they threw me into the pit with Phil, Jacob, and Bud."

Michael nodded, chewing loudly. "It great insult to Uati to turn down gift. He say Jack not *his* god."

"But we weren't giving up." Bud smiled. "Uati wanted to learn English. So, being the god of wisdom myself," he chuckled, "I volunteered to teach him. Every day, they took me out of the pit to sit with him and every day, he trusted me just a little bit more. Jacob taught me the language, and I made a bet with Uati that if he could catch three enemies, I could kill my opponent faster with wisdom than Jack could kill his own with strength. I told him that Phil, the god of trickery, could fool his opponent and win his own battle faster than Jack or I combined. We were gods, after all... And he was fascinated by this idea. I told him that if I was right, he had to let us walk free. And if I was wrong, he could kill us all."

Captain Cook smiled, his chin rested on his palm as he listened intently.

"It didn't take long for three more men to join us in the prison," Bud continued. "Collectively, we agreed to put on a show, and we'd perform it well enough to fool them all. The native tribesmen, with a bit of coaxing, agreed to fake their deaths at our hands, and we agreed in turn to keep Uati's people from going near them. We would then wait and leave with them under cover of night to the opposite side of the island where the men would give us a canoe to return to our island."

Jack stretched his legs out in front of him. "It was an imperfect plan—

"Oh, it was never going to work!" Bud laughed.

Jack smiled at that. "No, it wouldn't have worked at all, but coincidentally, your ship was headed toward our shore at the exact moment we were let out. It offered just enough distraction for all of us to escape into the woods. The natives we'd been imprisoned with led us to another beach, and you know the rest."

"Incredible," the captain marveled. "Absolutely extraordinary. It is a remarkable story to be certain! I shall tell it for all of my days."

Jack smiled. "It was Bud's quick thinking that saved us all."

Bud laughed. "I may be an old man, but I've got some fight in me yet."

The captain stood and removed his hat. "I'm afraid I am quite beside myself to be amongst all of you this night. Your tales of perseverance and adventure have warmed my heart and I shan't say the last time I've ever enjoyed the company more. Let us share one final drink to your good fortune before I retire for the evening!"

He pulled several bottles of wine from a basket at his feet, handing them to two servants who then circled the group to administer it. I noticed Phil place up a palm when they'd stopped at him. "None for me, thank you." And I watched Kyle as he observed the encounter, a momentary expression of hope lighting his features before he dismissed it.

"Chris," Captain Cook raised his glass to him. "tell us again about the coconut crab. I'm sure your comrades will be delighted to hear it!"

I looked over at him as he began telling the story. I watched the familiar way his hands moved to illustrate each point, smiling when his lip curled upward in amusement. I'd forgotten it did that. How I wanted to love him the way I once had. There was a time when my heart had been completely consumed by him. And while it no longer was consumed, it still beat a little faster at the sight of him. I wanted him to be happy, and I wished I could give him that. I knew I couldn't.

I peered across the flames at Maria, who couldn't make her desire for him any less obvious. She was leaning forward with that far-off gaze that told me she was lost in a daydream of him. She, in contrast, *could* give him that…

Would I be able to let him go; to watch him give her the love he'd once given me?

As Chris finished his story, the captain stood and stretched. "I must excuse myself and retire for the evening lest I fall upon my face right here in the sand. Thank you all for an unforgettable day. I hope we shall share many more like it during our time together."

Alongside him, Isaac and William both rose as well, removing their hats to bow.

"Goodnight," the captain said, lowering his head for a moment in a bow before he returned his hat to its place and the three of them turned toward the tents.

We waited until they'd disappeared into the encampment before any of us spoke.

It was Johann that started us off. He rose to his feet. "Let us not waste any time with pleasantries. We need to stay in Otaheite. Anna and I have spoken at length throughout the day and have one concept we think might serve us well."

He cleared his throat as he paced before the fire. "On the first voyage, Joseph Banks came back speaking of little else but the natives' abilities to heal in Otaheite. He said their surgeons' methods of treating illness were unlike anything he'd ever seen. Since Isobel is the sole descendant of two very important members of society, would it not be believable that you might travel to great lengths if there was a chance she could be cured? Would it not also explain why you travel with a midwife so well versed in herbal medicines and a native translator?"

"I'd believe that story," the lieutenant offered. "But mightn't the duchess have mentioned the true purpose of her trip once she had come to trust us? I would ask that of her if presented with the tale myself."

"It wasn't for the duchess to tell." Lilly wrapped an arm around Isobel and pulled her against her. "Maybe we were afraid we might be judged for chasing after less traditional methods of treatment;

that we might be accused of witchcraft. I can't imagine society is any less judgmental in this time than it is in our own."

"That's good." Johann nodded. "It could work... but should the captain offer to stay with us? Surely he would not be willing to abandon a duchess and her cousins with no way to return home?"

"When we were last there," Maria squinted in thought, "there was a Spanish ship that had come in just before us. What if we said we didn't want to expose Isobel's ears to the cold of the Arctic and risk jeopardizing her treatment? We could ask them to return for us after they have finished exploring the south. But upon their return, we could hide and have Hitihiti tell the captain we left on a Spanish ship."

Johann considered it. "Do you think Hitihiti would do this? Or that Otou would go along with it?"

Chris nodded. "Hitihiti will help us. He's a friend."

"But what reason would we *all* have to stay with them?" Bruce asked. "Particularly you, Johann. You don't have any personal attachment to Isobel."

Johann smiled. "I am a naturalist, my friend. The captain knows it is curiosity that leads me to any given location. My son shall be quite capable of performing my duties aboard the ship whilst I stay behind to study the Otaheite methods of healing."

The lieutenant paced with a hand behind his back. "But if we were to return to Otaheite and find you gone with them... You wouldn't abandon Georg."

"I would if the Spanish took me prisoner. Lieutenant, it is no great secret that I am wanted for unpaid debts all over the world. The captain would surely not find it uncharacteristic of me to have a debt with the Spaniards as well. If there was word that I'd been taken prisoner, the captain might have a sense of urgency that would serve as just cause to abandon an extended stay in Otaheite to return and negotiate my release. You, Lieutenant, could of course inform Georg as to my whereabouts once returned, and he is wise enough to fool the captain into believing he'd worked out a deal for my release."

"Very clever," the lieutenant surmised. "So the duchess will not leave her cousins... and since the rest of you serve either the duchess or her cousins, none of you would have cause to abandon them, except..." He looked at Jack. "The ship's master... What reason have you to stay? The captain has seen your maps. So far as he knows, you were only aboard the ship to serve the illusion that they had been exploring the Pacific, and so, given this new story, I cannot fathom an explanation that could warrant your willingness to stay behind."

I noticed a hint of defensiveness in the tone the lieutenant took with Jack. He and Chris were friends then. I wondered how much he knew.

Jack leaned casually back on his hands. "Well, that's assuming those maps were even made by me." He grinned. "The captain knows I'm no ship's master. He said so after the hunt today. My build isn't one that comes from years of sitting behind a desk. I never said the maps were mine, or that I was the ship's master. He made the assumption after I pulled out the map and I went along with it as part of the illusion. I am better suited as a soldier sent to serve as guard to Lord James."

"A soldier?" The lieutenant raised an eyebrow. "And where is your sword, sir? If given one, would you even know how to use it?"

Jack matched his condescending tone. "Care to loan me yours and find out?"

"Ay," Jim looked between the two of them. "We ain't got time for a pissin' match right now. Both of yuns knock that off."

"A soldier does make much more sense than a ship's master, Lieutenant... the man is a giant." Johann informed him. "Now, are we all agreed on the story, then? Have we left out anything?"

"Just one small detail." Magna finally spoke. She'd been sitting to one side, listening carefully. "As great as their treatment might be, do the Tahitians actually have a way to treat Isobel? And is that something we want to expose her to? Surely the captain will want to see what it is we are staying for. He'll be curious about the treatment. What do we do if they turn her away or if we don't think it is safe?"

"I'll talk to Hitihiti," Chris said. "Even if there is no safe way to treat her, perhaps he can convince some of his people to make it appear as if there were."

"But," I pursed my lips, "what if the Tahitians don't want us to stay? What if we aren't welcome there? We're making a pretty big assumption that we would not be a burden to them."

"I'll talk to Hitihiti," Chris said again. "Whatever we need to do to make our stay convenient for them, we'll do."

"Do we tell Hitihiti the truth?" Maria asked. "Wouldn't we need his help if Tahiti is supposed to be Magna's home? Someone would need to recognize her, and he's the only person who could make that possible. Wouldn't he want to know why we were suddenly asking him for all these favors?"

Chris ran a hand over his beard. "Maybe parts of the truth, but not all of it. He's been a good friend. I think some of our secrets would be safe with him."

Jim held his hands out. "Well now, wait just a minute. Let's say this all works and Hooty-hotty helps us out and the Tahitians let us stay. They's a much bigger issue that none of us are talkin' 'bout. Our whole plan revolves around Lieutenant Edgecumbe returnin'... But it's 1774... and by the time ye' return to England, the British will be at war with America. As a lieutenant, ye' gonna' be expected to join 'at fight. Even if you get made captain once ye' get there, you'll still be expected to fight."

"You're right." The lieutenant nodded, turning to resume his pacing. "I wouldn't be able to desert if called upon to serve."

"Wait..." I help up my palm. "Why can't we just tell the captain the truth? He seems like a reasonable man. We have a whole cave full of evidence to prove it... Wouldn't that be easier than lying? Couldn't we just explain everything to him and ask *him* to help us find a way back? Discovering a way to travel through time might be a hell of a lot more valuable to him than discovering Antartica."

Lieutenant Edgecumbe shook his head. "That would mean Maria and Chris would have to confess to masquerading as the duchess and her guard for nearly a year. He would feel as though he'd been slighted. If there is one thing I've learned about the captain during our travels, it is that the man is not one to be made a fool of. He is reasonable, to be certain. However, when his pride is at stake, he will abandon all reason to protect it. It is my belief that making such a confession could put us all in a considerably great deal more danger. With an entire army at his command, should he respond negatively, we could risk far more than never finding the way back."

"But we are risking *so much* by lying," I argued. "We are leaving a lot to chance with this plan. You get on that ship and disappear and we wait and hope that you not only are made captain and given your own ship, but that you are somehow able to escape the war with that ship and come back here. We are assuming that the Tahitians will be accommodating of our extended stay should it take you years to return... and what do we do if you don't? What if you can't escape the war or aren't given a ship? We wouldn't know... We would be stranded there... And what happens when we have worn out our welcome and they want us to leave? Isn't that a much bigger risk than at least attempting to tell the captain the truth?"

I exhaled, aggravated, as the lieutenant made a move to argue. "Lieutenant, some of us don't have time to wait for years. Some of us need to go home... to have access to modern technology and medicine now."

He glanced down at my belly and I saw the acknowledgement in his expression. Chris had told him already... and by the distaste that washed over his features, I concluded the lieutenant did not think highly of me for it.

"Madam," he held his chin high, "forgive my forwardness, but would you risk the lives of us all to save only the one?"

"I just—

"He would have us all hung..." He continued, disregarding any rebuttal I might offer. "He has introduced Maria to many great leaders along our voyage as the duchess. Kings and chiefs all along our path now sit taller for having dined with royalty. We would not only be making a mockery of him, but he would be, in his own eyes, a fraud to the many men he holds in high regard. He would have made a mockery of the Royal Society. I beg of you, madam, consider that we have already explored this endeavor and would have previously acted upon it had we come to the conclusion that it was safe to do so."

Johann cleared his throat. "*I* have an alternative idea."

We all fell silent and looked toward him as he pulled the small leather journal from his bag and thumbed through it.

"According to your journal, this man, Zachary, came through time similarly. He experienced the same storm and landed upon the same island. I have been pondering this entry all night, attempting to determine a commonality between his entry date of September 3rd, and yours of March 3rd, and I've only just recently formed a new hypothesis. Aside from being precisely six months apart, both months also share one other similarity: the equinox. Now generally, the equinox falls around the twentieth day of March and the twenty-third day of September."

He closed the journal and held it behind his back as he paced. "The equinox is the moment at which the center of the sun aligns directly above the equator. What if twenty or so days *prior* to the equinox, a gap in time is allowed to open due to the relation of the earth's equator to the sun? One gap could lead backward. The other, forward. And I can only assume that the time span is running parallel. It could be that such a specific time and location would render the event rare for anyone else to have found themselves caught inside it. Today is the fifth of April. We've missed the window of opportunity to catch the spring equinox, but come September—or rather, the end of August, we could plan to be anchored in the very place you came through."

"How?" I asked. "Cook will be halfway to Antartica in September."

Johann smiled. "Madam, the duchess cannot be expected to sit idle in a foreign land with no transportation to move her comfortably about the islands! I shall ask for a cutter to be left behind. It will not be so comfortable as the ship, but it will navigate us to the location even in rough waters."

The lieutenant narrowed his eyes at Johann. "And if your theory is incorrect? Or if it is correct and I return to find you all gone?"

Johann shook his head. "Fear not, my friend. If I succeed in traveling forward, I shall promptly return backward the following fall to greet you here. If my theory is incorrect, then you shall return to find us all waiting for you just the same."

"Are you saying we could potentially navigate between the times at will?" Phil asked. "We could rewrite history... We could change the world as we know it."

"It does not come without risks." Johann peered around the fire at each of us. "The lightning in both occurrences caused a considerable amount of damage and much death. This man, Zachary, lost his entire crew, and you yourselves lost a great deal of passengers. There would be no amount of preparations that could ensure our safety for such a rare and unstudied phenomenon. Some of us may very well not make it through... for all we know, human life is a required price for others to be able to pass through."

"I'm willing to take that risk," Anna said decidedly. "I have to at least try to get to my son."

"I'm not." Jack looked at my belly and I saw in his expression, he'd come to the realization, just as I had, that the baby would already be born by that time. "Not unless I know we're *all* safe."

"September is a ways away," I assured him. "We've got time to plan; to try to remember anything from the crash that could help us prepare for it... We need to at least try."

There was a silence that fell upon us as we all considered it and, I assumed, based on my own mind racing, remembered the first time through.

I remembered the shaking of the plane and the odd sense of weightlessness that came over me; the lack of sound and the look on Jack's face. I'd never seen him so scared. I wasn't afraid the first time, mostly because I didn't comprehend what was happening until it was over, but the second time… knowing the danger… going in with a newborn baby… I would be terrified.

Lilly stood with Izzy wrapped in her arms. "We have plenty of time before September to work out the rest of the details. I'm gonna go say goodbye to gramma while I've got the chance. I might never be here again."

Jim immediately stood beside her, as did Bud.

"Thank ye.'" Jim nodded at Johann, then at the lieutenant. "Both of ye.' I know it cain't be without its own risks helpin' us like ye' are. I want ye' both to know, we all appreciate what y'all are doin' for us."

The lieutenant bowed his head. "It's my honor, sir."

Johann grinned. "Mine as well, selfishly so. I'm afraid I am indebted to you all for giving my life new meaning. Discovering this gap in time will become my life's achievement."

Jim winked. "Well, don't go tellin' nobody about your *life's achievement* after ye' find it. I like the future just like it is and don't need it changin' every other day cause' too many folk travel back to muck it up!" He followed Bud and Lilly out of the circle. "Night y'all."

Anna yawned. "I think I'll go to bed. Is there a tent for each of us or should I head up to our old camp?"

Johann smiled at her. "We've all got our own tents set up for the night. Come, I'll escort you to yours."

Bruce rose from his seat alongside Anna. "I'll come as well."

One by one, Magna, Phil, Kyle, Jacob, and Michael all joined them, each saying their own goodnights before heading toward the tents, leaving only myself, Chris, Jack, John, and Maria at the fire to awkwardly avoid eye contact.

"Maria," the lieutenant extended a hand to her. "Might I escort you to your own tent? Surely these three have much to discuss and I'd like a word with you before we depart tomorrow."

She yawned before taking his hand and rising. "Sí. I need to get this dress off before I suffocate, anyway. We can grab Fetia on our way." She looked over her shoulder at the three of us remaining. "Goodnight."

Chapter Thirty Seven

Alaina

I could feel my cheeks burning as we all sat in silence, listening to the fire crackle between us. None of us wanted to have the conversation that was coming and so none of us opted to be the one to initiate it.

I watched as a single Kolea feather was lifted from its basket in the breeze, floating up over the flames. The escaping embers that danced over the fire clung to its edges, quickly searing the white threads of its edges to burn inward and curl the feather into itself until it fell as ash into the flames.

In so many ways, I felt like a feather floating through ember, my edges searing as I waited for the conversation to start, my insides burning away as I envisioned having to make the choice between them.

The minutes dragged on as I stared at my feet, uncomfortably shoved into black wool shoes with silver buckles that were not built with comfort in mind. In truth, none of the attire I'd been forced to wear was comfortable. The corset top was burning my sides, and every part of my body was sore from wearing it. Even the stockings itched on my legs. I couldn't wait to be out of it all.

I looked first at Chris who was poking a small stick into the flames, staring dazedly at its glowing end. I couldn't imagine how difficult the situation must've been for him.

Across from me, Jack was sitting with his elbows rested on his knees, staring down at his hands as he balled them into fists and released them.

I knew them both so well and yet; I had no idea how either man would handle the upcoming conversation. The Chris I knew was much more patient than Jack. Where Jack was explosive when it came to his emotions, Chris was reserved and would normally handle conflict in a mature and neutral manner. Earlier that day, however, he had surprised me in the way he'd spoken to Jack; in the way he'd demanded he leave and even threatened him by placing a hand on his sword. Would this conversation go similarly?

"You are my wife." Chris finally spoke, not looking away from the stick he twisted over the flame. "You'll be expected to sleep in my tent... in my cabin on the ship... If we're going to pull this story off, we can't risk them catching you coming out of another man's bed. I have no expectations for you to actually share my bed, but you'll have to sleep there until they're gone."

Jack didn't look up from his hands. "I agree." The words were forced through gritted teeth and I could tell how much it pained him to have to say them. "We won't get to the doctors you need... we won't have a hospital if you need a surgery..."

Chris dug the glowing end of his stick into the sand, then placed it back over the fire. "I know what I'm asking of you and how hard it would be, but given the risks... have you considered an abortion?"

"No," I said simply. "You know why I can't do that."

Chris nodded. "I know, I just... don't see many other options. Ally, you could die."

I placed a hand protectively over my stomach. "Johann says the Tahitians are known for their medicine and surgeons... *That's* an option. It might sound silly, and I don't know how to explain it, but it's different this time."

"And so what if it is?" Chris finally looked up at me. "I didn't experience that storm like the rest of you, but I remember it being awful. How do we go back with a newborn? Or with Isobel? Do we really want to risk the lives of children just to get to a time we're familiar with?"

"No," Jack said, flexing his hands. "We can't go back. Not until we know no one will get hurt in the process."

Chris shook his head. "What if we never know for certain? What if there is no guarantee?"

"Then we stay. We find a place and make a life here."

Chris closed his eyes and took a deep breath. "Do you know how to use a sword?"

"Yes," Jack responded.

"A real one?" Chris peered across the fire at him. "That ship is full of a hundred lonely and desperate men. Even with the duchess's name and the threat of being hanged for it, one of them went after Maria. A servant, however…" He looked at me. "They would not be afraid to go after… If the captain decides on an extended stay in Tahiti like he did the last trip, a time may come when you'll would need to defend one of these women. If you are a soldier, you'll need to know how to fight like one."

"I said I know how," Jack grumbled.

"If that is pride, there's no place for it here," Chris said bluntly. "John could train you if you need—

"It's not pride," he muttered. "I know how to use one. My first movie role was set in the 16th century. I joined a swordplay guild to play a more believable role. Even afterward, I spent years in the guild, studying and practicing historical European swordplay with real steel blades."

Chris's nose twitched at this and he looked back down at his stick where the end had started to char and curl. "Al, you'll need to learn how to defend yourself in case you're ever alone."

"Maybe Maria could teach me." I could feel the small bit of disdain in my voice as I'd said the words, a tinge of jealousy at the thought of the two of them together, and I adjusted my tone. "She mentioned she killed a man?"

"She did. The single time she was alone, a soldier pinned her down and attempted to rape her. She stabbed him…" He grinned as he looked up into the flames, a small airy laugh escaping him. "... in his dick."

I'd told Jack just hours prior I wasn't in love with Chris, and yet, I couldn't help myself resenting the look of pride on his face as he'd said the words. What was I aiming to achieve in bringing her into this conversation? Was I looking for feelings on his part? Was I hoping to find out he had spent the past year doing the *very thing* I had in developing feelings for another? How hypocritical could I possibly be for envying her in that moment?

"I don't want to be the bad guy in all this," he said, letting the stick fall into the fire and straightening his back. "You know," he snickered, "I actually thought I was coming to your rescue..." He ran a hand over his face. "Jesus Christ, I never expected this."

Jack looked up at him then. "Neither did I."

Chris bit his lower lip, narrowing his eyes at the flames that were now dying down in front of us. "Didn't you though? When I went into the restroom," he made eye contact with Jack, "*you* were awake. Even if you didn't see who went in, you had to notice the light when the door opened... I know you have replayed the crash over and over in your mind, reliving every single little detail before and after, just as I have. I know you had to see the light... And I know you've wondered about it. Did the thought ever cross your mind, while you were chasing my wife, that *I* could've potentially been the one to go in that bathroom right before the crash... that I might be out there trying to get to her?"

"It crossed my mind, yes." Jack admitted.

And suddenly it was I that was replaying moments... moments on the beach when I'd sworn he felt alive and Jack dismissed it... Moments up on the summit when I'd broken down and he'd consoled me... All the while he'd been aware there had been someone unaccounted for... I felt a stab of betrayal slash through my heart.

He saw it in my eyes and looked back down at his feet. "But I told myself there was no way anyone could've survived that crash without the seatbelt to hold them in... And if they had, there was no way they could fight that ocean. I told myself whoever had been in there surely must be dead. What was I going to do? Add salt to the wound by giving her that same image? She cried night after night after night, assuming you'd blown up in the airplane. I wasn't going to paint her a picture of you drowning in the ocean or smashing your skull in the bathroom."

"That wasn't your picture to keep from me," I blurted out, finding it difficult to breathe with the corset squeezing my ribs even tighter. I stood to place my hands on my head in an attempt to slow my breathing. "How could you keep that from me? When I'd told you he didn't feel gone… how could you not tell me someone had gone into that bathroom?"

"Red, I—"

"Don't you dare call me that right now," I growled. "All this time, you knew there was a possibility—even if it was slim—it was possible he could be out there, and you kept that from me. You let me let go of him… So you could what? Move in on me once I'd gotten over it?!"

"No, I swear—"

"I think I'll go to bed now." I took a very deep breath in and out and turned toward the tents, realizing I had no idea which one I would be going to, but walking toward them all the same.

"Wait," Jack pleaded behind me, and I heard Chris step in.

"Enough," he said, and I slowed my pace just in case things got physical. Upset as I was with Jack in that moment, I didn't want them fighting.

"You did this," Jack snarled.

"No," Chris said cooly, "*you* did this by keeping secrets you knew would change things. I get why you did it, and I can't say I wouldn't have done the same thing if the roles were reversed and I saw a chance to be with her… but don't blame me for exposing *your* secret."

I could hear his footsteps crunching the dead leaves as he hurried to catch up to me.

"I didn't mean for that to happen," he said softly, placing a hand on the small of my back. "Or.. hell, maybe I did, I don't know. I certainly didn't mean for it to upset you like this."

I leaned against him, his familiarness instantly comforting as my body remembered exactly where to land against his side to walk easily together.

"I let you go, love. I let you go, and I gave all of my heart to him… and now you're alive, and all I want is to do the right thing; to run right back into your arms because that's what you deserve… He watched me let go of you. And he knew all along there was a chance this could happen…"

He curled his arm around me, but I felt him stiffen as he did so. I couldn't blame him for being uncomfortable. I couldn't imagine how he must've felt. He opted not to speak and escorted me quietly into the encampment, stopping at a tent to pull the flap open.

A single straw-filled mattress sat on a cot inside. He looked down at me and frowned. "You take the bed. I'll sleep on the ground."

"We can share the bed, Chris, I—

"I'll sleep on the ground," he repeated. "I heard you earlier when you told him you were *in love* with him. I know where I stand in all this."

"I didn't mean for you to hear that," I said sheepishly, sitting down on the bed as he pulled a blanket from it and laid it neatly on the ground.

"I didn't need to hear it to know it."

"It could be temporary… Like I said, I let you go… maybe it's just—

"It's not." He sat down in the center of the pallet he'd made. "Ally, you have never looked at me the way you look at him."

I could feel fresh tears spill down my cheeks. "What a terrible thing for you to have to notice! Every single day of our lives, I should've looked at you that way. You gave me an amazing life. I should've been so much more than I was to you."

He patted my hand, nodding, then swung his legs to lie on his back on the blanket. "It's been a very long day, and I'm too tired to have this conversation now. Get some sleep."

Chapter Thirty Eight

Chris

Chris laid on the ground, staring up at the blue of the tent's white fabric ceiling where the moon's light shined through it. He knew she was still awake in the bed by the quietness in her breathing, but he didn't want to speak to her anymore that night.

He felt like a fool. He should hate her after what he'd heard. He should've run away from her years ago. Even in that moment, when she'd ripped his heart out of his chest, he hadn't.

He'd spent the day convincing himself she would somehow change her mind and willingly choose him by the night's end... But then he saw the way she'd looked at Jack over dinner and he knew she wouldn't change.

She *hadn't* been the woman he'd fallen in love with in... And he wondered if, after he'd asked God for a sign, he hadn't been sent to that moment to question whether or not he had ever known who she actually was.

He thought back to their relationship and tried to remember it without the rose-colored glasses he tended to put on when it came to her.

He'd always shown up with flowers, surprises, or romantic dinners. Even the first kiss, he'd been the one to initiate... He thought hard about the early days of what he'd always considered the perfect love; the good times he was so anxious to get back to...

Was it always him initiating things? Had she ever surprised him with some sweet gesture to make him feel loved in return?

He remembered all the work he'd put into finding her that perfect house, then making it match the dream she'd had... He remembered staying behind at the hospital to cut a small piece of hair from Evelyn's head; how difficult it was for him to touch her lifeless body but how he'd done it anyway, thinking only of how happy it would make Alaina to have it...

But not once in all of that had she gone out of her way for him. He couldn't think of a single moment where she'd shown any signs of feeling even remotely close to the way he'd felt about her.

How had he never seen it before?

He needed air. He needed to get out of the tent to be alone with his thoughts, but she was still awake and he didn't want to risk her following him out. He wanted to be angry; to let himself feel the contempt he held and not be softened by her nearness.

He waited. And as he waited, his thoughts naturally drifted to Maria. She, in contrast, would've loved him fiercely had he let her, and he could've returned that love had he not been so intent on being reunited with Alaina; had he not been so blinded by the picture of perfection he'd painted of her in his mind.

He could feel his muscles tense as he imagined Maria down there in that pit, asking him to tell her there was nothing between them. She'd loved him then. He squeezed his eyes tightly shut as he saw himself letting her go, despite his mind pleading with him not to.

He remembered the morning on the ship; the squeeze of his hand that meant goodbye. She hadn't given John an answer, but after today... would she? After seeing him run up that trail, would she run to John?

He wondered if John was with her now; if he peeked in Maria's tent, would he find them snuggled up together in her bed?

He rolled onto his side. It didn't matter. He'd made his own bed and now he was lying in it. He'd chosen wrong, and that was that. The only thing he could do now is try to carry out the plan; try to get them back home, and once there, attempt to start over in life.

'*Show me how a husband kisses his wife,*' his mind teased him. Even those words... the words he had held onto for so long... sounded wrong now in his mind. Why did it have to be him doing the kissing?

Ten years of his life she'd wasted. *Ten years.* He wanted to hate her—needed to hate her for wasting so much of his time. He could feel his blood boiling as he laid there getting angrier with every breath she took.

Jack Volmer... what a tool.

He recalled seeing his face on the tabloids while standing in line with her at a grocery store; the headline reading: '*7 days, 7 different dates. Fairview nights star not so fair in love.*'

This was the type of man she wanted? A man that thought love was sleeping with whichever woman was within his reach? He huffed. How long, once they'd returned, before he abandoned her for the next pretty girl that batted her eyes at him? Did it even matter? If Jack Volmer decided to leave her for the next woman, wasn't that what she deserved for having chosen him?

After what felt like an eternity confined inside with her, he heard her breathing relax into the subtle rhythm of sleep. Quietly, he eased himself up and crept out into the fresh air.

He needed to walk; needed to clear his mind and get rid of the anger, so he headed toward the water's edge. None of these men would touch *Der Mutige's* wife, he knew, but he scanned the campsite once just to be sure.

In the shadows just beyond the first set of tents, he caught sight of the silhouette of a man lingering, leaned up against a tree.

He looked back toward the center of camp where the largest tent was erected for Maria. Slowly, he pulled his sword from its sheath and crept toward the shadow.

"Did you enjoy that?" The shadow whispered as Chris grew closer. "Making yourself the good guy? Is it your goal to upset her so much that she loses the baby and runs back to you?"

He recognized the voice as Jack's and the rage that had been building inside him boiled hotter.

He threw the sword off to one side, not trusting himself not to use it, as he stepped within inches of him. "And what if she did? How long before you'd run off with the next? You think I don't know what kind of man you are?! How easily you could replace her?!"

Jack narrowed his eyes. "Not many to choose from here." He raised a defiant eyebrow. "I suppose Maria would have to do."

And that was all it took. Chris saw red, and before he could process what he was doing, he was on the ground, rolling against the dead palm leaves into the brush with Jack wrapped up in his grip as he attempted to get enough leverage to land a punch.

"Oh, so you're no saint yourself then!" Jack panted, pinning him to the ground by forcing his weight down on the center of his back. "You make her feel an insurmountable amount of guilt for moving on from you, but you didn't exactly remain the devoted husband you're pretending to be, did you? Wouldn't be the first time you cheated on her though, would it?"

Chris bucked him off long enough to spin around and get ahold of his shirt, balling his hand into a fist and landing one satisfying blow to his mouth before Jack wrestled him back down to roll further into the trees.

"You sonofabitch," Chris managed through gritted teeth. "Piece of shit…" He couldn't think of coherent words, so he poured out whatever obscenities he could muster as they both grappled for leverage, both of them throwing fists, elbows, knees, and grabbing at whatever they could to overpower the other.

All the while, Chris's mind was echoing the word *'Jack'* as it escaped Alaina's lips on the trail earlier. He remembered how her voice had cracked; how her eyes had watered…

He grabbed Jack's head with both hands and pounded it against the ground, freeing Jack's fist to land a punch on his jaw and nearly knock him out, his eyes filling with yellow fuzz as he fell to one side.

"What are you fighting for, anyway?" Jack hissed, pinning Chris down to press his face against the dirt once again. "You made her miserable. Is that what you want? For her to be miserable with you again? Or is it the other one you want to make miserable?"

"Fuck you," Chris spat against the dirt, rolling from one side to the other until he was able to elbow Jack in the nose and get his feet underneath him.

Jack sprung on him, throwing fists into his gut as Chris wrapped him in a headlock and landed jab after jab to his face.

"Fuck *you*," Jack spat back, freeing his head from his grip and kicking Chris in his ribs, forcing him to roll to one side. "Acting high and mighty when you're just as guilty as she is!"

Chris stood. "Quit talking and fight me." He held his fists out and ready, motioning for Jack to stand.

Jack rose to balance on one knee. He shook his head, spitting blood to one side. "You think that's going to earn either of us any points with her?"

"To hell with points," Chris growled, his chest heaving. "You've already won her. This is for me. Stand up."

Jack looked past him toward camp. "Wouldn't exactly be a fair fight now, would it?"

Chris followed his gaze to see two soldiers inside camp already looking toward the trees that kept them concealed. He turned back to find Jack holding up both hands in surrender.

"I should've told her," he said, wiping the blood from his lip with the back of his hand. "I knew I should've given her the chance to come to the same conclusions I had about whatever possibilities might've been tied to that bathroom light, but I couldn't. And the more time that passed without me telling her, the more I thought she'd hate me for it if I finally got around to it. It wouldn't change anything. You *had* to be dead… We barely made it on a life raft full of supplies. It would only give her hope she didn't need and make her hate me for keeping it a secret… At least, that's what I thought, anyway. I never imagined you'd come sailing up with an army a year later."

Chris's adrenaline was wearing off and he could feel the emotion that always followed a fight burning his nose. He sat down hard on his butt, balancing his forearms on his knees. His fingers throbbed from being balled so tightly into fists and his jaw was on fire. "I never imagined her being anything but relieved to see me when I sailed up. I hate you for taking that away from me."

"I know." Jack sat back on his butt as well, rubbing his nose and checking his fingers for blood. "I'd hate me too." He sighed. "I came up here looking for a fight... Needed to fight just to get out of my head. She's the only thing I've ever felt sure of in my whole life... and then you come back from the dead and threaten to take that away... I've never hated anyone more."

Chris ran a hand hard over his face. "I'm no threat to you. She made that fact *perfectly* clear today... Ten years, she was the only thing *I* felt sure of... and now it's all lost on some actor. What the hell do I do now?"

"We can keep fighting if you want," Jack offered.

Chris shook his head. "That's not going to change it, though, is it?"

"You...uh... want a drink then?" Jack raised his eyebrows.

Chris let his muscles relax and rolled his head from one shoulder to the other. "You got any more of that whiskey?"

"By the fire." Jack leaned to one side and grunted as he attempted to push himself off the ground. "Jesus Christ," he groaned. "I think you bruised a rib."

"Good." Chris followed suit, struggling with his own body aches and doing his best to hide the fact that he would be paying for this fight in the morning.

"You know," he slowly straightened, wincing as he did so, "I never touched Maria."

"I know." Jack grimaced and rubbed his shoulder as they turned toward the almost completely extinguished fire. "But I assumed it would be a sore enough subject to get you to throw the first punch."

Chris nodded. "It was going to happen eventually... might happen again before the night's over."

"Just watch the face next time," Jack noted. "We might be able to pull this off as injuries from the hunt today, but if the others wake up and find us completely bloodied and bruised, they'll look at Alaina as the reason. It's not hard to notice the bump if you're looking for it."

Chris looked over at him then, observing the swelling in his nose and lip in the dim moonlight. "I do believe we've already taken it too far... they'll know a boar didn't do that to you."

Jack inspected the damage he'd inflicted on Chris and nodded in agreement. "You're right... a boar wouldn't do this... They'll be looking at her, anyway. She's already showing... You mentioned he stayed in Tahiti for two months last time. We can't hide it for that long. Is the truth so far-fetched in this century we couldn't use it? I mean, I thought she was a widow, and we were stranded together for a year... Is it so unbelievable that a man could make that mistake in this time? Couldn't we just be honest? It might be just one thing we wouldn't need to lie about. It wasn't anyone's fault."

"Out of wedlock? It's a crime."

"We made Jim and Lilly married. Why not she and I? A marriage vow is a marriage vow in the eyes of God, isn't it? We could've exchanged vows on that island, assuming no one was coming for us. And I would've if I thought she was up for it, you know. She wears my ring on her finger... I'm sure they've seen it."

"I'll think about it," Chris muttered. He knew it was entirely possible and believable that such a thing could've happened... and telling the truth would free Alaina from their marriage. It would allow her to be with the man she actually wanted without having to hide it behind the facade of a marriage to Chris. Could that be his one final gesture to her? Could he sacrifice his own pride to give her that one last thing?

They walked down to the fire silently, and Chris sat down on a log as Jack stoked the fire back to life, then knelt to grab the bottle of whiskey from where he'd been seated.

Chris took the bottle when he offered it, tilting it back to let it warm his throat. He passed it back. "That story earlier… you really killed a man?"

Jack nodded, taking a swig and exhaling heavily as it burned his throat.

"What was it like?"

"Thinking about killing me?" Jack teased, handing the bottle back.

"I can't say the thought hasn't crossed my mind a few times today. How'd you do it?"

"I strangled him."

Chris watched as Jack relived it and his face distorted in thought. "Terrible way to die… begging for air… I closed my eyes thinking maybe I could forget it if I didn't look down at him… But I can still feel the life inside him convulsing as it tried not to be put out. I can still feel his pulse slow and stop against my arm." He ran his palm over the spot on his forearm. "It haunts me every night. The dreams… It's like I kill him over and over again every single time I go to sleep. I'll never be able to forget it."

Chris couldn't help but think of Maria. Was she, too, reliving the moment she'd killed Sergeant Harris every night? Was it haunting her the way this man's death was haunting Jack? He took a sip of the whiskey, holding it in his mouth and closing his eyes.

"Do you wonder what it'll be like to go back to our time?" Jack asked. "After all this?"

Chris opened his eyes and squinted into the flames as he swallowed. "I think about it all the time… What would I even do once we get there? Go back to work? Pay a mortgage? Would I forever be aware of the lack of meaning my life would have? Here… I feel like I'm at least serving some purpose."

Jack took the offered bottle and held it in front of his lips. "Serving a purpose trying to plan a way back to the future you don't fit into anymore?" He smirked, tilting the bottle to his lips.

"What will you do when you go back?"

Jack shrugged. "Pray I still have enough money left to my name to buy a place tucked away from it all."

Chris's head was starting to swim and he could feel his body warming from the whiskey. "Ironic, isn't it? Working so hard to get off these islands to want to go back to seclusion…"

"I'd only be going back for her and the baby. There, they'd have access to medicine, hospitals, grandparents, education… I couldn't *not* give that to them."

"I've got no reason to go back," Chris said, surprising himself at the ease with which the words fell out. "Not anymore, anyway. Wherever I go, I'll have to start over… why not do it here where I feel like my life has some kind of meaning?"

"You gonna take this or not?" Jack shook the bottle he'd been holding out toward him. Chris took it as Jack leaned back on his hands. "What would you do here? Where would you go?"

"Wherever I wanted." Chris took another drink, hiccuping after he swallowed. "Seeing the world in this time with the captain has been fulfilling in a sense. I might hop from ship to ship and explore more of it. Stay in whichever place I decide I like best."

"What about your family?"

Chris hiccuped again. "Well… if Johann is right… if we figure out a way to cross through safely, maybe I'll come visit."

Jack laughed. "Right… Because there'd be no attention on anyone for coming back into the United States years after we'd all been presumed dead. How would we ever explain what happened to us?"

"Amnesia?" Chris chuckled, handing Jack the bottle. "Wouldn't that be one hell of a way to complete this friggin' soap opera we're all living in?"

"I see you two been talkin' things out like mature adults," Jim called out as he and Lilly approached. "Ye' both look like ten miles of bad road. Lordt almighty, cain't leave ye' alone for five minutes! Ye' done squabblin' or do I need to sit here and babysit ye' before you both blow our dang cover?"

"Jesus," Lilly breathed, kneeling down at Chris to pull his forehead with her thumb and inspect a cut on his eyebrow. "What were you two thinking?!"

Chris hiccuped and grinned at her. "He stole my wife."

Jack scoffed. "He threatened me with a sword."

"You're lucky I didn't use it."

"Shut up," Lilly hissed, tilting Chris's head back. "You're both idiots. I don't even know *you,* and I know you're an idiot. Do you know how closely they're all watching us?!"

"Ye' couldn't wait to punch him?" Jim inspected Jack similarly. "Until maybe after they left?"

"We can't hide it, anyway," Jack slurred. "They're gonna see she's pregnant."

"Well, they will now, numbnuts!" Jim shook his head. "Christ, if ye' had a thought between the two of ye' it might die of loneliness! What we gonna' tell 'em now?"

Chris sighed as Lilly dabbed at his eyebrow with her kerchief. "We'll tell them the truth... at least about the island... They thought I was dead... But we'll have to tell them they married each other there. It's the only way they'll accept it. You both witnessed them taking vows. We tell them that, then she won't have to pretend to be happily married to me and we wouldn't have to hide the pregnancy."

Lilly raised an eyebrow, her expression softening. "You'd do that for her?"

He hiccuped a little loudly. "I don't see how I have any other choice. I can't exactly force her to stay married to me. Plus..." He blinked. "It'd give me a reason to beat the shit out of him again if I felt the need to."

"PFFF," Jack rebutted. "You're in much worse shape than I am, buddy. Count your blessings I stopped the fight when I did."

"I wouldn't say either of yas' came out a winner." Jim sat down beside Jack and took the whiskey bottle from him, inspecting the small bit left before taking a sip. "Ain't got no sense, neither of yuns. Ye' feel good about what ye' done here?"

Chris smiled across the fire at the sight of Jack's busted lip and swollen nose. "Wouldn't change a thing."

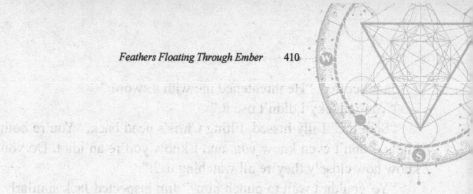

Chapter Thirty Nine

Alaina

I opened my eyes, surrounded by darkness. I knew, even without looking down at his pallet on the ground, I was alone in the tent. I squeezed my eyes closed as I'd remembered the night before; the disappointment in Chris's voice as he'd confessed to overhearing me and Jack.

I hated hurting him; hated seeing that familiar disappointing look on his features. I needed to apologize, needed to find some way to make things right between us.

I sat up in the bed, wondering where he'd disappeared to.

I blinked heavily to try to clear my eyes enough to find my discarded clothing. Having grown accustomed to sleeping in the back cave for so long, my eyes quickly adjusted, and I scooped up the pile of clothing from the foot of the bed.

I layered on what I remembered, lazily tying the corset and covering the sloppy job with the apron tied at my waist.

Barefooted, I tiptoed out of the tent, scanning the camp around me for signs of life. All was quiet.

I crept through camp and down the sand in the faded morning light where I could just make out a few shadows moving at the water's edge. As I moved closer, I could see one body laying still in the sand while two others waded in the water. My chest suddenly heavy, I hurried my pace.

Just as I reached Chris's unconscious body, Jim grinned at me from the water where he was holding Jack's head under the water.

"Mornin' sugar. Don't you worry your pretty little head about nothin,' I got this all under control." Jack came up in a gasp for air and Jim smacked his back hard. "That oughta sober ye' up right quick. Come on, help me get the other one."

As they trudged through the water toward me, I could see the busted lip, black eye, and bruised nose on Jack. I looked down at Chris where he laid at my feet; his hair matted and full of leaves with dried blood on his eyebrow and a massive bruise on one cheek. I sighed and ran a hand through my hair. "What happened out here?"

"Had us a hell of a night." Jim winked at me, then knelt over Chris to slap him across his already bruised cheek. "Ay Gigantor... wake yer ass up."

He pulled Chris up to a sitting position and draped his lifeless arm across his shoulders. "Ye' couldn't date normal sized humans, huh?" He grunted. "Come on, Hoss, grab the other side. I cain't lift the summbitch by myself."

Jack looked at me, then back down to Chris, kneeling to drape Chris's other arm across his shoulders and help Jim lift. Collectively, they dragged him into the ocean, fully clothed, where Jim promptly pushed him into the water and held his head there.

"These two decided to have a wrestle," Jim said casually as Chris came alive and began to flail. "Then decided to polish off an entire bottle of whiskey and go at it again..." He released him and Chris came up spitting and gasping for air.

"What the hell?!"

Jim grinned. "Ye' can sleep all ye' want just as soon as ye' get somewhere no one can see ye.' Come on.'"

Jack smoothed the hair from his face as he stumbled out of the water to stand before me. "Red... I can explain everything."

"Donn' be mad," Chris called as he hobbled toward the beach alongside him. "I punched him..." He held a fist up. "In the face."

I raised an eyebrow, glancing between the two of them as they attempted to compose themselves after a night of fighting and heavy drinking. "More than once from the looks of it…?"

"Didn't keep count…" Chris said. "But I hit him a couple two… four… a few times."

"We should get them up to their tents," I said to Jim as the two men swayed heavily. "We can't let the others see them like this."

"That's the plan, darlin.' One wrong word from either of these two idiots could throw the whole dang thing cattywampus. I's just wakin' 'em up to get 'em up to camp. Lordt knows I cain't lift neither one of these behemoths. Princess is down by the fire. Since yer up, why don't ye' go and keep her company while I get these two fools up to bed? I've got some things I need to discuss with ye' before we ship off."

I walked with them halfway to camp, then split off to join Lilly by the fire. She smiled at me from where she sat in the sand, a blanket wrapped around her shoulders.

"You enchantress!" she teased, unfolding one side of the blanket in invitation. "Whatever you've got that makes men do that to each other, I want some of it."

"No, you don't." I yawned, sitting down beside her and letting her cover my shoulders with the blanket. "What happened?"

"Ugh. When we came back, they were just sitting by the fire drinking whiskey… they were all bloody and bruised but at least they were talking. We were *all* talking… about how we'd explain this to the captain… I thought maybe they'd gotten it out of the way and things would be okay. Chris even agreed to tell the truth about you and Jack; tell the captain you'd both exchanged vows here. He said it would be best for you if you didn't have to pretend to be married to him and hide the baby. I was actually impressed by how selfless he was."

She shook her head. "But then Jack said something under his breath and Chris just… idunno… leapt on him. Lainey, I've never seen two grown men fight like that. They fought from here all the way down to the beach… Jimmy finally managed to pull them apart. They were both so drunk they couldn't even stand up. As soon as they sat down, they both just passed out cold right there in the sand. We left them for a few hours but thought it'd be best to get them up to camp before people started to wake up."

"Jesus," I muttered.

She squeezed me against her shoulder. "I shouldn't have told you all that. I don't want to upset you."

"I was going to find out one way or another. I'm alright," I assured her. "Oh God, where's Izzy? She didn't see them fighting, did she?"

"No. She went to camp with Grandpa after we left gramma's grave."

I exhaled a sigh of relief. "Good. I'm worried about her. I don't like the idea of using her as a part of our story. I don't want anyone experimenting on her, you know?"

"I don't either." She laid her head against my shoulder. "But it *is* a believable story… and the best one any of us could come up with. Magna won't let anything happen to her. She speaks the language, and she'd make sure no one was going to hurt her. And if their medicine is that advanced, who knows… maybe they can actually help."

"How good could their medicine possibly be in this century?"

"Better than whatever we could come up with on this island, I imagine. They could help with the birth. Magna and Anna could train some of their surgeons… teach them how to do a c-section if you need it. Maybe they have a medicine to help with that?"

"Maybe." I yawned. "So Chris really offered to tell the truth about me and Jack?"

"He did. It was very admirable. He said no one should be forced by marriage to stay with someone they don't want to be with. And let's be honest, there's no way we're hiding this pregnancy much longer." She patted my stomach. "You're getting bigger by the hour."

"But what if I *do* want to be with him? I mean… I loved him very much once. I should want to be with him after everything he's done for me; everything he's gone through to be with me. Did Jack tell you he knew someone had been in the bathroom when we crashed? He knew all along there was a chance it could've been Chris and never mentioned it. What kind of woman am I to turn down a great man for one that could keep that kind of secret from me?"

Lilly shook her head. "Would telling you have changed anything? You still would've thought he'd died, just under a different circumstance." She slid her palm down to rub my lower back. "Do you remember that night after Jack left? When you and I slept on the beach, just the two of us? Do you remember what you said to me?"

"I remember rambling…"

"You said you never liked who you were with Chris and didn't realize it until you'd met Jack. You said you were a better person because of him and it took meeting him to make you understand you didn't like who you were because you were trying to make a relationship work with someone you just weren't meant to be with. It's not your fault you feel more passionately about one than the other; even if the other is a great person. You love Jack. We all saw that connection long before it happened."

"But I love Chris in my own way… and I hate doing this to him."

She nudged my shoulder with hers. "Chris is a big, tough guy. I've seen it for myself. He'll be alright. You know, deep down, which one you want. Don't torture them both by being indecisive."

I took a deep breath. "You're right… But the truth… do you think these men would accept that and not try to retaliate?"

Lilly shrugged. "It's nobody's fault you both thought Chris was dead. They'd have to understand that. And you're carrying Jack's child. Surely they'd understand why you'd feel the need to stay with him."

"Hopefully."

"Would ye' get a look at you two…" Jim called from across the fire as he joined us, his face lit up in a smile. "All snuggled up and lookin' fit to eat. If a sight like that don't start a man's fire, his wood must be wet."

We both laughed as he sat down on the opposite side of Lilly.

"Thank you Jim," I said. "For handling all that. Who knows what would've happened had you not been out here."

"It's nothin' darlin.' It needed to happen. Better now than later."

I huffed. "Grown men... fist fighting! And how long before they're at it again?"

"I wouldn't worry 'bout it happenin' again sweetheart. Them two wasn't made to talk things out. Now that they've beat it out of each other, they'll be alright... So long as Hoss can learn when to keep his trap shut."

"What'd he say to him to set it off the second time?"

Jim smirked. "Now, I ain't a perfect gentleman, but I also ain't one to speak those kinds of words when there's ladies present. Let's just say he was lookin' to get punched in the mouth. If it'd been directed at me, I'd have had a piece of him too."

"Men." Lilly rolled her eyes.

"Now," Jim leaned forward. "I think the idea of tellin' the captain about you and Jack is the right one. And I'd like to be the one to tell it. The captain's a good ole' boy deep down and he likes me, I can tell. I'll tell him what happened here; tell him yuns got married right here on this beach, then I'll tell him about Izzy and our plan to stay in Tahiti."

"Otaheite," Lilly corrected.

"Whatever." Jim waved her off. "And then it's done. You are free to choose whichever one of 'em ye' want, and ye' won't have to wear them string thingies and risk squeezing the baby to death."

I laughed. "It's a corset. And I hate it."

"I like it." Lilly grinned.

"Well, I don't." He rolled his eyes. "T'ain't natural to be all tied up and sucked in like 'at. Yer squishin' all yer insides! Hell, it'll take me two days if I want to get ye' naked!"

"Oh, but it'll be worth it," she flirted. "It'd do you good to have to work a little harder for it."

"Woman, I love ye,' but you're already 'bout as much work as a man can take." He snickered. "Yuns hungry? I could whip us up some bacon and eggs if ye'd like. Maybe some bread and jam?"

"I'm always hungry," I said.

"I'll help," Lilly offered, sliding out of the blanket and wrapping it around me.

The sun was just beginning to rise and the bacon just starting to sizzle when the captain, dressed to perfection, strolled down the beach to join us.

"Good morning, Lord James! Lady Lillian! Mrs. Grace! I thought I smelled bacon! We have plenty of cooks and servants to do that for us! You needn't be burdened with preparing your own meals."

Jim quickly slipped into his proper English accent. "It's no bother at all, Captain. We've all grown quite accustomed to cooking over a fire. Would you care for some?"

"I do not wish to inconvenience you, sir."

"Not at all." Jim prepared a clay bowl for the captain. "We've plenty."

"Captain..." Jim balanced on his haunches after the captain had taken the bowl from him. "There's something I wish to discuss with you before the others join us... regarding the reason for our voyage as well as... an urgent matter I'd like to seek your advice on regarding Mrs. Grace. Might we speak openly?"

The sound of Jim's English impression was difficult for Lilly and I not to laugh at. Despite the seriousness of what was happening, I could feel her shaking with the effort of holding in her amusement beside me.

The captain flashed a concerned look in my direction, then bowed his head at Jim. "Of course, sir. I am quite humbled you should seek my counsel at all and I certainly hope it can serve some use to you."

"Well," Jim sighed, "I'm afraid there have been... some developments... since last we saw our cousin and Mr. Grace a year ago. You see, we all presumed them both dead... perished in the sea."

The captain leaned in, listening intently with his untouched breakfast in his lap.

Jim frowned, searching for the right way to word things. He spoke slowly, picking out the phrasing between sentences. "There's no easy way to say this, Captain, but I'm afraid Mrs. Grace, who we all assumed was a widow, has now become Mrs. Jack Volmer. Presuming we might never be rescued, she and Mr. Volmer exchanged vows right here on this beach. As man and wife, they have only recently learned she is… with child."

The captain's eyes went wide, and he looked at me. "Most surprising news indeed, madam!"

"As you can imagine," Jim continued, "Mr. Grace did not take the news lightly. No man could. He and Mr. Volmer resolved their differences with fists last night… But I'm afraid I am at a loss as to which marriage should be recognized. After so much time together here, I consider these people my family, and as family, I am inclined to recognize Jack as her husband. However, as their lord, I wonder if this type of favor over the other might reflect poorly on my character?"

"Indeed." The captain frowned, looking down at his bowl.

"And you have traveled with Mr. Grace for a year," Lilly added. "Your men know him and respect him. Might she be in danger if the men begin to notice a pregnancy that is not his?"

"The men shall not lay a hand on her, you've my word." He made eye contact with me. "This must be a most trying time for you, my dear."

I nodded.

He furrowed his brow. "Christopher cannot be expected to rear another man's child. It would be a stain upon his honor. While both men have a legitimate claim to her, given the child, I suppose her marriage to Mr. Volmer would hold precedence over the prior. If she has taken a new vow under the assumption Christopher was dead, those vows would nullify, in the eyes of God, the marriage between them. Her Grace shall have to authorize it since they are under her employ, but I cannot see how she could possibly remain married to one when she has exchanged vows before God with another."

"I will speak with my cousin," Lilly agreed, laying a hand on my shoulder. "Do you see? It's going to be alright. You haven't done anything wrong."

She looked back at the captain. "She's been very afraid of the judgement she might face for having married another. The guilt is eating away at her."

"Let your heart not be troubled." He smiled warmly. "You cannot be blamed after so long for believing him dead. No man could judge you for it."

"Speaking of judgement," Jim cleared his throat. "I've a confession to make to you, sir."

"Oh?" Captain Cook held a piece of bacon in front of his lips, too intrigued to move it any further. "Pray tell."

"I'm afraid Her Grace has been lying to you about our journey. She's done this out of our insistence she keep our true intentions for the voyage quiet."

The captain smiled. "She's not a very good liar, sir. I'm afraid we all found her explanation quite unbelievable."

Jim nodded. "I presumed so. She's never been very good at concealing the truth." He paused in thought for a moment, then continued. "You have met our daughter, Isobel?"

The captain nodded.

"And you are aware she's recently lost her hearing?"

"I've been informed of it, yes. My apologies, sir."

"Well, we weren't on that voyage to map the islands. We stole that story from you. We heard tales of your first trip all the way in Milan. When we learned of the advanced medicine Joseph Banks witnessed on the islands of Otaheite, my wife and I thought we might bring Isobel there, under cover of a scientific voyage much like your own, to inquire as to a remedy for her hearing. We've seen countless doctors and surgeons in Milan and have been unable to find any answers. We didn't want anyone to judge us or accuse us of seeking out ungodly medicine, so we begged our cousin to assist us in creating a cover. Her Grace was all too happy to get away from Parma."

"Since you are going to Otaheite," Lilly said softly, "I thought I might beg you to let us stay while you journey south. I wouldn't want to expose Isobel to that kind of cold, and perhaps we could find a cure for her lost hearing while we wait for your return? I realize it is out of the way for you to return to the islands, but I would be indebted to you for all my life if you would. In exchange, we would offer you the finest homes in both Milan and Parma for any time you wished to come and stay."

The captain's eyes lit up at that. "You are too generous, Lady Lillian." He pursed his lips as he weighed her offer. "I hadn't considered how dangerous it might be for a person so young as she to travel through such unforgiving conditions... but the men will be anxious to return to England after such a long journey... To return would add several more months to our expedition..."

He bit into his bacon, waiting until he was thoroughly finished chewing before he dabbed the corners of his lips with a kerchief and continued. "But I can see you have gone to great lengths and suffered a great deal in order to reach Otaheite. I shall speak with King Otou upon our arrival. If accommodations can be made, I shall do all that is within my power to assist, including adjusting course to return for you."

Lilly, a natural actress, fanned her watering eyes. "Thank you, Captain. You have no idea what this means to us."

"OYE!" Maria shouted from near the camp. "What the hell have you done to yourself?"

We all turned to find her standing before Chris, his face held tightly in her grip as she turned his head from one side to the other to inspect the damage.

"I suppose I should go and explain everything to my cousin," Lilly said, hopping up from her seat. "Thank you again, Captain."

She hurried up toward camp where Maria was becoming increasingly boisterous as she spouted off a trail of what sounded like Spanish obscenities. Tiny as she was, I was terrified of her... so was Chris, I presumed, by the expression on his battered face.

Jack had exited his own tent and joined the two before Lilly could make it there. Maria, a fraction of his size, released Chris's face to spin and face Jack, pushing him hard in the chest and knocking him back several steps, shouting several more Spanish words in the process.

"Her Grace is quite a lively specimen," the captain observed, grinning as he turned back to focus on his breakfast. "I daresay even I should be quite petrified to cross her."

"She's somethin,'" Jim agreed, letting his accent slip for only a second.

The captain seemed too invested in his bite of bread and jam to notice the slip. "This jam is exquisite. I must have your cook show mine his recipe!"

"I'm sure he would be delighted to." Jim picked up his own toast and took a bite, winking at me.

We finished our breakfast in silence as Lilly filled the others in on our conversation with the captain. For the first time since their ship had arrived on our shore, I felt my entire body relax. We'd pulled off the story, and we just might make it to Tahiti.

The relaxation was gone almost as quickly as it had come when we were ushered onto the ship in a frenzy of packed bags, rolled up tents, bedding, wine, whiskey, and crates filled with hogs and Kolea.

I stood on the stern with Lilly as the others worked out sleeping arrangements and pulled the anchor to set us on course.

My eyes watered and my throat grew heavy as I looked back at our island for the last time. Lilly slipped her hand into mine and squeezed.

The island had been our home for a year. It had fed us and taken care of us. It had guided us and given us family in each other. We both had fallen in love and I had a child inside of me because of that island. I couldn't help but cry as we slowly moved away from it.

"I'll never forget it," Lilly whispered.

"Me neither."

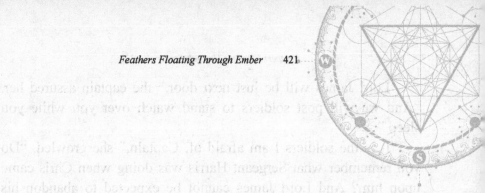

Chapter Forty

Chris

"He is my guard, is he not?" Maria spat hatefully to the captain. "And since his wife has taken a new husband, she cannot be expected to share a cabin with him. Whenever we are in camp, he has slept on a cot in my tent. What is the difference if he sleeps on a cot in my cabin?"

Chris stared at his feet, fidgeting on the deck of the ship as Maria argued over his placement in light of the news of Alaina's pregnancy. He could feel John's eyes on him as Maria insisted he sleep in her own cabin.

"Mightn't he be more comfortable on the lower deck with the soldiers, Your Grace?" John offered. "It would be frowned upon in such confined quarters for a man to share a room with a woman not his wife. It is much different than sharing a tent where there is no door."

"It's really no problem," Chris said. "I don't mind sleeping down there."

"Well, *I* do mind," she argued. "You and I both know Der Mutige is above sleeping down there with those men. He deserves a room. Besides, he is here to guard me. What happens if someone breaks into my room and he is on the lower deck? If I cry out, with no guard next door, who will come to assist me?"

"Lord James will be just next door," the captain assured her. "And we will post soldiers to stand watch over you while you sleep."

"It is the soldiers I am afraid of, Captain," she growled. "Do you remember what Sergeant Harris was doing when Chris came upon him? And Lord James cannot be expected to abandon his wife to look after me!"

"I'll stand guard," Chris said. "Just outside. That way no one can question my intentions and you will be safe."

"And I shall come to relieve him." John bowed to her. "So he may get some sleep through the night."

"Fine." She rolled her eyes and looked up at Chris. "Are you sure you are alright with this? I don't need to recognize their marriage if it makes you unhappy."

"I'm alright." He could see the lingering question in her eyes. "I promise. This is for the best."

"Okay then." She curtsied to the captain. "I think I would like to go and lie down for a while. Chris, come and help me unpack my things. I have some more questions about this marriage announcement. I will see you all at dinner."

The captain and John bowed and Maria led him down to her cabin, pulling him inside and closing the door.

"Mi amor." She shook her head, reaching up to lightly touch the gash on his eyebrow. "Are you sure you're alright with all this? I could have him killed, you know."

He huffed. "I've been so blind for so long when it comes to her. She's never going to love me the way she does him... and honestly, she never has. I don't know how I wasn't able to see it until now, but I can't unsee it. She's not the person I thought she was. Let him have her. I'm done hurting for it."

"Aye. Lo siento mucho, mi amor." She wrapped her arms around his waist and hugged him hard. "I'm so sorry. You deserve so much better. At least you messed up that pretty face of his more than he messed up yours."

He snickered. "At least there's that."

"Come and sit down." She let him go and motioned to the bed. "I want to hear all about the fight. Oh, wait." She spun away from him. "Untie me first. I have been stuck in this thing for more than twenty-four hours. We left Fetia on the ship yesterday!"

He smiled, loosening her stays until she was able to slide the corset off. She sighed audibly the moment she was free. He reached down to pick it up from the floor, inspecting the stiff interior. "I don't know how you do it. I can't imagine how uncomfortable this thing must be."

She plucked it from his grasp. "Do you want to try it?!" She grinned mischievously, holding it over his abdomen. "I bet it hurts worse than that eyebrow!"

"No, thanks." He sat down on the bed, wincing as it felt like someone had jammed a knife into his side.

"Oye, what's wrong?" She frowned.

"I'm fine. Just sore." He held his side and let out a long exhale.

"Let me see," she demanded, crossing her arms over her chest.

"I'm fine, Maria. It was just a fight. Nothing's broken."

She rolled her eyes and hopped into the bed beside him, scooting back on her bottom to rest her back against the headboard and cross her legs in front of her. "Tell me about the fight. Who started it?"

He turned to face her, his side burning as he did so. "I did."

"I knew it!" She tapped the spot beside her. "I'm not going to bite you. Come and relax, superman. Did it feel good to hit him?"

He kicked off his boots and very carefully slid back to sit beside her, their shoulders touching. He held up his swollen right hand, the knuckles all scabbed over. "It felt great at the time... Not so much anymore."

"¡Ay Dios mío!" She took his hand and turned it over, running her fingers along the scabs. "How hard did you hit that man?!"

"Pretty hard, I guess." He laughed, returning his hand to his lap. "It's hard to remember... One minute he was running his mouth, the next minute we were on the ground."

"But you let him win?" She looked up at him.

"He didn't win. Did you see his face?"

"No, I mean, you gave her to him. Isn't that what you were fighting for?"

He shook his head, laughing at the memory. "Actually, no... Strange as it sounds, it was *your* name on his lips that set me off."

"My name?" She raised an eyebrow. "What reason would that man have to say my name?"

He shrugged. "He was looking for a fight... When he couldn't get the reaction he wanted using her name, he thought he'd try yours. It worked."

"Hmmf." She laid her head against his shoulder. "My hero." She sighed. "What will you do now that you do not have a wife to search for?"

"Idunno... I guess I'll just start over somewhere... Who knows, maybe I'll join the navy and travel the world with Captain Cook."

"You're gonna stay in this time?"

He looked down at her. "Are you?"

"If I agree to marry John, I'll have to." She uncrossed her ankles and crossed them in the opposite direction.

"You haven't given him an answer yet?"

She frowned up at him. "No... But I can't very well turn down his marriage proposal when he has agreed to come back for us, can I? If I turn him down now and Johann doesn't find the way back, we could be stranded in Tahiti forever."

She grinned. "Although, then I might be freed up to marry the naked man with the giant pinga."

He laughed loudly as she bounced her eyebrows at him. "I thought you'd forgotten about him."

"Mi amor, no woman could ever forget about him." She laid her hand over his, curling her fingers into his. "Seriously, though... are you alright? You can talk to me. I know this is hurting you."

He squeezed her hand and caved at the opportunity to talk. "It hurts like hell. All this time... like I was living a lie. Last night, I tried to think of a single instance where she went out of her way to make me feel appreciated the way I did her... I tried to remember if she'd saved something sentimental or surprised me with some romantic gesture. I couldn't come up with a single thing. And as much as I want to be angry at her for it, I'm more angry at myself."

He stretched out his legs. "She didn't go out of her way because she never felt that strongly about me. Sure, she loved me, but not passionately... She loved me the way you love a family member, you know? And maybe she never realized there was more to it than that, but I knew there was because I felt it for her... or at least, I felt it for the person I thought she was. I never knew my own wife... I'm an idiot for thinking I did."

"You're not an idiot, Kreese. Not for that, anyway." She ran the fingers of her free hand over his swollen knuckles. "You are an idiot for lots of other things, though. Will you fight him again?"

"No." He laughed. "Once was enough."

"Good." She grinned up at him. "Because you look like shit."

"I feel like shit."

"I know. Come on." She tugged him toward her. "Lay down for a bit with me."

He looked toward the door. "But what if—"

"Pshh," she scoffed. "No one's coming in here. Lay down and I will hold on to you the way you have done for me when I am hurt. Oye, but I will only do this for you this once. You are allowed to fall apart for the next few hours, but then you will be the man I know so well and you will pull yourself back together when we get up. Understand?"

"Understood."

"Good." She smiled, pulling him with her to lie down as she wrapped her arms around his neck and coddled him, softly stroking his hair. "No one should ever have to feel this way." She scratched softly at the base of his skull. "You sulk all you want now."

He smiled as she softly kissed the top of his head. "It's a good spot to sulk in." He playfully rubbed his cheek against her breast.

"Oh, are you comfortable, pervertido?" She joked, smoothing her palm down the nape of his neck and back up. "Don't get any ideas. I am no man's second best."

Chris frowned, pulling himself back to look at her. "You know that's not—

"Your Grace?" John called from outside the door. "Might I have a quick word?"

She groaned, leaning in to whisper. "Can we not have five minutes in this stupid place without someone coming to interrupt?! Hide. Under the bed."

"Just a moment," she called as Chris eased out of the bed. "I've taken off my stays and need to find a robe!"

He slid awkwardly beneath the bed, his legs too long to fit without angling them at a very uncomfortable position. His insides boiled as he forced them into the confined space.

She quickly adjusted the bed skirt to keep him concealed, then he heard the door open.

"What is it?" She asked.

"May I come in?"

"Be alone with a man behind a *door*?" She smirked. "Would that not be frowned upon?"

"Maria, please," he whispered, but even then, his voice was full of desperation. "Why do you insist on keeping me in such a state of torture? I must have an answer. I simply cannot go on with this plan, risking my title, my honor, my life, without some sign you would have me."

"John," her voice shook as their footsteps moved into the room, "let go."

Just as Chris prepared to launch himself out from beneath the bed to defend her, John's voice softened. "I'm sorry. But I don't understand you. One minute, you are mad about me, and the next, you are a stranger... You haven't even looked at me since we found the others. Do you not love me anymore? Is there history with one of the men from the island I should know about?"

"No," she said sweetly. "Of course not."

"No?" His voice shook. "You lie about so many other things... how should I know when to believe you? How could I know I am not risking everything for a woman who is only toying with me?"

"John, I do not give you an answer because I am not the type of woman to *toy* with a man. Marriage is forever. I want to be sure the forever I would have here with you is the one that would make me happy. I would not just be agreeing to become your wife, I would be agreeing to leave everything I know. I would change everything. And if I would not be happy, then you would not be happy... I cannot say yes if there is a chance I could make you miserable."

"Kiss me then. Kiss me the way you did that morning in Queen Charlotte Sound. Make me believe none of this is a lie."

Chris could feel his body tense. The image of her lips on his that morning drove a fresh knife into his heart that hurt ten times more than the one Alaina had placed there the day before.

"I will not kiss any man who demands me to. I will do nothing to prove I am telling the truth," she huffed. "If you cannot trust me, then why would you marry me?"

"I love you." There was a shuffling of her skirts as they moved closer, her feet at the very edge of the bed. "I am bewitched entirely, jealous of every man who your eyes land upon that is not me. You are driving me mad, and I cannot go on with this charade without my answer."

"Oye, what are you trying to say? That I owe you this because you are helping us?"

"I didn't say that."

"But you are implying it." She stomped. "What if my answer is no?"

"Is it?"

"I did not say that. But what if it was?"

"Then I would be sacrificing my entire life for nothing."

She blew out. "So you *are* saying I owe this to you."

Again there was a shuffling of her skirts and he felt the mattress above him dip as John's voice grew more demanding. "I am saying I have been patient long enough. I am telling you I love you and I will not be made a fool of. I am begging you, yes or no, Maria."

"You're scaring me," she said softly. "You have never acted like this before. Is this what marriage to you would be like? Kreese will be here soon to stand guard. What would he say if he found you like this?"

"Chris," John echoed, his tone heavy with contempt as the weight on the mattress lightened while he turned to pace the room. "Is it him? Now that his wife has run off with another, are you attempting to decipher whether or not you could fit into her place? Is that why you refrain from giving me an answer? Do you keep me as an alternative should your desire for him prove unreciprocated?"

"No! He is my friend! He is your friend too. Have you forgotten?"

"I haven't forgotten... Nor have I forgotten finding you in his bed that morning he was arrested. What were you doing there?"

She growled. "John, I told you, I was scared. When I got scared on the island, he was there to hold on to me. I can't begin to explain the type of friendship that develops from being stranded like we were. Being close like that... there was nothing wrong with it. He was married, and he held me out of necessity, not out of wanting. We kept each other warm, comforted each other when we were sad or lonely. He has never done anything to imply there was more to it. He is only my *friend*."

Chris could feel his pulse quickening. He'd never done anything to give her that impression, but he'd felt it. All along, he'd wanted her, and John knew it too. Was John becoming more insistent on an answer because of this knowledge?

Even when he'd been kissing his wife, he'd fought with his desire for Maria in the back of his mind. Now, with John all but forcing himself upon her, he wanted to scream. He wanted to burst out of his hiding place and expose himself for what he was.

"How am I to know what to think?" John asked. "You've given me no indication you feel any certain way about me. You've barely spoken to me these last few weeks. If you are indeed attempting to determine whether or not you could be happy before giving me an answer, should you not want to spend as much time by my side as possible?"

"You're right." She stood from the bed. "I *should* be spending more time with you. I've been so caught up in forming this story... and then I was worried about Kreese after his wife rejected him.

He's a very dramatic man. I had to make sure he wouldn't throw himself into the ocean. I have let myself become too distracted from what matters. Come and help me put on my stays. We'll call for tea and sit together on the deck. I will devote the rest of our time together to getting to know this life with you, and I promise to give you an answer before you leave Tahiti."

He could hear their movement as she gathered her stays from the floor. He could hear the dropping of her robe and the effort of John's attempt to secure the corset around her.

"I'm sorry," John said quietly, "if I have been too forward. I did not mean to frighten you."

"I am not afraid of you, John." She grunted as her stays were pulled tight. "I do not want to keep you waiting... But I have seen what an unhappy woman can do to a man. And I will not be that to anyone."

"I could go with you... to the future... if you couldn't be happy here."

She laughed out loud at that. "No. I could surely never make you happy there!" She shuffled around quickly.

"What are you looking for?"

"My pockets... they must've come untied..."

Chris stiffened as he felt the little strips of fabric beneath his forearm.

She sighed. "Ah well. I guess I don't *need* them for tea. Come on. Let's get some air."

He listened as the door opened and closed, their footsteps growing quiet as they disappeared down the hall.

He slid out from underneath the bed, dragging the fabric of her pockets with him. He winced as he rose up on his knees, cursing himself for deciding on a second fight the night before. His head was pulsing.

As he lifted the pockets to place them on her bed, a small round object fell from one, clanking and rattling loudly as it rolled and spun on the floorboards. He froze, staring at the partially open door for signs of anyone coming to check on the noise.

After a few minutes with no indication anyone had heard the raucous, he reached down to grab the object and place it back into her pocket, when the lettering on its surface caught his eye.

Engraved in a circle around the small brass button were the words *'Dunning Jean Co.'* and he laughed to himself at the gesture. It was the button from the jeans he'd given her their first night on the island. Mortified after the events of that night, she'd thrown the jeans into the ocean so he could never see them, but even then, after less than twenty-four hours, she'd valued the moment enough to keep the button. Now she carried it with her in her pocket.

What did that mean? He wondered, depositing the pockets onto the bed as he rose and stared at the button between his fingers. Was she in fact waiting to give John an answer because she held onto feelings for him? Could it be possible that while he was fighting to hide his own love for her, she was doing the same? Was she waiting for him to get over Alaina to see if she indeed could stand in her place? He tucked the button into his pocket and hurried out the door.

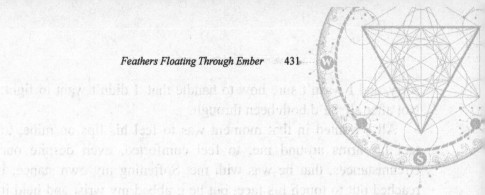

Chapter Forty One

Alaina

Jack closed the door to our cabin, slowly turning to face me. We hadn't spoken since early that morning. With all the hustle to load up the ship and then the ensuing argument about sleeping arrangements followed by the explanation to the soldiers as to why we needed to make said arrangements, we hadn't had a single opportunity to be alone until that moment.

He stood before me, his hands balled into fists and his chest moving beneath his button-up shirt with visible effort to keep steady. Where the others had changed into clothing that suited the century, Jack remained in his navy shirt and jeans.

"The decision is made then?" he asked, an unrecognizable evenness in his tone that made me wonder if he was somehow angry with me.

Angry with me? For what? I was the one that was allowed to be angry in that moment. Wasn't I?

I raised my chin and crossed my arms over my chest. "Why didn't you tell me about the bathroom? And what were you thinking going off and fighting him like that?"

"Is the decision made?" he repeated.

I swallowed, recognizing in his stance that he was, in fact, angry. I hadn't been prepared for anger. I was expecting him to be sorry; to come in and apologize profusely, but I saw he wasn't sorry, and I wasn't sure how to handle that. I didn't want to fight. Not after all we'd both been through.

All I wanted in that moment was to feel his lips on mine, to feel his arms around me, to feel comforted, even despite our circumstances, that he was with me. Softening my own stance, I reached out to touch his face, but he grabbed my wrist and held it there.

"Is it me that you want or him?"

I frowned, my heart beating in my throat as his grip tightened. "There was never a decision to make, Jack. It was always going to be you."

He moved closer then, his other hand sliding up my cheek to tilt my face up toward him. His eyes were swollen and tired. "Does he know that? Did you tell him?"

"He knows," I said.

"But did you tell him?" He asked, his expression softening a little.

"He heard us yesterday. He knows I'm in love with you and not him."

"And last night, when you walked away with him, it was *I that knew* you were in love with him and not me. Did you know what that did to me? To watch you leave with *him*?"

I could see it was not anger, but hurt that was causing his shoulders to stiffen and his breathing heavier. I'd hurt him, and I wanted to crumble as I watched him fight with the tears inside him.

"You cannot tell me you choose me and then run to him if we fight. If the decision is made, it is final. If you tell me you want me, you cannot change your mind tomorrow. I realize this is not an easy decision to make, and I would never force you to make it if you weren't ready. But I'm begging you, if you are indecisive in any way, do not tell me what I want to hear now, then run to tell him the same later. It won't prevent either of us from getting hurt. I would rather you say nothing than say it is me if you are unsure."

"It's you," I blurted. "Of course it is you. I'm so sorry." My eyes stung from the tears that rapidly filled them. I felt ashamed at my lack of empathy for him; ashamed for letting him think I would ever let him go; for walking away, knowing full well I had left him there to think I had chosen Chris. "I was angry, and I wasn't thinking. It's you. It will always be you."

His shoulders relaxed and he let go of my wrist, keeping my face cupped in his hand as his other slid around my back to pull me closer.

"You never hurt me like that before. After everything we've been through; everything I did to get back to you, to see you leave with him... Red, it broke me."

The fingers at my back began to untie the laces of the corset top. "If you are angry with me, you will stay and fight with me. We will not ever leave each other feeling abandoned. If you are mine," he pulled the corset loose, tossing it onto the floor, "you are mine. And you'll never let me doubt that again, as I will never let you. If you tell me now the decision is final, you cannot take that back."

"It's final," I breathed, standing on my toes to attempt to kiss him.

He wound his fingers into my hair, pulling my head back softly before I could, and he spoke against my exposed skin. "I'm not a jealous man, Alaina, but I couldn't bear the thought of what might be happening in that tent... I wanted to hurt him last night... to give him a glimpse of the pain he'd caused me." He pulled my hair tighter, his breath hot against the skin at my throat. "Wanted him to hurt me to erase the pain *you'd* caused me when you walked away."

I curled my arms around him as he arched me back further. "I have done things..." he whispered, forcing a shiver down my entire body as his lips grazed the sensitive skin. "Things I'd never imagined myself capable of... But Christ, I'd do them all over if I had to just to have you in my arms."

He aid teasing kisses along the nape of my neck. "Promise me, no matter how angry you are, you will stay and fight with me before you'll ever walk away again."

"I promise," I managed, my entire body trembling in his grasp. "I'll never be so stupid again, I swear."

He turned us then and my back hit the door as his mouth came down fervently on the skin at my neck, forcing me to gasp and grab onto him. His body pressed against mine, he slid a palm up my thigh, dragging the fabric of the skirt up with it.

"I love you," he breathed, his mouth hovering over mine, "and so help me God, I'll never leave you again."

He covered my lips with his, pushing them open with a demanding possession that rendered me powerless, commanding my mouth to submit to his will. I curled my fingers into his hair, urging him closer as his lips moved with more ferocity; as his fingers grasped at the skin on my outer thigh, urging my legs apart so his body could mold against mine.

I was putty beneath him, and my fingers quickly worked the buttons of his shirt until it hung open and I could slide my palms over the expanse of his chest, anxious to feel his skin against my own.

His hands left me only long enough to shrug the shirt off his shoulders before returning to push the shift up to my neck so he could pull my exposed body tightly against his and feel the desperation surging through him.

He pulled me off my feet, wrapping my legs around him as he carried me to the bed, lying me on my back as he removed his jeans.

There would be no teasing, and no additional play. It wasn't needed, and neither of us had the patience for it in that moment. We both knew it, and I cried out in complete ecstatic relief as he pushed himself inside me.

He held there for a moment, his eyes meeting mine, and I saw all the pain that was behind them melt away just before he pressed his lips back to mine.

In that moment, there was a profound understanding that came over me. It wasn't a conscious thought, but more just a knowing that I would never be the same woman again. I would never hurt this man again. I would do anything, go anywhere, and be whatever he wanted me to. I would be the type of woman who takes care of a man, not the woman who waited to be taken care of.

I wrapped my arms tightly around him as he moved more steadily.

This man was everything, and I would be better for him. He made me feel like a woman, and I, in turn, would make him know the man he was to me.

Our bodies trembling, he held me tighter, pulling me against him as we both found our climax.

He collapsed at the side of me, and I rolled into his side, clinging to him for fear that the wholeness I felt might somehow escape if I let go.

As I ran my palm over his chest, I felt the multiple gashes that covered his upper body. I raised up on my forearms over him and gasped as I inspected the markings covering his chest and ribs, blue and black bruises with long deep cuts covering his skin.

"Jesus Jack. Why didn't you tell me you were hurt this bad? Chris did this??"

"Those aren't *all* from him." He winced as I touched a spot near his shoulder. "Escaping that island wasn't without its costs."

I pressed on his ribs and his face distorted with the effort of hiding the pain it caused him. "And you thought it'd be a good idea to add more injury by fighting? Some of these cuts are deep. Have you had Anna look at you?"

He shook his head, sliding his palms along each of my cheeks. "There was only one person I needed to see when I got off that boat." He combed the hair from my face. "And it has all been worth it to be here with you now."

The cuts had scabbed over and it was too late for stitches, but they looked painful and infected, and the bruising was dark and widespread. I shook my head. "This looks really bad. I can go get Anna... have her just look really quick—

"Tomorrow," he said, covering my hand with his own to stop it from exploring further. "I've waited too long for this moment."

I stared down at him with a new sense of appreciation for him. He was such a strong man that it was easy for me to forget he could be hurt just as easily as the rest of us. And he had been hurt. He'd been hurt physically and then I'd hurt him even worse. He'd killed someone to be here, and as he'd told that story, I could see it had weighed heavily on him. I should've run to him the moment I saw him. I should've never let him feel anything but my relief he was there. Should've asked him immediately about everything instead of making things about me.

"Tell me about that island... about what happened."

He shook his head, smoothing his thumb over my lips. "Not now." He smiled as he wrapped my hair around his finger. "Tell me about the baby." He frowned. "I didn't hurt it, did I?"

I laughed. "No. The baby is fine. He's been moving around more and more. I think maybe I'm further along than we thought. It's more movement than it should be for nineteen weeks... At least, from what I remember."

"If you are, he'll *definitely* be here before September." He watched his fingers as they moved over my collarbone. "If Johann is right... We will have been missing for a year and a half by the time September rolls around. For a commercial airliner to just disappear... Well, they will have been searching nonstop for us. Whoever goes back is going to be in the spotlight... There'll be questions. It's not like others can just show up afterwards. Whoever goes, goes. Whoever stays..."

"Stays," I whispered, kissing his knuckles as they swept over my lips.

"Red, I can't willingly put either of your lives at risk. We lost so many before... And Zachary lost a whole crew... What if we stayed here? Do you think we could build a life in this time?"

I considered it for a moment. "If he got sick... or if one of us got sick... In our time, we'd have money, access to medicine, family... I could work there and so could you..." I sighed. "But if staying here means all of us stay alive and together... we could find a way to make it work. If you think we should stay, I'll stay. If you think we should go, I'll go. I trust you, and I will follow you anywhere..." I grinned. "We could always sacrifice Phil if we need a sacrifice."

He bit his lip as his eyes met mine. "I'm so sorry... I never meant for you to have to see his face again." He frowned, shaking his head. "But the things they would've done to him on that island... As much as I hate the man, I couldn't bring myself to leave him. We can keep him away from you—lock him up somewhere in Tahiti once Captain Cook leaves."

I smiled, running my fingers over his cheek. "You're a good man, and I trust whatever decisions you make to be the right ones. I'm not afraid of him. I'm not afraid of anything when I'm with you."

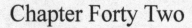

Chapter Forty Two

Alaina

It was a strange thing to be living as a maid on an 18th century ship. For the most part, I was ignored. I got the impression that, after finding out I was married to Jack, the ship's inhabitants wanted little to do with me or him.

They loved Chris, and even though the captain had recognized our fake marriage as legitimate, the soldiers and crew still viewed us as having betrayed him.

We were allowed to roam the ship freely, but after several weeks of side-eye glances and non-discreet whispering as we passed by, I preferred the privacy of the cabin below deck.

The cabin was far too small to accommodate more than two people, so we didn't see our island family all that often.

Lilly, Izzy, and Jim were always invited to join the captain for tea, breakfast, dinner, or drinks in the great cabin. Chris, Maria, Johann, and the lieutenant were also part of the captain's primary party, so we would go days without seeing many of them.

Anna came to our cabin daily to check on me, and Bruce found his place immediately alongside the ship's cook.

We'd been informed there was coffee onboard; a detail Jim nearly jumped out of his skin for. After being served the thick mucky drink they'd *called* coffee, Bruce volunteered to make his own brew in the mornings. Bud, Bruce, Jack, and Jim then made a ritual out of meeting on the top deck for coffee in the early mornings. Lilly, not a coffee drinker herself, took the early morning opportunities to come down and visit me.

Michael and Kyle, being so close in age, had formed a friendship right away and spent a lot of time on deck, always quick to volunteer to help with the various duties on the ship. Kyle avoided Phil entirely, as did we all, and when they were not helping on deck, they were both quite taken with Lieutenant John Edgecumbe. He and Chris were all too happy to offer both Kyle and Michael lessons in swordplay during their downtime.

I'd watched them a few times as they sparred on deck, but it was difficult to see Chris as a stranger. He avoided me; wouldn't even make eye contact with me most days. I understood why, and I wouldn't push for him to accept me as his friend, but it hurt nonetheless.

I'd loved him once, and we'd been so close for so long it was a sort of torture to see him from the outside and not be able to talk to him the way I once had. To see him and not know how he was, what he was feeling, or share any given thought we'd once shared so freely would always leave me with a sense of loneliness.

I knew Jack was where I belonged, but there was a place in my heart that had been momentarily filled with the knowledge Chris was alive, and that place was empty again.

Where Chris avoided me, Maria seemed more and more interested in me. Since I was technically her maid, she wasted no time in summoning me to come and dress her in the mornings, then undress her in the evenings.

Jack hadn't been a fan of it, but I appreciated having something to do, and I was intrigued by her. She was fascinating in so many ways; the way she spoke her mind without pause; the way she commanded people by simply looking at them. Adding all her allure with her interest in Chris, I couldn't wait to get to her cabin to learn more about her.

She wasn't a person to beat around the bush. She would ask direct questions about my life, the pregnancy, our time on the island, Jack, and more often than not, Chris. Her forward manner was infectious, and I found myself in turn asking openly about her life, her experiences leading up to our rescue, John Edgecumbe, and more often than not, Chris.

I tapped on her door that morning, yawning. I had been dreaming about ice when I'd been summoned, and I found myself longing to get back to the dream just to satisfy the craving.

My pregnancy cravings were torture. I craved 21st century things I could never have access to in this time. I needed the distraction of Maria to pull my mind from ice, potato chips, and chocolate cake.

She pulled the door open, smiling uncharacteristically. She was not normally cheerful in the mornings.

"¡Buenos dias!" She grabbed my hand and pulled me into her room, the rising sun shining bright orange through her window and forcing me to blink the sleep from my eyes.

"Eat." She motioned to a tray of food and tea beneath the window as she sat down on the edge of the bed. "I called for some bread and jam for you. You are too skinny for a pregnant woman."

There was something about the way she watched me that made me nervous. I, of course, knew she wasn't a duchess and I wasn't a servant, but playing those roles left an impression of unequal hierarchy between us. My stomach growled in response as I shook my head. "I don't want to take your food. I can eat breakfast downstairs with the others."

She clicked her tongue and leaned back on the bed. "You can eat *more than one* breakfast, Flaca. I will eat with the captain. Take it and sit down. I can see you are hungry. Besides, it is rude to turn down food from a Latin person."

Hesitantly, I took the plate of bread and jam from the tray. She patted the bed next to her, insisting I sit. As I did, she lightly tugged on a piece of my hair. "Hair for days." She smiled. "That's how he described you… and it is accurate. Look at all this hair."

"How is he?" I asked, taking a bite and closing my eyes as the guava jam awakened my tastebuds.

"He is fine." She swung her foot casually where it hung off the bed. "His mind is always going. He wants to bring Hitihiti and

Magna in here tonight for a secret meeting. We are getting closer to Tahiti and he wants to make sure they have their backstory straight before we get there. He's been spending more time with Hitihiti. He thinks the people there will be more welcoming of our stay if he offers to help build houses with them. They're very interested in building things."

"That's smart," I said with my mouth full, waiting until I'd swallowed to continue. "He's very good at it but, I meant... How is he... with everything?"

"Oh." She stopped swinging her leg and frowned. "He doesn't talk about it. I think he is keeping his mind busy with other things. You know?"

I nodded, sighing. Chris always tended to find things to distract him from dealing with difficult situations.

Maria straightened. "I can tell you care for him... The way you ask about him all the time. Are you doubting you made the right choice?"

I shook my head. "No... It's just, well, he was such a big part of my life... And I just... I care about him and want to make sure he's going to be alright."

"Such a martyr you are," she teased. "Flaca, you are not the last woman he will ever love. He'll be fine. You hurt him. We all hurt each other. And we all heal and live better lives for it. Stop thinking he is defeated. It will take much more than you to defeat a man like Kreese."

Feeling more brazen than normal with food in my belly, I decided to contend with her that morning. "Me, a martyr? And what about you?"

"What about *me*?" She snapped back defensively, her scowl throwing a wrench in my newfound bravery.

"I just meant... well..." I looked at her then, raising my eyebrow. "It's obvious who *you* want. Are you not making yourself a martyr by choosing the lieutenant instead?"

She looked up at the ceiling. "¡Ay Dios mío! Who is this woman sitting in my bed thinking she knows everything now?" She huffed. "You don't know anything, mi amiga. What kind of woman would I be, eh? To chase after a man who has been chasing after someone else all this time? Like I am what? The leftovers? No gracias. I will take the one that wants me, thank you."

"Oh, come on Maria," I blurted. "Don't act like you don't see it. Of course he wants you. He chased me out of obligation and avoided you out of love. I saw it right away. I know you're not stupid, so don't act like you don't see it too."

She stood up from the bed, crossing her arms over her chest. "Are you done eating yet?" She spun around to look at herself in the vanity. "I don't have time to be talking this nonsense with you. I need to get dressed."

I laughed, biting into my toast. "No. I'm not. What's the matter? Uncomfortable?"

She groaned, pulling her dark hair to one side in the mirror. "I never thought I would miss Fetia. Maybe I should call for her to come and dress me instead. You talk too much now."

"So you can ask me all the questions you want, but I can't ask you direct questions in return?"

She turned slowly around. "Not that question."

"Why not?"

"Because you cannot begin to understand the answer."

"Try me." I smiled.

"Okay fine." She flipped her hair behind her shoulder. "Let's say I turn down John's proposal to chase after Kreese, and John sails off with the captain... What reason would he have to come back for us? Eh? Why would he ever help us again after I had strung him along for so long? And if he did not return and Johann is wrong... What would that do to that poor woman who wants to get to her son? Or that little deaf girl who probably has family somewhere looking for her?"

She shook her head. "No. I cannot take the chance of ruining this for her... For Kreese... for all of us. I do not have the luxury of choosing the one I want like you did. I *have* to choose John. For all of us. It doesn't matter what I want. You all want to go home. Who am I to take that from any of you by acting selfishly?"

I cleared my throat. "Martyr."

"Ay, sí. I am the martyr because I am thinking about more than just myself... Do you see? You are too full of yourself to understand the answer. You cannot relate to it because *you* could never do it."

I set the plate down on the bed, frowning. "I am not full of myself. I don't even like myself most of the time."

She laughed. "Oh, honey, you don't have to like yourself to be self-centered. You are living the Alaina show and we are all just extras. Your life is the main story line and you don't see what the extras do in it."

"That's not true," I argued, "you don't even know me." I stood from the bed, feeling her words sting. "How can you say that?"

"I know enough about you."

She took a deep breath, adjusting her tone. "I am too blunt. I don't mean it as offensive. Many people live this way and they live happy lives in their main story line... I'm not saying I don't like you for it. I envy you for it. I wish I could live this way sometimes. If I had even a hint of self importance, I would've taken him for my own a year ago on that island, wife be damned."

My eyes watered then, and I felt my nostrils burn. I sat back down on the bed, unable to remain standing as I played out a lifetime of memories to determine whether or not there was truth to her judgement.

"I'm sorry." She clicked her tongue, kneeling down to take my hand in hers. "I do not know how to talk to women. I call you here so you will be my friend and then I say mean words to you. Please don't cry. I'm sorry. I shouldn't say those things."

"No, you're right," I admitted, aggravated with myself that even my tears seemed conceited. "I have been living the Alaina show my whole life... I've never even noticed."

She smiled, squeezing my hand. "If that's not who you want to be, the beautiful thing about this life is you can change yourself anytime you want."

She tugged on my arm. "Come. Stop crying now because I cannot stand that I have made a pregnant woman cry. You are a good person, I can tell. If you weren't, there'd be no reason for all of us, even me, to want a part in the Alaina show. Besides, that baby will become the new star of the show the instant it shows up here, and we will all volunteer to be its extras, showering it with every bit of love we have. Come on." She pulled me up onto my feet and motioned to the stool at her vanity. "Sit down here and I will braid your hair. Okay?"

I nodded, taking a deep breath as she forced me to sit down at the vanity. I looked up at her reflection. "I didn't mean for the conversation to go that way. I just... I really want to see Chris happy, you know? He deserves that."

She mindlessly began brushing my hair back from my temples. "He does deserve happiness. If I could, I would give everything I had to make him happy. I have never in my—

She stopped brushing and raised an eyebrow at my reflection. "Oye, have you seen a little brass button anywhere? I have been looking all over for it. I must have dropped it somewhere... unless maybe you grabbed it?"

"Woah woah woah... you can't just switch the subject mid-sentence like that. You *have never in your* what?"

"Did you grab it?" she repeated, scowling in the mirror.

"No. I haven't seen anything. Seriously, what were you about to say?"

"It was in my pockets... It must've fallen out when we took them off..." She proceeded to divide my hair into sections, avoiding eye contact with my reflection.

"I have looked everywhere in here. It is too big to go through the floorboards, I think. Fetia doesn't have it... and if you don't have it... The only other person who has been in here is..." She narrowed her eyes as a realization washed over her. "Nevermind... I know where it is."

She began pulling the hair at my temples up into a high braid. "How do you live with all this hair? It is too much, no?"

"How do *you* manage to change the subject every time the subject is about you?"

She grinned at me in the mirror. "You are very much like him, you know that? The questions you ask and the things you notice… You must miss him after being together so long."

"This isn't my show anymore, remember? You were about to say something meaningful before you went off about a button and my hair."

"You're too pushy. You must not have many girlfriends either, eh?"

I could feel myself inherently wanting to go off topic to talk about myself. She'd been right. I'd been caught up in my own story for far too long. It was amazing to me that someone who'd known me for so short a time could deliver me such a hard lesson about myself. I refused to let myself be deterred and only stared patiently at her reflection in anticipation of an answer.

She raised her chin. "It isn't natural for you and I to talk about him like that. It's weird."

"Why else would you want to be friends with *me*? As far as I can tell, he is the single thing we have in common. Of course you wanted someone to talk to about it with… You chose to befriend me for that very reason. I'm not stupid either, Maria. You wanted someone to talk to and I'm here. So talk."

She rolled her eyes, focusing on the braid as she worked down the back of my head. "I am regretting that decision now."

I watched as she worked it over in her mind, then ultimately resigned as her shoulders eased a little. "Fine… I was just going to say that… I have never known anyone like him… Never felt the way I feel about him for any person in my life. I want him to be happy too… I wish more than anything in this world it was me that could be the person to give that to him."

I pursed my lips in thought. "No one should be forced to marry out of obligation. Especially when you want someone else. It's not fair for you to carry this all on your shoulders. There's got to be something else we can do."

She huffed. "Like what?"

"Before we found out we were back in time, we used to talk about how much money we would have when we got off the island... We would never need to work again after we sued the airline, you know? And if we find a way back... that means we should be able to return... what if there was a promise of money? *Lots* of it."

"How would you bring money to this time? You know how much those old coins cost? Just to get a dollar's worth, you'd spend a fortune." She shook her head. "No, that won't work."

"Gold," I suggested. "We'll buy gold and bring it here. I'm pretty sure gold is just as valuable in this time as it is in ours. You wouldn't have to turn him down yet... Lilly could talk to him about the gold... Get a feel for whether or not that might be enough. And if it is... you would be free to be with whoever you wanted."

She kept her eyes on her fingers as she wound the braid up and pinned it into a bun on my head. "Maybe," she said softly.

"Maybe... as in yes, I should talk to Lilly?"

She nodded. "Okay... I think yes."

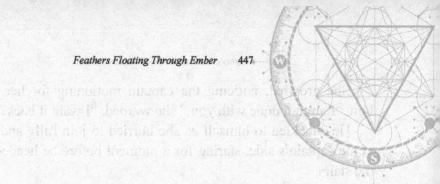

Chapter Forty Three

Chris

"Do you hate her now?" Kyle asked. He was seated beside Chris on the deck's rail eating an apple as Alaina, Maria, and Lilly emerged from below.

Chris sighed. "No, I don't hate her." He placed a hand on Kyle's head and messed his hair as he hopped off the rail, chucking his own finished apple into the ocean. "Come on, we've got leaks to fix in the hull this morning."

Chris had taken a liking to Kyle. The boy was unhindered by his handicap, determined to be as capable as any other boy his age to handle a sword and perform the required duties of a sailor, despite having only one arm with which to do them. He could tell Kyle instantly had chosen him as a mentor and it gave him a sense of pride to be someone a kid as willful as he could look up to.

Kyle followed behind him as he avoided eye contact with Alaina when they passed the three women on their way to the stairs. Maria, trailing behind the other two, grabbed Chris's forearm and stopped him in his tracks.

"Did you take something of mine?" She hissed.

He hid a smile as he looked down at her. "Something of *yours*?"

"You did take it, didn't you?" Her eyes narrowed.

"Take what?" he teased.

She growled, noticing the captain motioning for her to join him. "I am not done with you," she warned. "I want it back."

He chuckled to himself as she hurried to join Lilly and Alaina at the captain's side, staring for a moment before he headed down the stairs.

"You don't look at her," Kyle said, pulling him from his amusement to bring him back to their previous conversation. "If you don't hate her, why don't you look at her?"

Chris shrugged. "I just need some time."

"A year wasn't enough time?" he asked, his low teenage voice cracking.

Chris shook his head. "When a woman hurts your pride, it's hard to look at her and still feel like a man. You'll understand that someday."

"You think?" he asked, motioning to his missing arm.

Chris placed a hand on his shoulder as they descended the last set of stairs. "It's just an arm. The arm is not who you are and you know that. Women will notice the man who is unaffected by it. Fetia, for instance... I have caught her noticing you on more than one occasion. Yes, I absolutely think you'll have plenty of opportunities to have your heart broken."

Kyle leaned in, glancing around them scandalously. "Did you know Michael is younger than me and he's already had sex with four women? Four!"

"Four?!" Chris couldn't help the surprise in his voice. "He looks like he's twelve!"

"He's fifteen."

"Four women..." Chris repeated incredulously as he trudged through the inch of water to the ship's hull, grabbing two rolls of oakum from a basket and handing one to Kyle before he lit the oil lantern that hung on one wall. "I was lucky to get to first base at fifteen!"

He watched proudly as Kyle positioned the roll beneath the armpit of his wounded arm, tearing a chunk of the thin fibers from it to place into a small crack in the wood. "Was it weird... the first time?"

Chris grinned, pulling a wad of oakum from his own roll to place into a small gap where a beam of sunlight was shining into the dark space. "Everyone's first time is weird. Don't stress out about it. You've got plenty of time to master it throughout your life."

As he'd said the words, he was reminded of his previous stay in Tahiti and wondered if Kyle might find out first-hand sooner than later with so much promiscuousness in the native culture there. "How old are you, anyway?"

"Sixteen," he said. "Almost seventeen."

He remembered his own sixteen-year-old self combing the mall for girls and thinking almost round the clock about the possibilities of sex. He couldn't imagine being that age and being stranded on an island, losing a limb, and then being stuck on an old wooden ship in a time other than his own. The fact that Kyle still maintained his optimism was beyond impressive.

"You look at Maria," Kyle poked, his eyes focused on his work.

"So? I look at lots of people," Chris responded, pulling a wooden wedge from the basket to use to fill a larger crack.

"You don't look at them like you look at her." He bounced his dusty blonde eyebrows. "I mean... why wouldn't you? She's *smokin'* hot... I think she likes you."

"You think?" Chris hid a smile. "I think I annoy her... at least, I try to anyway."

"Ay!" Jim called from behind them. "I thought I heard yuns down here. Mind if I join ye' fer a bit?"

Kyle turned toward the voice. "What are *you* doing down here?"

"Hidin.'" Jim grinned, pulling a lit cigarette from behind his back. "...and smokin.' Lordt help me, Princess would kill me if she caught me doin' it, but I needed one after all this. I tell ye,' half the time I don't know whether to check my ass or scratch my watch, I'm so caught up in these damn lies. And the accent, Christ almighty, it ain't natural to talk like 'at all damn day. My dang tongue hurts."

He took a drag, closing his eyes as he inhaled deeply and stifling a cough as he blew out. "What you two doin?"

"Fixing cracks in the hull," Kyle informed him, glancing up at Chris. "And hiding too."

Jim inspected Chris, offering him the cigarette. "For good reason, I suspect. How ye' holdin' up, Beanstalk?"

Chris took the cigarette—he hadn't had one since he was in his twenties—and heedlessly inhaled it, instantly choking on the rancid smoke as it entered his lungs. He handed it back to Jim and bent over in a coughing fit.

Jim smacked the center of his back a few times. "'Ain't fer everyone. Take 'at as a lesson in life, Kyle. Don't touch these things. They'll kill ye.'"

Chris inhaled carefully as he straightened, exhaling a sigh of relief to find his lungs clear again.

Kyle pulled a piece of oakum from his roll, bunching it between his fingers. "Have you seen my dad at all?"

Jim balanced the cigarette between his lips, taking a roll of oakum for himself and inspecting it. "I got my eye on him, don't ye' worry none about that. He knows to keep away from ye' less ye' ask fer him. He's been in with the ship's master yammerin' on about the maps. I feel sorry for the men in there with him. Lordt knows yer daddy talks enough for four sets of teeth." Jim frowned at the fabric in his hands. "What in the hell is this stuff?"

"Tarred rope fibers," Chris said, taking it from him. "Probably not a good idea to smoke around it."

Jim took a cautious step backward, puffing on the cigarette. "What ye' thinkin' about Johann's theory? Ye' reckon he might be right?"

Chris leaned against the wall, absentmindedly picking at the oakum fibers. "Did you see the drawing he made?"

Jim shook his head.

"He showed me a few nights ago. There's a straight line that runs between the spot we went down and the spot we came through that creates a perfect triangle to the sun at exactly the time we came through. I think he might be onto something."

"That's what I's afraid of." Jim bent to distinguish the cigarette with a hiss in the water at their feet, rising slowly to lean against the opposite wall. "How many people ye' think died in that airplane?"

Chris tried to think of the number of seats... he tried to remember the number of rows... he'd been seated in 28C which was a little past the halfway point between the front and back of the plane. "I'm not sure... there might've been what... fifty rows of seats? But Maria said we weren't even at half capacity so... That'd be roughly a hundred people total... Give or take a few."

"That's about right," Jim noted. "That would mean only about fifteen percent lived. Zachary had twenty men on board, and only three made it out... fifteen percent." He sighed. "Now I might be pullin' at strings here, but there ain't nothin' normal about where we are and how we got here, so I gotta weigh the risks, even the more far-fetched ones. Let's say, just like the position of the sun, the ratio of dead to alive has got to stay the same. If we *all* try to go back... with Johann, that's thirteen of us. If the fifteen percent rule applies, then only two of us might make it."

"I've thought about that too... not the exact numbers, but similar," Chris agreed. "I don't like our odds."

"We lost two," Kyle reminded them. "We lost two on this side. Five if you count Zachary, Dutch, and Frankie."

Chris and Jim fell silent, both of them considering it.

"Think about it," Kyle said simply. "If crossing over to one side requires death on the opposite side, then we already have five."

"Ain't you a little Einstein, eh? It's not a bad theory... What you think, big man?"

"What if we're just not seeing the numbers correctly?" Chris asked, not quite ready to accept so dire a hypothesis. "There's got to be a way to safely pass through. Maybe in our case only fifteen were meant to make it... and maybe that has something to do with the different months? What if the fifteen percent rule is just a coincidence? What if only fifteen people were meant to pass through in March and only three in September?"

"Sixteen," Kyle said, not turning his attention from where he was pushing the fabric into a small seam. "The pilot was alive for a few days."

"But it was the accident that killed him," Jim corrected. "I think fifteen is right... I think we orta call a meeting with Johann tonight... see if we cain't work these numbers into his triangle somehow."

Chris nodded. "Magna and Hitihiti are meeting in Maria's room tonight to get their backstory straight. I can ask Johann to join us. I relieve John of guard duty at 1a.m. every night in front of her door. So far, no one has come down that hallway any earlier than 5a.m. We should be safe to convene there."

"I hear yuns switchin' shifts at night. Them walls are paper thin. I'll come over when ye' give me a signal."

"Do you mind staying here while I go find Johann?" Chris asked Jim, smiling at Kyle as he worked meticulously to expel sunlight from a larger crack.

Jim winked. "Take yer time, I'd be happy to stay down here all day."

The plan had been set in motion. Chris had given instructions to Johann, Hitihiti, and Magna to await his signal and then to convene a half hour afterwards in Maria's cabin.

Hitihiti and Magna would then take Jim and Lilly's cabin while the others would gather in Maria's. He'd signaled them with a knock on each door, then headed up and relieved John of his watch.

John had been particularly exhausted after the day of rain that kept him busy on deck, and was all too pleased to hurry off to his cabin downstairs for much needed sleep.

He waited ten minutes to be sure John would not return, glancing in the direction of the great cabin where the captain had set up his own cot, before tapping on Jim's door and creeping into Maria's room.

She'd been waiting for him. As soon as he entered the candlelit room, she launched herself at him, shoving him hard against the wall. "Give it back."

"Keep your voice down," he hissed. "Do you want to wake up the captain?"

She pressed her side against him, attempting to keep him pinned as she patted down his pockets. "I know you took it. Where is it?"

Finding himself suddenly on the edge of arousal, he pulled her hands from him and spun them away from the wall. "Stop." He tried to calm her as she fought to free her arms. "The others will be here any second."

"So give it back and I will, asshole."

"Are we interruptin' something?" Jim whispered at the open door. "We can come back..."

Chris let go to find Jim and Lilly both standing in the doorway in their robes, suspicion washed across both their features. "No, come in... We were just... finishing an argument."

"It's not finished," Maria huffed. "Yet." She reached out to take Lilly's hands in hers, her entire demeanor shifting to pleasant. "Come in." She led Lilly to sit beside her on the bed. "Do you want some tea? It's a little cold..."

"No, thank you." Lilly yawned. "The captain said we'll be in Tahiti tomorrow. I want to get some sleep at some point tonight."

Jim half-sat on the edge of the bed beside Lilly. "Ay, I been thinkin' about somethin.' Your island..." He looked up at Chris. "Ye' said it was right there where we crashed, right?"

Chris nodded. "Yes."

The door opened, and they all froze. Johann grinned as he entered and shut the door behind him. "It is only I. And I can see you have begun without me. I must insist you all start again." He plucked a biscuit from Maria's tea tray and took a seat on the stool at her vanity.

"We's just gettin' started." Jim eyed the tray of biscuits. "I's sayin' that island where these two landed was right next to the crash site." He turned his attention back to Chris. "Did ye' ever see any signs of the back of the plane? Any dead bodies or parts of the plane wash ashore?"

Chris frowned. "No. Just a suitcase… that's it."

Jim nodded. "Ye'd have seen bodies floatin' if they came through, and so would we. I don't think they did. I think whatever time warp we got tangled in only brought the front part of the plane with it. And that would make for a different theory. What if it's not death at all that's required? What if it's just a certain amount of people that can make it through? We don't know what happened to Zachary's men. We just know they disappeared. What if they all found themselves floatin' in the ocean in 1928 while that ship and the others crossed to the other side? In our case, there was death because we were up in the air, but we don't know his people died."

"I hadn't thought of that," Chris said, hearing Hitihiti and Magna whispering in the room next door. "That's a good point. We should've seen some signs of the plane on that island."

Jim patted Lilly's leg. "I cain't take the credit. Was all Princess's thinkin' there."

She smiled. "And if that's right, we could take more than one boat… we could all wear our life jackets—I brought them… With the spyglass, we could watch from a safe distance to see if the first group goes through or if there are people left in the water. If they make it through, we should be able to see them disappear… and we could follow behind."

"And what if people on the second boat are left in the water?" Chris asked. "The life jackets aren't enough to keep us alive in that water."

"We bring three boats," she said simply. "Someone has to commit to staying here. And that person will have to have the spyglass. They'll be the one that will have to collect whoever is left when the storm clears. The raft has to go with whoever goes through first in case the first boat gets damaged."

"Three boats?" Chris shook his head. "It's going to take a lot of coercing just to get the captain to give us one, let alone three. And we don't know anything about navigating these waters to get back to Tahiti."

Jim raised his palm. "We don't need strong boats to go to the other side. There'll be shipping routes to find us on that raft. We just need somethin' to take us from the main cutter to the center of the storm and some supplies while we wait for rescue."

Maria looked up at Chris and he recognized a hopelessness behind her eyes. "I might have to stay, anyway. I can be the lookout. But someone will need to teach me to drive a boat."

Chris took a deep breath and shook his head. "If you're staying, I'm staying too. With a compass, I can navigate us back to Tahiti."

And there, in her eyes, was the answer he'd been looking for when he'd found that button. The hopelessness in her features faded and pouring from her were all the very same feelings he'd been harboring for her in himself. He felt them, as if there was a pulse sent directly from her into him, and was taken aback by the overwhelming sense of wholeness he found in it.

No, she wouldn't marry John. From the word *'might'* in her sentence, and the energy radiating off her now, he understood a life with John wasn't what she wanted. And for so long as he lived, he would never again let her feel forced to do anything she didn't want to do.

Johann stood and helped himself to a cup of tea, dropping a sugar cube into the cup and stirring it without regard to the silence he'd rendered in rising up.

He took a loud sip and sat back down. "That's all a fine plan, assuming we are correct in the assumption no one will die and there even is such a safe distance away to anchor without being pulled into the storm."

He looked at Lilly and Jim's joined hands. "But what if one of you goes through and the other does not? Have you considered what you will do?"

Jim squeezed her hand. "If she goes through without me, she knows I'll spend every single March and September tryin' to get through behind her."

"And if it is *she* who is left in this time?"

Jim shook his head. "Ain't happenin.' I'll be on the second boat. Only way I'm gettin' anywhere near 'at storm is if she's already disappeared inside it."

"We didn't talk about that." She frowned at him. "I'm not going without you, Jimmy."

"Yeah, ye' are."

She shook her head. "No, I'm not. We can't have random plane crash survivors just showing up at different times. The ones who make it are the ones who go. Remember? Otherwise, border patrol is going to hound us for questions we can't answer."

Jim raised her hand to his lips and kissed it. "Ye' really think that's gonna' stop me from gettin' back to *you*? Sugar, there ain't no amount of questioning can keep me from it. I'll write up a will that leaves you all my lottery winnings. If you get there before I do, you go find us a place to live and I'll be there just as soon as I can get there. Now hush. We got bigger fish to fry right now."

"She does have a point though," Chris noted, leaning against the door. "How will we explain ourselves if we come through separately?"

"Yer assuming the United States government don't already know there's a time portal there." Jim raised his eyebrows. "What if we get to that spot and find we're not the only ones lookin' to go for a ride through time?"

"And if we're not?" Chris straightened. "Do you really think the United States government would want to risk anyone else finding out about it? That information in the wrong hands could be deadly... it could change the entire course of history."

"Wait a minute," Maria interjected. "You're all getting *way* ahead of yourselves. It's much more possible we're wrong about the whole triangle equinox thingy. Shouldn't we be thinking more about what we'll do if there is not a way home than talking about it as if there is?"

"Show her the drawing," Chris said.

Johann set his teacup on the vanity with a clank and pulled a scroll from the inside pocket of his jacket. He stood and smoothed it out on the bed for Jim, Lilly, and Maria to examine.

Chris didn't need to look. He'd seen the straight lines and the perfect triangle himself. It was the single thing that made sense out of their predicament. His theory *had* to be correct.

"You see." Johann smoothed his finger over the lines on the paper. "You came through here, went up and through to end up here. I've run some calculations based on the distance and the angle with which the triangle is formed, and do you know what the resulting number came to be?"

Jim titled his head to one side. "Two hundred, forty-four?"

"Correct." Johann nodded. "The exact number of years you travelled backward. And so, one can only assume that if you go through here," he placed his pointer finger on the paper, "you shall return forward two hundred, forty-four years to the year 2018."

Maria frowned. "If there were others that knew about this," she looked between Jim and Chris, "they would've been there when we came through. We would've seen them in the storm. Wouldn't we?"

"Say they don't." Jim rose from the bed to finally grab one of the biscuits he'd been salivating over. "We cain't tell 'em. We tell 'em we were stuck on an island. Everything that happened there can be truth. But beyond that, we need a story that allows for more to come through. Maybe we left some behind?"

Lilly shrugged. "But they'll have satellites to search if we tell them people are out there. Won't they? And if people show up six months or a year later… they'll know there's more to it."

Jim took a bite of the biscuit, snarling at the taste as he chewed miserably. "So what if they do? As far as we know, we was stuck on an island and we left to find help. Both times we run into a storm. If the captain hadn't shown up, we'd never know we was in another time so we act like he didn't."

"And Johann?" Maria asked. "He has no identity there. There's nothing to explain him. They'll have the flight log and will know he wasn't on the plane."

Chris nodded. "She's right. Johann. Identity isn't as simple in the future as giving your name. There are files and photos and evidence of an existence you won't have. There's no way to explain you."

Johann sighed. "That's what I have surmised myself based on previous conversation. For as much as I would like to see this future of yours, I believe my place must be in the third boat. It will have to be enough to see you all go through."

He looked at Maria. "And my dear, forgive my saying so, but I believe your place is on the first. Every day you spend in this time, you bring yourself closer to the danger of being exposed as a fraud. They could have you hanged if they discover you are not the duchess, and the lieutenant will be hanged alongside you."

"I agree," Chris said.

She turned her focus back to him, and he found the same look again; this time seeming to ask the question of whether he would go with her if she did. He could feel Lilly's eyes scanning them both, noticing the unspoken exchange pass between them.

"We should all try," Lilly said. "None of us belong here. We *all* need to go home."

"Hoss won't do it," Jim said pointedly. "He won't risk the baby. It'll be born before September. Even with this new theory, they could risk being separated from their child and neither of 'em will take that chance."

"I'll talk to her," Lilly assured him. "They could give that baby a much better life in the future than the life it would have here. I could convince them. If they somehow got separated, I would promise to take care of the baby until they got there…"

Jim laughed and pet her head. "Honey, that's mighty sweet of ye,' but they won't never agree to it."

"How will they live here?" she argued. "They've got nothing… no identity… no job… no home… no income. What would they do?"

"Gold," Maria said. "She mentioned if Johann is right, someone could buy gold and send it back to this time… She said surely, once we have gone and given our story, we would be compensated for the crash and free to go on with our lives. Who's to stop any of us from buying gold and a yacht and traveling to and from the past at our will? We could bring them gold to start a life here if they decide to stay. They could wait in Tahiti until the war is over and settle in America."

"Oh, yeah?" Jim smiled at her. "You gonna' willingly go in and out of that storm regularly, Firecracker?"

Maria raised her chin. "Sí. I would do that for her."

"You would?" Lilly tilted her head to one side. "You barely even know her."

Maria frowned back at Lilly. "She is one of us. It doesn't matter how long I have known her. What kind of woman would I be to go on with my life and do nothing to make their life better here when I have the means? Wouldn't you do this as well?"

Lilly huffed. "Of course I would. She's my best friend... I just... I didn't get why *you* would think you needed to be the one to do it."

"She is my friend too, you know." Maria said, smiling wryly as Chris noticed a hint of possessiveness in Lilly pertaining to Alaina.

"Well then, we'll both come," Lilly said with finality. "We'll have to bring two yachts, anyway."

Jim laughed, curling his arm around Lilly. "Alright, alright... let's take on one thing at a time. I think we've got a plan, and sounds like we're gonna' have a few months to iron it out. We'll talk to Hoss and see if we cain't get 'em on board. If not, we'll *all* make sure they're cared for."

A loud crack of thunder forced them all to jump.

"We'd best get on back now." Jim rose and extended a hand to Lilly. "That'll have woke the captain up."

Johann stood as well. "He's right. If it's another bad storm, everyone will be awake in minutes."

Without another word, they all spilled quietly out into the corridor, hurrying back to their prospective rooms.

Chris had been hopeful, after what had exchanged between them, to catch a moment alone with Maria before the night was over, but the storm picked up momentum as the others fled for the stairs and he saw the light of a lantern illuminating the great cabin to signify the captain was awake. He would have to wait. He closed her door, resuming his position as guard outside it just as the boat began to rock.

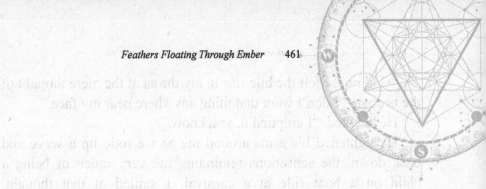

Chapter Forty Four

Alaina

I was comfortably curled into Jack's chest when he was pulled suddenly out of the bed to land hard on the floor against the door.

I could hear the thunder roaring outside as he groaned into consciousness.

"Are you alright?" I asked, clinging to the headboard to prevent the same fate as the ship rocked violently from side to side.

"I'll live," He managed.

I couldn't see him in our pitch black room, but I could hear him moving to get a grip on something. "I'm tired of being on this damn ship, that's for sure. The minute we get close to land, I'm jumping off and swimming to shore. Are you alright?"

I held on as I felt my stomach rise up to my throat. "Oh… I'm fine, I might throw up all over you, but otherwise… perfectly fine."

He extended an arm out toward me, touching my leg. "Here, come down here. I don't want you falling out of the bed."

Carefully, I crawled down, and he wrapped me in his arms.

Bracing his legs against one wall, he pressed his back against the opposite wall to keep us secure. "There. I've got you now. Do you want the bedpan in case you throw up?"

"God no." I felt the bile rise in my throat at the mere thought of the bedpan. "I don't want that thing anywhere near my face."

He laughed. "I emptied it, you know."

He tightened his arms around me as we rode up a wave and back down, the sensations reminding me very much of being a child on a boat ride at a carnival. I smiled at that thought, remembering my sister beside me as we both watched for the other to raise her arms into the air before doing the same.

I missed Cece. I missed all of my family. Knowing I might stay in this time forever, I found myself thinking of them more and more frequently.

I thought about what Maria had said to me earlier that day and wondered if I'd ever really paid attention to their own story lines; the paths in their lives that meant something to them that had nothing to do with my own. Had I ever really known what they were going through? I wished I could see them again... to really get the chance to know them the way I should've.

"Jack, tell me something about your life I don't know."

He kissed the top of my head and laughed. "Right now?" He stiffened as we rocked up and down again. "Sweetheart, now's not exactly a good time to reminisce. You should try to get some sleep."

I clung to him as the waves grew higher and threatened to send both of us tumbling to the opposite wall. "I haven't asked you enough about your life. I want to know everything about you. You know that, right?"

"I know." He scratched the back of my head. "What's this really about?"

"Nothing."

"Something." He hugged me tighter as the ocean roared outside our room. "What's going on?"

I nuzzled my face into his chest. "I just... Maria pointed out a trait in me today I really never noticed. I live my life and don't pay enough attention to the lives of the people around me. I think it's why I've always had a hard time with friendships. I don't have empathy the way other people do. And I don't want to be self-centered anymore."

He chuckled. "You're not self-centered, Red."

"Yes, I am."

"No, you're not. A self-centered person wouldn't have made sure I was breathing when I had pneumonia on that island... wouldn't have risked her life and jumped down in that pit to save Izzy or pulled the boulders off that wall to help get Jim out of that collapse. You've asked and listened to the stories about all of our lives. You're not self-centered. Maybe a little neurotic and indecisive," he snickered, "but not self-centered."

"You think I'm neurotic?"

"Just a tad, but I love you for it." He pulled me closer. "Why are you listening to that woman, anyway? She doesn't know anything about who you are deep down."

I huffed. "I suppose that's the picture Chris painted of me. He's not wrong... Everything about our relationship was centered around me. I hate that I didn't see it. I don't want ours to ever be that way. I don't ever want you to wake up one day and see me as this self-absorbed woman who stole part of your life away."

"If that's how he sees you, he's just as guilty for creating that atmosphere. It takes two people to make a relationship what it is. You and I will *never* be that. I tell you when you're being ridiculous, just like you tell me when I'm being an asshole. We hold each other up; make each other better. We are both at the center of this relationship."

I sighed. "She called it the Alaina-show. She said I walk around living the main storyline without really noticing anyone else." I traced the pocket of his shirt with my finger. "And she's right."

He tilted my face up to him. I couldn't see him in the darkness, but I could tell he was smiling. "Alaina, my dear, you are being ridiculous." He laid his lips softly over mine. "Knock it off." He gently pulled my head down against his shoulder. "And go to sleep."

I closed my eyes and let the rocking of the ship lull me into sleep inside his arms.

I woke up still in his arms on the floor, and every part of my body ached for having spent the night in that position. I stretched my legs out and straightened my burning back, an act which caused him to stir as well.

"Did you get any sleep?" I asked.

He yawned and stretched his arms out. "I got enough. We should head up and see if we can see the islands yet."

Jack, unlike me, had been to Tahiti several times. He knew it well and knew exactly how it should appear. I think part of him was holding onto a small shred of hope that everything was an act, and we'd somehow manage to arrive in a century we recognized. I knew we wouldn't, but I also knew Jack was a man that needed to see something before he could believe it.

I echoed his yawn and gradually rose to my knees. "Jesus," I groaned, crawling toward the bed and feeling around for the lantern and matches so I could get a look at my pulsing feet. "My feet feel like they're going to explode."

Jack moved alongside me and I heard the box of matches shake as he found them first. I sat on my butt, stretching my aching legs out in front of me while he scratched the match and lit the lantern.

As the warm glow grew and illuminated our small room, I got a glimpse of my swollen feet. They were almost double in size, looking very cartoonish, and the image forced me back to the morning of the day I'd gone into early labor with my first child. I'd been sitting up in bed staring at the same comical looking feet.

Terror swept over me as I considered how close I now was to the point I'd been before. I'd been twenty-seven weeks pregnant then. Based on the very sizable swell of my belly now, I imagined I was somewhere around twenty-one or twenty-two weeks pregnant. Could I make it this time? Would my body hold out or would it fail him, too?

Jack slid on his butt across from me to take my feet in his lap. "You know," he said, kneading the sole of my foot to relieve the pressure, "when you've got something on your mind, you always have that same look. What's wrong? Are you still thinking about what Maria said?"

I shook my head. "No... No, I was just thinking of the last time." I ran my palms over my stomach. "There's no way to know for sure how far along I am right now... I could be twenty-one weeks or maybe even twenty-three or twenty-four... I'm certainly big enough... and I'm so close to where I was last time. I'm just a little scared the closer we get, you know? I don't know if my body will hold up."

He worked his thumbs up my calf. "It will hold, and you're going to do fine. Don't lose hope on me now. Are you feeling alright? Does something feel off?"

"Everything feels fine." I frowned. "But it all felt fine then too... until it wasn't."

"You said it feels different this time. You said you just know it's going to be alright. Do you not feel that way now?"

"I don't know what I feel. I just know I'm scared. I'm bigger than I was at twenty-one weeks before, and he's moving around a lot. What if I'm way further along than I thought? If I don't go to term... then any day now I could—

"Shhh." He crawled to sit beside me and put his arm around me. "Don't talk like that. It's going to be alright. We just have to wait and see what happens. Please don't talk like that."

I laid my head against him. "You're right. I'm sorry. I think the hormones might be getting to me."

"Well, don't be sorry either." He kissed my temple. "It scares me when you mention it, and that's not fair to you. You're allowed to be scared, especially after losing Evelyn. I'm just scared too... horrified to be honest."

"Horrified?" I looked up at him. "That I'll lose him?"

He nodded. "Or that you won't and I won't know how to be a father... and he'll grow up resenting me the way I did my dad... waiting for me to die so he can get on with his life."

I laughed at that. "Jack, honey, you're going to be a wonderful father. Look at how you are with Izzy. She adores you. I'm sure he will too."

I laid my head against his shoulder, relaxing just in time to be startled by the knock on our door.

"Mrs. Volmer?" The familiar voice of the man who was always sent to summon me to Maria's room called from the opposite side.

"I'll be right up," I called back, groaning.

"You don't have to go, you know," Jack said. "Look at you, you're all swollen. She doesn't need you today."

"I know, but I want to go." I kissed his cheek and forced myself up off the floor, holding my back as I stretched. "It keeps my mind busy. Plus, I kinda' like her." I plucked my clothing from the edge of the bed.

Jack stood alongside me, frowning. "Are you sure?" He looked down at my swollen feet. "Your feet look terrible."

"I'll be fine." I tied my petticoat loosely around my waist. "Come on, help me put the stays on."

"I don't think you should be wearing this anymore." He scowled at the corset top in his hands. "It can't be good for the baby."

"Just tie the top half. We'll leave it loose at the waist and pin the apron over it."

He sighed, surrendering to wrap it around me as I turned my back to him. I regretted the decision instantly as my already tender breasts ached the minute they were squeezed inside.

He noticed them as I turned to face him and he grinned as he ran his thumb along the crease of my newly developed cleavage. "I like you pregnant."

I laughed. "Oh you do, huh? Enjoy them while they last. I'll go back to being flat as a pancake in no time."

"I like you that way too," he said, leaning down to lay a kiss where his thumb had been before he began pinning the apron over my stays. "I like you all the ways."

I smiled up at him, smoothing the hair from his face while he focused on his fingers. "I suppose I like you all the ways too, Mr. Volmer."

"Mmm." He kissed my wrist as it passed over his lips. "And I especially like you when they call you Mrs.Volmer."

I grinned. "I do too. I don't think I've ever liked my name more."

"I suppose we haven't had a chance to talk about our *actual* wedding. I'd like to have something before..." He trailed off, pinning the final edge of the apron.

"Before they all go?" I asked. "I would too... If we decide to stay. Have you decided?"

He shrugged. "I don't see many other options. We've got time still to think about it, though."

I raised on my toes to kiss his lips. "I may be the neurotic one, but I'm not the only one who is indecisive. I'll see you in a little while."

"Hey," he grabbed my hand as I turned to go. "Don't let her make you feel bad about yourself. Some people see fault in others where they are different from themselves. There's absolutely nothing wrong with you. You're different than her, and I like it that way."

I smiled. "You wouldn't like me more if I had just a hint of her feistiness?"

He shook his head. "You're perfect as you are."

I rolled my eyes. "Okay. But you gotta admit, the accent is sexy."

"If you could see what I'm looking at, you'd know what sexy was." His eyes once again found their way to my cleavage, and he slowly licked his lower lip. "You should probably go... I don't know how much longer I can go without ripping that thing back off you."

I laughed at that, blowing him a kiss as I pulled the door open. "Rip it off me later though, okay?"

"I was planning on it."

"For real." I leaned against the door frame, doing my very best as a pregnant woman to pose seductively. I lowered my voice to a whisper. "I *want* you to rip it."

His eyes lit up, and I turned proudly to make my way toward the stairs, more anxious than ever to get back to him.

I smiled all the way up the steps until I hit the corridor and a familiar tightening in my abdomen rendered me motionless.

'No,' I begged in my mind, placing one hand protectively over my belly and the other on the wall as my insides tightened further.

'Please don't do this. Please.'

I squeezed my eyes closed and took several deep breaths, feeling the tears spill down my cheeks.

'Please, God. Please don't do this to me again.'

"Ally?" Chris called ahead of me in the hallway.

I opened my eyes to find him jogging toward me. "Al, you okay?" He reached my side and immediately began rubbing my back. "Is it like before?"

I nodded. "Yes." And I could hear the lump in my throat forcing the word to crack. "It's *exactly* like before."

"Can you walk? Do you want me to carry you?"

"I can walk," I snapped, unable to stop the tears and letting them fall as I felt the tightening ease.

"Here, let me help you." He offered me his arm to lean on, and I was relieved to have it. I knew, without a doubt, what this feeling was. My entire world was about to crumble again and I needed to hang on to something.

He led me to Maria's door and didn't knock before pushing it open. "Help," he said as he led me inside.

Maria leapt off the bed to the other side of me. "¡Ay Dios mío!" She crossed herself. "No, no no, it is too soon for this. Put her in the bed!"

Chris led me to the bed, and I sat down hard, tears streaming down my cheeks.

"I don't wanna do this again," I said to him, and I saw, just like me, the memory of the first time was playing out in his mind.

"Go and get the nurse right now!" Maria ordered, shooing him away as she sat down beside me to massage my shoulders.

"Maybe it is nothing, cariño. Don't cry. Not yet. Nothing is lost yet." She pulled me against her and stroked my hair. "It's alright. Shhh…" She rocked softly. "Oye, what are you doing?" she spat at Chris, who stood staring dumbfounded in the center of the room. "Go and get the nurse!"

He blinked back to reality and rushed out of the room.

"Look at me," she said, pulling me from her. "Let me see you, mama. Is it hurting right now?"

I sniffled, taking a deep breath in. "No. Not now… But it was just like before… The same tightening… The same length of time… and I know what's coming next."

"No, you don't." She swept the hair from my face. "You don't know for sure. Only God knows what's next."

Lilly hurried through the door, her robe lazily tied, hair a mess, and her feet bare on the wood floorboards. "I heard shouting. What's going on?" She looked from Maria to me. "Lainey? What happened?"

"Nothing," Maria said pointedly. "She just had a little cramp, probably nothing. Chris is going to get the nurse to check it out. We're not panicking." She looked at me. "Isn't that right?"

I nodded.

"Come on, lie back now and put your feet up," Maria cooed, stroking my hair. "Lilly, take those shoes off her."

Lilly pulled off my shoes and stockings, gasping as she revealed my swollen feet. "Oh my God."

Maria shook her head. "Aye, it's just a little swelling. No big deal. Come on, put your feet up here."

She patted the bed, hopping off it to collect all the pillows and place them under my head and back as I laid down. "Are you in pain?"

"Not now… but if it's like last time, it'll come soon."

Lilly took my hand in hers. "Is it like before then?"

"Yes."

Maria rustled around near her vanity with her back turned to us, speaking softly to herself in Spanish. She spun around and returned with a wet cloth, placing it on my forehead.

"You should've stayed in bed today. I only call for you to have someone to talk to, and you can always say no. You're in no condition to be going up and down those stairs all the time."

Lilly smoothed her hand over my belly. "It's gonna be okay. Anna's coming. You'll see. It's going to be fine. You're fine."

"Are you hungry?" Maria asked, sitting down at the foot of the bed to massage my feet. "Do you want me to call for breakfast?"

"No," I said softly, feeling defeated and helpless as I waited for the next contraction. I knew this feeling. I recognized it instantly. It was the same. I had to find a way to come to terms with it this time. I couldn't let it destroy me like it had before, but I could feel, deep down, it already had.

I heard Anna long before she entered the room. They were running, and she was questioning Chris.

"How long did it last?" She panted.

"I don't know," he responded breathlessly.

"Was that the first one? How long ago did it happen?"

"I *don't* know," he said again as they reached the doorway.

"I'm here," she announced "Tell me everything. When did it happen? What were you doing?"

"Just a few minutes ago. I had just come up the stairs."

"Okay." She felt my stomach. "Are you wearing a corset?! Lilly, help me take this off her."

"It's not tied all the way," I assured her as I sat up. "I left it loose in the waist."

Lilly went to work unlacing it while Anna felt my forehead. "Any bleeding or discharge?"

"No."

"Was it painful or just uncomfortable? Like sharp pains or just tightening?"

"It was like my whole stomach just suddenly tightened. Exactly like it did when I went into labor last time."

"What about lower back pain? Not like the contraction, but more consistent and dull?"

I nodded. "Yes. I have that too. We slept on the floor because of the storm, and at first, I thought the back pain was just from that, but now I know it's not..."

"Okay, when was the last time you drank water?"

I squeezed my eyes closed, trying to remember. Water rations on the ship weren't what they should've been. I'd learned pretty quickly that 18th century sailors hydrated with beer instead of water. "Last night at dinner."

Anna snapped her fingers at Chris, and he ran into the hall toward the great cabin.

The corset came loose and Anna pressed on each side of my stomach. "Does that hurt?"

I shook my head. "No."

She furrowed her brow as she worked downward. "How bout now?"

"No."

"And have you felt the baby moving today?"

"Yes."

She smiled and nodded. "Show me about where you feel it?"

I laid my hand over the familiar spot.

"So..." She placed her hand over the same spot, closing her eyes as she pressed gently. "You slept all night on the floor, then climbed a flight of stairs and haven't had any water since last night with an active kicking baby? I think what you are experiencing is Braxton Hicks contractions."

I shook my head, my throat tightening with panic. "No. That's what I thought last time, but I was in labor. I'm in labor now, I know it. It felt just like this one did. Exactly the same."

"Do you know what a Braxton Hicks contraction is, sweetie?" Anna tilted her head to one side. "It is your uterus essentially practicing for labor. It feels very similar, and sometimes exactly the same. We'll keep you in bed just to be safe, and I'll stay here with you. If the contractions do not come on a schedule, and if they do not worsen, I would say, your baby is just fine."

"How can you know that?" I asked, still convinced I recognized what was going on with my *own* body.

She patted my belly softly. "Braxton Hicks is generally set off by changes in the mother's activities. If you slept in an uncomfortable position, you could've inadvertently been putting pressure on your abdomen. This can cause Braxton Hicks. Increases in physical activity, such as *climbing several flights of stairs*, can also cause Braxton Hicks. And more frequently than not, a lack of water will set it off every time. Honey, you've done it all."

"You see, mama?" Maria smiled from the foot of the bed where she'd been meticulously working her thumbs into the balls of my feet. "I told you it was nothing. I will stay with you, too."

"Me too." Lilly said, combing my hair.

I felt fresh tears spill down my cheeks and groaned. "Ugh, well I feel like an idiot now."

Maria clicked her tongue. "Anything that could feel like the last time would be scary for *any* person. It doesn't make you an idiot."

Chris plowed through the door with a pitcher and a glass of water. He handed Anna the glass and stood with the pitcher, awaiting further instruction.

"Sit up and drink a little," Anna encouraged, helping me up as I took the glass and drank the entire thing.

"Superman, you can put the pitcher down there." Maria pointed to her tea tray. "And then you can go and find something else to do. The baby is fine."

"Are you sure?" He stared down at me with his brows furrowed.

Anna nodded. "False alarm. But we're gonna keep an eye on her and make sure she doesn't have any more. She's just had a little too much excitement this week."

She laid her hand on my stomach. "You really need to be taking it easy with your condition. I don't know much about it, but I'd guess it's not a good idea for you to be wearing corsets and climbing stairs as often as you've been."

"Y'all alright?" Jim whispered, creeping slowly inside with Izzy wrapped in his arms.

"We're fine, Jimmy." Lilly smiled, outstretching her arms. "You can leave her with us today. Go have your coffee. We're gonna have a girls' day today."

"She's tuckered out," Jim said, stroking her hair and rocking her before he handed her sleeping body to Lilly. "She didn't sleep with the ship knockin' around last night." He frowned at me. "Should I go get Hoss?"

"No, we'll come find him if something happens," Lilly assured him, pulling Izzy against her shoulder. "Poor baby," she murmured. "You can snuggle up with Lainey today."

"We should tell him," Chris said, still staring nervously down at me. "He would want to know, even if it's nothing. I know I would."

I looked up at him and smiled, mouthing the words *'thank you.'*

Lilly laid Izzy down beside me, and despite being half-asleep, she immediately draped her little arm around my neck. "Just make sure he knows it's a false alarm. No sense in getting everyone panicked this morning."

"Oye, but there are already too many men in my room full of undressed women now! Go and do your man things. We will come and find you if anything changes."

While Maria stood and escorted the men to the hallway, I wrapped an arm around Izzy, pulling her closer as I watched the rain fall softly on Maria's window.

I'd been so confident in my body this time around. I had trusted all the little sensations and had learned to read them. How had I not trusted this one? How had I not even thought about Braxton Hicks? Why had I immediately assumed the worst?

I couldn't let every little ache or pain cripple me like this had. That kind of anxiety would most definitely force him to come sooner than he should.

I waited for signs of another contraction, stroking Izzy's hair as she tucked her face into the crook of my neck. My heart warmed as all three women positioned themselves in the bed surrounding me.

Lilly climbed over to sit on one side of Izzy, Anna on the other side of me, and Maria at my feet.

For someone who had been living so aimlessly stuck in my own little world, I wondered what I'd done to deserve these kinds of friends who would drop everything to watch over me.

As I looked between them, I noticed Anna's appearance for the first time. She was wearing only her shift and had wrapped Chris's jacket around herself. Her thin blonde hair was disheveled, and her eyes were still puffy from being woken abruptly from her sleep. "Oh, I'm sorry Anna. I didn't mean to pull you out of bed like that."

She smiled, evidently realizing herself what she must look like as she ran a hand over her hair. "Don't be. When I was pregnant with Liam, every time he would so much as kick, I would have to call my mother just to make sure it was normal. I'd call her at all hours of the night and morning. I can't imagine having to go through it without her. You can wake me up anytime. Day or night."

"Thank you. All of you," I said. "I didn't mean to get us all panicked." I patted Lilly's leg. "You wanted to see Tahiti on the horizon today. You don't have to stay with me."

"Don't be crazy." She yawned. "I'm not going anywhere. Besides, Maria's bed is so much more comfortable than mine." She flashed Maria a sarcastic grin. "You're gonna have to drag me out of it."

Maria smiled. With the absence of men and the abundance of females now in her room, I noticed she'd grown timid. I remembered her saying she hadn't had many girlfriends, and I wondered if she didn't feel a bit like an outsider among us. She hadn't spent the time we had together. She didn't have the bond we had, and suddenly outnumbered, I imagined she felt out of place and uncomfortable.

"So," I nudged her with my foot, "you guys had a meeting with Johann here last night? Tell me what happened."

I watched her as she gradually came out of her shell while she and Lilly recalled the details of the conversation from the night before. They ran through the new theory about the fifteen percent possibly being just a number that can pass through and not necessarily a life or death option, and they told me about the plan to bring multiple boats. Both of them encouraged me to come along, if for nothing else than to watch from the third boat, and by the time they were done, Maria resembled more of herself.

We had just shifted into more casual conversation about what it might be like to go home when Jack, soaking wet from the rain, came barreling through the door.

He'd run down, I could tell by the heaving of his chest as he scanned the bed, and he instantly placed a hand on my stomach. "Is she alright?" he asked Anna. "Is the baby alright?"

Anna nodded. "They're both fine. The baby is moving around in there like crazy and it hasn't dropped at all. It's just a false alarm. You're going to have those more and more frequently."

As if he couldn't stand a second longer, he sat down heavily on the edge of the bed, his palm still rested on my stomach. "You're sure?"

"I'm sure." She smiled. "But I want to keep her here for the day. She really shouldn't be going up and down those stairs with as much risk as we already have with her condition. Assuming that's alright with you, Maria?"

"Of course!" Maria said, as if the idea of Anna even having to ask was offensive to her.

"We'll be in Tahiti before the end of the night." He took my hand and kissed it. "I'll make sure we have a place on land when we drop the anchor. I want you off this boat. I never should've let you go with your feet looking like they did."

"I'm fine," I promised him. "It was something perfectly normal I just overreacted to. I should've known what it was."

He shook his head. "There's no such thing as normal with this pregnancy and I want to be there to go through all of it with you. If you're scared, I should be there beside you. You shouldn't have been alone."

"It's alright, really. And I'm not alone." I looked at the women surrounding me. "My girls took care of me."

He nodded, glancing at each of them. "Thank you... What can *I* do? Do you need anything? Are you hungry? Should I have Bruce fix you some breakfast?"

I grinned. "I'm always hungry."

"I think it's oatmeal this morning, but if you'd like something else—

"Oatmeal sounds wonderful."

"You don't have to go get it," Maria said, hopping out of the bed. "I can call for it."

She went to the door, opening it to send the servant posted there off with instructions. "We're taking breakfast in here," she ordered. "There are four of us. Bring enough for all." She shut the door and returned to her place at my feet. "There. It is done."

"Well, I need to do something," he said, his shoulders slumping. "I can't just go on with the day knowing you're in here in the bed."

I squeezed his hand. "You can help the captain get us to that island and set us up a spot at camp. The faster you can get me on dry land and away from the constant movement of this ship, the better. I'm alright, and I promise, one of these women will come find you if anything changes."

He leaned in to kiss my forehead before he rose from the bed. "If anything happens," he looked at Lilly, "anything at all, come find me."

"I will," she promised.

He looked at me a moment more before he left the room, and I think we all let out a sigh once we were alone again.

An hour passed with no contractions, and then another as Lilly and Maria styled our hair and filed each of our nails. We chatted about boys and life experiences; I about Jack, Lilly about Jim, Anna about her ex, and Maria talked about some man named David.

I imagined, had I ever actually had one, this was what it was like to have a *'spa day,'* and I felt myself more relaxed than I'd been in months. I fell asleep surrounded by women I trusted, and I didn't care what year it was. I was just grateful to have them there with me.

Chapter Forty Five

Alaina

"Red." Jack whispered, pulling me from a deep sleep. "We're in Tahiti."

I opened my eyes to a candlelit room. The women were all gone. I'd slept the entire day away. I could see the night sky outside the window beside the bed.

"The captain has met with some of the chiefs here," he said, combing the hair from my face. "They've just finished building a few houses right on the bay and they've agreed to give us the biggest one so we can all sleep comfortably. Come on, let me get you on land before the rain starts up again. Everyone's waiting for us."

I yawned, and before I could slide my legs over the edge of the bed, he'd already scooped me up into his arms. "I can walk, you know."

He shook his head, holding me against his chest. "I know, but I need to carry you."

I laughed, wrapping my arms around his neck as he carried me out of the room. "I'm sorry I scared you. It was a false alarm. I'm alright."

"False alarm or not, I should've been there." He kissed the top of my head as he carried me up the stairs.

"How did the captain manage to get us the biggest house?"

His arms tightened around me as he took the second flight of stairs. "Chris and I agreed to help them build more."

I smiled and laid my head against his chest, smoothing my palm over the fabric of his shirt. "So you're speaking to each other then?"

"Not on purpose." He chuckled. "But I suppose we'll have to acknowledge each other on occasion if we'll be working together."

"They're going to let us stay? Long-term?"

He slowed his pace as he proceeded to the final set of stairs. "Not sure yet. We haven't spoken to the king. This agreement was just for the house with a man named Tu... he seems to be important, and the captain thinks he might become the new king in Tahiti."

I could feel my skin cooling as we approached the top deck, and I curled in closer.

"Jack... today... what happened... it was so much like the first time. And with all the risks, there's a real chance I could lose this one too. We can't go into denial. The risks have to be a reality. I don't want to fall apart like I did before. I ruined everything that was good in my life after I lost her. I can't do that this time. I can't ruin us."

He pulled me closer. "I've got you now, and I won't let anything happen to us."

"I don't want to get excited." I touched the pendant on my necklace. "Last time, I got too excited. But I don't want to steal your excitement away..."

He smiled down at me. "I know very well what the risks are. I am not, nor have I ever been, in denial. The risk to you and to our baby is ever present in my mind. For as much as I will love having a son, I love having you more. Every day that *you* wake up excites me. You're not stealing anything, Alaina. You *are* my excitement."

"Aye, so romantic!" Maria teased as we emerged on the top deck. "Look at this man and how he carries his woman! This is a man in love!"

She hurried to our side. "How are you feeling? Did he tell you they built houses since the last time we were here?! Kreese and

John are already down there preparing it for us! We're going to sleep in a real home with real beds! Are you excited?"

I blinked heavily. I wasn't entirely sure whether she was addressing me or simply talking through her own excitement. I laughed. "I'm very excited, yes."

"Well, come on!" She danced toward the sloops where Lilly, Jim, Magna, and Izzy were already waiting. "I am dying to see our new home!"

"Where are Anna, Bruce, and Kyle? Where's Bud?" I asked as Jack lowered me down onto the boat.

"On that boat over yonder." Jim pointed to a sloop already in the water rowing toward the shore, the moonlight's reflection on the water outlining their silhouettes.

"And Phil?" Jack asked stiffly, looking around the top deck for signs of him.

"That summbitch is stayin' on the ship where he belongs." Catching his slipped accent, Jim straightened, eyeing the two soldiers who had paid him no mind. He cleared his throat, returning to proper English to add. "Good riddance."

Jack assisted Maria down from the ledge, and she batted her eyes at him. "Gracias, querido." Snickering at herself and at the momentary discomfort she'd implanted in Jack's facial expression, she nudged my elbow, sitting down beside me as Jack climbed in behind her.

"You've got to be starving, Lainey," Lilly said sweetly. "You've slept all day." She reached into a small basket and produced a chunk of bread and cheese.

As if her words brought my hunger to life, my stomach grumbled in response, and I took the food happily. "Oh my God, thank you."

I took a bite of bread entirely too big for mouth and held my hand over my lips in an attempt to hide it.

"¡Que linda!" Maria marvelled, pulling my hand into the lantern light. "What a beautiful ring!"

Mid-chew, I froze. The ring she was admiring was Chris's, and my cheeks burned as I became painfully aware of everyone else's eyes on my finger.

Thankfully, Lilly caught my discomfort. "Maria, tell us about the arctic. The captain said you sailed it with him? Is it as beautiful as the pictures?"

"Oh." She grinned, abandoning my hand to paint a picture. "It is the most marvelous place I have ever seen."

She continued in detail, but I was too distracted to hear her. I stared down at the ring on my finger. It had made sense to keep the ring when I'd thought Chris was dead, but now it felt wrong to have a part of his family history on my finger. It had been there for so long it had become a part of me. I touched it all the time as a means to ensure I was still together. It didn't belong to me, though. I needed to give it back to him so he could give it to someone else someday… To Maria even…

I'd watched them over the weeks on the ship, and I'd teetered between jealousy and amusement as I noticed the way they looked at each other; the way they danced around feelings they both wore on their sleeves.

Given the abundance of desire I could see welling in his eyes for her, I wondered if he might not have turned me down if I'd chosen differently. He was in love with her. I knew this because I'd seen that same look once directed at me. And she was so evidently in love with him even a blind person could see it.

John had seen it. On several occasions, I'd watched him notice them, just as I had, and it pained me to watch as he awkwardly interjected himself into their conversation.

I could see he was struggling to force a smile more and more each day, and I wondered how much longer he would pursue her before giving up. It was obvious to all of us they were mad about each other. I could see in the devastation John wore on his shoulders that it was obvious to him as well.

What would it be like to see them together as a couple? Could I be happy for them? Would I stand in their wedding one day and offer my congratulations? Would I be a part of their life or would we be strangers bound only by a fading history?

Again, I looked down at the ring and tried to imagine it on her finger. The thought made me smile. She would be good to him, and she deserved it far more than I ever had.

I looked at the ring on my right hand, and again, I smiled. This ring needed to sit on that finger. We needed to make our marriage official. Being called Mrs. Volmer was one thing... *being* Mrs. Volmer would be everything.

Cheese and bread devoured, the soldiers pulled us onto the shore. Jack, still unwilling to let me walk on my own, immediately pulled me off my feet.

"Jack, seriously. I can walk just fine."

"I know." He grinned down at me as he followed the others up the beach toward a large house just off the sand, lanterns already lit in each of the windows. "But I like carrying my family in my arms. Makes me feel like I'm doing something important."

He leaned in, tilting me up so he could whisper. Evidently sharing similar thoughts as a result of the ring fiasco, he nuzzled my cheek. "I'd like to marry you sooner than later."

I reached up to pull his lips to mine. "Me too."

Chapter Forty Six

Chris

Chris woke up as he was thrust backward by the sudden opening of Maria's door, forcing him to fall flat on his back.

She glared down at him with her arms crossed over her chest. "Give it back."

He grinned up at her. "Give what back?"

"You know *what*, estupido! I know you took it! Give it back!"

Carefully, he rose, grunting as his stiff body straightened. He placed a hand on her door frame and leaned in to whisper. "First, tell me why you have it."

"Hijo de puta, I don't need to tell you anything. It's mine and I want it back."

He raised an eyebrow. "Technically, it's mine. *Why* do you have it?"

She pulled her robe tighter around her body and growled. "You know what? Keep it. What do I care about some stupid button, anyway?"

"Okay, I will," he beamed, pulling the button from his pocket to roll it between his thumb and forefinger. "Your loss, I guess."

She sprung at him, reaching for the button as he held it up high over her head. "Give it to me!"

"No!" he teased, placing his other palm on her forehead to keep her at a distance. "Tell me why you have it!"

"You know why I have it you stupid man!" She swatted his hand away from her face. "Now give it back!"

She reared back to throw a slap, and he grabbed her wrist mid-swing, leaning into the room. "Tell me this doesn't mean something to you."

She glared at him, attempting to free her wrist. "You are full of yourself, you know that?"

"Am I?" he taunted her. "Why else would you keep it?"

Her cheeks flushed red. "Maybe to remind myself to never drink water from a puddle again!"

He leaned closer, his face inches from hers. "Are you sure that's it?"

She narrowed her eyes at him. "Yes, I am sure *that's it*. Stop flattering yourself and give it back."

"Fine." He smiled, releasing her wrist and extending his palm to her. As she moved to take the button from it, he curled his fingers tightly around hers. "But you might as well take this too."

He reached into his jacket pocket with his free hand and pulled out her red and blue silk scarf. "To remind yourself not to go cracking your skull open as well."

She took the scarf and her mouth dropped partially open. "Why do you have this?"

He followed into her room as she slowly backed inside it, letting the door close behind him. "You know why I have it, *you stupid woman*."

Unable to keep himself from it, he reached out to touch her, but she held up a palm. "Wait. Stop." She stared down at the contents of her palm as she took another step back, her face distorting between happiness and hopelessness. "You know I can't do this now... If John—

"Do you want to marry him?"

"It doesn't matter what I want." She tightened her fingers around the scarf and button. "I have to."

With a single finger beneath her chin, he tilted her face up so her eyes would meet his. "Do you want to marry him?" he asked again softly, keeping his forefinger in place as he inched closer.

She squeezed her eyes closed. "We are too far in now for me to turn him down. I have let it go on for too long. It would be cruel to say no."

"Maria." He let his fingers glide along the side of her jaw. "You are not a payment owed to any man. Do you understand? Look at me."

He reached out to hold her face in both his hands. "Look at me," he whispered.

She opened her eyes then, and a single tear slid down her cheek.

"You are so much more than that. I will not let you marry him out of debt. I will not let anyone force you to do something you don't want to do ever again. It was me that promised *I* would get us home, and I will. This is my burden, not yours. Now tell me the truth, do you *want* to marry him?"

She shook her head. "No," she whispered.

"And *why* don't you want to marry him?" He could feel his heart beating out of his chest as he closed the gap between them.

She placed her palm over his where it sat against her cheek. "You know why, Kreese… They are only words…"

He leaned down to hover over her lips, every inch of his body shivering with restraint. "I need you to say them, Maria. I need you to tell me what you want."

"You," she whispered. "*You* are all I have ever wanted."

He softly brought his lips to hers then, every nerve and hair in his body coming alive as her lips instantly responded to his.

He loved her, he knew, but he hadn't realized the entirety of it until that very moment as she moved her hands over his cheeks and forced a tear to escape from his closed eyes.

She wrapped her arms around his neck to pull him closer, and he bent to her will, letting himself forget the world around them and be completely lost in the sensations of her.

Curling his fingers into her hair, he parted her lips ever so gently, an act which forced a single ecstatic sound to emit from her throat. That single sound was all it took for his breathing to quicken; for his muscles to release the restraints he'd been keeping them in; for his pulse to race with the need for more, and for his hands to explore the lengths of her.

Everything had a meaning. Every move of his hand or touch of his tongue against hers was a statement. He needed to show her, in that moment, all the words he had never been able to say to her; needed to show her all the emotions that had filled him throughout their time together; that were all but overflowing from him now.

He needed her to know it was always there, that she was everything to him all along, and not acting upon it had been torturing him for almost an entire year.

Her hands glided over his cheeks as her lips matched his, all the same emotions pouring from her. A million words passed unspoken between them, and he couldn't have enough. He pulled her body against his, realizing that no matter how much of her he had, he could never have enough.

"MARIA?!" John banged loudly on the door. "Maria? Is Chris in there?!!"

Chris stiffened as Maria pulled away. He'd known, in the back of his mind, he wouldn't have this moment with her uninterrupted. They were never entirely alone with the captain and crew still on the island. He hadn't planned for this to happen; never intended for John to find them out, but as his hand went for his sword to find it left carelessly in the hall, he realized John already had.

"Hide," she whispered.

"No," he whispered back, taking her hand in his.

"Please." She attempted to drag him toward the bed. "He is already suspicious."

"No," he repeated, setting his feet as he pulled her behind him. "My sword is in the hall. He knows." He straightened and cleared his throat before calling out. "I'm here."

Without invitation, John pushed through the door, one hand on the hilt of his sword as he observed the two of them, his eyes lingering on their joined hands.

"It is as I thought then," he said, narrowing his eyes at Chris. "All this time... even after I offered to stand aside. Why?" he demanded. "Why would you let me shower my affections upon her when you knew all along you would take her from me?"

"John, it's not that simple," Chris said, attempting to keep the situation neutral. "I didn't think—

"You didn't think your wife would turn up with child by another?" John spat hatefully. "Yes, I am aware. I am not a complete fool. I knew the instant we found her that this would be where you would run to. I'd been mistaken to assume you might seek the consent of your most devoted friend before you stole away with his betrothed."

"John, I'm sorry. I never meant for this to hurt you," Chris said, relaxing a little as Maria squeezed his hand. "It was not my intention to hide it from you, but I—

"I love him," Maria blurted, forcing Chris to look back at her. Her gaze softened as his eyes met hers and she whispered between them, "I love you."

'They are only words,' she'd said, but he'd never remembered a moment where mere words had rendered such a powerful physical effect on him.

Knees suddenly trembling, his whole body felt like it had been brought to life, as if the words had sent a lightning bolt straight through him and awakened every sense inside. These words could never be unheard—unfelt. He could never go back to who he was before he'd heard them, and as he stood looking at John's heart break before them, he knew he would sacrifice far more than friendship to be able to hear those words from her lips over and over again.

John cleared his throat, barely making eye contact with Maria. "I knew you did. I had hoped you might love me more."

Chris glanced at John's hand where it rested on the hilt of his sword, wondering what he might do next. Maria, evidently thinking the same, stepped forward to stand at Chris's side. "I'm sorry. I really hoped I would too, and I tried to. I didn't mean for you to get hurt. Will you expose us now?"

John let his hand fall to his side. "No." He frowned in thought and straightened, taking a deep breath as he regained his formality.

"I've come to summon Chris on behalf of the captain. We have been invited to join him on his trip to Oparre. He says he will grant you audience with Tu and his chiefs to make a deal for your stay on their land."

Taken aback by the sudden change in John's demeanor, Chris nodded slowly. "I'll... uh... I'll gather my things and be right out."

John stood inspecting the two for a long moment before he bowed his head in return and turned back into the hallway.

Chris waited in place, his eyes on Maria, until he heard the sound of the front door opening and closing to signify they were once again alone in the house.

His body pulsing with a current that could only be calmed by her, he pulled her off her feet to cover her mouth with his. Fingers wrapped in her hair, he held her tightly to him, relishing in the sweetness of her lips, in the feel of her body pressed against his own.

"Don't go," she breathed. "Stay here with me."

"You know that's all I want to do." He laid kisses along her jaw, to her neck, and back to her lips. "God, that's all I want to do... But I have to make sure we can stay, and I have to make things right with John. We can't afford for him to turn on us when we are so close."

"Sí. I know," she groaned. "I want to go home. I want to go home and I want to be alone with you for as long as I want without anyone coming to interrupt us. I want to lock a door and stay behind it with you for days if I feel like it."

"I do too." He softly kissed her forehead. "Maria, I have to tell you that I lo—"

"No." She pressed her finger to her lips, lowering her feet to the floor. "You will not say those words to me and then leave me here to wait for you. I have waited my whole life for what comes after. You will say them to me when we have the time. Understand?"

He smiled, running a hand over her hair. "At least let me tell you—

"No," she repeated, placing both hands over her ears. "I do not want to hear anything you have to say when you are leaving."

He pulled her hands from her ears and held them in his, running his thumbs over her fingers. "I'll make it quick then."

"You'd better." She smiled menacingly. "You do not want to keep me waiting much longer. I have not forgotten about that handsome naked man in Oparre, you know."

He hurried after John, his boots heavy with mud as he made his way down toward the beach.

"John, wait!" he called once he was within earshot. "Please, let me explain."

John stopped and spun around, waiting until Chris caught up to him. "Your explanation is not needed," he said pointedly, his expression cool and even. "You confessed your feelings for her months ago, and I have known since we came upon your wife with another that my time with Maria was ended."

Chris took a deep breath. "I should've talked to you first. Should've told you... but I didn't know the feelings were mutual until now. I'm so sorry."

John narrowed his eyes. "So you'd deny that she came down to your prison to tell you she might love me and ask if there was anything between you before she allowed herself to?"

Taken aback, Chris frowned. "She told you that?"

John shook his head, looking down at his feet as they walked slowly toward the ship. "Do you think me the sort of man to promise to watch over her and then *not* follow her when she sneaks off toward danger in the night?"

He raised his chin. "I was there. I heard every word. When she said she could love me; that she might stay here in this time with me... Why do you think I asked for her hand the minute you were released? I thought it honorable you would turn her away out of devotion to your wife. I also assumed, *foolishly*, that such an honorable man would surely fight for his wife instead of so quickly surrendering to pursue a woman who was betrothed to another—another who had been his most loyal friend."

"If she'd said yes to you, I never would've pursued anything further," Chris assured him. "But the fact that she hadn't... And the fact that she did come down that night... I had to know. I didn't mean for that to hurt you, but I couldn't just leave her to stay in this time if I thought she might regret it."

John refused to look at him, keeping his eyes ahead of him as they reached the sand. "And so it is done now."

The tone was far too cold for his liking. There was deep resentment and anger behind every evenly toned word John spoke. It made Chris nervous that a man that held all of their fates so tightly in his hands could harbor animosity toward him. "Where do we go from here then?" he asked. "You and I?"

"You have delivered me a grave injustice, sir. Make no mistake, a wound upon my pride shall not go unresolved. You and I shall find a way to settle this matter before the day is done."

Before Chris could respond to such a grim sounding warning, the captain, standing at the shore among a small group of soldiers, noticed their approach, and waved them in to his circle to put an end to the conversation.

"Christopher. We have been invited to Oparre to take lunch with Tu and inspect his naval fleet. I believe this trip shall be most beneficial in securing temporary residence for Her Grace and her family. I have brought no small amount of red parrot feathers from Tonga to trade. These, alongside building supplies and your willingness to assist in the erecting of additional dwellings for his people, should encourage him to be most welcoming of your extended stay here. I daresay the homes they have already managed to construct with our materials are a vast improvement upon their growing economy."

"They are very impressive, sir," Chris noted, still cautiously watching John out of the corner of his eye.

"Let us not keep him waiting then." The captain smiled, gesturing toward the cutter to encourage them onboard. "I am anxious to see what kind of fleet they have been able to assemble after seeing such architectural marvels here!"

As Chris climbed inside, Edmund grinned from where he'd been adjusting the sail. "Der Mutige! I hadn't realized you would be joining us today! What a happy surprise!"

Chris felt a bit of relief in seeing the familiar faces of Edmund and Hitihiti onboard. They had both shown signs of loyalty toward Chris over the others, and he hoped they might be allies should John decide upon revenge.

"Edmund." He bowed his head, keeping a wary eye on John as he assisted the captain into the boat. "It's good to see you. Are you enjoying your time in Otaheite so far?"

Edmund winked, tapping his pocket to rattle the nails kept inside. "Oh, aye, sir. I daresay any man might find himself remiss to leave a place *so enjoyable* as this."

"Christoph!" Johann called, grinning as he and Georg stepped into the cutter, his presence adding to Chris's sense of relief to be so surrounded by friends. "A fine day for a *naval display*, is it not?"

Chris noticed a sense of sarcasm around the words *'naval display.'*

Johann rolled his eyes. "I can't imagine we'll find more than a few rafts in the water. I am more excited for the roast pig!"

Once the remaining soldiers had boarded, they set sail, moving away from Matavi Bay toward Oparre. The captain spent the duration of the short trip expressing to Johann how impressed he'd been with the rapidness with which the natives had been able to build homes in their absence. He spoke about Tu and how he was certain Tu would be the king soon, then went on and on about their good luck securing red feathers in Tonga.

Hitihiti sat quietly at the front of the ship listening with the other soldiers while Chris's mind raced between the excitement of returning to Maria and the suspicion of what John's ominous words might've meant.

John had always been even-tempered and kind toward him. He'd never shown even a hint of the callousness with which he was now radiating. His willingness to become quick friends had made it easy for Chris to overlook the fact that he was indeed a lieutenant of the British marines.

A man in this century did not wear such a title if he was incapable of brutality. John could be ruthless if he had to be. He'd seen it a time or two in his handling of the marines, but had never considered what it might be like to be on the opposing side of John's temper.

What could John be capable of doing to *'settle this matter before the day is done?'* He certainly wouldn't kill him over a wounded ego, would he? Maybe he would fight him?

The love John claimed to have for Maria had to be infatuation more than anything. There was no passion between them. They'd shared a few kisses and nothing more. He didn't know her; not really, not the way Chris knew her.

He could still taste her on his lips, and that taste brought a chill of excitement to his skin. She would be worth whatever beating John could give him. There was no amount of pain or torture he wouldn't endure to get back to her. He would take whatever John gave and wear the scars proudly, just as he had with Captain Furneaux.

He wouldn't fight back. In the end, he would have Maria, and they would both get in that boat and go home to build a new life together. He wondered what a life with Maria might look like.

What he wouldn't give to have had the insight he had now before they'd been rescued from the island. He sat quietly in the boat, considering every opportunity he could've had uninterrupted with her there; every moment cuddled up together on that island or during their first trip to Tahiti.

Even on board the ship, he could've snuck into her room and confessed his feelings for her at any point in time. He'd had so many chances to tell her, but had wasted them out of obligation to a wife he'd known all along wouldn't be relieved to find him still alive.

Alaina. He'd loved her once, but now that he'd heard the words from Maria, he could hardly remember why he'd loved her at all.

Had it just been attraction? Had it been convenience? Had they ever really known each other or were they just comfortable going through the motions of what you were supposed to do in life? Marriage, a home, kids... What were they doing together? Where would they have ended up if the plane hadn't crashed?

As the small cutter came around the inlet, he was pulled from his thoughts, and every man stood in sudden awe at the spectacle before them.

Hundreds of canoes took over the waters around the beach with thousands of natives aboard, armed with clubs, pikes, and stones, all of them wearing turbans, breastplates and helmets. There were at least three hundred double canoes, most of them sporting a small hut at the rear. Several hundred more vessels were lined front to back with rowers, and the men aboard each chanted loudly; the most distinctive word among them being *'Towha.'*

"Miraculous," Cook said under his breath. "Absolutely remarkable!" He laughed, looking back to Johann. "When Tu invited me to inspect his fleet, I had never imagined it could be this impressive!"

Johann was rendered speechless. His eyes darted from one vessel to the next as they made their way to the shore.

The shore was lined with at least a hundred more men, all of them also dressed for war and echoing the battle cries of the men aboard the canoes. Each group of men was crowded around their own chief, and as they all hopped out of their boat, two men hurried through the crowd to greet the captain.

The first was an older man, his dark curling hair and thick black eyebrows intimidatingly masculine. He said a few words and Hitihiti translated. "This Tee. He uncle of Tu. He take you to Tu."

Tee grabbed Cook's hand to lead him through the crowd when the other man took his opposite hand to pull him back.

The factions of men suddenly swarmed them and Chris found himself being pulled back into the mass as more and more bodies swarmed to fill the space between himself and the captain.

There was shouting, and he heard John order the men back, to no avail. Chris was wedged between several natives and unable to see anyone in his group. He attempted to force his way back through the crowd, and was nearly mowed over when gunfire forced the group to scurry backward, Chris dragged with them.

"Get back!" He heard John shout ahead of him. "Captain, get back on the boat!"

The captain said something in response, but Chris couldn't hear it for the agitation in the crowd he was trapped in. He could feel himself being pushed even further away as more gunshots blasted and the men backed up.

"I will find him!" John answered, his voice heavy with frustration. "Go! Edmund, take the captain back. It is not safe for him here. Once I have Chris, we shall locate Tu and join you and the others on the Resolution! Go!"

"I'M HERE!" Chris shouted among the raised voices of the surrounding men, growing anxious that he might end up stuck in Oparre and away from Maria for a longer amount of time than he'd hoped. "OVER HERE!!"

His cries went unanswered and once he'd finally forced his way back through the crowd, he found only John and Hitihiti still standing on the shore, the captain and the crew already out on the open water.

"I'm here," he said breathlessly, his heartbeat racing as he watched the captain sail away. "Call them back in."

John shook his head. "This is Towha," he said, presenting the large native man standing at his side. It was the same man who had started the raucous by taking Cook's hand to pull him the opposite direction. "He is the navy's admiral, and the captain has offended him by refusing his invitation to inspect the fleet alongside him. We cannot call the captain back now."

The man spoke a few short words and Hitihiti translated. "Towha say he put on great display for captain and captain turn his back. He say English no friend to Otaheite."

"He didn't mean it," John assured him, allowing Hitihiti the time to relay the message between sentences. "He didn't know who you were. We thought he might be in danger. I promise to make this right and return with him to inspect the fleet properly."

Towha spoke, his eyes lingering on the rifle in John's hand.

Hitihiti frowned. "Towha say you make right by sending guns to Eimeo with Towha's navy. Guns help defeat our enemy faster."

John shook his head. "The captain will never agree to it. We are not to engage in any act of war without the crown's authority. My apologies, but this we cannot agree to."

Towha spoke again, holding his pointer finger up as he raised his voice slightly.

"Towha say you send *one* gun then. He send man tonight for spy on Eimeo. You send man with his man to see enemy fleet. If his man found, gun help escape."

Towha interrupted, smiling as he spoke in his low baritone.

"He say this make right with him. He forgive captain if you help."

John frowned. "The captain will have my head if he were to learn we have assisted in any endeavor to wage war. We are prohibited from sympathizing with anyone without the crown's authority; even those that would be considered our allies. I'm sorry, but I cannot agree to this."

Towha looked at Chris and spoke, his tone forcing Chris to wait nervously for the translation.

"Towha say he not tell captain. Tu see you as friend and give you anything. Tu wants men to go. He say…" Hitihiti looked at Chris. "You send this man. He come back by daylight."

Chris took a step back. "No, I can't—

"Actually…" John narrowed his eyes in thought. "This might be a way to secure residence here for your extended stay." He turned to Hitihiti. "If I agree to send this man and a rifle along with him, can Towha convince Tu to allow Her Grace and family to stay on the island for a few months until we can return to collect them? They cannot make the trip to the southern continent."

Hitihiti translated and Chris could feel his palms beginning to sweat. He wasn't sure he trusted Towha.

Towha smiled and nodded, speaking in a much friendlier tone now.

"Towha say yes. He give you many houses for your stay and even a goat."

Chris frowned. "How do we know we can trust him? We've never met this man. I don't remember even seeing him last time we were here."

John pursed his lips, ignoring Chris as he continued. "The captain can never know. No matter the circumstance, he mustn't find out. Might I make the acquaintance of the man you will send with him? I must know I can trust him with one of my best soldiers before I can allow it. Do you have a man who can speak English?"

Towha bowed his head once Hitihiti had translated. He motioned beyond the dissipating crowd toward a set of huts far up the beach.

"You wait here," John said to Chris. "I shall go and make certain tthis man can be trusted to provide for us should I agree to send you. For now, you are a dutiful marine under my command. It should be easy for you to masquerade as such. You are *quite* good at deception. Speak to no one until I have returned."

Chris watched as John, Hitihiti, and Towha headed up the beach, unsure if he should obey, follow, or flee toward the safety of Matavi Bay.

On one hand, if this man did hold Tu's ear, he could ensure they would have a place to stay if he went on this mission. On the other, this man could be lying, and if the captain found out he'd conspired behind his back, he could very well end up flogged and stuck down in that prison once again for nothing.

He shuddered at the thought of his back being ripped open a second time; at the idea of the complete isolation and psychosis that came with being locked in the ship's prison cell, but he couldn't very well turn down the possibility to secure their place here strictly to save himself.

He watched as the men ducked into one of the huts. Could he trust John in his absence? If he were to go on this mission, where would John be? Would he have it in him to return and force himself upon Maria? Is that how he would '*settle this matter before the day is done?*'

He sat down in the sand to consider it.

No. John might have it in him to be ruthless when need be, but he was still a gentleman and a good man at his core. He might try to plead with Maria, but he wouldn't lay a hand on her. Even if he did, the others were with her in the house, and as much as he despised Jack Volmer, he couldn't imagine the man not rushing to her aid if she cried out.

Jack could take John down if he needed to. Even despite the weeks that had passed, his own ribs still ached from their fight. Maria would be safe.

He waited, his mind racing for the hour that passed, until finally John and a very large native man carrying John's rifle against his shoulder exited the hut. Chris stood quickly, brushing the sand from his breeches while the men approached him.

"Chris," John said casually, "this is Oro. He speaks a little English. I was able to confirm from Tu that Towha is, in fact, the admiral. Tu is aware of this mission and has agreed to offer multiple homes in Matavi Bay in exchange for your assistance. This is strictly a spy mission and should be quite simple. Tu desires to know the size of the Eimeo navy fleet. You are to accompany this man on a small canoe under cover of darkness to Eimeo. It is several hours from here by canoe, so you'll need to get going soon. You will count the number of vessels they have and be returned by tomorrow morning. If you are discovered and if the Eimeo pursue too closely, you may use the rifle to create distance. You are not to fire under any other circumstances. Oro is afraid of us. He has insisted that he hold the rifle until the time comes when you must use it. Understand?"

Chris nodded slowly, inspecting Oro's large stature and finding himself stifling a laugh at the idea that this giant man would be afraid of anyone.

He was dauntingly wide and tall, which would've been intimidating had he not had the face of a small child. His friendly expression and full, youthful cheeks made him appear nonthreatening and docile, and Chris could feel his shoulders relax a little with the knowledge he would be traveling with this particular man. He extended his hand to him. "Chris."

Oro looked at the offered hand confusedly. "We go," he said, his voice significantly higher-pitched than what Chris had expected from a man his size. "Take long time. Want be back soon." He motioned toward the naval fleet.

Chris nodded, glancing back at John. "You're sure this is a good idea? If the captain finds out—

"I shall handle the captain should he ever find out. It is my authority under which you go. It will be my burden to withstand any punishment for it."

"And Maria?" Chris asked, noticing Oro was impatiently inching backward toward the fleet. "How will we settle this now?"

John smiled. "Our quarrel can wait. The plan is more important right now, and this will ensure that we will be capable of carrying it out."

Chris took a deep breath, attempting to find some sign of deception in John's demeanor and discovering none. "Alright then. Where will you tell them I am when you show up without me?"

John frowned. "Surely, you do not think I would return to the Resolution without you? Tu has agreed to return us *both* to the captain tomorrow. He's given his word that he shall inform the captain he insisted we stay in Oparre as his guests for the night."

He pulled his pocket watch from his breeches and clicked it open. "If you wish to return by morning, you must go now."

"Okay. I will see you tomorrow then…" Chris said, hesitantly.

"Fairwell," John replied, tucking his watch back into his pocket and turning back toward the hut.

Oro paddled silently, the rifle laying across his lap. He avoided eye contact with Chris as they moved out into the open water, and Chris assumed it was an attempt to deter him from engaging in conversation. Oro's English was terrible and he could see in the few words the man had spoken it was a struggle for him to form the words.

Chris didn't mind the silence. It gave him time to think.

He thought almost exclusively about Maria. He'd been relieved to find out John would be staying in Oparre to wait for him. He didn't like the idea of John returning and begging her to change her mind.

He never should've turned her away in that prison; never should've let her go on with her plan for John. She'd always been able to see through him, and she'd known deep down his feelings were there.

That's why she'd come down. What an idiot he'd been to turn her away. And now... now she might think she was his second choice... She might think he'd only run to her because Alaina had turned him down. In a way, he had, but it wasn't for a lack of loving her.

Despite his mistakes in the past, Chris believed a marriage meant something. He took his vows seriously. He had promised to remain faithful to only Alaina, and he had given everything to honor the promises he'd made to her to never cheat again. For as much as it hurt him to find his wife with another, it was also a relief to be freed from those vows. Being free meant he would no longer have to feel guilt for the way he longed for Maria.

If he'd been in their own time, he would've waited. He would've waited long enough to ensure whatever lingering affection he might've had for Alaina was long gone before he'd shared his heart with Maria. Even though he loved her, he wouldn't risk her doubting him.

Here, though, he needed to intervene. He couldn't let her marry John. He couldn't let her stay in this time with a man she so obviously was settling for. If he had to, he would spend his whole life making sure any inferiority she might feel as a result of his hasty decision to move on from Alaina to her would be diminished.

As the day turned to evening, Chris could see they were actually moving closer to Moorea. He recognized the tall peaks of Mount Tohivea towering in the clouds above it. He could see

Moorea from Tahiti, but hadn't put it together that this was their destination.

He pointed. "That's Eimeo?"

Oro nodded.

"How close will we get? Can they see us?"

Oro stopped rowing and waved his hand toward a tiny island about a mile off Moorea's coast. "Go there. No one see."

Oro proceeded to row them toward it, returning to his silence.

Chris wondered if the captain might return to Oparre when he and John hadn't returned. What would he do if he found John without him? Would John turn him in as the mastermind behind this plan? Pretend he had gone without authority? Would that be his way of settling the matter?

The silence was almost deafening as they rowed in the darkness. At long last, Oro stopped and lit a small oil lantern at his feet.

"Won't they see the light?" Chris asked.

Oro did not respond.

Chris motioned in the direction of Moorea. "They'll see us."

Oro shook his head, reaching into a fabric satchel at his hip. He pulled from it a rolled up parchment, and extended both the scroll and the lantern to Chris.

"What is this?" Chris frowned, the hairs on the back of his neck standing on edge as he took them.

Oro's docile demeanor had disappeared, and suddenly Chris felt exposed and vulnerable. Had it all been a facade just to get him away from Maria long enough for John to make a move? He'd been very hasty to make a decision to send Chris. What had he really sent him off for?

Oro remained quiet, waiting patiently.

Chris set the lantern down on his seat and leaned down into the light to unroll the paper. There, in fine cursive, were written four words:

'Now it is settled.'

Slowly, Chris turned his attention toward Oro and found him pointing the musket directly at his chest.

Not leaving a second to chance, Chris leapt over the side of the canoe, hearing the bang and seeing the flash of the shot fired from the corner of his eye as he did so. He swam deep beneath the water in the direction of the island.

His chest and shoulder were on fire with the salty water. He'd been hit. He could feel the wounds, like a hot poker in his chest, even submerged under the water. He swam on in the darkness, praying he could hold his breath long enough to make it to land and hide before Oro could figure out how to reload.

Chapter Forty Seven

Alaina

Anna had a hand on my stomach, both of us grinning as the baby put on a concert of gentle percussion against my skin. It was dark, and we'd lit a few oil lanterns in the house, all of our island family gathered alone together at last in the small living room area while Maria was off dining with the captain.

A stone fireplace was built in the center of the room and its warm glow illuminated the space with a soothing ambiance that prompted us all to speak a little softer so as not to disturb its crackling.

"You are definitely further along than we thought," Anna said, smiling up at me and Jack.

"How much further?" Lilly asked from her seat across from us where she was snuggled against Jim's side, Izzy asleep across both their laps. "It seems like her belly is doubling in size every few days."

"Thanks, jerkface!" I teased, and she stuck out her tongue.

"Well, I can't be sure," Anna started, pursing her lips as she moved her hand over the swell, "but if I had to guess, I'd say she's at least *four weeks* further along than we thought. I've never felt a more active baby."

"Four weeks?!" I echoed, incredulously. "But... that would mean—

Maria suddenly burst through the front door, her chest heaving from having evidently run from the ship.

"Kreese is missing!" she said, bending against the corset of her elaborate silk gown to catch her breath. "He left this morning with John and never came back. Something happened. I know it—I can feel it. We have to go find him."

"What do you mean, missing?" I asked, sitting up straighter. "Where were they going?"

She leaned against the door, still out of breath. "They went to Oparre with the captain. He said he'd come right back. John came back and so did the captain... but Kreese is gone. John says they got separated, and he doesn't know what happened to him. But I know he is lying. He did something to him. Kreese wouldn't just leave me. He wouldn't disappear. And the captain is in a rage because one of the rifles is missing. Why would a gun be missing the same time as Kreese? John had to do something to him."

Jim frowned. "Them two's been thick as thieves since we got here. Why would John wanna' go and do somethin' to his best bud?"

"Because he found us together," Maria said softly, her eyes watering as she looked at me. "And he was angry. I could see it in his eyes he wanted to hurt him. I know he did something... I could tell when I asked him where he was. He is lying."

I could feel my skin chill as terror swept over me to replace the small bit of jealousy that had momentarily appeared when she'd said *'found us together.'* "Was anyone else with them?"

She furrowed her brow. "I don't know... The captain doesn't go anywhere without Hitihiti. Maybe he knows something? We have to find him. If a gun is missing, Kreese could be hurt somewhere in Oparre. Please. *Please* help me find him."

"Where's John now?" Jack asked, rising from his place beside me to stand.

"I don't know," she said between tears. "I slapped his face and told him I never wanted to see him again, and he left."

"Do you know where Hitihiti is?" Jack inquired as he slid his socked feet into his boots.

"He has a hut not far from here, but I don't know which one it is. Maybe Fetia would know? She is in camp somewhere."

"I know where to find her. You stay here," he instructed. "*All* of you," he added, turning toward me as I'd begun to stand. "I will bring Hitihiti back and we'll get to the bottom of it."

"I want to help," I argued.

He shook his head. "You can help by staying right here in this room and staying calm." His eyes darted down to my abdomen. "You don't need to be running around in a panic when he's probably fine. I'll be right back." He turned toward Jim. "You have the pistol?"

Jim gestured to a small side table where a pistol the captain had gifted him sat. "Ain't nobody comin' in here without a fight."

Jack headed toward the door, stopping at Maria's side. "Try to relax. I'm sure he's alright. He's probably just stuck in Oparre without a ride back. We'll get the truth from Hitihiti." He pulled the door open and disappeared into the night.

"Come and sit down," Magna said to Maria, her motherly tone strong as she patted the blanket beside her where she sat on the floor.

I could see Maria's hands shaking as she stayed in place. I, too, was shaking. I'd thought he was dead once, and I didn't think I could bear grieving him again. I could see the same panic in her I'd had the first time I'd thought him dead, and I attempted to calm her despite my own sense of doom. "He's alright, Maria. You'll see. He's fine."

"He's not fine!" she snapped. "I know it in my heart something terrible has happened." She paced the floor near the door. "He is hurt somewhere. That is the only thing that could keep him from coming back to me!"

"Come on now," Jim cooed, "we don't know what's goin' on yet. Ain't no sense in gettin' all worked up till' we do. Go on and sit down. Hoss'll find him."

"I don't want to sit down!" She growled, pulling at her hair where it was wound up and pinned. "I want to hurt someone. I want to scream and cry and punch things." She looked at me, an unrecognizable rage filling her eyes. "Does he mean nothing to you at all anymore? How can you, of all people, be so calm? Can't you feel something is wrong?"

I could, actually. As soon as she'd said he was missing, a feeling in the pit of my stomach told me something terrible might've happened.

Chris was my past. He was every memory I had up until that island, and more family to me than any person in the room. In truth, I was horrified, but I was attempting to keep those feelings subdued until Jack could return with Hitihiti. "Jack will find him," I said softly.

"*Jack*," she mocked. "He is not half the man Kreese is." She paced angrily. "This is all your fault."

"My fault?" I frowned. "I didn't tell him to go to Oparre."

Maria glared at me. "If you'd just loved him the way he loved you... If you'd known the man he is instead of being so caught up in yourself... He wouldn't have come to me. He wouldn't even look at me if you loved him back."

"That's enough," Lilly said with more ferocity than I'd ever heard from her. She eased Izzy off her lap and stood. "I get you're upset, but attacking her isn't going to change things. This isn't her fault, and you know it. It's yours. You knew what you were getting yourself into by seducing the lieutenant. And you knew what could happen if he caught you with Chris. His anger is on you, not her."

"All of you, stop it," Bud said, placing himself between them. "Nobody is at fault, and you're all getting worked up before any of us has had the chance to find out what's happened. Have you forgotten that Chris's sole objective in Tahiti is to secure us a place to stay while the captain sails south? It is likely he is with Tu doing just that in Oparre. Both of you sit down," he said with authority. "now."

Lilly obeyed her grandfather, sitting silently back down in her place beside Jim. Maria, surprisingly, also seemed affected by the order, quietly making her way to the edge of the room to sit on the floor beside Kyle.

"Huh." Jim raised an eyebrow. "I ain't never seen anyone quiet a woman like that before." He winked at me. "Will ye' teach me how to do that sometime?"

Despite Jim's attempt to neutralize the situation, the room was thick with tension as Lilly, Maria, and I all sat sulking. The others could feel it too, and we stayed in silence for a long while.

Bud, still standing, took a deep breath. "All of you need to remember what we're doing here. I don't think any of you understands the gravity of what it might mean to stay trapped in this time. Chris does. He's had a lot more time to spend thinking about it than we have. We've spoken at length about the dangers of staying; war, plague, and a lack of identity being the least of them. If he has not come back, he is likely focusing on whatever must be done to get us all home safely."

He looked down at Maria. "You need to understand his mission to get us back to our time will take importance over any romantic moments he might share with you. He is determined to find the way home and will do anything to get us there. You can't let your emotions fog your judgment, dear. Rushing to conclusions and placing blame on others—*the lieutenant especially*—might throw a wrench in the whole plan."

"But I know something is wrong," she said softly. "Have you ever had a connection so strong to someone you just know when they are in trouble?"

I swallowed, remembering my own terror while Jack had been stranded on the devil's island. I knew then something terrible had happened to him… just as I knew something terrible had happened to Chris now. She was right.

Bud nodded. "And if something's happened, we will know soon enough. Panicking will not save him if he is already in trouble. When Hitihiti arrives, we will get all the details. I know Jack, and if Chris is in trouble, he will not rest until he is safely returned. We are all in this together; you and Chris included. There's not a person among us that wouldn't go to any length to rescue him if he needs it."

At that, Bud took a seat at the small table, and we all sat anxiously waiting for Jack to return, listening to the fire crack from the small stone fireplace.

Rain began to pour outside, lightly tapping on the thatched roof over our heads and growing more steady the longer we waited.

"I am sorry," Maria finally whispered, her eyes meeting mine. "I didn't mean to say those things to you. I cannot control the things I say when I am angry, and I didn't mean that."

"Yes, you did," I said softly, offering a smile. "It's alright. You're not wrong. I struggle with those same thoughts every day. You're wrong about one thing, though. I *know* the man he is—I've always known how amazing he was... and the fact that I didn't love him the way I should've eats away at me."

"Cain't nobody help who they love, sweetheart," Jim said, pulling Lilly tighter against his shoulder. "Hell, look at me," he grinned wide, "I am a tall drink of ice tea and ye' ain't fallin' over yourself to get a drink now, is ye? A person can be wonderful and have all the good intentions in the world, but that don't mean ye' owe 'em feelings ye' ain't got."

Lilly laughed, resting her chin on his chest as she looked up at him. "A tall drink of ice tea?"

He smiled down at her. "Means I'm a catch, darlin.'"

She rolled her eyes. "You're something, that's for sure."

The front door opened, Jack and Hitihiti soaked to the bone as they hurried inside.

"Where's Kreese?" Maria demanded before they'd even closed the door, rising to stand in front of them.

"He go Eimeo for Tu. Count enemy boats. Come back morning."

"See?" Jack said. "I told you he was probably alright."

Maria frowned. "The lieutenant. Did he know they went?"

Hitihiti nodded. "He one who *send* Der Mutige. He tell Tu give you house here for sending Der Mutige with rifle. Tu say yes."

Maria shook her head. "Why would he lie then when I asked him where Kreese was?"

"He say captain be angry. They keep secret. Even Tu keep secret."

She stomped her foot. "But he wouldn't need to keep it a secret from me!" She placed her hands on her hips, blocking the pathway into the room and keeping both men confined to the entryway.

"Something else is going on here, I know it." She turned to face me. "John said he didn't know what happened to him. He lied. Why would he hide that from me?" Her brow furrowed in thought. "Were you with John when he spoke to Tu?"

Hitihiti nodded. "I talk for him."

"Did John talk to anyone else separately?"

"Tu send Oro with Der Mutige. He speak little English. Lieuten..." He frowned as he tried to remember the word, then giving up, continued, "...he go outside alone with Oro. I not talk for them. I not hear their words."

"Oro," she said, tapping her foot. "You know this man?"

Hitihiti shook his head. "Only little. He Towha soldier. Not same."

"But you could recognize him if you saw him, yes? You know what he looks like?"

He smiled. "Yes."

"They will return to Oparre by morning, you say?" She crossed her arms over her chest. "Will you take me there to wait for them?"

"But captain—

"*I* will deal with the captain. He knows Kreese did not come back. He is concerned for him, too. I will tell him I went to Oparre to search for him. Will you take me?"

Reluctantly, Hitihiti agreed.

"I want to come too," I said, standing from my seat. "I have a bad feeling about all this, and I need to see him come back. I can't sit here and wait."

"Red," Jack looked disapprovingly in my direction as Maria pulled the door open, "you need to stay here and rest. If you're a whole month further along than we suspected, you'll need to stay close to Anna. Any little thing could set you into early labor."

"No." I looked from Jack to Maria. "I can't sit here and worry. She's right. Something feels wrong. I want to go with to make sure he's alright. Besides, if he really is in some kind of trouble, you'll need Anna. And since I need to stay close to her, I *have* to come."

"It's raining," he argued weakly.

"Then I'll get wet," I answered decidedly, sliding my swollen feet into my shoes. "You're not talking me out of this. Anna, are you coming?"

She plucked up the bag housing our first-aid kit and secured it across her body. "Right behind you."

Chapter Forty Eight

Alaina

Under a dark, cloudy sky, Hitihiti rowed us silently in the pouring rain from our beach to the beach at Oparre. No one spoke during the trip, and Jack held me against him, attempting to block the rain that drenched me nonetheless.

Maria was unaffected by the storm. She sat at the front of the canoe, scanning the water for signs of them, her dark hair plastered to her skull and face while her elaborate blue gown turned almost black with the dampness.

When we came around the bend and into the inlet, we could see the light of a single lantern far down the beach. In its glow, the silhouette of a tall man stood with a sword at his hip.

"KREESE!" Maria shouted, leaping off the boat and into the waist-deep water to sprint toward him.

"Maria, wait!" Jack cautioned, hopping into the water to chase after her. "Wait!"

I watched the two of them race onto the beach, disappearing behind the wall of rain, and the instant our canoe came ashore, I too climbed out and hurried after them, leaving my shoes in the sand that pulled them off as I jogged toward the light.

Ahead of me, Maria had stopped short, allowing both Jack and me time to catch up to her, Anna and Hitihiti trailing behind us.

"John," Maria said through gritted teeth, her eyes focused on the man in front of her. "What have you done? Tell me now!"

John did not move. He stood staring out at the water with his arms slack at his sides, the rain pouring over his face. "I'm so sorry, Maria. I am afraid I've done something quite terrible."

He pulled the sword from its sheath, an act which forced Jack to place himself in front of us all, but he took the blade in his hand, offering the hilt to Maria as he dropped down to his knee.

Maria pushed Jack aside and took the sword, the weight of it unexpected in her grip, forcing the steel to fall into the sand. With a second hand on the hilt, she shakily raised the pointed edge to his throat. "Tell me what you've done."

"I ordered him shot," he said with a quivering voice.

"SHOT?!" Maria and I both shouted in unison.

John nodded, rain dripping from his nose. "I'd gone quite mad with jealousy. I meant only to separate you from him—not to kill him, I swear it. The man I sent with him, Oro, was explicitly instructed to shoot him in the arm and leave him in Eimeo. It was my intention only to keep him away long enough to win back the love you'd once had for me. I'd hoped, after a while, you might forgo the plan to return to your time and sail south with me. But I'm afraid I have underestimated your feelings for him."

He lowered his head. "I came here to wait for Oro's return to be informed of Chris's location so I might go to Eimeo myself and return him to you as a token of my love."

"You stupid man!" Maria growled. "No, not a man… a *boy*! You cannot say you love me if you would steal away the only thing in this world that matters to me! You do not know what love is! ¡Hijo de puta, comemierda! You do not deserve the death I would give you!" She threw the sword to one side. "This man, Oro, has he ever fired a gun before?"

"No."

"You stupid, stupid coward of a man! You sent someone else to do what you were too afraid to do yourself! How do you know this man who has never shot a gun before didn't shoot him by accident somewhere other than his arm?! He could've killed him!"

She turned toward Jack, her chest heaving. "I cannot wait for Oro to come back. I must go now and find him. If he is shot..." Her eyes watered. "He won't have much time." Screaming into the sky, she spun on her heel to stomp back down the beach toward the canoe. "Hitihiti! Which direction is Eimeo?"

"The captain will be looking for you!" John called after her, not looking up from his trembling hands. "You are expected to take breakfast with him in the morning. If he finds out... The whole plan could be ruined."

She stopped and turned angrily back around to shout over the rain. "I suggest then that you make up a reason why I, *too,* have gone missing. And you had better pray I find him alive. If I do not, then I give you my word, you will beg for the captain to kill you before I can get my hands on you!"

One by one, Jack, Anna, and Hitihiti turned away from John to follow Maria. I glanced at the sword and back to John's quivering body, considering for the first time in my life actually killing someone. I was shaking with anger. In that moment, every happy memory of Chris played out in my mind within seconds. Every morning beside him in bed, playful afternoon banter, every romantic moment or shared laugh flashed before my eyes.

As suddenly as those visions had come, they were gone, and I saw him lying in the dark, blood pooling in the sand around him. All I could see was red. I wanted to hurt John; wanted desperately to injure him in some way to make him feel the pain he'd just sent through me.

"Come on, Red," Jack whispered, his fingers curling softly around my shoulders. "We have to go."

"Coward," I said down to him before letting Jack turn me back to follow the others.

"Leave the lantern burning," Jack said over his shoulder. "So we can gauge our direction. It is the least you can do."

Back on the canoe, Jack and Hitihiti each took oars, both of them rowing in unison. We travelled quietly for an hour, all of us scanning the dark water for signs of Oro's return.

Beside me, I could feel Maria shivering. The rain had cleared, but she was soaked through. I draped my cloak over her shoulders and took her hand in mine in my lap. "We'll get to him," I said between us. "He's still alive, I can feel it."

"I love him, you know," she whispered, squeezing my hand. "What will that mean for you and I? I could see that it hurt you earlier when I said we'd been found together. I do not want to be your enemy."

I had been possessive for a single fleeting moment when the image of Chris wrapped in a kiss with Maria had played out in my mind. It was unfair and unwarranted. I'd dismissed it, but however short-lived that moment was, Maria had noticed.

"You will never be my enemy, Maria. I want him to be loved. If I was jealous, it is only because I had grown so used to him only ever loving me. And I know I have no right to feel that way. I'll get used to him loving you. Even if it still hurts a little to see, I'm happy it's you. I swear."

"I told him I loved him," she said. "After all this time, I felt like I finally could say the words to him without being afraid he would choose you... and then having him in my arms... the way I'd always dreamt of him... It was like a fairytale. I knew what it might do to our plan and to John, but I couldn't stop myself. I know I did this to him. But God help me. I can't ever undo it. Now that I know what it's like to be his, I cannot go back to being on my own. And if something has happened to him... how can I ever go on living without him?"

As we'd carried out our hushed conversation, I could feel Jack's eyes on me; his presence near me, and I recognized the depths with which I loved him were no different than those with which she loved Chris.

I couldn't go on without him, and that's why I'd chosen him over my estranged husband. It hadn't been selfishness; it had been necessity. I knew what I had done in loving him, and I could never undo it.

"He's going to be alright," I assured her. "Anna is an amazing nurse. She'll get him right back to himself in no time. She's brought all of us back from the edge of death."

She leaned over the edge of the canoe, squinting to see further. "Where's the moon? I can't see anything." She looked back toward the direction we'd come from, the dim glow of John's lantern a small yellow dot on the horizon. I wondered if he was still sitting where we'd left him, waiting for us to come back.

Maria groaned, "Oro could be right in front of us and we wouldn't be able to see him."

"It's pretty late," Jack said. "Or... early. Probably close to two in the morning if I had to guess... Maybe even later. Hitihiti, how much further?"

Hitihiti looked up to the sky. "After sun come up. Many more hour to go."

"You know, if we had a motor," Jack yawned, pulling the rows at a steady pace, "or even a sail... we could be there in an hour— two tops."

Across from us, Anna echoed his yawn. "I'm going to close my eyes for a while. If I need to stitch him, I'll need to have my wits about me."

"You should all try to sleep a little," Jack suggested. "I have a feeling we're going to have a long day ahead of us."

"I will sleep when I know he is safe," Maria said. "I cannot close my eyes now for fear I might be the one to see Oro and miss him."

"Are we in danger going to Eimeo?" I asked Hitihiti. "If you are enemies, how will they have received Chris? Would they hurt him? What will they do to us if they find you among us?"

Hitihiti rowed steadily as he processed the question and the English response. "Eimeo not want war. Towha one want war with Eimeo. Peaceful people. They not hurt Der Mutige or us."

I felt my shoulders relax with that knowledge. I had been hasty to tag along on the search for Chris, assuming he'd only been in Oparre and we would be back before the night was over. Fear had driven us all back onto the canoe and out to sea, and the closer we got, the more anxious I became about the safety of my child. I hadn't meant to put him in danger, nor had Jack, and I knew he too had been having the same thoughts as I heard him let out a sigh of relief.

"When home, I take to my mother." Hitihiti added, apparently reading my mind. "She help with many our baby. She say she want help."

"That's wonderful," I said softly. "I would love to meet her."

"I tell her everything." He smiled proudly. "She say you not be afraid now. She give you food help baby be healthy."

I smiled to myself. I'd never met Hitihiti's mother, but somehow I instantly felt safe; like I was right where I was supposed to be. I remembered Bertie's last words to me. She'd said, *'you're going to have a healthy baby, I know it. I'm close to death and I've seen it for you.'* Never being one to believe in supernatural phenomena, it had come as a surprise to me that I'd believed her entirely. I felt closer to her suddenly, like she'd seen this for me as well.

"What about Izzy?" Maria asked, not pulling her attention from the water. "The captain has asked us if we have found someone to help with her hearing."

Hitihiti nodded. "My mother speak to Temanu. He best healer. He say he try help. Ear very hard fix. Maybe some sound."

I grinned, feeling grateful for our newfound friend in Hitihiti. Sliding down a bit to rest my head against the canoe's edge, I rolled part of my cloak to support my head and closed my eyes. I wouldn't be able to sleep, I knew, not with the ever present dread that sat in the back of my mind telling me Chris was hurt somewhere, but I listened to the oars flowing in and out of the water as we rowed along in silence then.

I let the soft sound lull me into a half sleep, and in that state, my mind took me to a memory I'd completely forgotten. I was sitting in our bedroom at the vanity that was positioned to the side of the French doors that overlooked our backyard. I'd gone to see Dr. Moore secretly. Chris, after all we'd been through with Evelyn, wanted nothing to do with a second chance at pregnancy. I, however, felt the missing presence of children in our home, and I needed to know if IVF would be possible.

The doctor hadn't given me the news I'd hoped for, and when I returned home, I had gone straight to our room to cry. I remembered sitting at the vanity staring at my reflection, wondering what I was doing in this life. My mother and uncle were coming for dinner, and I was filled with a sense of dread that I would have to tell her the grandchild she wanted so badly from me would never come.

I remembered how selfish I'd been in that moment. I wasn't thinking about my mother, my uncle, my sister, or Chris—not in the right way, that is.

Staring at my swollen reflection, I was only thinking of myself and how pointless my existence was in the life I'd been living. Chris had stopped touching me entirely, and I was beyond lonely in the home we'd made together. I had no meaning. My life was made up of working, cleaning, and sleeping. There was nothing that gave my life any value. And I'd thought, what was the point?

I shuddered as the memory came pouring in. I'd stood from the vanity to pull the gun out of Chris's bedside table. With the case in my hand, I'd convinced myself of all the reasons I needed to end my life. I told myself he wasn't happy. And since he would never leave me willingly, I would be giving him the freedom to find a life that *would* make him happy. I would be ridding the world of my miserable existence.

My mother would be free to move to Minnesota to be close to my sister without feeling stuck there to look after me. I would be free of the sadness that was slowly eating away at me. I could see how ridiculous I'd been, but in that moment I couldn't see anything but the pointlessness of carrying on.

Opening the case, I'd held the unloaded gun in my hand. I remember the coolness of it; the unexpected weight against my wrist when I held it to my head and wondered if I had enough courage to pull the trigger once I'd loaded it.

I'd taken the clip and the gun back to the vanity. Too afraid to load it, I once again held the gun to my head and stared at myself in the mirror.

'Do it,' my mind had tormented me. *'Do it if you're going to do it, you miserable asshole. You are obviously too chicken to do anything else to fix this life. Go on and do it. Put yourself and everyone around you out of this misery.'*

Could I do it? And if I did, what would happen then? Would I burn in hell for having taken my own life? I think that thought was the single thing that stopped me. That, and the spaghetti.

"Al?" Chris had called from the downstairs foyer. "Al, the sauce is boiling over. Do you want me to turn it off?"

And just like that, I had snapped back to reality. For some reason, not ruining the spaghetti sauce became infinitely more important than ending my life, and I'd taken the gun back to the case, tucking it and the memory away for good.

When I'd gone to the stove, I'd started to confess. I'd told Chris I went to the doctor, but before I could get to what I'd almost done upstairs, my mother and uncle had arrived for dinner.

Not long after they had arrived, we'd been pulled from dinner to rush to Minnesota after Maddy had fallen through the ice. So caught up in the events that followed, I let the memory fade away, and I hadn't thought of it since.

But now, it was all I could think of. What would I have done if Chris hadn't called for me? What would he have said if I'd had the chance to tell him what happened? Did I ever put the clip away?

I couldn't believe I'd been that person once. It'd felt like an entirely different lifetime. Less than two years later, I was going to marry a man I could never imagine being unhappy beside. I would never let myself be that unhappy again. No matter what.

"There he is!" Maria cried out, waking me from my half sleep to find the sun had begun to rise, the water around us was now cast with a dim grey light, and I could see Eimeo on the horizon.

"ORO!" She called to a large man in a canoe ahead of us. "ORO!" She waved her hands over her head, standing. "WAIT!"

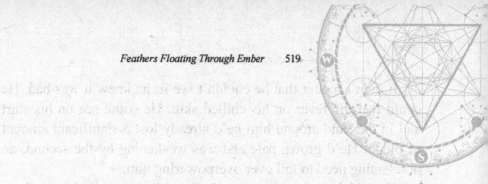

Chapter Forty Nine

Chris

The sun had risen. Chris could feel its warmth on his closed eyelids. His chest was on fire, and memory returning to him, he sat up quickly in the sand to search for signs of Oro coming to finish him off.

The pain that shot through his body with the motion was unlike any other he'd felt in his life. A jolt of electricity raced through his chest and shoulder into the rest of him. He looked down to find his white shirt soaked entirely red with blood.

His mouth was dry—drier than it had ever been—and he could feel his body trembling despite the warm sun.

He looked up at the sky. "I'm going to die, aren't I?"

Looking around the small island for Oro or the boat and finding himself completely alone, he carefully unbuttoned his shirt and slid it off his shoulders to inspect the damage. The blast had sent the round lead bullet straight through his back and into his upper chest, just under his collarbone. He could see the small hole the bullet had made upon exiting, a dark black ring surrounding the opening where blood was slowly oozing out.

He attempted to get a look at his back to see if the damage was worse where it had initially struck him. Reaching behind him with his other hand, he felt for a hole with his fingertips. There was something there, and he winced when his fingers found it.

It didn't matter that he couldn't see it; he knew it was bad. He could feel the fever on his chilled skin. He could see on his shirt and in the sand around him he'd already lost a significant amount of blood. He'd grown pale and was weakening by the second; an unrelenting need to fall over overpowering him.

He laid back on the sand, letting his heavy limbs go limp. "That's all you got for me?" He laughed, rolling his eyes. "Seems about right, I suppose. Every single time I get close to happiness, you manage to steal it away from me. Should've known it'd happen now too."

He could feel his eyes getting heavier, and that made him angry. "Actually, you know what? No. I'm not ready. You can't have this one!" He sat up, jerking his shirt off the sand and ripping it into strips. "I'm not dying yet."

Wrapping the fabric around his upper chest and pulling it tight, he cursed himself for not dressing the wound the night before. The truth was he had no memory of actually coming ashore. All he could remember was reading John's message, jumping off the boat, and swimming. The rest was a blur.

He glanced through the trees toward Moorea, his mouth like cotton as he envisioned the fresh water that was almost within reach. What were the natives like there? Would they help him or would he be worse off if he came ashore on their land? He was dwindling fast, he knew, and if he didn't seek help, he would surely die. He couldn't afford to wait for rescue.

Rescue? He looked out toward Tahiti. What would John have told the others? Would they all assume he was dead? Would anyone even think to come to search for him? And if they did, how would they know where to find him? John wouldn't tell them the truth; wouldn't tell them his location or how he'd come to be there.

What was Maria doing right then? How would she have reacted when he hadn't returned? She wouldn't accept that he'd died, and she'd know Chris would never abandon her. She'd fight. Was she fighting John in that very instant for details?

John. He narrowed his eyes. His most *'devoted friend.'* How could he do this? How could he live with himself after doing such a thing? Did *he* assume Chris was dead? Surely, Oro must have thought he'd killed him with the shot and that's why he hadn't pursued him onto the island.

If he somehow made it back to Tahiti, would John or Oro attempt to finish what they'd started? Would John make up a crime, as he'd offered to do to Jack, to have him imprisoned once again?

He was shivering, and had been for so long that his bones ached from the constant movement. Again, he looked toward the shore of Moorea and wondered if he could make it that far. He didn't think he had the strength to swim, but could see the turquoise waters stretching close to where he was indicating mostly shallow water. Was he strong enough to walk through the water? It had to be a mile between the shore he was on to the beach there.

He attempted to stand and was forced down onto his knee as thick static filled his vision and rendered him blind. When the fuzz cleared, he crawled in the sand toward the water's edge.

"I can't die here," he said to himself. "Stand up and be a man. Stand up!"

He forced himself up, and despite his swaying body, he refused to fall back over. Suddenly Moorea seemed miles away as he stood at the edge of the water, looking toward it. He didn't have the strength to cross. He would die in the water.

He scanned the scene before him.

Boats!

There were canoes out on the ocean between him and the shore, native fishermen with lines in the water sitting patiently in each one. If he shouted loud enough, could he get their attention?

"HELP!" He cried out, his voice cracking and coming out in just barely a whisper. "HELP!" He shouted again and again, each time his voice growing a little stronger.

The fishermen did not notice his cries, but feeling himself fading, he took a deep breath and shouted with all the strength he could muster one final time. "HEEEEEELP!!!!!"

He collapsed in the sand; the water touching his calves where his breeches had risen up from his boots to tease his dry mouth.

He wasn't sure how long he'd been unconscious, but when he opened his eyes, he found an old man with dark, sun-wrinkled skin frowning down at the wound in his chest. His long gray hair blew with the subtle breeze and he was focused on his hands as they prodded the bullet hole in Chris's chest.

He'd been chewing something, and he pulled the paste he created from his mouth to place on the wound, then added green leaves from his side into his mouth to create more.

"Water," Chris whispered. "Do you have any water?"

The man smiled delightedly, bits of green mush showing through his teeth as he said something in his native tongue.

Chris slowly motioned toward his lips. "Water?"

The man made a noise indicating he understood and disappeared momentarily before returning with a clay jug from his boat.

Chris didn't have the strength to sit up. He tried to will his arms to move in order to push his upper body off the sand enough to be able to drink, but they refused to move.

The old man was talking in his own language as if Chris could understand him, and he gently laid a hand on the back of Chris's head to pull it up to where he was holding the jug to take a drink.

When the jug reached his lips, in the first sip, he could feel the water reviving each piece of him it touched; first his lips, his gums, and his tongue, and then moving slowly down his throat to wash away the heaviness that had been trapped there.

He didn't need a translator to understand the man was urging him to go slow as he pulled the jug away between each mouthful. But the little bit he'd taken was enough for his arms to come alive, and he raised his trembling hands to the bottle to tip it back.

For as much as he wanted to be mindful of the man's own water supply, he couldn't stop drinking. Growing more confident, he took larger swigs and eventually chugged until he felt more like himself. He exhaled in relief, letting his head grow heavy again and allowing the man to lower it back down against the soft sand.

"Thank you," he breathed.

The man spoke again, but this time, he wasn't addressing Chris. His attention was focused on someone else on the beach and Chris's heartbeat quickened, visions of Oro pointing the rifle at his chest filling his mind as he forced his head back up to inspect his surroundings.

He saw a young native boy standing a few feet from him, his dark eyes wide as he took in Chris's appearance.

Again, the old man spoke to the boy, this time raising his voice a little, and the boy blinked before scurrying off toward their canoe.

"Are you from Moorea—Eimo?" Chris managed, looking up at the man as he pulled another glob of green from his lips to place onto the wound.

The man bowed his head once in a sign of confirmation.

"I have to get back to Otaheite," he said, praying the word wouldn't send his caretaker away. "I have a woman waiting for me there. Can you take me?"

This, the man did not understand, and he didn't attempt to clarify, returning his attention to Chris's chest.

"A woman," chris repeated, raising his hands to attempt the outline of a woman's silhouette in the air between them. "In Otaheite."

The man nodded and spoke conversationally as he poured a bit of water over the bullet hole.

The boy returned, and he handed the old man a patterned fabric that looked like a blanket, small bits of fringe framing the elaborate brown and black design.

Taking it, the old man pulled a small knife from a satchel at his side and cut the fabric into several strips. He said something to the child, and the boy hurried to Chris's opposite side, both of them grabbing a shoulder and pulling Chris to sit up.

Everything ached. His bones hurt. He had been shaking without end and he was physically exhausted. He was grateful that the boy positioned himself behind him to support his back. There was no way he could've stayed upright on his own.

The man went straight to work on the entry wound at his back, inspecting first for the bullet to make sure it was no longer inside before applying water and the cool paste to the puncture there.

He looked down at his chest and found that the thick green paste had hardened around the wound, spread wide over the area. The blood that had covered his upper body earlier had been cleaned off and the shirt he'd tied around himself was gone. His skin was ghostly pale and he could now see his entire body quivering beyond his control.

He swallowed the thick saliva that was torturing his mouth and wondered how much longer he would be able to stay alive. Was the old man doing all this for nothing? Why was he helping him, anyway?

He watched dazedly as the man began wrapping the fabric around him, his thoughts drifting to Maria. He hadn't thought John capable of this. What else could he be capable of? Was she in trouble? Despite his need to give in, a new surge of willpower filled him at the thought of John laying a hand on Maria. He needed to get to her; needed to make sure she was safe.

"Woman," he said again with more urgency, making the shape of one with his hands and then pointing toward Tahiti on the horizon. "I have to get back to her." He then pointed toward the man's canoe.

The man shook his head, tying a knot at his back, then tapping lightly on the fabric covering his chest to imply Chris would not be able to travel in such a condition.

"You don't understand," Chris insisted. "She could be in danger." He placed a hand over his chest where the bullet had been. "This. What they did to me…" He made the shape of a woman and pointed back to the wound. "They could hurt her."

It was clear in the apology on the man's wrinkled features that he'd understood, but he shook his head, tapping on the same location on his own chest as if to say *'they would shoot me too.'*

"I can go," Chris insisted, attempting to support himself by sitting up straighter. "If you give me the boat." He motioned toward the canoe and back toward Tahiti. "I can go alone."

The man spoke, shaking his head as he did so. He gestured toward Moorea, then back to his canoe. As Chris made a move to argue the man spoke louder, pointing to the canoe more determinedly, then Moorea, and then back his chest. "English," the man said, nodding at Moorea once more.

There was no use in arguing. The old man was right. Chris couldn't row himself back to Tahiti. He would have to accompany them back to their home and hope that once he'd recovered, he could convince them to loan him a canoe to return.

With food and rest, he might be able to make the trip back within a few days. Would Maria be safe among the others? Would Jack and Jim stand in John's way if he attempted to hurt her?

He blew out and nodded, surrendering to his circumstance as the boy pushed him straighter and the man gripped him under the arm.

"Wait, wait!" he insisted, wiggling free of their grip. "I have to leave them a sign I am alive. In case they come searching."

He looked around his body for something to indicate he was still alive. "My shirt... where's my shirt?" He used his hands to illustrate the missing article of clothing.

The man said something to the boy that sent him up the beach to collect the blood-soaked fabric. When he returned with it, Chris reached for the bag hanging at the man's side. "Your knife. Can I use it?" Growing frustrated with the lack of communication, he tried to illustrate a knife by making a stabbing motion.

The man obliged, pulling the knife from the satchel and handing it to him.

Still trembling, Chris spread the fabric flat on the sand, carefully cutting the word "alive" into it as best he could. It didn't look pretty, but he imagined they would understand the message.

He felt around in the sand and came up with a few rocks, securing them around the shirt to keep it in place.

Again, both of them positioned themselves at his sides, gripping him beneath the arms. They wanted him to stand, and with all the strength he could muster, he did his best to assist them in their efforts to pull him to his feet. He leaned heavily against the slender and frail frame of the old man as they led him into the water and rolled him into the canoe, where he landed on his back and let himself slip back into unconsciousness.

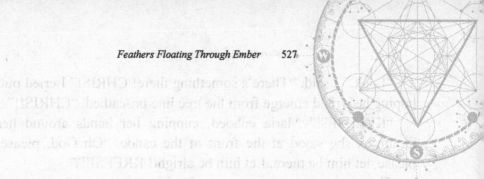

Chapter Fifty

Alaina

The sun now fully up above our heads, I could see the small island Oro had told us he'd left Chris at. He'd informed Hitihiti that he'd shot him and had seen the blood in the water when he held the lantern out to see where Chris had gone.

The act of shooting Chris had completely devastated him. He'd been crying, his face swollen and wet tears lingering on his large cheeks. He'd confirmed John's orders to merely shoot Chris in the arm, but said it was dark and he wasn't sure where the bullet had hit. I could see he was wrought with guilt, and I cursed John for forcing an innocent man to do such a horrible thing. I wondered what he'd promised him in exchange for the act.

Oro still had the rifle in his lap when we'd come upon him. We'd let him return home, encouraging him to return the rifle to camp when no one was around to see. He'd begged for our forgiveness, and Jack had assured him the fault lied entirely with John.

On edge after Oro's account of what had happened, Jack and Hitihiti rowed faster, and the smaller island was becoming increasingly visible. I could see the sand on its beach, the trees that surrounded it, and something out of place near the shore indicated human life.

"Look," I said. "There's something there! CHRIS!" I cried out, hoping he would emerge from the tree line unscathed. "CHRIS!!"

"KREESE?!" Maria echoed, cupping her hands around her mouth as she stood at the front of the canoe. "Oh God, please, please, let him be there. Let him be alright! KREESE!?"

There was no movement on the island, and as soon as we reached the shallow water, Maria leapt off the canoe to wade through the water toward the beach. Jack, too, jumped overboard to tow us the rest of the way.

A distance behind Maria, we hurried off the canoe once we'd reached the shore to find her knelt down in the sand. As we approached, I could see the pool of blood and the soaked red shirt that had once been white beneath her.

I grabbed Anna's arm, pointing toward it as I felt my knees weaken and my saliva thicken with the need to throw up. "Anna, that's too much blood…"

She frowned at the scene as we moved closer. Jack had already reached Maria's side and was kneeling down beside her.

"He's alive," Jack said.

"How do you know this?" Maria sniffled.

"Look at the cuts in the fabric." He ran his finger along the jagged lines. "A. L. I. V. E. Do you see?"

She laughed between sobs, touching the fabric lightly with one finger as if she might lose the message if she wasn't careful.

"He's alive…" She quickly scanned the landscape around us. "But where?" She stood, her once shiny silk dress now limp and drab as she bunched it up to run into the trees. "KREESE?" she called, disappearing beyond the brush. "KREESE??!"

Jack stood, his eyes on the ground as he followed the blood trail to the water's edge and back. "Someone helped him."

He pointed to three sets of footprints in the sand. "See…? One was a child… two came this direction from the water… then all three return to the water." He looked out to the larger island. "He's not here anymore. He's got to be there."

Anna remained on her knees in the sand, inspecting the blood that had spread over it. She looked up at me and shook her head slowly. "We need to get to him fast. He's lost *a lot* of blood."

"MARIA!" I called out in a panic. "MARIA! HE'S NOT IN THERE. HURRY!!"

She flew out of the tree line. "Did you find him?" she called, sprinting to rejoin us. "Where is he?"

Jack showed her the trails of footprints, quickly explained what they meant, and before any of us could say more, she began running to the canoe. "Come on! We don't have time to waste!!"

We all clambered back into the canoe and rowed toward the large island with our eyes focused forward. No one spoke, and I imagined, much like myself, everyone was plagued by the image of the blood-soaked sand.

As we moved closer, we could see natives on the shore watching our approach. More and more of them gathered at the water's edge in anticipation of our arrival. I prayed they knew where Chris was and would take us straight to him.

Joining the natives at the beach, however, a few finely dressed men worked their way to the front of the line. One man in particular stood out. He wore a black captain's hat with a bright red feather sticking out of it. His jacket was a rich red fabric adorned with glistening brass buckles, and a bright white collar at his neck.

The other non-native men stood alongside him, and I swallowed as we reached the shallows, afraid for unknown reasons of the very ominous-looking fellow. He approached ahead of all the native people, offering an arm to help us out of the boat.

Maria, fearless and determined, took the offered arm to quickly step onto the sand. She wasted no time in pleasantries. "We are searching for our friend. He was shot. We think he is here. Have you seen him? Tall, dark hair…"

The man tilted his head as he looked down at her, slowly taking in her silk gown, the sapphire pendant on her necklace, and the sparkling silver earrings that dangled from her ears.

He smiled beneath his short dark beard, his eyes full of menace, and he spoke to her in Spanish.

Taken aback, we all stiffened. The Spaniards were not known for their hospitality, and the language indicated this man was almost definitely a Spaniard.

Maria responded in Spanish, I assumed asking all the same questions, then introducing herself as the only words I understood were *'Maria Amelia, la duquesa de Parma.'*

The man's eyes went wide, and he smiled, taking her hand in his and bowing elaborately before it. "Your friend is here, Your Grace," he said with a thick Spanish accent.

I'd been watching from the canoe, standing daft in the center, and was pulled from the stare when Jack's hands met my sides to pull me down onto the sand.

Feet once again on solid ground, I watched the interaction continue. I didn't like the way he was looking at her. There was a sinisterness in him that made me uncomfortable.

"Take me to him," she said with the authority of a true duchess.

The man crossed his arms casually behind his back, raising a dubious eyebrow. "And who is this man to you? What makes this man so important that a woman so great as yourself would travel in most perilous conditions to retrieve him?"

"His identity is none of your business. Who are you, anyway?" she demanded.

Again, he grinned playfully. "My apologies, madam." He bowed again, removing his hat to expose thick black hair. "Juan Josef Perez Hernandez at your service."

She said something in Spanish that sounded like an order, then broke off into English to add, "and I am not in the mood for games. I must see him now. I must know he is alright. And I have to get him back to Otaheite before nightfall."

"Indeed," Juan Josef responded, scanning the rest of us for the first time. When he reached Jack, his eyes lingered on the dark blue denim pants, his expression puzzled.

"I'll tell you what I shall do for you. I shall have my men escort you to the village where he is, but in exchange, I insist you allow me and my men to return you to Otaheite. I cannot, in good conscience, allow you, your injured friend, or a woman so far along with child to travel back in such a way as you came."

She narrowed her eyes at him. "Why would I trust you? I don't know who you are! No, gracias. We are just fine in our canoe."

He frowned at this. "You do not know who *I* am? Your Grace, I am quite surprised you do not recognize my name."

Jack stepped forward. "Look, we don't have much time. We really need to get to our friend. We can talk after if you'd like, but he's injured and we need to get to him before he gets worse."

"And you must be the surgeon, then?" Once again, Juan Josef's attention went to Jack's jeans, his almost black eyes narrowing in wonderment at the fabric.

"No, I am," Anna said, holding her chin high.

Juan Josef laughed heartily at that. "A female surgeon?! Now, I can die and say I have seen it all! Tell me sir," he returned his attention to Jack, "is the duke aware that his wife has left in search of this man? Was it the duke who shot him in the back? Eh? Perhaps he found the two of them together?"

He flashed a knowing smile back at Maria. "I have heard tales of your promiscuity, madam. I daresay I never would have believed them had I not suddenly found myself caught up in a scandal of yours myself!"

"Please." She let her shoulders fall and adjusted her stance to be less standoffish. "I'm begging you. Take me to him. If you would like to escort me back afterward, I will not fight you. But I have to see him."

He bowed his head, holding a hand over his heart. "Alright then. I shall have my men make ready with the ship. Once you have retrieved your friend, we shan't waste any time in returning you to your English companions in Otaheite."

She took a deep breath. "Fine. Now take me to him."

"Not so fast, *Your Grace*." He glanced at his fingernails. "I have one more question. Tell me, my dear, what are you and your family doing so far from home? I'd not been aware of any Parmesan interest in these lands. What is it that you intend to accomplish here?"

She took a deep breath, and I could see she was making a considerable effort to remain calm. "Parma has no intentions here. It's my cousin. I have come along with her and her husband in the hopes they might find a cure for their daughter's lost hearing. We heard the tales from James Cook's first voyage, and we heard they had healing abilities unlike any other."

He furrowed his brow and scratched at his beard, once again examining Jack's jeans. "Indeed, they do. Your *friend* surely would have perished without their most miraculous intervention. You owe a great debt to these people. He was quite lucky to have caught the attention of Metua. Forgive my directness, *Your Grace*, but it would be rather insulting to leave without paying them the proper gratitude, don't you think?"

I could see Jack attempting to search beyond the crowd for signs of Chris as Maria continued to negotiate with Juan Josef. I, too, began to scan the island, looking for signs of blood that might lead us to his location if we could escape the present situation.

"I will thank them all personally," she promised, "just as soon as I see him. Please. Please show us where he is."

"I am to take lunch with the chief. I see you have brought with you a translator." His eyes zeroed in on Hitihiti. "As I've been unable to procure one for myself, I must ask that you and your translator join me—after, of course, you have been assured your *friend* is alive and well."

"Fine," she said without pause. "Can we go now?"

Juan Josef snapped his fingers, and the man at his side bowed.

"Take them to Metua," he instructed, "and after they have retrieved their man, escort them to the ship for refreshment before we accompany them back."

The man at his side and one other soldier bowed their heads in submission, then led the way through the crowd of natives to a trail that led up through the canopy.

"Maria," I whispered, curling my arm around hers, "I don't trust these men."

"I don't either," she said back, peering ahead of us at the backs of the two men in the lead. "I am not getting on a ship with that man. I'm not sure what he wants from us, but he has no intention of taking *me* anywhere. We have to find a way to lose them once we have Kreese."

Jack leaned in from the opposite side of me. "He knows where we are going," he whispered. "He could follow us to Tahiti.."

She shook her head. "The Spanish and the English are enemies. It would be unwise for him to come in direct contact with the captain and his army. If we can escape him, he will not follow."

"How will we do that?" I asked.

"I help," Hitihiti whispered, smiling. "I see this man before. He mean to our people. Eimeo help. More Eimeo people than Spanish people."

"Do you think he was telling the truth? About Kreese?" she asked. "These men could be taking us anywhere."

Hitihiti slowed his stride to chat with one of the many natives that walked along with us. They exchanged a few words before he returned to lean in. "Yes. Der Mutige just up there. He lie about translator. They take Eimeo woman speak for them."

We came out of the canopy to a small village of thatched huts. Wisps of smoke burned near several, and the smell of pork and banana wafted through the air around us to tease my pregnant appetite.

From one small hut, an old man appeared, a look of concern on his face as he took in the two Spanish soldiers who led us. I watched his tension fade as he noticed the rest of us, and he smiled at Maria as we moved closer.

Hitihiti moved to the front, addressing the man and speaking briefly. He pointed to each of us, apparently explaining who we were in relation to Chris and why we'd come, and the man nodded in approval. He frowned at the Spaniards and said something before heading back inside.

Hitihiti turned to us. "Metua have Der Mutige inside there. He say no soldiers inside." He looked up to the two men. "Soldiers stay here to wait."

Maria was bouncing from toe to toe with anticipation. I, too, was anxious to get inside. She spoke in Spanish to the two men, heatedly instructing them to stay put while we were inside. After a short exchange, they agreed and took a post on each side of the door. They were not going to let us leave.

Maria rushed inside, Anna at her heels. I took Jack's hand in mine, squeezing. "I know he is not your favorite person, but it's meant the world to me that you got us here."

He smiled down at me. "He's a part of you. Not my favorite part, but a part nonetheless. I wasn't going to sit idle when we all knew something was wrong."

"Thank you." I leaned against him, letting him lead me inside.

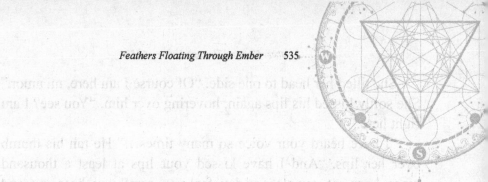

Chapter Fifty One

Alaina

And there he was. He was lying on a cot low to the ground on the far side of the hut. Maria was kneeling at his side, her fingers combing through the hair at his temple.

"Wake up, mi amor," she said softly. "Wake up, my superman. I have come to take you home."

I felt my heart skip a beat when his eyes slowly opened. Just as quickly as the relief had filled me, it was replaced by torment as I watched his hand reach up to caress her face in the same way he'd once caressed mine. I saw the look in his eyes that had once been reserved for me, an unyielding devotion to her in the way he smiled and pulled her lips to his own.

He'd been mine once, and I knew the jealousy was unfair, but I couldn't help feeling the loss of him, unable as I was to look away as he kissed her deeply.

"Maria," he breathed when she'd pulled away from the kiss to smile down at him. "You... How..." He noticed the rest of us for the first time, glancing from me to Jack to Anna, who'd rushed to his opposite side and was inspecting his chest.

He shook his head and let his eyes land back on Maria. "You're not really here."

She tilted her head to one side. "Of course I am here, mi amor." She softly kissed his lips again, hovering over him. "You see? I am right here."

"I have heard your voice so many times…" He ran his thumb over her lips. "And I have kissed your lips at least a thousand more. I can see you clear as day, feel you, smell you, hear you, and then suddenly I am awake again and you are gone."

He looked over at me. "And you. Before we found you, I had a hundred conversations with you… I could hear your voice, see your face as clear as I am looking at you now." He frowned. "I don't know what's real and what is a dream anymore. Have I dreamt it all?"

"No," Maria said. "Look at me. You are awake. You are awake and we are here and we are taking you back."

Anna took his hand in hers. "Chris. Tell me more about these dreams. When it happens, do you control it? Do you feel your mind forming the words; creating the vision?"

He closed his eyes as Maria swept her fingers over his cheeks. "No. Everything feels like it's really happening. I don't have any control over what happens."

"And did you ever have this happen before the crash? Can you remember having any lucid dreams or hearing voices that weren't there?"

"I see where you're going with this," he said. "No. But I'm not crazy."

"What about headaches? Have you had many recently?"

He opened his eyes, kissing Maria's wrist where it crossed over his face. "Yes. All the time." Unconcerned with her questioning, he curled his fingers into Maria's dark hair. "You're really here?"

She nodded. "And I'm not going anywhere."

"I'll be right back," Anna said, looking to me once she'd risen and tilting her head toward the door, encouraging me to follow her outside.

"Alaina," she said the moment I'd stepped into the sunlight, "do you notice anything different about Chris? Changes in his behavior… anything seem strange to you?"

"Everything about him seems strange to me after all this," I said, nervously looking back at the two Spaniards watching us.

She shook her head. "I mean, certain traits… Things he would never do before that he does now?"

"He was always patient," I offered. "He never yelled; not ever. Maria said he was temperamental when they were stuck on the island together. That's not like him at all. And that night with Jack… he went looking for the fight. He would never do that before."

Maria hurried out the door to stand beside me, unbothered by the soldiers whose eyes were glued to her. "What's going on? Why were you asking him those questions? You think something is wrong with him?"

Anna sighed. "I'm trying to figure that out. Hallucinations can be strictly the result of anxiety, trauma, or loneliness, but they can also be tied to a traumatic brain injury. If untreated, it could worsen over time. When we crashed, he hit his head?"

Maria nodded slowly. "Sí, but he has been normal since then. He wasn't in pain after the crash… except for a headache. He just dreams a lot at night or when he is alone. It's not like he hears voices or has these visions all the time."

"Yet," Anna clarified. "Honey, he could have a brain injury. He needs a real doctor."

Maria crossed her arms over her chest. "Well, we don't have one now, do we? Why are we even talking about this when there's nothing we can do? Shouldn't you be stitching him up before he bleeds to death? Shouldn't we be working on a way to get him back? That's what we can do now."

Anna shook her head. "He won't die from that wound. Not anymore. The mixture Metua put on there worked not only as a coagulant to stop the bleeding, but also as a disinfectant. He has no fever and no signs of infection. The brain injury, on the other hand, *could* kill him or cause him to harm someone unintentionally. He needs to be on that first boat when we go. He needs to get to a real doctor right away. Once we figure out how to get him back to

Tahiti, he needs to avoid any strenuous activity. He should be taking it easy. Any little thing could set him off."

Maria looked toward hut as if she could see through it to him, speaking under her breath. "Only three in September."

"What?" I asked.

She frowned. "The percentages... If they're wrong, it could be that only three can pass through in September... like the merchant's journal."

She held up three fingers, lowering each as she said a name. "Zachary, Dutch, and Frankie..." She held up the same fingers on her other hand, lowering each one as she added additional names. "Anna, Isobel, Kreese. I will have to live without him until March. If it is only three, could we go instead together in March? He has made it this long..."

Anna sighed. "I'm so sorry. I wish I could say with confidence I'm wrong in my assumption, but he's got all the signs of an injury. If he doesn't go... If he waits until March... Maria, he might not be recognizable. Plenty of people have survived traumatic brain injury to develop severe psychosis months or even years later."

I saw Maria accept it, even though her chin was raised in defiance. Her eyes were defeated, and I knew she would put his health over her desire to be with him.

"Come and stitch him up then," she said with an evident determination to hide the lump in her throat. "So I can have him back for the little time I have left."

We all hurried back inside. Maria and Anna went straight to work on Chris while I joined Hitihiti, Jack, and Metua on the opposite side of the hut.

Through Hitihiti, Metua explained how he'd found Chris and what steps he'd taken to keep him alive. Afterward, we expressed our concern with Juan Josef and his men. Jack explained the danger we might be in if we could not escape them.

Metua agreed to help us escape in exchange for one favor. He'd heard the stories of England and all the opportunity a man might have there. He begged us to take his grandson, Noona, to the captain so he might lead a better life in England than what the island could offer.

Jack attempted to negotiate around it, saying he could not guarantee the captain would agree to it, but Metua would not be deterred. This was his only requirement. He'd be putting his own life, his own people at risk by helping them. That kind of danger would only be worth it if Noona had the opportunity to build a new life. If we would agree, he would gather his people to help us escape. We could leave the hut from an opening in the back where the soldiers would not see. His people would be ready on the other side of the forest that sat at the hut's rear. They would keep us hidden until nightfall, where they would accompany us to a vacant cove and send us off on one of their own canoes. Metua had the authority among his people that would have them bend to his will.

Reluctantly, Jack made the deal, and Metua sent Noona off to set the plan in motion. We would need to leave soon. Juan Josef wanted Maria to join him for lunch and it wouldn't be long before the two soldiers forced their way inside to insist she accompany them back.

There was one little detail that could not be overlooked. Chris was in no condition to go running through the jungle. We would be going uphill over rough terrain with no path paved for easier navigation. He could barely stand, let alone walk.

With Metua's grandson returned and ready to go and Chris stitched up and re-bandaged, we all scrambled to get him out of the bed and on to his feet.

Jack sighed as he and Maria held him upright with their arms around his back. "I'll have to carry you."

"You're not carrying me," Chris argued, trying to stand on his own and falling into Jack's side.

"Mi amor," Maria said softly, "you cannot walk. Let him carry you. It is only until they can hide us. Do not be proud now. There is no other way to get away."

"*Can* you carry me?" Chris asked. "I weigh more than I look."

Jack pursed his lips in thought, scanning Chris to get an idea of his weight. "It'd be easiest over my shoulder." He looked at Anna. "Will that work with his injuries?"

Anna shrugged. "I don't want his head hanging down. Can you keep your head up?"

Chris nodded. "Yes."

"Alright." Jack took a deep breath. "Let's get going. Can you crawl through that hole?" He motioned to the small opening Noona knelt just outside of, holding the bamboo door open with his small figure.

"I'll manage," Chris said, wincing as he lowered himself to his hands and knees.

I watched the front door, terrified the soldiers might hear us shuffling around.

"You go next," Jack whispered in my ear, placing his hands on my shoulders to turn me toward the opening. "I'll be right behind you."

Maria had already gone through. I could see the blue of her dress just outside in the tall grass. I took Metua's hand in mine and squeezed it. "Thank you."

Metua bowed his head in acknowledgement, then motioned for me to get going. I lowered down to my hands and knees and crawled outside, immediately scanning my surroundings to be sure we were not exposed.

Jack followed behind me, as did Hitihiti. Holding a finger to his lips, Jack ordered us all quiet as he hoisted Chris over his shoulder and raised up onto his feet.

I could see the pain in Chris's face as he raised his head, and I filed in just behind them as we hurried deep into the woods, pushing silently through the thick, wet brush after Noona.

Noona amazed me as he led us through the jungle. He was young, maybe only a year or two older than Izzy, but somehow he seemed so much older.

He wore only a red cloth over his waist, his straight black hair sitting at his shoulders over already defined back muscles. His arms, too, were muscular, and I wondered how someone so young could seem more tough and fearless than most adults as he headed through danger toward an unknown future.

He stopped after an hour of walking at a small clearing. He spoke to Hitihiti, his facial expressions as serious as any adult.

"We wait here for others," Hitihiti said. "They come soon."

I looked behind me toward the village we had come from. Surely, the Spaniards would've realized we were missing already. Were they tracking us? How far behind us might they be? How many more men did Juan Josef have with him? Could they spread out on the beaches in search of us? Could they prevent us from safely escaping? What would they do if they found us?

Jack carefully set Chris down on a bolder, rolling his head from one shoulder to the other as he rose to stretch his back.

"You alright?" He asked Chris. It was strange for me to watch them interact. It made me happy to see them acting civilly toward one another. The fact that Jack had been concerned with Chris's well-being warmed my heart.

Chris rubbed his chest where the bandages were tightly wound around him, wincing a little. "I'm fine."

Maria sat down beside him, leaning to check the bandage on his back. "You stupid man," she said to him, smacking his face playfully. "Didn't I tell you before to never make decisions without me? Do you see what happens when you don't listen to me?"

He smiled. "Consider the lesson learned."

"Good, idiota!" She raised up on her knees on the rock to kiss his lips. "Don't ever do this to me again. I have never been so afraid in my life."

Feeling myself intruding on their very intimate moment, I turned and sat down behind Jack in the dirt, pulling him back toward me so that I could massage his shoulders.

"I love you for this," I whispered.

"It's all for you, you know," he said softly, letting his head fall forward as I worked the knots along his neck. "I can see this is hard for you... seeing the two of them together..."

I wound my arms around him and tucked my chin into the crook of his neck. "It's not hard. I'm glad he has her."

I could feel his cheeks move as he smiled. "Oh yeah? Is that why you scowl at them every time she touches him? It's understandable. You were with him forever. You chose me and I'm secure enough with that decision to be able to talk to you about it, you know. You don't need to hide anything from me."

I groaned, holding him tighter. "I don't want to be jealous," I said, looking over at the two of them snuggled up together. "I want to be happy for them. I like her for him."

"She's so different than you." He tilted his head back, laying a kiss on my temple. "To go from you to her... I mean, you can't get much more opposite than that. That has to be strange. I can see it bothering you."

"A little." I sighed. "But I have you and our child, and that is my whole world. Having him back in my world is a bonus. And seeing him happy, even if the woman is the complete opposite of me... well, it's worth whatever bit of jealousy I might have because of it. I'll get used to it."

The rustling of leaves nearby silenced us all. I saw Chris reach for the sword that was no longer at his hip, and Jack rose abruptly.

We all let out the breaths we'd been holding as a group of native women appeared in the clearing.

Hitihiti went straight to work communicating between the eldest among them, a tall woman with long silver hair.

There was a cove about a mile from where we were. They would lead us there to wait inside the caves for the cover of night to allow us to slip away unseen in a canoe.

This group of Spaniards was unknown to them. They'd never visited the island before and had only just arrived a day prior. Without extensive exploration, they wouldn't know of the cove's existence, and there weren't enough of them to spread out over the entire coastline.

One woman, a young, beautiful girl with dark wavy hair that reached her waist, had caught Juan Josef's eye right away. She would go to him with a claim she'd spotted us running away, and attempt to lead him to the beaches on the opposite end of the island.

Although my back was on fire, I rose to my feet. I was only a little envious of Chris when Jack placed him back over his shoulder. Pregnancy fatigue had settled in almost immediately and the exertion was wearing me down. I wished his arms were free to carry me instead, but I would tough it out. I could rest the minute we were on the boat.

The young woman took off ahead of us to navigate around to the opposite side of the village. The rest of us headed forward toward the cove, speaking quietly to pass the time.

We could hear Juan Josef's men far in the distance searching for us. Thankfully, they were moving away from our location. They were close enough, however, that I'd heard one shout, "the woman is not to leave this island. The captain wants her by any means necessary. Kill the rest if you must. Kill the natives if you must. But bring him the woman. She is our only way home."

We'd all heard him say it, and whatever he saw in Maria meant he would not be lost so easily. If she was his only way home, he would follow us... maybe not immediately, but he would undoubtedly continue to pursue her in Tahiti.

Jack didn't want to wait for nightfall. He and Hitihiti had only been able to navigate To Eimeo with the help of John's lantern the night before. Without it serving as a landmark at our backs, neither of them would've had a sense of direction in the dark.

"But they might see us," Maria argued.

Jack adjusted Chris's weight on his shoulder. "Yes, but by the time they did, we'd be too far gone. It would take hours for them to get their own ship out of the bay, and they'd never catch up to us by rowing. Their boats are all on the opposite side of the island, where we have a straight shot to our destination from this cove."

"They'll kill me if they catch us," she added. "You know that."

"If he were going to kill you, he'd have done it the moment we came ashore."

"He's right," Chris noted. "I don't think he wants to kill you."

"Well, what else would he want with me?"

"Bounty," Hitihiti said, keeping his eyes forward. "I see this man before. He not soldier. He care about riches only. Serve no king. He come to our land many time. Looking for old things."

"So they're pirates?" Jack asked.

"What this word mean?"

"Nothing. Just a word for men who serve no king and sail the seas in search of riches."

Maria looked around cautiously. "Do you think they'll come to Tahiti after the captain has sailed away?"

"Most likely," Jack observed. "Let's hope the captain decides to get comfortable and stay long enough to get us close to September. We'll have to find a place to hide out if Juan Josef comes sooner."

"What do we do about John?" Maria asked. "What if he tries to hurt you again?"

"It's settled now," Chris said. "I'll handle him if I have to."

"No you won't," Anna said softly. "No fighting for you. No more strenuous activity, period. You are going to need to take it easy until we can get you home."

Chris frowned. "Why?"

She sighed. "Because I think you might have a brain injury. I don't want you doing anything that could make it worse."

"Okay, mom," he teased, grimacing against the pressure of Jack's shoulder in his abdomen. "I'm fine."

"Oh, you are, are you?" she spat hatefully. "You hit your head in a horrific plane crash, started seeing things that aren't there, hearing voices that aren't there, and you're fine? Jesus Christ, I'm so sick of all your male egos. If you don't want to completely lose your mind, you'll lay low and do as I say."

I laughed to myself at Anna's innate ability to command men when she needed to. It was so rare that she spoke out, but Chris fell silent, as did the rest of us, and we walked along quietly for what felt like hours.

We came upon a cropping of rocks that led down into the cove and we cautiously made our way down into it. Nestled among the towering cliff faces, we were well hidden from view.

"Are you sure you don't want to hide in the caves just until evening?" Maria asked.

"I'm sure," Jack said, walking with purpose toward the single canoe in the water. "It took us nearly six hours to get here. I won't be able to get us back to Tahiti if I can't see it."

He deposited Chris into the canoe, a little harder than he intended to as he'd grown fatigued from the trip. Chris groaned as he forced himself to sit upright.

Jack motioned for us all to climb inside. "We can outrun them, I promise."

"You can barely hold your arms up," Maria noted. "How are you going to row for six more hours?"

"I'll manage," he said. "Let's go."

"No, you won't," she said, stomping ahead of him to climb in the boat. "I will row." She picked up an oar awkwardly, the length of it being almost as tall as she was. "Hitihiti, come and show me how to do this."

Jack rolled his eyes and let his head fall back in aggravation. "Come on, Red. You're going to have to keep me from throwing her overboard."

We all filed onto the canoe, Jack pushing Maria out of the way and taking the back set of oars for himself while Hitihiti took the front.

Maria climbed down onto the floor alongside Chris, encouraging him to lay his head in her lap. Anna found a seat beside me, and the women pushed us off into the deeper water.

"Are you alright?" Anna whispered, placing a hand on my belly. "This has been too much for you."

"I'm fine," I assured her, anxious to get back and lie down on a soft surface.

She gently rubbed my lower back. "You should try to get some rest. It's not good for you to go without sleep."

"Oh, I don't plan on staying awake for six hours on the water," I said, examining the ocean around us as Jack and Hitihiti rowed vigorously out of the safety of the cove. "I just need to know we're safe first. I won't be able to sleep until I do."

"The wind is working against us," Jack said, not breaking his stride. "If they try to sail, they won't be able to catch us."

We continued out further and further, the large island becoming smaller with no signs of Juan Josef or his men.

We all watched the shores until they became too faint to make out any movement upon them, and at long last, feeling like we were a safe distance from them to do so, I laid down in the floor of the canoe and closed my eyes.

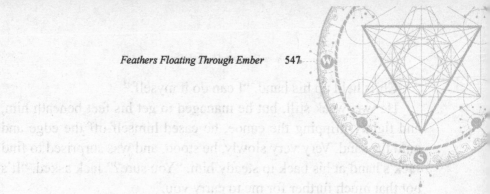

Chapter Fifty Two

Chris

"Mi amor." Maria whispered. "Wake up, my superman. We are safe. Look. We have made it to Tahiti."

Chris opened his eyes. Night had fallen and a bright full moon shone down upon the canoe. Maria was illuminated in the cool blue light, and he couldn't remember ever seeing anything quite so beautiful. He'd been so sure he would die on that island and never see her again. He could feel his whole body come back to life at the sight of her.

"Hello," she said softly, smiling down at him.

"Hello," he breathed, unable to stop himself from grinning.

Not ready or willing to be carried again, he pushed himself to sit up on his own. Everything hurt, but it was the pain of exhausted muscles now, not impending death, and he could deal with that.

"Feeling better?" Jack asked. It wasn't necessarily a friendly tone, but it wasn't the usual coldness Chris had grown accustomed to from him.

"A little," he said.

Jack nodded and stood, climbing over the side of the boat to tow them into the shores of Matavi Bay.

One by one, Jack assisted Alaina, Anna, Maria, and Noona off the canoe. Hitihiti jumped off to stand beside him.

"I help carry," Hitihiti said. "You tired."

Chris held up his hand. "I can do it myself."

He was weak still, but he managed to get his feet beneath him, and tightly gripping the canoe, he eased himself off the edge and onto the sand. Very very slowly, he stood, and was surprised to find Jack's hand at his back to steady him. "You sure?" Jack asked. "It's not that much further for me to carry you."

Chris shook his head. "My legs aren't broken."

He needed to walk. Needed to prove to himself that he could. He had no interest in playing the part of the damaged man for weeks on end. He'd dreamt of Maria endlessly, and there was no bullet or brain injury that would keep him from her now that he was returned.

He forced his legs to move, pushed his back straight, and with growing confidence, he kept pace with the others as they made their way up the sand toward the house.

It was strange to walk without the sword at his hip. It had grown to be as much a part of him as his phone had once been. He never went anywhere without it, and he felt almost lost without its weight. "What happened to my sword?"

"We found it with your shirt on the beach, but we left it in the first canoe." Jack said, his hand hovering at Chris's back in case he fell over. "I'm afraid you'll have to figure out a way to secure a new one. Perhaps you could get one for me as well? I'd feel a lot better if I had a weapon."

"Well, my sword supplier has just tried to kill me, so... it might be a bit more difficult to get one this time around. I'll see what I can do. You might have better luck with Jim."

He felt Maria's hand slip into his and he smiled. He would be alone with her within minutes, and he felt his shoulders relax. With renewed strength, he walked with more determination, anxious to have her alone at last.

"AY!" Jim called from the door of the big house as they approached. He hurried down to meet them.

Placing a hand on Chris's shoulder, he grinned widely. "It's good to see ye' Beanstalk. Ye' had us all worried sick."

"Has the captain been by?" Chris asked. "Or John?"

"Captain came by earlier. We got it covered, though. Hurry up and get in before someone sees ye.'"

He helped him the rest of the way inside. Stepping into the house, the warmth from the lit fireplace instantly filled him with a sense of safety. He was among friends, and at least for tonight, he was free from danger.

Jim continued, "Johann took Phil to climb the summit. It's a cover for yuns. We told the captain he took you and Maria with him and ye'd be back tomorrow. He wasn't too concerned to find the rest of ye' missing. Don't think he even noticed. Oh, but he was right pissed to find out Johann took the duchess on such a dangerous adventure."

Chris sighed. "Johann'll be fine. And John?"

Jim shook his head. "Ain't seen hide nor hair of him since ye' went missin.' Don't reckon he'll be showin' his face round here anytime soon."

"Welcome back," Kyle rose from his seat, a smile lighting his face as he crossed the room. "I'm so glad you're alright."

"Thanks kid," Chris affectionately messed his hair. "It'll take a lot more than that to kill me."

"Okay," Maria said loudly, shooing Kyle away. "You can all talk to him in the morning. Tonight, he is mine. Goodnight." She gripped his arm and began to pull him through the room.

"Wait," he said, setting his feet and turning. Swallowing the pride that had prevented him from doing so sooner, he extended his hand to Jack. "Thank you."

Jack looked surprised at the offered hand, but took it firmly.

"I mean it," Chris said, tightening his hand around Jack's. "Thank you... For everything."

Jack nodded. "You carried us this far. I was just returning the favor. It's nothing."

Chris smiled. "Well, it's something to me, and I appreciate it."

As soon as he'd released his hand, Maria tugged him beyond the living room to the bedrooms in the back of the house. "Goodnight!" She called out again loudly. He stifled a laugh as she pushed her door open and nearly pulled him off his feet into the room to close it behind her.

"I couldn't wait any longer to be alone with you." She said softly, the warm glow of the lit oil lamp reflecting in her brown eyes as she searched his.

"You said you'd be quick, and after just five minutes, I had grown tired of waiting." She ran her fingers along the bandages at his chest. "Are you hurting?"

He smiled, smoothing his palm over her cheek. "Not anymore."

"Do you need to sleep?"

"I'm done sleeping." He closed the gap between them, ignoring the pain in his chest as he gently covered her lips with his.

"But you're hurt," she whispered, her fingers gliding over his chest as he moved her backward toward the bed.

"Not anymore," he said again, curling his fingers into her hair to tilt her face up to him. "There is no pain when your face is in my sight. There is only you. And I'd like to spend whatever time I've got before I lose my mind making certain you know that."

He slowly led her down onto the bed, crawling over her to hover above her lips. "There is only you, Maria. The hurt Alaina delivered was to my pride only, *not to my* heart. She couldn't have hurt my heart because it has belonged to you since the last time we were in Tahiti. I need you to know you are not second best. You are everything. And I love you completely."

"Sí. I know." She bit her lower lip as she traced the lines of his face, outlining his brows, nose, and lips with the tips of her fingers.

He laid a soft kiss against her temple, returning to kiss the other side. "I've said that to you a hundred times in my mind. And it was the hardest thing I've ever done not to say it out loud... Seeing you with John—

"I know all this already too," she teased, running her thumb over his lower lip. "I know you, Kreese... all the way through. Stop telling me things I know and show me all the things I have been waiting my whole life to find out."

He smiled and kissed her then, prying her lips apart with his own as he moved his hips slowly against her. Despite his exhausted body, he was more aroused in that moment than he could ever remember being. He'd wanted her for so long, loved her so intensely, he could hardly contain himself. He too had grown tired of waiting five minutes after leaving her, and every instinct was urging him to rip the clothing from her body so he could immediately lose himself inside her.

He couldn't do that, though. This was Maria. This was a woman that needed more than just the words. She needed to feel loved. And showing her that love would be worth every second he'd had to wait.

She softly moaned against his mouth as he pulled her up against him, unlacing the corset at her back. "I don't want you to hurt yourself, mi amor," she whispered. "If you need to wait…"

"I can't wait any longer," he managed, reconnecting his lips with hers.

Her breathing quickened, and she gripped his face between her hands as he worked the laces loose, using her thumb to pull his lower lip and deepen the kiss. He felt the corset give way and tossed it away from her body, releasing her mouth so he could taste her skin.

He held her in place, slowly working his lips down her neck, enjoying the soft melody of her excitement singing in her throat and the thrill of her fingers growing more emboldened in his hair where she took hold, encouraging his mouth to move lower.

He could feel her breasts against him through the thin fabric of her shift. God, he'd dreamt of those breasts night after night on the island, and as he pulled the collar down and took the first in his mouth, he let out a sigh of relief almost in unison with her own.

He'd never wanted anyone more, had never enjoyed the taste of a woman quite like this. He couldn't have enough, and as she guided him to the other breast, he noticed that the pain in his chest had disappeared; the exhaustion was gone, and there was only the feel of her fingers in his hair, the sweet taste of her in his mouth, and the unyielding anticipation of all that would follow.

Keeping her in place with one hand, the other slid down her thigh to pull the fabric of her skirts up with it. She made a sound, low and deep, as his fingers danced lightly along her thigh until they reached the warmth between her legs.

"Kreese," she breathed, pulling his hair to bring his lips back to her own.

The sound of his name on her lips sent a chill up his spine, and he kissed her deeper, letting their mouths fall into rhythm with his fingers, petting her slowly at first, then quickening as her anticipation grew.

Her head fell backward in his grip as she gasped for air, allowing him access once again to the skin at her throat. Needing to hear her say his name again, he covered the skin with his mouth, becoming intoxicated with the sounds of her, his own excitement teetering near the edge the heavier she breathed against him.

He felt her quiver as she urged his fingers inside, and, hovering over her to gaze down upon her face, he felt a profound satisfaction as he watched the pleasure take over her, his name escaping her lungs with every exhale.

She began to shake, and he tightened his grip on her hair, arching her body so he could give her more. God, he needed to give her more. To give to her was more rewarding than any gift he'd ever received. He was hypnotized by the way she eased and tensed against his touch as she struggled to stay ahead of the climax building inside her.

He watched as her eyes closed and her skin flushed; as her entire body sank into the bed and, unable to fight it any longer, she released entirely.

Raising her head back to him, she opened her eyes and smiled before she kissed his lips. Gripping his shoulders, she urged him to lie back. Unaccustomed to doing so, he slowly relinquished control to her, letting her push him onto his back, where she quickly moved her mouth down his neck and over his chest.

Goosebumps covered his body, and he twitched with every pass of her tongue over his skin. She worked lower until she reached his stomach, grinning seductively up at him. "I have never undressed a man before."

She kissed him above his naval, then slowly slid down the bed to pull off his boots and stockings, ever so faintly laying kisses along his calf as she worked her way back up. "But I am going to enjoy undressing you."

Just as he'd done her, she smoothed her palm up his inner thigh until she stroked him in such a way that he trembled. "I have dreamt of touching you here," she admitted, "since the first time you held me in your arms."

She pulled the ties loose, smiling up at him. Gently, she curled her fingers into the fabric of his breeches, teasing him as her nails danced through the hairs just beneath the fabric for a moment before she pulled the pants off.

He watched her as she timidly let her fingertips glide up his legs, and he shook when they reached their destination, a feather's touch against the sensitive skin releasing a wave of uncontrollable desire through his entire body.

Unable to take a second more, he sat up and brought her back to him, pulling her knees to each side of his hips so he could feel her against him. He wrapped his arms around her, untying the skirts behind her back until they fell away and left only her shift.

She bit her lower lip as she raised her arms over her head in invitation. He laughed, pushing the shift up over her head to finally have her naked in the soft candlelight.

"I have dreamt of *this* so many times." He let his palm slide down in between her breasts, taking in the flawlessness of her naked body; the softness of her warm skin. "It was so real sometimes, I would wake up and wonder if it had actually happened." He scanned both of her eyes. "I am horrified I might wake up still and find you gone."

She smiled and shook her head. "No, mi amor. I am here. This is real." She took his hand in hers and led it to her lips. "However far your mind might go, I will always bring you back."

She kissed each of his knuckles softly. "I promise I will tell you what is real and what is not."

"And how do I know this is real now?"

"Porque no puedes hablar español, mi amor." She let go of his hand to smooth her palms wide against the expanse of his chest, careful of the bandage as she admired his body in the same way he'd been admiring hers. "And so I will always tell you first in Spanish since your mind doesn't know how to speak it."

"I love you," he whispered, his eyes watering as he led her gently down onto her back.

"Are you sure you're alright to do this?" she asked softly, her body contradicting her words as she moved against him in invitation.

"I've never been more sure of anything."

She inhaled audibly as he moved himself inside her, and he was instantly entranced by the warmth of her around him.

How could he ever again be cold now that he'd he felt her body surrounding him? She responded deep inside, tensing and releasing, pulling him deeper as her arms wrapped around his neck and she held him in a kiss that spoke a thousand words.

It was so much more than *I love you* that passed between them. It was all the words; all of her and all of him; two entire lifetimes exposed before each other as an offering.

In that moment, his existence and hers were no longer two, but one, and there was nothing else. He couldn't feel the weight of his own bones, the everyday aches of his muscles supporting them, there was only the rapture of being entirely bound to her.

They moved together, softly at first, both of them clinging to one another as each of them were lulled into a trance by the rhythm of their bodies' movement.

There was no fatigue as they moved more urgently; no effort in his lips as they took hers, no pain in his lungs as she took his breath away and forced him to gasp for air. He was not lost inside her, but found the deeper he explored her. He was whole, and he was filled with the knowledge that so was she.

He forgot about the world around them; about the people who resided just beyond their walls; about the year and the plans to escape, about Juan Josef and John and the captain; about his fading mind and the hole in his chest... there was nothing but his name on her lips, her warmth against his skin, and the sensation of being, for the first time in his life, exactly where he was meant to be.

He trembled as she did, both of their bodies convulsing as they reached the edge, and he cried out beyond his control as they plummeted over it together.

It was only then that the weight of his bones returned to him, the aches of his muscles supporting them forcing him to collapse on top of her. Finally able to breathe, he attempted to set a steady rhythm to it while he adjusted to the returning pain in his chest.

"Oye," she grunted. "Are you trying to kill me? I can't breathe."

Easing himself out of her, he rolled to one side and she let out a dramatic exhale as she turned to face him. She raised her eyebrows, gently running her pointer finger over his lower lip. "Mi amor, if I'd have known that was what it would be like, I would've taken you on that island, wife or not. I didn't hurt you, did I?"

He smiled, softly combing her hair. "No."

She grinned. "I love you."

"I—

"Shut up, I'm not done." She pressed her finger to his lips. "You know that I love you now. We gave each other that knowledge tonight. And I will give you everything I have for the rest of my life. I will never walk away from you and no man will ever catch my eye again. There is nothing, not even death, that could ever convince me to love another. There is only you, mi amor. Forever… And now you know that too."

She ran her fingers through the hair on his chest. "There are some words that *are* important. And I want you to know that I do not love you because we were stuck together. I love you because of who you are. Because you are a man, a *real* man, who stands up for what is right, who goes out of his way to take care of the people around him. I love you because you are good in your heart. Even when you are angry, you are good in your heart. You would never hurt someone on purpose. And I love you because of the way you look at me. No one has ever looked at me and seen me the way that you do. I do not need a mirror when I have your eyes upon me, because I know exactly who I am. You are the only man I have ever loved, and I can't imagine a man more deserving of love than you…"

She smiled widely. "Believe me, I have tried to imagine one many times… There, now I am done." She tugged on his arm. "Put your arm over me."

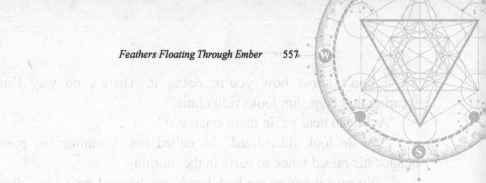

Chapter Fifty Three

Alaina

"Ay freckles," Jim called from the opposite side of our door. "Someone's here to see ye.'"

I blinked my eyes open, peeling my naked body from Jack's as he unwound his arms from me and groaned. "It's too early."

"I'll be right out," I called, laughing as Jack buried his face beneath the fold of his arm. "Go back to sleep. You've had a long night. I have no intention of staying awake for very long. I'll come right back… with food… and we'll sleep the rest of the day away."

"Don't make promises you can't keep, Red. I've got twenty bucks that says there's no way we're going back to sleep today."

"You're on, Volmer," I teased, pulling the shift over my head. "There's no way my pregnant ass is staying awake."

He chuckled beneath his arm. "I like your pregnant ass. It's very…" He glanced at my behind. "…plump."

I rolled my eyes, disregarding the corset and tying my petticoat over the shift. "Thanks."

I pulled an apron over my torso to hide the missing corset, tying it at my back, then added a jacket to hide the missing laces. "There. Done. I'm not even gonna bother with stockings and shoes. If they don't like it, well, that's too bad. I am too pregnant to deal with 18th century fashion today."

"I don't know how you're doing it. There's no way I'm wearing that crap. Jim looks ridiculous."

"Ay! I can hear ye' in there smartass!"

"You do look ridiculous!" he called out, squinting his eyes against his raised voice so early in the morning.

"Lilly says it makes me look handsome beyond my years," Jim muttered, his heavy footsteps making their way across the bamboo floorboards back to the living room.

I leaned down over Jack, pulling his arm from his eyes to kiss his lips. "I'll be right back."

"No, you won't." He sighed. "But I'll wait for you, anyway."

I laughed, pulling the door open and hurrying out into the living room.

Standing near the door was Hitihiti and a short plump woman with salt and pepper hair that I could only assume, based on their very similar facial expressions as I entered, was his mother. Anna was sitting on a chair near the fireplace. She was skeptical of the woman, but intrigued enough to allow her to examine me.

"This my mother, Raina," Hitihiti said. "She help many babies."

"Hi Raina, I am Alaina."

"Alaina," she repeated, smiling wide. She turned to Hitihiti and spoke a few words before turning back to me.

"She say you very beautiful."

"Oh!" I touched my hair self-consciously, realizing it might've been standing on end. "Thank you!"

She didn't need a translation to understand those words. She simply nodded her head once and crossed through the room to stand before me.

She held her hands up and over my belly, looking at me for permission to touch.

I smiled and nodded at her.

She said something and Hitihiti translated. "She say everyone quiet."

Immediately, she smoothed her palms over my belly, closing her eyes as she held them in place and applied pressure. Then she moved lower to hold and press. She did this all the way down and across my belly with her eyes squeezed tightly shut, and the only sound in the room that of the breath passing through her nose.

When she'd finished, she motioned to a chair beside Anna. I happily sat down and was a little surprised when she knelt to inspect my feet.

She clicked her tongue, shaking her head as she spoke at length to Hitihiti.

"She say you stay off feet now. Feet too big. Painful. Pain not good for babies. She make you drink help make feet small again."

She spoke again, placing a hand on my stomach and holding up two fingers.

"She say you have two babies. Both moving. Good sign."

"TWO?!" I asked breathlessly, shaking my head. "No, that's impossible. I shouldn't even be able to have one. Definitely not two."

Again they spoke, and I looked at Anna. She frowned at Raina and placed her own hand on my stomach. "Show me. Show me the two." She held up two fingers and Raina bowed in acknowledgement, placing a hand over Anna's to move it in the same way she'd just done. She pushed her hand softly and held up a finger. She then slid Anna's hand over and pushed again, holding up a second finger.

Anna bit her lip, closing her eyes as she returned to the first spot. "It does explain why you're so big already… but… This is… it's…" She slid her fingers to the second spot, pressing softly, and I saw she recognized something as her eyes opened wide. "Oh my God! It is twins! I have no idea how you're doing it, but you've got two babies in there!"

I felt like I might faint. I could feel my eyes watering as both women continued to feel each side of my stomach.

Two? I'd never thought there could be more than one. How was it even possible? I was both happy and terrified, and I couldn't stop myself from sobbing. Not something I did regularly in front of complete strangers, I was mortified.

"Oh honey, it's going to alright!" Anna assured me. "You've already made it this far. You'll just have to be extra careful now. Strict bed rest, alright?"

I sniffled. "I'm sorry. I don't mean to cry, and I don't even really know what I'm crying about!"

"That's the hormones, dear. You're allowed to cry. This is big news. I imagine it's a little overwhelming. Should I go get Jack?"

I wiped my eyes. "No. I'll tell him."

"Do you want me to show you?"

"Yes."

Just as Raina had done with her, she placed her hand over mine and moved it to one side of my belly, pressing down softly. "Do you feel the baby's movement there?"

"Yes," I said.

"Now, keep that hand there and give me your other."

I obliged, and she moved the other hand to the opposite side, again applying a little pressure. "Do you feel how this one is moving a little differently?"

Once again, I burst into tears. "Yes! I feel them! Oh my God! How is this even possible?"

Anna laughed, squeezing my hands where they rested beneath hers. "You are an anomaly, my friend!"

"Don't do that. Don't get excited for me." I sniffled loudly. "Bertie said I'd have a healthy baby. She didn't say anything about *babies*. I'm going to lose one."

"You don't know that." She turned to Raina. "Do you have any special way to tell when the babies might come?"

Hitihiti translated and Raina pursed her lips before she responded.

"She say lay down on back."

Crying uncontrollably with tears I couldn't decipher between happy or panicked, I eased myself onto the floor and laid down on my back.

She spoke again as she pulled a long, thick braided rope from her pocket.

"She say this not exact. It close."

I smiled at her, rolling my eyes at my ridiculousness as the tears continued to pour down both sides of my face.

She held one end of the rope down against my pelvic bone, then stretched it out over my stomach. She did this for each side of my belly where the babies were positioned alongside each other, each time holding the measurement up and counting the knots.

Anna watched her intently, holding my hand in hers. After her first discovery, both of us were completely absorbed in Raina's methods of examination.

She held up two fingers and spoke.

"She say two more month. If you go whole time."

"Two months?" I sat up, frantically dabbing my nose and eyes with the sleeve of my shirt. "I'm seven months pregnant? I thought I was maybe six months at the most…"

"If that's the case, you most definitely need to stay in bed," Anna said. "AND… you can start to get just a little excited now."

"I can?"

She smiled. "If Raina's right, then your babies can come anytime between now and August and have a really strong chance at survival. Raina, Magna, and I will need to really start planning for the delivery. And I'm serious. I'm ordering you to bed."

"Jack will be happy about that."

"Hello ladies…" Lilly called theatrically, making a grand entrance into the room by twirling her rich emerald green skirts loudly around her. She stopped mid-spin to tilt her head to one side. "Why are you on the floor? And why are you crying?"

"Alaina's having twins!" Anna said. "That's why she's gotten so big so fast and that's why they're moving as much as they are!"

"TWINS!" Lilly swooned, kneeling in floor beside me. "How do you know?!"

I sniffled, attempting to compose myself. "Lill, this is Raina." I presented the woman at my side. "She's Hitihiti's mother. Somehow, in less than ten minutes, with only her hands and a piece of rope, she's been able to determine that I am seven months pregnant with two babies."

"Two babies…" Lilly laughed and placed both hands on my stomach. "Oh my God, I'm so excited! That means there's one for me to hold while you're holding the other!"

"While you're here, anyway."

Lilly made the face she tended to make whenever I brought up not going back. Recognizing the ensuing argument, Anna rose, extending her hand to Raina and inviting her and Hitihiti outside to talk about the delivery.

Lilly shook her head. "Lainey, we don't belong here. *You* don't belong here. Those twins deserve the chance to know your sister, your mother, and your uncle. You have to at least try. Please."

"No," I said firmly. "I can't risk being separated from them. Not even for a little while. I'll find a way to belong here. Jack will find a way to make it work."

"But, your family—"

"I've been thinking about that." I rocked from side to side, grunting as I lifted myself off the floor and into a chair. "Frank's phone. How much battery do we have left?"

She frowned. "The last time we turned it on, it had about twenty-nine percent left. That was months ago, though."

"When the babies come… If we can get the phone to turn on… I'd like to make a video for my mother. I think we all should make something for our families. We can each send something back, even if we all can't make it back. You know?"

"Ooh, I love that idea!" She grinned. "But I still think you need to try. What if the first boat goes through… and then the second makes it… and no one is left behind? Will you try then?"

"No, honey." I shook my head. "You know I can't take that risk. I'll be alright, I promise."

She pouted. "But I don't want to go without you. I love you."

"I love you, too. And I'll write to you. I'll write to you all the time. We have the coordinates to our island now. I will make sure hose letters make it to our cave. I'll bury them in the back cave where my bed was and you can read one every time you miss me. Okay?"

"It's not the same."

"I know. But it'll have to be enough."

"Ay sugar." Jim smiled sweetly as he leaned against the front door frame. "Ye' bout ready? The captain's just had Oro flogged for stealin' a gun and the natives seem right pissed about it. We gonna' have to do some damage control today." He frowned as he looked between us. "What's goin' on?"

"Lainey's having twins," she said softly, her expression still pleading with me to reconsider.

"Twins?!" He grinned from ear to ear. "Well slap my ass and call me Sally! Congratulations darlin! And here I thought today'd already gone to shit!"

He frowned at Lilly, recognizing exactly what was going on between us. "Ay Princess, give it a rest. Come on and fix yer face now. This is good news."

She huffed, standing from her seat. "Gramma told you you'd have a healthy baby, but do you remember what she said to us both after?" She took a deep breath. "She said *'You'll need each other more than ever in this place... In this time... you'll both live happy lives so long as you watch over each other.'* Do you remember?"

I nodded.

"So... if you aren't going, we're not going. Isn't that right, Jimmy?"

Jim sighed. "Let's not give away the bank now. We weren't gonna' say nothin,' remember?"

"Lil—

"No. You don't get to argue with me if I don't get to argue with you. If you guys are staying, we're staying with you. And that is that." She spun away from me. "Come on Jimmy. Let's go fix whatever the captain has screwed up for us." She didn't look back at me, but hurried out the door.

"Jim..." I shook my head. "You can't stay here. She can't be serious."

He raised his eyebrows high on his forehead, blowing out as he ran a hand over his hair. "I ain't goin' against her so don't even try. If she's says we're stayin,' we're stayin.' We got plenty of time to argue about it later. You go on and enjoy your good news with

Hoss. We'll deal with her later." He winked and called after Lilly, closing the front door behind him as he hurried after her.

Not quite ready to return to the room I would likely be confined to for the next two months, I leaned back in the chair, closing my eyes and placing both hands over my stomach.

Deep down, I loved the idea of Lilly and Jim staying behind with us. I would love to have my babies know them as family and grow up with their influence. But that was selfish. They both had lives waiting for them, and I wouldn't rob either of them of that. I wouldn't let them stay.

That's if staying was even an option. If the captain had angered Tu, we might not be able to stay. Or worse… the captain might have worn out his welcome and be forced to leave… giving Juan Josef the opportunity to come searching for Maria.

"Good morning," Chris said softly from the doorway that led to the back bedrooms. "You okay?"

"I'm fine." I sighed, turning toward him. He hadn't bothered with a shirt. With his bandage stretched across his chest and around his back, he hardly needed one. He wore only his black breeches, his hip bones exposed as they hung a little low. The image was so familiar, I'd almost forgotten we were strangers now. "How are you feeling?"

He came into the room and sat down in the chair across from me. "I'm alright. More than alright, actually." He smiled. "I've never been better."

"I like her," I said, surprised at how freely I'd said it.

He looked back toward her room and grinned. "I do too. Is it weird? Talking like this?"

I shook my head. "Not as weird as it should be."

He looked at my belly, then back up at me. "I'm sorry… for letting things get the way they did between us."

"Me too."

He pulled at a loose thread on his pant leg. "Do you remember that night we rushed out to leave for Minnesota? Before we left…" He swallowed and looked up at me. "I saw the gun clip on your vanity."

I could feel my cheeks burn with embarrassment. "I didn't mean for you to see that... I—

"Just... let me say this before someone can come in and interrupt us." He held his hand up. "It's been eating away at me. You asked me when we were there if I knew you... and the truth is Al, right then, I didn't. I didn't come to you that night because I didn't recognize the woman who I'd made so miserable that she would consider ending her life. I was mad at you; mad at myself for not seeing it. I didn't want kids *because* of that clip on the vanity... And... I realized just recently I hadn't *tried* to know you after Evelyn."

He smiled at my belly. "I wanted to go backwards and you... standing in that hotel room... all you wanted was to move forward. It wasn't you holding onto what happened. It was me. I thought, all that time, Evelyn had ruined you. And I spent all that time waiting for my wife to come back to me. But you were there all along. It wasn't you she ruined, it was me. I stopped knowing you after it happened, and I'm sorry. I had to say that to you. And I have to tell you I'm happy you're moving forward. He seems like a good man, and you deserve that."

"She ruined both of us." I looked down at his grandmother's ring still on my finger, touching it with my thumb. With a considerable amount of effort, I pulled it off my swollen finger. "You should have this back," I said, offering it to him. "It doesn't belong to me."

"Al, you don't have to give it back."

"No, I do. It was your grandmother's, and it belongs in your family."

He took it, holding it between his hands to inspect the intricate design. "You're still my family, Al."

I tried to smile, but I could feel fresh tears already spilling down my cheeks. "And you're still mine."

He tucked the ring into his pocket. "You hungry?"

Embarrassedly wiping the tears from my eyes, I forced a smile, ignoring the returning wall he'd put back up between us. "I'm always hungry. There's some salt pork and oats by the fireplace. I can heat some up for you if you'd like."

"No, you relax. You've all done enough for me. The least I can do is heat up some breakfast for everyone."

He stood from his seat and knelt at the fireplace, turning his bare back to me as he unwrapped the oats and pork.

"Oh my God, Chris. Your back!" My stomach turned as I observed the dark, scarred lines that spanned from one shoulder to the other.

I saw him tense for a moment, then his shoulders eased with acceptance. "Took a pretty nasty beating." He looked over his shoulder at me and winked. "It was worth it that he couldn't do it to her instead. Doesn't hurt anymore."

"Are those all from Furneaux?" I asked, still staring at the scars. Maria had told me about Sergeant Harris and what Chris did for her. I hadn't realized the severity of the beating until I'd seen the marks for myself.

"Yes." He carefully took the water pitcher and poured a cup into our iron pot. "Jim and Lilly are having breakfast with the captain... and Jacob and Michael are on the ship... so that leaves... eleven...?" he said to himself, adding additional scoops of oats to the pot and hanging it over the fire.

Dusting off his hands, he hung several thin strips of pork along the spindle that held the pot. "Might be out of my mind, but I can still make breakfast."

I squinted to see through his thick dark hair for signs of the wound to his head. "Are you afraid?"

He balanced on his heel, furrowing his brow as he spun to face me. "Am I afraid I'll completely lose my mind?" He scratched at the bandage over his chest. "I suppose, but we'll worry about that later. For now, we are only worrying about feeding everyone. Want to go wake up the others?"

Frustrated with his unwillingness to open up to me, I sighed. "I can do that." I groaned as I rose from my seat. "I know it's hard for you, but I'm glad we got a chance to talk... and I'm glad to have you back. I was worried sick when you went missing."

He hung a few more pieces of pork on the spindle, not looking up at me. "Glad to be back. We don't have to be strangers, you know."

'But we will be,' I thought, forcing a smile at his turned back. We would never be as close as we once were. It made me sad that we would forever be a little awkward with one another, but he was happy and so was I. That would be enough.

I tapped on Lilly and Jim's door, opening it to find Kyle and Izzy asleep on a pallet in the floor. "Good morning!" I called.

Kyle opened his eyes, blinking heavily. "Morning," he managed, his voice cracking as he yawned.

"Chris is making breakfast for everyone. Can you wake her up and then go outside and collect the others for me? They shouldn't be far."

He smiled and stretched his one arm before softly scratching Izzy's head. "Yeah, I'll get them. I'm starving."

"Thanks."

I hurried to Maria's door and knocked softly. "Maria. There's breakfast."

"I'll be out in a minute," she spat hatefully from the other side, grunting as she attempted to dress herself.

I grinned, rolling my eyes, then opened the door to my own room. Jack was still lying on the bed just as I'd left him, one heavy arm draped over his eyes. I watched him sleep for a few minutes, admiring the image of this man that was all mine, before I crept into the bed to curl up at the side of him.

"You want breakfast?" I whispered, laying a kiss against his chest.

He groaned. "Only if you feed it to me while I sleep."

I chuckled. "I have something to show you."

He uncovered his eyes and looked up at me, twisting a piece of my hair around his finger. "Is it twenty bucks?"

"No... and I still intend to come back in here and sleep after we eat something. Actually, I don't have a choice in the matter. Doctor's orders."

He tilted his head to one side, his brow furrowing. "Everything alright?"

I smiled. "I think so. Here, sit up so I can show you."

He quickly slid up in the bed, looking me over as if I was about to tell him I was dying.

"Give me your hand."

I took his hand and moved it over my belly, showing him, just as Anna had done for me, the movement of two babies instead of one.

His eyes went wide. "Two of them?"

I nodded. "I have no idea how, but yes, there are two." I scooted in close and wrapped my arms around his waist. "Anna wants me to stay in bed. She thinks we're close to being in the clear. Raina thinks I'm closer to seven months pregnant... much further along than we thought... and the babies get a stronger chance at survival every day that passes now, even if they come early."

"But your condition? What about the delivery? If you need a cesarean..."

"Anna is working that out with Raina as we speak. She's got this handled, and I trust her entirely. We'll be alright. This is good news. Let's not spoil today worrying."

"Two babies..." he said breathlessly. "I was terrified to have just one."

I smiled as the smell of freshly cooked bacon began to waft into the room. "And they will both love you like crazy."

He kept his hands on my stomach, pressing softly to feel each one again. He laughed as each one protested the touch separately. "You're happy?"

I nodded. "Very."

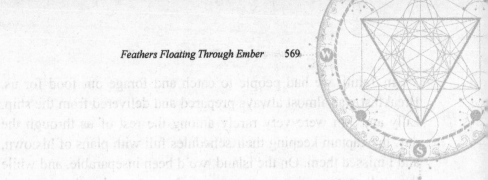

Chapter Fifty Four

Alaina

The captain, through no small amount of gifts and apologies, had made amends with Tu after the flogging. Within a week, routines resumed to what they'd been.

Being restricted to bed rest and unable to leave the big house meant time moved excruciatingly slow. With no television or internet, my mind had nothing to fill the gaps of time between visitors but sleep.

I'd made it to July. My stomach was significantly bigger than it had been during the first pregnancy and with every day that passed, I allowed myself to get a little more excited about meeting my children.

I'd refused, in the months leading up to Raina's examination, to speak to them the way I once had Evelyn. Feeling their movement as the due date drew closer, I let myself begin to love them, telling them stories about my mother and Cece and uncle Bill. I sang to them constantly, which was something I hadn't done since we'd been rescued, and it made me happy to have my voice returned for them.

While life in Tahiti wasn't completely unlike our lives on the island, I did miss the closeness of all of us being together in the little cave. I missed the quietness in the mornings when we'd all gather around the fire for breakfast. I missed our daily routines.

In Tahiti, we had people to catch and forage our food for us. Breakfast was almost always prepared and delivered from the ship. Lilly and Jim were very rarely among the rest of us through the day, the captain keeping their schedules full with plans of his own, and I missed them. On the island, we'd been inseparable, and while they still came to visit me the minute they returned in the evenings, every day they felt a little further away.

I supposed I needed to get used to them being gone. Despite Lilly's insistence that she and Jim would stay behind with us in the 18th century, I knew Jack would make sure they were on the boat to go through. He and I had spoken at length about their lives and there was no way we were robbing them of the future we knew they'd been planning for.

Most days, I spent hours on end with Anna, Magna, Bruce, and Kyle. Bud was always out searching for more answers while Jack was stealthily building up our supplies for our journey. He'd stolen a water cask from the Resolution, and had been slowly collecting bits of oats and honey. Because the natives were known for petty theft and tended to steal for sport, the captain hadn't been suspicious of our involvement at all.

Confined to my bed, my only connection to the world outside our house was through the stories my visitors would share.

Juan Josef was at the top of everyone's minds. Unsure of what exactly he may want from us or Maria, our group was constantly on the lookout for signs of him or his men.

Kyle watched the water religiously through the spyglass, all of us ready to flee for the innermost parts of the island should any signs of him arise.

Hitihiti had confirmed he was a "bad man," and after we'd all heard his man refer to Maria as their only way home, we were sure they would show up within days of the captain's departure. We couldn't afford to be detoured by an 18th century Spanish pirate when we were so close to potentially going home.

Our anxiety over his nearness had only gotten worse as July crept in and the captain had begun to pack up the encampment in preparation of sailing south. Without the English ship anchored in the shallows, there would be nothing to stop Juan Josef from traveling to Tahiti.

Hitihiti had mentioned he'd been there before, and I wondered if he didn't have a few local spies already implanted among us. We knew his ship hadn't left Moorea, and he had to be waiting for the captain to leave. Did he know already we were staying? And if he did, what would his punishment be for our running away?

Part of me wondered if Lieutenant Edgecumbe wasn't one of his spies. He spoke only to Johann and avoided all of us since Chris had returned. He was close enough that we were all forced to see him in passing; Chris and Maria had even been obligated to dine at the same table with him a time or two, but he wouldn't look any of us in the eyes after what he'd done.

Through Johann, he'd informed us that he would see the plan through and would return to ensure that we'd made it home. He promised he would seek us out when he and the captain returned from the southern continent.

Filled with remorse that was visible even at a distance, he would not come to us uninvited, nor would he speak to us unless he was spoken to. His shoulders slumped and head bowed in shame. He was a broken man, but he'd nearly killed Chris, and none of us had been ready to make amends.

I didn't know him the way Chris and Maria had, so I didn't trust his promises the way they did. To send Chris off the way he had; to form a plan so quickly out of pure jealousy made him more dangerous in my mind than even a ruthless pirate such as Juan Josef. If he could do that to a friend, what else could he be capable of? Spying on us wasn't something I considered outside of his capacity, even if Chris disagreed.

Chris was the only person in our group who didn't come to visit me. I understood why he didn't, but it left a place in my heart empty nonetheless. Maria kept me informed of his well-being, sometimes sharing too much with her eagerness to have someone close to talk to.

Much like she'd done me, Anna had ordered Chris to rest. Through Maria, I learned that it was during the times his mind was at rest that it most often slipped away from him. Not ready to go insane, he'd refused to *'take it easy'* and had insisted on keeping his mind occupied.

He'd promised on the day of our arrival to assist the natives in building homes in exchange for our extended stay. Even though Anna begged him not to, and even after Towha had assured him his debt was already paid, he worked morning to night building homes alongside the natives. In the month that had passed, they'd already erected four larger houses and several small homes.

When he was finished with his work, he joined Jim and Johann to obsess over the journals. One night, he mapped out the entire journey, calculating the speed we would need to travel, water rations we would need to keep, and the exact places and allotted times we could stop to restock our supplies before reaching our destination.

He secured a larger cutter from the captain, a canoe from Towha, and we had the inflatable raft. He thought endlessly about the possibilities and risks, and he and Jack had decided that, with no way of knowing that we'd end up in the future together, it wouldn't be wise to send any of the children. Instead, a few would go—Anna could not be persuaded to wait—and, if they made it, they would return in March to inform us of their travels.

Whoever came out on the other side would stick to the truth as far as the island went, explaining to whoever might question them we'd hit a storm and others were left on the island. This would allow more of us to come through if they returned in March with good news.

I could hear Chris already up and building that morning, the sounds of hammers nearby preventing me from going back to sleep.

The house was empty. Jack and Bud had left after breakfast to gather more supplies and Magna was serving as a translator between William Hodges and a few locals at Point Venus, where he'd setup his easel to paint the landscape one final time.

She'd taken Noona with her, hoping to secure him a place in England as William's assistant.

Lilly and Jim had taken Izzy to her regular appointment with the local healer, Temanu. His treatments didn't hurt her, nor did they help with her hearing, but she enjoyed the attention and it solidified our reasons for remaining on the island.

My body ached from both the pregnancy and from being stuck in bed, and I rolled onto my side to attempt to alleviate some of the pain in my back.

"Are you awake?" Lilly whispered from the door to my room.

"Yes," I sighed, sliding up in the bed. "What are you doing back so soon? Why aren't you with Temanu?"

She half-skipped into the room to plop down on the bed beside me. "He wasn't there today. You're not going to believe what I've just witnessed."

"What?"

She grinned mischievously. "Oh, but I shouldn't say…"

"What?!" I laughed. "Come on, don't tease me!"

"I just caught two somebodies locked in a very intimate kiss behind our house."

"Who?" I asked.

"Guess."

"Chris and Maria?" I rolled my eyes.

"Ew. No, that's not even gossip anymore. Guess again."

I pursed my lips. "Anna and Johann?"

She snarled. "No! Johann is married! Why would you think it was them??"

I groaned. "I don't know. She seems to have a little crush on him. Stop stalling and tell me who!"

Lilly crossed her legs, folding her hands over her knees. "I can't just tell you. That would make me a gossip. You'll have to guess before I can say any more. I'll give you a hint. One of them is missing an arm."

I gasped loudly before I leaned in the whisper. "Kyle?!"

"MMMHMMMM…. And??"

"And…?" I raised my hands in surrender.

"Fetia!" She looked around the room to be sure no one was listening. "And it wasn't a little peck on the lips either! I think our little sweet Kyle might be in loooooove."

"Shut up! Are you being serious?!"

She nodded, doing her best impression of Jim. "Serious as a heart attack." She giggled. "Who knows where his second hand might've been if he had one! The one he's got was getting rather... adventurous."

I laughed. "With Fetia?! She doesn't even speak English! Do we even know how old she is?"

She shook her head. "From the looks of things, they were able to communicate just fine. And I think she's probably closer to his age. Maybe 18 or 19?"

"Dammit, I'm so tired of being stuck in this room and missing everything! How long has this been going on?"

"This was the first time I saw them, but I imagine it's been going on for a while now. That definitely looked like more than a first kiss. Chris or Michael might know more. I'll get to the bottom of it." She smoothed her palm over my sizable belly. "Lainey... since we're less than a month away from our departure date, and since we're not entirely sure how far along you are... what if there's a chance you could go through before you have the babies? There might still be time to get you to a real doctor... We haven't decided who's on that first boat yet outside of Anna. We all agree it's too dangerous to send Izzy. What if you were on it?"

I smiled, laying my hand over hers. "These babies aren't sticking around for another month. I can tell I'm getting close. And Anna says we need to send Chris. She's worried about his head. I wouldn't want to separate him and Maria if only three can go through. Whoever we send will come back in March to confirm it worked. If we know more then about the risks and can feel confident, maybe we'll all go home together."

"But if the babies don't come naturally... If you need surgery... Anna doesn't feel good about a caesarean. If you're still pregnant, you should go. *Not* Maria."

"It's alright." I patted her hand. "I've already talked to Anna about this. I'm not afraid. If something happens where it comes down to my life or the babies', I'm alright knowing it's theirs."

"But—

"Lilly, I won't make it another month. And even if I did, I'd risk giving birth to these babies on a raft in the ocean, or worse—in a time that's not the future we know. I won't do that either. Your grandma said we'll be alright. That's enough for me. It should be enough for you, too."

She sighed, scooting back on the bed to lay her head against my shoulder. "I won't go without you, ya know. I'll wait with you until March… And if you decide after they come back that you still don't want to go, I don't wanna go either."

"Lill… if something does happen to me… you'll make sure they're okay?"

"Of course I will. I won't leave them either, I promise."

I smiled, laying my head against hers. "I've been thinking… you know those videos we talked about sending home? I think… just in case… I'd like to shoot mine soon."

She took a deep breath. "How soon?"

"Right after the captain leaves." I placed both hands on my stomach. "I think the babies are coming soon and…" I didn't say I was terrified I might die in childbirth because I didn't need to. She understood. "Anyway, I think we should find a spot outside… away from everything and everyone."

She raised her head from my shoulder. "Anna will kill us if you leave this room."

I turned to face her. "When our people show up out of thin air, they'll be questioned and everything in their possession will be inspected as evidence. We'll all need to avoid talking about time travel. And we should shoot it somewhere where you can't identify the landscape, where you can't make out any of the native people or homes… Candles… lanterns… hell, even a noise in the background can work against us. If anyone asking questions knows about the portal, we can't risk them becoming suspicious of our people and detaining them. We have to make it seem like we know nothing. If they *don't* know about time travel, we can't have them recognize Tahiti and come searching. You know?"

She looked around the room. "Bamboo walls aren't a giveaway... You could stay in this room and we could eliminate anything that might give us away—clothing, lanterns, candles... You can't be hiking around this island anyway and there are more background noises out there than in here. We'll make it work here."

"And what about them?" I tilted my head toward the sounds of hammers just outside.

"Everyone will stop working in order to say goodbye to the captain tomorrow. They'll all be at the ship. We'll shoot your video then."

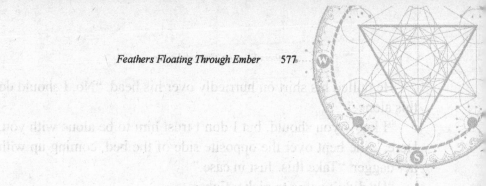

Chapter Fifty Five

Chris

A sound like knocking forced Chris's eyes open. His arms were wrapped around Maria's sleeping body, the warmth of her skin against his comforting in the pitch black room. Not trusting his mind at night, he held her tighter and listened closely for another sound.

Again, the light tapping of knuckles against bamboo came from the door.

"Maria," he whispered, laying a kiss against her bare shoulder, "am I awake?"

She yawned. "Sí, mi amor. Estás despierto. You are awake."

"Someone's here." He unwound his arms from her and eased out of the bed, pulling on his pants before he pressed his ear against the door. "Who is it?"

"…It's John."

He let out a long exhale. With Juan Josef on everyone's minds, he was relieved it was only John. He'd known John would come eventually and had expected him much sooner than the night before their departure. "I'll meet you outside."

He struck a match to light the oil lantern that hung beside the door, instantly illuminating the room in a soft orange glow. Maria sat up in the bed and was holding the sheet over her body. "You want me to come?" she asked softly.

He pulled his shirt on hurriedly over his head. "No, I should do this alone."

"I know you should, but I don't trust him to be alone with you. Here." She bent over the opposite side of the bed, coming up with her dagger. "Take this. Just in case."

"He didn't come to pick a fight."

"I know that too," she said, urging him to take it. "But I will feel better if you have a weapon."

He took the dagger from her, bending to kiss her softly on the lips. "My hero."

She smiled, holding his face over hers. "My big strong man... Will you forgive him?"

He nodded, smoothing his palm over her hair. "I already have."

"You *are* a saint."

"If I were a saint, there'd be nothing to forgive him for. I hurt him first, and I did this after he'd already done so much for us; after he'd risked so much to keep us safe. I can't begrudge him for acting impulsively when he felt betrayed by the people he was working so hard to protect."

"I can," she said hatefully, letting go of his face. "He almost killed you."

He tucked the dagger into the waist of his pants. "He didn't intend to."

"It doesn't matter what he intended, he almost did! And then he waits until the night before he is leaving to show up at our door to apologize to your face?" She furrowed her brow. "He is a coward and he does not deserve your forgiveness, mi amor."

He slid his bare feet into his boots and grinned down at her. "If you want to stay mad at him, then you can be mad for the both of us. I have all I want in this world, and I'm far too happy to carry around a grudge for the rest of my life."

"Don't do that."

"Do what?"

She held the sheet tighter against her chest. "Make your love greater than mine by saying things like that. I do not carry a grudge because I am unhappy. I carry a grudge because I was there. I was there when he lied about not knowing where you were. I watched him lie to me and the captain and everyone around him, knowing full well you could be dead if we didn't get to you. I saw the blood spilled out all over the sand and I cannot tell you how terrified we all were we wouldn't get to you in time. I was there when he let Oro take a beating for the gun he gave him to shoot you with. He did that. He put that fear inside me. I cannot get rid of that fear, and neither can you. It is because of him you scream in your sleep, and it is because of him the rest of us sleep with one eye open. Juan Josef is a threat to us because of what he did. I have everything I want in this world, too. But I will hate that man my whole life for almost taking that from me."

He couldn't help himself from smiling. Sitting in the center of the bed with a scowl affixed to her perfect little face, she looked so small and yet so fierce. When she felt strongly about something, her energy could fill a room so rapidly it consumed everyone in proximity to her. And when there was love behind that energy, it was powerful enough to bring a grown man to his knees.

He'd never been loved the way she loved him; never felt loved so entirely and had never loved anyone in return the way he loved her. This love wasn't a tug of war; nothing was withheld, and neither would ever have to guess whether their own feelings were reciprocated because it was all-knowing.

They saw each other entirely and loved everything they saw. It wasn't perfect, as neither of them were, which made it that much more real. She would fight him to always be better, and he would fight her to do the same.

He took her chin between his fingers, tilting her face up as he bent to meet her lips with his. "You really are my hero, you know."

Despite her attempts to stay angry, she smiled. "Sí. I know." She kissed his lips once more. "And you are mine. Go on then. Hurry up and forgive him so they will all leave sooner. I am tired of their interruptions. I swear to God though, if he tries anything…"

"He won't."

She laid down in the bed, winding the blankets around her body. "I love you."

He grinned. "I know. I love you too."

He stood staring for a moment longer as she closed her eyes and pulled the blankets up to her chin. He'd never remembered being as happy as he was right then, and for the first time since they'd found her, he was grateful Alaina had chosen Jack.

"Oye, will you go already?" she huffed, not opening her eyes. "I can hear you standing there breathing and I can't sleep with you looking at me all creepily, weirdo. Go!"

Laughing to himself, he hurried out of the room, navigating quietly through the house and out the front door.

John was leaning against a tree waiting, the moon reflected on his jacket buttons and on the hilt of his sword.

"Shall we take a walk?" Chris asked.

John nodded, pushing himself off the tree and unfastening the belt that held his sword. He wrapped the belt around the hilt and offered both to him. "You are unarmed, sir, and I cannot expect you to walk with me at such a disadvantage. I want you to have this. You'll need it in our absence."

Chris took it without argument, quickly pulling it around his waist before they both turned toward the beach. It felt like a part of him suddenly restored to have the familiar weight of the sword returned to his hip.

"I do not expect your forgiveness," John said once they were a safe distance from the house. "For I cannot even forgive myself." He turned toward him, stopping his pace. "But I could not leave without expressing to you my most sincere apology. I loved her, and that is no excuse, but I tell you now that the actions I took were unconsciously done. So in love was I that I acted foolishly, in preservation of myself and upon impulse in an attempt to salvage what I thought was her returned love."

He shook his head. "I knew deep down she could never love me the way she loved you, so, out of desperation, I regretfully decided to remove you from her sight. It was never my intention to cause the harm I did. And I have prayed over and over that I could open my eyes to find myself still standing upon that shore to make a different decision. You were my friend, and I betrayed you. She was my heart, and I betrayed her. The guilt shall be my burden to bear for the rest of my life. It has taken me too long to tell you how deeply sorry I am. Because I *am* a coward, and facing what I have done to you has been more terrifying than any battlefield I have ever stepped onto."

Chris took a deep breath. "I should be angry with you, but I can't be, because I betrayed you first. You were my friend, and you'd done so much for me. I told you back in Queen Charlotte Sound I approved, and I gave you my word I would not act upon whatever desires I held for her. It's not your fault you reacted the way you did. I took her from you, and I know the feeling well. I wanted to kill Jack when we found them. I fought him to preserve what little pride he hadn't stolen from me, and while I wish you would've just punched me, I cannot see your reaction any differently than my own."

"You didn't send someone else to do it," he said solemnly.

"I considered it. Had I not already had feelings for Maria, I might've let you place him in irons just long enough for me to plead my case. It's no different."

"I knew you loved her. I knew that first night at dinner... the way you spoke on her behalf; gave yourself away when she could not form the story... I knew you loved her then. We all assumed you were her lover for that very reason. Even the captain made remarks about your secret affair with her. I, however, held out hope we were all mistaken. When you insisted upon finding your wife; when you pleaded with the captain for a sloop to take you to the devil's islands; when you set about the islands in search of any signs of your wife... I thought we were all misled in our assumptions, and since I knew she most assuredly was not the duchess, and because I was instantly captivated by her, I thought I might find in her, my wife. But I knew... I knew you loved her and she loved you... I chose to ignore it. I knew what I was getting into, and still I reacted poorly."

"I didn't." Chris said, kicking the sand around his feet. "I thought it was infatuation from being stranded together for so long. I was fighting it. If I'd known what it was then, I never would've given my consent. I carry my own guilt for that, and I'm sorry that I hurt you."

John crossed his arms over his chest, looking out toward the ocean, where the moon shone over the gentle waves. "There is nothing for me to forgive. Not after what I did to you. I'm sorry."

"You are forgiven." Chris offered his hand.

John looked at the hand and frowned as he took it. "You are not obligated to give your forgiveness only because I have begged for it. I'd no expectations of a restored friendship. I meant only to express my remorse to you before I leave, and to assure you I would return as we had planned."

Chris smiled as he shook John's hand. "I had no intentions of staying angry with you, although I cannot say the same for Maria. I know what you've done for us, and all you'll be sacrificing to return to us. You made a mistake, but so did I in holding back my true feelings for her. We are men, and we cannot be blamed for the things we do when a woman stands between us. You are still my friend, and I assure you, you are forgiven. I hope you'll forgive me as well."

"Of course I do! Of course."

"Good, then it is settled." Chris let go of his hand. "Now, there's another matter I'd like to speak to you about before you go. Juan Josef. Do you know of him?"

John nodded. "Aye. Johann's informed me of your encounter with the man. I daresay he is a most ruthless man, notorious for taking what he wants from whosoever he chooses. I must only assume he has not come to place an attack on the captain because he is outmanned. Johann says you are worried he may join you after our departure?"

Stretching his back, Chris sat down in the sand. "Kyle's been watching the shores around Eimeo. His ship has not left. We're not sure if he knows Maria is not the duchess or if he believes she is and is interested in some kind of bounty. We all got the feeling he was interested solely in her, and I'm worried he is waiting for the right opportunity to come and take her. We cannot keep track of all the natives here as they come and go from these shores. He could very well have someone spying on us. If he knows we are staying... he'll be here the instant the captain leaves. We can't abandon our plan, and there are only so many places we can hide for the month we have left."

"Perhaps I could stall the captain?" John sat down beside him. "If some of the sailors should fall ill... surely he would not disembark with a threat to the health of all of his men? We could ask Temanu for a concoction to induce a sickness..."

"It's too late for that," Chris noted. "They've already packed the ship and are ready to pull the anchor at first light. Besides, I can't risk the captain seeing us leave. I only meant to get a better understanding of the man's character and motive. He said *'she is my only way home,'* and I'm hoping to understand what that meant. Have you met him?"

"Once. He dined at our table as a guest to Frederick Howard of Carlisle. He's a very boisterous man. The Earl took notice of the man's incapacity to adhere to even the most elementary of good manners. He spoke of himself almost exclusively, boasting on his many great accomplishments and riches, not allowing many of the others at the table the opportunity to speak themselves. While he did not address me directly, it was my belief that he has a desire for rank and title that would gain him acceptance in society. He has not been received at many tables and I believe he wishes for nothing more. His piracy may be merely a means to establish himself as an equal to the great men he attempts to associate with."

John frowned. "His reputation at sea, however, is very contradictory to the man I encountered. He's known to be ruthless and savage. He'll kill for what he wants... The man I met only wished for acceptance. I wonder if he sees Maria as a means to wedge himself into society by either winning her affection— assuming he believes she is the duchess—or by exposing her to the real duchess for the imposter she is."

"I didn't meet him myself," Chris said, "but I got the feeling it was the latter."

"Then you have good reason to be concerned. He could very well have eyes upon you this moment. Mightn't you leave sooner? Find solace on a more deserted island along your route?"

Chris sighed. "That's the plan... but Alaina can't leave until she's given birth. I'd hoped she would've had the babies before the captain left. We need to stay until the babies come."

"Juan Josef will not be after *her*. Could you not slip away with Maria and await the others in a safer location? Surely you would not risk Maria's life in order to save the woman who has abandoned you?"

"If he is as ruthless and desperate as you say, and assuming he has spies here already, he could use the others to get to us. They would be just as much at risk as her, and I can't willingly put any of us in danger."

"There is a place, deeper inland and hidden away from view. Fetia knows of it. Her family resides there. I have been there once before. Perhaps you could conceal yourselves there until Alaina's given birth. It might buy you a bit of time to convince Juan Josef you have left with the captain... but if he has a spy..."

Chris shrugged. "The natives surround us at all times. I wouldn't know how to decipher one's behavior from the next. They are all curious about us. It could be anyone."

"So don't tell the natives. Let me assist you. I know the way. Gather your people and I shall take you there now before I leave."

"We can't do that either," Chris insisted. "The captain will expect us all to say goodbye, and we can't move Alaina that far in her condition."

A man cleared his throat behind them, causing both Chris and John to jump up from the sand. Chris pulled the sword from its sheath and spun to face the shadows behind them.

"It's just me," Jack said, stepping into the moonlight. "Take Maria inland tonight. Show me the way."

"But, the captain—

"Go," Jack insisted. "I saw the look on that man's face and I know he is dangerous. He's not interested in anyone but Maria. The rest of us are safe if she is gone. If you slip away now, no one among us, not even our own people, will know you are still here. I'll tell them you've left with the captain to save us from Juan Josef. The natives around us will all believe it if our people believe it. They themselves will inform the captain you must already be onboard the ship."

Chris frowned. "Won't the captain come looking for us inside the ship?"

John pursed his lips. "He'll be too preoccupied with his goodbyes to Tu and Otou to seek you out until after he has sailed off. I can inform him that you changed your mind just before we set sail… it might work."

Jack peered around them to be sure no one was listening. "It has to work. If Juan Josef comes and finds her here, our whole plan is ruined. He'll take us all for bounty and we'll never make it to the portal. If he learns she has sailed off, then he might shift his course to seek her out elsewhere. We have to come back here to wait for the return of the ones we send. If he believes she's gone with the captain, we may just be able to continue with our plan. Go and get Maria. The sun will be up soon so we'll need to leave now." He looked at John. "You're sure you know the way?"

"Positive."

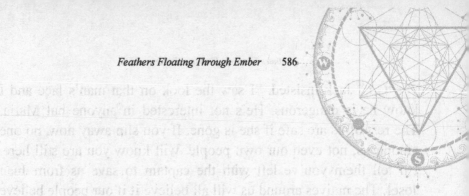

Chapter Fifty Six

Alaina

The house was empty, and I was alone in my room while the others were down at the bay saying their goodbyes to the captain. I'd been awake most of the night with a backache and, finally able to sleep a little, was too exhausted to join the others for breakfast before they left.

Lilly had assured me she would return quickly so we could make our video. I needed to get out of the bed, find a shirt made in the 21st century, and make myself appear somewhat presentable so my family could know I was alright.

I forced myself to stand when suddenly my back seized up, a feeling like my entire torso was being sucked backward into my spine, and the pain was so intense I cried out loud.

I was wet. I could feel it on my legs as I bent over to try to ease the pain. My water must've broken at some point unnoticed and as no amount of bending or maneuvering could ease the pulling, twisting pains engulfing my body, I knew I was in labor.

"HELP!" I tried to shout, praying someone could hear it. I couldn't even make it to my bedroom door. The contraction had me paralyzed where I stood.

I tried to breathe through the pain as they'd taught me during my first pregnancy, but this was crippling. This was nothing like the last time. The last time was quick. She'd been small and while it was painful, it was manageable. I remembered, at one point, thinking to myself *'this is it? This is what women make such a big fuss about?'* I hadn't known yet I'd lose her, and the pain then was comparable to very bad constipation cramps.

Now I understood. I felt as if my insides were being pulled out of me. The only thing I could do was shout. It felt good to scream, and I had to get someone's attention. I screamed through the pain, hoping it would ease long enough for me to lie back down. I wouldn't be able to walk.

'Please, Jack,' I thought. *'Please be close by.'*

Very slowly, the tensing eased, and I was able to straighten my legs and sit down on the bed. Taking several very deep breaths, I told myself I needed to get outside. I needed to get help. Someone had to get Anna and Raina. I couldn't go into labor alone. I needed to get dressed and get myself outside.

I pushed myself up off the bed, holding my lower stomach for fear one might fall out, as I waddled around the room to collect my shift and a jacket. Slowly and shakily, I pulled the shift on over my head.

'We're alright,' I promised myself. *'We've got plenty of time.'*

Sliding a jacket over my shoulders, I pulled it around myself to hide my shift and tottered to the bedroom door. Pulling it open, I was instantly paralyzed as my entire midsection twisted into a knot, threatening to rip all of my inner organs out of me. Again, I cried out, holding onto the door as a means not to fall over.

Fetia ran into the living room, her eyes wide as she took me in. "Jack," I panted, wincing as my back tightened further. "Please. Go get Jack. I need help."

As quickly as she'd appeared, she disappeared, leaving me clutching the door and praying my muscles would ease.

'They're too close together,' I thought. *'That wasn't even five minutes... was it?'*

The pain intensified, creeping from my lower back around to the front and top of my stomach. I couldn't even cry out. My throat felt like it was clutched in the grips of the contraction. I couldn't breathe, couldn't move, all I could do was wait for the muscles to release me.

Very very slowly they did, and I crept carefully back to the bed and laid on my back. My babies were coming… *soon.* I prayed Fetia could get to Anna in time.

I took several deep breaths, reminding myself all was completely natural. "It's okay. We're okay…"

Part of me wanted to stop the labor. I was terrified. The pain had been so intense and unexpected; I didn't think I could continue on. The other part of me had spent the last eight months getting to know my babies and couldn't wait to see their faces. Two conflicting emotions raged inside me as I both looked forward to the next sign of their arrival and dreaded the pain of it at the same time.

I waited and waited and finally, it came, this time feeling less like pulling and more like someone had dug a knife into the top of my stomach and pulled it all the way down to my pubic bone.

My body wanted to push, and try as I might to wait until Anna could get there, I could feel my muscles inherently pushing on their own. I cried out again, and this time, someone responded.

"Alaina?" Magna's voice called from the living room.

I couldn't speak, so I shouted again, and she burst into the room to sit at my side. "I'm here, baby," she cooed, pulling my back up from the bed so she could massage it. "Breathe… it's alright. Breath."

"Where's Anna?" I managed through tears as the pain slowly fizzled out with the movement of her fingers. "Fetia… I sent her to get Anna and Jack."

"I haven't seen any of them," she said, adjusting several pillows behind my back to replace her as she moved to the foot of the bed. I tensed as she pulled my shift up.

"It's alright," she reminded me, gently spreading my legs to take a look.

It was a strange feeling to have her down there. I felt like I was suddenly on display, and nothing was my own. As much as I loved Magna, I was horrified that her face was so near to the area where my body was doing things I couldn't control. Pushing could've resulted in any matter of mess I wasn't comfortable with anyone seeing in that moment. I needed to make sure I hadn't done the unimaginable before anyone else could see.

"Magna..." I leaned forward, trying to get a peek over my massive belly. "Did I, umm..." I cleared my throat. "Have I... umm... well... there's no other way to say it... Did I poop on myself?"

"No, honey." She hid a laugh. "But it's alright if you do. We all do it and it's perfectly natural. You don't have much time, though. You're fully dilated and I believe the first one is coming now. You're going to need to push through the next contraction. We don't have time to get Anna."

"But..." Tears welled in my eyes. Anna was always the one who was supposed to be there. I'd played it in my mind over and over. Anna would be at my feet and Jack would be by my side, holding my hand. I wasn't ready to do this without them. "But I needed Anna... I don't know if I can—

The pressure came again, like a giant fist tightening around my entire torso.

"Push," Magna instructed, pushing my knees back toward me with her upper arms as she pulled the upper half of me toward her. "Come on baby, push and breathe. You can do this."

I did push, my body immediately recognizing what to do. I could feel all of it; a life inside me moving through my insides, its legs and arms threatening to pull out my intestines as it slowly inched lower. It was excruciating and euphoric at the same time. When I couldn't push any harder, I stopped, and the pain became unbearable, as if its little hand was curled around my lower spine and squeezing with the strength of a grown man. I had to push until it was out.

"Keep going," Magna encouraged. "Keep pushing."

I did, my entire body trembling beneath the effort, as if I were attempting to lift a thousand pounds and hold it there with only my pelvic muscles. The longer I pushed, the further the pain moved away, like a noise in the background, one that became fainter and fainter as I felt my child moving through me.

"One more," Magna said. "Her face buried beneath the edge of my shift. "I can see it. You're almost there."

I was exhausted. Everything ached. My abdomen burned and my entire body was trembling with fatigue, but I could feel how close my child was... just barely hanging onto me. She pushed my legs inward and pulled me toward her, and with every bit of strength I had, I squeezed my eyes closed and pushed until I felt the sting of its head and the immediate emptiness of its life being pulled out of me.

I collapsed onto the pillows as I heard my baby make his first sound. His cries were like the highest and most perfect note in an opera, sending a chill through my soul that forced tears into my eyes. Sobbing just as heavily as he was, I reached out for him, and Magna placed him in my arms as she hurried to collect a washrag to clean him with.

He was perfect. His eyes were squeezed shut, and he was covered in fluid, but he was mine and he was perfect. I held him against the skin at my collar and wept.

Magna sat at my side, wetting the washcloth from a basin. "Don't get too comfortable, dear. You've still got one more to go. You're doing great." She gently wiped the slime from his face and body, not daring to pull him away from me.

"Thank you, Magna," I sobbed, unable to pull my eyes from my son—my son! "I'm so glad it was you who was here with me."

And I really was. I hadn't been scared with her there. At no point had I worried about my life or the lives of my babies. The minute it started, I had been too focused on pushing to worry about anything. And Magna had a motherly energy that made me calm and comfortable enough to focus only on my body.

It had hurt like hell, but it was natural and I couldn't have imagined going through it with anyone else. Even my own mother couldn't have made me feel any safer than I'd felt right then. I wasn't the least bit concerned with having to do it again. Part of me was looking forward to delivering my second child now that I knew what I was doing... now that I knew I was in the right hands.

She returned to her place at my ankles, checking for signs of the second baby. "We'll need to swaddle him, and then you need to push again. We don't have much time."

I nodded.

"Which means," she smiled warmly, "you're going to have to give him to me, baby."

I half-laughed, half-cried as I stared down at his wrinkled little red face against my skin. "Magna, you're gonna have to pry him out of my arms. I don't think I can let him go on my own."

She laughed her deep rich laugh, and obliged, pulling him gently away from me to wrap him tightly in the fabric of one of my skirts.

I watched her as she did so, keeping my eyes on his limbs as they all moved in perfect protest against her. "What will you name him?" She asked, smiling down at him as she placed him on the bed beside me.

"I don't know..." I sniffled, attempting not to break down. "I wouldn't give him a name until I knew he was alive and well." I winced as the familiar tightening came again in my lower back.

"Shall we meet the other one now?"

I did break down then and nodded as the tears fell uncontrollably down my cheeks with the subduing of the contraction. "Yes!"

"You really are doing great," she said as she returned to the foot of the bed. "If your mother were here, she'd be proud of how strong you are. I know I am."

She pushed my knees back upward. "Just a little bit more and you can rest. When the next one comes, you gotta push, okay?"

I sat up and prepared myself for the next round, taking several deep breaths as I waited for the familiar pull of the next contraction. "Having you here, Magna, is like having her with me. You've been a mother to us all this past year... and... I love you very much."

She smiled wide. "I love you too, honey. And I'm not leaving you either. These babies are gonna need a gramma to spoil them. Anna's gonna find the way home, and when she comes back in March, we're all gonna go back together. You'll see. And when we get back home, these babies will always have this gramma watching over them."

I laughed, taking her hand in mine to squeeze it. "I can't wait. Are you anxious to get back to Haunui? Being married as long as you've been, I can't imagine how hard this has all been for you."

She sighed, looking at me but not quite seeing me. "I am anxious to get back to him yes, but he will not be there waiting for me. He died several years before our plane crashed."

"Oh, Magna, why didn't you say so? I'm so sorry! I just assumed—

"Sorry?" She shook her head. "No honey. I will see him again. Do not be sorry for me. He was in pain and death took that pain from him. Death will take that pain from me as well one day. Until then, I will be mother and grandmother to the people I have been left behind to care for. I am not without company as I wait to join him."

I squeezed her hand again. "He would be proud of you... for how strong you are."

We sat in silence then and her words sank in deep. As I looked down at my healthy little boy, I thought of Evelyn for the first time since we'd left the island. She'd been in pain, unable to breathe or eat, and death had taken that pain from her.

I had been selfish to get as upset as I had back then. Death was a relief to her and I should've seen it that way instead of as an attack on me. I would be with her one day, and until then, I was not without company. I smiled at the little squirming body that laid beside me. I would be mother and grandmother to the people I had been left behind to care for.

The second baby, unlike the first, was stubborn. The contractions intensified, and I'd been pushing off and on for thirty minutes before Lilly rushed into the room.

"Lainey!" she shouted, her voice far off in the distance as I focused only on pushing to alleviate the excruciating pain in my lower stomach. "Lainey! Oh my God! Where's Anna? Where's Jack?"

"She sent Fetia off almost an hour ago to find them," Magna responded, not looking away from me as she coached me through breathing. "Can you go get them? We have a boy already."

"A boy!" Her eyes darted to the little bundle at my side. "Oh my God! And—That's a lot of blood… Is she—

"Lilly," Magna said calmly, nodding her head with each breath to remind me to keep breathing, "go and get the others. I promise you, she is better than fine."

Blood? I could feel my heart pounding as Lilly rushed out of the room. Was something wrong? Had I lost the second one? Is that why it was taking so long? Was Magna attempting to keep me calm just long enough for Anna to get there and do something different? Would I need surgery for the second one? Was I going to die?

Magna recognized the terror and slowly shook her head, smiling. "Look at me. I will tell you if there is something wrong. There is nothing wrong, okay? Do not let that panic you. Blood is normal. You've just had a person come out of you and another one on its way. You're fine. Keep going."

I pushed as hard as my tired body would allow until I couldn't push any harder and I was forced to lay back, accepting the increased level of pain it caused me to stop just to give my trembling muscles a moment of rest. "I don't know how much more I've got left."

Magna was exhausted, too. I could see it in her eyes. "I'm just going to check really quick."

I felt her reach inside but was too tired to be self-conscious. I didn't mind. I prayed she could feel the second baby, begged God to let her pull it out of me. If I didn't push, my body would clench in a knot of stabbing pain. If I did push, I ran out of breath and my muscles ached. I was tired of pushing. For as much as I was anxious to hold both of my children, I needed to sleep, and I selfishly closed my eyes, hoping I could ignore the pain of labor for just five minutes of rest.

"No, baby, wake up," Magna cooed as she removed her hand and repositioned herself. "You have to give it everything you have on this next one. I know it's hard, but you've got to find the strength somewhere. He's breech, and it's too late to turn him. Listen to your body. If it's telling you to keep going, you have to."

Strength was found with the panic that my child could be in danger. I knew what breech meant, and I knew if I were in my own time, I'd be taken into surgery. If Anna was on her way, I would need to try everything now before she did what she promised me she would do and save my child over me.

Holding the first one in my arms, I wasn't ready to die. I wasn't willing to let go of him. With renewed strength, I leaned forward, and a sound came out of my throat I didn't think myself capable of as I used every muscle in my body to force the baby out.

"Keep going. Keep going! Almost there!"

My hips felt like they were breaking, my insides felt like they had spilled out on the bed beneath me, and everything inside me was either on fire or tied in a knot, but I leaned further in, feeling the little body move ever so slowly through me.

"One more big one. One more."

I could feel the baby, right there, just like the first one had been before she'd pulled him out, and I knew all I needed was to push one more time, but my entire body felt like it had shriveled into itself. I had nothing left. I couldn't even support my head.

"Red."

My eyes were closed, and I didn't even have the strength in my eyelids to pull them open. All of me was exposed on the bed and God only knew what it must've looked like. I heard him right there in the room, and I knew I needed to keep going. I needed to find the energy for just one more round.

I felt him take my hand in his, felt his weight on the bed as he sat down beside me. "Red," he whispered, pulling me up so he could position himself behind me. "I'm here."

Magna remained where she'd been, even though I could hear Anna and Raina in the room. "Push, baby," she said softly. "I know you can do it."

And some part of me did. I wasn't there for it, but I knew I was pushing. I knew my organs were on fire and my muscles were trembling. I knew my body was bent forward, and I was crying out loudly as the baby was pulled from me, but I wasn't there. I was in Jack's arms, high up on the edge of the summit, looking out at a red sky.

I could hear the baby crying far away and I smiled in relief as I laid my head against Jack's chest. I'd done it. Both of our children were alive and well. I could die if I needed to. But I felt him pull me closer, and I knew I wasn't dead. His voice came to my ear. "We have a baby girl."

I blinked my eyes open to find I was still in Jack's arms, a baby cradled against my chest by each of his hands.

"How long have I been asleep?" I whispered, gently petting each of their tiny heads.

"About an hour." He kissed my temple. "How are you feeling?"

I smiled down at the two little breathing bodies rested on my bare breasts. "Elated... and exhausted. They're both healthy?"

"Very." He rested his chin on my shoulder to look down at them. "Thank you... for them... For you."

I grinned as one of the babies moved. "I don't think I've ever loved anything more."

"Me neither."

I looked down to where Magna once sat, finding the foot of the bed empty and realizing my shift had been removed and I was naked beneath the blanket. Whatever blood might've been there once was now gone, and I'd been cleaned. "Did everyone see me when I was all... out there?"

He laughed softly. "No. No one has been allowed in here except me, Anna, and Magna. Once they got you cleaned up, I shooed them out, too. The others can have their moment later. This one is for us." He smoothed his thumb over one of the babies' cheeks. "Do you think you can feed them yet? Anna was pretty adamant you should feed them as soon as you were awake."

I nodded. Tired as I was, I'd been looking forward to feeding them.

"The boy has been trying, I think," he said, sitting up a little straighter behind me.

"The boy..." I looked between them as Jack helped me position them lower on each breast. "We should probably name them, eh?"

Before Jack could respond, the boy, who'd been searching for the nipple, found it and latched on immediately. I gasped as he locked on, not quite ready for the sensation. It was strange. I'd expected it to be pleasurable, and I supposed it was in a way, but it was also a little strange. It pinched and pulled, but it was a relief as well. Watching his little eyes open for a moment as they rolled back in his head was worth it. I laughed out loud.

"Is it weird?"

"So weird."

He lowered the girl, and I cradled my other arm to support her. Anna had told me it should be natural and so I waited for her to latch on as our son had. She took longer, attempting and missing several times before she found the right spot.

Jack kept his hands beneath my cradled arms, resting his chin against my shoulder. "God, I've never seen anything so beautiful in my life."

I watched as her eyes opened and she looked at me. I knew she couldn't really see me yet, but it felt like she had and a tear rolled down my cheek.

"What should we name them?" Jack asked, laying kisses down my neck.

"I was thinking we could name her after my sister Cecelia? But if you have a name...

"Cecelia is perfect. Look at her." He smiled. "She already looks like a Cecelia. What about her middle name?"

"You pick."

He sighed. "How about Bertie?"

"I love that. Cecelia Bertie Volmer... and your son? What should we call him?"

"My son," he echoed breathlessly. "How about Zachary? Since the man has been guiding us this whole time, it might make sense to honor his name."

"Zachary it is." I closed my eyes, letting the gentle tingle and pull of the two babies relax me. "Zachary William Volmer?"

"It's perfect." He kissed my shoulder, an act which mixed with the sensation of the babies was oddly arousing in a non-sexual way. I couldn't describe the closeness I felt to all three of them in that moment, but it was unbreakable and unlike anything I'd ever felt in my life.

"They're perfect," he said. "And so are you. I love you so much."

I sighed for the hundredth time, entirely content in the moment. "And I love you."

We stayed like that until both babies had had their fill, then each of us took a baby against our shoulder to softly rub and tap their backs.

Both of us exhausted, we laid down together, placing both babies between us, and we slept off and on for the next several hours, waking only when the babies needed to eat.

He'd gotten up to light the lanterns as the night set in and I sat up, finally feeling a little more like myself.

"What took you so long to get here?" I asked as he took a fussing Cecelia into his arms.

He frowned. "I came as soon as Lilly called for us. She said you'd already had the first. I ran as fast and as hard as I could to get here in time for the second."

"I sent Fetia long before the first one came."

He shook his head. "I never saw Fetia."

"Now, Got dammit Hoss. I can hear yuns in there talkin.' Ye' cain't keep us out here waitin' all night!" Jim called from the opposite side of the door. "We wanna' see 'em!"

Jack laughed, naturally smoothing his palm, which appeared gigantic, over Cecelia's back as he sat back down beside me in the bed. "I suppose we're going to have to let them in at some point."

"I'll need to put something on. Here. Take him." I placed Zachary against his other shoulder and smiled at the sight of my big handsome man with two tiny little humans in his hands.

I stood, forgetting that I'd just given birth, and I caught myself as my legs refused to support me. "Oh... or maybe I'll just cover myself." I crawled back into the bed.

"Are you alright?"

I pulled Cecelia from his chest to place against my own as I repositioned myself in front of him. "I'm fine. Just a little too weak still to function."

I adjusted the blankets and triple checked that nothing was exposed before I called out. "You can come in now."

And in a wave of baby talk and kissy faces, we were surrounded by our island family.

Both babies were naked save for their linen diapers, and Magna and Anna hurried to take each of them and wrap them tightly in linens.

"Give me that baby," Lilly demanded, taking Cecelia into her arms to gently rock her from side to side. "I love you and I don't even know you yet," she said softly to her. "Auntie Lilly is never ever, ever letting you go. Not ever."

"Easy Princess," Jim teased, looking over her shoulder and smiling at my daughter. "If we're gonna' steal one of 'em, we cain't make it that obvious." He winked at me before returning his attention to the baby.

Anna rocked Zachary in her arms, and I saw her eyes water, as I'm sure she thought about a time when she'd held her own son that way. I understood her that much more as I watched both my babies be showered with love. I couldn't imagine being separated from them for even a moment, let alone an entire year.

I scanned the room and found only two were missing. "Where are Maria and Chris?"

Lilly stopped rocking and looked at Jack. "You haven't told her?"

I frowned, pulling the blanket up to my chest so I could turn around to face him. "Told me what?"

"They're gone," he said softly, taking my hand in his. "They thought it'd be better to leave with the captain... hoped Juan Josef might follow them and give us a chance to get to the portal."

I shook my head. "No... You're lying."

"I'm not," he said, unable to meet my eyes. "They boarded the ship this morning before the sun came up."

"No, they didn't." I looked from him to Lilly. "Tell me this isn't true. Maria says Chris's mind is getting worse. She wouldn't do that. She knows better than all of us he has to go home. He needs a doctor. Tell me they didn't get on that ship."

Lilly gave me an apologetic look. "I'm so sorry, Lainey. They're gone."

"Well, they can't be far. We can still catch up to them in a cutter, can't we?"

"No, Red. It's too late now." He refused to look at me as he spoke. "Chris promised he would come back here with the captain and wait with us for March. He just wanted to lure Juan Josef away. He'll still go home, just not the first round."

He was lying. I knew Maria would never agree to it. She and I had spoken every day, and every day she was more and more concerned about Chris. He would scream in his sleep and he would ask her more frequently whether or not he was awake.

I placed my finger on Jack's chin and tilted his head so his eyes would meet mine. I saw my answer there. Chris was here somewhere and Jack was hiding him. "Where's Fetia?"

"I haven't seen her since this morning," Kyle said. Anna was carefully placing Zachary into his arm, and he was grinning from ear to ear as he looked down at him. "Why?"

"When I went into labor, she was here. I sent her to find you all, but Jack said she never came to the shore... where'd she go?"

Kyle frowned and looked up from the baby. "What are you saying? You think she purposely didn't come for us?"

I took a deep breath. "Well, you weren't exactly hard to find... and she wouldn't need to speak English to understand I needed help. I want to know why she didn't send help. I want to know where she went."

"I saw her," Phil was leaning against the bedroom door, cautious not to come too close to any of us as he tried to sneak a peek at my babies. "I was down by the beach and I saw her go running up the trail that leads inland. Looked like she was in a hurry."

"You were on the beach?" I asked. "You didn't hear me screaming?"

He shook his head. "No. I haven't been able to hear much of anything since that gun went off beside my ear." He glanced at Kyle. "That's *my* fault, not yours."

"Why would she run inland when I was clearly in labor? And why hasn't she come back?"

"Maybe she got scared and went to get her mother?" Kyle offered. "Her family lives that way. Maybe they came back and found you were already taken care of?"

Jack straightened. "You know where her family lives?"

Kyle shook his head, making a funny face at the baby in his arm. "No. I just know it's up that trail."

"What's going on with you two, anyway?" Lilly asked, handing Cecelia to Jim, who took her expertly into his cradled arms. "I saw you yesterday all wrapped up in a kiss."

"Oh... nothing. It's nothing," he answered nervously, offering Zachary to Bud, who happily took him.

"That wasn't nothing."

Kyle blushed, rubbing the back of his neck. "Well, it's... she doesn't even speak English... it's nothing."

Jack cleared his throat. "How much time have you been spending with her?"

"I don't know... little bits here and there." His cheeks flushed red.

"Have you told her anything about us? Even though she doesn't speak English, do you talk to her, anyway?"

Kyle shook his head. "We don't do much talking when we're together. Why are you so concerned with what I do with her?"

Jack took a deep breath. "Because she acted strangely, and we don't know who we can trust here. Anything that is strange should be suspicious with Juan Josef so close by."

Kyle laughed at that. "Fetia is not a spy."

Lilly tilted her head to one side. "How do you know?"

"I just know. She's not a spy."

Lilly stared at him for a long moment before she gasped and covered her mouth. "You slept with her!"

Even in the candlelight, I noticed Kyle's face as it became dark red. He looked down at his feet and stifled an uncomfortable smile.

"Kyle," Jack softened his tone. "It's alright. Did you tell her anything about us?"

Kyle shook his head. "Not really."

"Not really or not at all?"

Kyle slowly raised his head. "Not really."

Jim held Cecelia against his shoulder. "Now hold on. Fetia's been with 'em for almost a year. And she's been right here beside us this whole time. She ain't had a chance to get caught up in Juan Josef's nonsense. We just came upon him a few months ago, anyway. She cain't be involved."

"Her family could be," Bud said, and I noticed Jack stiffen.

"Magna," Jack rose from the bed. "I need you to come with me to translate."

I tilted my head to one side as I looked up at him. "Going to get Chris and Maria?"

He rolled his eyes, letting his shoulders fall. "Yes."

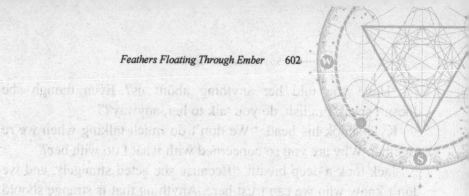

Chapter Fifty Seven

Alaina

"Wakey, wakey…"

I knew that voice the instant I heard it. Juan Josef. He was here. Rapidly, I opened my eyes and sat up in the bed to find him two feet away. The dim morning light shining through the small windows made his dark features ever the more sinister, and he stood over the baskets that held my babies; a dagger pointed at each.

"Please. Oh God, please. Whatever you want, it's yours. Just… please don't hurt them."

"I have questions," he said. "And you're going to answer them."

Heart beating in my throat, my eyes stayed fixed upon each dagger. If either blade moved any lower, I would have to launch myself on him. Could I get to him in time? How did he get into our room? Where were the others?

"What are you doing here?" he asked.

"We already told you." I said, searching the room for any sign of Jack. "We heard about the healing—

"In 1774!" He shouted, waking one of the babies and causing it to whimper. "How did you get here?! And what year did you come from?!"

Taken aback, I frowned. How could he possibly know about that? Every instinct inside me needed to console my now wailing child, but I also needed to keep my wits about me. This man with that knowledge was dangerous. "What…What are you talking about?"

"Do not toy with me, woman! I have spent the last twenty years sailing this damn ocean looking for a way back home. You can imagine my surprise when I was sent to these islands in search of a stolen Nikora boy, only to find a man wearing denim! Now tell me, what year did you come from?"

"You…?" I sat up straighter. "You're from our time? How…?" I swallowed as his eyes narrowed. "It was March of 2017 when we came through."

He cringed as the babies cried louder. "Tell me how to get back or I'll kill them both." He tightened his fingers around both daggers.

"I don't know," I said frantically. "We've been trying to figure that out ourselves. We don't know how it works. We just know the locations and have an idea of the dates you can pass through. Please, put the daggers down. We can talk all you want. I'll tell you everything I know."

He raised an eyebrow. "*Locations?* You know where you came through then?"

"Yes," I breathed, my heart breaking as both babies began to howl. "Why are you asking *me* these questions?" I asked, watching his hands. "I haven't been involved with the research. The others will have more answers than me. Where are they?"

"They're a little tied up at the moment." He grinned, looking down at the babies. "And I chose you long ago, my dear. *You* have more to lose than any one of them. You might not have come up with the answers, but you'll know them all the same, and you'll tell them to keep these two safe, won't you? How many of you came through?"

I closed my eyes and shuddered. He hadn't been waiting for the captain to leave, as we'd suspected. He'd been waiting for me to give birth. I'd never even spoken to the man, but he knew he could use my babies as leverage to get me to agree to anything he wanted. He hadn't sailed here. We'd have seen his ships or cutters on the water. He'd been here; likely hiding inland among Fetia's family, waiting for the right time to show himself.

"How many of you came through?" he repeated, raising his voice.

"Fifteen," I said, defeatedly.

"Fifteen?" He frowned. "How is that possible?"

"I don't know. Please, put the daggers down. We had no idea you were one of us. If you'd said so, we never would've run from you. We can learn from each other. I'll tell you everything we've figured out so far. You're the only other person we've met in-person who's crossed through. There's no reason for us not to help each other. Please, let me take my babies. I swear, I won't fight you."

"Your husband swore the same thing…" He tapped a cut above his eyebrow with one of the daggers. "And that didn't work out so well for me."

"Look at me and look at you. I've just given birth. I couldn't fight you if I tried. I can barely stand up. Please. I have no weapons, as you can see." I held both of my hands up to prove it. "Just let me hold them so they'll stop crying. I can't give you answers with two screaming babies between us."

I could see their screams were annoying him the longer the encounter went on, and I could see him pondering which he wanted more, to frighten me or to have them quieted.

As if he'd understood the argument I was trying to make, Zachary increased his volume, bellowing with every bit of air in his tiny lungs.

"Alright!" he said, sliding the daggers into his belt and pinching the bridge of his nose. "Hurry up. I can't take that sound any longer!"

I rushed from the bed to the baskets, quickly pulling Zachary to my chest as I reached down to take Cecelia in my other arm. "They're hungry," I said, returning to the safety of the bed. "If you could just… look away for a second?"

Much to my surprise, he did, turning his back to me and facing the door. "If you try anything…"

"It would be stupid to try anything now. I won't."

As quickly as I could on my own—it was the first time I'd attempted it without Jack's help—I positioned each baby beneath each breast, bashfully watching Juan Josef's back as I pulled my shift open for each one to latch on. It took a lot of juggling, but at long last, both babies were attached, and I sighed in relief as they slowly alleviated the pressure the milk had created. I draped a blanket over them and triple checked for any exposure before clearing my throat. "Okay. You can turn around now."

His demeanor was a little softer when he faced me. He lacked the menacing look as he observed the blanket and the subtle movement of the babies beneath it.

I didn't like his eyes on them, so I hurried to restart the conversation. "Did you come through in March or September?"

He frowned at me. "How could you know I came through in September?"

"We found a journal," I said. "It was dated 1928, and the man had come through in September. We came in March. How many were with you?"

"Six were on my yacht," he said, still staring at the blanket. "Only three of us came through, though. I don't know what happened to the others. What does March or September have to do with it?"

'Three in September.'

It wasn't a percentage. It was a set number, and that set the gears in my head spinning. I needed to tell him as much of the truth as was necessary to keep my babies safe, but I could fudge parts of it to keep our plan secure.

"Were you in the front of the boat?" I asked, a new theory forming.

"The three of us were all in the cockpit… So I suppose we would've been closer to the front than the rest. What does that have to do with anything? You promised answers!"

"I'm getting to them!" I matched his irritable tone. "We were on an airplane. Fifteen of us made it and we were all in first-class. We were in the front. The man whose journal we found... he came in September. I'm guessing he too was in the front of his ship."

I couldn't tell him only three would be able to go through in September... he might try to beat us to it. With no way of knowing who he'd talked to before me, I couldn't afford to lie.

"We're not sure how it works. Not everyone who gets caught in the storm makes it through. I'm not sure if it's a percentage or something to do with the year, and there's no way to know if it works the same going forward as it does backward, but I think the people in the front go through first."

"What does March or September have to do with it?"

"We think that's when it opens... something to do with the sun... we're not sure, though. It could be that there are other dates and other numbers, or a moving target... But so far September and March are both consistent."

"And you know the location?"

"The journals have the exact coordinates of where we disappeared and where we reappeared."

He scratched his dark beard. "Hmm... I could ask you for the coordinates, but what reason would you have to give them to me? If my three go, that's three less of yours to make it through... That leaves only one viable option." His menacing grin returned. "*You* will accompany me there on the date we must pass through."

I held my children tighter against me, attempting to make myself look bigger by sitting straighter. "I have no more of a reason to *accompany* you to the right coordinates than I do to tell you them."

He tilted his head to one side and smiled. "Oh, but I think you do. I have your people already on their way to my ship to be detained. I will kill them, one by one, if I should find myself sitting idle in the sea with no signs of a storm."

"There's no need for threats," I said, attempting to sound calm and hide my growing anxiety. "We can be of use to each other. If you've been able to detain all of my friends, I'm guessing there are more than three of you. There are several of us who want to stay in this time. If it *is* a percentage, with more people, you can guarantee those of my group who want to go home can go. And in exchange, the ones in my group who want to stay can guarantee that your three can return. We know that's how it should work... we just have to wait for the storm."

He laughed out loud at that. "Now I *know* you are lying. What possible reason could anyone have to want to stay here?"

Finding the perfect opportunity to buy my people their freedom, I did so, using the truth to my advantage. "Fear," I said simply. "We don't know how it works going forward, or if it works at all. Many of us have decided that it's safer to stay here than to risk the unknown. I wouldn't want to go through time with my babies and find my arms empty on the other side. Our plan was to send three and wait for them to return in March to verify it worked. If they came back to us, then we'd return the following September so we could all go back home."

I watched him mull it over, weighing the options of staying in the 18th century for another year or taking the chance at going home.

"There's more if you'd like to hear it," I said, adjusting Cecelia's head.

As I'd sat observing Juan Josef, I noticed the gold rings on his fingers, the emeralds and rubies that sat encased inside each. It was evident there was only one thing that could be more important to him than going home; the promise of money.

"Go on then," he said, taking a seat in the chair near the door.

"We were on a commercial airplane when we crashed. There's a lawyer among us. He says the lawsuit that could be filed against the airline would be enough to offer, not only my people, but yours as well, the opportunity to live like royalty for the rest of our lives; for the rest of our children's lives... And we could share that with you, assuming you let my friends go and help us... Think about it." I met his eyes. "You've been as good as dead for twenty years. You'll need money if you want to go back."

"An intriguing offer." He combed his beard. "You're smarter than I'd given you credit for. How do I know you're telling the truth?"

"Let us send our three. You can wait with us for their return. What's another year after you've been away this long? If, in six months, they do not return with money for each of you, *then* you can kill us, one by one. Either way, you'll have the location and the date. If I am telling the truth, you'll have a future to go back to. If I am not, you'll still have a way home. And you wouldn't need to be the first person to take the risk of going through."

"Most intriguing indeed..." He slowly scanned me from head to toe. "What's to stop your friends from going on with their lives and keeping all the money for themselves?"

"They wouldn't. Not if they knew the rest of us would die without their return. Can you..." I attempted to adjust the babies beneath the blanket. They'd stopped suckling and were beginning to fuss. "Can you look away for just a second, please?"

Once again, to my surprise, he did, turning in the chair to face the door as he continued the conversation. "Which three did you intend to send?"

"We haven't reached a decision yet... but I'd like to send the blonde woman, Anna. The tall man with dark hair, Chris, and Maria, the woman posing as the duchess."

"No," he said simply. "We should send the men. We can't keep them locked up for a year, and they'll fight us the instant they're set free. I've seen it for myself."

"They won't fight." I pulled the blanket from my chest, balancing Cecelia over my thighs on her stomach and Zachary over my shoulder as I adjusted the collar of my shift to hide my breasts. "Not if I talk to them first." I gently began patting each of their tiny backs, my hands working in perfect unison. "You can look now."

He turned slowly back around, his eyes lingering on the outline of my breasts beneath the shift. "You have that kind of control over your men?"

"One is my husband, and the other is my fiancé." I gave him a wry smile, attempting to seem much more controlled on the outside than I was on the inside. "I have that kind of control over two of them."

"Quite a fearsome little thing, you are." He leaned back in his chair. "You want to send one of them so you may be with the other?" His lip curled upward in a dubious smile. "Women are cruel, scheming little creatures... Even now, with a man threatening your life, you plot to send one away..." Pursing his lips, he shook his head. "I'm sorry. I cannot accommodate you. Your men will have to go."

I shrugged. "Then they *would* fight."

"This isn't a negotiation. You forget you are at a disadvantage, madam."

"Am I?" I raised an eyebrow, lowering Zachary from my shoulder to lay him on his back on the bed. Keeping my hands busy would hide the fact they were shaking. "You may have my friends, but I have your future."

I pulled Cecelia up to my shoulder to finish burping her. "Besides, there's a much stronger chance the women will return with the money where the men might try to come up with a scheme to trick you."

He crossed his arms over his chest. "The men go, and that's that... When in September?"

"The second or third," I said cooly, laying Cecelia on the bed beside Zachary. "It'll take about three weeks to get there from here. We were planning to leave in two weeks."

I could see in his stance he wouldn't be deterred. If, in the time between now and when we came upon the portal, I could somehow make a case for why Anna, Chris, and Maria should leave, perhaps I could make him think it was his idea to send them.

"Fifteen you say came through?" He frowned. "You are missing a few. Where are they?"

"Dead," I said, not looking up from my babies. He'd been watching us for quite some time. I had no clue how many he had detained, and I didn't want to give numbers without knowing his.

"We lost a few to injuries from the crash. We were all injured pretty badly, as you can imagine, after our airplane fell out of the sky."

I searched the room for the linens that served as diapers.

He reached down and separated two squares from a pile near his seat, extending them to me. "How long have you been in this time?"

"A little more than a year," I said, somewhere baffled by his willingness to assist me while still attempting to frighten me. Returning to the task of changing and cleaning both my children, I focused on keeping my hands busy.

"And now I have a bit of information for you," he said, leaning forward and waiting until I looked over at him to clear his throat and continue. "A little over twenty years ago, I crossed into March of 1754... from September of 1977."

CPSIA information can be obtained
at www.ICGtesting.com
Printed in the USA
LVHW041112150622
721313LV00008B/1177